UnSouled

Also by Neal Shusterman

NOVELS

Antsy Does Time

Bruiser

The Dark Side of Nowhere

Dissidents

Downsiders

The Eyes of Kid Midas

Full Tilt

The Schwa Was Here

The Shadow Club

The Shadow Club Rising

Ship Out of Luck

Speeding Bullet

What Daddy Did

THE UNWIND DYSTOLOGY

Unwind

UnWholly

UnStrung (an e-novella)

THE SKINJACKER TRILOGY

Everlost

Everwild

Everfound

THE STAR SHARDS CHRONICLES

Scorpion Shards

Thief of Souls

Shattered Sky

THE DARK FUSION SERIES

Dreadlocks

Red Rider's Hood

Duckling Ugly

STORY COLLECTIONS

Darkness Creeping

Kid Heroes

MindQuakes

MindStorms

Visit the author at storyman.com and facebook.com/nealshusterman

Neal Shusterman

UnSouled

BOOK 3 OF THE UNWIND DYSTOLOGY

SIMON & SCHUSTER BFYR

New York London Toronto Sydney New Delhi

An imprint of Simon & Schuster Children's Publishing Division
1230 Avenue of the Americas, New York, New York 10020
For information about special discounts for bulk purchases, please contact Simon &
Schuster Special Sales at 1-866-506-1949 or business@simonandschuster.com.
The Simon & Schuster Speakers Bureau can bring authors to your live event.
For more information or to book an event,
contact the Simon & Schuster Speakers Bureau at 1-866-248-3049
or visit our website at www.simonspeakers.com.
Book design by Hilary Zarycky based on a design by Al Cetta.
Jacket photographs copyright © 2013 by Jeremy Samuelson/Getty Images
The text for this book is set in Fairfield.
Manufactured in the United States of America
4 6 8 10 9 7 5 3
Library of Congress Cataloging-in-Publication Data
Shusterman, Neal.
Unsouled : book 3 of the Unwind dystology / Neal Shusterman.
pages cm
Sequel to: UnWholly.
Summary: After the destruction of the Graveyard, Connor and Lev are on the run, seeking
a woman who may be the key to bringing down unwinding forever, while Cam, the rewound
boy, tries to prove his love for Risa by bringing Proactive Citizenry to its knees.
ISBN 978-1-4424-2369-5 (hardback)
ISBN 978-1-4424-2371-8 (eBook)
1. Fugitives from justice—Fiction. 2. Survival—Fiction. 3. Revolutionaries—Fiction.
4. Identity—Fiction. 5. Science fiction.] I. Title.
PZ7.S55987Uns 2013
[Fic]—dc23
2013022703

For Jan, Eric & Robby, Keith & Thresa,
Chris, Patricia, Marcia, Andrea, Mark,
and all of my friends, who were there
when I needed them most

ACKNOWLEDGMENTS

Like Camus Comprix, this book, and all the books and stories in the Unwind world, are given life by many people. First and foremost, I'd like to thank my editor, David Gale; associate editor, Navah Wolfe; and publisher, Justin Chanda, for their support, and for continuing to allow me to divide a sequel into a trilogy, and now into a four-book "dystology." Many thanks to everyone at Simon & Schuster, including Jon Anderson, Anne Zafian, Paul Crichton, Lydia Finn, Michelle Fadlalla, Venessa Carson, Katrina Groover, and Chava Wolin. Many thanks also to Chloë Foglia who designed this wonderfully creepy cover!

I'd like to thank everyone who has supported me through this very eventful year—especially my children, Brendan, Jarrod, Joelle, and Erin; their mom, Elaine Jones; my "big sister," Patricia McFall; my assistant, Marcia Blanco; and my good friend, Christine "Natasha" Goethals.

Thanks to the wonderful people who keep my career on track; my book agent, Andrea Brown; my entertainment industry agents, Steve Fisher and Debbie Deuble-Hill; my manager, Trevor Engelson; and my lawyers, Shep Rosenman and Lee Rosenbaum.

I am deeply indebted to Marc Benardout, Catherine Kimmel, Julian Stone, Charlotte Stout, and Faber Dewar, whose tireless efforts and belief in Unwind have resulted in a film deal for the entire book series—which couldn't have happened without Robert Kulzer and Margo Klewans at Constantin Films, and their passion for these books.

Thanks to Michelle Knowlden, for her collaboration on "Unstrung," and upcoming short stories in the Unwind world; Matthew Dierker and Wendy Doyle, for their work on my website; and Symone Powell, Tyler Hotlzman, Annie Wilson, Meara McNitt, Matthew Setzekorn, and Natalie Sommors, who began as fans and have gone on to help maintain a Facebook and Twitter presence for the Unwind world and its characters!

Спасибо to Ludovika Fjortende and Michelle and Artie Shaykevich for translating Russian phrases, and to Stephanie Sandra Brown for her expertise in Portuguese.

And lastly I owe a debt of gratitude to all the teachers and librarians who are bringing these books to kids and adults alike, as well as the readers and fans. It is your passionate word-of-mouth that makes all the difference in the world!

UnSouled

Part One
Flightless

"Surely this new medical technology will free us rather than enslave us, for it is my firm belief that human compassion outweighs human greed. To that end, I hereby found Proactive Citizenry to be a stalwart watchdog over the ethical use of neurografting. I am confident that abuses will be the exception rather than the rule."

—Janson Rheinschild

"I am become death, the destroyer of worlds."

—J. Robert Oppenheimer

The Rheinschilds

"They signed it. The Heartland War is over."

Janson Rheinschild closes the front door, throws his coat on the sofa, and collapses into an armchair, as if all his joints have become internally undone. As if he's been unwound from the inside out.

"You can't be serious," Sonia says. *"No one in their right mind would sign that hideous Unwind Accord."*

He looks at her with a bitterness that isn't meant for her, but it has nowhere else to go. *"Who,"* he asks, *"has been in their right mind for the past nine years?"*

She sits on the arm of the sofa as close to him as she can get and takes his hand. He grasps it with a sort of desperation, as if her hand is the only thing keeping him from the abyss.

"The new chairman of Proactive Citizenry, that narcissistic weasel Dandrich, called me before they made any official announcement, to let me know the accord was signed. He said that I should know first 'out of respect.' But you know as well as I do, he did it to gloat."

"There's no sense torturing yourself, Janson. It's not your fault, and there's nothing you can do about it."

He pulls his hand away from her and glares. *"You're right—it's not my fault. It's our fault. We did this together, Sonia."*

She reacts as if he's slapped her across the face. She doesn't just turn away from him. She gets up and moves away, beginning to pace the room. Good, *thinks Janson. She needs to feel a little bit of what I feel.*

"I did nothing wrong," she insists, *"and neither did you!"*

3

"We made it possible! Unwinding is based on our technology! Our research!"

"And it was stolen from us!"

Janson gets up from his chair, unable to bear even one sedentary moment. Sitting feels like acceptance. It feels like admitting failure. Next he'll be lost in that armchair with a drink in his hands, swirling the ice to hear it clink, feeling the alcohol numbing him into submission. No, that's not him. It will never be him.

There's some shouting in the street. He looks out the living room window to see some neighborhood kids being rowdy with one another. "Ferals," the news now calls them. Feral teens. "Something must be done about the feral teens this war has created," the politicians bleat from their legislative pens. Well, what did they expect when educational funding was diverted to the war? How could they not know public education would fail? With no schools, no jobs, and nothing but time on their hands, what did they think these kids would do other than make trouble?

The mob in the street—barely a mob at all, numbering only four or five—passes without incident. They've never had trouble at their house even though theirs is the only home on the street without window bars and an iron security gate. On the other hand, several of the security doors on the street have been vandalized. These kids, they may be lacking in education since the school closures, but they're not stupid. They see distrust all around them, and it makes them want to deliver their anger all the more. "How dare you distrust me?" their violence says. "You don't know me." But people are too wrapped up in their own fearful security measures to hear it.

Sonia comes up behind him now, wrapping her arms around him. He wants to accept her comfort, but can't allow himself. He can't be consoled or find a sense of peace until he's undone this terrible wrong.

"*Maybe it will be like the old Cold War,*" Sonia suggests.

"*How do you figure?*"

"*They have this new weapon,*" she says, "*unwinding. Maybe just the threat of it is enough. Maybe they'll never actually use it.*"

"*A cold war implies a balance of power. What do these kids have if the authorities start unwinding them?*"

Sonia sighs, finally seeing his point. "*Not a chance in hell.*"

Now at last he can take some comfort that she understands. That he's not alone in seeing the murky depths to which this new law could lead.

"*It still hasn't happened,*" she reminds him. "*Not a single feral teen has been unwound.*"

"*No,*" Janson says. "*Because the law doesn't take effect until midnight.*"

And so they decide to spend the rest of their evening together, holding each other close like it's the last night of civilization. Because in a very real sense, it is.

1 · Connor

It begins with roadkill—an act so random and ridiculous that it boggles the mind to consider the events to which it leads.

Connor should have pulled off the road to sleep—especially on a windy night like this. Certainly his reflexes behind the wheel would be much better in the morning, but the burning need to get himself and Lev to Ohio keeps pushing him harder each day.

Just one more exit on the interstate, he tells himself, and although he had resolved to stop once they crossed into Kansas, that marker came and went half an hour ago. Lev, who is good at talking sense into Connor, is no help tonight, slumped in the passenger seat, fast asleep.

It's half past midnight when the unfortunate creature leaps into Connor's headlights, and Connor has enough time only to register a brief impression of it as he jerks the wheel in a desperate attempt to avoid a collision.

That can't be what I think it is. . . .

Even though he swerves wide, the stupid thing bolts right into the car's path again as if it has a death wish.

The "borrowed" Charger slams into the creature, and it rolls over the hood like a boulder, shattering the windshield into a million bits of safety glass. Its body wedges in the windshield frame, with a twisted wiper blade embedded in its slender neck. Connor loses control of the steering wheel, and the car leaves the asphalt, careening wildly through the roadside chaparral.

He screams and curses reflexively, as the creature, still clinging to life, rips at Connor's chest with its talons, tearing fabric and flesh, until finally Connor pulls enough of his wits together to slam on the brakes. The abominable creature dislodges from the windshield, launching forward as if shot from a cannon. The car keels like a sinking ship, comes to a sudden stop in a ditch, and finally the air bags deploy, like a faulty parachute opening upon impact.

The quiet that follows feels like the airless silence of space, but for the soulless moan of the wind.

Lev, who woke up the second they hit the thing, says nothing. He just gasps for the breath that was knocked out of him by the air bag. Connor has discovered Lev to be more of an opossum than a screamer. Panic makes him freeze.

Connor, still trying to process the previous ten seconds of his life, checks the wound in his chest. Beneath the tear in his shirt is a diagonal gash in his skin maybe six inches long. Oddly, he's relieved. It's not life-threatening, and flesh wounds can be dealt with. As Risa would have said when she ran the infirmary at the airplane graveyard, "Stitches are the least of all evils." This wound will take about a dozen. The biggest problem will be where a fugitive-presumed-dead AWOL can get medical attention.

Both he and Lev get out of the car and climb up from the ditch to examine their roadkill. Connor's legs are weak and wobbly, but he doesn't want to admit it to himself, so he concludes that he's merely shaky from the adrenaline rush. He looks at his arm—the one with the shark tattoo—and pumps the hand into a fist, coopting the brutal strength of that stolen arm for the rest of his body.

"Is that an ostrich?" asks Lev, as they look down on the huge dead bird.

"No," snaps Connor, "it's the freaking Road Runner." Which was actually Connor's first irrational thought when the giant bird had first loomed in his headlights. The ostrich, which had still been alive enough to rip into Connor's chest a minute ago, is now very dead. Its torn neck is twisted at a severe angle, and its glassy eyes stare at them with zombielike intensity.

"That was some bird strike," Lev says. He seems no longer fazed by it, just observational. Maybe because he wasn't driving, or maybe because he's seen things far worse than a roadkill raptor. Connor envies Lev's calm in a crisis.

"Why the hell is there an ostrich on the interstate?" Connor asks. His answer comes with the rattle of a fence in a sudden gust of wind. Passing headlights illuminate the limb of an oak tree brought down by the wind. The bough was heavy enough to take out a piece of the chain-link fence. Long-necked shapes move behind the fence, and a few ostriches have already come through the breach, wandering toward the road. Hopefully they'll have better luck than their comrade.

Connor has heard that ostrich farms were becoming more common as the price of other meat soared, but he'd never actually seen one. He idly wonders whether or not the bird's death was suicide. Better roadkill than roast.

"They used to be dinosaurs, you know?" says Lev.

Connor takes a deep breath, only now realizing how shallowly he's been breathing—partially from the pain, partially from the shock of it all. He shows Lev his cut. "As far as I'm concerned, they still are. The thing tried to unwind me."

Lev grimaces. "You okay?"

"I'll be fine." Connor takes off his windbreaker, and Lev helps him fix it tightly around his back and across his chest as a makeshift tourniquet.

They look back at the car, which couldn't be more totaled if it had been hit by a truck rather than a flightless bird.

"Well, you did plan to ditch the car in a day or two, right?" Lev asks.

"Yeah, but I didn't mean in an actual ditch."

The waitress who was kind enough to let them take her car said she wouldn't report it missing for a few days. Connor can only hope she'll be happy with the insurance money.

A few more cars pass on the interstate. The wreck is far enough off the road not to be noticed by someone who's not looking. But there are some people whose job it is to look.

A car passes, slows a hundred yards up, and makes a U-turn across the dirt median. As it makes the turn, another car's headlights illuminate its black-and-white coloring. A highway patrol car. Maybe the officer saw them—or maybe he just saw the ostriches, but either way, their options have suddenly been cut short.

"Run!" says Connor.

"He'll see us!"

"Not until he shines his spotlight. Run!"

The patrol car pulls to a stop by the side of the road, and Lev doesn't argue anymore. He turns to run, but Connor grabs his arm. "No, this way."

"Toward the ostriches?"

"Trust me!"

The spotlight comes on, but it fixes on one of the birds nearing the road and not on them. Connor and Lev reach the breach in the fence. Birds scatter around them, creating more moving targets for the patrolman's spotlight.

"Through the fence? Are you crazy?" whispers Lev.

"If we run along the fence, we'll get caught. We have to disappear. This is the only way to do it."

With Lev beside him, Conner pushes through the broken fence, and like so many other times in his life, he finds himself running blind into the dark.

FOLLOWING IS A PAID POLITICAL ADVERTISEMENT

"Last year, I lost my husband of thirty-five years to a burglar. He just came in through the window. My husband tried to fight him off and was shot. I know I can never bring my husband back, but now there's a proposition on the ballot that can finally make criminals truly pay for their crimes, flesh for flesh.

"By legalizing the unwinding of criminals, not only do we reduce prison overcrowding, but we can provide life-saving tissues for transplant. Further, the Corporal Justice law will allow for a percentage of all proceeds from organ sales to go directly to victims of violent crime and their families.

"Vote yes on Proposition 73. United we stand; divided criminals fall."

—Sponsored by the National Alliance of Victims for Corporeal Justice

---

They can't stay at the ostrich ranch. Lights are on in the farmhouse; more than likely the owner has been notified of the problem on the interstate, and the place will be crawling with farmhands and police to wrangle the birds.

Down a dirt road, a half mile from the farm, they come across an abandoned trailer. There's a bed with a mattress, but it's so mildewed, they both decide their best bet is to sleep on the floor.

In spite of everything, Connor falls asleep in minutes. He has vague dreams of Risa, whom he hasn't seen in many months, and may never see again, as well as dreams of the battle at the airplane graveyard. The takedown operation that routed the place. In his dreams, Connor tries dozens of different tactics to save the hundreds of kids in his care from the Juvenile Authority. Nothing ever works. The outcome is always the same—the kids are all either killed or put in transport trucks bound for harvest camps. Even Connor's dreams are futile.

When he wakes, it's morning. Lev isn't there, and Connor's chest aches with every breath. He loosens the tourniquet. The bleeding has stopped, but the gash is red and still very raw. He puts it back on until he can find something other than his bloodstained Windbreaker to cover it.

He finds Lev outside, surveying their surroundings. There's a lot to survey. What at night appeared to be just a lone trailer is actually the central mansion of an entire rust-bucket estate. All around the trailer is a collection of large, useless objects. Rusted cars, kitchen appliances, even a school bus so old it retains none of its original color, not a single window intact.

"You have to wonder about the person who lived here," Lev says.

As Connor looks around the veritable junkyard, it strikes him as disturbingly familiar. "I lived in the airplane junkyard for more than a year," he reminds Lev. "Everyone's got issues."

"Graveyard, not junkyard," Lev corrects.

"There's a difference?"

"One is about a noble end. The other is about, well . . . garbage."

Connor looks down and kicks a rusted can. "There was nothing noble about our end at the Graveyard."

"Give it up," says Lev. "Your self-pity is getting old."

But it's not self-pity—Lev should know that. It's about the kids who were lost. Of the more than seven hundred kids in Connor's care, over thirty died, and about four hundred were shipped off to harvest camps to be unwound. Maybe no one could have stopped it—but it happened on Connor's watch. He has to bear the weight of it.

Connor takes a long look at Lev, who, for the moment, seems content to examine a wheelless, hoodless, roofless Cadillac so overgrown by weeds inside and out, it looks like a planter.

"It has a kind of beauty, you know?" says Lev. "Like how sunken ships eventually become part of a coral reef."

"How can you be so stinking cheery?" Connor asks.

Lev's response is a toss of his overgrown blond hair and a grin that is intentionally cheerful. "Maybe because we're alive and we're free," Lev says. "Maybe because I singlehandedly saved your butt from a parts pirate."

Now Connor can't help but grin as well. "Stop it; your self-congratulation is getting old."

Connor can't blame Lev for being upbeat. His mission succeeded with flying colors. He walked right into the middle of a no-way-out battle and not only found a way out, but saved Connor from Nelson, a disgraced Juvey-cop with a grudge who was hell-bent on selling Connor on the black market.

"After what you did," Connor tells Lev, "Nelson will want your head on a stake."

"And other parts, I'm sure. But he's got to find me first."

Only now does Lev's optimism begin to rub off on Connor. Yes, their situation is dire, but for a dire situation, things could be worse. Being alive and free counts for something, and the fact that they have a destination—one that may just give them some crucial answers—adds a fair amount of hope into the mix.

Connor shifts his shoulder and the motion aggravates his wound—a reminder that it will have to be taken care of sooner rather than later. It's a complication they don't need. Not a single clinic or emergency room will do the work without asking questions. If he can just keep it clean and dressed until they get to Ohio, he knows Sonia will get him the care he needs.

That is, if she's still at the antique shop.

That is, if she's even alive.

"The last road sign before we flipped the bird said there was a town just ahead," Connor tells Lev. "I'll go jack a car and come back for you."

"No," says Lev. "I traveled across the country to find you—I'm not letting you out of my sight."

"You're worse than a Juvey-cop."

"Two sets of eyes are better than one," says Lev.

"But if one of us gets caught, the other can make it to Ohio. If we're together, then we risk both of us getting caught."

Lev opens his mouth to say something, but closes it again. Connor's logic is irrefutable.

"I don't like this at all," Lev says.

"Neither do I, but it's our best option."

"And what am I supposed to do while you're gone?"

Connor offers him a crooked grin. "Make yourself part of the reef."

It's a long walk—especially for someone in pain. Before leaving, Connor had found some "clean" linens in the trailer, as well as a stash of cheap whiskey, perfect for cleaning a wound. Painful, too, but as all the world's sports coaches say, "Pain is weakness leaving the body." Connor always hated coaches. Once the stinging had stopped, he created a more secure dressing, which he now wears under a faded flannel shirt that belonged to the trailer's final resident. It's too warm a shirt for such hot weather, but it was the best he could do.

Now, sweating from the heat and aching from the wound, Connor counts his steps along the dirt road until it becomes paved. He has yet to see a passing car, but that's fine. The fewer eyes that see him, the better. Safety in solitude.

Connor also doesn't know what to expect ahead of him in this small town. When it comes to cities and suburbs, Connor has found that most are fairly identical—only the geography changes. Rural areas, however, vary greatly. Some small towns are places you'd want to come from and eventually go back to: warm, inviting communities that breathe out Americana the way rain forests breathe out oxygen. And then there are towns like Heartsdale, Kansas.

This is the place where fun came to die.

It's clear to Connor that Heartsdale is economically depressed, which is not that uncommon. All it takes these days for a town to give up the ghost is for a major factory to shut down or pick up its skirt and do an international waltz for cheaper labor. Heartsdale, however, isn't just depressed; it's ugly in a fundamental way and on more than one level.

The main drag is full of low, flat-faced architecture, all in shades of beige. Although there are farms in abundance that Connor had passed, thriving and green in the July sun, the town center has no trees, no green growth except for weeds between pavement cracks. There's an uninviting church built out of institutional mustard-colored bricks. The sermon message on the billboard reads WHO W LL ATONE FOR YOUR S NS? B NGO ON FR DAYS.

The town's most attractive building is a new three-story parking garage, but it isn't open for business. The reason, Connor realizes, is the empty lot next to it. There's a billboard for a modern office building to be erected there, which may one day need three levels of parking, but the forlorn state of the lot betrays the fact that the office complex has been in the planning stages for perhaps a decade and will probably never be built.

The place isn't exactly a ghost town—Connor sees plenty of people going about their morning business, but he has an urge to ask them, "Why bother? What's the point?" The problem with a town like this is that anyone with even a rudimentary survival instinct managed to get out long ago—perhaps finding themselves one of those other small towns in which to live. The kind with the heart that Heartsdale lacks. Left behind are the souls that kind of got stuck to the bottom of the pan.

Connor comes to a supermarket. A Publix. Its blacktop parking lot shimmers with waves of heat. If he's going to jack a car, there are plenty here to choose from, but they're all out in the open, so he can't do it without the risk of being exposed. Besides, his hope is to find a long-term parking lot where a stolen car might not be missed for a day or more. Even if he manages to get away with a car from this lot, it will be reported stolen within the hour. But who is he kidding? A long-term parking lot implies the owners of the vehicles parked there had somewhere to go. The folks in Heartsdale don't seem to be going anywhere.

It's hunger, however, that pulls him toward the market, and he realizes he hasn't eaten in half a day. With twenty-some-odd dollars in his pocket, he reasons that there's nothing wrong with buying something to eat. It's easy to remain anonymous in a market for a whole of five minutes.

As the automatic door slides open, he's hit with a blast of cold air that is at first refreshing, then makes his sweaty clothes cold against his body. The market is brightly lit and filled with shoppers moving slowly through the aisles, probably here to get out of the heat as much as they are to shop.

Connor grabs premade sandwiches and cans of soda for himself and for Lev, then goes to the self-checkout, only to find that it's closed. No way to avoid human contact today. He chooses a checker who looks disinterested and unobservant. He seems a year or two older than Connor. Skinny, with straggly black hair and a baby-fuzz mustache that just isn't working. He grabs Connor's items and runs them across the scanner.

"Will that be it for you?" the checker asks absently.

"Yeah."

"Did you find everything all right?"

"Yeah, no problem."

He glances once at Connor. It seems he holds Connor's gaze a moment too long, but maybe he's been instructed to make eye contact with customers, as well as ask his standard rote questions.

"You need help out with that?"

"I think I can handle it."

"No worries, man. Keep cool. It's a scorcher out there."

Connor leaves without further incident. He's back out in the heat and halfway across the parking lot, when he hears—

"Hey, wait up!"

Connor tenses, his right arm contracting into a habitual fist. But when he turns, he sees that it's the checker coming after him, waving a wallet.

"Hey, man—you left this on the counter."

"Sorry," Connor tells him. "It's not mine."

The checker flips it open to look at the license. "Are you sure? Because—"

The attack comes so suddenly that Connor is caught off guard. He has no chance to protect himself from the blow— and it's a low one. A kick to the groin that registers a surge of shock, followed by a building swell of excruciating pain. Connor swings at his attacker, and Roland's arm doesn't fail him. He connects a powerful blow to the checker's jaw, then swings with his natural arm, but by now the pain is so overwhelming, the punch has nothing behind it. Suddenly his attacker is behind him and puts Connor in a choke hold. Still Connor struggles. He's bigger than this guy, stronger, but the checker knows what he's doing, and Connor's reaction time is slowed. The choke hold cuts off Connor's windpipe and compresses his carotid artery. His vision goes black, and he knows he's about to lose consciousness. The only saving grace is that being unconscious means he doesn't have to feel the agony in his groin.

PUBLIC SERVICE ANNOUNCEMENT

"I used to make jokes about clappers until three of them senselessly targeted my school and detonated themselves in a crowded hallway. Who would have thought that the simple act of bringing your hands together could create so much misery? I lost a lot of friends that day.

"If you think there's nothing you can do to stop clappers, you're wrong. You can report suspicious teens in your neighborhood, since it's been documented that most clappers are under twenty. Be aware of people who wear clothing too heavy for the weather, as clappers often try to pad themselves so that they don't detonate accidentally. Also be aware of people who appear to walk with exaggerated caution, as if every footfall might be their last. And don't forget to lobby for a ban on applause at public events in your community.

"Together we can put an end to clappers once and for all. It's our hands against theirs."

—Sponsored by Hands Apart for Peace®

Connor snaps awake, fully conscious, fully aware. No bleary-eyed moments of uncertainty; he knows he was attacked, and he knows he's in trouble. The question is how bad will this trouble be?

The wound on his chest aches, his head pounds, but he pushes thoughts of the pain away and quickly begins to take in his surroundings. Cinder-block walls. Dirt floor. This is good: It means he's not in a jail cell or a holding pen. The only light is a single dangling bulb above his head. There are food supplies and cases of bottled water piled against the wall to his right, and to his left, concrete stairs lead to a hatch up above. He's in some sort of basement or bunker. Maybe a storm cellar. That would account for the emergency supplies.

He tries to move but can't. His hands are tied to a pole behind his back.

"Took you long enough!"

Connor turns to see the greasy-haired supermarket checker sitting in the shadows by the food supplies. Now that he's been spotted, he scoots forward into the light. "That choke hold I gave you knocks people out for ten, maybe twenty minutes usually—but you were out for nearly an hour."

Connor doesn't say anything. Any question, any utterance, is a show of weakness. He doesn't want to give this loser any more power than he already has.

"If I held you ten seconds more, it woulda killed you. Or at least given you brain damage. You don't got brain damage, do you?"

Connor still gives him nothing beyond a cold stare.

"I knew who you were the second I laid eyes on you," he says. "People said the Akron AWOL was dead, but I knew it was all lies. 'Habeas corpus,' I say. 'Bring me his body.' But they couldn't do it, because you're not dead!"

Connor can't hold his tongue any longer. "That's not what habeas corpus means, you moron."

The checker giggles, then pulls out his phone and takes a picture. The flash makes Connor's head pound. "Do you have any idea how cool this is, Connor? I can call you Connor, right?"

Connor looks down and sees that the wound on his chest has been redressed with actual gauze and surgical tape. The fact that he can see the bandage brings to his attention the fact that he's shirtless.

"What did you do with my shirt?"

"Had to take it off. When I saw the blood, I had to check it out. Who cut you? Was it a Juvey-cop? Did you give as good as you got?"

"Yeah," says Connor. "He's dead." Hopefully his continued glare implies, *And you're next.*

"Wish I coulda seen that!" said the checker. "You're my hero. You know that, right?" Then he goes off into a twisted reverie. "The Akron AWOL blows the hell out of Happy Jack Harvest Camp, escaping from his own unwinding. The Akron AWOL tranqs a Juvey-cop with his own gun. The Akron AWOL turns a tithe into a clapper!"

"I didn't do that."

"Yeah, well, you did the rest, and that's enough."

Connor thinks about Lev waiting for him back at the field of junk and begins to feel sick.

"I followed your career, man, until they said you died—but I never believed it, not for a minute. A guy like you don't get taken down so easy."

"It wasn't a career," Connor says, disgusted by this guy's particular brand of hero worship, but it's as if he doesn't hear Connor.

"You tore up the world. I could do that too, y'know? Just

need the opportunity. And maybe a partner in crime who knows what he's doing. Knows how to mess with the powers that be. You know where I'm going with this, right? Sure you do—you're too smart not to know. I always knew if we'd met, we'd be friends. We'd click—kindred spirits and all that." Then he laughs. "The Akron AWOL in my storm cellar. Can't be an accident. It was fated, man! Fated!"

"You kicked me in the nuts. That wasn't fate; it was your foot."

"Yeah, sorry about that. But, see, I had to do something or you'd just leave. It hurts, I know, but there's no real damage. I hope you won't take it the wrong way."

Connor laughs bitterly at that. He can't help himself. He wonders if anyone saw the attack happen. If someone did, they didn't care, or at least they didn't care enough to stop it.

"Friends don't tie friends up in a cellar," Connor points out.

"Yeah, sorry about that, too." But he makes no move to untie him. "Here's the quandary. You know what a quandary is, right? Sure you do. See, if I untie you, you'll probably bolt. So I have to convince you I'm the real deal. A decent guy in spite of knocking you out and tying you up. I gotta make you see that a friend like me is hard to find in this screwed-up world and that this is the place where you want to be. You don't gotta run anymore. See, nobody looks for nobody in Heartsdale."

His captor stands and paces, gesturing with his hands. His eyes get wide as he talks as if he's telling a campfire story. He's not even looking at Connor anymore as he weaves his little fantasy. Connor just lets him talk, figuring in his verbal diarrhea, he might expel some piece of information that Connor can use.

"I got it all figured out," he continues. "We'll dye your hair as dark as mine. I know a guy who'll do pigment injections in your eyes on the cheap so they'll look the same hazel as mine—

19

although I can see one of your eyes is slightly different from the other, but we can get them to match, right? Then we'll tell folks you're my cousin from Wichita, on account of everyone knows I got family in Wichita. With my help, you'll disappear so good, no one'll know you're not dead."

The thought of being made to look like this guy in any way is almost as unpleasant as a kick to the groin. And disappearing in Heartsdale? That's the stuff of nightmares. Yet in spite of everything, Connor dredges up the warmest smile he can muster.

"You say you want to be friends, but I don't even know your name."

He looks offended. "It was on my name tag at the market. Don't you remember?"

"I didn't notice."

"Not too observant, are you? A guy in your situation should learn to be more observant." And then he adds, "Not your situation here. I mean your situation out there."

Connor waits until his captor finally says, "Argent. Like Sergeant without the S. It means money in French. Argent Skinner at your service."

"Of the Wichita Skinners."

Argent looks a bit shocked and increasingly suspicious. "You heard of us?"

Connor considers toying with him, but decides that Argent won't look kindly upon it once he figures it out. "No—you said so before."

"Oh, right."

Now Argent just stares at him, grinning until the trapdoor swings open and someone else clambers down the steps. The woman looks somewhat like Argent, but a couple of years older, taller, and a little doughier—not fat, but a bit heavyset and unshapely. Dowdy—if a woman so young could be called dowdy. Her expression is a bit vaguer than Argent's, if indeed that's possible.

"Is that him? Can I see him? Is it really him?"

Suddenly Argent's whole demeanor changes. "You shut your stupid hole!" he shouts. "You want the whole world to know who we got visitin'?"

"Sorry, Argie." Her broad shoulders seem to fold at the reprimand.

Connor quickly sizes her up to be Argent's older sister. Twenty-two or twenty-three, although she carries herself much younger. The slack expression on her face speaks of a dullness that isn't her fault, although Argent clearly blames her for it.

"You want to keep us company, then go sit in the corner and be quiet." Argent turns back to Connor. "Grace has got a problem using her indoor voice."

"We're not indoors," Grace insists. "The shelter's in the yard, and that's outside the house."

Argent sighs and shakes his head, giving Connor an exaggerated long-suffering look. "You see how it is?"

"Yeah, I see," says Connor. He logs one more bit of information. This cellar is not in the house, but in the yard. Which means if Connor manages to escape the cellar, he's maybe a dozen yards closer to freedom. "Won't it be hard to keep it a secret that I'm down here," Connor asks, "once everyone else gets home?"

"No one else comin'," Argent says. This was the news Connor was fishing for. He's ambivalent about it. On the one hand, if there were other members of this household, someone might be rational enough to stop this before it gets any further. But on the other hand, a rational person would most likely turn Connor over to the authorities.

"Well, I figured you've got a house, so you must have a family. Parents maybe."

"Dead," says Grace. "Dead, dead, dead."

Argent throws her a severe warning look before turning back to Connor. "Our mother died young. Our father kicked the ghost last year."

"Good thing too," adds Grace, grinning. "He was gonna unwind Argent's sorry ass for the cash."

In one smooth motion, Argent picks up a water bottle and hurls it at baseball speed at Grace. She ducks, but not fast enough, and the bottle careens off the side of her head, making her yelp with pain.

"HE WAS JUST SAYING THAT!" yells Argent. "I WAS TOO OLD TO BE UNWOUND."

Grace holds the side of her head, but remains defiant. "Not too old for parts pirates. They don't care how old you are!"

"DIDN'T I TELL YOU TO SHUT IT?" Argent takes a moment to let his fury dissipate, then looks for an ally in Connor. "Grace is like a dog. Sometimes you gotta shake a can at her."

Connor can't hold back his own seething fury. "That was more than shaking." He looks over at Grace, still holding her head, but Connor is sure her spirit is hurt more than anything else.

"Yeah, well, unwinding is nothing to joke about," says Argent. "You know that more than anyone. Truth be told, our father woulda unwound us both if he could, so he didn't have our mouths to feed. But Grace wasn't ever eligible since there's laws against unwinding the feebleminded, and not even parts pirates'll do it. He couldn't do me either, because he needed me to take care of Grace. You see how it is?"

"Yeah, I see."

"Low-cortical," grumbles Grace. "I ain't feebleminded. I'm low-cortical. It's the less insulting way."

Although low-cortical always sounded pretty insulting to Connor. He twists his wrists, gauging the tightness of the knots. Apparently Argent is very good with knots, because the ropes don't give at all. His hands are tied individually, so he'll have to squirm out of both sets of bonds to free himself. It makes Connor think of how he had tied Lev to a tree after Connor had first rescued him. He had kept Lev against his will to save his life. *Well*, thinks Connor, *what goes around comes around*. Now he's at the mercy of someone who believes he's holding Connor captive for his own good.

"Did you happen to keep the sandwiches I bought?" Connor asks. "Because I'm starving."

"Nah. They're still in the parking lot, I imagine."

"Well, if I'm your guest, don't you think it's rude not to feed me?"

Argent considers this. "Yeah, that is rude. I'll go fix you something." He orders Grace to give Connor some water from their stockpile of survival rations. "Don't do anything stupid while I'm gone."

Connor's not sure if he's talking to him or to Grace, but decides it doesn't really matter.

After Argent is gone, Grace visibly relaxes, freed from her brother's sphere of influence. She holds out the water bottle for Connor to take, then realizes he can't take it. Grace unscrews the cap and pours it into Connor's mouth. He gets a good gulp, although most of it spills on his pants.

"Sorry!" says Grace, almost in a panic. Connor knows why.

"Don't worry. I'll tell Argent that I pissed myself. He can't get mad at you for that."

Grace laughs. "He'll find a way."

Connor looks Grace in the eye. There's an innocence there that's slowly breaking. "He doesn't treat you too well, does he?"

"Who, Argie? Nah, he's okay. He's just mad at the world, but the world isn't around to be mad at. Just me."

Connor smiles at that. "You're smarter than Argent thinks."

"Maybe," Grace says, although she doesn't seem too convinced. She looks back toward the closed cellar door and then to Connor again. "I like your tattoo," she says. "Great white?"

"Tiger shark," Connor tells her. "Only it's not mine. It belonged to a kid who actually tried to strangle me with this same arm. He couldn't do it, though. Chickened out at the last second. Anyway, he got unwound, and I wound up with his arm."

Grace processes it and shakes her head, getting a little red in the face. "You're making that up. You think I'm dumb enough to believe the Akron AWOL would take an Unwind's arm?"

"I didn't have a choice. They slapped this thing on while I was in a coma."

"You're lying."

"Untie me and I'll show you the scar where it was grafted on."

"Nice try."

"Yeah, it would have worked better if I had my shirt on and you couldn't see the scar for yourself."

Grace comes closer, kneeling down, examining Connor's shoulder. "I'll be damned. It *is* a grafted arm!"

"Yeah, and it hurts like hell. You can't tie a grafted arm back like this."

Grace looks at him—maybe searching Connor's eyes the way Connor searched hers.

"You got new eyes, too?" Grace asks.

"Just one of them."

"Which one?"

"Right. The left one is mine."

"Good," says Grace. "'Cause I already decided that's the

honest one." She reaches behind Connor for the ropes. "I'm not gonna untie you—I'm not that dumb—but I'll loosen the rope on this arm a little so it don't pull at your shoulder so much."

"Thank you, Grace." Connor feels the rope loosen. He wasn't lying. His shoulder was burning from the strain. As the rope gives, Connor tugs his hand. It slips through the loop, and his hand—Roland's hand—is free. It closes reflexively into a fist ready to swing. Connor's own instinct is to do it, but Risa's voice, ever present in his head, as if it has been transplanted there, stops him. *Think*, Risa would say. *Don't do anything rash.*

The fact is, only one of his hands is free. Will he be able to knock Grace out with one blow, then free his other hand and escape before Argent gets back? In his current state, will he be able to outrun the two of them, and what will the consequences be if he fails? All this flashes through Connor's mind in a fraction of a second. Grace still stares at Connor's freed fist in shock, not knowing what to do. Connor makes a decision. He takes a deep breath, loosens his fingers, and shakes his hand. "Thanks. That feels much better," he says. "Now quick. Tie up my hand again before Argent comes back—only not as tight this time."

Relieved, Grace redoes the bonds, and Connor allows her to do it without resisting. "You won't tell him I did that, will you?" Grace asks.

Connor smiles at her. It's easier to pull off a smile for Grace than for Argent. "It'll be our secret."

In a few moments, Argent returns with a BLT heavy on mayo and light on bacon. He feeds it to Connor by hand, never noticing the subtle shift in dynamics. Grace now trusts Connor more than she trusts her own brother.

2 · Clapper

The clapper has misgivings, but he's beyond the point of no return.

For many months before today, he had suffered on the streets. The things he had to do to survive were horrifying and demoralizing. They were dehumanizing to the point that there wasn't much left of him that felt remotely human anymore. He had surrendered to the shame of it, resigning himself to a marginal life on the seediest back streets of Sin City.

He'd gone to Las Vegas thinking an AWOL Unwind could more easily disappear there, but Las Vegas treats no one who lands there well. Only those who are free to leave get VIP treatment—and although most of them leave with empty pockets, it's better than remaining as an empty shell.

By the time he was recruited, the clapper had lost his ability to care. It had been pounded out of him on every level. He had been perfectly ripe for picking.

"Come with me," the recruiter had said. "I'll teach you how to make them pay."

By "them," he meant everyone. The universal "not me" who was responsible for ruining his life. Everyone else was at fault. Everyone must pay. The recruiter understood that, and so the deal was made.

Now, two months later, he walks gingerly with the girl of his dreams into a neighborhood sports club in Portland, Oregon. It's far from Las Vegas, far from what had once been his life before that. The farther the better. This new life, brief though it may be, will be bright. It will be loud. It will be impossible to ignore. This random target was chosen for them by someone farther up the clapper chain. Funny, but he never thought of clappers as being so organized—but there is definitely a structure and a hierarchy behind the chaos. It gives him some comfort to think that there's a method behind the madness.

His is a cell of two. He and the girl have been prepped, primed, and pointed by a gung-ho trainer who must have been a motivational speaker in a previous life.

"Randomness will change the world," they'd been told. "Your act will be smiled upon years from now—and in the meantime, your revenge will be sweet."

The clapper cares less about changing the world and more about revenge. He knows he would have died ignobly on the streets, but now at least his bitter end will have meaning. It will be under his control by the sheer power of his applause. Or is he just deluding himself?

"Are you ready for this?" the girl asks as they approach the gym.

He doesn't share his doubts with her. He wants to be strong for her. Resolute. Brave. "Maximum carnage," he says. "Let's do this."

They go into the gym. He holds the door for her, and she smiles at him. Such smiles and gentle moments between them is the furthest their relationship will ever go. They wanted more, but it was not to be. Their explosive blood had made intimacy an impossibility.

"Can I help you?" asks the guy at the front desk.

"We'd like to talk to someone about a gym membership."

"Excellent! Let me get someone to help you."

The girl takes a deep, shuddering breath. The boy holds her hand. Gently. Always gently, because you don't always need a detonator to set yourself off. The detonators make it quick and clean, but accidents do happen.

"I want to be with you when we . . . complete our mission," she tells him.

"Me too, but we can't. You know that. I promise I'll be thinking about you." Their orders are to be at least ten meters apart. The farther apart they are, the more effective they'll be when their mission completes.

A ripped dude with an expensive smile approaches them. "Hi, my name is Jeff. I'm the new member coordinator. And you are?"

"Sid and Nancy," the clapper says. The girl chuckles nervously. He could have said Tom and Jerry; it didn't matter. He could even have given their real names, but fake names somehow add to the authenticity of the deception.

"Come on. Let me give you both the grand tour." Jeff's wholesome smile is reason enough to blow the place sky-high.

He leads them past the manager's office. The manager, on the phone, glances out at the clapper, catching a moment of eye contact. The clapper looks away, feeling read. He feels as if every stranger he sees can read his intentions, as if his hands are already spread wide, ready to swing together. But the manager has a real air of suspicion. The clapper moves out of his sight range quickly.

"Over here we have our free weight area. Our resistance machines are to the right. All state of the art, of course, with holographic entertainment consoles." Neither of them is listening, but Jeff doesn't seem to notice. "Our aerobics deck is upstairs." Jeff beckons for them to follow him up the stairs.

"You go, Nancy," the clapper says. "I'm going to check out the free weights." They share a brief nod. Here is where they put distance between themselves. Here is where they say good-bye.

He moves away from the stairs and toward the free weight area. It's five o'clock—a crowded time. Does he feel remorse for coming at this time of day? Only when he looks at people's faces, so he tries not to. They are not people—they are ideas. They are just extensions of the enemy. Besides, he didn't choose to come at the gym's most crowded time. They were told to come precisely now, precisely on this day—and when an event is this big, it's easy to hide behind "I'm just following orders."

Stepping behind a pillar, he reaches into his pocket and pulls out the circular Band-Aid-like detonators, affixing them to his palms. This is real. This is going down. *Oh my God. Oh my God—*

And as if to echo his thoughts, he hears, "Oh Jesus."

He looks up to see the manager standing there, catching him with the penny-sized detonators glaring from the clapper's palms like stigmata—there's no mistaking what he means to do.

The manager grabs his wrists, keeping his hands apart.

"Let go of me!"

"There's something you need to know before you do this!" the manager hisses in a loud whisper. "You think this is random, but it's not. You're being used!"

"Let go or I swear—"

"You'll what? Blow me up? That's what they want. I'm an organizer with the Anti-Divisional Resistance. Whoever sent you here has been targeting us! This isn't about chaos. It's about taking us out! You're working for the wrong side!"

"There are no sides!"

He pulls away, ready to swing his hands together . . . but suddenly not as ready as he was a moment ago. "You're ADR?"

"I can help you!"

"It's too late for that!" He can feel his adrenaline surge. He can feel his heartbeat in his ears and wonders if a pounding heart is enough to detonate him.

"We can clean your blood! We can save you!"

"You're lying!" But he knows it's possible. They disarmed Lev Calder, didn't they? But then the clappers came after him and tried to kill him for not clapping.

Finally one of the various self-absorbed weight lifters notices the nature of the conversation and says, "Clappers?" and backs away. "CLAPPERS!" he yells, and makes a beeline to the door. Others quickly size up the situation, and the panic begins—but the manager doesn't take his eyes off the clapper.

"Let me help you!"

Suddenly an explosion rocks the gym, and the cardio deck comes crashing down upon the first floor. She did it! She did it! She's gone, and he's still here.

Bloody people stumble past him coughing, wailing, and the manager grabs him again almost hard enough to detonate him. "You don't have to follow her! Be your own man. Fight for the right side!"

And although he wants to believe there *is* a right side—that this hint of hope is real, and not false—his head is as confused as the burning rubble still raining down around him. Can he betray her? Can he close the door that she opened and refuse to finish what she has begun?

"I can get you to a place of safety. No one has to know you didn't detonate!"

"Okay," he says, making his decision. "Okay."

The manager breathes a gasping sigh of relief, letting him go—and the instant he does, the clapper holds his hands wide and swings them together.

"Nooo!"

And he's gone, along with the ADR organizer, the rest of the gym, and any question of hope.

3 · Cam

The world's first composite human being is in black-tie attire.

His tailored tuxedo is of the highest quality. He looks handsome. Impressive. Imposing. He looks older in the tux—but as age is a fuzzy concept for Camus Comprix, he can't quite say how old he should look.

"Give me a birthday," he says to Roberta as she works on his tie. Apparently of all the sundry bits and pieces of kids in his head, not a single one of them knew how to tie a bow tie. "Assign me an age."

Roberta is the closest thing he will ever have to a mother. She certainly dotes on him like one. "Choose your own," she tells him as she tucks, tugs, and tightens the bow tie. "You know the day you were rewound."

"False start," Cam says. "Every part of me existed before I was rewound, so it's not a day to celebrate."

"*Every* part of *everyone* exists before they are presented to the world as an individual."

"Born, you mean."

"Born," Roberta admits. "But birthdays are random. Babies come early; babies come late. Defining one's life by the day one was cut from an umbilical cord is completely arbitrary."

"But they *were* born," Cam points out. "Which means *I* was born. Just not all at the same time, and to multiple mothers."

"Very true," says Roberta, stepping back to admire him. "Your logic is as impeccable as your looks."

Cam turns to look at himself in the mirror. The many symmetrical shades of his hair have been cut and combed into a perfect style. The various skin tones bursting forth from a single point in the center of his forehead only add to the stunning nature of his looks. His scars are no longer scars, but hairline seams. Exotic, rather than horrible. The pattern of his skin, his hair, his whole body is beautiful.

So why would Risa abandon me?

"Lockdown," he says reflexively, then clears his throat and tries to pretend he didn't say it. Lockdown is the word that comes out of him lately whenever he wants to purge a thought from his mind. He can't stop himself from saying it. The word brings an image of iron blast doors falling into place, locking the thought in, refusing to give it purchase anywhere in his mind. Lockdown has become a way of life for Cam.

Unfortunately, Roberta knows exactly what the word means.

"October tenth," Cam says quickly, before Roberta has a chance to commandeer the conversation. "My birthday will be October tenth—Columbus Day." What could be more appropriate than a day commemorating the discovery of a land and people who were already there and didn't need discovering? "I will be eighteen on the tenth of October."

"Splendid," says Roberta. "We'll throw you a party. But right now we have another party that requires our attention." She gently takes him by his shoulders, forcing him to face her, and she adjusts the angle of his tie the way she might straighten a picture on the wall. "I'm sure I don't need to tell you how important this gala is."

"You don't, but you will anyway."

Roberta sighs. "It's not about damage control anymore, Cam," she tells him. "Risa Ward's betrayal was a setback, I'll admit, but you've moved past it with flying colors. And that's all I'll say on the matter." But apparently not, because she adds, "Public scrutiny is one thing, but now you are under the scrutiny of those who actually make things happen in this world.

You cut a striking image in that tuxedo. Now show them you are as glorious inside as out."

"Glory is subjective."

"Fine. Then subject them to it."

Cam looks out of the window to see their limousine has arrived. Roberta grabs her purse, and Cam, always the gentleman, holds the door for her as they leave Proactive Citizenry's lavish Washington town house and head into a steamy July night. Cam suspects that the powerful organization owns residences in every major city throughout the nation—maybe throughout the world.

Why has Proactive Citizenry put so much of their money and influence behind me? Cam often wonders. The more they give him, the more he resents it, because it makes his captivity increasingly apparent. They have elevated him on a pedestal, but Cam has come to understand that a pedestal is nothing more than an elegant cage. No walls, no locks, but unless one has wings to fly away, one is trapped. A pedestal is the most insidious prison ever devised.

"A penny for your thoughts," Roberta asks coyly as they pull onto the beltway.

Cam grins, but doesn't look at her. "I think Proactive Citizenry can afford more than a penny." And he shares none of his thoughts with her, regardless of the cost.

It's dusk as the limo rides along the Potomac. Across the river, bright lights already illuminate the monuments of DC. Scaffolding surrounds much of the Washington Monument, while the Army Corp of Engineers struggles to correct the pronounced tilt it's taken on over the past few decades. Bedrock erosion and seismic shift has given the city its own leaning tower. "From Lincoln's chair, it leans to the right," political pundits have been known to say, "but from the Capitol steps, it leans to the left."

33

This is Cam's first time in DC—but he has memories of being here nonetheless. A memory of riding a bike down the paths of the National Mall with a sister who was clearly umber. Another memory of a vacation with parents of Japanese descent, who are livid that they can't contain the irascible behavior of their little boy. He has a color-blind memory of a huge Vermeer canvas hanging in the Smithsonian—and a parallel memory of the same work of art, but in full color.

Cam has come to enjoy comparing and contrasting his various recollections. Memories of the same places or objects should be identical, but they never are, because the various Unwinds represented in his brain each saw the world around them in very different ways. At first Cam had found this confusing and disconcerting—a cause for panic and alarm—but now he finds it curiously illuminating. The varied textures of his memories give him mental parallax on the world. A sort of depth perception beyond the limited point of view of a single individual. He can tell himself that and it would be true—yet beneath it, there is a primal anger brewing at each point of conversion. Each time merging memories contradict, the dissonance reverberates to the very core of his being, as a reminder that not even his memories are his own.

The limo turns up the semicircular driveway of a plantation-style mansion that is either very old or very new but made to look old, like so many things are. Town cars and limos line the driveway. Valets scramble to park the cars of the nonchauffeured guests.

"You know you're in the highest echelon of society," Roberta remarks, "when having to valet park a car is an embarrassment."

Their limo stops, and the door is opened for them.

"Shine, Cam," Roberta tells him. "Shine like the star you are." She gives him a gentle kiss on the cheek. Only after they step out and her attention is on the path ahead of them, does he wipe off the remnants of the kiss with the back of his hand.

"Is it true what they say about you?" the pretty girl asks.

She wears a dress that's a little too short for an event filled with gowns and tuxedos. She's one of the only people Cam's age at the gala.

"That depends," he tells her. "What do they say?"

They are in a den in the mansion, away from the hustle and bustle of the crowded party. There's a wall of leather-bound legal books, a comfortable chair, and a desk too large to be of any practical use. Cam wandered in here to escape from "shining" for the various rich and powerful guests. The girl had followed him in.

"They say that everything you do, you do like no other."

She moves toward him from the door. "They say that every part of you was handpicked to be perfect in every way."

"That's not me," he says slyly. "I believe it's Mary Poppins who claims to be practically perfect in every way."

She chuckles as she gets closer to him. "You're funny, too."

She is beautiful. Clearly she is also starstruck. She wants to bask in his light, and he wonders if he should let her.

"What's your name?"

"Miranda," she says gently. "Can I . . . touch your hair?"

"Only if I can touch yours . . ."

She reaches for him tentatively at first, patting his hair, then running her fingers through the varied textures and colors.

"You're so . . . exotic. I thought I'd be frightened to see you in person, but I'm not."

She smells of vanilla and wildflowers—a scent that pings his memories in several nonspecific places. It's a popular perfume among popular girls.

"Risa Ward is a bitch," she tells him. "The way she dumped you on national TV. The way she played you, then tossed you away. You deserve someone better. Someone who can appreciate you."

"Lockdown!" Cam blurts.

She smiles and saunters to the door. "There's no lock," she says, "but I can certainly close it."

She shuts the door and is back in his airspace in an instant. He can't even remember her moving there; it's like she dissolved from the door into his embrace. He's not thinking clearly. There's too much input to handle, but for once that's a good feeling.

She undoes his bow tie. He knows he can't tie it again, but he doesn't really care. He holds her in his arms, and she leans forward, kissing him. When she pulls away from the kiss, it's only for a moment to catch her breath. She looks at him with intense mischief in her gaze. She leans in for another kiss that is far more explorative than the first. Cam finds he's no slouch when it comes to this. Muscle memory, he supposes, for the tongue is most definitely a muscle.

She pulls away again, even more breathless than before. Then she presses her cheek against his, with her lips by his ear, and she whispers so quietly he can barely hear her.

"I want to be your first," she says. She presses closer to him, the fabric of her dress hissing on the fine weave of his tuxedo.

"You seem like a girl who gets what she wants."

"Always," she tells him.

Cam didn't come here looking for this. He could turn her away, but why? Why refuse this when it's offered to him so freely? Besides, he finds that the mention of Risa has made him defiant. It's made him want even more to be here in the moment with this girl whose name he's already forgotten.

He kisses her again, matching her building aggression.

That's when the door swings open.

Cam freezes. The girl steps away from him, but it's too late. Standing in the doorway is a distinguished man looking even more intimidating in his tuxedo than Cam looks in his.

"Get your hands off my daughter!"

As his hands are already off the man's daughter, there's not much more he can do but stand there and let this play out.

"Daddy, please! You're embarrassing me!"

Now others arrive, curious at the building drama. The man's glare never falters, as if he's practiced it professionally. "Miranda, get your coat. We're leaving."

"Daddy, you're overreacting. You always overreact!"

"You heard me."

Now waterworks abound. "Why do you always have to ruin everything!" Miranda wails, then stomps out in tears, wearing her humiliation like a war wound.

Cam is not sure how to respond to all this, so he doesn't. He slips his hands into his pockets, lest he still be accused of having them all over Miranda as she races down the hall, and he keeps a resolute poker face. The furious man looks like he might spontaneously combust.

Roberta arrives, hesitates, and asks, "What's going on here?" She sounds uncharacteristically weak and powerless, which means this must be even worse than Cam thinks it is.

"I'll tell you what's going on," growls the man. "Your . . . *thing* . . . was trying to have its way with my daughter."

"Actually, *she* was trying to have her way with *me*," Cam says. "And she was succeeding."

That brings forth muted laughter from several in attendance.

"Do you expect me to believe that?" He stalks forward, and Cam pulls his hands out of his pockets, ready to defend himself if necessary.

Roberta tries to come between them. "Senator Marshall, if you'll just—"

But he pushes her aside and wags a finger in Cam's face. Part of Cam wants to reach up and break that finger. Part of him wants to bite it. Another part wants to turn and run, and yet another part wants to laugh. Cam reins in all those conflicting impulses and holds his ground without flinching as the senator says:

"If you come anywhere near my daughter, I will see to it that you are taken apart piece by bloody piece. Do I make myself clear?"

"Any clearer," says Cam, "and you'd be invisible."

The senator backs off and turns his rage to Roberta. "Don't

come looking for my support for your little 'project,'" he hisses, "because you won't get it." Then he storms out, leaving an air of oppressive silence in his wake.

Roberta speechlessly looks to Cam with helpless disbelief. *Why?* Those eyes say. *Why have you spat on all I've tried to give you? You're ruined, Cam. We're ruined. I'm ruined.*

And then in the silence one man begins to applaud. He's slightly older and larger around the middle than Senator Marshall. His heavy hands let loose a frightful peal as he brings them together. Clappers must envy him.

"Well done, son!" says the large man with a heavy Southern drawl. "I've been trying to get under Marshall's skin for years, and you've managed to do it in a single evening. Kudos to you!" Then he lets loose a grand guffaw, and the tension bursts like a soap bubble.

One woman in a shimmering gold gown and a champagne glass in hand puts her arm around Cam and speaks with a slight alcoholic slur. "Trust me. You're not the first boy Miranda Marshall has tried to devour whole. The girl is an anaconda!"

That makes Cam giggle. "Well, she did try to wrap herself around me."

Laughter from all those gathered. The large man shakes his hand. "But we haven't properly met, Mr. Comprix. I'm Barton Cobb, senior senator from Georgia." Then he turns to Roberta, who looks as if she's just stepped off a roller coaster. "You have my unconditional support for your project, Miss Griswold, and if Marshall doesn't like it he can stick it where the sun don't shine 'cept Tuesday." He guffaws again, and as Cam looks around, it seems as if the entire party has moved into the library. Introductions are made—even people he's already shaken hands with step forward to introduce themselves again.

Cam had arrived at the party as a novelty—a decorative mascot to add some flavor—but now he's the very center of everyone's attention. That's a role he's much more at home with, and so the more attention he gets, the more relaxed he becomes. The more spotlights, the fewer shadows.

Roberta is also at her best when he's the center of attention. A tiger moth beating about his light. He wonders if she has the slightest clue how much he despises everything she stands for. And the odd thing of it is, he doesn't even know what she really stands for, which makes him despise it even more.

"Cam," she says, gently taking his elbow and manipulating him toward a man in uniform who clearly doesn't move for anyone. "This, Cam, is General Edward Bodeker."

Cam shakes the man's hand and gives a polite obligatory bow. "An honor, sir."

"Mutual," says the general. "I was just asking Miss Griswold if you've considered a future in the military."

"I don't rule out anything, sir," Cam tells him. It's his favorite nonanswer.

"Good. We could put a young man like you to good use."

"Well, sir, the only problem with that is that there are no 'young men like me.'"

And the general laughs warmly, clapping a fatherly hand on his shoulder.

The tension from just a few minutes ago is completely forgotten. Apparently he's made the right enemy, because now he has many, many friends.

4 · Night Manager

It's a disease, plain and simple, rotting out the world from the inside out. Clappers! Goddamn clappers. Everywhere. A disease.

The night manager of the 7-Eleven on Palm Desert Drive has nothing much to do for most of his nights but mull over the state of his middle-aged life, the modern-age world, and the tabloids, which, aside from alien and dead celebrity sightings, just love to report on clapper carnage. Blood and gore at a fifth-grade reading level for your entertainment and pleasure. An office building taken out here, a restaurant blown sky-high. The latest clapper attack was at a freaking fitness club, for God's sake. They just walked into the gym without as much as a hello-how'dya-do, and boom! Poor bastards working out didn't stand a chance. Not much you can do to escape lead weights flying like shrapnel.

At 2:15 a.m. a customer shuffles in and buys a ToXin Energy drink and a pack of gum. Shady-looking guy. But then, anyone who shows up at a roadside 7-Eleven at this time of night looks questionable and has got a story you don't want to hear.

The man notices the tabloid the night manager is reading. "Crazy, huh? Clappers. Where do they come from, right?"

"I know where they go," says the night manager. "They oughta take all the clappers and AWOLs and ferals, put 'em on a plane and crash it."

He had thought he'd found a sympathetic ear, but the customer looks at him with shock. "All of 'em, huh? Didn't a planeload of AWOLs go down in the Salton Sea a couple of weeks ago?"

"Good riddance. I wish I'd been close enough to see it." There's an awkward silence between them. "That'll be $5.65."

The customer pays, but makes a point of making chilly eye contact with the night manager as he drops all of his change in the charity box for Runaway Rescue, which helps straighten out feral teens before someone can shove an unwind order up their worthless asses. It's a cause the night manager despises, but keeping that charity box there is company policy.

The customer leaves, and the night manager has something else to grumble to himself about. Bleeding hearts. Way too many people are not willing to take a hard line on the unwindable. Sure there are ballot measures up the wazoo this year. Shall we set aside X billion to construct new harvest camps? Yes or no? Shall we allow for partial unwinding and slow sequential division? Yes or no? Even the constitutionality of the Cap-17 law is being challenged.

But with the population evenly divided in their support of unwinding, it all comes down to that huge 30 percent who either don't have an opinion or are afraid to voice it. "The wishy-washy masses," the night manager calls them, too weak to take a stand. If the glacier huggers and feral forgivers start to outnumber sensible folk, all the hard-line unwinding legislation could fail, and then what?

At 2:29 a woman with more baggage under her eyes than stuffed in her cluttered car buys chips and flashes a medical tobacco license for a pack of Camels.

"Have a good one," he says as she leaves.

"Too late for that."

Her rust bucket of a Volkswagen drives off with a backfire and spews thick blue smoke that the night manager can smell inside. Some people oughta be unwound just to protect the environment. It makes him chuckle. Protect the environment—who's the glacier hugger now?

The night becomes unusually quiet. Nothing but crickets and the occasional rumble of a passing car. Usually he enjoys an empty shop, but tonight there's an air of tension about that silence. Intuition being a night manager's most useful tool, he checks beneath the counter to make sure that his sawed-off shotgun is there. He's not supposed to have one, but a man's gotta protect himself.

At 3:02 the ferals descend on the 7-Eleven out of nowhere, pouring in through the door. Dozens and dozens of them, swarming like a cloud of locusts as they grab things from the aisles. The night manager reaches for the shotgun, but before he can grab it, there's a gun aimed at his face, and another, and another. The three kids hold their aim steady.

"Hands where I can see them," one of them says. It's a tall girl with short hair and man shoulders. She definitely looks tough enough to blow his brains out without a second thought. Still he says, "Go to hell!"

It makes her smile. "Be a good little lowlife and do as you're told, and you might live to sell more chips tomorrow."

Reluctantly, he puts his hands up and watches as kids flood in and out, filling trash bags with everything they can get their hands on. All the drinks from the coolers, the snacks from the aisles, even the toiletries. Then suddenly he realizes who these kids must be. These must be the survivors from that plane that went down in the Salton!

A kid saunters in wearing an unpleasant musk of superiority. Clearly he's the one in charge. He's not tall, but he's muscular, with a mop of red hair with much darker roots. There's also something about his left hand. It's bandaged with layer after layer of gauze, as if he had slammed it in a car door, or worse. He comes up to the counter, and offers the night manager a smile.

"Don't mind us," he says jovially. "We'll be on our way in a minute. Your convenience store was just too convenient to pass up."

The cashier would spit in his face if he thought it wouldn't get him killed.

"Now comes the moment where I ask you to open the register and you point to the sign that says 'Cashier Does Not Have More Than Twenty Dollars in Change,' but I make you open it anyway."

The night manager opens the cash drawer to reveal the sign is true to its word. "See? All the money goes into the cash box, and I don't have a key, scumbag."

The kid is unfazed. "Your attitude reminds me of our pilot. If you'd like to visit him, he's at the bottom of the Salton Sea."

"We could send you there too," says the girl, still holding her gun on him.

The kid in charge reaches over to the cash drawer and grabs a dime. Then he grabs a few lotto scratchers, lays them on the counter, and with his good hand, he uses the coin to scratch away the silver boxes. All the while, the three other kids keep their guns aimed at the night manager's face, and the swarm of kids behind them continue their relentless ransack, carrying everything off in their greedy little arms.

"Look at that!" says the kid in charge. "I won five bucks!" Then he flicks the winning scratcher card at the cashier. "Keep it," he says. "My gift to you. Buy yourself something nice."

Then he leaves, followed by the rest of his brood. Only the girl with the gun remains until everyone else is gone; then she backs out, keeping the gun trained on the night manager until she's out the front door. The second she leaves, he goes for the rifle and hurries out after them. He fires into the dark at the retreating shapes, but no one goes down. He wasn't fast enough. He screams after them, curses, swears he'll get them, but knows he won't and that just angers him even more.

He turns to go back into the store and just stares. There's virtually nothing left. The store hasn't just been robbed. It's been gutted of everything not nailed down. They chewed through the place like piranhas.

There on the floor, having fallen behind the counter, is the Runaway Rescue box. To hell with it—the night manager reaches in and pockets whatever money it has. The ferals it tries to save don't deserve that money any more than these

AWOLs do, and he'll be damned if he'll let them get any of it. Lock 'em up, cut 'em up. Let them serve society in pieces rather than tear it down whole.

Shall we give more power to the Juvenile Authority? Yes or no? There's no question where the night manager's vote is going.

5 · Lev

He should never have agreed to let Connor go off alone to get them a car. He wasn't back by the afternoon, or by the evening, or during the night. Now it's dawn of the following day. Connor's been gone for twenty-four hours, and Lev's anxiety grows, as well as his aggravation at both himself and at Connor. A better plan would have been to tail Connor at a distance so that if something did go wrong, at least Lev would see it and would know. Now it's the uncertainty that's killing him. He gets out his frustration by kicking the side of a rusty old industrial dryer lying half-buried in the weeds. He has to stop because the thing rings out like a bell with each kick, and he knows people can probably hear it for miles. He sits down in the shade of the dryer, trying to figure out what to do now. He has very few choices. If Connor doesn't show up soon, he's going to have to go on alone to Ohio, to find an antique store where he's never been, to speak to an old woman he doesn't know about a man who disappeared before Lev was born.

"Sonia could be the key to everything," Connor had told Lev. Connor explained how the old woman—a key player in the Anti-Divisional Resistance—ran a safe house for AWOL Unwinds, getting them off the street. She had given shelter to Connor and Risa during those early days on the run. What Connor hadn't known at the time was that her husband was

Janson Rheinschild—the scientist whose advances in medical science made unwinding possible . . . and a man who was meticulously and systematically erased from history by the very organization he founded to prevent the misuse of his technology.

"If she knows something worth knowing," Lev had asked Connor on their long drive from Arizona, "why didn't Proactive Citizenry make her disappear as well?"

"Maybe they don't see her as a threat," Connor had answered. "Or maybe they don't know she's alive any more than they know I'm alive."

Proactive Citizenry isn't exactly a household name to Lev. He's heard of them, though. Everyone's *heard* of them, but no one pays much attention. They're just one of many charitable organizations you hear about but have no idea what they actually do. Or how powerful they really are.

No matter how powerful Proactive Citizenry is, though, one thing is certain: They're afraid of Janson Rheinschild. The question is, why?

"If you want to mess with things," Connor had said, "that's where we start."

But as far as Lev is concerned, he's messed—and has been messed with—enough. He had turned himself into a bomb but chose not to detonate. He had been the target of a clapper vengeance attack. He had been coddled and sequestered and treated like a god by a mansion full of tithes saved from their unwindings. And he had entered a battle zone to save a kid whom he considered to be his truest, and maybe only, friend.

With all that behind him, what Lev wants more than anything else is normality. His dreams aren't of greatness or of power, wealth, or fame. He's had all of those things at one time or another. No, what he wants is to be a kid in high school, with no more worries than what teachers he'll get stuck with and whether or not he'll make the baseball team.

Sometimes his fantasies of the simple life include Miraco-lina, the tithe who was so determined to be unwound, she despised him and everything he stood for. At least at first. His current fantasies put them at the same suburban school—it doesn't matter which suburb. They do class projects together. Go to the movies. Make out on the couch when her parents aren't home. She cheers for him at his baseball games, but not so loudly that she's heard above the crowd, because she's not that type.

He has no idea where she is now, or if she's even alive. And now he's facing the same uncertainty with Connor. Lev has come to realize that he's strong, but there's only so much he can take.

Lev resolves to wait one more hour before heading out alone. Unlike Connor, he doesn't know how to hot-wire a car. Technically, he doesn't know how to drive either, although he's done it before with marginal success. His best bet for getting to Ohio would be to stow away, which means going into town and finding a truck, bus, or train headed in the right direction. No matter what, though, it would put him at serious risk. He broke the terms of his parole, so he's a fugitive. If he's caught, there's no telling what will happen to him.

Lev is still hemming and hawing, building up the fortitude it will take to leave Connor behind, when a visitor arrives. Lev does not have the option of hiding—he's spotted the second the car pulls up and the woman steps out. Rather than run-ning, Lev calmly goes inside the old trailer and looks through the drawers until he finds a knife large enough to do damage but small enough to conceal.

Lev has never stabbed anyone. He had once, in a moment of sheer fury, threatened to beat a man and woman with a base-ball bat. They had unwound their son—and a part of their son's brain had come back in another kid's body, begging their forgiveness.

This is different though, Lev tells himself. This isn't about righteous rage; it's about survival. He resolves he will use the knife only in self-defense.

Lev comes out of the trailer but stands on the lip of the doorway because he knows it makes him look taller. His visitor stands ten feet away, shifting weight from one leg to the other and back again. She's in her early twenties by the look of it. Tall and just a little pudgy. Her face is reddened from the sun, probably from driving around in the convertible—a T-Bird in a condition too poor for the car to be considered classic. There's an off-center bruise on her forehead.

"This is private property," Lev says with as much authority as he can muster.

"Not yours, though," says his visitor. "It's Woody Beeman's— but Woody's been dead for two years now."

Lev pulls a fiction out of thin air. "I'm his cousin. We inherited the place. Right now my dad's in town renting a forklift to get rid of all this junk and clean the place up."

But then the visitor says: "Connor didn't tell me it would be you. He just said a friend was here. He shoulda told me it was you."

All of Lev's spontaneous lies evaporate. "Connor sent you? Where is he? What's happened?"

"Connor says he wants you to go on without him. He's staying with us here in Heartsdale. I won't tell no one you were here. So you can go."

The fact that Connor has managed to get Lev a message gives Lev a wave of intense relief. But the message itself makes no sense. Clearly it's a distress signal. Connor is in trouble.

"Who's 'us'?" Lev asks.

The visitor shakes her head and kicks the ground almost

like a child might. "Can't tell you that." She looks at Lev and squints against the rising sun. "Can you still blow up?" she asks.

"No."

The woman shrugs. "Right. Anyway, I promised I'd tell you what I told you, and I did. Now I gotta go before my brother finds out I'm gone. Nice to meet you, Lev. It is Lev, right? Lev Calder?"

"Garrity. I changed my name."

She nods approvingly. "Figures. Guess you wanted no part of a family that would raise you to want your own unwinding." Then she turns and lumbers back to the car.

Lev considers going after her—telling her he wants to stay in Heartsdale too—but even if she falls for it, getting in that car would be a bad idea. Whatever trouble Connor is in, it would be folly to volunteer for more of the same.

Instead Lev hurries to the old crumbling school bus and climbs to the hood and then to the roof, avoiding patches that have rusted all the way through. From his high vantage point, he watches the T-Bird kick up dust on the dirt road until it turns left onto a paved road. Lev tracks it as long as he can until it disappears into Heartsdale. Now that he knows the general direction the T-Bird has gone, he can wander the streets until he finds it again.

Maybe Connor wants Lev to go on without him, but Connor knows Lev better than that.

---

thousands of seventeen-year-old incorrigibles back into the streets and severely limits the age for which parents can choose unwinding.

"Last week a boy on my block was stabbed by one of them on his way to school, and I'm afraid I'll be next.

"Call or write your congressperson today. Tell them you want the Cap-17 law repealed. Let's make the streets safe again for kids like me!"

—Sponsored by Mothers Against Bad Behavior

Lev heads out into the scorching day on his reconnaissance mission. He keeps his head low but his eyes wide open. The T-Bird, Lev had observed, was dirty enough to suggest it was left out in the elements instead of in a garage—but Heartsdale is a rat's warren rather than a grid, and a systematic search of the streets proves difficult.

By two in the afternoon, he's desperate enough to risk contact with the citizens of the town. He prepares himself by buying a Chevron baseball cap at a gas station and a pack of gum. He wears the cap to further hide his face and chews several sticks of gum until the sugar is blanched out. Then he spreads half of the gum wad in his upper gums above his front teeth and the other half in his lower gums. It's just enough to change the shape of his mouth without making him look too weird. Maybe his paranoia that he will be recognized is a little extreme, but as AWOL Unwinds are fond of saying, "Better safe than severed."

There's a Sonic that he had passed that morning, where pretty servers on roller skates bring food to parked cars, as they have done since the beginning of recorded fast-food history. If anyone knows the cars of this town, it will be the Sonic servers.

Lev goes to the walk-up window and orders a burger and

a slushy, faking an accent that sounds way too deep-South drawly to be from Kansas, but it's the best he can do.

After he gets his food, he sits at one of the outdoor tables and zeroes in on one of the roller girls who sits at the next table, texting between orders.

"Hey," says Lev.

"Hey," she says back. "Hot enough for ya?"

"Five more degrees, you can fry an egg on my forearm."

That makes her smile and look over at him. He can practically read her mind in her facial expressions. *He's not a regular. He's cute. He's too young. Back to texting.*

"Maybe you can help me," Lev says. "There was this car with a 'for sale' sign parked by the side of the road the other day, but now I can't find it."

"Maybe it sold," she suggests.

"Hope not. See, I'm gettin' my license in a couple of months. I was really hoping for that T-Bird. It's a green convertible. Do you know it?"

She continues texting for a moment, then says, "Only green convertible around here belongs to Argent Skinner. If he's selling it, he must be having a harder time than usual."

"Or maybe he's buying somethin' better."

She gives a dubious chuckle, and Lev gives her a winning smile with slightly puffy lips. She takes a moment to reassess, decides even with a driver's license he's still too young for her attention, and says, "He's on Saguaro Street, two blocks up from the Dairy Queen."

Lev thanks her and heads off with his burger and slushy. If he appears overeager, it'll just play into his cover story.

Having passed the DQ earlier that morning, he knows exactly where to go—but as he reaches the corner, he hears something that sounds out of place in a town like Heartsdale. The rhythmic chop of an approaching helicopter.

Even before it arrives, a series of police cars pull onto the street. Their sirens are off, but their speed speaks of urgency. There are more than a dozen vehicles. There are Juvey squad cars, black-and-whites, and unmarked cars as well. The helicopter, now overhead, begins to circle the neighborhood, and Lev gets a sick feeling deep in the pit of his gut.

Rather than following the cars, he comes at the scene from an adjacent street, cutting through a few backyards, so as not to be seen. Finally he finds himself peering through the slats of a wooden fence at an unkempt ranch-style house that is in the process of being surrounded.

A house with a green convertible T-Bird parked on the driveway.

6 · Connor

That same morning, Argent comes down with a TV and plugs it into the outlet attached to the single dangling light fixture.

"All the comforts of home," he happily tells Connor.

Argent, who must watch bad TV and infomercials all night long, didn't wake up until after Grace had been gone and back, delivering her message to Lev. "Mum's the word," she had said. Connor has never known anyone else who actually used that expression. Now, as she enters behind Argent, she gives Connor a surreptitious zipped-mouth gesture.

The little TV pulls in a weak wireless signal from the house that makes everything painful to watch.

"I'll figure out how to make it work better," Grace tells Conner.

"Thanks, Grace. I'd appreciate that." Not that Connor has any interest in watching TV, but showing Grace more appreciation than Argent shows her is key.

"No worries," Argent says. "We don't need a signal or cable to watch videos."

By Connor's reckoning, he's been in captivity for about twenty-four hours now. Lev better have gone on without him. An antique shop near the high school in Akron where they first got separated. That should be enough for Lev to find it.

Argent, who called in sick at the supermarket, spends the morning playing his favorite videos, his favorite music, his favorite everything for Connor.

"You've been out of circulation for a while," Argent tells him. "Gotta reeducate you on what's cutting-edge in the world," as if he thinks Conner was literally hiding under a rock for two years.

Argent's theatrical tastes lean toward violent. Argent's musical tastes lean toward dissonant. Connor's seen enough real violence not to be entertained by it much anymore. And as for music, knowing Risa has broadened his horizons.

"Once you let me out of this cellar," Connor tells Argent, "I'll take you to see bands that will blow you away."

Argent doesn't respond to that right away. Since yesterday, Connor's been mentioning things that they might do together. As buds. Connor suspects that whatever time frame Argent has in his head for Connor's conversion, the turning point has not yet been reached. Until it is, anything Connor says will be suspect.

Argent leaves Connor with Grace to run some errands, and she is quick to bring out a plastic chessboard, setting up the pieces. "You can play, right? Just tell me your move, and I'll make it for you," Grace tells him.

Connor knows the game but never had patience to learn strategy. He won't deny Grace the game, though, so he plays.

"Classic Kasparov opening," she says after four moves, suddenly not sounding low-cortical at all. "But it's no good against a Sicilian Defense."

Connor sighs. "Don't tell me you have a NeuroWeave."

"Hell no!" says Grace proudly. "The brain's all mine, such as it is. I just do good at games." And then she proceeds to trounce Connor with embarrassing speed.

"Sorry," says Grace as she sets up a second game.

"Never apologize for winning."

"Sorry," says Grace again. "Not for winning, but for being sorry for winning."

Throughout the next game, Grace gives a blow-by-blow analysis, pointing out all the moves Connor should have made and why.

"Don't worry about it," Grace says, capturing Connor's queen with a bishop hiding in plain sight. "Morphy made that slip against Anderssen, but still won the freaking match."

Connor isn't so lucky. Grace wipes the floor with him again. Actually, Connor would have been disappointed if she didn't.

"Who taught you to play?"

Grace shrugs. "Played against my phone and stuff." Then she adds, "I can't play games with Argent. He gets mad when I win, and even madder when he wins, because he knows I let him."

"Figures," Connor says. "Don't let me win."

Grace smiles. "I won't."

Grace leaves and returns with an old-fashioned backgammon board—it's a game Grace has to teach Connor how to play. She's not very good at explaining, but Connor gets the gist of it.

Argent comes back during the second game, and with a single finger, flips the board. Brown and white pieces scatter everywhere.

"Stop wasting the man's time," Argent tells Grace. "He doesn't want to do that."

"Maybe I do," Connor tells him, making sure to force a smile when he says it.

"No, you don't. Grace just wants to make you look stupider than her. And anyway, she's useless. She couldn't once get her game on in Las Vegas."

"I don't count cards," mumbles Grace morosely. "I just play games."

"Anyway, I got something much better than board games right here." And Argent shows Connor an antique glass pipe.

"Argie!" says Grace, a little breathless. "You shouldn't be using great-grandpa's bong!"

"Why not? It's mine now, isn't it?"

"It's an heirloom!"

"Yeah, well, form follows function," says Argent, once more completely missing the actual meaning of the expression. This time Connor doesn't bother to point it out.

"Wanna smoke some tranq?" Argent asks.

"I've been tranq'd enough," Connor tells him. "I don't need to smoke the stuff."

"No—see it's different when you smoke it. It doesn't knock you out. It just throws you for a loop." He pulls out a red and yellow capsule—the mildest kind used in tranq darts—and puts it in the bowl with some common yard cannabis. "C'mon, you'll like it," he says as he lights it.

Connor had done his share of this sort of thing before his unwind order was signed. Being hunted kind of killed his taste for it.

"I'll pass."

Argent sighs. "Okay, I'll admit something to you. It's always been one of my fantasies to do tranq with the Akron AWOL and talk some deep spiritual crap. Now you're actually here, so we have to do it."

"I don't think he wants to smoke tranq, Argie."

"Not your business," he snaps without even looking at Grace. Argent takes a hit from the pipe, then puts it over Connor's mouth, holding Connor's nose so he has no choice but to suck it in.

The physiological response is quick. In less than a minute, Connor's ears feel like they're shrinking. His head spins, and gravity seems to reverse directions a few times.

"You feeling it?"

Connor doesn't want to dignify him with a response. Instead he looks to Grace, who just sits helplessly on a sack of potatoes. Argent takes a second hit and forces Connor to do one as well.

As Connor's mind liquefies, memories of his life before unwinding come rushing back to him. He can almost hear his parents yelling at him and him yelling back. He can remember all the things—both legal and otherwise—that he did to numb the feeling of being troubled and troubling in a dull Ohio suburb.

He sees a little bit of his old self in Argent. Was Connor ever this much of a creep? No—he couldn't have been. And besides, he got past it, but Argent never did. Argent is maybe twenty, but he's still wallowing in the loser mud hole, letting it turn into a tar pit beneath his feet. The anger that Connor feels toward Argent dissolves into the liquid of his thoughts, spreading into a thin, wide layer of pity.

Argent takes another hit and reels. "Oh man, this is good stuff." He looks bleary-eyed at Connor. The combination of tranq and weed have made Connor emotional. He knows it's about his own past, but Argent takes it as a connection between them.

"We're the same, Connor," he says. "That's what you're thinking, right? I coulda been you. I can still be you." He starts giggling. "We can be you together."

The giggle is contagious. Connor finds himself giggling uncontrollably as Argent makes him take another hit.

"Gotta show you this," Argent says. "You'll get mad, but I gotta show you anyway." Then Argent pulls out his phone and shows him one of the pictures he took with Connor yesterday.

"Good one, right? I put it up on my Facelink profile."

"You . . . did what?"

"No big deal. Just for my friends and stuff." Argent giggles again. Connor giggles. Argent laughs, and Connor finds himself laughing hysterically.

"Do you know how bad that is, Argent?"

"I know, right?"

"No, you don't. The authorities. The Juvenile Authority. They've got facial tracing bots on the net."

"Bots, right."

"They'll take down this house. I'll get taken in. You'll both get five to ten for"—Connor can't control his laughter—"for aiding and abetting."

"Ooh, this is bad, Argie," says Grace from the corner.

"Who asked you?" Argent says. Being wasted doesn't temper his treatment of his sister.

"We gotta get out of here, Argent," Connor says. "We've gotta go now. We're both fugitives now."

"Yeah?" Argent still doesn't quite grasp it.

"We'll be on the run—you and me."

"Right. Screwing with the world."

"It was fated, just like you said."

"Fated."

"Argent and the Akron AWOL."

"Triple A!"

"But you have to untie me before they come to take us out!"

"Untie you . . ."

"There's no time. Please, Argent."

"I can really trust you?"

"Did we or did we not just do tranq together?"

That's enough to clinch the deal. Argent puts the pipe down, then goes behind Connor to undo his hands. Connor flexes his fingers and rolls his aching shoulders. He doesn't know whether the numbness in his arms is from being tied up or from the tranq.

"So where do we go?" Argent asks.

Connor's response is a glass pipe to the head. The pipe catches Argent just above his jaw and shatters, cutting the left side of Argent's face in at least three places. Argent's legs slip out from under him, and he hits the ground, groaning—still half-conscious, but unable to get up. His face gushes blood.

Grace stands staring at Connor, dumbfounded. "You broke great-grandpa's bong."

"Yeah, I know."

She doesn't go to help Argent. Instead she just looks at Connor, unsure whether she's just been betrayed or liberated.

"Is it true what you said about the police coming after us?" she asks.

Connor finds he doesn't need to answer. Because he can hear cars screeching to a halt outside and the steady beat of a helicopter overhead.

7 · Grace

Grace Eleanor Skinner fears death as much as anyone else. She fears pain even more. Once, a long time ago, Argie had made her go up to the high-dive platform while they were on vacation. She had squandered her willpower, mustering the guts for waterslides and such, but once she had made the climb to the ten-meter platform, she found herself weak. The pool below looked small and very far away. Hitting the water would hurt. As she stood on the edge, toes curled on the concrete lip, Argie had heckled her from down below.

"Don't be a stupid wimp, Gracie," he yelled for all to hear. "Don't think about it—just jump."

Behind her, others were getting impatient.

"Gracie, jump already! You're making everyone mad!" In the end, Grace had backed away and gone down the ladder in shame.

That's what this feels like today. Only now the threat is far more real. Argie's words from that day come back to her. *Don't think about it—just jump.* She follows the advice this time.

She pushes open the cellar door and bursts forth into the light of day. *This is a game*, she tells herself. *I win games.*

There are sharpshooters in the yard, but they don't see her at first. Their rifles are trained on the house, and the cellar is at the far back of the yard. They haven't gone in yet. The force is still positioning.

"Don't shoot! Don't shoot!" she yells, running out into the weedy yard, pulling the sharpshooters' attention. Immediately all the rifles turn to her. She doesn't think they're loaded with tranqs.

"Don't shoot," she says again. "It's this way. He's over here. Don't shoot!"

"On the ground!" one of the sharpshooters orders. "On the ground now!"

But no. Rule one—never allow capture unless it gives you an advantage.

"This way! Follow me!" She turns around, hands still flailing in the air as she runs back to the cellar. She half expects to be shot, but the other half wins; they don't fire. She races down the stairs into the cellar and waits. In a moment, the sharpshooters are there, covering one another, aiming at her and into the dim light of the cellar like soldiers in hostile territory. Although her heart feels like its exploding and she wants to scream, she says calmly, "You don't need guns. He's unarmed."

The marksmen still hold their ground, covering for an officer in a suit who follows them down the stairs.

"I knew it was a bad idea," Grace tells him. "I told Argie, but he wouldn't listen."

The officer sizes Grace up quickly, dismissively, just as everyone does. He guesses she's low-cortical and pats her shoulder. "You've done a good thing, miss."

More officers come into the cellar, making it crowded.

The figure tied to the pole is limp and semiconscious. The lead officer grabs his hair to lift his head and looks into his face.

"Who the hell is this?"

"My brother, Argent," Grace says. "I told him not to steal all this stuff from the supermarket. I told him he'd be in big trouble. I knocked him out and tied him up. I had to hurt him, see, so he wouldn't get shot. He's not resisting, right? So you'll go easy on him, won't you? Won't you? Tell me you'll go easy on him!"

The officer is no longer kind to Grace. Instead he glares at her. "Where's Lassiter?"

"Who?"

"Connor Lassiter!" Then he pulls out the picture of Argent with the Akron AWOL that he must have downloaded off the net.

"Oh, that? Argie made that up on the computer. It was a gag for his friends. Looks real, don't it?"

The other officers look to one another. The lead man is not pleased in the least. "I'm supposed to believe that?"

Grace shakes her brother's shoulder. "Argie, tell them."

Grace waits. Argie might have a lot of faults, but he's pretty good at self-preservation. Like Conner said, "aiding and debating"—or whatever it's called—is a serious crime. But only if you get caught.

Argent glares at Grace through his blood-clouded eyes. He radiates a sibling hatred that could kill if it were set free. "It's the truth," he growls. "Gag photo. For my friends."

It's not what the officer wants to hear. The other men chuckle behind his back.

"All right," he says, trying to seize what's left of his authority. "Untie him and get him to a hospital—and go through the house anyway. Find the original file. I want that picture analyzed."

Then they cut Argie's ropes and haul him out. He doesn't complain, doesn't resist, and he doesn't look at Grace.

After the others leave, one of the local deputies lingers, looking around at the stockpile of food. "He stole all this huh?"

"You still gonna arrest him?"

The deputy actually laughs. "Not today, Gracie."

Now she recognizes him as a man she went to school with. She recalls he used to tease her, but he seems to have mellowed—or at least redirected his bad into good.

"Thank you, Joey," she says, remembering his name, or at least hoping she remembered it right.

Grace thinks he's going to leave, but he takes a second look around at the stockpiles of emergency supplies. "That's an awful lot of potatoes."

Gracie hesitates and shrugs. "So? Potatoes is potatoes."

"Sometimes they are, and sometimes they're not." Then he pulls out his pistol, keeping his eyes trained on the large pile of potato sacks. "Out of the way, Gracie."

8 · Connor

The deputy only suspects Connor's presence, but doesn't really believe it. Clearly he doesn't give Grace credit enough to be harboring a fugitive. He thinks she's too dim-witted to pull it off. Once he finds Connor, he's just as likely to shoot him on the spot as not, because killing the Akron AWOL is just as good as capturing him. All Connor has in his favor now is the element of surprise, but that will be gone once he's discovered—so the instant the deputy begins poking around the potato sacks, Connor makes his move, lunging out of the sack he's hiding in, grabbing him by the ankles, and pulling his feet out from under him.

The man goes down, shouting in surprise, and his weapon, which he was not holding on to the way a deputy should, flies free. Grace goes for the weapon as the man lands in a stack of water bottles, sending them bouncing and rolling all over the ground.

Connor's arms are still wrapped around the guy's ankles, and he finds there's only one thing he can say under the circumstances.

"Nice socks."

Grace stands above them, aiming the gun at the deputy's chest. "Don't move and don't call to the others or I swear I'll shoot."

"Hold on there, Gracie," he says, trying to charm himself out this. "You don't want to do this."

"You shut up, Joey! I know what I do and don't want to do, and right now I want to see you in your underwear."

"What?"

62

Connor laughs, immediately getting what Grace has in mind. "You heard the lady. Strip down!" Connor wriggles the rest of the way out of the burlap sack and begins stripping down too, exchanging his clothes for the deputy's. While Connor had thought he'd be in charge of his own escape, he lets Grace take the lead. He's awed by what she's managed to accomplish up till now, and as the Admiral once told him, "a true leader never puts his ego ahead of his assets." And Grace Skinner is an asset of the highest order.

"What's the game, Grace?" Connor asks, as he puts on the deputy's pants.

"The kind we win," she says simply. Then to the deputy, "Go on—the shirt too."

"Grace . . ."

"No backtalk or I'll fill ya full a' lead!"

Connor chuckles at the silver-screen gangland cliché. "Technically bullets aren't made of lead anymore—and let's not even mention the ceramic ones they use on clappers."

"Yeah, yeah—no backtalk from you, either."

Joey the deputy, Connor notes, wears plain gray boxers that have seen better days, sitting limply under a pale belly that has probably gone from six-pack to kegger since his high school days. If Grace really did have an interest in seeing him in his skivvies, she must be disappointed.

"Where d'ya think you're gonna run, Gracie? You've never been out of Heartsdale. This guy'll dump you at the first rest stop, and then what?"

"Why should you care?"

"Put your back against the pole, please," Connor says. Connor ties him as tightly as he can, but then Grace grabs a jagged piece of the broken bong from the floor and puts it into the deputy's bound hands so that he can eventually cut himself free.

"They'll all be after you the second I get loose. You know that, don't you?"

Grace shakes her head. "Nope. The second you get loose, you're gonna scoot yourself upstairs and hide in the bushes."

"What?"

"That's right—you'll hide there till everyone else is gone. Then you're gonna stroll on over to the Publix parking lot and collect your car, because that's where we're gonna leave it, keys and all. Then you're gonna go about the rest of your day like nothin' ever happened, and when people ask where you were, you were out gettin' lunch."

"You're crazy! Why would I do that?"

"Because," says Grace, "if you don't keep this a secret, everyone in Heartsdale is gonna know you were outsmarted by dumb old Grace Skinner, and you'll be a laughingstock till the cows come home, and they ain't comin' home anytime soon!"

Connor just smiles, watching the deputy's face get beet-red and his lips purse into angry slits. "*You low-cortical bitch!*" he growls.

"I should shoot you in the kneecap for that," Grace says, "but I won't because I'm not that kinda girl."

Connor puts on the deputy's hat. "Sorry, Joey," he says. "It looks like you've been double-gammoned."

9 · Lev

It's only a hunch. And if he's wrong, his actions will make things worse—but he foolishly acts on his gut, because he *needs* it to be true. Because if it's not true, then Connor is done for.

There is a whole series of observations that are feeding into this hunch:

—The fact that the deputy comes from behind the house rather than walking out through the front door.

—The fact that he seems to intentionally avoid the other officers.

—The fact that his hat is pulled low on his forehead, shielding his face like a sombrero.

—The easy way he grips the arm of the woman he's taking into custody—the same one who came to give Lev the message. The deputy escorts her to a police car by the curb, and Lev can tell that her behavior is off too. It's as if she's anxious to get to the car, rather than resistant.

And then there's the way that officer walks—with one arm stiff and pressed to his side, as if he's in pain. Maybe from a wound on his chest.

The two get in the police car and drive off—and although Lev can't get a clear enough look at the deputy's face, the hunch is pinging Lev's brain on all frequencies. Only after the squad car has driven away does Lev convince himself that this is Connor in disguise, effecting a clever escape right beneath the noses of law enforcement.

Lev knows that when the car reaches the end of the street, it will have to turn right on Main, and now he's thankful that he had spent most of the day searching the town, because he knows things he might not otherwise know. Such as the fact that Main is in the midst of heavy construction, and all traffic will be diverted down Cypress Street, two blocks away. If Lev can cut through a series of front and back yards, he can get there first. He takes off, knowing if he makes it there, it will only be by seconds.

The first yards have no fences. Nothing dividing one property from another except for the state of the grass—well tended in one yard, neglected in the next. In a moment, he's tearing across an adjacent street to the second set of yards. There's a picket fence in the front yard of the next house, but it's a low one, and he's quickly able to get over it, onto artificial turf of a weird aquamarine shade.

"Hey, whad'ya think you're doing?" a man shouts from the porch, his toupee as artificial as his lawn. "This here's private property!"

Lev ignores him and runs down the side yard to the back, coming to his only major obstacle: a wooden fence six feet high that divides one backyard from another. On the other side of that fence a dog begins barking as Lev climbs. He can tell it's no small dog either.

Can't think about that now. He reaches the top and drops down so close to a huge German shepherd mix, the dog is taken aback. It barks its head off, but its brief hesitation gives Lev the advantage. He bolts down the side yard, through an easy latched gate, and to a front yard, where the owner opted for low-maintenance river stones instead of grass. This is Cypress Street, where more traffic flows than would usually be the case when the main drag isn't closed for construction. Lev can see the police car accelerating down the street toward him. The only thing between him and the street is a dense hedge, just high enough to be a problem, and he thinks how stupid if, after everything, he's screwed because of some lousy bush. He hurdles the hedge, but all that adrenaline-pumped momentum takes him too far, and there are no sidewalks on these streets. He lands on the asphalt of Cypress Street, right in the path of the approaching police car.

10 · Connor

"Of all the freaking days to have roadwork!" Connor had been certain that they were going to be made. That one of the other drivers caught in the construction traffic was going to look into the car and see that he's not deputy Joey at all.

"It's not just today," Grace tells him. "They been diggin' up that sewer pipe for weeks. Stinks to high heaven too."

Connor had been careful to avoid the traffic cones and any eye contact with the utility workers. Having followed the detour arrows, he now floors the accelerator down Cypress Street, speed limit be damned. Who's gonna pull over a cop car for speeding?

Then suddenly some kid leaps into the road in front of him, and he immediately flashes back to the damnable ostrich—but if there's roadkill today, it will be a lot worse than a dead bird. Connor slams on the brakes. He and Grace lurch forward. He hears the *thud* as the reckless kid connects with the front bumper. The car finally stops, and mercifully there is no telltale lurch of the car climbing over the kid's body. He was hit, but not run over. He had been hit pretty solidly, though.

"Ooh, this is bad, Argie!" Grace says, probably not even realizing she just called Connor Argie.

Connor considers just speeding off and leaving the scene—but he considers it for only a fraction of a second before dismissing it. That's not him. Not anymore. Some things have grown larger in him than primal self-preservation. Instead he gets out of the car to assess how bad this is and makes a pact with his survival instinct. If the kid is dead, then Connor will speed off and add hit-and-run to his list of offenses. Staying at the scene will not help a dead kid. But if he's alive, Connor will stay and do what must be done until help arrives. And if it means capture, then that will be that.

The figure lying sprawled on the road is groaning. Connor is relieved that he's alive but gripped with the fear of what will happen now. Then those feelings are slapped out of his head by shock and absolute disbelief when he sees who it is.

Lev's face is a grimace of pain. "It *is* you," Lev says. "I knew it."

Speechless doesn't even begin to describe Connor's state.

"Is he dead?" Grace asks, stepping out of the car and covering her eyes. "I don't wanna look—is he dead?"

"No, but . . ." Instead of saying anything more, he lifts Lev up, and Lev releases a helpless wail. Only now does Connor notice that Lev's shoulder is bulging forward in a very unnatural way. Connor knows he can't allow himself to think about that now.

"It's *him*?" says Grace, having uncovered her eyes. "What's *he* doing here? Did you plan this? It wasn't a very good plan, if you did."

On porches around them, people have come out to observe the little drama. Connor can't think about that now either. He gingerly puts Lev into the backseat and has Grace sit with him. Then he gets back in himself, feigning calm, and drives off.

"Hospital's up on Baxter," Grace says.

"Can't," Connor tells her. "Not here." Although he knows he means not anywhere. Medical attention brings other attention, too. If they bring Lev to a hospital, they'll know who he is within minutes. Not only did Lev break house arrest; he ran from the people protecting him from the Juvenile Authority. Which means there's no place safe to take him between here and Sonia's.

Grace leans closer to Lev, looking at his shoulder. "Dislocated," she says. "Happened to Argent once. Playing Ping-Pong. Rammed his shoulder into a wall. Blamed me for it, a' course, since I sent him chasing the ball. Won the point too." She puts both her hands on Lev's shoulder. "This is gonna hurt like a son of a bitch." Then she shoves with the full force of her weight.

Lev releases a siren wail of pain that makes Connor swerve

out of his lane. Then Lev sucks in a breath and screams again. The third one is more of a whimper. When Connor looks back, he sees that Lev's shoulder has popped into place.

"Like diving into a cold pool," Grace says. "Gotta do it quick before you start thinkin' on it."

Even in his pain, Lev has the presence of mind to actually thank her for fixing his shoulder, but there must be more going on inside that they can't see, because Lev grimaces in pain every time he shifts position.

Following Grace's plan, they pull into the supermarket parking lot and leave the squad car there, along with the keys and the deputy's gun—because a missing gun will beg too many questions. Leave the man his car and his gun, and he might just keep quiet to save himself from humiliation.

Connor hot-wires a blue Honda, out in the open, caution be damned, and in two minutes they've switched vehicles and are on the road again, heading for the interstate. It's not a pleasant vehicle. The entire car smells of ass sweat and stale potato chips. The steering wheel shimmies, betraying poor alignment. But as long as it gets them the hell out of Heartsdale, it's a magic coach as far as Connor is concerned. The town itself, however, seems to have taken umbrage against them. They hit every vindictive pothole and every pointless red light Heartsdale has to offer. Lev groans, grimaces, and hisses at every jolt.

"It'll get worse before it gets better," Grace says, stating the obvious, and Connor must suppress an urge to yell at her the way Argent might. Unlike Argent, Connor knows that it's not Grace he's frustrated with; it's the entire situation.

At the last stop light before the interstate, Connor turns to look at Lev and asks him to lift his shirt.

"Why do you want him to do that?" asks Grace.

"Because there's something I need to see."

Lev lifts his shirt, and Connor grimaces as his worst fear is realized. The accident didn't just dislocate Lev's shoulder. His whole side has turned sunset purple. There's internal bleeding, and there's no way to know how bad it is.

"Lordy, lordy, lordy," Grace says, her voice shaky. "You shouldn't a' hit him! You shouldn't a' hit him!"

"Okay," Connor says, feeling himself getting light-headed. "Okay, now we know."

"What do we know?" warbles Grace in a panic. "We don't know nothin'!"

"You know my deep dark secret," Lev says lazily. "I'm turning into an eggplant." He tries to laugh at his own joke, but the laugh is aborted because it causes him too much pain.

Risa would know what to do, Connor thinks. He tries to hear her voice in his head. The clarity of her thought. She ran the infirmary at the Graveyard better than a professional. *Tell me what to do, Risa.* But today she's mute and feels farther away than she ever did. It only increases Connor's longing for her and his despair. When they get to Sonia, she'll have a whole list of physicians supporting the cause, but this is still Kansas. Ohio never felt so far away.

He glances at the glove compartment. People sometimes keep ibuprofen or Aspirin in there, although he doesn't expect that much luck, considering how his luck has been running lately. Luck, however, is too dumb to remain consistent, and as he reaches over and opens the glove box, a clatter of orange vials spills out.

Connor releases a breath of sheer relief and begins tossing them to Grace in the back. "Read me what they are," Connor says, and Grace almost preens at the request. Whatever developmental issues she has, difficulty in reading complicated words is not one of them. She rattles off medication names Connor probably couldn't even pronounce himself. Some of them he recognizes; others he is clueless about. One thing's for sure—whoever belongs to this car is either very sick, a hypochondriac, or just a druggie.

Among the medications in the dashboard pharmacy are Motrins the size of horse pills and hydrocodone caplets almost as big.

"Great," he tells Grace. "Give Lev those two. One of each."

"With nothing to drink?" asks Grace.

Connor catches Lev's gaze in the rearview mirror. "Sorry, Lev—either swallow them dry or chew them. We can't stop for drinks right now, and better you get those meds in your system now than wait."

"Don't make him do that!" Grace complains. "It'll taste bad."

"I'll deal," Lev says. Connor doesn't like how weak his voice sounds.

Lev works up some saliva, pops both pills at once, and manages to swallow them with just a little bit of gagging.

"Okay. Good," says Connor. "We'll stop in the next town and get ice to help with the swelling."

Connor convinces himself that Lev's situation isn't all that bad. It's not like bone is poking through the skin or anything. "You'll be fine," Connor tells Lev. "You'll be fine."

But even after they get ice ten miles down the road, Connor's mantra of "you'll be fine," just isn't ringing true. Lev's side is darkening to a dull, puffy maroon. His left hand and fingers are swelling too, looking cartoonish and porcine. *It'll get worse before it gets better.* Grace's words echo in Connor's thoughts. He catches Lev's gaze in the rearview mirror. Lev's eyes are wet and rheumy. He can barely keep them open.

"Stay awake, Lev!" Connor says a bit too loudly. "Grace, make him stay awake."

"You heal when you sleep," Grace tells him.

"Not if you're going into shock. Stay awake, Lev!"

"I'm trying." His voice is beginning to slur. Connor wants to believe it's because of the medication, but he knows better.

Connor keeps his eyes fixed on the road. Their options are slim and the reality severe. But then Lev says, "I know a place we can go."

"Another joke?" asks Connor.

"I hope not." Lev takes a few slow breaths before he can build up the strength, or perhaps the courage, to tell them. "Get me to the Arápache Rez. West of Pueblo, Colorado."

Connor knows Lev must be delirious. "A ChanceFolk reservation? Why would ChanceFolk have anything to do with us?"

"Sanctuary," Lev hisses. "ChanceFolk never signed the Unwind Accord. The Arápache don't have an extradition treaty. They give asylum to AWOL Unwinds. Sometimes."

"Asylum is right!" says Grace. "No way I'm going to a Slot-Monger rez!"

"You sound like Argent," Connor scolds. That gives her pause for thought.

Connor considers their options. Seeking asylum from the Arápache would mean turning around and heading west, and even if they pushed the car, it would take at least four hours to get to the reservation. That's a long time for the state that Lev's in. But it's either that, or turn themselves in at the nearest hospital. That's not an option.

"How do you know all this about the Arápache?" Connor asks.

Lev sighs. "I've been around."

"Well," says Connor, more than a little bit nervous, "let's hope you're around a little while longer." Then he turns the car across the dirt median and heads west, toward Colorado.

11 · Rez Sentry

In spite of all the literature and spin put forth by the Tribal Council, there is nothing noble about being a sentry at an Arápache Reservation gate. Once upon a time, when the United States was just a band of misfit colonies, and long before there were fences and walls marking off Arápache land, things were different. Back then, to be a perimeter scout was to be a warrior. Now all it means is standing in a booth in a blue uniform, checking passports and papers and saying *híísi' honobe*, which roughly translates to "Have a beautiful day," proving that the Arápache are not immune to the banality of modern society.

At thirty-eight, the rez sentry is the oldest of three on duty today at the east gate, and so, by his seniority, he's the only one allowed to carry a weapon. However, his pistol is nowhere near as elegant and meaningful as the weapons of old, in those times when they were called Indians rather than ChanceFolk . . . or "SlotMongers," that hideous slur put upon them by the very people who made casino gaming the only way tribes could earn back their self-reliance, self-respect, and the fortunes leeched from them over the centuries. Although the casinos are long gone, the names remain. "ChanceFolk" is their badge of honor. "SlotMongers" is their scar.

It's late afternoon now. The line at the nonresident entry gate just across Grand Gorge Bridge is at least thirty cars deep. This is a good day. On bad days the line backs up to the other side of the bridge. About half of the cars in the line will be turned away. No one gets on the rez who doesn't either live there or have legitimate business.

"We just want to take some pictures and buy some

ChanceFolk crafts," people would say. "Don't you want to sell your goods?" As if their survival were dependent upon hawking trinkets to tourists.

"You can make a U-turn to your left," he would politely tell them. *"Hiísi' honobe!"* He would feel for the disappointed children in the backseat, but after all, it's their parents' fault for being ignorant of the Arápache and their ways.

Not every tribe has taken such an isolationist approach, of course, but then, not many tribes have been as successful as the Arápache when it came to creating a thriving, self-sustaining, and admittedly affluent community. Theirs is a "Hi-Rez," both admired and resented by certain other "Low-Rez" tribes who squandered those old casino earnings rather than investing in their own future.

As for the gates, they didn't go up until after the Unwind Accord. Like other tribes, the Arápache refused to accept the legality of unwinding—just as they had refused to be a part of the Heartland War. "Swiss Cheese Natives," detractors of the time had called them, for the ChanceFolk lands were holes of neutrality in the midst of a battling nation.

So the rest of the country, and much of the world, took to recycling the kids it didn't want or need, and the Arápache Nation, along with all the rest of the American Tribal Congress, proclaimed, if not their independence, then their recalcitrance. They would not follow the law of the land as it stood, and if pressed, the entire Tribal Congress would secede from the union, truly making Swiss cheese of the United States. With one costly civil war just ending, Washington was wise to just let it be.

Of course, court battles have been raging for years as to whether or not the Arápache Nation has the right to demand passports to enter their territory, but the tribe has become very adept at doing the legal dance. The sentry doubts the issue will ever be resolved. At least not in his lifetime.

He processes car after car beneath an overcast sky that threatens rain but holds its water like an obstinate child. Some people get through; others get turned away.

And then he gets a car of AWOLs.

He can spot AWOLs the second they pull up. Their desperation wafts out at him like a musk. Although no tribe supports unwinding, the Arápache is one of the few that gives sanctuary to AWOL Unwinds, to the constant consternation of the Juvenile Authority. It's not something they advertise or openly admit, but word gets around, so dealing with AWOLs is just another part of his day.

"Can I help you?" he asks the teenage driver.

"My friend is injured," he says. "He needs medical attention."

The sentry looks in the backseat, where a kid in poor shape rests his head in the lap of a girl in her early twenties who looks a little bit off. The kid in back doesn't appear to be faking it.

"Best if you turn around," the sentry tells him. "There's a hospital in Cañon City—it's much closer than the reservation's medical lodge. I'll give you directions if you like."

"We can't," says the driver. "We need sanctuary. Asylum. Do you understand?"

So he was right after all. They're AWOLs. The sentry scans the line of cars waiting to get through the bottleneck. One of the other guards looks at him to see what he'll do. Their policy is very clear, and he must set an example for his coworkers. Being a rez sentry is not noble.

"I'm afraid I can't help you."

"See?" says the girl in the back. "I knew this was a bad idea."

But the kid driving won't be deterred. "I thought you take in AWOLs."

"AWOLs must be sponsored before we can let them in."

The kid can't hold in his frustration. "Sponsored? Are you serious? How would AWOL Unwinds get sponsored?"

The sentry sighs. Does he really have to spell it out? "You have to have a sponsor to enter *officially*," he says. "But if you can find your way in *unofficially*, chances are you'll find someone to sponsor you." Only now does the sentry notice something familiar about his face, but he can't place where he's seen him before.

"We don't have time for that! Do you think he's going to climb a fence?" The driver indicates the semiconscious kid in the back, who, come to think of it, also looks familiar. Considering that kid's sorry state, the sentry considers stepping forward to sponsor them himself, but he knows it will cost him his job. He's paid to keep people out, not find ways to let them in. Compassion is not part of his job description.

"I'm sorry, but—"

And then the injured kid speaks up, as if out of a dream. "Friend of Elina Tashi'ne," he mumbles.

That surprises the sentry. "The medicine woman?" There are many thousands on the rez, but there are those whose reputation is well known. The Tashi'ne family is very highly regarded—and everyone knows about the terrible tragedy they endured. Cars in line begin to honk, but he ignores them. This has gotten interesting.

The kid driving looks back at his delirious friend, as if this is a surprise to him as well.

"Call her," the injured kid says; then his eyes flutter closed.

"You heard him!" says the driver. "Call her!"

The sentry calls the medical lodge and is quickly transferred to Dr. Elina. "Sorry to bother you," he tells her, "but there are some kids here at the east gate, and one of them claims to know you." He turns to the kid in the back, but he's gone unconscious, so he asks the driver, "What's his name?"

The driver hesitates, then finally says, "Lev Garrity. But she probably knows him as Lev Calder."

The sentry does a double take. All at once he recognizes Lev, and the driver, too. He's that kid they call the Akron AWOL. Connor something-or-other. The one who's supposed to be dead. As for Lev, he was infamous on the rez before he became "the clapper who wouldn't clap." You can't speak the name of poor Wil Tashi'ne without also thinking of Lev Calder and his involvement in that tragedy. And his friends here probably don't even know. He imagines Lev wouldn't talk much about what happened that awful day.

The sentry tries to hide his shock, but he doesn't do a good job of it. Connor registers mild disgust. "Just tell her, okay?"

"Brace yourself," he says into the phone. "It's Lev Calder. And he's injured."

A long pause. The honking cars continue to build into a dissonant chorus. Finally Dr. Elina says, "Send him in."

He hangs up the phone and turns to Connor. "Congratulations," he says, feeling just the slightest bit noble. "You've got yourselves a sponsor."

Part Two

Fine Young Specimens

GLOBAL ORGAN HARVESTING A BOOMING BLACK MARKET
BUSINESS; A KIDNEY HARVESTED EVERY HOUR

By J. D. Heyes

NaturalNews / Sunday, June 3, 2012

In this age of instant, mass communication, it's hard to cover up virtually anything, and yet there's one story that has yet to be told on a wide
scale—how organ trafficking has ballooned into a global business and
that the practice is so widespread, one organ is sold every hour.

That's according to the World Health Organization, which said recently
in a report that there are new fears the illegal organ trade may once
again be rising. . . .

Kidneys are in high demand

The World Health Organization says wealthy patients in developed
nations are paying tens of thousands of dollars for a kidney to India-,
China-, and Pakistan-based gangs, who harvest them from desperate
people for as little as a few hundred dollars.

Eastern Europe, the U.N.–based health organization says, is becoming
fertile ground for black-market organs; recently the Salvation Army said
it rescued a woman who had been brought to the United Kingdom to
have her organs harvested.

The illicit kidney trade makes up 75 percent of the black-market organ
trade . . . experts say that is likely due to the diseases of affluence such
as diabetes, high blood pressure and heart problems.

And, since there is such disparity between wealthy and poor countries,
there isn't much chance the illicit trade will end anytime soon.

The full article can be found at:

http://www.naturalnews.com/036052_organ_harvesting_kidneys_black_market.
html

The Rheinschilds

It's begun. The newly established Juvenile Authority, as its first official act, has announced its first unwinding facility. Cook County Juvenile Temporary Detention Center, in Chicago, the largest facility for juvenile incarceration in the country, is to be retrofitted with three operating rooms and a thirty-three member surgical staff.

Janson Rheinschild reads the article in his research office, nestled in a building named for him and his wife on the campus of Maryland's Johns Hopkins University. The article about the unwinding center is small and buried so deep in the newsfeed, no one who's not looking for it will find it.

Unwinding creeps in on the hushed feet of angels.

There is no call from Proactive Citizenry to gloat. They have dismissed him and Sonia as irrelevant. He looks to the gold medallion across the room sitting in a clear glass display case. What does a Nobel Prize in science mean when your lifesaving work has been transformed into an excuse to end life?

"But life doesn't end," the smiling proponents of unwinding all insist. "It just transforms. We like to call it 'living in a divided state.'"

As he prepares to leave his office, on sudden impulse he punches the display case and the glass shatters. Then he stands there feeling stupid for what he's done. The medallion lies amid the shards, knocked off its base. He rescues it, shoving it into his jacket pocket.

• • •

As he pulls up his driveway, he sees that the pickup is gone. Sonia is at it again. Garage sales and flea markets, which means it must be Saturday. Janson has lost track of the days. Sonia drowns her disillusionment by hunting for knickknacks and old furniture that they don't need. She hasn't been to her own research offices for weeks. It's as if she's given up on medical science completely and has retired at forty-one.

The front door is unlocked—careless of her to leave it that way. But a moment later, as he crosses from the foyer into the living room, he learns in no uncertain terms that it wasn't her doing. He's hit in the head with one of his wife's heavier knick-knacks and falls to the ground. Dazed, but still conscious, he looks up to see the face of his attacker.

It's just a kid of maybe sixteen. One of the "ferals" the news and neighbors keep complaining about. The lawless, vicious by-product of modern civilization. He's gangly and malnourished, with an anger in his eyes that was only partially relieved by smashing a stranger in the head.

"Where's the money?" he demands. "Where's the safe?"

Even in pain, Janson can almost laugh. "There is no safe."

"Don't lie to me! A house like this always has a safe!"

He marvels at how the boy can be so dangerous and so naive at once. But then again, ignorance and blind cruelty have been known to go hand in hand. On a dark whim, Rheinschild reaches into his coat pocket and tosses the kid his medal.

"Take it. It's gold," he says. "I have no use for it anymore."

The kid catches the medal in a hand that's missing two fingers. "You're lying. This ain't gold."

"Fine," says Rheinschild. "So kill me."

The kid turns the medallion over in his hands a few times. "The Nobel Prize? I don't think so. It's fake."

"Fine," says Rheinschild again. "So kill me."

"Shut up! I didn't say anything about killing you, did I?" The teen hefts it, feeling its weight. Rheinschild pulls himself up to a sitting position, still feeling his head spin from the blow. He may have a concussion. He doesn't care.

The kid then looks around the living room, which is filled with awards and citations that Janson and Sonia received for their groundbreaking work. "If this is real, whad'ya win it for?"

"We invented unwinding," Rheinschild says. "Although we didn't know it at the time."

The kid lets loose a bitter, disbelieving guffaw. "Yeah, right."

The young burglar could leave with his prize, but he doesn't. Instead he lingers. So Rheinschild asks, "What happened to your fingers?"

The kid's distrustful gaze notches toward anger again. "Why is that your business?"

"Was it frostbite?"

His attacker is taken aback, surprised by Rheinschild's guess. "Yeah, it was. Most people think it was fireworks or something stupid like that. But it was frostbite last winter."

Rheinschild pulls himself up into a chair.

"Who said you could move?" But they both know the kid's posturing is now all for show.

Rheinschild takes a good look at him. It appears he hasn't been introduced to a shower in this lifetime. Rheinschild can't even tell the color of his hair. "What is it that you need?" Rheinschild asks him.

"Your money," he says, looking down his nose at him.

"I didn't ask you what you want. I asked you what you need."

"Your money!" he says again, a little more forcefully. Then he adds a bit more gently: "And food. And clothes. And a job."

"What if I gave you one of the three?"

"What if I bashed your head in a little deeper than I already did?"

Rheinschild reaches into his pocket, pulls out his wallet, intentionally revealing that there are a few bills in there, but instead of the bills he tosses the boy his business card.

"Come to that address at ten on Monday. I'll put you to work and pay you a livable wage. If you want to buy food and clothes with it, that's fine with me. If you want to squander it, that's fine with me too. Just as long as you show up every day, five days a week. And you take a shower before you do."

The kid sneers at him. "And you'll have the Juvey-cops waiting there for me. Do you think I'm stupid?"

"There's not enough empirical evidence to make that judgment."

The kid shifts his weight from one foot to another. "So what kind of work is it?"

"Biological. Medical. I'm working on something that could end unwinding, but I need a research assistant. Someone who isn't secretly on Proactive Citizenry's payroll."

"Proactive Who?"

"Good answer. As long as you can say that, you'll have job security."

The kid considers it, then looks at the medallion in his three-fingered hand. He tosses it back to Rheinschild. "You shouldn't walk around with this. You should frame it or something."

Then he leaves with nothing more than he had when he broke in, except for a business card.

Rheinschild is sure he'll never see the kid again. He finds himself pleasantly surprised when the boy shows up at his research office on Monday morning, wearing the same filthy clothes, but freshly showered beneath them.

12 · Risa

She cannot believe the position she's put herself in.

All this time surviving against overwhelming odds and now, thanks to her own stupidity, she's going to die.

She blames her own arrogance for her downfall. She was so certain she was too clever, too observant, to be snagged by a parts pirate—as if somehow she existed on a higher plane.

A crumbling barn on a marginally functional farm in Cheyenne, Wyoming. She had found it in the midst of a storm and had gone in to take shelter from the rain. In one stall there was a shelf stocked with food.

Stupid, stupid, stupid! What was food doing in a deserted barn? If she had been thinking, she would have run and risked the lightning, but she was tired and hungry. Her guard was down. She reached for a bag of chips, hit a trip wire, and a spring-loaded steel cable wrapped around her wrist. She was caught like a rabbit. She tried to tug free, but the slipknot cable was designed to ratchet tighter and tighter the more she pulled.

The parts pirate had been careless enough to leave various farm tools within her reach, but none of them were of the type to cut a steel cable. After an hour of struggling, Risa realized there was nothing to do but wait—and envy wild animals who had the good sense to gnaw off their own limbs to escape from traps.

That was last night. Now as morning comes, Risa, having not slept at all, must face a fresh hell. The parts pirate comes an hour after sunrise. He's a middle-aged man with a bad scalp job. His mop of boyish blond hair doesn't make him look boyish, just creepy. He practically dances a jig when he sees that his trap has done the job.

"Been there for months and nothing," he tells Risa. "I was ready to give up—but good things come to those who wait."

Risa seethes and thinks of Connor. She wishes she could have been more like him last night. Connor would never be so foolish as to allow himself to be captured by an imbecile.

Clearly this guy's an amateur, but as long as he's got the goods, the black-market harvesters won't turn him away. He doesn't recognize her. That's good. The black market pays more for the infamous—and she doesn't want this man to get paid what she's worth. Of course that assumes he gets that far. Risa has had all night to come up with a plan of action.

"Selling you might just get the banks off my back," he tells her jovially. "Or at least get me a decent car."

"You have to cut me loose first before you can sell me."

"Indeed I do!"

He looks at her a little too long, his grin a little too wide, and it occurs to Risa that selling her to a black-market harvester is only at the end of his list of planned activities. But whatever his plans, he's the type who has to have everything just right. He goes around the stall and begins cleaning up the mess Risa made in her frustrated attempts to escape.

"You sure were busy last night," he says. "Hope you got it out of your system."

Now Risa begins to taunt him. She knows what sorts of things will push this man's buttons—but she begins with some easy, glancing blows. She begins with slights against his intelligence.

"I hate to kill the dream," she says, "but the black market won't deal with morons. I mean, you have to know how to read if you're going to sign a contract."

"Very funny."

"Seriously, maybe you should have gotten some brains to go along with that hair."

It only makes him chuckle. "Bad-mouth me all you want, girlie. It's not gonna change a thing."

Risa thought there was no way she could possibly hate this man more . . . but calling her "girlie" opens up a whole new level of loathing. She begins her next round of attacks—this time against his family. His gene pool. His mother.

"So did they slaughter the cow that gave birth to you, or did it die of natural causes?"

He continues his stall tidying, but his focus is gone. Risa can tell he's getting rankled. "You shut up. I don't gotta take crap like that from a dirty Unwind bitch!"

Good. Let him curse at her. Because the angrier he gets, the more it plays in Risa's favor. Now she delivers her final salvo. A series of cruel assertions about the man's anatomy. Assertions of severe inadequacy. At least some of them must be true, because he loses it, getting red in the face.

"When I'm done with you," he growls, "you ain't gonna be worth what you are now—that's for sure!"

He lunges for her, his big hands out in front of him—and as he throws himself forward, Risa raises the pitchfork that she's concealed in the hay. She doesn't have to do any more than that: just hold the thing up. His weight and momentum do all the work.

The amateur parts pirate thoroughly impales himself and pulls back, taking the pitchfork with him.

"Whad'ya do to me! Whad'ya do!"

The pitchfork flails back and forth like an appendage in his chest as he curses and screams. Risa knows it's hit some vital organ because of all the blood and the speed at which he goes down. In less than ten seconds, he collapses against the far wall of the stall and dies with his eyes open and staring not quite at her, but off to her left, as if maybe in his last moments he saw an angel over her shoulder, or Satan, or whatever a man like him sees when he dies.

Risa considers herself a compassionate human being, but she feels no remorse for this man. She does, however, begin to feel a deepening sense of regret. Because her hand is still caught in the cable. And the only human being who knows she's here is now lying across the stall, dead.

And Risa cannot believe the situation she's put herself in. Again.

ADVERTISEMENT

"You wonder who I am? Yeah, sometimes I do too. My name is Cyrus Finch. My name is also Tyler Walker. At least one-eighth of me is. See, it's like that when you get jacked up on some other dude's gray matter, dig? Now I don't feel like me or him, but less than both of us. Less than whole.

"If you've gotten yourself an unwound part and regret it, you're not alone. That's why I started the Tyler Walker Foundation. Call us at 800-555-1010. We don't want your money; we don't want your vote—we just want to fix what's broken. That's 800-555-1010. We'll help you make peace with your piece."

—Sponsored by the Tyler Walker Foundation.

The parts pirate, who had no intention of dying, had left the barn door open. A coyote comes to visit that night. When Risa first sees it, she yells at it, throws hay, and heaves a garden hoe. The hoe hits it on the nose hard enough to make it yelp and leave in a hurry. Risa knows nothing of wild animals, their natures, or habits. She does know that coyotes are carnivorous but she's not sure if they hunt alone or in packs. If it returns with its mangy brethren, she's done for.

It comes back an hour later, alone. It takes little interest in her, other than to note whether or not she's still in a throwing mood. The point is moot, since there's nothing left in her reach to throw. She yells at it, but it ignores her, focusing all of its attention on the parts pirate, who isn't putting up any resistance.

The coyote dines on the man, who is already beginning to grow rancid in the summer heat. Risa knows the stench will only get worse until, in a day's time, maybe two, the stench of her own flesh will join his. Perhaps the coyote is smart enough to know that she will eventually die as well and is prioritizing. As far as the coyote is concerned, her continued life is better than refrigeration. It can make several meals of the parts pirate, knowing that, when all is said and done, fresh meat will be waiting.

Watching the coyote eat eventually desensitizes her to the horror of it. She finds herself objective, almost as if watching from a safe distance. She idly wonders which is crueler, man or nature. She determines it must be man. Nature has no remorse, but neither does it have malice. Plants take in the light of the sun and give off oxygen with the same life-affirming need that a tiger tears into a toddler. Or a scavenger devours a lowlife.

The coyote leaves. Dawn breaks. Dehydration begins to take its toll on Risa, and she hopes the thirst will kill her before the coyote finds her alive but too weak to fend off its advances. She slips in and out of consciousness, and her life begins to scroll before her eyes.

The flashing of one's life, Risa finds, is by no means complete; nor does it take into account the value of memories. It is as random as the stuff of dreams, just a little more connected to what once was.

The Cafeteria Fight

She's seven years old and fighting another girl who insists that Risa stole her clothes. It's a ridiculous assertion, because everyone in the state home wears the same basic utilitarian uniforms. Risa's too young at the time to know that it's not about clothes but about dominance. Social position. The girl is larger than her, meaner than her—but when the girl pins her to the ground, Risa gouges the girl's eyes, flips her, and spits in her face—which is what the girl was trying to do when she pinned Risa. The girl cries foul when the teachers pull them apart, claiming Risa started it and that she fights dirty. But no adult really cares who started it as long as it ends, and as far as they're concerned, all fights among state home orphans are dirty. The interpretation among the kids, however, is much different. What matters to them is that Risa won. Few people pick fights with her after that. But the other girl gets no peace from her peers.

A Practice Room

She's twelve and playing piano in a small acoustic-tiled room of Ohio State Home 23. The piano is out of tune, but she's used to that. Risa plays the Baroque piece flawlessly. In the audience, disembodied faces observe, stony and impassionate, in spite of the passion with which she plays. This time she does fine. It's only when it matters four years later that she chokes.

The Harvest Camp Bus

The administration has decided that the best way to deal with budget cuts is to unwind one-tenth of the home's teen population. They call it forced downsizing. The glitches and clunkers in Risa's pivotal piano recital leave her firmly placed within that 10 percent. Sitting next to her on the bus is a mealy boy by the name of Samson Ward. An odd name for a scrawny kid, but since all state home orphans are, by law, given the last name of Ward, first names tend to be, if not entirely unique, at least fairly uncommon and often ironic because they're not chosen by loving parents, but by bureaucrats. The kind who might think giving a sickly premature baby the name "Samson" is droll.

"I'd rather be partly great than entirely useless," Samson says. This memory has the perspective of hindsight. Samson, she discovered much later, had a secret crush on her, which expressed itself in the person of Camus Comprix. Cam had received the part of Samson's brain that did algebra and apparently also had fantasies about unattainable girls. Samson was a math genius—but not enough of one to keep him out of the unlucky 10 percent.

Looking at Stars

Risa and Cam lying on the grass on a bluff on a Hawaiian island that had once been a leper colony. Cam announces the names of the stars and constellations, his accent suddenly tweaking New England as he engages the piece of the person in his head who knows everything about stars. Cam loves her. At first she despised him. Then she endured him. Then she came to appreciate the individual he was becoming—the spirit that was exerting itself above and beyond the sum of his parts. She knows she will never feel for him what he feels for her, though. How could she when she is still so in love with Connor?

Connor.

Months before that stargazing night in Molokai. He's massaging her legs as she sits in a wheelchair in the shade of a stealth bomber in the Arizona desert. She cannot feel her legs. She doesn't know that in a few short months her spine will be replaced and she'll walk again. All she knows in the moment is that Connor can't truly be with her the way she wants him to be. His mind is too full of responsibilities. Too full of the hordes of kids he's hiding and protecting in the airplane graveyard.

The Graveyard.

Now true to its name. Violently emptied of its occupants as thoroughly as a World War II ghetto. All those kids were either killed or sent off to harvest camps to their eventual unwinding—or "summary division," as the paperwork officially calls it. And where is Connor? She knows he must have gotten away, because if he had been caught or killed, the Juvenile Authority would have had a field day with it in the media. It would be a death blow to the Anti-Divisional Resistance—which has become as effective as a flyswatter against a dragon.

And it is dusk once more in the barn. The coyote comes back again, this time with a mate to share in the feast. Risa yells so as to not appear weak and to remind them that she still has some strength left, although it's waning quickly. They don't bother with her. Instead they tear cruelly at the dead man, and as they do, Risa realizes something. From where she's caught— even when she stretched herself as far as she could—she was still two feet away from the dead man.

But the coyotes have pulled him away from the wall.

With all the energy that she has left, she stretches herself across the ground toward him. Reaching with her left hand, she manages to snag the cuff of his pant leg with her forefinger.

She begins to tug him closer, and as he begins to move, the coyotes realize that tomorrow's meal has become a threat to today's. They bare their teeth and growl at her. She doesn't stop. She pulls on him again. This time one of the animals bites her arm, clamping down. She screams and uses her old trick of gouging its eye. The animal is hurt enough to loosen its grip, and Risa breaks free long enough to pull the dead man closer. She can reach the edge of his pocket—but the other coyote leaps for her. She has only a second. She reaches into the dead man's pocket hoping, for once, that luck is in her favor, and she finds what she's looking for just as the second coyote grabs on to her upper arm. But the pain is only secondary to her now. Because she has his phone.

Risa pulls away and withdraws into the corner. The coyotes yap and snarl angry warnings. She stands on shaky legs and they back off, still intimidated by her height. Soon they'll realize that there's no fight to this foe and they'll do to her what they've done to the parts pirate. Her time is limited.

She turns on the phone to find it has only a tiny bit of battery life left, which means her life now depends on the capricious whim of a lithium battery.

Who does a fugitive call? There's no one she personally knows who would take such a call, and the standard emergency numbers will rescue her right into a world worse than death. There is one number she knows, however. It's a number she thinks she can trust, even though she's never called it before. She dials. The battery holds out for one ring . . . two rings. Then a man answers on the other end.

"The Tyler Walker Foundation. Can I help you?"

A deep breath of relief. "This is Risa Ward," she says. Then she speaks the three words she despises above all others. "I need help."

13 · Cam

There are many Mirandas.

An endless glut of girls, all bored with the dull familiarity of ordinary boys, hurl themselves at Cam as if they're hurling themselves off a cliff. They all expect his strong rewound arms to catch them. Sometimes he does.

They want to run their fingers along the symmetrical lines of his face. They want to lose themselves in the depths of his soulful blue eyes—and knowing the eyes really aren't his at all makes them want to lose themselves even more.

Cam has very few events as fancy as the Washington gala, so a tuxedo is rarely required. Mostly it's speaking engagements. He wears a tailored sports coat and tie, with slacks that are just casual enough to keep him from looking too corporate. Too much like the creation of Proactive Citizenry—who silently bankrolls everything he does.

Cam and Roberta are on a tour on the university lecture circuit. Fairly small events since most universities are quiet in the summer—but the upper faculty still have their research to oversee, and it's those highly esteemed academics on whom they are focusing.

"We need the scientific community to see you as a worthwhile endeavor," Roberta has told him. "You've already won the hearts and sympathy of the public. Now you must be respected on a professional level."

The speaking events always begin with Roberta and her flashy multimedia presentation laying out in fine academic fashion the nuts and bolts of how Cam was created—although she doesn't call it that. Proactive Citizenry's spin doctors have decided that Cam was not created; he was "gleaned." And his rewound bits and pieces are all part of his "internal community."

"The gleaning of Camus Comprix took many months," Roberta tells their audiences. "We first had to identify the high-level qualities we wanted his internal community to have. Then we had to find those qualities within the population of Unwinds awaiting division. . . ."

Like the opening act at a concert, Roberta primes the audience for the main event, and then—"Ladies and gentlemen, I give you the culmination of all of our medical and scientific efforts: Camus Comprix!"

A spotlight appears, and he steps into it to the sound of applause—or snapping in the places where public applause has been banned due to clapper attacks.

At the podium Cam delivers his prepared speech, written by a former presidential speech writer. It is thoughtful, intelligent, and memorized word for word. Then comes the Q and A—and although both he and Roberta are on stage to receive questions, most are directed at Cam.

"Do you find you have problems with physical coordination?"

"Never," he answers. "My muscle groups have all learned to get along."

"Do you remember the names of any of the constituents of your internal community?"

"No, but sometimes I remember faces."

"Is it true you speak nine languages fluently?"

"*Da, no v moyey golove dostatochno mesta dlia escho neskolkikh*," he says. *Yes, but there's room up here for a few more.* That brings chuckles from any Russian speakers in the room.

He has mastered all of his answers—even to questions that are intentionally belligerent and incendiary.

"Admit it—you're nothing but a kit-car," one heckler says during his appearance at MIT. "You're just a model put together from parts in a box. How can you call yourself human?"

Cam's response to questions like this is always tactful and puts the heckler in his or her place.

"No, I'm more like a *concept* car," Cam tells the man, without any of the animosity with which the question was asked. "The sum of the imaginations of all the experts in the field." Then Cam smiles. "And if by 'model,' you mean something worth striving toward, I agree."

"What about those who gave their lives so that you might live?" someone shouts out from the audience of his UCLA event. "Do you feel any remorse for them?"

"Thank you for asking that," Cam says in the charged silence that ensues. "Remorse would imply I had anything to do with their unwinding, and I did not. I'm just on the receiving end. But yes, I do grieve their loss—so I choose to honor them by giving voice to their hopes, their dreams, and their talents. After all, isn't that what we do to honor those who came before us?"

When the time for questions ends, each event is wrapped up with music. Cam's music. He brings out a guitar and performs a classical piece. His music is so flawless and so heartfelt, it often brings forth a standing ovation. Of course, there are those in the audience who will never stand—but their numbers are diminishing.

"Come fall, we should speak in bigger theaters," he tells Roberta after one highly successful evening.

"Would you prefer a stadium?" Roberta offers with a twisted grin. "You're not a rock star, Cam."

But he knows otherwise.

LETTER TO THE EDITOR

With regards to your recent editorial "THE CONTROVERSY OF CAMUS COMPRIX," forgive me, but I don't see anything that should be controversial at all. Indeed, I think the members of the media have, as usual, stirred up a tempest in a teapot. I attended one of Mr. Comprix's presentations, and I found him to be eloquent, personable, and respectful. He appears both intelligent and humble—the kind of young man I wish my daughter could, for once, bring home instead of the string of miscreants that continue to grace our doorstep.

Your editorial implied that his parts were gleaned without permission, but I ask you—other than tithes, what Unwind ever gives permission to be unwound? It's not a matter of permission. It's a matter of social necessity, as unwinding has always been, since its inception. So why not avail ourselves of the finest attributes of these Unwinds to build a better being? If I, in my youth, had been designated for unwinding, I should think I'd be honored to know that a part of me was worthy to be chosen for inclusion in Mr. Comprix.

Proactive Citizenry, and Dr. Roberta Griswold in particular, are to be commended for their vision and for their selfless commitment to the betterment of the human condition. Because, if even our most incorrigible youth can be rewound into such a fine young specimen, it gives me hope for the future of mankind.

Every event has its greenroom—a guarded space designed for the comfort of those about to go on stage, or to relax after the blare of spotlights and barrage of questions. Roberta always busies herself with the bigwigs in the theater lobby, shaking hands and making those critical personal connections. This has allowed Cam to become the master of the greenroom, picking and choosing who gets to keep him company as he winds down after an event. His guests are almost always female. An endless parade of Mirandas.

"Play something just for us, Cam," they would say with a gentle pleading lilt to their voice as if their hearts hang on his answer. Or they would invite him to some party he knows he can't attend. Instead he tells those girls that the party is right here. They always like the sound of that.

He entertains three such girls in the greenroom after his successful MIT presentation. Now he sits between two of them on a comfortable sofa, while a third occupies a chair nearby, giggling and starstruck as she awaits her turn, like a little kid waiting for Santa's lap. Cam has, at the request of his guests, removed his shirt to show his curious seams. Now one of the girls explores those seams and the varied skin tones of his chest. The other girl snuggles with him and feeds him Jordan almonds, sweet and crunchy.

Eventually Roberta pops in, as he knew she would. It is, in fact, something he counted on. It has become their pattern.

"Look, it's my favorite party pooper!" Cam says jovially.

Roberta glowers at the girls. "Playtime is over," she says coldly. "I'm sure you young ladies have places to be."

"Not really," says the one with her hand on Cam's chest. In the nearby chair, the giggler giggles some more.

"Aw, please, Grand Inquisitor," says Cam. "They're so cute—can't I take them home?"

Now all three girls giggle as if they're drunk, but Cam knows the only thing they're drunk on is him.

Roberta ignores him. "You girls have been asked to leave. Please don't make me get security."

As if on cue, the guard steps in, looking guilty but ready to throw them out in spite of the cash Cam paid him to let them in.

Reluctantly, the girls get up. They all leave in their own personal manner, one strutting, another strolling, and the third sneaking, trying to suppress her unending case of the giggles. The guard follows to make sure they don't linger and closes the door behind him. Now Roberta's glare is aimed at Cam. He tries to hide his smirk.

"Spanking? Time out? Bed without supper?" Cam suggests.

But Roberta is certainly not in a teasing mood. "You should not be objectifying those girls."

"Double-edged sword," Cam says. "They objectified me first. I was just returning the favor."

Roberta growls in exasperation. "Did you believe anything you said out there about being a 'model' for others to strive for?"

Cam looks away. The things he tells audiences is certainly what Roberta believes—but does he believe these things himself? Yes, he is made of the best and the brightest—but those are just parts, and what do parts truly say about the whole? What he wants more than anything is to make the question go away.

"Sure I believe it."

"Then show some common comportment." She takes his shirt and tosses it to him. "You're better than this. So act it."

"And what if I'm not better?" he dares to suggest. "What if I'm nothing more than ninety-nine compounded adolescent lusts?"

"Then," says Roberta, taking the dare, "you can slice yourself back down into ninety-nine pieces. Shall I give you a knife?"

"Machete," he answers. "Much more dramatic."

She sighs, shaking her head. "If you wish to impress General Bodeker, this type of behavior won't fly."

"Ah yes, General Bodeker."

Cam isn't quite sure what to make of the man and his intentions, but he can't deny that he's intrigued. Cam knows he would be shepherded through his training directly into officership, like some American prince. Then, once he was wearing the crisp, sharp dress of an officer, all pressed linen and brass buttons, the bitter voices that suggest he has no right to exist would be silenced. No one can hate an honored Marine. And he'd finally have a place to belong.

"Irrelevant," Cam says. "The general won't care about my personal downtime adventures."

"Don't be so sure," Roberta tells him. "You need to be more

discerning about your choice of companions. Now get your shirt on. The limo is waiting."

Cam jolts awake at thirty-six thousand feet. For a moment he thinks he's in a dentist's chair, but no. He had fallen asleep before extending the chair to its full reclining position.

Proactive Citizenry has provided this richly appointed private jet for his speaking tour, although it's not all that private. Roberta slumbers in her own sleeper chair in the alcove behind his, her breathing steady and regulated, just like everything else in her life. There is a concierge—which is the private aircraft equivalent of a flight attendant—but he is also asleep at the moment. The time is 3:13 a.m., although Cam is not sure what time zone that's reflecting.

He tries to bring back his dreams for analysis, but can't access them. Cam's dreams have never made sense. He has no idea how much sense the dreams of normal people make, so he can't compare. His dreams are plagued by snippets of memories that lead nowhere, because the rest of those memories are in other heads, living different lives. The only memory that is clear and consistent is the memory of being unwound. He dreams of it way too often. He dreams not of just one unwinding, but many. The bits and pieces of dozens of divisions blend together into one unforgettable, unforgivable whole.

He used to wake up screaming from those dreams. Not from the pain of it, for unwinding is, by law, painless. But there are things worse than physical pain. He would scream from the terror, from the sheer helplessness each of those kids felt as the surgeons moved closer, limbs tingled and went numb, medical stasis coolers were carried away in their peripheral vision. Each sense shutting down and each memory evaporating, always ending with a silent cry of hopeless defiance as each Unwind was shuffled into oblivion.

Roberta is in the dream, for she was there at each unwinding—the only person in the room not wearing a surgical mask. *So you would see me, hear me, and know me when the parts were united* she had told him—but she hadn't counted on how horrible that knowledge would be. Roberta is part of the terror. She is the author of hopelessness.

Cam has learned to bite back the scream in his dreams, holding it inside until he drags himself from the rancid soup of his nightmare and into the living, breathing world, where he is himself and not the particulated bits of his "inner community."

Tonight he is alone. He knows there are people around him, but in a private jet soaring through an icy black sky, he cannot help but feel alone in the universe. It is in these moments of profound loneliness that the questions posed by the more judgmental audience members haunt him, for their questions are his own.

Am I truly alive? Do I even exist?

Certainly he exists as organic matter, but as a sentient being? As a some*one* rather than a some*thing*? There are too many moments in his life when he just doesn't know. And if, in the end, each individual faces judgment, will he stand to face it too—or will the constituents of his inner community return to their true owners, leaving a void where he once stood?

He curls his hands into fists. *I am!* he wants to shout. *I exist.* But he knows better than to voice these concerns to Roberta anymore. Better if she thinks his weaknesses lie in youthful lust.

This is the fury that fills him when no one is watching. Fury that the hecklers in the audience may be right and he may be nothing more than medical sleight of hand. A trick of the scalpel. A hollow shell mimicking life.

In these dark nihilistic moments when the universe itself seems to be rejecting him the way people's bodies used to reject transplanted organs, he thinks of Risa.

Risa. Her name explodes into his mind, and he fights the urge to put his mind in lockdown. Risa did not despise him. Yes, at first she did, but she came to truly know him and to see him as an individual who is more than the sum of his parts. In the end, she came to care for him in her own way.

When he was with Risa, Cam felt real. When he was with her, he felt more than a patchwork of science and hubris.

He cannot deny how much he loves her—and the pain of that longing is enough to make him know that he lives. That he *is*. For how could he feel such anguish if he had no soul?

Yet in many ways he feels as if she took his soul with her when she left.

Do you know what that feels like, Risa? he wants to ask her.

Do you know what it's like to be un-souled? Is that how you felt when your precious Connor died at Happy Jack Harvest Camp? Cam knows beyond a shadow of a doubt he could fill that void in her, if only she loved him enough to let him. It would be the one thing that would make him feel whole.

Mild turbulence rattles the jet, sounding so much more ominous than it really is. He hears Roberta stirring, then settling back into the depth of sleep once more. The woman has no idea how fully she has been duped. She, so clever, so shrewd, so aware, and yet so blind.

He knows she will see though any pretense he puts forth, so all his deceits must be thickly coated with truth, like the candy coating of a Jordan almond.

Yes, it's true Cam does enjoy the attention of pretty girls who are drawn to his unique gravity. And yes, it's true that in his more glorious moments Cam does feel inebriated by his own existence, drunk on a heady brew of human ambrosia—the humanity that was unwound to create him. He has learned how to summon that feeling—to draw it like a bath and luxuriate in it when he needs to. It is the candy coating on the kernel of truth that only he knows, but shares with no one.

I am nothing without Risa.

So he will play the role of the spoiled star, allowing Roberta to think his hedonistic ways are real. And he will enjoy himself just enough to fool her and make her think arrogance and excess are all she needs to wrangle.

The plane begins its descent to wherever it is they're going next. More audiences. More Mirandas. A pleasant way to bide his time. Cam smiles, remembering the secret pledge he made with himself. If the one thing that Risa wants more than all else is the utter destruction of Proactive Citizenry, then Cam will find a way to provide it for her. More than just undermining Roberta, he will wedge himself in the gears of the entire Proactive

Citizenry machine. He will find a way to shut it down, and Risa will know that he was the one who did it.

Then she will truly love him, returning every last bit of his affections. And she will restore to him his soul.

14 · Manager

The Redwood Bluff Campground is sold out.

The manager of the Northern California campground should be happy, but he's troubled in the worst way. For him, the worst way means in his wallet.

A huge portion of the campground is taken up by Camp Red Heron—a summer camp for underprivileged kids. The bright crimson camp shirts are everywhere.

The afternoon before they're scheduled to leave, the manager comes into the midst of the campground of teens, who all admittedly look underprivileged. There are at least a hundred of them. They seem a little stressed when they see him, but quickly get back to their business. Mostly they act like kids on vacation, throwing balls, climbing trees—but there's a fear in their eyes and a sense of distrust in their actions. It betrays something their camp T-shirts are trying to hide.

"Excuse me. Who's in charge here?"

A girl who could have been a bouncer in a previous life comes forward. "He's busy," she tells him. "You can talk to me."

"I'll talk to the person in charge," the manager insists. "And I'll talk to him in private."

The big girl sneers. "You won't get much privacy among our campers." She folds her arms in defiance of his request. "I'll tell him you came by."

"I'll wait," he says.

Then from behind the girl, he hears, "It's okay, Bam. I'll talk to him."

From a gaggle of kids, emerges a teen—couldn't be any older than sixteen. He's short, but well built. Red hair with substantially long brown roots. He, like the girl, wears a red polo shirt with a logo indicating camp staff. He also wears a leather glove on one hand, but not the other. For all intents and purposes, he appears like a fine young man—but appearances are often deceiving.

He gestures to the manager. "Walk with me."

They leave the clearing, taking a path through the redwoods. The massive, ancient trees never cease to amaze the manager—one of the reasons why he took the job, even though it pays so little. Today, however, he's confident his fortunes will change.

He knows the path by heart and takes it only as far as the nearest campsite that's not occupied by Red Herons. A large family with lots of toddlers running around in diapers. He makes sure to keep the campsite, and the people there, in sight, because he suspects it's not a good idea to go any deeper into the woods alone with this young man.

"If you're worried about us cleaning up the campsite," the kid says, "I promise it will be done."

"I didn't get your name," the manager says.

He smirks. "Anson." The smirk is so blatant and broad, it's clear that this isn't his real name.

"Awfully young to be in charge of all these kids, aren't you?"

"Looks are deceiving," he says. "I got the job because I look closer to their age."

"I see." He looks down at the young man's left hand. "What's with the glove?"

The kid holds up his hand. "What's the matter? You have a problem with Louis Vuitton?"

The manager notes that the fingers of that hand don't seem to move. "Not at all. It just seems like an odd accessory for a camping trip."

The kid puts down his hand. "I'm a busy man, Mr. Proctor. It is Proctor, isn't it? Mark Proctor?"

The manager is caught off guard that this kid knows his name. Most people who book campsites at Redwood Bluff barely know he exists, much less know his name.

"If it's about payment," the young man says, "we already paid in full, and we paid in cash. I'm sure that's better than most people."

The manager decides to get to the point, because he's beginning to feel that the longer he draws this out, the more likely this kid will find a way to squirm off the hook.

"Yes, you did. One problem, though: I did some checking, and there is no Camp Red Heron. Not in this state or any other."

"Well," says the kid in a slick, condescending tone, "you obviously haven't been looking in the right place."

Mark Proctor will not be mocked. "As I said, there is no Camp Red Heron. What there are, however, are reports of a gang of renegade Unwinds. And one of them is an AWOL cop killer named Mason Michael Starkey. The picture looks an awful lot like you, 'Anson.' Without the red hair, of course."

The boy only smiles. "How can I help you, Mr. Proctor?"

Proctor knows he's in the driver's seat now. He's got this Starkey kid by the short hairs. He gives the kid back his mocking, condescending tone. "I would be shirking my civic responsibility if I didn't turn you and your little menagerie over to the Juvenile Authority."

"But you haven't done it yet."

Proctor takes a deep breath. "Maybe I could be persuaded not to."

He has no idea how much money these kids have, or where it comes from, but clearly they have enough to keep their little charade going. Proctor doesn't mind relieving them of some of that cash.

"All right," says Starkey. "Let me see if I can persuade you, then." He reaches into his pocket, but instead of producing a billfold, he produces a photograph. He deftly flips it in the fingers of his ungloved hand like a magician presenting a playing card.

The picture is of Proctor's teenaged daughter. It appears to have been taken recently, from right outside of her bedroom window. She's in the middle of doing her evening aerobic exercises.

"Her name is Victoria," Starkey says, "but she goes by Vicki—did I get that right? She seems like a nice girl. I sincerely hope nothing bad ever happens to her."

"Are you threatening me?"

"No, not at all." The picture seems to vanish before Proctor's eyes as Starkey moves his fingers. "We also know where your son goes to college—he's there on a swimming scholarship, because you certainly can't afford Stanford on your salary, can you? It's sad, but sometimes the best of swimmers have been known to drown. They get a little too sure of themselves, from what I understand." Starkey says nothing more. He just smiles with false pleasantness. A bird high above in the redwoods squawks as if amused, and a toddler in the nearby campsite begins to cry, as if mourning the loss of Mark Proctor's dignity.

"What do you want?" Proctor asks coldly.

Starkey's smile never loses any of its warmth. He puts his arm around Proctor's shoulder and walks them back the way they came. "All I want is to persuade you not to turn us in— just as you suggested. As long as you say nothing about us— either now or after we've left—I can personally guarantee that your lovely family will remain just as lovely as ever."

Proctor swallows, realizing that the sense of power he had only a few moments ago was nothing but an illusion.

"So do we have a deal?" Starkey prompts. He holds out his gloved hand for Proctor to shake, and Proctor grabs it, shaking it with conviction. Starkey grimaces as Proctor pumps his hand, but even the grimace is a show of strength rather than weakness.

"As you said, you're paid in full," Proctor says. "Nothing more is needed at this time. It was a pleasure to have Camp Red Heron here, and I hope to see you next summer." Although both of them know that's the last thing he wants.

As Proctor leaves, his legs a little wobbly, he realizes something. The picture of his daughter that seemed to have vanished during their conversation has now appeared in his shirt pocket. As he gazes at it, tears come to his eyes. Rather than feeling anger, he feels gratitude. Gratitude that he was not so much of a fool as to bring harm to her or to her brother.

15 · Starkey

"Don't move," Bam says. "If this stuff gets in your eyes, it burns like you can't believe."

It's after dark at the campsite now. Starkey sits in a lawn chair, his head leaning back. One kid holds a bucket of water; another kid is ready with towels. Bam, wearing rubber gloves, smears a sharp-smelling solution into Starkey's hair, massaging it into his scalp, all beneath the collective spotlight of four other kids holding flashlights.

"Can you believe it? The guy actually tried to blackmail us," Starkey tells Bam, closing his eyes.

"I wish I could have seen his face when you turned it around on him."

"It was classic—and it proves that our backup plan works."

"Jeevan deserves a medal," says one of the flashlights.

"But Whitney took the picture," says the kid with the water bucket.

"But Jeevan thought of it."

"Hey," says Starkey. "I didn't ask either of you."

Actually, it was Starkey who decided to put Jeevan in charge of intelligence. He's a smart kid with computer know-how who's good at thinking ahead. It's true that it was Jeevan's idea to gather information on the people they deal with—but what to do with that information is entirely up to Starkey. In this case blackmail for blackmail was the right move, and the man caved, just as Starkey had known he would. Even the hint of harm to his precious children was too much for the man. Incredible. It never ceases to amaze Starkey how far society will go to protect the children it loves and to discard the ones it doesn't.

"So where do we go now?" asks the kid with the towel. Starkey opens one eye, because the other one is already starting to sting. "It's not for you to worry about. You'll know when we get there."

As leader of the Stork Club, Starkey had learned the art of information control. Unlike Connor—who held nothing back when he ran the Graveyard—Starkey metes out information in bite-sized rations and only when absolutely necessary.

Since their plane crashed in the Salton Sea almost three weeks ago, things have not been easy for the Stork Club. Not at first anyway. Those first days, they hid out in the bare mountains above the Salton Sea, finding shallow caves and crevices to huddle in, so they couldn't be seen by reconnaissance aircraft. Starkey knew a ground search would be mounted, which meant they had to get far away, but they could travel only at night and on foot.

He had not thought of how to provide food or shelter or first aid for the kids who were injured in the crash, and they resorted to ransacking roadside convenience stores, which kept giving away their position to the authorities.

It was a trial by fire for Starkey, but he came through the flames, and thanks to him they remained alive and uncaptured. He kept those kids safe in his fist, in spite of his shattered hand. His hand is now the kind of war wound that legends are made of and has brought him even greater respect, because if he was tough enough to break his own hand in order to save them, he's tough enough to do anything.

In Palm Springs, they came across a hotel that had shut down but had not yet been demolished, and their fortune began to change. The place was isolated enough that they could hole up there and take the time to come up with a survival plan more effective than stripping 7-Elevens to the bone.

Starkey began to send kids out in small teams, choosing kids who didn't have an innately suspicious look about them. They stole clothes from unattended laundry rooms and groceries right from supermarket loading docks.

They stayed there for almost a week, until some local kids spotted them. "I'm a stork, too," one of the kids said. "We won't tell on you; we swear."

But Starkey has never trusted kids who come from loving families. He has a particular dislike of storks whose adoptive parents love them like their own flesh and blood. Starkey knows the basic statistics of unwinding. He knows that 99 percent of all storked kids are in warm loving homes, where unwinding would never be an issue. But when you're in that remaining 1 percent, and you're surrounded by other throwaway kids, those loving homes seem too distant to matter.

Then Jeevan came up with a stroke of genius. He tapped into the bank account of the Stork Clubs' parents—because quite a few of the kids either knew, or could figure out, their adoptive parents' passwords. The operation went down all at once, with a few computer clicks—and by the time anyone knew what was going on, the Stork Club had amassed more than seventeen thousand dollars in an offshore account. Accessing it was as simple as linking a counterfeit ATM card.

"Somebody somewhere is investigating this," Jeevan told Starkey. "In the end it won't lead them to us, though. It will lead them to Raymond Harwood."

"Who's Raymond Harwood?" Starkey had asked.

"A kid who used to pick on me in middle school."

That had made Starkey laugh. "Jeevan, have I ever told you that you're a criminal genius?"

He hadn't seemed too comfortable with the thought. "Well, I've been told I'm a genius. . . ."

Starkey often wonders why Jeevan's parents would choose to unwind a kid so bright—but it's an unspoken rule that you just don't ask.

The money gave the storks a little bit of freedom, because money buys legitimacy. All they needed was a simple subterfuge—an illusion that no one would question—and if there's one thing that Starkey knows as an amateur magician, it's the art of illusion. Misdirection. Every magician knows that an audience will always follow the hand that moves and will always believe what is presented to the eye until there's a reason not to.

Camp Red Heron was Starkey's own brainstorm. All it took to make the illusion real was an order of 130 camp T-shirts, staff shirts, and a few matching hats as icing on the cake. As Camp Red Heron, they were able to travel on trains and even charter buses, because the illusion ran on the power of assumption. People saw a camp on a field trip, and it became part of their reality without a second thought. Ironically, the more boisterous, the more visible they were, the more powerfully the illusion held. Even if people were watching a news report about the band of fugitive Unwinds, Camp Red Heron could march right past them, loud and obnoxious, and no one—not even law enforcement—would bat an eye. Who knew that hiding in plain sight could be so gratifying?

The first order of business was getting out of Southern California to a place where the authorities would not be searching for them. Having had enough desert for a lifetime, Starkey deemed that they take the Amtrak north to greener, lusher pastures. At their first campsite, near Monterey, they had no trouble whatsoever. Then they continued north, reserving their space at Redwood Bluff. All had gone well until today—but even so, today's crisis was easily managed.

Bam finishes rinsing the bleaching solution out of Starkey's hair, and the towel boy hurries to dry it.

"So, if the campground manager squeals, will you really hurt one of his kids?" Bam asks.

Starkey is annoyed that she's asked such a question in front of the flashlights, the towel, and the water bucket.

"He won't squeal," Starkey says, tousling his hair.

"But if he does?"

He turns to the towel kid. He's one of the younger groupies who's always trying to win Starkey's favor. "What do I always say?"

The kid takes on a terrified pop-quiz look. "Uh . . . smoke and mirrors?"

"Exactly! It's all smoke and mirrors."

That's the only answer he gives Bam—and even the answer is a foggy deflection, a nonanswer that avoids the question. Would he hurt them? Although Starkey would rather not think about it, he knows he'll do whatever is necessary to protect his storks. Even if it means making an example of someone.

"Speaking of mirrors, have a look," Bam says, and hands

him a mirror that she tore off the side of someone's car.

It's hard to get a full view of himself—he keeps having to shift the mirror to catch the entire visual effect. "I like it," he says.

"You look good as a platinum blond," she tells him. "Very surfer dude."

"Yeah, but surfer dude doesn't exactly inspire trust from adults," Starkey points out. "Cut it. Make it short and neat. I want to look like an Eagle Scout."

"You'll never be an Eagle Scout, Starkey," she says with a grin, and some of the other kids laugh. It actually hurts, although he won't show it. He first got interested in magic when he was younger because of its value as a Boy Scout merit badge. Funny how things change.

"Just do it, Bambi," he says. Which makes her scowl, as he intended. The other kids know not to laugh at her actual given name, lest they face her formidable wrath.

When Bam is done, Starkey could pass for the boy next door when he smiles, or a Hitler Youth when he doesn't. His scalp still stings from the bleaching solution, but it's not a bad feeling. "You know, I'm not the only one who needs to change identities," he tells Bam, after the other kids have left.

She laughs. "Nobody's touching my hair."

Bam has hair just short enough to be low maintenance. Her clothes are mannish, but only because she detests prissiness. Once and only once she made a pass at Starkey, but it was quickly deflected. Another girl might have folded and turned painfully awkward around him, but Bam took it in stride and carried on. Even if Starkey had been attracted to her, he knows acting on it would have been a bad idea. He's not foolish enough to think that a relationship here in the relative wild will last, and adding that kind of complication to his relationship with his second in command would be foolhardy.

As for other girls, the fact that he can have any girl he wants is a perk of his position he knows he must apply with careful discretion. He gives the same eye contact, the same lingering smile to every girl—and even to the boys that he can tell have an interest. It's all part of his subtle control. Keep them all thinking they're special. That they can be more than just a face in the crowd. These little touches carry big weight. The illusion of hope, combined with a healthy fear of him, keeps all his storks in line.

"I don't mean changing *your* identity, Bam," Starkey says. "I mean our identity. This guy did figure out who we are. To be safe, we can't be Camp Red Heron anymore."

"We could be a school—that way it won't just get us through the rest of the summer, but will work once the school year starts too."

"Excellent idea. Let's make it a private school. Something that sounds exclusive." Starkey runs through his mind all the storklike species he knows. "We'll call ourselves the 'Egret Academy.'"

"I love that!"

"Get that artsy girl what's-her-face to design the shirt again—but not so bright as the camp's. The Egret Academy will be all about beige and forest green."

"Can I come up with the school's history?"

"Knock yourself out."

There is a fine line between hiding in plain sight and flaunting their status as a fugitive band—Starkey knows how to ride the edge of illusion like a tightrope walker.

"Make it sound legit enough to fool the Juvies, if we come across any."

"The Juvenile Authority is a pack of idiots."

"No, they're not," Starkey tells her, "and that kind of thinking will get us caught. They're smart, so we need to be smarter. And when we do strike, we have to strike hard."

Since their ill-fated flight, there have been no stork liberations. Starkey had rescued several storked kids about to be unwound back during their stay at the airplane graveyard, but Connor was the one with the lists of kids about to be rounded for unwinding. Without a list, there's no way to know who needs to be rescued. But that's all right—because while saving individual kids and burning their homes as a warning is fine and dandy, Starkey knows he is capable of far more effective measures.

He has a brochure for a harvest camp that he keeps in his pocket. He pulls it out when he needs reminding. Like all harvest camps brochures, it features pictures of beautiful bucolic scenery and teens that are, if not happy, at least at peace with their fate.

A *bittersweet journey*, the brochure proclaims, *can touch many lives*.

"Finally giving up, Starkey?" Bam asks, when she catches him studying it later that night. "Ready to be unwound?"

He ignores the suggestion. "This harvest camp is in Nevada, north of Reno," he tells her. "Nevada has the weakest Juvenile Authority in the nation. It also has the highest concentration of storks waiting to be unwound. But check this out: This particular harvest camp has a shortage of surgeons. The population is bursting, and they can't unwind them fast enough." Then he gives her the boy-next-door grin. He's kept this to himself long enough. Time to start sowing the seeds of glorious purpose. He might as well begin with Bam.

"We're not going to take down individual homes and liberate one stork at a time anymore," Starkey proudly tells her. "We're going to liberate an entire harvest camp."

And God help anyone who gets in his way.

16 · Risa

HUMAN INTEREST NEWS CLIP

Today Eye-On-Art focuses on the provocative sculptures of Paulo Ribeiro, a Brazilian artist who works in a radical medium. As you can see from these images, his work is stunning, intriguing, and often disturbing. He calls himself an "Artist of Life," because every piece of work is crafted from the unwound.

We caught up with Ribeiro at a recent exhibition in New York.

"It is not so unusual what I do. Europe is full of cathedrals adorned in human bones, and in the early twenty-first century, artists like Andrew Krasnow and Gunther Von Hagens were known for their work in flesh. I have simply taken this tradition a logical step further. I hope not just to inspire but to incite. To bring to art patrons an aesthetic state of unrest. My use of the unwound is a protest against unwinding."

Pictured here is what Ribeiro considers to be his finest piece—both haunting, and intriguing, the piece is a working musical instrument he calls Orgão Orgânico, which now resides in a private collection.

"It is a shame that my greatest work should be privately owned, for it was meant to be heard and seen by the world. But like so many unwound, it now will never be."

Risa dreams of the stony faces. Pale and gaunt, judgmental and soulless as they gaze at her—not from a distance this time—but so close she could touch them. However, she can't touch them. She's sitting at a piano, but it will not bring forth music because Risa has no arms with which to play. The faces wait for a sonata that will never come—and only now does she realize that they are so close to one another they cannot possibly have bodies attached. They truly are disembodied. They are lined up in rows, and there are too many for her to count. She's horrified, but can't look away.

Risa can't quite discern the difference between the dream and waking. She thinks she might have been sleeping with her eyes open. There's a TV turned low, directly in her line of sight, that now shows an advertisement featuring a smiling woman who appears to be in love with her toilet bowl cleanser.

Risa rests on a comfortable bed in a comfortable place. It's a place she's never been, but that's a good thing, because it can only be an improvement over the places she *has* been lately.

There's a lanky umber kid in the room, who just now turns his gaze to her from the TV. It's a kid she's never met, but she knows his face from more serious television ads than the one on now.

"So you're the real deal," he says when he sees she's awake. "And here I thought you were some crazy-ass crank call." He looks older than he does in the commercials. Or maybe just wearier. She guesses he's about eighteen—no older than her.

"You'll live. That's the good news," the umber kid says. "Bad news is your right wrist is infected from that trap."

She looks to see her right wrist puffy and purple and worries that she might lose it—perhaps the pain being the cause of her armlessness in the dream. She instantly thinks of Connor's arm, or more accurately, Roland's arm on Connor's body.

"Give me someone else's hand, and I'll brain you," she says.

He laughs and points to his right temple and the faintest of surgical scars. "I already got brained, thank you very much."

Risa looks to her other arm, which also has a bandage. She can't remember why.

"We also gotta test you for rabies because of that bite. What was it, a dog?"

Right. Now she remembers. "Coyote."

"Not exactly man's best friend."

The bedroom around her is decorated in gaudy glitz. There's a mirror in a faux-gold frame. Light fixtures with shimmering chains. Shiny things. Lots and lots of shiny things.

"Where are we?" she asks. "Las Vegas?"

"Close," her host says. "Nebraska." Then he laughs again.

Risa closes her eyes for a moment and tries to mentally collate the events that led her here.

After she made the call, two men had come for her in the barn. They arrived after the coyotes had left and before they came back. She was semiconscious, so the details are hazy. They spoke to her, but she can't remember what they said and what she said back. They gave her water, which she threw up. Then they gave her lukewarm soup from a thermos, which she kept down. They put her in the backseat of a comfortable car and drove away, leaving the coyotes to find their next meal somewhere else. One of the men sat in the backseat with her, letting her lean against him. He spoke in calming tones. She didn't know who they were, but she believed them when they said she was safe.

"We got a pair of lungs with a doctor attached, if you get my meaning," the umber kid tells her. "He says your hand's not as bad as it looks—but you might lose a finger or two. No big thing—just means cheaper manicures."

Risa laughs at that. She's never had a manicure in her life, but she finds the thought of being charged by the finger darkly funny.

"From what I hear, you really did a number on that parts pirate."

Risa pulls herself up on her elbows. "I just took him out; it was nature that wolfed him down."

"Yeah, nature's a bitch." He holds out his hand for her to shake. "Cyrus Finch," he says, "But I go by CyFi."

"I know who you are," she tells him, shaking his hand awkwardly with her left.

Suddenly his face seems to change a bit, and so does his voice. It becomes harsher and loses all of its smooth style. "You don't know me, so don't pretend you do."

Risa, thrown for a bit of a loop, is about to apologize, but CyFi puts his hand up to stop her before she does.

"Don't mind my lips flapping: That's Tyler talking," he says. "Tyler don't trust folks far as he can throw 'em—and he can't throw no one, as his throwing arm has left the building; get me?"

It's a little too much for Risa to process, but the cadence of his forced old-umber speech is soothing. She can't help but smile. "You always talk like that?"

"When I'm me and not him," CyFi says with a shrug. "I choose to talk how I choose. It pays respect to my heritage, back in the day, when we were 'black,' and not 'umber.'"

Her only knowledge of Cyrus Finch, aside from the TV commercial, is from what little she saw of his testimony to Congress—back when it was all about limiting the age of unwinding to under seventeen, instead of eighteen. Cyrus helped push the Cap-17 law over the top. His chilling testimony involved Tyler Walker describing his own unwinding. That is to say, the part of Tyler that had been transplanted into Cyrus's head.

"I gotta admit I was surprised to get your call," CyFi tells her. "Big shots with the Anti-Divisional Resistance don't usually give us the time a' day, as we just deal with folks *after* the unwinding's done, not before."

"The ADR doesn't give anyone the time of day anymore," Risa tells him. "I haven't been in touch with them for months. To be honest, I don't know if they still exist. Not the way they used to."

"Hmm. Sorry to hear it."

"I keep hoping they'll reorganize, but all I see in the news are more and more resistance workers getting arrested for 'obstructing justice.'"

CyFi shakes his head sadly. "Sometimes justice needs obstructing when it ain't just."

"So where exactly in Nebraska are we, Cyrus?"

"Private residence," he tells her. "More of a compound, actually."

She doesn't quite know what he means by that, but she's willing to go with it. Her lids are heavy, and she's not up for too much talk right now. She thanks CyFi and asks if she can get something to eat.

"I'll have the dads bring you something," he says. "They'll be happy to see you've got your appetite back."

FOLLOWING IS A PAID POLITICAL ADVERTISEMENT

"Hi, I'm Vanessa Valbon—you probably know me from daytime TV, but what you might not know is that my brother is serving a life sentence for a violent crime. He has put himself on a list for voluntary cranial shelling, which will happen only if Initiative 11 is passed this November.

"There's been a lot of talk about shelling—what it is and what it isn't, so I had to educate myself, and this is what I learned. Shelling is painless. Shelling would be a matter of choice for any violent offender. And shelling will compensate the victim's family, and the offender's family, by paying them full market value for every single body part not discarded in the shelling process.

"I don't want to lose my brother, but I understand his choice. So the question is, how do we want our violent offenders to pay their debts to society? Wasting into old age on tax payers' dollars—or allowing them to redeem themselves, by providing much-needed tissues for society and much-needed funds for those impacted by their crimes?

"I urge you to vote yes on Initiative 11 and turn a life sentence . . . into a gift of life."

—Sponsored by Victims for the Betterment of Humanity.

Risa sleeps, then sleeps some more. Although she usually loathes lethargy, she decides she's earned little bit of sloth. She finds it hard to believe it's been barely three weeks since the Graveyard take down—and the night she exposed Proactive Citizenry's devious endeavors on national news. Truly, it was another lifetime ago. A life of being in the media spotlight had become a life of hiding from searchlights.

It had been the shadowy movers and shakers of Proactive Citizenry that had gotten the charges against her dropped and allowed her to come out of hiding in the first place. But—big surprise—new charges were filed after the night she made herself their enemy. There are claims that she had stolen huge sums of money from the organization—which she had not. There are claims that she had helped to arm the AWOL Unwinds at the Graveyard—which she did not. All she had done during her tenure at the Graveyard was administer first aid and treat colds. The truth however, is of no interest to anyone but her.

CyFi's fathers—both of whom are as sienna-pale as CyFi is dark—dote on her in equal measure, bringing her meals in bed. They were the ones who came all the way out to Cheyenne to get her, so they've taken a vested interest in her health. Being treated like a delicate flower tires for Risa quickly. She begins to pace the room, still amazed every time she swings her feet out of bed and walks on her own. Her wrist is stiff and aches, so she carries it carefully, even after the doctor-in-residence concludes that her fingers are fine and she will have to pay full price for any future manicures, and happily, she doesn't have rabies either.

Her window gives her a view of a garden and not much more, so she really doesn't know how big the place is and how many are here. Occasionally there are people tending the garden. She would go out to meet them, but her door is locked.

"Am I a prisoner?" Risa asks the taller, kinder-looking of CyFi's dads.

"Not all locks are about restraint, dear," he tells her. "Some are merely about timing."

On the following afternoon, the timing must be right, because CyFi offers to give her the grand tour.

"You've got to understand, not everyone here is sympathetic to you," CyFi warns. "I mean, yeah, people know all that whack campaigning you did in favor of unwinding was bogus. Everyone knows you were being blackmailed—but even so, that interview where you talk about how unwinding is the least of all evils?" He grimaces. "It's a dish that sticks to your bones, if you know what I mean."

Risa can't meet his gaze. "I do."

"You best be reminding people that the new spine you got is something you didn't ask for and something you regret having. That's a sentiment we can all relate to."

As CyFi had said, the place is more than just a home; it's a full-fledged compound. Risa's room is in the main house—but the house has large wings that were clearly added on recently, and across the large garden are half a dozen sizeable cottages that Risa couldn't see from her window.

"Land is cheap in Nebraska," CyFi tells her. "That's why we came here. Omaha's close enough for folks that got business to go about it and far enough out that strangers leave us alone."

Some of the people she passes glance at her, then look away without a greeting. Others give her a solemn nod. A few smile, although the smile is forced. They all know who she is—but no one knows what to make of her, any more than she knows what to make of them.

This afternoon there are several people tending to the garden as Risa and CyFi stroll through. On closer inspection, the garden isn't just ornamental—there are vegetables growing in rows. Off to the left are pens with chickens and maybe other animals Risa can't see.

CyFi answers her question before she asks it. "We're fully sustainable. We don't slaughter our own meat though, 'cept for the chickens."

"Who, may I ask, is 'we'?"

"The folk," CyFi says simply.

"ChanceFolk?" Risa guesses—but looking around, none of the people here look Native American.

"No," CyFi explains. "Tyler-folk."

Risa doesn't quite catch his meaning yet. It seems quite a lot of the people she sees have grafted bits about them. A cheek here, an arm there. It isn't until she sees one bright blue eye that perfectly matches someone else's that it begins to dawn on her what this place is.

"You live in a revival commune?" Risa is a bit awed and maybe a bit frightened, too. She's heard rumors of such places, but never thought they were real.

CyFi grins. "The dads were the first to call it a 'revival commune' when we got started. I kinda like it, don't you? It sounds kinda . . . spiritual." He gestures to the cottages and land around him. "Most everyone here got a part of Tyler Walker," CyFi explains. "That's what the Tyler Walker Foundation is all about. Putting together places like this, for people who feel the need to reunite the Unwind they share."

"Cyrus, that's twisted."

CyFi doesn't seem fazed by her judgment. "A lot less

twisted than some other things. It's a way to cope, Risa—cope with something that never shoulda happened in the first place." Then his jaw tightens, his gaze turns dodgy, and she knows it's Tyler talking now.

"You go put yourself in a room with the arms, legs, and thoughts that belong to that spine of yours, and you'll look at this place a whole lot differently."

Risa waits a moment for Tyler to go back to drafting behind CyFi again, as CyFi's much more pleasant to talk to.

"Anyways," says CyFi, not missing a beat, "this place was the first, but now we've set up more than thirty revival communes across the country—and there's more on the way." He folds his arms and smiles proudly. "Pretty cool, huh?"

Out in front of one of the cottages, Risa spots the doctor who's been tending to her wrist. CyFi calling him "a pair of lungs," suddenly makes more sense now. The man is throwing a ball with a young boy who is clearly his son.

"So people just dropped everything and came here with their families?" Risa asks.

"Some brought families with them; others left families behind."

"All to join the cult of Tyler Walker?"

CyFi takes a moment before answering. Maybe it's a moment to keep Tyler from shouting out something they might both regret. "Maybe it's a cult, and maybe not—but if it fills a need and doesn't hurt anyone, who are you to judge?"

Risa holds her tongue, realizing the more she talks the more she insults her host.

CyFi is happy to change the subject. "So, how's the Fry?"

"Excuse me?"

He rolls his eyes, like it should be obvious. "Our mutual friend. How is he? Do you hear from him?"

Risa is still at a loss.

CyFi looks at her incredulously. "The one, the only Levi Jedediah Small-Fry Calder. He never told you he knew me?"

Risa finds herself stuttering. "Y-you know Lev?"

"Do I know Lev? Do *I* know *Lev*? I traveled with him for weeks. He told me all about you and Connor kidnapping him and stuff. The way you saved him from getting tithed." CyFi gets a little wistful. "I took care of him until he had to take care of me. He took care of me real good, Risa. No way I'd be here today if it weren't for him. Life woulda hit me like a train if he hadn't been there to stop it." CyFi stops walking. He looks down. "When I saw he became a clapper, I nearly crapped my pants. Not Fry—not that good kid."

"He didn't blow himself up."

He snaps his eyes to her. She doesn't know whether it's CyFi or Tyler. Maybe it's both of them. "Of course he didn't! You think I don't know that?" CyFi takes a moment to mellow. "Do you have any idea where he is now?"

Risa shakes her head. "There was an attack on his home. Last I heard he went into hiding."

CyFi purses his lips. "Poor little Fry. Hope he turns out less screwed up than the rest of us."

Risa knows that, as horrifying as it was that Lev had become a clapper, she would have been unwound long ago if his clapper friends hadn't taken down Happy Jack Harvest Camp. "Small world, isn't it?" she tells CyFi. "Lev's still here because of us—but we're both here because of him."

"See, we're all interconnected," CyFi says. "Not just us Tyler-folk."

As they pass the last of the cottages, a middle-aged woman with no outward surgical signs smiles warmly at Risa from her porch, and Risa smiles back, finally beginning to feel comfortable with the idea of this place. CyFi touches his chest, indicating to Risa that the woman has Tyler's heart.

They round back toward the main house, and Risa's wrist begins to ache, reminding her that she'll have to take it easy for a while. Her running from the powers that be will have to slow to a walk for a while. She could think of worse places than this to have to lie low.

FOLLOWING IS A PAID POLITICAL ADVERTISEMENT

"This is actor Kevin Bessinger, asking you to vote no on Initiative 11. Initiative 11—the 'pound-of-flesh' law—is not what it appears. It says it will allow for the voluntary shelling of inmates—in other words, the removal and disposal of their brains, followed by the unwinding of the rest of their bodies. It might seem like a sensible idea—until you read what the initiative actually says.

"Initiative 11 states that shelling would be voluntary— but it also allows prison administrators to override that and mandate the shelling of any prisoner they choose. In addition, it brings into the mainstream the unethical black-market practice of selling unwound parts at auction. Do you really want our lawmakers in the black market?

"Vote no on Initiative 11. The pound-of-flesh law is not a solution we can live with."

—Sponsored by the Coalition for Ethical Unwinding Practices

Dinner that night for Risa is not room service but a feast in the large dining room of the main house. The long table seats two dozen, and Risa is seated toward the middle, after refusing to be seated at the head. CyFi's fathers, who, Risa learned, had given up lucrative law and dental practices to run the Tyler Walker Foundation, are not present.

"Twice a week we have a special dinner," CyFi explains. "Just Tyler-folk—no spouses or family. It's a time just for us— and tonight you get to be one of us."

Risa's not sure how to feel about that.

The doctor takes it upon himself to introduce Risa, stealing CyFi's thunder. He offers Risa up in the best possible light. A loyal member of the ADR forced by the enemy to testify against her own conscience. "She believed that by doing their bidding, she was saving hundreds of kids from being unwound," the doctor explains, "but in the end she was double-crossed, and those kids are now in harvest camps awaiting 'summary division.' Risa is a victim of the system, as we all are, and I, for one, welcome her with open arms."

Those gathered applaud, although there's still some reluctance. Risa supposes that's the best she's going to get.

The meal is brisket and flavorful home-grown vegetables. It's like Sunday dinner among a big family. Everyone eats with minimal conversation until CyFi says, "Yo, maybe you all oughta introduce yourselves."

"Names, or sharings?" someone asks.

"Sharings," someone else answers. "We might as well tell her the Tyler."

CyFi begins. "Right temporal lobe." Then he looks to his left.

Reluctantly the man next to him says, "Left arm." He holds up his hand and waves.

Then the woman beside him says, "Left leg below the knee." And around the table it goes:

"Right eye."

"Left eye."

"Liver and pancreas."

"A substantial part of the occipital lobe."

Part after part is announced until it comes all the way around the table, back to Risa. "Spine," she says awkwardly. "But I don't know whose."

"We could find out for you," the woman who received Tyler's heart offers.

NEAL SHUSTERMAN

"No, that's all right. I'd rather not know," Risa tells her. "At least not now, anyway."

She nods with understanding. "It's a personal choice—no one will pressure you."

Risa looks around the table. They're all still eating, but now the attention is focused on her.

"So . . . every single piece of Tyler Walker is at this table?"

CyFi sighs. "No. We don't got spleen, left kidney, intestinal tract, thyroid, or any part of his right arm. And there's also a bunch of smaller brain bits that didn't have enough of him to feel the pull—but about seventy-five percent of him is here around the table."

"And the other twenty-five percent can take a flying leap," says left-auditory-tract man. Everyone laughs.

Risa also learns that the garish decor in every room is also for Tyler. He had an overwhelming attraction to shiny things. Stealing them was part of the reason he was unwound.

"But everything here is bought and paid for," the Tyler-folk are quick to tell her.

"Does the Tyler Walker Foundation pay you all to stay here?"

"More like the other way around," the doctor says. "Sure, when we first heard the idea, we were all dubious"—his eyes go a little euphoric—"but when you're here, in the presence of Tyler, you realize you don't want to be anywhere else."

"I sold my home and gave everything to the foundation," someone else says. "They didn't ask for it. I just wanted to give it."

"He's here with us, Risa," CyFi tells her. "You don't have to believe it, but we all do. It's a matter of faith."

It's all too strange, too foreign for Risa to embrace. She thinks of the many other "revival communes" that have sprung up, thanks to the Tyler Walker Foundation. Their existence is another unexpected consequence of unwinding—a convoluted solution to an even more convoluted problem. She doesn't fault CyFi or any of these people. Instead she blames the world that made this place necessary. It galvanizes her more than ever to bring an end to unwinding once and for all. She knows she's only one girl, but she also knows she's a larger-than-life icon now. People love her, fear her, despise her, revere her. All these elements can make her a force to be reckoned with, if she plays her cards right.

That night, before everyone goes to bed, there's a ritual that CyFi lets her witness.

"We played with a bunch of ideas—silly stuff mostly—like lying on the ground in the shape of a body, in our respective positions. Or huddling together in a little room, all squeezed in like clowns in a car, to reduce the space between us. But all that crap just felt weird. In the end we settled upon this circle. Simpler is better."

The circle, which is at the center of the garden, is marked by stones, each one engraved with the name of a part—even the parts that aren't there have a place. Everyone sits in front of their respective stone, and someone—anyone—begins to speak. There seem to be no rules beyond that. It's a free-for-all, and yet they never seem to speak over one another. Risa notices that it's the people who got Tyler's brain that seem to motivate most of the conversation, but everyone participates.

"I'm pissed off," someone says.

"You're always pissed off," someone else responds. "Let it go."

"I shouldn't have stolen all that stuff."

"But you did, so get over it."

"I miss Mom and Dad."

"They unwound you."

"No! I can stop them. It's not too late."

"Read my lips: They . . . unwound . . . you!"

"I feel sick to my stomach."

"I'm not surprised the way you scarfed down that brisket."

"It tasted like Grandma's."

"It was. I convinced Mom to give us the recipe."

"You talked to her?"

"Well, to her lawyer."

"It figures."

"I remember Mom's smile."

"I remember her voice."

"Remember how cold she was toward the end?"

"Sorry, not part of my memory."

"There's so much stuff I wanna do, but I can't remember what it was."

"I remember at least one thing. Skydiving."

"Yeah, like that's gonna happen."

"Maybe it will," says CyFi. Then he asks, "How many of you would skydive for Tyler?"

About half the hands go up immediately, then a bunch more with mild reluctance. There are only a couple of hold-outs.

"Great," says CyFi. "It's a done deal. I'll have the dads make the arrangements. Tyler's going skydiving!"

Risa feels like the ultimate outsider, and she can't help but feel these people are deluding themselves . . . but she also can't help but wonder if maybe, just maybe, Tyler is really here in some real but immeasurable way. Whether it's an illusion or not, she'll never know. Like CyFi said, it's a matter of faith.

One thing's for sure, though. If Tyler really is "present," then he's got a lot of growing up to do. Risa wonders if a divided person *can* grow up. Or if they're stuck at the age at which they were unwound.

When the circle chat is through, CyFi walks Risa back to

her room, and Risa can't keep herself from giving at least one opinion.

"It's all well and good what you're playing at here, Cyrus," Risa says, "but when you stood in front of Congress and fought for the Cap-17 law, you were doing something truly important."

"Yeah—and look what good it did. We got Cap-17 through, and now there are even more crackdowns by the Juvies and ads convincing people what a good thing unwinding is. They use all our good intentions against us—you should know that more than anyone. I'm pretty damn smart, but no way am I smart enough to beat that."

"That doesn't mean you give up trying. Now what are you doing? Nothing but indulging the childish whims of a troubled unwound kid."

"Watch yourself, Risa," CyFi warns. "People have given up a lot to indulge that troubled kid."

"Well, then, maybe Tyler needs someone to tell him to man up."

"And that person is you, I suppose?"

"I don't see anyone else doing it. You're all fixated on what Tyler was and what he wanted before he got himself unwound. Why don't you start thinking about what he'd want three years later?"

For once, CyFi has no wisecrack answer. But Tyler does.

"You suck," Tyler says out of CyFi's mouth. "But yeah, I'll think about it."

---

and the initiative has a provision allowing burn victims to receive them for free. When you've been in the field as long as I have, you know how important that is.

"Opponents of Initiative 11 claim some sort of 'moral high ground'—but you want to know the truth? They're the ones with an unethical agenda. They, and the Juvenile Authority, want Initiative 11 to fail, because they want to repeal the Cap-17 law instead. Not only that, but these same self-serving billionaires are fighting for a constitutional amendment that would bump the legal age of unwinding all the way up to 19, allowing even more kids to be unwound— which would increase their profits and their stranglehold on the organ industry.

"I don't know about you, but I'd rather see a killer unwound than the kid next door. Vote yes on Initiative 11!"

—Sponsored by Patriots for Sensible Shelling

Although Risa had resolved to stay a second week, her antsiness, and desire to *do* something becomes overwhelming. On her eighth day, she decides to leave.

"Where will you go?" CyFi asks as he escorts her to the main road. "If the ADR is the full-on mess you say it is, do you even have a place to go?"

"No," she admits, "but I'll take my chances out there. There's got to be someone left in the ADR. If not, I'll start my own Anti-Divisional Resistance."

"Sounds pretty iffy to me."

"My whole life's been iffy—why should this be any different?"

"All right, then," says CyFi. "You take care of yourself, Risa, and if you happen to run into Lev, tell him to come on by. I'll cook some nice old-fashioned smorgasbash." CyFi smiles. "He'll know what it means."

17 · Argent

Argent Skinner's left cheek is torn. Not beyond repair, but beyond any repair he can afford. Three jagged rifts, now stitched together like a baseball, spread out from beneath his eye to below his ear. Another inch and it would have cut his carotid artery. Maybe he wishes it had. Maybe he wishes his hero had taken his life, because then, in some twisted way, Argent and Connor Lassiter would be connected forever. Then he would not have to face the fallout from what should have been the greatest event of his meager existence.

The idea of Grace on the run with Connor is something he just can't wrap his mind around. The two of them taking off like some ridiculous Bonnie and Clyde would make Argent laugh if he weren't so lethally pissed off. He had the Akron AWOL in his damn cellar! For just a moment he had the world at his feet—or at least in kicking distance. Now what does he have?

When he showed up for his shift the next morning, half his face in a bandage, customers and coworkers all feigned to care.

"Oh my, what happened?" they all asked.

"Gardening accident," he told them, because he couldn't come up with anything better at the time.

"Wow, musta been one nasty hedge."

At home he stews, he curses, then stews some more, for what else can he do? Argent knows he can't tell the police the truth of what happened. He can't tell anyone, because his fool friends have bigger mouths than he does. The Juvenile Authority and FBI have dismissed him as a dumbass yokel who concocted a lie and almost made it stick. They see him as a joke.

Even his own half-wit sister managed to turn him into a joke of a man, and all because of Connor Lassiter.

Can you despise your personal hero?

Can you long to share in his light and at the same time want to slit his throat the way he almost slit yours?

Argent's only consolation is that Grace is no longer his problem. He doesn't have to feed her; he doesn't have to scold her and make her mind. He doesn't have to worry about her leaving the water running, or the gas on, or the freaking back door open for the raccoons. He can have his own life. But what is that life, really?

Argent knows that these thoughts will fill his head for months to come as he mindlessly scans canned corn and pocket-damp coupons. "Did you find everything okay?" his mouth will say. "Have a good one!" But his heart will be wishing them worms in their meat, disease in their produce, and swollen, rancid canned goods. Anything that will inflict upon them a small fraction of the misery that now resides within him.

A week after Connor's escape, a visitor shows up at Argent's door just before he's about to leave for his morning shift.

"Hello," the man says. His voice is a little bit ragged and his smile suspiciously broad. "Would you happen to be Argent Skinner?"

"Depends on who's asking." Argent figures this might be one of the feds, come to tie up loose ends. He wonders if he's going to be arrested after all. He wonders if he cares.

"May I come in?"

The man steps forward a bit, and now Argent can see something that was hidden by the oblique morning light. There's something wrong with the right half of the man's face. It's peeling and infected.

"What's the deal with your face?" Argent asks, point-blank.

"I could ask the same of you," he answers.

"Gardening accident," Argent volunteers.

"Sunburn," the man counters—although to Argent it looks more like a radiation burn. A person would have to lie beneath an unforgiving sky for hours to get a burn that bad.

"You oughta take care of that," Argent says, not even trying to mask his disgust.

"I will when time allows." The man steps forward again. "May I come in? There's something I need to discuss with you. Something of mutual interest and benefit."

Argent is not so stupid as to let a stranger into his house at the crack of dawn—especially one who looks as wrong as this man does. He blocks the threshold and takes a stance that would resist any attempt for the man to barge his way in. "State your business right there," Argent tells him.

"Very well." The man smiles again, but his smile seems like a silent curse. Like the smile Argent gives people in the ten-items-or-less line who violate the limit. The smile he gives them while wiping just a little bit of snot on their apples.

"I happened to catch that picture you posted of you and Connor Lassiter."

Argent sighs. "It was a fake, all right? I already told the police." Argent steps back to close the door, but the man moves forward, planting his foot in just the right spot to keep the door from budging.

"The authorities may have fallen for your story—mainly because they truly believe that Lassiter is dead—but I know better."

Argent doesn't know what to make of this. Half of him wants to run, but the other half wants to know what this guy is all about.

"Yeah?" he says.

"Just like you, I caught him, yet he managed to slither away.

And just like you, I want to make him pay for what he's done."

"Yeah?" Now Argent begins to get the slightest glimmer of hope. Maybe his life won't be all about ringing up groceries in this town.

"Now can I come in?"

Argent steps back and lets him enter. The man closes the door gently and looks around, clearly unimpressed by the lived-in look of the house.

"So did he screw up your face too?" Argent asks.

The man glares at him, but then his gaze softens. "Indirectly. This was the fault of his accomplice. He left me unconscious by the side of the road, and when morning came, I roasted in the Arizona sun. Not a pleasant thing to wake up to."

"Sunburn," says Argent. "So you were telling the truth."

"I'm an honest man," Nelson says. "And I've been wronged, just like you. And just like you, I want to settle the score. That's why you're going to help me find Connor and his little friend."

"And my sister," Argent adds. "She took off with Connor."

The idea of going after Connor and Grace had crossed Argent's mind, but not seriously. It's not the kind of thing you do alone. But now he wouldn't be alone. Then it occurs to Argent what this man is.

"Are you some kind of parts pirate?"

That smile again. "The best there is." He tips an imaginary hat. "Jasper T. Nelson, at your service."

Parts pirates, Argent knows, are like cowboys of old. Lawless bounty hunters who play by their own rules, bringing in AWOL Unwinds and collecting official rewards—or better yet—selling those Unwinds for more money on the black market. Argent can see himself living life on the edge like that. He lets the idea linger, trying on the label like a new pair of jeans. Argent Skinner, parts pirate.

"The fact is, you're in a lot of trouble, son. You just don't know it yet," Nelson tells him. "You may think the authorities are done with you, but tomorrow, or the next day, or the day after that, someone in some lab is going to run a routine forensic analysis of that picture you took, and they're going to discover that it's not a fake after all."

Argent tries to swallow, but his throat is too dry. "Yeah?"

"Then you will be arrested. And interrogated. And interrogated some more. You will be charged with obstruction of justice, harboring a known criminal, and maybe even conspiracy to commit terrorism. You'll end up in prison for a good long time. You might even get unwound if one of those new laws pass allowing the unwinding of criminals."

Argent feels the blood drain from his sore face. He has to sit down, but doesn't, because he's afraid he might not have the strength to get up. So instead he locks his knees and sways a little bit on feet that suddenly feel too far away from the floor.

And all this because of Connor Lassiter.

"I'm sure if they interrogate you, you'll sing to them everything Lassiter told you. But I would much prefer it if you sang for me instead. And you do have things to sing about, don't you?"

Argent racks his brain for anything useful Connor might have said, but nothing comes to mind. Still, that won't be what the parts pirate wants to hear.

"He told me some stuff," Argent says. Then more forcefully, "Yeah. He told me stuff. Maybe enough to figure out where he's going."

Nelson laughs gently. "You're lying." He pats the good side of Argent's face. "That's all right. I'm sure there are things you know that you don't even know you know. And besides, I need an associate. Someone to whom catching Connor Lassiter is personal, because that's the only kind of person I can trust. I would have preferred someone a bit higher on the evolutionary ladder, but one takes what one can get."

"I'm not stupid," Argent tells him, intentionally avoiding the word "ain't" to prove it. "I'm just unlucky."

"Well, today your luck has changed."

Perhaps it has, Argent thinks. *Maybe this partnership is fated.* The right side of Nelson's face is ruined, as is the left side of Argent's. They both bear the marks of their struggle with the Akron AWOL. It makes them a team perfectly suited for the mission.

Nelson looks toward the window, as if checking to see if the coast is still clear. "Here's what you're going to do, Argent. You're going to fill a backpack with only the things you need, and you'll do it in less than five minutes. Then you'll come with me to take down the Akron AWOL once and for all. What do you say to that?"

Argent offers a feeble smile on the side of his face that still can. "Yo-ho, yo-ho," Argent says. "A pirate's life for me."

Part Three

Sky-Fallers

Documented cases of cellular memory being transferred to heart transplant recipients:

CASE 1) A Spanish-speaking vegetarian receives the heart of an English speaker and begins using English words that were not part of his vocabulary but were words habitually used by the donor. The recipient also begins craving, and eventually eating, meat and greasy foods, which were mainstays of the donor's diet.

CASE 2) An eight-year-old girl receives the heart of a ten-year-old girl who was murdered. The recipient begins having nightmares about the murder, remembering details that only the victim could know, such as when and how it happened and the identity of the murderer. Her entire testimony turns out to be true, and the murderer is caught.

CASE 3) A three-year-old Arab child receives the heart of a Jewish child, and upon waking, asks for a Jewish candy the child had never heard of before.

CASE 4) A man in his forties receives a heart from a teenaged boy and suddenly develops an intense love of classical music. The donor had been killed in a drive-by shooting, clutching his violin case as he died.

CASE 5) A five-year-old boy receives the heart of a three-year-old. He talks to him like an imaginary friend, calling him Timmy. After some investigation, the parents discovered the name of the donor was Thomas. But his family called him Timmy.

A total of 150 anecdotal cases have been documented by neuropsychologist Paul Pearsall, PhD.

http://www.paulpearsall.com/info/press/index.html

The Rheinschilds

She's worried about him. He's always been obsessed with their work, but she's never seen him like this. The hours he spends in his research lab, the dark circles beneath his eyes, all the mumbling in his sleep. He's losing weight, and no wonder; he seems to never eat anymore.

"He's like this superbrain with no body," says Austin, his research assistant, who has grown from an emaciated bean-pole to a much more healthy weight since Janson hired him six months ago.

"Will you tell me what he's working on?" Sonia asks.

"He said you didn't want any part of it."

"I don't. But I have a right to know what he's doing, don't I?" It's so like Janson to take everything she says literally. Shutting her out to spite her, like a child.

"He says he'll tell you when he's ready."

It's no sense trying to get anything out of the boy—he's got the loyalty of a German shepherd.

She supposes this obsession of Janson's is better than the despair he felt before. At least now he has something to focus on, something to take his thoughts away from the cascade of events that the Unwind Accord has brought about. Their new reality includes clinics that have popped up nationwide like mushrooms on an overwatered lawn, each of them advertising young, healthy parts. "Live to 120 and beyond!" the ads say. "Out with the old and in with the new!" No one asks where the parts are coming from, but everyone knows. And now it's not just ferals that are being unwound—the Juvenile Authority has actually come up with a form that parents can use to send their "incorrigible" teen off for unwinding. At first she doubted anyone would use the form. She was convinced its very existence would finally spark the outcry she'd been waiting for. It didn't. In fact, within a month, there was a kid in their own neighborhood who had been taken away to be unwound.

"Well, I think they did the right thing," one of her neighbors confided. "That kid was a tragedy waiting to happen."

Sonia doesn't talk to either of those neighbors anymore.

Day to day, Sonia watches her husband waste away, and none of her pleas for him to take care of himself get through. She even threatens to leave him, but they both know it's an empty threat.

"It's almost ready," he tells her one evening as he moves his fork around a plate of pasta, barely putting any into his mouth. "This'll do it, Sonia—this will change everything."

But he still won't share with her exactly what he's doing. Her only clue comes from his research assistant. Not from anything the boy says, but because he began his employment with three fingers on his left hand. And now he has five.

18 · Lev

He bounds through a dense forest canopy, high up where the leaves touch the sky. It's night, but the moon is as bright as the sun. There is no earth, only trees. Or maybe it's that the ground matters so little, it might as well not exist. Stirred by a warm breeze, the forest canopy rolls like ocean waves beneath the clear sky.

There is a creature leaping through the foliage in front of him, turning back to look at Lev every once in a while. It has huge cartoonish eyes in its small furred face. It's not fleeing from Lev, he realizes; it's leading him. *This way*, it seems to say with those soulful eyes that reflect twin images of the moon.

Where are you leading me? Lev wants to ask, but he can't speak. Even if he could, he knows he won't get an answer.

Branch to branch Lev leaps with an inborn skill that he did not possess in life. This is how he knows he's dead. The experience is too clear, too vivid to be anything else. When he was alive, Lev never cared much for climbing trees. As a child, it was discouraged by his parents. Tithes need to protect their precious bodies, he was told, and climbing trees can lead to broken bones.

Broken.

He was broken in a car accident and left with deep damage inside. That damage must have been worse than anyone thought. His last memory is a cloudy recollection of pulling up to the eastern gate of the Arápache Rez. He remembers hearing his own voice telling the guard something, but he can't remember what it was. His fever was soaring by then. All he wanted to do was sleep. He was unconscious before he learned whether or not the guard would let them in.

But none of that matters now. Death has a way of making the concerns of the living feel insignificant. Like the ground below, if indeed there is ground.

He leaps again, his pace getting faster. There is a rhythm to it, like a heartbeat. The branches seem to appear right where he needs them to be.

Finally he reaches the very edge of the forest at the very edge of the world. Star-filled darkness above and below. He looks for the creature that was leading him, but it is nowhere to be seen. Then he realizes with a dark sort of wonder that there never was a creature. *He* is the creature, projecting his anima before him as he launches through the treetops.

Up above, the full moon is so clear, so large, that Lev feels he could reach out and grab it. Then he realizes that is exactly what he is meant to do. Bring down the moon.

It will be a devastating thing if he plucks the moon from the sky. Tides will change, and oceans will churn in consternation. Lands will flood, while bays will turn to deserts. Earthquakes will re-form the mountains, and people everywhere will have to adapt to a new reality. If he tears down the moon, everything will change.

With infinite joy and absolute abandon, Lev leaps to his purpose, soaring off the edge of the world and toward the moon with his arms open wide.

Lev opens his eyes. There is no moon. There are no stars. There is no forest canopy. Only the white walls and ceiling of a room he hasn't seen for a long time. He feels weak and wet. His body hurts, but he can't yet identify the location of the pain. It seems to come from everywhere. He's not dead after all—and for a moment he finds himself disappointed. Because if death is a joyous jaunt through a forest canopy for all eternity, he can live with that. Or *not* live, as the case may be.

This room is where he hoped he'd find himself when he awoke. There's a woman sitting at the desk across the room, making notes in a file. He knows her. Loves her, even. He can count on one hand all the people in his life whom he would be happy to see. This woman is one of them.

"Healer Elina," he tries to say, but it comes out like the squeak of a mouse.

She turns to him, closing the file, and regards him with a pained smile. "Welcome back, my little Mahpee."

He tries to smile, but it hurts his lips to do it. Mahpee. "Sky-faller." He had forgotten they had called him that. So much has changed since he was last here. He's not the boy he was when they first took him in as a foster-fugitive. That was the beginning of his dark days—between the time he left CyFi and the time he showed up at the airplane graveyard.

Elina comes over to him, and immediately he notices the gray infiltrating her braid. Was it there a year and a half ago and he hadn't noticed, or is it new? She certainly has reason to have new gray hairs.

"I'm sorry," he rasps out.

She seems genuinely surprised. "For what?"

"For being here."

"You should never apologize for existing, Lev. Not even to all those people out there who wish you didn't."

He wonders how many of those people are right here on the reservation. "No . . . I mean I'm sorry I came back to the rez."

She takes a moment to look at him. No longer smiling, just observing. "I'm glad you did."

But Lev notices that she didn't say "we."

"I decided that once you were stable, you were better off here in my home than in the medical lodge." She checks the IV leading into his right forearm. He hadn't even noticed it was there before. "You're looking a little puffy, but you're probably just overhydrated. I'll turn this off for a bit." She shuts down the fluid infuser. "That's probably why you sweat so much when your fever broke." She looks at him for a moment, probably assessing what he needs to know, then says, "You have two broken ribs and suffered quite a lot of internal bleeding. We had to give you a partial thoracotomy to stop the bleeding—but it will heal, and I have herbs that will keep it from scarring."

"How's Chal?" Lev asks. "And Pivane?" Chal, Elina's husband, is a big-shot Arápache lawyer. His brother Pivane isn't one to leave the rez.

"Chal has a major case in Denver, but you'll see Pivane soon enough."

"Has he asked to see me?"

"You know Pivane—he'll wait until he's invited."

"My friends?" Lev asks. "Are they here?"

"Yes," Elina says. "It seems my household is overrun by mahpees this week." Then she goes to an entertainment console, fiddles with it a bit, and music begins to play. Guitar music.

He recognizes the piece from his first time on the rez, and it pulls at his heartstrings. That first time, he had climbed over the southern wall to get in and was injured in the fall. He woke to find himself in this same room. An eighteen-year-old boy was playing guitar with such amazing skill, Lev had been mesmerized. But now all that remains of him is a recording.

"One of Wil's songs of healing," Elina says. "Wil's music goes on, even if he doesn't. It's a comfort to us. Sometimes."

Lev forces a smile, his lips not hurting quite so bad this time. "It's good to be . . . here," he says, almost saying "home" instead of "here." Then he closes his eyes, because he's afraid to see what her eyes will say back.

19 · Connor

"He's awake," Elina says. That's all, just "he's awake." She is a woman of few words. At least few words for Connor.

"So, can I see him?"

She folds her arms and regards him coolly. Her lack of response is his answer. "Tell me one thing," she finally says. "Is it because of you he became a clapper?"

"No!" says Connor, disgusted by the suggestion. "Absolutely not!" And then he adds, "It's because of me that he didn't clap."

She nods, accepting his answer. "You can see him tomorrow, once he's a little stronger."

Connor sits back down on the sofa. The doctor's home—in fact, the entire rez—is not what he expected. The Arápache have steeped themselves in both their culture and modern convenience. Plush leather furniture speaks of wealth, but it is clearly made by hand. The neighborhood—if one can call it that—is carved into the red stone cliffs on either side of a deep gorge, but the rooms are spacious, the floors are tiled with ornate marble, and the plumbing fixtures are polished brass or maybe even gold—Connor's not sure. Dr. Elina's medical supplies are also state of the art, although different in some fundamental way from medical supplies on the outside. Less clinical, somehow.

"Our philosophy is a little different," she had told him. "We believe it's best to heal from the inside out, rather than from the outside in."

Across the room, the boy playing a board game with Grace growls in frustration. "How can you keep beating me in Serpents and Stones?" he whines at Grace. "You've never even played it before!"

Grace shrugs. "I learn quick."

The boy, whose name is Kele, has little patience for losing. The game, Serpents and Stones, appears to be a lot like checkers, but with more strategy—and when it comes to strategy, Grace cannot be beat.

Once the kid storms away, Grace turns to Connor. "So your friend the clapper is gonna be okay?" she asks.

"Please don't call him that."

"Sorry—but he's gonna be okay, right?"

"It looks like it."

They've been here for nearly a week, and Connor has yet to feel welcome. Tolerated is more like it—and not because they're outsiders, for Elina and her brother-in-law, Pivane, have been more than kind to Grace—especially after they realized she's low-cortical. Even when she stitched up Connor's ostrich wound, Elina was cool and impassionate about it. "Keep it clean. It'll heal," was all she said. She offered no "you're welcome," to Connor's "thank you," and he couldn't tell whether it was a cultural thing, or if her silence was deliberate. Perhaps now that Elina knows he wasn't responsible for Lev becoming a clapper, she might treat him with a little less frost.

Kele returns with another board game, fumbling with black and white pieces of different sizes.

"So what do you call this game?" Connor asks.

He looks at Connor like he's an imbecile. "Chess," he says. "Duh."

Connor grins, recognizing the pieces as he places them. Like everything else on the rez, the game is hand carved and the pieces unique, like little sculptures—which is why he didn't recognize it right away. Grace rubs her hands together in anticipation, and Connor considers warning the kid not to get his hopes up, but decides not to: He's much too entertaining as a sore loser.

Kele is twelve, by Connor's estimate. He's not family, but Elina and her husband, Chal, took him in when his mother died a year ago. While Elina has offered Connor no information on anything, Kele, whose mouth runs like an old-time combustion engine, has been filling Connor in on a part of Lev's life that Lev never spoke about.

"Lev showed up here maybe a year and a half ago," Kele had told Connor. "Stayed for a few weeks. That was before he got all scary and famous and stuff. He went on a vision quest with us, but it didn't turn out so good."

Connor placed Lev's weeks at the rez somewhere between the time he and Risa lost Lev at the high school in Ohio and the time he showed up at the Graveyard, markedly changed.

"He and Wil became good friends," Kele told Connor, glancing at a portrait of a teenaged boy who looked a lot like Elina.

"Where is Wil now?" Connor asked.

It was the only time Kele got closemouthed. "Gone," he had finally said.

"Left the rez?"

"Sort of." Then Kele had changed the subject, asking questions about the world outside the reservation. "Is it true that people get brain implants instead of going to school?"

"NeuroWeaves—and it's not instead of school. It's something rich stupid people do for their rich stupid children."

"I'd never want a piece of someone else's brain," Kele had said. "I mean, you don't know where it's been."

On that, Connor and Kele were in total agreement.

Now, as Kele concentrates intently on his game of chess with Grace, Connor tries to catch him off guard enough to get some answers.

"So do you think Wil might come back to the rez to visit with Lev?"

Kele moves his knight and is promptly captured by Grace's queen. "You did that on purpose to distract me!" Kele accuses.

Connor shrugs. "Just asking a question. If Wil and Lev are such good friends, he'd come back to see him, wouldn't he?"

Kele sighs, never looking up from the board. "Wil was unwound."

Which doesn't make sense to Connor. "But I thought ChanceFolk don't unwind."

Finally Kele looks up at him. His gaze is like an accusation. "We don't," Kele says, then returns to the game.

"So then how—"

"If you wanna know, then talk to Lev; he was there too."

Then Grace captures one of Kele's rooks, and Kele flips the board in frustration, sending pieces flying. "You eat squirrel!" he shouts at Grace, who laughs.

"Who's low-cortical now?" she gloats.

Kele storms off once more, but not before throwing Connor a glare that has nothing to do with the game.

20 · Lev

Lev sits in shadow on the terrace, looking out at the canyon. It's nowhere near as dramatic as the great gorge that separates Arápache land from the rest of Colorado, but the canyon is impressive in its own way. Across the dry stream bed, the homes carved into the face of the opposing cliff are filled with dramatic late-afternoon shadows and activity. Children play on terraces with no protective rails, laughing as they climb up and down rope ladders in pursuit of one another. When he was first here, he was horrified, but he quickly came to learn that no one ever fell. Arápache children learn a great respect for gravity at an early age.

"We built America's great bridges and skyscrapers," Wil had told him proudly. "For us, balance is a matter of pride."

Lev knew he had meant that in many ways—and nowhere in his own life had Lev felt more balanced than when he was here at the rez. But it was also here that he was thrown so off-kilter that he chose to become a clapper. He hopes that maybe he can find some of the peace he once had, if only for a little while. Yet he knows he's not entirely welcome. Even now, he sees adults across the canyon eying him as he sits there.

From this distance, he can't tell if it's with suspicion or just curiosity.

Lev's shoulder itches, and there's a faint throbbing with every beat of his heart. His left side feels hot and heavy, but the pain he had felt in the car has subsided to a dull ache that only sharpens when he moves too fast. He has not seen Connor or Grace since awakening. As long as he knows they're all right, he's fine with that. In a way, his life has been compartmentalized into discrete little boxes. His life as a tithe, his life as a clapper, his life as a fugitive, and his life on the rez. He had been here for only a few weeks that first time, but the experience looms large for him. The idea of merging this delicate oasis of his life with the rest of his tumultuous existence is something he must get used to.

"When the council cast you out, it broke my heart."

Lev turns to see Elina coming out onto the terrace, carrying a tray with a teapot and a mug, setting it down on a small table.

"I knew you weren't responsible for what happened to Wil," she tells him, "but there was a lot of anger back then."

"But not now?"

She sits in the chair beside his and hands him a mug of steaming tea instead of answering. "Drink. It's getting chilly."

Lev sips his tea. Bitter herbs sweetened with honey. No doubt a potent brew of healing steeped by the modern medicine woman.

"Does the council know I'm here?"

She hesitates. "Not officially."

"If they know officially, will they cast me out again?"

Unlike her tea, her answer is honest and unsweetened. "Maybe. I don't know for sure. Feelings about you are mixed. When you became a clapper, some people thought it heroic."

"Did you?"

"No," she says coldly, then with much more warmth says, "I knew you had lost your way."

The understatement is enough to make Lev laugh. "Yeah, you could say that."

She turns to look across the ravine at the lengthening shadows and the neighbors trying to look as if they're not looking. "Pivane took it very hard. He refused to even speak of you."

Lev is not surprised. Her brother-in-law is very old-school when it comes to dealing with the world outside of the rez. While her husband, Chal, seems to spend more time off the rez than on, Pivane is a hunter and models his life much more on ancestral ways.

"He never liked me much," Lev says.

Elina reaches out to touch his hand. "You're wrong about that. He wouldn't speak of you because it hurt too much." Then she hesitates, looking down at his hand clasped in hers rather than in his eyes. "And because, like me, he felt partially responsible for you becoming a clapper."

Lev looks to her, thrown by the suggestion. "That's just stupid."

"Is it? If we had gone against the council. If we had insisted you stay—"

"—then it would have been horrible. For all of us. You would look at me and remember how Wil sacrificed himself to save me."

"And to save Kele and all the other kids on that vision quest." The doctor leans back in her chair. Still unable to look at him for any length of time, she looks across the arroyo and waves to a staring neighbor. The woman waves back, then self-consciously adjusts the potted plants on her terrace.

"Look at me, Elina," Lev says, and waits until she does. "When I left here, I was on my way to a terrible place. A place

where all I wanted to do was share my anger with the world. You didn't make that anger. My parents did. The Juvies did. The lousy parts pirates who took Wil did. Not you!"

Lev closes his eyes, trying to ward off the memory of that one awful day. Like Pivane, Lev finds the pain of it too much to bear. He takes a deep breath, keeping the memory and all the emotions it holds at bay, then opens his eyes once more. "So I went to that terrible place inside. . . . I went to hell. But in the end I came back."

Elina grins at him. "And now you're here."

Lev nods. "And now I'm here." Although he has no idea where he'll be tomorrow.

Lev comes out to the great room after the sun sets.

"You're alive," Connor says when he sees him. Connor is tense, but his stress level does look a little bit lower.

"Surprised?"

"Yeah, every time I see you."

Connor wears a designer Arápache shirt with a coarse weave and a tailored fit, to replace the rank shirt he had taken from the deputy. It looks good on him, but it's also an odd disconnect. Lev finds it hard to allow Connor and the rez to share the same space in his mind.

"Love the ponytail," Connor says, pointing at his hair.

Lev shrugs. "It's just because my hair is so tatted. But maybe I'll keep it."

"Don't," Connor tells him. "I lied. I hate it."

That makes Lev laugh, which makes his side hurt, and he grimaces.

The greetings now begin to feel like a receiving line. Kele comes up to Lev, looking awkward. He was a head shorter than Lev when they last saw each other. Now he's almost the same height.

"Hi, Lev. I'm glad you came back and that you didn't come back dead."

Kele will continue to grow, but Lev will not. Stunted growth. That's what he gets for lacing his blood with explosive chemicals.

Pivane is there, cooking dinner. A stew of fresh meat—something he probably shot in the wild today. Pivane's greeting, reserved at first, ends in a hug that hurts, but Lev doesn't let on. Only Grace keeps her distance, ignoring Lev. Even after their desperate road trip here, she's still not sure what to make of him. It isn't until the middle of dinner that she finally speaks to him.

"So how do you know you won't still blow up?"

And in the awkward silence that follows, Kele says, "I was kinda wondering that too."

Lev makes his eyes wide. "Maybe I will," he says ominously, then waits a few seconds and shouts "BOOM!" It makes everyone jump—but no one quite as much as Grace, who spills her stew and lets loose a stream of curses that makes everyone burst out laughing.

After dinner everyone goes about their own business, and Connor gets him alone.

"So what's the deal here?" he asks quietly. "How do you know all these people?"

Lev takes a deep breath. He owes Connor an explanation, although he'd rather not give it. "Before I showed up at the Graveyard, I came here, and they gave me sanctuary for a while," Lev tells him. "They almost adopted me into the tribe. Almost. It all got ruined by parts pirates. They cornered a bunch of us out in the woods, and Elina's son—"

"Wil?"

"Yes, Wil. He offered himself in exchange for the rest of our lives."

Connor considers this. "Since when do parts pirates negotiate?"

"They were looking for something special. And Wil *was* something special. I've never heard anyone play guitar like he played. Once they had him, they didn't care about the rest of us. Anyway, since I was there, and I was an outsider, I kind of became the scapegoat. There was no staying after that."

Connor nods and doesn't press for more details. Instead he looks toward the window. Outside not much can be seen in the dark but the lights of other homes across the ravine. "Don't get too comfortable here," Connor warns.

"I'm already comfortable," Lev tells him, and leaves before Connor can say anything more.

The cliff-side home is spacious. The individual bedrooms are small but numerous, and all of them open to the great room, which serves as living room, dining room, and kitchen. Perhaps out of morbid curiosity, Lev checks out the room that was Wil's. He thinks they might have kept it as it was, but they haven't. They haven't redesigned it for anyone else either. Wil's room is now empty of furniture and decorations. Nothing but bare stone walls.

"No one will use this room again," Elina tells Lev. "At least not in my lifetime." As everyone begins to settle down for the night, Lev goes looking for Pivane. There's been more awkwardness between them than Lev has found with anyone else, and Lev hopes he can bridge the gap. He expects to find the man down on the first floor, creek-bed level, in the workroom, tinkering with something. Perhaps preparing hides for tanning. Instead he finds someone he wasn't expecting.

She sits there at the workbench, her hair pulled back in a colorful tie, looking exactly the same as Lev remembers. Una.

Una was Wil's fiancée and must have been more devastated

than anyone when Wil was taken by the parts pirates and unwound. After that, his petition to join the tribe was quickly denied, Pivane had driven him to the gate, and Lev was set loose without ever saying good-bye to Una. Lev had been glad for that at the time. He'd had no idea what to say to her then, and he has no idea what to say now, so he lingers in the shadows, not wanting to step into the light.

Una is absorbed in cleaning a rifle that Lev recognizes as Pivane's. Does she know that he's here on the rez? Elina was very clear that his presence was to be kept low-key. His question is answered when Una says, without looking up, "Not very good at lurking, are you, Lev?"

He steps forward, but Una keeps her attention focused on the rifle without looking at him.

"Elina told me you were back," she says.

"But you didn't come to see me."

"Who says I wanted to?" Finally she spares a look at him, but she keeps her poker face. "Anyone ever teach you how to clean a bolt-action rifle?"

"No."

"Come here. I'll show you."

She takes Lev through the steps of removing the bolt and scope. "Pivane has been teaching me to shoot, and I've been finding a desire to do it," Una tells him. "When he gets his new rifle, he'll give me this one."

"A little different from making guitars," Lev says, which is what Una does.

"Both will have their place in my life," Una tells him, then directs him in cleaning the inside of the rifle barrel with solvent and a copper brush. She says nothing about what happened the last time he was on the rez, but it hangs as heavy and as dark as gunmetal between them.

"I'm sorry about Wil," he finally says.

Una is silent for a moment, then says, "They sent back his guitar—whoever 'they' is. There was no explanation, no return address. I burned it on a funeral pyre because we had no body to burn."

Lev holds his silence. The idea of Wil's guitar turned to ash is almost as horrifying as the thought of his unwinding.

"I know it wasn't your fault," Una says, "but Wil would not have helped lead that vision quest if it hadn't been for you and would never have been taken by those parts pirates. No, it wasn't your fault, little brother—but I wish you had never come here."

Lev puts down the rifle barrel. "I'm sorry. I'll go now."

But Una grabs his arm. "Let me finish." She lets go of him, and now Lev can see the tears in her eyes. "I wish you had never come, but you did—and ever since you left, I wished you would come back. Because you belong here, Lev—no matter what the council says."

"You're wrong. There's nowhere I belong."

"Well, you certainly don't belong out there. The fact that you almost blew yourself up proves it."

Lev doesn't want to talk about his days as a clapper. Not to Una. Instead he decides to share something else. "I haven't told anyone this, but I had a dream before my fever broke. I was jumping through the branches of a forest."

Una considers it. "What kind of forest? Pine or oak?"

"Neither. It was a rainforest, I think. I saw this animal covered in fur. It was leading me."

Una smiles, realizing what Lev is getting at. "Sounds like you've finally found your animal spirit. Was it a monkey?"

"No. It had a tail like a monkey, but its eyes were too big. Any idea what it could have been?"

Una shakes his head. "Sorry. I don't know much about rain forest animals."

But then Lev hears a voice behind him. "I think I know." He turns to see Kele standing in the doorway "Big eyes, small mouth, really cute?"

"Yeah . . ."

"It's a kinkajou."

"Never heard of it."

Una smirks at Lev. "Well, it's heard of you."

"I did a report on kinkajous," Kele says. "They're like the cutest animals ever, but they'll rip your face off if you mess with them."

The smirk never leaves Una's face. "Small, cute, and not to be messed with. Hmm . . . Who does that remind me of?"

That makes Kele laugh and Lev scowl.

"I am not cute," Lev growls.

"Matter of opinion, little brother. So tell me, did your guide give you any sort of task?"

Lev hesitates, but then decides to tell her, no matter how ridiculous it sounds. "I think he wanted me to pull the moon from the sky."

Una laughs. "Good luck with that one." Then she snaps the rifle closed with a satisfying clang.

21 · Cam

Cam and Roberta's Washington town house becomes *the* place to be invited to. Dinner soirees abound with international dignitaries, political movers and shakers, and pop culture icons, all of whom want a proverbial piece of Camus Comprix. Sometimes their attention is so aggressive, Cam wonders if they actually do want a piece of him as a souvenir. He dines with the crowned prince of a small principality he didn't know existed until the entourage showed up at the door. He does an after-dinner jam with none other than music super-star Brick McDaniel—the artist who comes to mind when you think of the words "rock star." Cam is actually so starstruck, he becomes a gushing fan—but when they jam side by side on guitar, they are equals.

The heady lifestyle he leads is addictive and all-encompassing. Cam keeps having to remind himself that this is not the prize—nor is it the path to the prize. All this glitz and glamour are merely distractions from his purpose.

But how can you bring down the people who've given you this extraordinary life? he occasionally asks himself in weaker moments. Like the moment when Brick McDaniel actually asked for his autograph. He knows he must be careful to ride the tornado—and not be drawn into it.

"I'm needed back on Molokai," Roberta tells him one evening. She's come down to the basement where they've set up a full gym for him. His old physical therapist, back when he was first rewound, used to say that his muscle groups didn't work and play well with others. If only he could see Cam now.

"I'll return in a couple of days. In time for our luncheon with General Bodeker and Senator Cobb."

Cam doesn't let her announcement interrupt his set at the bench press station. "I want to come," he tells her, and finds that it's not just posturing—he does want to go back to the compound on Molokai, the closest thing to home that he knows.

"No. The last thing you need after all your hard work is Hawaiian jet lag. Rest up here. Focus on your language studies so you can impress General Bodeker with your Dutch."

Dutch, one of the various languages that wasn't included in the nine he came with, has to be learned by Cam the old-fashioned way. His knowledge of German helps, but it's still a chore. He prefers when things come easier.

"Just because Bodeker has Dutch ancestry doesn't mean he speaks it," Cam points out.

"All the more reason for him to be impressed that you do."

"Is my whole life now about impressing the general and the senator?"

"You have the attention of people who make things happen. If you want them to make things happen for you, then the answer is yes—impressing them should be your primary focus."

Cam lets the weights drop heavily, with a resounding slam.

"Why do they need you on Molokai?"

"I'm not at liberty to say."

He sits up and looks at her with something between a grin and a sneer. "'Not at liberty to say.' They should put that on your grave. 'Here lies Roberta Griswold. Whether or not she rests in peace, we're not at liberty to say.'"

Roberta is not amused. "Save your morbid sense of humor for the girls who fawn over you."

Cam blots his face with a towel, grabs a sip of water, and

asks, as innocently as he can, "Are you building a better me?"

"There is only one Camus Comprix, dear. You are unique in the universe."

Roberta's very good at telling him the things she thinks he wants to hear—but Cam is very good at getting past that. "The fact that you're going to Molokai says otherwise."

Roberta is careful in her response. She speaks as if navigating a minefield. "You are unique, but my work doesn't end with you. It is my hope that yours will be a new variation of humanity."

"Why?"

It's a simple question, but Roberta seems almost angered by it. "Why do we build accelerators to find subatomic particles? Why did we decode the human genome? The exploration of possibility has always been the realm of science. The true scientist leaves practical application to others."

"Unless that scientist works for Proactive Citizenry," Cam points out. "I want to know how creating me serves them."

Roberta waves her hand dismissively. "As long as they allow me to do my work, their money is far more important to me than their motives."

It's the first time Roberta has referred to Proactive Citizenry as "they" instead of "we." Cam begins to wonder if the whole debacle with Risa has put Roberta in the organization's dog house. He wonders how far she'll go to get back into their good graces.

Roberta goes upstairs, leaving Cam to finish his workout, but his heart is no longer in it. He does take a moment, though, to examine his physique in the mirrored wall.

There were no mirrors when Cam was first rewound— when the scars were thick ropy lines all over his body and horrible to look at. Those scars are now gone, leaving behind smooth seams. And now there can never be enough mirrors for him. His guiltiest pleasure is how much he enjoys looking at himself and this body they've given him. He loves his body, yet that still falls short of loving himself.

If Risa loved me—truly and without coercion—then I could bridge that gap and feel it myself.

He knows what he has to do to make that happen—and now that Roberta will be five thousand miles away, he can begin the work necessary to bring this about without fear of her persistent scrutiny of everything he does. He's been stalling for much too long.

As soon as the limo spirits Roberta off the following morning, Cam gets to work on the computer in his room, moving his hands across the large screen as if casting a spell. He creates a nontraceable identity on the public nimbus—the global cloud so dense it would plunge the world into eternal darkness were it real instead of just virtual. He knows all his activity is monitored, so he piggybacks on an obsessive gamer somewhere in Norway. Anyone monitoring him will think he's developed an interest in Viking raids on drug-dealing trolls.

Then, obscured within the nimbus, he tweaks and strokes the firewall of Proactive Citizenry's server until it opens for him, giving him access to all sorts of coded information. But for Cam, making sense of the random and disjoint is a way of life. He was able to create order within the fragmented chaos of his rewound brain, so pulling order out of Proactive Citizenry's protective scramble will be a walk in the park.

22 · Risa

Omaha. Arguably the geographic center of the American heartland. But Risa does not feel very centered. She needs to be elsewhere, but has no destination, no plan. More than once she has felt that leaving the protection of CyFi's little commune was a mistake—but she was an outsider among the people of Tyler. Now Risa must live in the shadows. She sees no way out of it. She sees no future that doesn't involve hiding.

She keeps hoping she'll see signs of the Anti-Divisional Resistance—but the ADR has fallen apart. *Today,* she keeps thinking. *Today I'll find a path to follow. Today I'll be hit by a revelation and I'll know exactly what I need to do.* But revelation has become a scarce commodity in Risa's solitary existence. And beside her, she hears:

"It's a birthday gift, Rachel—one that your father and I will be paying a pretty penny for. At the very least you could be grateful."

"But it's not what I asked for!"

Risa has come to realize that train stations like this one have two layers that don't mix. They don't even touch. The upper layer are the wealthy travelers like the mother and daughter down the bench from her, taking high-speed trains with every amenity to get them from one exclusive place to another. The lower layer are the dregs who have nowhere else but the station to hang their hat.

"I said I wanted to *learn* violin, Mom. You could have gotten me lessons."

Risa knows she cannot board any of these trains. There's too much security, and too many people know her face. She would be met at the next stop by a phalanx of federal officers who would be thrilled to take her into custody. The train, just like any other legitimate mode of transportation, is nothing but a dream for Risa.

"No one wants to *learn* an instrument, Rachel. It's grueling repetition—and besides, you're too old to start. Concert violinists who learn the traditional way begin when they're six or seven."

Risa can't help but listen to the irritating conversation between the well-dressed woman and her fashionably disheveled teenaged daughter.

"It's bad enough they'd be messing in my brain and giving me a NeuroWeave," the girl whines. "But do I have to have the hands, too? I like my hands!"

The mother laughs. "Honey, you've got your father's stubby, chubby little fingers. Trading up will only do you good in life, and it's common knowledge that a musical NeuroWeave requires muscle memory to complete the brain-body connection."

"There *are* no muscles in our fingers!" the girl announces triumphantly. "I learned that in school."

The mother gives her a long-suffering sigh.

The most troubling thing about this conversation is that it's not an isolated incident. It's becoming more and more common for people to get vanity transplants. You want a new skill? Buy it instead of learn it. Can't do a thing with your hair? Get a new scalp. Operators are standing by.

"Think of them like a pair of gloves, Rachel. Fancy silk gloves, like a princess wears."

Risa can't stand it anymore. Making sure her hood is low enough so that her face can't be seen, she gets up, and as she walks past them, she says, "You'll have someone else's fingerprints."

Princess Rachel looks horrified. "Ew! That's it! I'm not doing it."

Leaving the train station, Risa goes out into the steamy August evening. She knows she has to look like she's occupied. Like she's going somewhere with purpose. Looking indolent will make her a target for Juvies and parts pirates—and after her last run-in with a parts pirate, she does not want to repeat the experience.

She has a pink backpack she stole from a school playground, featuring hearts and pandas, slung over her shoulder. A police officer is coming down the street in her direction, so she pulls out a phone that doesn't actually work and makes fake conversation into it as she walks.

"I know. Isn't he just the cutest! Oh, I would die to sit next to him in math."

She must appear to have a place to go and vapid people to talk to about her vapid life. She knows the look of an AWOL and has to give the impression of anything but.

"Ugh! I know! I hate her—she is such a loser!"

The officer passes and doesn't even glance at Risa. She's got this illusion down to a science. It's exhausting though—and as the night ticks away, it will be too late for any respectable girl to be on a downtown Omaha street. No matter what image she tries to push forth, she'll draw suspicion.

The train station was good for about an hour, but it's a classic hangout for kids on the run. She knew she couldn't stay very long. Now she reviews her options. There are some older landmark office buildings with old-fashioned fire escapes. She could climb up and find an unlocked window. She's done that before and has always managed to avoid the nighttime cleaning staff. The risk is being spotted while breaking in.

There are plenty of parks, but while older vagrants can get away with sleeping on park benches, a young fugitive can't. Unless she can break into a maintenance shed, she wouldn't risk staying in a park. Usually she'll scope out such places earlier in the day. When the shed is open, she'd replace the lock with one that she has the key to. Then when the groundskeeper locks up, he'll have no idea he's only locked himself out. But she was lazy today. Tired. She didn't do her due diligence, and now she's paying for it.

There's a theater on the next street playing a revival of *Cats*, which mankind will likely have to suffer through for the rest of eternity. If she can pickpocket a single ticket, she can get in, and once inside, she can find a place to hide. Hidden space high above the flies. Basement crannies filled with props.

She cuts through a back alley to get to the theater. Mistake. Halfway down the alley, she encounters three boys. They look to be eighteen or so. She pegs them right away as either AWOLs who lived long enough to outgrow the threat of unwinding, or maybe they were among the thousands of seventeen-year-olds set free from harvest camps when the Cap-17 law passed. Sadly most of those kids were just hurled out into the streets with nowhere to go. So they got angry. Rotten, like fruit left too long on the vine.

"Well, well, what do we have here?" says the tallest of the three.

"Really?" says Risa, disgusted. "'What do we have here?' Is that your best line? If you're going to attack a defenseless girl in an alley, at least try not to be cliché about it."

Her attitude has the desired effect. It catches them off guard and makes the leader—a prime douche, if ever there was one—take a step back. Risa makes a move to push past, but a beefy kid, fat enough to block her way, eclipses her view of the end of the alley. Damn. She really hoped this didn't have to get messy.

"Porterhouse don't like uppity girls," says the Prime Douche. He smiles, showing two of his front teeth are broken.

The fat kid, who must be Porterhouse, frowns and solidifies his mass like a nightclub bouncer. "That's right," he says.

It's kids like these, thinks Risa, *that made people think unwinding was a good idea.*

The third kid lingers, saying nothing, looking a little bit worried. Risa marks him as her possible escape route. None of them have recognized her yet. If they do, their motives will instantly compound. Rather than trying to have their way with her, then leaving her there in the alley, they'll have their way, then turn her in for the reward.

"Let's not get off on the wrong foot, now," Prime Douche says. "We could be of service to you."

"Yeah," says Porterhouse. "If you're of 'service' to us."

Sleaze number three snickers at that and moves forward, joining the other two. So much for an escape route. Prime Douche takes a bold step toward her. "We're the kind a' friends a girl like you needs. To protect you and such."

Risa locks eyes with him. "Touch any part of me, and I break a part of you."

She knows that a guy like this, with more bravado than brain, will take that as a dare—which he does. He grabs her wrist—then braces himself for whatever she might try to do.

She smiles at him, lifts her foot, and jams her heel into Porterhouse's knee instead. Porterhouse's kneecap breaks with an audible crunch, and he goes down, screaming and writhing in pain. It's enough to shock Prime Douche into loosening his grip. Risa twists free and elbows him in the nose. She's not sure if she's broken it, but it does start gushing blood.

"YOU THTINKING BITH!!" he yells. Porterhouse is in such agony, he can only wail wordlessly. Sleaze number three takes this as his cue to exit, running off down the alley, knowing he'll be next if he doesn't.

Then Prime Douche produces more bad news. He pulls out a knife and starts swinging at Risa, trying to cut any part of her he can. His sweeping slashes are wild, but deadly.

She uses her backpack to block, and he slices it open. He swings again, coming dangerously close to her face. Then suddenly she hears—

"In here! Hurry!"

There's a woman poking her head out of the back door of a shop. Risa doesn't hesitate. She lurches into the open door, and the woman tries to close it behind her. She almost gets it closed, but Prime Douche gets his hand in, stopping it—so the woman slams the door on his hand. He screams on the other side of the door. Risa throws her shoulder against the door, slamming it on his fingers again. He screams even louder. She releases the tension just enough for him to pull his swelling fingers back, then pushes the door fully closed while the woman locks it.

They endure the furious barrage of bile—a vitriolic burst of curses that sound increasingly impotent, until the douche and Porterhouse stumble off, vowing vengeance.

Only now does Risa look at the woman. Middle-aged, wrinkles she tries to hide with makeup. Big hair. Kind eyes.

"You all right, hon?"

"Fine. My backpack might not pull through though."

The woman throws a quick glance at the backpack.

"Pandas and hearts? Hon, that thing needed to be put out of its misery."

Risa grins, and the woman holds her gaze just a moment too long. Risa can clock the exact moment of recognition. The woman knows who she is—although she doesn't let on right away.

"You can stay here until we're sure they're gone for good."

"Thanks."

A pause, then the woman drops all pretenses. "I suppose I should ask you for your autograph."

Risa sighs. "Please don't."

The woman gives her a sly grin. "Well, being that I'm not turning you in for the reward money, I figured I could sell the signature someday. It might be worth something."

Risa returns the grin. "You mean after I'm dead."

"Well, if it was good enough for van Gogh . . ."

Risa laughs, and her laughter begins to chase away the anxiety of just a few moments ago. She still feels adrenaline making her fingers tingle. It will take longer for her physiology to recognize safety.

"Are you sure all the doors are locked?"

"Hon, those boys are long gone, licking their wounds and icing their bruised egos. But yes. Even if they came back, they couldn't get in."

"It's boys like that who give the rest of us teenagers a bad name."

The woman waves her hand at the suggestion. "Bottom-feeders come in all ages," she says. "I should know. I've dated my share of them. You can't just unwind the young ones, 'cause once they're gone, others'll sink down to take their place."

Risa carefully gauges the woman, but she's not all that easy to read. "So you're against unwinding?"

"I'm against solutions that are worse than the problem. Like old women who want their hair dyed the color of shoe polish to hide the gray."

Risa finally takes a moment to look around and quickly understands why the woman made the comparison she did. They're in the back room of a salon—a retro kind of place with big hair dryers and notched black sinks. The woman introduces herself as Audrey, the proprietor of Locks and Beagles— an establishment specializing in salon services for people who absolutely, positively must bring their dog with them everywhere.

"You'd be surprised how much some of these ladies will pay for a shampoo and cut if their Chihuahua can sit in their lap."

Audrey looks Risa over, like a prospective client. "Of course, we're closed now, but I wouldn't be disagreeable to an after-hours makeover."

"Thank you, but I'm good," Risa says.

Audrey frowns. "Come now. I thought you'd have better survival instincts than that!"

Risa bristles. "Excuse me?"

"What, do you think hiding under a hood is doing you any good?"

"I've done fine until now, thank you very much."

"Don't get me wrong," Audrey says. "Smarts and instinct go a long way—but when you get too proud of how very clever you are at outwitting the powers that be, bad things are bound to happen."

Risa begins to subconsciously rub her wrist. She had thought she was too good to fall for a trap—which is why she ended up getting caught. Changing her look would play to her advantage, so why is she so resistant?

Because you want to look the same for Connor.

She almost gasps at the realization. He's been on her mind more and more, clouding her judgment in ways she never even considered. She can't let her feelings for him get in the way of self-preservation.

"What kind of makeover?" Risa asks.

Audrey smiles. "Trust me, hon. When I'm done, it'll be a whole new you!"

The makeover takes about two hours. Risa thinks Audrey must be bleaching her hair blond, but instead she gives Risa just a lighter shade of brown with highlights and a light perm.

"Most people think it's hair color that changes a person's looks—but it's not. It's all about texture," Audrey tells Risa. "And hair's not even the most important thing. The eyes are. Most people don't realize how much of recognition is in the eyes."

Which is why she suggests a pigment injection.

"Don't worry. I'm a licensed ocular pigmentologist. I do it every day and never had complaints, except from the people who'd complain no matter what I did."

Audrey goes on to talk about all her high-society patrons and their bizarre requests, from phosphorescent eye colors that match their nails, to midnight-black pigment injections that make it look like the pupil has swallowed the iris altogether. Her voice is soothing and as anesthetic as the drops she puts into Risa's eyes. Risa lets her guard down and doesn't notice until it is too late that Audrey has clamped her arms against the arms of the chair and has secured her head in place against the headrest. Risa begins to panic. "What are you doing? Let me go."

Audrey just smiles. "I'm afraid I can't do that, hon." And she turns to reach for something Risa can't see.

Now Risa realizes that Audrey's agenda has nothing to do with helping her. She wants the reward after all! A single call and the police will be here. How stupid Risa was to trust her! How could she have been so blind!

Audrey comes back with a nasty-looking device in her hand. A syringe with a dozen tiny needles at the tip, forming a small circle.

"If you're not immobilized, you might move during the process—even grab the device reflexively, and that could damage your cornea. Locking you down is for your own protection."

Risa releases a shuddering breath of relief. Audrey takes it as anxiety from the sight of the injection needles. "Don't you worry, hon. Those eye drops I gave you are like magic. I promise you won't feel a thing."

And Risa finds her eyes welling with tears. This woman truly does mean to help her. Risa feels guilty for her burst of paranoia, even though Audrey never knew. "Why are you doing this for me?"

Audrey doesn't answer at first. She focuses on the task at hand, injecting Risa's irises with a surprise shade that Audrey promised Risa would like. Risa believed her because the woman was so overwhelmingly confident about it. For a moment Risa feels as if she's being unwound, but wills the feeling away. There is compassion here, not professional detachment.

"I'm helping you because I can," Audrey says, as she works on her other eye. "And because of my son."

"Your son . . ." Risa thinks she gets it. "Did you—"

"Unwind him? No. Nothing like that. From the moment he arrived on my doorstep, I loved him. I would never dream of unwinding him."

"He was a stork?"

"Yep. Left at my door in the dead of winter. Premature, too. He was lucky to survive." She pauses as she checks how the pigments are taking, then goes for a second layer of injections. "Then, when he was fourteen, he was diagnosed with cancer. Stomach cancer that had spread to his liver and pancreas."

"I'm so sorry."

Audrey leans back, looking Risa in the eyes, but not to gauge her own handiwork. "Honey, I'd never take an unwound part for myself. But when they told me the only way to save my boy's life was to basically gut him and replace all his internal organs with someone else's, I didn't even hesitate. 'Do it!' I said. 'Do it the second you can get him in that operating room.'"

Risa says nothing, realizing this woman needs to give her confession.

"You want to know the real reason unwinding keeps going strong, Miss Risa Ward? It isn't because of the parts we want for ourselves—it's because of the things we're willing to do to save our children." She thinks about that and laughs ruefully. "Imagine that. We're willing to sacrifice the children we don't love for the ones we do. And we call ourselves civilized!"

"It's not your fault that unwinding exists," Risa tells her.

"Isn't it?"

"You had no other way to save your son. You had no choice."

"There's always a choice," Audrey says. "But no other choice would have kept my son alive. If there were any another option, I would have taken it. But there wasn't."

She releases Risa's bonds, then turns away to clean up her injection tray. "Anyway, my son's alive and in college, and he calls me at least once a week—usually for money—but the fact that I can even get that call is a miracle to me. So my conscience will ache for the rest of my life, but that's a small price to pay for having my son still on this earth."

Risa offers her a nod of acceptance, no more, no less. Can Risa blame her for using every means at her disposal to save her son's life?

"Here you go, hon," Audrey says, turning her around to face the mirror. "What do you think?"

Risa can hardly believe the girl in the mirror is her. The perm was gentle enough that her hair, rather than being wide and poofy, falls in a gentle cascade of auburn ringlets, lightly highlighted. And her eyes! Audrey did not give her the obnoxious sort of pigmentation so many girls go for these days. Instead she boosted Risa's eyes from brown to a very natural, very realistic green. She's beautiful.

"What did I tell you?" Audrey said, clearly proud of her handiwork. "Texture for hair, color for eyes. A winning combination!"

"It's wonderful! How can I ever thank you?"

"You already did," Audrey told her. "Just by letting me do it."

Risa admires herself in a way she's never taken the time to do before. A makeover. That's something this misguided world is long overdue for as well. If only Risa knew how to make that happen. Her mind goes back to Audrey's heartfelt tale about her son. It used to be that medicine was about curing the world's ills. Research money went into finding solutions. Now it seems medical research does nothing but find increasingly bizarre ways to use Unwinds' various and sundry parts. NeuroWeaves instead of education. Muscle refits instead of exercise. And then there's Cam. Could it be true what Roberta said—that Cam is the wave of the future? How soon until people start wanting multiple parts of multiple people because it's the latest thing? Yes, perhaps unwinding is kept alive by parents desperate to save their children, but it's the vanity trade that allows it to thrive with such gusto.

If there were any other option . . . It's the first time Risa truly begins to wonder why there isn't.

23 · Nelson

J. T. Nelson, formerly of the Ohio Juvenile Authority, but now a free agent, considers himself an honest man making due in a dishonest world. Nelson came by his current van legitimately. He bought it in cash from a used-car dealer in Tucson the day after he was so unceremoniously tranq'd by a fourteen-year-old. The tithe-turned-clapper who left him unconscious by the side of the road to be gnawed on by scavengers and, come morning, to fry in the Arizona sun, hadn't thought to relieve Nelson of his wallet. Thank heaven for small miracles. It allowed Nelson the luxury of remaining an honest man.

The used-car dealer was, by definition, a swindler and was happy to part Nelson from more money than the ten-year-old blue whale of a van was worth—but Nelson didn't have time to dicker. All the money he had made from his last two Unwind sales went into the purchase, but stealing a set of wheels was out of the question, for when one is involved in such an illicit business as parts pirateering, it's best to keep oneself legit in other ways. Crimes will compound. At least now he doesn't have to look over his shoulder for the highway patrol.

When Nelson saw the picture on the news—the one that Argent Skinner had so obliviously posted—it was treated as a farce. Something to laugh at—because it had already been dismissed by the Juvenile Authority and the FBI as a hoax. Nelson, however, knew that it wasn't. Not just because he knew Connor was still alive—but because in the picture he was still wearing the same ridiculous blue camouflage pants he had worn at the Graveyard. He did his research on Argent before paying him that fateful visit. A dim bulb with a menial job and a pathetic little criminal record of drunk driving and bar-room brawling. Still, he could be of use to Nelson—and in the shape he's currently in, Nelson could use someone on his side. Although he tries not to show it, those hours unconscious in the Arizona wild have taken a toll that goes deeper than the painful molting burns on his face. There are the animal bites. Infected, some of them are. And who knows what diseases those animals carried. But he can't let himself be sidetracked by that now. Not until he has his prize.

24 · Argent

He must be smart. Smarter than anyone gives him credit for. Smarter than even he believes himself to be. He must rise to the occasion . . . because if he doesn't, he may end up dead.

"Talk to me, Argent," Nelson says. "Tell me everything Lassiter said while you had him in your basement."

It's day one: They've just left Heartsdale not half an hour ago, heading north. This man behind the wheel—this parts pirate—is intelligent and knows his business. But there's something about his eyes that hints that he's lingering near the edge of the world. Balancing on the brink of sanity. Driven there, perhaps, by Connor Lassiter. If Nelson has truly lost his edge, perhaps he and Argent are on even footing.

"Tell me anything you remember. Even if you think it's insignificant, I want to know."

So Argent starts talking and doesn't stop much. He goes on and on about the things Connor said and a whole lot of things he didn't say.

"Yeah, we got to be tight," Argent brags. "He told me all this crap about his life before. Like how his parents changed the locks on him during his last stint at juvey, before they signed the unwind order. Like how he resented his kid brother for being such a goody-goody all the time." These are things Argent had read about the Akron AWOL long before he turned up to buy sandwiches at Argent's register. But Nelson doesn't need to know that.

"You were so tight that he cut up your face, huh?" Nelson says.

Argent touches the stitches on the left side of his face—bare now that the gauze has been removed. They itch something terrible, but they ache only when he touches them too hard. "He's a mean son of a bitch," Argent says. "He don't treat his friends right. Anyway, he had places to go, and I wouldn't let him unless he promised to take me with him. So he cut me, took my sister hostage, and left."

"Left where?"

Now comes the part Argent has to sell. "Never talked much about it except, of course, when we were high on tranq."

Nelson looks over at him. "The two of you smoked tranq?"

"Oh yeah, all the time. It was our favorite thing to do together. And the good stuff too. High grade, prime tranq."

Nelson eyes him doubtfully, so Argent decides to pull back on his story a little bit. "Well, I mean, as prime as you can get in Heartsdale."

"So he talked when he was high. What did he say?"

"Ya gotta remember, I was buzzing up there too, so it's all kind of fuzzy. I mean, it's still up in my noggin, I'm sure, but I gotta tease it out."

"Dredge is more like it," Nelson says.

Argent lets the insult slide. "There was this girl he talked about," Argent offers. "'Gotta get there; gotta get there,' he said. She was gonna give him stuff. Not sure what, though."

"Risa Ward," Nelson says. "He was talking about Risa Ward."

"No, not her—I would have known if he was talking about her." Argent wrinkles his brow. It hurts to do it, but he does it anyway. "It was someone else. Mary, her name was. Yeah, that's it. Mary, something French. LeBeck. Or LaBerg. LaVeau! That's it. Mary LaVeau. He was gonna meet with her. Drink themselves some bourbon."

Nelson is silent after that, and Argent doesn't give him anything more. Let him chew on that for a while.

Day two: Crack of dawn. Cheapo motel room in North Platte, Nebraska. To be honest, Argent had expected better. Nelson wakes Argent when the sky is still predawn gray.

"Time to go. Get your lazy ass out of bed; we're turning around."

Argent yawns. "What's the rush?"

"Mary LaVeau's House of Voodoo," Nelson tells him. He's been a busy boy doing his research. "Bourbon Street, New Orleans—that's what Lassiter was talking about. For better or worse, that's where he's headed, and he's got a week-long lead. He's probably there already."

Argent shrugs. "If you say so." He rolls over and presses his face into the pillow, hiding his smile. Nelson has no idea how thoroughly he's been played.

Day three: Fort Smith, Arkansas. The blue piece-of-crap van breaks down in the afternoon. Nelson is furious.

"Cain't get parts for that on a weekend," the mechanic says. "Gotta special order it. Get here Monday, maybe Tuesday."

The more Nelson blusters, the calmer the mechanic gets, extracting a kind of spiritual joy from Nelson's misery. Argent knows the type. Hell, he *is* the type.

"The way to deal with this guy is to beat the crap out of

him," Argent advises Nelson, "and tell him you'll do the same to his mother if he don't fix the car."

But Nelson doesn't take his sound advice. "We'll fly," he says, and he pays the mechanic to drive them to Fort Smith Regional Airport only to find out that the last flight out—a twenty-seat puddle jumper to Dallas—leaves at six, and although there's four open seats, the airport's security gate closes at five. TSA officers are still in their office eating corn dogs, but will they open security for two passengers? Not on your life.

Argent suspects Nelson might kill them if they didn't have weapons of their own.

In the end Nelson uses one of his false IDs to rent a car that they have no intention of returning anytime soon.

Day four: Bourbon Street after dark. Argent has never been to New Orleans, but had always wanted to go. Not a place he could take Grace, but Grace isn't his problem anymore, is she? He strolls down Bourbon Street with a hurricane in his hand and beads around his neck. Raucous catcalls and laughter fill the street. Argent could do this every night. He could live this. Half the hurricane is already swimming in his head. Imagine! Drinking in the street is not only legal, but encouraged. Only in New Orleans!

He and his buds talked about coming here for Mardi Gras, but it was always just talk 'cause none of them had the guts to get out of Heartsdale. But now Argent has a new bud. One who was more than happy to take a road trip to New Orleans, thinking it was his own idea. Argent's apprenticeship won't last for long, though, if he doesn't earn his keep. Prove himself useful. Indispensable.

Argent isn't sure where Nelson is now. Probably harassing whoever runs Mary LaVeau's House of Voodoo. He will find no answers there. No leads as to the whereabouts of Connor

Lassiter, no matter what methods of information extraction a parts pirate is apt to use. It's a wild-goose chase if ever there was one. He will be furious and will blame Argent.

"Hey, you're the one who said go to New Orleans, not me," will be Argent's response, but Nelson will still hold him responsible. So Argent needs a peace offering. One that will open Nelson's eyes to Argent's true value.

Instead of going back to their Ramada, which smells like disinfectant and burnt hair, Argent looks for trouble. And finds it. And befriends it. And betrays it.

Day five: Nelson sleeps off a binge of the alcohol and painkillers he doused himself in when his search for Connor Lassiter came up short. Argent, out all night, returns to the Ramada at dawn, to wake him.

"I got something for you. Something you're gonna like. You gotta come now."

"Get the hell out of here." Nelson is not cooperative. Argent didn't expect he would be.

"It won't keep for long, Jasper," Argent says. "Trust me on this one."

Nelson burns him a killer gaze. "Call me that again, and I'll slit your throat." He sits up, only slightly successful in his battle with gravity.

"Sorry. What should I call you?"

"Don't call me anything."

After pumping a pot of hotel room coffee into the man, Argent brings Nelson to an old burned-out bar in a crumbling neighborhood that looks postapocalyptic. Probably hasn't been inhabited by legitimate folk since the levies last failed.

Inside are two AWOLs, bound and gagged. A boy and a girl.

"Made friends with them while you were dead to the

world," Argent proudly tells Nelson. "Convinced them I was one of them. Then I used my choke hold on them. Same hold I used on you-know-who."

The two AWOLs have since regained consciousness. They can't speak through their gags, but their eyes are a study in terror. "They're prime," Argent tells Nelson. "Gotta be worth good money, you think?"

Nelson regards them with hangover-subdued interest. "You captured them yourself?"

"Yep. Coulda got more if I'd found more. Whatever you get for them, keep the money. They're my gift to you."

And Nelson says, "Let them go."

"What?"

"We're too far from my black-market contact, and I'm not going to haul them all around creation."

Argent can't believe it. "I put them right into your lap and you're just gonna throw good money away?"

Nelson looks at Argent and sighs. "You get an A for effort. It's good work, but we're after a bigger catch." Then Nelson just walks out.

Furious, Argent spews vitriol at the gagged kids, who can't answer back. "I oughta just leave you here to rot, is what I oughta do." But he doesn't. He doesn't free them either. Instead he makes an anonymous call to the Juvies to come pick them up, giving away his first payday as parts pirate for free. His only consolation is that Nelson was maybe a little bit impressed by the catch.

He heads back to the Ramada, all the while scheming up the next leg of their wild-goose chase and ways to make Nelson think that he's driving it. There are plenty of places besides New Orleans that Argent would like to go. Plenty of places Nelson will take him, as long as Argent is skillful in dropping bread crumbs.

25 · Connor

He does not want to be on the reservation. He has nothing against the Tashi'ne family; they seem accommodating enough, if somewhat cool toward him—and they genuinely care for Lev—but the rez should have been nothing more than a quick pit stop on the way to their destination. The days here, as slow as they seem to pass, also pass at an alarming speed somehow. Their pit stop has stretched to two weeks. Yes, Lev needed a lot of healing time, but he's well enough to be on the road now. Just because things on the rez don't change, that doesn't mean the rest of the world stops spinning. The harvest camps keep unwinding, Proactive Citizenry continues lobbying for stricter laws against Unwinds. Every day they remain here is another day for things to get worse out there.

The solution, or at least part of it, has to lie with Janson Rheinschild. Trace, Connor's right-hand man at the Graveyard, was convinced of it, and Trace was right about so many things. Since the moment Connor learned that Rheinschild had been Sonia's husband, the man sat heavy in Connor's gut like bad meat. The sooner they get to Sonia, the sooner he can purge it.

"What's so important about getting to Ohio anyway?" Grace asks him as she snacks on Arápache fry bread. "Argent says it's nothing but cold and full of fat people."

"You wouldn't understand," Connor tells her.

"Why? Because I'm stupid?"

Connor grimaces. He hadn't meant it that way, but he knows that's how it came out. "No," he tells her, "it's because you're not an AWOL. You've never had to face unwinding and until you have, you'll never understand why it's worth risking everything to stop it."

"I might not be an Unwind, but I'm AWOL, sure enough. AWOL from my brother, who'll kill me soon as look at me if he ever finds me."

Connor tries to dismiss that, but can't entirely. Clearly Argent has hit her quite a lot in the past—beaten her, maybe—but is Argent a killer? Maybe not an intentional one, but Connor can imagine him beating Grace to death in blind fury. And even if he's not capable of that, it's a very real threat in Grace's mind. Like him and Lev, she's a fugitive, but for a different reason.

"We'll never let him hurt you again," Connor tells her.

"Ever?"

Connor nods. "Ever." Although he knows it's a promise with no teeth, because he and Lev won't be in her life forever.

"So who is this guy you're chasing after?"

Connor considers giving her a "just some guy," sort of response, but instead decides to give her the kind of respect she's never gotten before. He tells her what he knows. Or, more accurately, what he doesn't know.

"Janson Rheinschild developed the neural-grafting technology that made unwinding possible. He founded an organization called Proactive Citizenry."

"I heard of them," Grace says. "They save poor children in India and stuff."

"Yeah, probably so they can harvest their organs. The thing is, Rheinschild didn't intend his work to be used for unwinding. In fact, he set up Proactive Citizenry as a watchdog organization to prevent any abuse of his technology. But in the end, other people took control, and it became just the opposite. Now it promotes unwinding, it manipulates the media—and there are rumors that it even controls the Juvenile Authority."

"That sucks," Grace says with a mouth full of food.

"Right—and what sucks even more is that they vanished Rheinschild off the face of the earth."

"Killed him?"

"Who knows? All we know is that he's been deleted from history. We were able to find him only because one article misspelled his name. Anyway, Lev and I figure an organization like that wouldn't make the man disappear for just speaking out against them. We think he knew something so dangerous, he had to be snuffed. And anything dangerous to Proactive Citizenry is a weapon for us. Which is why we have to get to his wife, Sonia, who's been living in secret all these years."

Grace licks grease from her fingers. "I knew a Sonia once back in Heartsdale. She had a mean temper and a thing on her face the size of dog turd. She went in to have it removed, but had a heart attack on the table and died before they could get her a replacement heart. Argent says he was surprised she even had a heart to begin with. Made me sad, though. It's stupid to die because of a turd growing on your face."

Connor has to smile. "Truer words were never spoken." As far as he's concerned, Proactive Citizenry is like a turd on the face of humanity. But whether or not it can be excised without killing the patient, only time will tell.

"So who's in charge of Proactive Citizenry now?" Grace asks.

Connor shrugs. "Damned if I know."

"Well, tell me when you find out. 'Cause that's someone I'd love to play in Stratego."

The dynamic between Connor and Lev has changed. Before, they were a team, single-minded in purpose, but now their relationship is strained. Any talk of moving on is met by Lev's thinly veiled impatience, or a quick exit from the room.

"After all he's been through, he deserves a little bit of peace," Una tells him after one such exit. Connor likes Una. She reminds him of Risa—if not in appearance, then in the way she won't take crap from anyone. Risa, however, would be urging Lev to get on with it rather than planning his vacation.

"We don't deserve peace until we've earned it," Connor tells her.

She smirks. "Did you read that on a war memorial somewhere?"

He glares at her, but says nothing because, actually, he did. The Heartland War Memorial. Sixth-grade field trip. He knows he's going to need a better argument than granite-carved clichés if he's going to stand toe-to-toe with Una.

"From what I understand," says Una, "he saved your life, and you came pretty close to ending his when you hit him with that cop car. At the very least, you could cut him enough slack to recover from his wounds."

"He threw himself in front of the car!" says Connor, beginning to lose his temper. "Do you honestly think I meant to hit him?"

"Race headlong and blind, and you're bound to hit something. Tell me, was nearly killing your only friend the first obstacle in your journey, or were there more?"

Connor pounds the wall with Roland's hand. He holds a clenched fist, and although he doesn't release it, he forces the fist down to his side. "Every journey has obstacles."

"If the universe is telling you to slow down, maybe you should listen instead of putting your head in the ground like an ostrich."

He snaps his eyes to her, wondering if Lev told her about the ostrich—but nothing in her expression gives away whether she said it intentionally or if it's only a coincidence. He can't say anything about it, though, because if he did, she'd probably insist that there are no coincidences.

"He feels safe here," insists Una. "Protected. He needs that."

"If you're his protector," Connor asks, "where were you when he was turning himself into a bomb?"

Una looks away, and Connor realizes he's gone too far. "I'm sorry," he says. "But what we're doing . . . it's important."

"Don't flatter yourself," says Una, still stinging from his jab. "Your legend might be larger than life, but you're no bigger than the rest of us." Then she storms off so quickly, Connor can feel a breeze in her wake.

That night he lay in bed, his thoughts and associations spilling into one another, a product of his exhaustion. The small stone room feels more like a cell, in spite of how comfortable the bed is.

Perhaps it's just because he's an outsider, but to Connor, the Arápache live a life of contradiction. Their homes are austere and yet punctuated by pointed opulence. A plush bed in an undecorated room. A simple wood-burning fire pit in the great room that's not so simple because logs are fed and temperature maintained by an automatic system so that it never goes out. With one hand they rebuke creature comforts, but with the other they embrace it—as if they are in a never-ending battle between spiritualism and materialism. It must have been going on so long, they seem blind to their own ambivalence, as if it's just become a part of their culture.

It makes Connor think of his own world and its own oxymoronic nature. A polite, genteel society that claims compassion and decency as its watch cry, and yet at the same time embraces unwinding. He could call it hypocrisy, but it's more complex than that. It's as if everyone's made an unspoken pact to overlook it. It's not that the emperor has no clothes. It's that everyone's placed him in their blind spot.

So what will it take to make everyone turn and look?

Connor knows he's an idiot to think he can do anything to change the massive inertia of a world hurtling off its axis. Una's right—he's no bigger than anyone else. Smaller really—so small that the world doesn't even know he exists anymore, so how can he hope to make a difference? He tried—and where did that get him? The hundreds of kids he'd tried to save at the Graveyard are now in harvest camps being unwound, and Risa, the one good thing in his life, has gone as far off the radar as him.

With the impossible weight of the world on their shoulders, how tempting it must be for Lev to imagine disappearing here. But not for Connor. It's not in his nature to be one with nature. The sound of a crackling fire doesn't calm him, only bores him. The serenity of a babbling brook is his version of water torture.

"You're an excitable boy," his father used to say when he was little. It was a parent's euphemism for a kid out of control. A kid uncomfortable in his own skin. Eventually his parents weren't comfortable keeping him in his skin either and signed the dread unwind order.

He wonders when they truly made the decision to unwind him. When did they stop loving him? Or was lack of love not the issue? Were they conned by the many advertisements that said things like "Unwinding—when you love them enough to let them go," or "Corporeal division; the kindest thing you can do for a child with disunification disorder."

That's what they call it. "Disunification disorder," a term probably coined by Proactive Citizenry to describe a teen who feels like they want to be anywhere else but where they are and in anyone else's shoes. But who doesn't feel like that now and then? Granted, some kids feel it more than others. Connor knows he did. But it's a feeling you learn to live with, and eventually you harness it into ambition, into drive, and finally into achievement if you're lucky. Who were his parents to deny him that chance?

Connor shifts positions in his bed and punches his swan-down pillow with his left fist, but switches, realizing it's far more satisfying when he uses Roland's hand for punching. Connor has built up his left arm so that it's almost a match to his right, but when it comes to sheer physical expression, Roland's arm is the one that makes his brain release endorphins when violently used.

He can't imagine what it would be like to have an entire body wired to wish damage on everyone and everything around it. Sure, Connor had a little bit of that in him all along, but it only came in fits and starts. Roland, however, was a bashing junkie.

Sometimes, when he knows no one's watching or listening, Connor will say things to his surgically grafted limb. He calls it "talking to the hand."

"You're a basket case, you know that?" he'll say, when the hand won't stop clenching. Occasionally he'll give himself the finger and laugh. He knows the impetus for the gesture is his, but imagining that it's Roland's is both satisfying and troublesome at the same time, like an itch that gets worse with each scratch.

Once, at the Graveyard, Hayden had slipped Connor some medicinal chocolate to get him to mellow out a bit. Pharmacologically compounded, genetically engineered cannabis, Connor learned, packs a hallucinogenic wallop much more severe than smoking tranq. The shark on his arm spoke to him that night, and in Roland's voice, no less. Mostly it spat out strings of cleverly conceived profanities—but it did say a few things of note.

"Make me whole again, so I can beat the crap out of you,"

it said, and, "Bust a few noses; it'll make you feel better," and "Spank the monkey with your own damn hand."

But the one that keeps coming back is "Make it mean something, Akron."

What exactly did the shark mean by "it"? Did it mean Roland's unwinding? Roland's life? Connor's life? The shark was maddeningly vague, as hallucinations often are. Connor never told anyone about it. He never even acknowledged to Hayden that the chocolate had any effect on him. After that, the shark, its jaw fixed in a predatory snarl, never spoke to Connor again, but its enigmatic request for meaning still echoes across the synapses between Roland's motor neurons and his own.

Roland's fury at his parents had been far more directed than Connor's. A nasty triangle of pain there. Roland's stepfather beat his mother, so Roland pummeled the man senseless for it—and then his mother chose the man who beat her over the son who tried to help her, sending Roland off to be unwound.

Make it mean something. . . .

The fury that Connor feels against his own parents burns like the ever-burning fire pit in the great room, but unlike Roland's, Connor's fury is as random as leaping flames in search of purchase. His fire isn't fueled by their choice to unwind him, but by the unanswered questions surrounding that choice.

Why did they do it?

How did they make the decision?

And most important: What would they say to him now if they knew he was alive . . . and what would he say back?

He's rushing to Ohio to find Sonia, but in the back of his mind, Connor knows that it also brings him painfully close to home. He wonders if, beneath everything, that's the real reason he's making this trip.

So he furiously tosses and turns in a luxurious bed, in a Spartan room, emotionally unwinding himself with his own ambivalence.

26 · Lev

Lev knows staying on the rez ticks off Connor—but hasn't he earned the right to be selfish just this once?

"You can stay as long as you want to," Elina had told him.

Pivane, on the other hand, was a little more practical. "You can stay as long as you *need*." So the question is—how much of Lev's desire to stay is need, and how much is want?

His side is still badly bruised, and without speed-healing agents—which the Arápache don't use—his ribs and bruised organs will take time to heal. He can make an argument that he needs to stay that entire time, but he knows Connor won't hear of it—and his frustration would be justified. They have a mission and can't be sidetracked by the lures of comfort. What Lev needs is a mission of equal magnitude.

Then, toward the end of their second week on the rez, the entire situation takes a sharp turn that leaves everyone more than a little shell-shocked.

It's dinnertime. A small gathering tonight—just the three guests, joined at the table by Elina, Kele, and Chal, Elina's husband, who is finally back from his court case. From the moment he arrives, he treats Lev with lawyerly reserve and courtesy, as if he's afraid to commit to any specific action or emotion with regards to Lev. "Elina told me everything. I'm glad you're here," Chal says when he greets Lev—but whether he means it or is just being obliging is something Lev can't read in his voice. The man's response to Connor and Grace is also reserved and measured.

Pivane arrives late for dinner today, wearing a look of concern that diffuses Elina's irritation. "You need to see this," he says. First to Elina and Chal, but then he turns to Lev and Connor. "All of you need to see this."

As everyone rises from the dinner table, Pivane turns on the TV across the great room. He flips through channels until finding a news station.

If there was any question as to what kind of evening this will be, all doubts are chased away by what they see:

Connor's face is on a screen behind the news anchorman.

"*. . . and the Juvenile Authority, putting an end to rumors and wild speculation, has confirmed that Connor Lassiter, presumed dead for over a year, is actually alive. Lassiter, also known as the 'Akron AWOL' was a key figure in the Happy Jack Harvest Camp revolt that resulted in nineteen deaths and the escape of hundreds of Unwinds.*"

Connor and Lev can only stare in disbelief. The anchorman continues.

"*It is believed that he may be traveling with Lev Calder and Risa Ward, both of whom played prominently in the revolt.*"

Risa and Lev's pictures appear on the screen as well. Not Lev as he is now, but as he was in the old days. Clean-cut, innocent, and ignorant.

"Is this bad?" Grace asks, then answers her own question. "Yeah, this is bad."

The news cuts to an interview with a pompous representative of the Juvenile Authority, holding a picture of Connor with a grungy-looking guy, who Lev assumes is Grace's brother. The Juvey rep appears irritated that he must divulge this information, yet needy for the public's help.

"*Our analysts have determined that this picture is authentic and taken a little over two weeks ago. The young man in this picture, Argent Skinner, and his sister, Grace Skinner, are now missing, and we believe Lassiter either kidnapped them or killed them."*

"What!" It comes out of Connor like a quack.

"Anyone who has any information on this fugitive should contact the authorities immediately. Do not try to approach him as he is considered armed and dangerous."

Lev turns his attention from the TV to Connor, who is quickly slipping into fury mode. To anyone who doesn't know him, he would look pretty dangerous at this moment.

"Take it easy, Connor," Lev says. "They want you to be angry. The angrier you are, the more mistakes you'll make and the easier you'll be to catch. The fact that they felt a need to go public with it means they have no clue where you've gone, which means you're still safe."

But right now, it seems Connor won't hear anything but the turmoil in his own head. "Damn them! If they could pin the whole goddamn Heartland War on me, they would. Sure, I wasn't even born then, but they'd find a way to blame me for it!" Connor punches the wall with his grafted arm and grimaces from the pain of it.

"A lie," Elina says calmly, "is a powerful weapon that the Juvenile Authority certainly knows how to wield."

Grace looks at each of them, a little bit frightened. "Why's Argent missing? What happened to him?"

And then from behind them. "Who's Argent? Is he really dead? Did Connor kill him?"

They turn to see Kele, who, in these reeling moments, had been forgotten.

Lev and Elina's logic could not calm Connor down, but apparently the fearful look on Kele's face does the trick.

"No, he's not, and no, I didn't," Connor tells him, his voice a little more under control. "Wherever he is, I'm sure he's fine."

Kele seems only half-convinced, and that worries Lev. He

knows the kid is a bit of a loose cannon. While Lev's presence here is "unofficially" known, no one knows that the infamous Akron AWOL is here as well. Kele had promised to keep his presence here a secret, but could he still, now that the secret looms so large?

"So what do we do?" Lev asks Elina, knowing what she'll say—or at least hoping.

"You'll stay in our care, of course," Elina says.

Lev releases his breath. He hadn't even realized he'd been holding it.

"Like hell we will!" snaps Connor.

Lev grabs his shoulder to keep him from storming away. "It's the smart thing to do. No one out there knows we're here. We can lie low until we're out of the news."

"We'll never be out of the news, Lev! You know that."

"But it won't always be the big story like it is today. Give it a few weeks. And maybe by then we can keep under the radar. Taking off now is the stupidest thing we could possibly do."

"While we're sitting here, kids from the Graveyard are being unwound!"

"And how much will it crush their spirit if you're caught?" Lev points out. "As long as you're free, they have hope."

"Cowards hide!" says Connor.

"But warriors lie in wait," Elina says. "The only difference is whether you're motivated by fear or purpose."

That shuts Connor up, at least for the moment. Elina is always good at choking people on food for thought. His eyes burn for a moment more; then Connor drops into a dining room chair, resigned. He looks at his knuckles—*Roland's* knuckles—which are bleeding and raw. It must hurt, but he seems to draw some satisfaction from the pain.

"They think we're with Risa," Connor says. "I wish we were that lucky."

"If she's sees the report," Lev points out, "then she'll know that you're still alive—so that's a good thing."

Connor throws him a quick and mildly disgusted glance. "Your ability to see the bright side of everything makes me sick."

The news has gone on to the clapper attack of the week, and Pivane turns off the TV. "How long can we realistically keep Connor's presence here a secret?"

Lev notices that Kele has taken on a growing look of silent guilt, so Lev asks him point-blank. "Who did you tell, Kele?"

"No one," he says, and when Lev doesn't look away, Kele tells the truth. "Just Nova. But she promised not to tell, and I trust her." Then he adds, "I figured he was safe, since it's the Juvenile Authority that's after him, and Connor's not juvenile anymore, right?"

"It doesn't matter," Chal explains. "His so-called crimes happened when he was under their jurisdiction, which means they can chase him into old age."

Pivane begins pacing, Elina rubs her forehead, as if getting a headache, and Kele looks miserable and forlorn like his dog just died. Lev can already see this beginning to cascade like a rock slide.

"If word does get out," Chal says, "and the Juvenile Authority calls for us to give him and Lev over, we can refuse. I can make a case for political asylum—and without an extradition treaty, there's nothing the Juvenile Authority can do."

Elina shakes her head. "They'll put pressure on the Tribal Council and the council will give in, like they always do."

"But it will buy time—and I can keep throwing up roadblocks to stall things."

And then Grace chimes in. "You know what's better than roadblocks?" she says. "Detours!"

Lev and the others take it as Grace being obtuse, but Connor, who knows her better, takes it seriously.

"Explain what you mean, Grace."

Now that she's the center of attention, she gets animated and excited, gesturing with her hands so much, it almost resembles old-world sign language. "See, if you stop them with roadblocks, they'll break through each one soon enough. A better strategy would be to send them down some winding path that goes on and on, so's they think they're makin' progress, but really they're just spinnin' their wheels."

Stunned silence for a moment, and Pivane grins. "That actually makes sense."

Lev looks to Connor, raising his eyebrows. Clearly there's more to Grace than meets the eye.

Chal gets a far-off, but intense look, like he's pondering an equation. "The Hopi are desperate for me to represent them in a major land dispute. I could agree to do it, and in return, the Hopi council could agree to announce that they're giving Connor and Lev asylum."

"So," says Connor, putting it all together, "even if people around here start talking, the Juvies won't hear it, because they'll be all over the Hopi—and when they finally find out we're not there, they'll be back to square one!"

The mood, which just a moment ago lay flat with despair, is quickly rebounding toward hope. Lev, however, feels a sizeable lump in his throat. "Would you go out on that much of a limb for us?" he asks his hosts.

They don't answer for a moment. Pivane won't meet his eye, and Elina defers to Chal. Finally Chal speaks for all of them. "We did wrong by you before, Lev. This is a chance to make things right."

Pivane grasps Lev's shoulder hard enough that it hurts, but Lev doesn't let it show. "I must admit I take a little bit of pride to be harboring modern folk heroes."

"We're not heroes," Lev tells him.

At that Elina smiles. "No true hero ever believes that they are one," she tells him. "So you go ahead, Lev, and keep denying it with every fiber of your being."

27 · Starkey

Mason Starkey knows he's a hero. He knows this beyond any shadow of doubt. The many lives he's saved proves it. The evidence is all around him—his storks, all spirited from the death throes of the airplane graveyard, kept alive and safe through cleverness and well-placed sleight of hand. But it's only a beginning. The groundwork has been laid for a great work— and for his own personal greatness, which he will more than earn. Starkey knows that there's a grand destiny waiting for him, and his first foray into the limelight of history is about to begin.

"The Egret Academy," says the pleasant woman, reading the logo on his forest-green T-shirt, as Starkey signs the guest registry. "Is that a parochial school?"

"Nondenominational," Starkey tells her. "I'm the youth minister."

She smiles at him, taking him at his word. How could she not? His clean-cut, blond, well-groomed appearance reeks of honesty and integrity.

"Is the school here in Lake Tahoe?"

"Reno," he says without hesitation.

"Too bad. I'm looking for a good school for my own kids. One with the right moral values."

Starkey gives her his most winning smile. He knows the names of her kids and her home address. Not that he'll need the information this time, but it's turned out to be a solid protective policy for the storks.

This time it's not a campground but a high-end retreat. The Egret Academy has rented all ten cabins for the next four days. It's an expense, but Jeevan has managed to squeeze even more money from the storks' parental accounts, more than enough to pay for four days of comfort . . . and considering what's coming next, his storks deserve it.

While the storks explore their new environment themselves, all in their new Egret Academy shirts, the woman gives Starkey the grand tour.

"The dining hall is to the left—you provide your own food of course, but the kitchen is fully stocked with cookware, dinnerware, and everything you'll need. Tennis court and pool is up the hill. Come. I'll show you the clubhouse. It's down by the lake. We have a theater-quality TV, a classic arcade—even a bowling alley."

"And a cloud connection?" Starkey asks. "We have to have a high-speed connection to the public nimbus."

"Well, that goes without saying."

BROCHURE

For more than twenty years, **The Egret Academy** has brought together knowledge and character in order to inspire our students to be leaders of the future. Our **strong academic program** is designed to pull information from the widest variety of sources and impart learning through **experiential hands-on experience.** At the Egret Academy, we strive to give every student a unique and personal education.

Through spiritual retreats and eye-opening field trips, we expose our students to the past, present, and future—all in a **nurturing environment that encourages self-reliance** as well as trust and camaraderie among fellow egrets.

Our emphasis on personal accountability and social responsibility is exemplified in our **Peer Leadership Program,** in which our youth ministers organize and run retreats of up to a hundred students at a time. By combining **traditional education** with special programs, projects, and activities, our faculty is dedicated to creating **well-educated, well-rounded, ethically responsible students** with the ability and the confidence to take on the world!

"You really outdid yourself this time, Mason. This place is fantastic." Bam peers over Starkey's shoulder at the computer screen that he and Jeevan strategize over. "I mean a bowling alley? I can't even remember the last time I bowled."

Starkey can't help but be irritated by Bam's intrusion, but he tries not to show it. "Enjoy it while you can," he tells her. That sobers her up a bit.

"When are we going to tell the others the whole plan?"

"Tomorrow," he tells her. "It will give them time to prepare themselves."

Yet another clatter of bowling pins from the other side of the clubhouse sets Starkey's nerves on end. The clubhouse is one big open space. He would much prefer quiet privacy right now.

"Bowl a game for me," he tells Bam. I would but"—he holds up his stiff hand—"I bowl lefty." It isn't true, but it gets her to leave them alone.

On screen is a schematic of Cold Springs Harvest Camp, north of Reno. "I think I've figured out a way to jam communications," Jeevan says. "I'll need a few kids to help me out, though. Smart ones."

"Choose whoever you want for your team," Starkey tells him. "And anything you need, just let me know."

Jeevan nods but, as always, seems nervous, concerned. He's a kid who can never just relax and go with the flow.

"I've been thinking of after," he says, "and how, after we hit

Cold Springs, we won't be able to be out in public anymore. At all."

"So give me options."

Jeevan pecks at the computer, swipes various windows off the screen, and pulls up a map covered in blinking red dots. "I've isolated a few possibilities."

Starkey clasps him on his shoulder with his good hand. "Excellent! Find us a new home, Jeevan. I have every faith in you."

Which only makes Jeevan squirm.

As Starkey strolls through the clubhouse, the cacophony of his storks enjoying themselves transforms from a distraction to a testimony of all he has accomplished for them. But it's only a glimpse of what he has planned for their future.

Yes, Mason Starkey is a hero. And in just a few days, the entire world will know.

28 · Risa

"Close your eyes," Risa says. "I don't want to get soap in them."

The woman leans back, her Pomeranian in her lap. "Check the water first. I don't like it too hot."

This is Risa's fourth day residing in Audrey's salon. Each day she tells herself she's going to leave, yet each day she doesn't.

"And make sure you use the shampoo for dry hair," the woman commands. "Not the kind for very dry hair, the kind for mild to moderately dry hair."

It all stems from that first night. Audrey had spent the night there in the shop with Risa, because "a girl shouldn't be alone after a thing like that." Which she supposes is true for girls who have the luxury of not being alone. Risa rarely has that luxury, so she was glad for the company. Apparently, the attack in the alley affected Risa much more deeply than she thought, because she had a string of nightmares all night. The only one she can recall is her recurring dream of countless pale faces looming over her and a sense that she could not escape them. On that night, dawn could not come soon enough.

"You're not the usual shampoo girl, are you? I can tell because the other one has the most hideous breath."

"I'm new. Please keep your eyes closed while I lather you up."

Until today, Risa had paid for Audrey's kindness by organizing the stockroom, but when one of her stylists called in sick today, she begged Risa to man the shampoo sink in a back alcove.

"What if someone recognizes me?"

"Oh, please!" Audrey had said. "You have a totally new look. And besides, these women don't see anything past their own reflections."

So far Risa has found that to be true. But washing the hair of wealthy women is not exactly her job of choice and is even more thankless than dispensing first aid at the Graveyard.

"Let me smell that conditioner. I don't like it. Get me another."

Tonight I'll leave, Risa tells herself. But nighttime comes and, again, she doesn't. She's not quite sure if her inertia is a problem or a blessing. Even though she didn't have a specific destination before arriving here, she always had a vector—a direction to be moving. True it changed from day to day depending on what seemed the most likely direction of survival, but at least there was momentum. Now her momentum is gone. If she leaves here, where will she go? A place of greater safety? She doubts there is one.

That evening when Audrey closes shop, she treats Risa to something special.

"I've noticed your nails are in pretty bad shape. I'd like to give you a manicure."

That makes Risa laugh. "Am I your Barbie doll now?"

"I run a beauty shop," Audrey says. "It comes with the territory." Then she does the oddest thing. She comes to Risa with scissors, snips off an inconspicuous lock of hair and shoves it into the compartment of a small machine that looks like an electric pencil sharpener. "Have you ever seen one of these?"

"What is it?"

"Electronic nail builder. Hair and nails are basically made of the same stuff. This device breaks down the hair, then applies it in fine layers on top of your nails. Put your finger in." The hole, Risa now realizes, is not pencil-sized, but large enough for a woman's fingertip. She's hesitant, as putting one's finger into a dark hole is a very counterintuitive thing, but in the end she acquiesces, and Audrey turns it on. It buzzes, vibrates, and tickles for a minute or two, and when she pulls her finger out, her nail, which had been uneven and ragged, is now smooth with a perfect curve.

"I programmed it for the shortest setting," Audrey tells her. "Somehow I can't imagine you with long nails."

"Neither can I."

Risa endures the process for all ten nails. It takes almost an hour.

"Not very efficient, is it?"

"No. You'd think they'd make one that can do a whole hand at once, but they don't. Something to do with limitations on the patent. Anyway, I use it only when someone has patience and can actually appreciate the thing."

"So it doesn't get much use at all, does it?"

"Nope."

Audrey, Risa realizes, is probably around the same age as her own birth mother, whoever she is. She wonders if a mother-daughter relationship would be something like this. She has no way to judge. All the kids she knew growing up didn't have parents, and after she left the state home, she only knew kids whose parents had thrown them away.

Audrey leaves for the night, and Risa settles in the comfortable niche she's made herself in the storeroom, complete with a bedroll and comforter that Audrey provided. Audrey has offered her the foldout in her apartment, and even the stylists, who are all as kind as Audrey, have offered to take her in, but there's only so much hospitality Risa's willing to accept.

That night she dreams of the cold, impassive multitude again. She's playing a Bach étude much too fast on a piano that's hopelessly out of tune, and right in front of her are the countless looming faces lined up and stacked like shelves of trophies. Deathly pale. Disembodied. Alive and yet not alive. They open their mouths but they don't speak. They would reach for her but they don't have hands. She can't tell if they mean her ill, but they certainly don't mean her well. They reek of need, and the deepest terror of the dream is not knowing what it is they so desperately desire from her.

When she pulls herself out of it, her fingers, new nails and all, are drumming against her blanket, still struggling to play the étude. She has to turn on the light and leave it on for the rest of the night. When she closes her eyes, she can still see those faces like afterimages on her retina. Is it possible to have the afterimage of a dream? She can't help but feel she's seen these faces before, and not just in a dream. It's something real, something tangible that she can't place. Whatever it is, she hopes she never sees it—never sees *them* again.

• • •

First thing in the morning—just five minutes after opening, two Juvey-cops come into the salon, and Risa's heart nearly stops. Audrey's already there, but none of her stylists are. Risa, knowing that turning and running will not go over well, hangs her hair in her face and turns her back to them, pretending to stock one of the stylist's stations.

"You open for business?" one of them asks.

"That depends," says Audrey. "What can I do for you, Officer?"

"It's my partner's birthday. I'm giving her a makeover."

Now Risa dares to look. One of the Juvies is a woman. Neither of them takes much notice of her.

"Perhaps you could come back when my stylists arrive."

He shakes his head. "Shift starts in an hour. Gotta do it now."

"Well, I guess we'll have to work with that, then." Audrey comes over to Risa, speaking sotto voce. "Here's some money; go get us doughnuts. Go out the back way and don't come back until they're gone."

"No," Risa says, not realizing she would say it until she does. "I want to do her shampoo."

The Juvie doesn't have a dog on her lap, but she does have a chip on her shoulder. "I don't go for nothing foo-foo," she says. "Just keep it simple."

"I intend to." Risa drapes her with a smock and leans her back toward the sink. She turns on the water, making sure it's nice and hot.

"I'd like to personally thank you," Risa says. "For keeping the streets safe from all those bad boys and girls."

"Safe and clean," says the Juvey-cop. "Safe and clean."

Risa glances out to the waiting area, where her partner obliviously reads a magazine. Audrey peers in at Risa nervously, wondering what she's up to. With this woman leaning her head back, totally at Risa's mercy, Risa feels like the Demon Barber of Omaha, ready to slit her throat and bake her into pies. But instead she just dribbles shampoo into the corners of her closed eyes.

"Ah! That stings."

"Sorry. Just keep your eyes closed. You'll be fine."

Risa then proceeds to wash her hair with water so hot she can barely stand it herself, but the woman doesn't complain.

"Catch any AWOLs yesterday?"

"As a matter of fact, yes. Usually we just patrol the detention facility, but a kid slated for unwinding went AWOL on our watch. We brought him down, though. Tranq'd him from fifty feet."

"My, that must have been . . . thrilling." It's all Risa can do not to strangle her. Instead she opts for concentrated bleaching solution, rubbing it unevenly into her dark hair after rinsing out the shampoo. That's when Audrey intercedes, a moment too late to stop her.

"Darlene! What are you doing?" Darlene is Risa's salon pseudonym. Not her choice, but it works.

"Nothing," she says innocently. "I just put in some conditioner."

"That wasn't conditioner."

"Oops."

The Juvie tries to open her eyes, but they still sting too much. "Oops? What kind of Oops?"

"It's nothing," Audrey says. "Why don't I take over from here?"

Risa snaps off her gloves and drops them in the trash. "Guess I'll go get those doughnuts now." And she's gone just as the woman begins to complain about her scalp burning.

"What were you thinking?"

Risa doesn't try to explain herself to Audrey, and she knows

Audrey really doesn't expect her to. It's a motherly question though, and Risa actually appreciates it.

"I was thinking that it's time for me to go."

"You don't have to," Audrey tells her. "Forget about this morning. We'll pretend it never happened."

"No!" It would be so easy for Risa to do that, but being that close to a Juvey-cop—hearing what she had to say, the blatant disregard for the fate of the AWOL they took down— it's knocked Risa out of this local eddy and given her a vector again. "I need to find whatever's left of the ADR and do what I can to save kids from cops like the ones we saw this morning."

Audrey sighs and nods reluctantly, already knowing Risa well enough to know that she can't be dissuaded.

Now Risa understands her awful recurring dream of the disembodied faces. It is the faces of the unwound that haunt her, forever separated from everything that they were, looming over her in desperate supplication, begging her, if not to avenge them, then to make sure their numbers do not increase. She's been complacent for too long. She can't deny their pleas anymore. The mere fact that she's alive—that she survived— bonds her to their service. And giving a spiteful hairdo to a Juvey-cop, while satisfying to her, does nothing to save anyone from unwinding. Her place is not in Audrey's salon.

That afternoon Risa says her good-bye, and Audrey insists on stocking Risa up with supplies and money and a sturdy new backpack that has neither hearts nor pandas.

"I guess now is as good a time as any to tell you," Audrey says, just before she leaves.

"Tell me what?"

"It was just on the news. They announced that your friend Connor is still alive."

It's the best news Risa's gotten in a long time . . . but then she quickly comes to realize the announcement is not a good thing at all. Now that the Juvenile Authority knows he's alive, they'll be beating every bush for him.

"Do they have any idea where he is?" Risa asks.

Audrey shakes her head. "No clue. In fact, they think he's with you."

If only that were true. But even when Connor shows up in her dreams, he's not with her. He's running. He's always running.

29 · Cam

Lunch with the general and the senator is in the dark recesses of the Wrangler's Club—perhaps the most expensive, most exclusive restaurant in Washington, DC. Secluded leather booths, each in its own pool of light, and a complete lack of windows gives the illusion that time has been stopped by the importance of one's conversation. The outside world doesn't exist when one dines in the Wrangler's Club.

As Cam and Roberta are walked in by the hostess, he spots faces he thinks he recognizes. Senators or congressmen, perhaps. People he's seen at the various high-profile galas he's attended. Or maybe it's just his imagination. These self-important folk, wheeling and dealing, all begin to look alike after a while. He suspects that the ones he doesn't recognize are the real power brokers. That's the way it always is. Lobbyists for surreptitious special interests he couldn't begin to guess at. Proactive Citizenry does not have a monopoly on secret influence.

"Best foot forward," Roberta tells Cam as they are led to their booth.

"And which one is that?" he asks. "You'd know better than me."

She doesn't respond to his barb. "Just remember that what happens today could define your future."

"And yours," Cam points out.

Roberta sighs. "Yes. And mine."

General Bodeker and Senator Cobb are already at the table. The general rises to meet them, and the senator also tries to slide out of the booth, but he's foiled by his copious gut.

"Please, don't get up," says Roberta.

He gives up. "The burgers win every time," he says.

They all settle in, share obligatory handshakes and obsequious niceties. They discuss the unpredictable weather, raining one minute, sunny the next. The senator sings the praises of the pan-seared scallops, which is today's special.

"Anaphylactic," Cam blurts out. "That is, I mean, I'm allergic to scallops. At least my shoulders and upper arms are. I get the worst rash."

The general is intrigued. "Really. But just there?"

"And I'll bet he can't do any brown-nosing on account of his nose is allergic to chocolate," says Senator Cobb, and guffaws so loudly it rattles the water glasses.

They order, and once the appetizers arrive, the two men finally get down to the business at hand.

"We see you as a military man, Cam," says the general, "and Proactive Citizenry agrees."

Cam moves his fork around in his endive salad. "You want to make me into a boeuf."

General Bodeker bristles. "That's an unfair characterization of young people who are military minded."

Senator Cobb waves his hand dismissively. "Yes, yes, we all know the official military opinion of the word—but that's not what we're saying Cam. You'd bypass traditional training and go straight into the officer program—and on the fast track, to boot!"

"I can offer you any branch of the military you like," Bodeker says.

"Let it be the Marines," Roberta says, and when Cam looks

at her, she says, "Well, I know you had that in mind—and they have the crispest uniforms."

The senator puts out his hand, as if chopping wood. "The point is, you would float through the program, learn what you need to learn lickety-split, and emerge as an official spokesperson for the military, with all the perks that come with it."

"You'd be a model for young people everywhere," adds Bodeker.

"And for your kind," adds Cobb.

Cam looks up at that. "I don't have a 'kind,'" he tells them, which makes the two men look to Roberta.

She puts down her fork and composes her response carefully. "You once described yourself as a 'concept car,' Cam. Well, what the good senator and general are saying is that they like the concept."

"I see."

The main course arrives. Cam ordered the prime rib—a favorite of someone or another in his head. The first taste brings him back to a sister's wedding. He has no idea where, or who the sister is. She had blond hair, but her face did not make the cut into his brain. He wonders if that kid—if any kid inside him—would have ever been offered a crisp uniform. He knows the answer is no, and he feels insulted for them.

Brakes in the rain. He must apply them slowly, so as not to set this meeting fishtailing out of control. "It's a very generous offer," Cam says. "And I'm honored to be considered." He clears his throat. "And I know you all have my best interests at heart." He meets eyes with the general, then with the senator. "But it's not something I want to do at this"—he searches for a suitably Washingtonian word—"at this juncture."

The senator just stares at him, all jovialness gone from his voice. "Not something you want to do at this juncture . . . ," he repeats.

And, predictable as clockwork, Roberta leaps in with, "What Cam means to say is he needs time to consider it."

"I thought you said this would be a slam dunk, Roberta."

"Well, maybe if you were a little more elegant in your approach—"

Then General Bodeker puts up his hand to silence them.

"Perhaps you don't understand," the general says with calm control. "Let me explain it to you." He waits until Cam puts down his fork, then proceeds. "Until last week you were the property of Proactive Citizenry. But they have sold their interest in you for a sizeable sum. You are now the property of the United States military."

"Property?" says Cam. "What do you mean, 'Property'?"

"Now, Cam," says Roberta, working her best damage control. "It's only a word."

"It's more than a word!" insists Cam. "It's an idea—an idea that, according to the history expert somewhere in my left brain, was abolished in 1865."

The senator starts to bluster, but the general keeps his cool. "That applies to individuals, which you are not. You are a collection of very specific parts, each one with a distinct monetary value. We've paid more than one hundred times that value for the unique manner those parts have been organized, but in the end, Mr. Comprix . . . parts is parts."

"So there you have it," says the senator bitterly. "You wanna leave? Then go on; git outta here. Just as long as you leave all those parts of yours behind."

Cam's breathing is out of control. Dozens of separate tempers inside of him join and flare all at once. He wants to dump the table. Hurl the plates at their heads.

Property!

They see him as property!

His worst fear is realized; even the people who venerate

him see him as a commodity. A thing.

Roberta, seeing that look in his eyes, grabs his hand. "Look at me, Cam!" she orders.

He does, knowing deep down that making a scene will be the worst thing he can do for himself. He needs her to talk him down.

"Thirty pieces of silver!" he shouts. "Brutus! Rosenbergs!"

"I am not a traitor! I am true to you, Cam. This deal was made without my knowledge. I'm as furious as you, but we both must make the best of it."

His head is swimming. "Grassy knoll!"

"It's not a conspiracy either! Yes, I knew about it when I brought you here—but I also knew that telling you would be a mistake." She throws an angry glare at the two men. "Because if it were your choice, the technical issue of ownership need never have come up."

"Out of the bag." Cam forces his breathing to slow and his flaring temper to drop into a smolder. "Close the barn door. The horses are gone."

"What the hell is he babbling about?" snaps the senator.

"Quiet!" Roberta orders. "Both of you!" The fact that Roberta can quiet a senator and a general with a single word feels like some sort of victory. Regardless of who and what they own, they are not in charge here. At least not at this juncture.

Cam knows that anything out of his mouth will be just another spark of metaphorical language—the way he spoke when he was first rewound, but he doesn't care.

"Lemon," he says.

The two men glance around the table in search of a lemon. "No." Cam takes a bite of prime rib, forcing himself to calm down enough to better translate his thoughts. "What I mean is that no matter what you paid for me, you've thrown away your money if I don't perform."

The senator is still perplexed, but General Bodeker nods. "You're saying that we bought ourselves a lemon."

Cam takes another bite. "Gold star for you."

The two men look to each other, shifting uncomfortably. Good. That's exactly what he wants.

"But if I *do* perform, then everybody gets what they want."

"So we're back where we started," says Bodeker, with waning patience.

"But at least now we understand each other." Cam considers the situation. Considers Roberta, who is all but wringing her hands with anxiety now. Then he turns to the two men. "Tear up your contract with Proactive Citizenry," he says. "Void it. And then I'll sign *my own* contract that commits me to whatever you want me to do. So that it's my decision rather than a purchase."

That seems to baffle all three of them.

"Is that possible?" asks the senator.

"Technically he's still a minor," Roberta says.

"Technically I don't exist," Cam reminds her. "Isn't that right?"

No one answers.

"So," says Cam. "Make me exist on paper. And on that same paper, I'll sign over my life to you. Because I choose to."

The general looks to the senator, but the senator just shrugs. So General Bodeker turns to Cam and says:

"We'll consider it and get back to you."

Cam stands in his room in his DC residence, staring at the back of the closed door.

This town house is the place he comes back to after the various speaking trips. Roberta calls it "going home." To Cam this does not feel like home. The mansion in Molokai is home, and yet he hasn't been back there for months. He suspects he may never be allowed to go back again. After all, it was more a nursery than a residence for him. It was where he was rewound. It was where he was taught who he was—what he was—and learned how to coordinate his diverse "internal community."

General Bodeker, for all of his ire at the use of the word "boeuf" for military youth, apparently had no problem skirting euphemisms and calling Cam's internal community "parts."

Cam does not know who to despise more—Bodeker for having purchased his quantified flesh, Proactive Citizenry for selling it, or Roberta for willing him into existence. Cam continues to stare at the back of his door. Hanging there—strategically placed by some unknown entity while he was out—is the full dress uniform of a US Marine, shiny buttons and all. Crisp, just as Roberta had said.

Is this a threat, Cam wonders, or an enticement?

Cam says nothing about it to Roberta when he goes down for dinner. Since their meeting with the senator and the general last week, all their meals have been alone in the town house, as if being ignored by powerful people is somehow punishment.

At the end of the meal, the housekeeper brings in a silver tea service, setting it down between them—because Roberta, an expat Brit, must still have her Earl Grey.

It's over tea that Roberta gives him the news. "I need to tell you something," Roberta says after her first sip. "But I need you to promise that you'll control your temper."

"That's never a good way to begin a conversation," he says. "Try again. This time full of springtime and daisies."

Roberta takes a deep breath, sets down her cup, and gets it out. "Your request to sign your own document has been denied by the court."

Cam feels his meal wanting to come back, but he holds it

down. "So the courts say I don't exist. Is that what you're telling me? That I'm an object like"—he picks up a spoon—"like a utensil? Or am I more like this teapot?" He drops the spoon and grabs the pot from the table. "Yes, that's it—an articulate teapot screeching with hot air that no one wants to hear!"

Roberta pushes her chair back with a complaint from the hardwood floor. "You promised to keep your temper!"

"No—you asked, and I refuse!"

He slams the teapot down, and a flood of Earl Grey ejects from the spout, soaking the white tablecloth. The housekeeper, who was lurking, makes herself scarce.

"It's a legal definition, nothing more!" insists Roberta. "I, for one, know that you're more than that stupid definition."

"Sweatshop!" snaps Cam, and not even Roberta can decipher that one. "Your opinion means nothing, because you're little more than the sweatshop seamstress who stitched me together."

Indignation rises in her like an ocean swell. "Oh, I'm a little more than that!"

"Are you going to tell me you're my creator? Shall I sing psalms of praise to thee? Or better yet, why don't I cut out my stolen heart and put it on an altar for you?"

"Enough!"

Cam slumps in his chair, a twisted rag of directionless anger.

Roberta puts down her napkin to help blot the tea, a task beyond the abilities of the tablecloth. Cam wonders if the tablecloth would resent the napkin's absorbency were it legally granted personhood.

"There's something you need to see," Roberta says. "Something you need to *understand* that might give you some perspective on this."

She gets up, goes into the kitchen, and returns with a pen and a blank piece of paper. She sits down beside him, folds back the tablecloth, and puts the paper down on a dry patch of wood.

"I want you to sign your name."

"What for?"

"You'll see."

Too disgusted to argue, he takes the pen, looks down at the paper, and writes as neatly as he can "Camus Comprix."

"Good. Now turn the paper over and sign it again."

"Your point?"

"Humor me."

He flips the paper, but before he signs, Roberta stops him. "Don't look," she says. "This time look at me while you're signing. And talk to me too."

"About what?"

"Whatever is in your heart to say."

Looking at Roberta, he signs his name while delivering an appropriate quote from his namesake: *The need to be right is the sign of a vulgar mind.*" Then he hands the page to Roberta. "There. Are you happy?"

"Why don't you look at the signature, Cam?"

He looks down. At first he thinks he sees his signature as it should be. But a switch seems to flick in his head, and the signature he sees is not his at all. "What is this? This isn't what I wrote."

"It is, Cam. Read it."

The letters are a bit scrawled. "Wil Tash . . . Tashi . . ."

"Wil Tashi'ne," Roberta says. "You have his hands, and his corresponding neuro-motor centers in your cerebellum, as well as crucial cortical material as well. You see. It's *his* neural connections and muscle memory that allow you to play guitar and accomplish a whole host of fine-motor skills."

Cam cannot look away from the signature. The switch in his head keeps flicking on and off. *My signature. Not my signature. Mine. Not mine.*

Roberta regards him with infinite sympathy. "How can you sign a document, Cam, when not even your signature belongs to you?"

Roberta hates when Cam goes out alone, especially at night, but on this night, there's nothing she can say or do that will stop him.

He strides fast, down a street still wet with the day's rain, but feels like he's getting nowhere. He doesn't even know where he wants to go—only away from whatever spot he occupies at the moment, unable to feel right in his own skin. What is it the advertisements call it? That's right—Biosystemic Disunification Disorder. A bogus condition that conveniently can be cured only by unwinding.

All his scheming, all his daydreams of bringing down Proactive Citizenry—of being the kind of hero Risa requires—it all amounts to nothing if he is just a piece of military property. And Roberta's wrong. It's more than just a legal definition. How can she not see that when you are defined, you lose the ability to define yourself? In the end he will become that definition. He will become a thing.

What he needs is some sort of proclamation of existence that trumps anything legal. Something he can hold on to in his heart in the face of anything they have on paper. Risa could give that to him. He knows she can, but she's not here, is she?

But there might be other places he could find it.

He begins to scour his memory, seeking out moments that ring with a spiritual connection. He had First Communion, a Bar Mitzvah, and a Bismillah ceremony. He saw a brother baptized in a Greek Orthodox church and a grandmother cremated in a traditional Buddhist funeral. Just about every faith is represented in his memories, and he wonders if this was intentional. He wouldn't put it past Roberta to have, as part of her criteria for his parts, that all major religions be represented. She's just that anal.

But which one will give him what he needs? He knows if he speaks to a rabbi or a Buddhist priest, he'll get very wise responses that point to more questions instead of an answer. "Do we exist because others perceive our existence, or is, indeed, our own affirmation enough?"

No. What Cam needs is some meat-and-potatoes dogma that can give him a concrete yes or no.

There's a Catholic church a few blocks away. An old one with impressive stained-glass windows. He puts together from his internal community a sizeable posse of believers—enough to give him a sense of reverence and awe as he steps into the sanctuary.

There are a few people present. Mass is over, and confessions are winding down. Cam knows what he has to do.

"Forgive me, Father, for I have sinned."

"Tell me your sins, child."

"I've broken things. I've stolen things. Electronics. A car—maybe two. I may have become violent with a girl once. I'm not sure."

"You're not sure? How could you not be sure?"

"None of my memories are complete."

"Son, you can confess only to the things you remember."

"That's what I'm trying to tell you, Father. I have no complete memories. Just bits and pieces."

"Well, I'll accept your confession, but it sounds like you need something more than the sacrament of the confessional."

"It's because the memories are from other people."

". . ."

"Did you hear me?"

"So you've received bits of the unwound?"

"Yes, but—"

"Son, you can't be held responsible for the acts of a mind that isn't yours, any more than you can be responsible for the acts of a grafted hand."

"I have a couple of those, too."

"Excuse me?"

"My name is Camus Comprix. Does that name mean anything to you?"

". . ."

"I said my name is—"

"—yes, yes, I heard you, I heard you. I'm just surprised you're here."

"Because I'm soulless?"

"Because I very rarely hear confessions from public figures."

"Is that what I am? A public figure?"

"Why are you here, son?"

"Because I'm afraid. I'm afraid that I might not . . . *be*. . . ."

"Your presence here proves you exist."

"But as what? I need you to tell me that I'm not a spoon! That I'm not a teapot!"

"You make no sense. Please, there are people waiting."

"No! This is important! I need you to tell me. . . . I need to know . . . if I qualify as a human being."

"You must know that the church has not taken an official position on unwinding."

"That's not what I'm asking."

"Yes, yes, I know it's not. I know. I know."

"In your opinion as a man of the cloth . . ."

"You ask too much of me. I am here to give absolution, nothing more."

"But you have an opinion, don't you?"

". . ."

"When you first heard of me?"

". . ."

"What was that opinion, Father?"

"It is neither my place to say, nor your place to ask!"

"But I do ask!"

"It is not to your benefit to hear!"

"Then you're being tested, Father. This is your test: Will you tell the truth, or will you lie to me in your own confessional?"

"My opinion . . ."

"Yes . . ."

"My opinion . . . was that your arrival in this world marked the end of all things we hold dear. But that opinion was borne of fear and ignorance. I admit that! And today I see the awful reflection of my own petty judgments. Do you understand?"

". . ."

"I confess that I am humbled by your question. How can I speak to whether or not you carry a divine spark?"

"A simple yes or no will do."

"No one on earth can answer that question, Mr. Comprix—and you should run from anyone who claims they can."

Cam wanders the streets aimlessly, not knowing or caring where he is. He's sure that Roberta has put out a search party already.

And what happens when they find him? They'll take him home. Roberta will soundly chastise him. Then she'll forgive him. And then tomorrow, or the next day, or the next, he'll try on the crisp uniform hanging on the back of his door, he'll like how it looks, and he'll allow himself to be transferred to his new owners.

He knows it's inevitable. And he also knows that the day that happens is the day any spark he has within him will die forever.

A bus approaches down the street, its headlights bobbing as it hits a pothole. Cam could take that bus home. He could take it far away. But neither of those choices is the idea pinioning his mind at that moment.

And so he prays in nine languages, to a dozen deities—to Jesus, to Yahweh, to Allah, to Vishnu, to the "I" of the universe, and even to a great godless void.

Please, he begs. *Please give me a single reason why I shouldn't hurl myself beneath the wheels of that bus.*

When the answer comes, it comes in English—and not from the heavens, but from the bar behind him.

"*. . . have confirmed that Connor Lassiter, also known as the Akron AWOL, is still alive. It is believed he may be traveling with Lev Calder and Risa Ward. . . .*"

The bus rolls past, splattering his jeans with mud.

Forty-five minutes later, Cam returns home with a new sense of calm, as if nothing has happened. Roberta scolds him. Roberta forgives him. Always the same.

"You must stop these reckless surrenders to your momentary moods," she chides.

"Yes, I know." Then he tells her that he's accepting General Bodeker's "proposal."

Roberta, of course, is both relieved and overjoyed. "This is a great step for you, Cam. A step you need to take. I'm so very proud of you."

He wonders what the general's response would have been had Cam not accepted. Certainly they would come for him anyway. Forced him into submission. After all, if he's their property, it's in their right to do anything they want to him.

Cam goes to his room and heads straight for his guitar. This is not an idle kind of playing tonight; he plays with a purpose only he knows. The music brings with it the impressions of memories, like an afterimage of a bright landscape. Certain fingerings, certain chord progressions have more of an effect, so he works them, changes them up. He begins to dig.

His chords sound atonal and random—but they're not. For Cam it's like spinning the dial of a safe. You can crack any combination if you're skilled enough and you know what to listen for.

Then finally, after more than an hour of playing, it all comes together. Four chords, unusual in their combination, but powerfully evocative, rise to the surface. He plays the chords over and over, trying different fingering, finessing the notes and the harmonies, letting the music resonate through him.

"I haven't heard that one," Roberta says, poking her head in his room. "Is it new?"

"Yes," Cam lies. "Brand-new."

But in reality it's very old. Much older than him. He had to dig deep to coax it forth, but once he found it, it's as if it was always there on the tips of his fingers, on the edge of his mind waiting to be played. The song fills him with immense joy and immense sorrow. It sings of soaring hopes and dreams crushed. And the more he plays it, the more memory fragments are drawn forth.

When he heard that news report coming from the bar—when he stepped in and saw the faces of the Akron AWOL, his beloved Risa, and the tithe-turned-clapper on the TV screen, he was stunned. First by the revelation that Connor Lassiter was alive—but on top of that, a sense of mental connection that made his seams crawl.

It was the tithe. That innocent face. Cam knew that face, and not just from the many articles and news reports. This was more.

He was injured.

He needed healing.

I played guitar for him.

A healing song.

For the Mahpee.

Cam had no idea what that meant, only that it was a spark of connection—a synapse within his complex mosaic of neurons. He *knows* Lev Calder—or at least a member of his internal community does—and that knowledge is somehow tied to music.

So now Cam plays.

It's two o'clock in the morning when he finally gleans enough from his musical memory to understand. Lev Calder had once been given sanctuary by the Arápache Nation. No one searching for him will know that, which means he has the perfect place to hide. But Cam knows. The heady power of that knowledge makes him dizzy—because if it's true that he's traveling with Risa and the Connor, then the Arápache Reservation is where they'll be—a place where the Juvenile Authority *has* no authority.

Had Risa known Connor Lassiter was alive all along? If she had, it would explain so many things. Why she could not give her heart to Cam. Why she so often spoke of Lassiter in the present tense, as if he were just waiting around the corner to spirit her away.

Cam should be furious, but instead he feels vindicated. Exhilarated. He had no hope of battling a ghost for her affections, but Connor Lassiter is still flesh and blood—which means he can be bested! He can be defeated, dishonored— whatever it will take to kill Risa's love for him, and in the end, when he has fallen from Risa's favor, Cam will be there to keep Risa from falling as well.

After that, Cam can personally bring the Akron AWOL to justice, making himself enough of a hero to buy his own freedom.

It's three a.m. when he slips out of the town house, leaving his semblance of a life behind, determined not to return until he has Risa Ward under his arm and Connor Lassiter crushed beneath his heel.

Part Four

The Scent of Memory

"FOUNDLING WHEELS" FOR EVERY ITALIAN HOSPITAL?

By Carolyn E. Price

Feb 28, 2007

Italy tests out the "foundling wheel," a concept first introduced in Rome in the year 1198 by Pope Innocent III.

A well-dressed, well-looked after three- or four-month-old baby, maybe Italian, or maybe not, and in excellent health, was abandoned on Saturday evening in the "foundling wheel," a heated cradle that was set up at the Policlinico Casilino. The foundling wheel was created for women to put their infants in when the child is unwanted or is born into seriously deprived conditions.

The baby boy is the first to be saved in Italy thanks to an experimental system that was devised to stop babies from being abandoned in the street. The baby "foundling" has been named Stefano in honor of the doctor who first took charge of him.

For health minister Livia Turco, the project is "an example to follow." Ms. Turco's colleague, family minister Rosy Bindi, wants a modern version of the foundling wheel "in every maternity ward in every hospital in Italy."

The head of the neonatology department at the Policlinico Casilino, Piermichele Paolillo, notes: "We wouldn't have been surprised to find a newborn in the cradle, but we didn't expect to see a three- or four-month-old baby. . . . Who knows what lies behind this episode . . . ?"

Published with permission of DigitalJournal.com

Full article at: http://www.digitaljournal.com/article/127934

The Rheinschilds

Finally a time to celebrate! Tonight the Rheinschilds dine at Baltimore's most expensive, most exclusive restaurant. This splurge is long overdue.

Sonia holds Janson's hand across the table. They've already sent the waiter away twice, not wanting to be rushed with their order. Bubbles rise in their champagne flutes while the bottle of Dom Pérignon chills beside them. This night must not pass too quickly. It must linger and last, because they both deserve it.

"Tell me again," Sonia says. "Every last bit of it!"

Janson is happy to oblige, because it was the kind of meeting worth reliving. He wishes he had found a way to record it. He tells her once more of how he went into the office of the president of BioDynix Medical Instruments and presented to him what he considers to be "his life's work"—just as he had presented it to Sonia a few days before.

"And he had vision enough to see the ramifications right away?"

"Sonia, the guy was sweating with greed. I could practically see fangs growing. He told me he needed to speak to the board and would get back to me—but even before I left the building, he called me back in to make a deal."

Sonia claps her hands together, having not heard that part before. "How perfect! He didn't want you to show it to his competitors."

"Exactly. He made a preemptive bid on the spot—and he didn't just buy the prototype; he bought the schematics, the patent—everything. BioDynix will have the exclusive rights!"

"Tell me you went straight to the bank with the check."

Janson shakes his head. "Electronic transfer. I confirmed it's already in our account." Janson takes a sip of champagne; then he leans forward and whispers, "Sonia, we could buy a small island with what they paid for it!"

Sonia smiles and raises her champagne glass to her lips. "I'll be satisfied if you just agree to take a vacation."

They both know it's not about the money. As it was once before, it's about changing the world.

Finally they order, their champagne flutes are refilled, and Janson raises his glass in a toast. "To the end of unwinding. A year from now it will be nothing but an ugly memory!"

Sonia clinks her glass to his. "I see a second Nobel in your future," she says. "One that you don't have to share with me."

Janson smiles. "I will anyway."

The meal comes—the finest they've ever had, on the finest evening they've ever shared.

It isn't until the following morning that they realize something's wrong . . . because the building in which they work—which had been named for them—is no longer the Rheinschild Pavilion. Overnight the big brass letters above the entrance have been replaced and the building renamed for the chairman of Proactive Citizenry.

30 · Hayden

Hayden Upchurch cannot be unwound. At least not today. Tomorrow, who can say?

"Why am I at a harvest camp if I'm overage?" he had asked his jailers after he had been deposited there along with the rest of the holdouts from the Communications Bomber at the Graveyard.

"Would you rather be in prison?" was the camp director's only answer. But eventually Director Menard couldn't keep the truth to himself—the truth being so delectably sweet.

"About half the states in this country have a measure on this year's ballot that will allow the unwinding of violent criminals," he had told Hayden with an unpleasant yellow-toothed grin. "You were sent to a harvest camp in a state where it's sure to pass and will go into effect most quickly—that is, the day after the election." Then he went on to inform Hayden that he would be unwound at 12:01 a.m. on November sixth. "So set your alarm."

"I will," Hayden had told him brightly. "And I'll make a special request that you get my teeth. Now that you good people have had my braces removed, they're ready for you. Of course, my orthodontist would suggest you wear a retainer for two years."

Menard had just grunted and left.

It boggles Hayden that he's been labeled a violent criminal when all he tried to do was save his life and the lives of other kids. But when the Juvenile Authority has a grudge against you, it can spin things any way it wants.

A year and a half ago, when Connor had arrived at Happy Jack Harvest Camp, he was paraded before all the Unwinds, a humbled, broken prisoner. They thought it would demoralize the other kids, but instead it practically turned Connor into a god. The falling, rising Unwind.

Apparently, the Juvenile Authority had learned from its mistake, and for Hayden they went about things differently. With Hayden's Unwind Manifesto still getting more hits online than a naked celebrity, they needed to damage his street cred.

Like Connor, they had immediately separated him from the other kids, but instead of making an example of him, Director Menard chose to treat Hayden to steak meals at the staff table and give him a three-room suite in the guest villa. At first Hayden was worried that the man was harboring some sort of romantic interest—but he had an altogether different agenda. Menard was spreading rumors that Hayden was cooperating with the Juvenile Authority and helping them round up the kids that escaped from the Graveyard. Although the only "evidence" was the fact that Hayden was being treated remarkably well, the kids at the harvest camp believed. The only ones who didn't fall for it were kids like Nasim and Lizbeth, who knew him from before.

Now when he's walked through the dining room, the kids boo and hiss, and his escort of guards—who at first were there to make sure he didn't escape, or tell anyone the truth—now are there to protect him from the angry mob of Unwinds. It's a masterful bit of manipulation that Hayden might appreciate were he not the butt of the joke. After all, what could be lower than a traitor to the traitors? Now, thanks to Menard, Hayden will leave this world shamed on all possible fronts.

"I won't bother taking your teeth," Menard had told him. "But I may put your middle finger on a key chain, to remind me of all the times you've flipped it at me."

"Left or right?" Hayden had asked. "These things are important."

But as summer pounds inexorably toward autumn and his postelection unwinding, Hayden finds it harder and harder to make light of personal impending doom. He's beginning to finally believe his life as he knows it will end in the Chop Shop of Cold Springs Harvest Camp.

31 · Starkey

There's an unwind transport truck on a winding road on a bright August day, and although it's painted in pastel blues, pinks, and greens, nothing can hide the ugliness of its purpose.

The northern Nevada terrain is arid and rugged. There are mountains that seemed to see where they were headed and gave up before they were fully pushed forth from the earth, deciding it wasn't worth the effort. Everything in the landscape is the neutral beige of institutional furniture. *Now I know why tumbleweeds roll,* Starkey thinks. *Because they want to be anywhere else but here.*

Starkey sits shotgun beside the driver of the transport truck. Although today it should be called "riding pistol," because that's the weapon he has pressed to the driver's ribs.

"You really don't need to do this," the driver says nervously.

"This thing is bigger than you, Bubba. Just go with it, and you might actually live." Starkey doesn't know the man's name. To him all truck drivers are Bubba.

As they come down into the valley toward Cold Springs Harvest Camp, Starkey gets a good view of the facility. Like all harvest camps, its calculated attention to design is part of the crime, putting forth an illusion of tranquillity and comfort. At a harvest camp, even the building where kids go in and never come out could be as inviting as Grandma's house. Starkey shudders at the thought.

The builders of Cold Springs Harvest Camp tried to take architectural cues from its surroundings, attempting a natural Western look—but a huge oasis of green artificial turf in the midst of stucco buildings is a glaring reminder that there is nothing natural about this place at all.

Bubba sweats profusely as they approach the guard gate. "Stop sweating!" says Starkey. "It's suspicious."

"I can't help it!"

To the guard at the gate, it's business as usual. He checks the driver's credentials and reviews the manifest. He seems not to care, or just doesn't notice the driver's perspiration. Nor does he pay attention to Starkey, who is dressed in the light gray coveralls of an Unwind transport worker. The guard goes back into his booth, hits a button, and the gates slowly swing open.

Now it's Starkey's turn to sweat. Until this moment it's all been hypothetical. Even coming down the valley toward the camp seemed surreal and one step removed from reality, but now that he's inside, there's no turning back. This is going down.

They pull up to a loading dock, where a team of harvest camp counselors wait to greet their new arrivals with disarming smiles, then sort them and send them to their barracks to await unwinding. But that's not going to happen today.

As soon as the back doors of the transport truck are swung open, the staff is met not with rows of restrained teenagers, but with an army. Kids leap out at them, screaming and brandishing weapons.

The instant the commotion begins, the driver leaps from the cab and runs for his life. Starkey doesn't care, since the man has done his job. The shouts give way to gunfire. Workers race away from the scene, and guards race toward it.

Starkey gets out of the cab in time to see some of his precious storks go down. The east tower has a clear view of the loading dock, and a sharpshooter is taking kids out. The first couple of shots are tranqs, but the sharpshooter switches rifles. The next kid to go down, goes down for good.

Oh crap this is real this is real this is—

And then the sharpshooter aims at Starkey.

He dodges just as a bullet puts a hole in the door of the truck with a dainty *ping*. Panicked, Starkey leaps behind a boulder, smashing his bad hand on the way down, spitting curses from the pain.

The storks are spreading out. Some are going down, but more are gaining ground. Some use the counselors as human shields.

I can't die, Starkey thinks. *Who will lead them if I die?*

But he knows he can't stay crouched behind a boulder either. They have to see him fighting. They have to see him in charge. Not just the storks, but the kids he's about to set free.

He pokes his head up and aims his pistol at the shadowy figure in the tower, who is now firing at kids running across the artificial turf. Starkey's fourth shot is lucky. The sharpshooter goes down.

But there are other guards, other towers.

In the end, salvation for all of them comes from the kids of the camp itself. The grounds are filled with Unwinds going about their daily activities—sports and dexterity exercises all designed to maximize their divided value and physically groom them for unwinding. When they see what's happening, they abandon their activities, overpower their counselors, and turn an attack into a revolt.

Starkey strides into the midst of it, amazed by what he's witnessing. The staff running in panic, guards overpowered, their weapons pulled from them and added to the storks' growing arsenal. He sees a woman in a white coat race across the lawn and behind a building, trying to use a cell phone—but the joke's on her. Even before the storks ambushed the transport truck, Jeevan and a team of techies had jammed the two wireless towers feeding the valley and took out the landline. No communication of any sort is getting in or out of this place unless it's running on two feet.

The rebellion feeds itself, fueled by desperation and unexpected hope. It grows in intensity until even the guards are running, only to be tackled by dozens of kids and restrained with their own handcuffs. *It's like Happy Jack!* thinks Starkey. *But this time it'll be done right. Because I'm the one in charge.*

Overpowered by sheer numbers, the staff is subdued, and the camp is liberated in fifteen minutes.

Kids are overwhelmed with joy. Some are in tears from the ordeal. Others tend to dead and dying friends. Adrenaline is still high, and Starkey decides to use it. Let the dead be dead. He must focus them now on life. He strides out into the middle of the common area, beside a flagpole poking out of the artificial turf, and draws their attention away from the human cost of their liberation.

He grabs a machine gun from one of his storks and fires it into the air until everyone is looking his way.

"My name is Mason Michael Starkey!" he announces in his loudest, most commanding voice, "and I've just saved you from unwinding!"

Cheers all around, as it should be. He orders them to separate into two groups. Storks to his left, the rest to his right. They are reluctant at first, but his storks wave their weapons and make the order stick. The kids divide themselves. There seem to be about a hundred storks and three hundred other kids. No tithes, thankfully. This is a titheless camp. Starkey addresses the nonstorks first, gesturing to the main entrance.

"The gate is wide open. Your path to freedom is there. I suggest you take it."

For a moment they linger, not trusting. Then a few turn and head toward the gate, then a few more, and in an instant it becomes a mass exodus. Starkey watches them go. Then he turns to the storks who remain.

"To you I give a choice," he tells them. "You can run off with the others, or you can become part of something larger than yourselves. All your life you've been treated like second-class citizens and then handed the ultimate insult. You were sent here." He gestures wide. "We are all storks here, condemned to be unwound—but we've taken back our lives, and we're taking our revenge. So I ask you—do you want revenge?" He waits and receives a few guarded responses, so he raises his voice. *"I said, do you want revenge?"*

Now primed, the answer comes in a single chorus blast. "Yes!"

"Then welcome," Starkey says, "to the Stork Brigade!"

32 · Hayden

Shortly before the liberation, Hayden takes a shower—which he now does almost obsessively three times a day, trying to wash off the filth of his situation. He knows no amount of scrubbing can do it, but it feels good all the same. The other Unwinds there hate him as much as they hate their jailers because they believe he's one of them. So smooth was Camp Director Menard in creating the spin—in making everyone there believe that Hayden had been turned and was now working for the Juvenile Authority. He would rather die, of course, than ever do anything to help the Juvenile Authority, but it's all about perception. People believe what they think they see. No, he'll never wash away Menard's lies, but they can't stop him from trying.

When he steps out of his shower today, however, he discovers that his world has completely changed.

He immediately hears the gunfire—round after round of staccato, arrhythmic blasts that seem to be coming from multiple directions. Although his lap-of-luxury suite has a veranda, he's not allowed on it, so it's locked. Still, he can see what's going on. The harvest camp is under attack by a team of kids with weapons—and each time a guard falls, a new weapon is added to their arsenal. Unwinds from the camp have joined with them, turning this into a full-scale revolt—and Hayden allows himself a glimmer of hope that perhaps the date set for his unwinding might be wrong after all.

A bullet catches the corner of the sliding glass veranda door, but leaves little more than a ding. It's bulletproof glass. Apparently the builders decided that anyone who would be invited to the visitor's suite of a harvest camp might be the kind of person likely to get shot at. His only way out is the door to the suite, but it's locked from the outside.

The sound of gunfire diminishes, until it's gone entirely—and the sight of kids still running outside tells Hayden that the invading force was victorious.

He pounds on his door over and over again, screaming at the top of his lungs, until someone comes.

It's a kid at the door, and he looks familiar. Hayden quickly recognizes him as a message runner from the Graveyard.

"Hayden?" the kids says. "No way!"

He is led by three fugitives he knew from the airplane graveyard out into the common area, where the artificial turf swelters in the midday sun. There are bodies strewn everywhere. Some are tranq'd; others clearly dead. Most are kids. A few are guards. To the left, the harvest camp workers are being bound and gagged. To the right, there are vast numbers of kids racing out the camp's gate, claiming their freedom. But not everyone is leaving.

The rest are being addressed by someone wearing the pastel-gray coverall uniform of an Unwind transport worker.

Hayden stops short when he realizes who it is.

Somewhere in the back of his mind, he was holding out hope that it was Connor come to rescue them. Now he wonders if it's too late to go back to his guest suite.

"Hey," the kid who unlocked his door shouts. "Look who we found!"

When Starkey lays eyes on Hayden, there's a moment of fear in Starkey's eyes, which is quickly engulfed by steel. He smiles a little too broadly. "What was it you always said at the Graveyard, Hayden? 'Hello. I'll be your rescuer today.'"

"He's one of them!" someone shouts before Hayden can come up with a clever response. "He's been working for the Juvies! They even let him pick who gets unwound!"

"Oh, is that the latest news? You know you can't trust a thing the tabloids say. Next I'll be giving birth to alien triplets."

Bam is there—she looks at Hayden, somewhat amused. "So the Juvenile Authority made you their bitch."

"Nice to see you too, Bam."

Shouts of "Leave him," and "Tranq him," and even "Kill him," spread through the crowd of Cold Springs Unwinds, but the kids who knew him rise to his defense enough to spread at least a few seeds of doubt. The crowd looks to Starkey for a decision, but he doesn't seem ready to make one. He's spared, though, because three strong storks approach with the struggling camp director.

The crowd parts, and someone has the bright idea to spit on Menard as he passes, and pretty soon everyone's doing it. Hayden might have done it if he had thought of it first, but now it's just conformism.

"So this must be the guy in charge," Starkey says. "Get on your knees."

When Menard doesn't obey, the three kids manhandling him push him down.

"You have been found guilty of crimes against humanity," Starkey says.

"Guilty?" wails Menard desperately. "I've had no trial! Where's my trial?"

Starkey looks up at the mob. "How many of you think he's guilty?"

Just about every hand goes up, and as much as Hayden hates Menard, he has a bad feeling about where this is going.

Sure enough, Starkey pulls out a pistol. "There's twelve in a jury, and that's definitely more than twelve people," Starkey tells Menard. "Consider yourself convicted."

Then Starkey does something Hayden was not expecting. He hands the gun to Hayden.

"Execute him."

Hayden begins to stammer, staring at the gun. "Starkey, uh—this isn't—"

"If you're not a traitor, then prove it by putting a bullet in his head."

"That won't prove anything."

Then Menard doubles over and begins to pray. A man who kills kids for a living praying for deliverance. It's enough to make Hayden aim at Menard's hypocritical skull. He holds it there for a good ten seconds, but he can't pull the trigger.

"I won't," Hayden says. "Not like this."

"Fine." Starkey takes back the gun, then points to a random kid in the crowd, who looks to be no older than fourteen. The kid steps forward, and Starkey puts the gun in the kid's hand. "Show this coward what it means to be courageous. Carry out the execution."

The kid is clearly terrified, but all eyes are on him. He's been put to the test and knows he must not fail. So he grimaces. He squints. He puts the muzzle of the gun to the back of Menard's head and looks away. Then he pulls the trigger.

The pop is not loud; it's just a pop. Like a single stray firecracker. Menard crumples, dead before he hits the ground. It's quick and clean. Just an entrance wound in the back of the head and an exit wound right beneath the chin, with the bullet itself claimed by the artificial turf. There are no exploding brain bits and pieces of skull—Starkey and the crowd seem disappointed that an execution, in the end, is far less dramatic than the buildup.

"All right, move out!" Starkey orders, giving instructions to commandeer any vehicle for which they can find keys.

"What about him?" Bam asks, sneering at Hayden.

Starkey spares Hayden a brief glance and the tiniest hint of a superior grin before saying, "We'll take him with us. He still might be useful." Then he turns back to all those gathered and says in a powerful voice, "I hereby announce that this harvest camp is officially closed!"

Starkey gets the cheers and adulation he's craving, and Hayden, looking at the dead director . . . and the dead guards . . . and the dozens of dead kids littering the grounds . . . wonders whether he should be cheering or screaming.

33 · Connor

Waiting is not in Connor's arsenal of personal skills. Even before his parents signed his unwind order, he was impatient and had little tolerance for downtime. Back then, quiet time made him think about his life, thinking about his life made him angry, and anger made him do the kinds of impetuous, irresponsible, and occasionally criminal things that always got him in trouble.

Since the day he ran from his home, however, there has been no downtime—at least not until arriving on the Arápache Reservation. Even when sequestered in Sonia's basement, there was a whole petri dish of viral angst to deal with. His guard had to be up at all times to protect himself, to protect Risa, and to keep an eye on Roland, who could have taken him out at any instant.

He still wonders if Roland, in the right circumstances, really would have killed him.

At Happy Jack, he had cornered Connor, pinned him against a wall, and tried to strangle him with the very hand that now is a part of Connor—but Roland couldn't go through with it. In the end, Roland could have been all bark and no bite—but no one will ever know.

Connor, on the other hand, *has* killed people.

He fired deadly weapons in a war against the Juvies at the Graveyard. He knows some of his bullets hit their mark and took people down. So does that make him a killer? Is there any way to be redeemed from that?

This is why Connor despises downtime. All that thinking can drive him mad.

His one consolation is a growing feeling of safety. Normalcy—if anything about this situation can be called normal. The Tashi'ne family have been kind hosts, in spite of their initial coolness to him. From the moment it became public that Connor is alive, they have truly made their home his.

During the day, however, no one is there. Kele is off at school—which is a good thing because Connor has little patience for Kele's lack of patience. Chal is off working his magic with the Hopi, Elina spends her days at the pediatric wing of the medical lodge, and Pivane, who does come over for dinner each night—is usually off hunting.

Connor, Grace, and Lev—who can't go out for fear of being spotted—are left to their own devices.

It's late afternoon a week into August—their twentieth day there. The light coming through the windows is a rich amber, reflected by the ridge across the ravine. Shadows become long quickly in these cliff-side homes, and when the sun sets, it's gone. There's little room for twilight in the ravine.

Grace, who is very good at entertaining herself, had proclaimed, "There's lots of stuff here," on their first day. Today
she's ransacked yet another closet, then reorganized it with
frightening precision. Lev, still recovering from the car accident, has a mat spread out on the marble floor in the middle of
the great room, doing some physical therapy Elina taught him,
while Connor sits on the overstuffed sofa nearby. Having found
a pocketknife that must have belonged to long-lost Wil, Connor has started carving wood, but for the life of him doesn't
know what to make, so he just ends up whittling larger sticks
into smaller ones.

"You should take this time to educate yourself," Lev told
Connor on the first day the three of them were left alone in
the Tashi'ne home. "You kicked-AWOL in, what, tenth grade?
You never finished high school; how do you expect to get a job
when this is all over?"

The thought of this "all being over" makes Connor laugh.
He tries to imagine what his life might be like in some alternate
universe, where staying whole was a given, rather than a privilege. He supposes his natural skill with electronics could have
eventually gotten him work as a repair technician somewhere.
So, when this is "all over," and if some miracle allows him to lead
a normal life, what will that life be about? Alternate-universe
Connor might be content repairing refrigerators, but the Connor
from this universe finds the idea vaguely horrifying.

All this *thinking* time is getting him angry again—an old
pattern coming back—and although he no longer misdirects
it into bursts of stupidity, he's troubled by the emergence of
this old mental subroutine because he knows there are other
things, other feelings that come with it.

"I hate this," Connor says, throwing down the useless stick
he's carving.

Lev uncurls himself from an awkward-looking stretch and

watches in that opossum way of his to see where this is going.

"I hate it here," says Connor. "Being in someone's house, being 'taken care of.' It's turning me into someone I'm not—or at least someone I'm not anymore."

Lev holds that long look at Connor, to the point that it's uncomfortable. Connor refuses to be stared down.

"You were never good at being a kid, were you?" Lev says.

"What?"

"You stunk at it. You were a total screwup. You were the kind of kid who would use a poor unsuspecting tithe as a human shield."

"Yeah," says Connor, more than a little indignant, "but don't forget I saved that tithe's life!"

"An added bonus—but that's not the reason why you first grabbed me that day, is it?"

Connor doesn't say anything, because they both know he's right—and it ticks Connor off.

"My point is that you're afraid of going back to being that same screwup you were two years ago—but I don't see it happening."

"And why is that, O wise clapper tithe?"

Lev throws him a dirty look, but lets it go. "You're kind of like Humphrey Dunfee. We both are. Torn apart by everything that's happened to us, then put back together again. Who you are now is nothing like who you used to be."

Connor considers it and nods, accepting Lev's observation. It's a comfort to know that Lev truly thinks he's changed, but Connor's not all that convinced.

Two things happen at dinner that night. Which of the two is worse depends on one's particular perspective.

Elina arrives home just after dark, followed by Pivane, who

brings a pot of rabbit stew he's had simmering all day. Connor is thankful he didn't have to see the animal skinned and prepared. As long as there's no bunny face in the stew, he'll be fine. At the dinner table, Kele is all blabber about how the kids with predatory animals as their spirit guides have started to bully the kids with tamer animal spirits.

"It's soooo unfair—and I know that half those kids made up their animals on their vision quest anyway."

It makes Connor think of Lucas—his own brother—who turned every little event in middle school into high drama. Connor gets a sudden chill from the memory. Not because he thought of his brother—but because he realizes how long it's been since he's thought about him at all. Lucas would now be getting close to the age Connor was when he kicked-AWOL.

"Could somebody pass the stew down this way?" Connor asks. Better to focus on the food than get caught in a minefield of reflection.

"They'll get over themselves," Pivane tells Kele. "And if they don't, they'll pay the price for it in the end. Birds fly north as well as south," which Connor assumes is the Arápache version of "What goes around, comes around."

"Hello!" calls Conner to the end of the table. "We need some stew down here."

While Lev has patience to wait, Connor's hunger demands attention.

Grace, who always sits right next to Elina, has filled her bowl to overflowing. The tureen is in front of Elina, but she doesn't notice because she's also involved in Kele's drama.

"I can't tell you how many injuries I see at the medical lodge because kids think their animal guides will protect them from broken bones."

Then Connor calls loud and clear: *"Mom!* Pass the stew!"

It's the way that Lev snaps his eyes to Connor that makes Connor realize what he's just said. The feeling of normalcy—the thoughts of family—somehow made the word surface like an unexpected belch.

Everyone looks to Connor like he just dropped a turd on the table.

"I mean, just—pass the stew. Please."

Elina passes the stew to him, and Connor thinks his slip can just slip on by until Kele says, "You let him call you Mom now? I don't even get to call you Mom."

After that, no one knows where to pick up the conversation, and so Elina decides to drive the nail home rather than let it sit halfway to nowhere.

"Do I remind you of her, Connor?"

Connor ladles himself stew and answers without looking at her. "Not really. But dinner's kind of the same."

"Betcha didn't have rabbit," says Grace through a mouthful of stew.

Connor wishes that some sort of black hole could suck away everyone's attention from this embarrassing faux pas. About five seconds later, Connor gets schooled in being careful for what he wishes.

The main window in the great room suddenly shatters, and stone chips fly from a small hole in the back wall—a hole that hadn't been there a second ago.

"Down!" Connor yells. "Under the table! Now!" He has instantly flipped into battle mode and takes charge. He doesn't know if anyone else realizes it was a bullet, but they'll figure it out. What matters is that he gets them out of harm's way. Everyone does as they're told. "Kele—no, over here—out of the window's sight lines!"

As Kele moves closer, Connor bolts across the room to the

light switches and turns them off, leaving them in darkness, so the shooter can't see them. With sudden adrenaline pumping through his retinas, his eyes adjust remarkably quickly to the dark.

"Pivane!" cries Elina. "Call the police."

"We *can't* call the police," he says. That realization hits them all at once. If they call the police, they'll have to explain why they were shot at. Connor, Lev, and Grace will be exposed.

Then Pivane stands up and strides toward the shattered window.

"Pivane!" yells Connor. "What are you, crazy? Get down!"

But Pivane just stands there. It's Grace who points out what only she and Pivane have come to understand.

"That shot was all the way across the room," Grace says. "Kinda like in old war movies. A shot across our bow. They didn't mean to kill no one."

"A warning?" suggests Lev.

"A message," answers Pivane. Still, the rest are reluctant to move from under the table.

Connor steps away from the light switch to stand next to Pivane, looking out into the darkness. There are some lights in the homes across ravine. It could have come from just about anywhere. There is no second shot.

"Someone knows we're here," Connor says, "and wants us gone."

"I'm sorry!" Kele pleads. "Nova promised she wouldn't tell anyone, but she must have. It's my fault."

"Maybe so and maybe not." Pivane turns to Connor. "Either way, it's not safe for you in this house. We'll need to move you."

"The old sweat lodge?" suggests Kele, which somehow sounds appropriate, since this is making them all sweat.

Pivane shakes his head. "I know a better place."

34 · Una

The knock on the shop door is so quiet, Una barely hears it from upstairs. She has just put a steak on the skillet. Had the skillet been sizzling any louder, she might not have heard the knock. She descends from her upstairs apartment into the luthier shop where she used to apprentice but now runs. As she crosses through the workroom, her bare feet smart from sharp wood shavings on the floor. She continues on through the show-room, where her handmade guitars hang from above like sides of beef.

Pivane is at the door with Lev, Connor, and Grace. She waits for an explanation before inviting them in.

"Something happened," Pivane tells her. "We need your help."

"Of course." She opens the door to allow them entrance.

Sitting on stools in the back room of the shop, Pivane explains the events of the evening. "They need a safe haven," Pivane tells her.

"It won't be for long," Connor says, although he probably has no idea how long it will be. None of them do for sure.

"Please, Una," says Pivane, holding intense eye contact. "Do our family this favor."

"Yes, certainly," says Una, trying to hide the trepidation in her voice. "But if whoever shot at them knows they're here—"

"I do not think any more shots will be taken," Pivane says, "but just in case, you should keep your rifle at the ready."

"That goes without saying."

"It's good that I gave it to you," Pivane says, "for if it's used in their protection, it will be used well."

Pivane gets up to go. "I'll be back to check on them tomorrow with supplies, food, anything they might need. If Chal is successful with the Hopi and it draws the Juvenile Authority off track, they'll be able to leave the reservation soon and continue their journey."

Una notices that Lev shifts his shoulders uncomfortably at the suggestion.

"I believe," says Pivane, giving her once again the all-encompassing full focus of his eyes, "that this is the safest place for them. Do you agree?"

Una holds his gaze. "Maybe you're right."

Satisfied, Pivane leaves, the bell on the shop door jingling behind him as he goes out. Una makes sure the door is locked, then escorts her guests upstairs.

Her steak is burning, filling the kitchen with smoke. Cursing, she turns off the burner, turns on the fan, and drops the skillet into the sink, dousing it with water. The steak is about as ruined as her appetite.

"Cajun Blackened Steak, my brother calls that," says Grace.

The small apartment has two bedrooms. She offers Grace her room, but Grace insists on the sofa. "The less space I have to bump around, the better I sleep," she says. She lies down and seems to be snoring instantly. Una covers her with a blanket and scares up blankets for the boys. "The spare bedroom has one bed and a bedroll on the floor."

"I'll take the bedroll," says Connor quickly. "Lev can have the bed."

"No argument," says Lev.

Una now notices that Connor is wearing one of Wil's shirts. The fact that he wears it so obliviously makes it all the more infuriating. He should apologize to every thread of the garment. He should apologize to her. But Una won't tell him this. All she says is, "You don't quite fill out that shirt, do you?"

Connor offers a smile that is apologetic, but not apologetic enough. "It's not like I had much of a choice, considering."

"Yes, considering," she echoes. She expects him to try to charm her, maybe sidle closer to her, because she assumes this is the kind of boy he is. When he doesn't, she is almost disappointed. She wonders when it was that she started looking for reasons to dislike people. But she knows the answer to that. It started the day she put Wil's guitar on the funeral pyre and watched as the guitar burned in his place.

She hands the two their bedding and fetches her rifle, leaning it against the wall near the stairs. "You'll be safe as long as you're here."

"Thank you, Una," says Lev.

"My pleasure, little brother."

She catches Conner smirking when she calls Lev that. Una doesn't care. Let him smirk. Outsiders always do.

35 · Lev

The bedroom has more pictures of Wil than in the Tashi'ne home, all from long before the brief time that Lev knew him. In fact, the room has the uneasy sense of being a shrine.

"Ya think she's got issues with her lost love?" says Connor blithely.

"Her fiancé," Lev corrects. "They knew each other all their lives—so try to be a little more sensitive."

Connor puts up his hands in surrender. "Okay, okay. I'm sorry."

"If you want to win her over, wash that shirt and leave it here when we go."

"Winning her over isn't high on my list of priorities."

Lev shrugs. "Guess you won't be getting any discounts on guitars."

After he's settled in his bed, Lev closes his eyes. It's getting late, but he can't sleep. He can hear Una in the kitchen, cleaning up her burned dinner, tidying up so that she can pretend the messy apartment they saw tonight was just their imagination come morning.

Although Connor isn't moving on his bedroll, it seems his head is far from sleep as well.

"Tonight at dinner was the first time I've said that word in almost two years," Connor confesses.

It takes Lev a few seconds to recall the moment, which was much more traumatic for Connor than for him. He notes that Connor won't even repeat the *M* word. "I'm sure Elina knows that and understands."

Connor rolls over to face Lev, looking up at him from the floor in the dim light. "Why is it that it's easier for me to deal with a sniper shot than to deal with what I said at the table tonight?"

"Because," offers Lev, "you're good in a crisis and you suck at normal."

It makes Connor laugh. "'Good in Crisis; Sucks at Normal.' That about sums up my whole life, doesn't it?" He's silent for a moment, but Lev knows there's more coming, and he knows exactly what it will be.

"Lev, do you ever—"

"No," Lev says, shutting him down. "And neither should you. Not now, anyway."

"You don't even know what I was going to ask."

"It's the parent question, right?"

Connor stews a bit, then says, "You were annoying as a tithe, and you're still annoying."

Lev snickers and flips his hair back. It's become a habit.

Anytime someone reminds him of his days as a tithe, he takes comfort in that shock of long, unruly blond hair.

"I'm sure my parents know I'm alive now," Connor says. "My brother must know too."

That catches Lev's attention. "I never even knew you had a brother."

"His name is Lucas. He got the trophies, and I got detention slips. We used to fight all the time—but you must know all about that. You've got a whole busload of siblings, right?"

Lev shakes his head. "Not anymore. As far as I'm concerned, I'm now a family of one."

"I think Una might see that differently, 'little brother.'"

Lev has to admit there's comfort in that, but not comfort enough. He decides to tell Connor something he's yet to tell anyone—not even Miracolina during the many desperate days they spent together.

"When the clappers blew up my brother's house, my father—who I hadn't seen for over a year—disowned me."

"That's harsh," says Connor. "I'm sorry."

"Yeah. He basically said I should have blown myself up that day at Happy Jack."

Connor offers no response to that. How could he? Yes, Connor's parents sent him off to be unwound, but what Lev's father did—that's a whole other level of heartless.

"It hurt more than anything, but I survived and changed my name from Calder to Garrity, after Pastor Dan, who died when the house blew. I disowned my family right back. I suppose if the hurt ever comes back, I'll deal with it, but I won't go looking for it."

Connor rolls away from him. "Yeah," he says with a yawn. "Probably best if we don't."

Lev waits until Connor's breathing is the steady and deep rasp of sleep; then he ventures out into the living room. Una sits in a comfortable chair with a cup of steaming tea—from the scent of it, one of Elina's herbal elixirs. Una appears lost in thought as complex as the flavorful brew.

"Which one is it?" Lev asks.

She's startled at first to hear his voice. "Oh—Elina calls it *téce'ni hinentééni*. 'Night Recovery.' Calms the soul and stomach. I think it's mostly chamomile and ginseng."

"Any left for me?"

She pours him a cup, and he lets the leaves steep, watching them rise and fall in the currents of the cooling liquid. Una sits across from him, content with silence. The only sound is Grace's gentle snoring across the room. Usually Lev is at peace with silence as well, but what hangs in the air between them demands words.

"Do you think Pivane knows you're the one who fired that shot through the window?"

Una makes no move of surprise at Lev's suggestion. She just slowly sips her tea. "I'm insulted by your accusation, little brother," she finally says.

"I've always respected you, Una," Lev says. "Respect yourself enough not to lie."

She glances at him—perhaps a dozen thoughts playing in her eyes before she puts down her cup and says: "Pivane knows. I'm sure he does. Why else would he have brought you here and make me promise to protect you?" She glances to the rifle beside her. "Which I will. Even if it's myself that I'm protecting you from."

"Why?" Lev asks. "Why did you do it?"

"Why?" Una mocks, beginning to lose her temper. "Why, why, and why! That's always the question, isn't it? I ask 'why' all the time, and the only answer I get are rustling leaves and the shrill chirps of mating birds."

Lev says nothing. He can see that her eyes are moist, but she doesn't allow tears to build.

"I did it because where you go, terrible things follow, Lev. The first time you came, the parts pirates came in your wake and took Wil. And now you bring the most wanted AWOL in the history of unwinding. I thought that shot would get the Tashi'nes to see reason and send you all on your way, but I suppose I got what I deserved."

"You said you wanted me to stay."

"I did and I didn't. I do and I don't. Today was a bad day. Today I wanted you and your friends gone."

"And tonight?"

"Tonight I'm drinking tea." And she goes back to sipping silently.

Lev can accept her ambivalence, although he can't deny it hurts. Is she betraying him by wishing he would leave . . . or is he betraying her by being here at all? Una leans closer, and Lev finds himself leaning away to maintain the distance.

"You, little brother, are the harbinger of doom," she tells him. "And I know, just as sure as we're sitting here, that because of you, something much worse is coming."

36 · Cam

Camus Comprix is amazed by the ability of music to change the world. Just a few simple chords. It is fuel more potent than uranium, and it powers his journey. It holds together fragments of memories like stars in a constellation. Connect the lines and you can see the whole image.

Now, as he moves through the dense pine forest, fifteen hundred miles away from the cushy town house in DC, he wonders what Roberta must be doing. Her favorite act of damage control, no doubt. He's an AWOL Rewind now—something new under the sun. He wonders if the Juvenile Authority will be called in to aid in the search. He is a fugitive, just like the fugitives he seeks. It's both frightening and empowering at once.

If he's right and Risa is on the Arápache Reservation, he wonders what she'll say to him and what he'll say back. What will he do when he comes face-to-face with the Akron AWOL? No matter how much he tries to plan for these moments, he knows nothing will prepare him.

Just as night begins to fall, he comes to something wholly out of place, yet wholly expected. A wall of stone, stretching endlessly left and right and rising thirty feet high.

The wall appears impenetrable at first, but as Cam gets closer, he can see that between many of the granite blocks that make up the wall are jutting pieces of shale. It could be just the aesthetics of the wall, but it seems more than just an attempt to make the wall pleasing to the eye. The more he looks at them, the more Cam realizes those jutting stones serve a different purpose. They are a message. A message that says "Go no farther . . . unless your need is greater than the wall is high."

He surveys the relative positions of the jutting stones, then begins to climb. It is not an easy task. The Arápache apparently give sanctuary only to AWOLs who can pass the test. He wonders if any have fallen and died in the process.

At the top of the wall, the sun, which has been blocked by the granite stones, strikes him with such intensity, he almost loses his grip. He thought it was already below the horizon, but instead it lingers on the treetops. He wonders if anyone can see him. There certainly isn't anyone nearby—the forest extends on the other side of the wall. In the distance, though, he can see a town in a valley. He can also see a gorge with what appears to be homes carved right into the cliff sides. He knows this place. Or at least a small part of him knows it.

He climbs down the other side of the wall and makes his way toward the village.

It's long after dark before he comes out of the forest. The town is both quaint and modern at once. Sparkling white adobe and brown brick, sidewalks not of concrete but of lacquered mahogany planks. Expensive-looking cars are everywhere, yet there are also hitching posts for horses. The Arápache live well and choose their technology rather than letting it choose them.

It's a small town, but not so small that it doesn't have some nightlife. The central part of town stays busy after dark. There, the restaurants and shops that cater to a younger crowd are bright, inviting, and full of people. He steers clear of them, but does dare to venture onto another commercial street with banks and other daytime businesses, all closed at this time of night. The occasional passerby offers him either hello, or *tous*, which he assumes means the same in Arápache—he can't be sure because he received no part of Wil Tashi'ne's language center. He returns the greeting, being sure to keep the hood of his dark sweatshirt pulled over his hair and dip his face so that it stays in the shadows.

Wil Tashi'ne will have memories of these streets. Most of them will be lost to Cam, part of other people's brains now. The rest drift within him like scents on the wind. They swirl, they eddy, they move his feet in directions his conscious mind can't fathom, but he knows to trust them.

One such eddy pulls him down a side street. He doesn't even remember making the turn—it just happened like something so habitual, it precluded any need for thought. The scent of memory is very powerful here. He lets it lead him to the rosewood door of a shop. The lights are off—the shop, like all the shops on this little side street, is closed.

He tries the doorknob, finds it locked, as he'd known it

would be. But there is something more to this door. Thinking about it doesn't solve the door's mystery, but he notices that his fingers tingle. He touches the brick of the building just beside the door. Yes—his fingers know something the rest of him does not! He slides a hand along the brick, feeling the rough texture and the rougher patches of cement in between the bricks until his fingers find what they're looking for. There is a spare key lodged in a mortar gap in the brickwork. The things his hands know! Even when he looks at the key, he has no memory of it.

He slips the key into the lock, turns it, and slowly opens the door.

Immediately he recognizes the shapes hanging from the ceiling. Guitars. Did Wil work here? Cam searches his memories, but can't find evidence of that. There are songs from this place, though. They've begun playing in his head, and he knows if he gives voice to them, more connections will be made.

A guitar sits on the counter. It must have been played recently because he finds it in decent tune. A twelve string. His favorite. He breathes in the woody, earthy smell of the guitar shop and begins to play.

37 · Una

She dreams of Wil again. She dreams of him way too often. At times she wishes he would leave her alone, because the waking is always so painful. This time, however, when she awakes, the music he played in her dream continues. It's faint, but it's still there.

At first she thinks she must have left one of his recordings playing in the living room. Or maybe Grace, who tends to dig out everything from every drawer, has found one and is playing it—but when she goes into the living room, she finds

Grace asleep on the sofa. Connor and Lev are asleep as well in the spare room, and the music, she realizes, is coming from downstairs.

Una opens the door, and the volume rises. She hears it echoing in the stairwell, ghostly, but very much real. It's not a recording; it's live—it's a song of Wil's that only he can play, and her heart nearly bursts from her chest. He's alive! He's alive, he's come home, and he's greeting her with a serenade!

She hurls herself down the stairs, her bathrobe billowing behind her. She knows what she's thinking can't be—but she wants so desperately for it to be true that it shuts down all logic within her.

Una bursts into the shop to see a figure sitting on a stool playing a guitar she had just prepared for a customer to pick up in the morning. Although she can't see his face, she can see the way he holds himself that it's not Wil.

"Who are you?" she demands, barely able to restrain her fury. *It's not Wil.* "What are you doing in my shop?"

He stops playing, looks at her just for a moment, then gets up. She notices something off about his face before he turns away. He puts the guitar down on the counter. "I'm sorry. I didn't know there was anyone here."

"So you think you can just break in?"

"It wasn't locked."

Which is a lie—ever since Lev and the others came to stay with her a few days ago, she's constantly checking that lock. Then on the counter beside the guitar, she sees the spare key. No one knew about that key. Even she had forgotten about it. So how did this intruder find it?

"I didn't mean to disturb you."

"Wait!"

Una knows she should let him go. She knows that if she

reaches to pull this strand of hope, any number of things could unravel. Everything could unravel. But she has to know. "That song you were playing . . . where did you hear it?"

"I heard it played once by an Arápache boy," he tells her, "and I remembered it."

But she knows this, too, is a lie. Even those with the skill to play something after hearing it only once could never capture the nuances and the passion. *That* belonged to Wil alone, and yet . . ."

"Come a little closer."

He's hesitant, but does as she asks. Now, as he steps into the light, she realizes what the oddness about his face was. His entire face is covered in thick pancake makeup—like a vain old woman trying to hide her wrinkles.

"I have a skin condition," he tells her.

His eyes are engaging. Persuasive. "Are you an AWOL? Because if you are, don't look for sanctuary from me. You'll have to find someone else to sponsor you."

"I'm looking for some friends," he tells her. "They mentioned this guitar shop."

"What are their names?"

He pauses before he speaks. "I can't tell you their names, or it would compromise their safety. But if you know them, then you know who I'm talking about. They're AWOLs. Notorious AWOLs."

So he's come for Lev and Connor. Or maybe he's there for Grace, to take her back to whatever life she was plucked from. His eyes speak of honesty, but so much about this visitor seems wrong. He could be working for the Juvenile Authority—or worse—a bounty hunter hoping to bring Connor and Lev in for a hefty reward. She decides not to telegraph her suspicion, though. Not until she has a better idea of his intentions.

"Well, if you can't tell me their names, tell me yours."

"Mac," he says. "My name is Mac," and he holds out his hand for her to shake.

It's the feel of his hand that gives him away. The firmness and texture of his grip. Sense memory knows that hand before she's even consciously aware of it. When she looks down at it, she almost gasps, but keeps it in. She turns the hand slightly in hers to notice a tiny scar on the third knuckle of the index finger—from when Wil cut himself as a boy. Now she has visual proof. She forces her breathing to stay calm and in control. She has yet to fully comprehend what this means, but she will.

Una releases his hand and turns away, for fear that something in her face might give her away. "I'll tell you about your friends, Mac—under one condition," she says.

"Yes, anything."

She grabs the guitar from the counter and holds it out to him. "That you play for me again."

He smiles, takes the guitar, and sits down on the stool. "My pleasure!"

He begins, and the song grabs the thread of hope that Una so foolishly tugged at and sails away with it, rending Una down to her very essence. The song is haunting. It is beautiful. It is Wil's music alive but in someone else. She lets the strains of melody and harmony caress her. Then she comes up behind him, kabongs him over the head with a heavy guitar so forcefully that it breaks, and he falls unconscious on the floor.

She listens to make sure there is no stirring from upstairs. She must not wake the others. Satisfied that no one has heard, she heaves "Mac" onto her shoulders like a sack of flour. Although she's a small woman, she's strong from working the lathe, plane, and sander. It tests the limit of her strength and endurance, but she manages to move through the night streets and finally into the woods.

Una knows the woods well. Wil was at home there, and

so she came to feel that way, as well. She carries him nearly a half mile through the forest with nothing to light her way but the moon, until she reaches the old sweat lodge—a place once used to begin the traditional vision quest for Arápache youth who were of age, before a more modern one was built.

Once inside, she tears off his jacket and shirt and uses them to string him up between two poles six feet apart. She knots the fabric so tightly only a knife could undo it. The rest of his unconscious body slumps on the ground, his arms outstretched above him in a supplicative Y.

This is how she leaves him for the night.

When she returns at dawn, she brings a chain saw.

38 · Cam

Cam knows this is not going to be a good day the moment he sees the chain saw.

His head hurts in so many places, he can't begin to know where he was actually hit. It feels as if all the members of his internal community have taken up arms against one another and are slicing his brain to bits.

The young woman sitting beside the chain saw hefts a rock in one hand.

"Good, you're awake," she says. "I was running out of stones."

He notices that there are rocks all around him. She's been throwing them at him to wake him up. Smaller aches on his body attest to that—and throbbing in his shoulders attest to the fact that his arms are tied to poles on either side—strung up with his own clothes. He gets up on his knees to relieve the strain on his shoulders, surprised that his seams haven't split—but then, Roberta always told him his seams were stronger than the flesh they held together.

He takes in his surroundings before speaking. He's in a large dome-shaped structure made of stones and mud—or at least made to look that way. Morning sunlight spills through gaps in the stone. It's far more primitive than anything else he's seen on the reservation. There's a washed-out pile of ashes in the middle, and on the other side of the ashes, sits the girl and her chain saw. The light pouring through the hole up above illuminates her face just enough for him to recognize her as the girl from the guitar shop.

His last memory was playing for her. And now he's here. He can only guess what transpired in between.

"I guess you didn't like my song."

"It wasn't *your* song at all," she responds. He can feel her anger from across the room like a blast of radiation. "And by the look of you, that's not the only thing that isn't yours." She gets up, grabs the chain saw, and steps over the pile of ashes toward him.

He struggles to get to his feet. She touches the silent chain saw to his bare chest. He can feel the cold steel of the dormant chain as it caresses his skin. She uses its curved tip to trace the seams.

"Up and down and around—those lines go everywhere, don't they? Like an old shaman's sand drawings."

Cam says nothing as she moves the chain saw along his torso and then across his neck. "The shaman's lines are meant to trace life and creation—is that what your lines are for too? Are you a creation? Are you alive?"

The question of questions. "You'll have to decide that for yourself."

"Are you that man-made man I've heard tell of? What is it they call you? 'Sham Complete'?"

"Something like that."

She takes a step back. "Well, you can keep all those other parts, Sham. But those hands deserve a proper funeral." Then she starts the chain saw, and it roars to life, puffing forth acrid, hellish smoke and releasing an earsplitting report that makes Cam's seams ache in alarm.

"Brakes! Red light! Brick wall! *Stop!*"

"Did you think I wouldn't figure it out when you came last night?"

His eyes are fixed on the deadly blade, but he tears his gaze away to focus on her—to get through to her. "I was drawn here. *He* was drawn here—and if you take these hands, you'll never hear him play again!"

It was the wrong thing to say. Her face contorts into a mask of sheer hatred. "I'd already gotten used to that. I'll get used to it again."

And she swings the blade toward his right arm.

Cam can do nothing but brace himself. He readies himself for the surge of pain, watching as the chain saw comes down— but then at the last instant, she twists her arm, aborting the attack, and the momentum veers sideways, cutting his knotted jacket, and setting his right arm free from the pole.

She hurls the chain saw across the room, screaming in frustration, and Cam thrusts his free arm toward her. He means to grab her by the neck and hurl her to the ground, but instead he finds his hand reaching behind her to the ribbon in her hair and pulling it free.

Her long dark hair flares out from behind her as the ribbon falls to the ground, and she backs away, staring at him in horrified disbelief.

"Why did you do that?" she demands. *"Why did you do that?"*

And Cam suddenly understands. "Because he likes your

hair free. He always pulled out your hair ribbons, didn't he?" He lets loose a sudden laugh, as the emotion of the memory hits him all at once like a sonic boom.

She stares at him—her face is hard to read. He doesn't know whether she's going to run in terror, or pick up the chain saw again. Instead she bends down to pick up her ribbon and rises, keeping her distance.

"What else do you know?" she asks.

"I know what I feel when I play his music. He was in love with someone. Deeply."

That brings tears to her eyes, but Cam knows they are tears of anger.

"You're a monster."

"I know."

"You should never have been made."

"Not my fault."

"You say you know he loved me—but do you even know my name?"

Cam searches his memory for her name, but there are neither words nor images in his personal piece of Wil Tashi'ne's psyche. There is only music, gestures, and a disconnected history of touch. So instead of a name, he shares with her what he does know.

"There's a birthmark on your back he would tickle when you danced," Cam says. "He liked toying with an earring in the shape of a whale. The feel of his guitar-callused fingertips in the crook of your elbow made you tremble."

"Enough!" she says, taking a step back. Then more quietly, "Enough."

"I'm sorry. I just wanted you to see that he's still here . . . in these hands."

She's silent for a moment, looking at his face, looking at his hands. Then she comes closer, pulls out a pocketknife, and cuts the shirt that ties him to the other pole.

"Show me," she says.

And so he reaches up, abandoning thought, and putting all trust in his fingertips the way he did when searching for the key to her shop. He touches the nape of her neck, moves a finger across her lips, and remembers the feel of them. He cups her cheek in his palm; then he brings the fingertips of his other hand drizzling down her wrist, over her forearm, to that singular spot in the crook of her elbow.

And she trembles.

Then she raises the heavy stone she's been hiding in her other hand and smashes him in the side of the head, knocking him out cold again.

When he regains consciousness, he's tied to the poles once more. And once again, he's alone.

NEWS UPDATE

In Nevada today, a coordinated attack on a harvest camp has left 23 dead, dozens wounded, and hundreds of Unwinds unaccounted for.

It began at 11:14 local time, when communication lines were cut to and from Cold Springs Harvest Camp, and by the time communication was restored an hour later, it was all over. Staff were tied up and forced to lie facedown while the armed attackers set loose hundreds of violent adolescents designated for unwinding.

Early reports suggest that the camp director was murdered execution style. While the investigation is ongoing, it is believed that Connor Lassiter, also known as the Akron AWOL, is responsible for the attack.

---

39 · Starkey

In the claustrophobic confines of the abandoned mine where the storks are holing up, Starkey kicks the dark stone walls. He kicks the rotting beams. He kicks everything in sight, searching for something breakable. After all his effort and all his risk, every last measure of his victory has been stolen from him and attributed to Connor Lassiter!

"You'll bring down the whole freaking mine if you keep kicking the beams like that," yells Bam. Everyone else is smart enough to stay deeper in the mine and keep their distance from him, but she always has to shove herself into his business.

"So let it come down!"

"And bury us all—that will really help your cause, won't it? All those storks you say you want to save, buried alive. Real smart, Starkey."

Out of spite, he kicks a support beam one more time. It quivers, and flecks of dust rain down on them. It's enough to make him stop.

"You heard them!" he yells. "It's all about the Akron AWOL." It should be *Starkey's* face on the news. *He* should be the one the experts are profiling. They should be camping out at *his* family's door, prying into what his private life was like before they cut him loose to be unwound. "I do all the work, and he gets all the credit."

"You call it credit, but out there it's called blame. You should be happy they're looking elsewhere after that bloodbath!"

Starkey turns on her, wanting to grab her and shake some sense into her, but she's taller than him, bigger than him, and he knows Bam is a girl who fights back. How would it look to the others if she floored him? So instead he smacks her down with words.

"Don't you dare accept their spin! I know you're smarter than that. What we did was a liberation! We freed nearly four hundred Unwinds and added more than a hundred storks to our number."

"And in the process more than twenty kids died—plus, we still don't have an accurate count of how many were tranq'd and got left behind."

"It couldn't be helped!"

He looks farther down the low-roofed tunnel to see, lit by the dim hanging incandescents, a cluster of kids eavesdropping. He wants to yell at them, too, but he's in control enough now to rein in that urge. He brings his voice down so only Bam can hear.

"We're at war," he reminds her. "There are always casualties in war." He steels his eye contact, trying to make her look away, but she doesn't. But she also doesn't argue. He reaches out, putting a comforting hand on her shoulder, which she doesn't shake off.

"The thing to remember, Bam, is that our plan worked."

Now she finally looks away from him, signaling her acquiescence. "That valley was pretty isolated," she says. "It was a long road out for those kids who went running through the gate. I don't know if you heard the latest, but nearly half of them have already been captured."

He moves his hand from her shoulder to her cheek and smiles. "Which means half of them got away. The glass is half-full, Bam. That's what we need to remind everyone. You're my second in command, and I need you to focus on the positive instead of the negative. Do you think you can do that?"

Bam hesitates; then her shoulders slump at his gentle touch, and she gives him a reluctant nod, as he'd known she would.

"Good. That's what I like about you, Bam. You take me to task, as you should, but in the end, you always see reason."

She turns to go, but before she leaves, she tosses him one more question. "Where do you see this ending, Starkey?"

He smiles at her even more broadly than before. "I don't see it ending. That's the beauty of it!"

40 · Bam

Bam moves through the tunnels and chambers of the mine, taking mental snapshots.

A kid in tears, mourning the death of a friend.

A terrified new arrival, calmed by an older stork.

A hapless fourteen-year-old "medic" trying to suture a leg wound using dental floss.

She sees scenes of hope and despair around her and doesn't know which to give more credence.

She passes one kid sharing his ration of food with another, while beside them a young girl teaches an even younger girl how to use one of the automatic rifles they confiscated from Cold Springs.

And then there's the boy who was forced to shoot the harvest camp director, sitting alone, staring off into nowhere. Bam would comfort him, but she's not the comforting type.

"Starkey's proud of all of you and happy with our victory today," she tells them. "We took the battle to the enemy, and we made history!"

She primes them, but she holds back, because she knows she mustn't steal Starkey's thunder. She's Bam the Baptist, preparing the way for the Savior of Storks.

"He'll be gathering everyone before dinner. He's got a lot to tell you." Of course it's really not about telling them anything; it's about rallying them and keeping them focused on the positive, just as he told Bam. He'll have gentle words for the dead, but will move past it. Gloss over it. Direct the audience's attention elsewhere. He's so very good at that. It's why they've gotten so far. Bam is in awe of the way Mason Starkey can work magic in the world around him. He's kept their hoard virtually invisible for more than a month now, keeping them clothed and fed with money that no one can trace. Yes, she's in awe of him, and she's also a little more afraid of him every day. That's normal, she decides. A good leader should be just a little bit frightening in the way he or she wields power.

When she's done priming the masses for Starkey, she turns down a side passageway that should be familiar, but she bumps her head for the umpteenth time on a jutting piece of stone. So many of these tunnels are alike; she always knows exactly where she is when she hits that damn stone. The walls begin to spread, opening into a wider cavern. The lights, which are strung around the edge, create an odd sense of darkness in the very center of the space, as if there's a black hole in the middle of the room.

This is the storage room, where food and supplies are kept. This is also where Hayden is currently stationed, with an armed guard at all times who is there for both his protection and to make sure he stays on his best behavior.

"He's a flight risk, but we can't make him look like a prisoner," Starkey had said. "We're not the Juvenile Authority."

Of course, Hayden *is* a prisoner—but God forbid they make him *look* like one.

It was Bam's suggestion that he be put in charge of food distribution. First because it was what he did when he first arrived at the Graveyard, so he had experience. Second because the kid who had been doing it was killed today.

She finds him taking inventory of their canned goods and

being very chatty with the guard, gleaning information about the plane crash and everything that happened since then from the 7-Eleven raids and their stint at the abandoned Palm Springs hotel to Camp Red Heron and the Egret Academy. Bam is going to have to make sure the guards know enough not to talk about anything with Hayden that doesn't involve Spam and canned corn.

The guard asks if he can go to the bathroom, which is quite a hike from this spot in the mine, and she lets him go. "I'll watch Hayden until you get back." He offers her his Uzi, but she refuses it.

Hayden has a pad and jots down notes about their food supply.

"You have way too much chili," he says, pointing to a stack of gallon-sized cans. "And it's not like you can disguise it to be anything but chili."

Bam crosses her arms. "I knew you'd already be complaining. In case you forgot, we just set you free. You should be grateful."

"I am. In fact, I'm ecstatic. But incarceration at a harvest camp must have left me a little brain damaged because suddenly I'm putting larger concerns ahead of my own."

"Like having too much chili?"

He doesn't respond to that—he just moves around the room continuing his inventory. Bam glances off, wondering when the guard will be back. She came here because she considers it her job to keep an eye on Hayden, but she doesn't like him—never did. Hayden's the kind of guy who gets in your head, but only goes there to amuse himself.

He looks up from his inventory pad, catching Bam's gaze. He holds it—longer than a glance, but shorter than a look. Then his attention is back on his pad again. But not really.

"You realize he's going to get you all killed, don't you?"

Bam is caught off guard—not by Hayden's comment, but by how it infuriates her. She feels her cheeks flushing in outrage. She must not allow him to put thoughts into her head. Especially when those thoughts are already there.

"Say one more thing about Starkey, and the next sound you hear will be your head cracking like an egg at the bottom of the nearest mine shaft."

Hayden just smirks. "That's clever, Bam. I had never counted you among the clever!"

She scowls, not sure whether to take that as a compliment or an insult. "Just keep your mouth shut and do what you're told, unless you want to be treated like a prisoner."

"I'll make a deal with you," Hayden says. "I won't say a thing to anyone else, but I get to speak my mind with you. Fair enough?"

"Absolutely not! And if you try, I'll rip your lousy tongue out and sell it to the highest bidder."

He guffaws at that. "Point for Bam! You truly do excel in disturbing imagery. Someday I may want to study under you."

She shoves him—not hard enough to knock him down, but enough to push him back and off balance. "What makes you think I'd want to hear anything that comes out of your mouth? And what makes you think you know better than Starkey? He's doing amazing things! Do you have any idea how many kids we saved today?"

Hayden sighs and looks to the stacks of canned food he's been counting, as if each can represents another kid saved. "I won't begrudge Starkey the statistics of salvation," he tells her. "But I wonder what it will mean in the long run."

"It means all those kids won't get unwound."

"Maybe . . . Or maybe it means they'll be unwound more quickly once they're caught—along with every other kid awaiting unwinding."

"Starkey's a visionary!" she yells. Her voice is so loud, she hears it echoing from the stone around her. She wonders who might be listening. In these tunnels there's always someone listening. She forces herself to use her indoor voice, although it comes out in an angry hiss. "To Starkey, it's not only about taking down harvest camps. It's about making a stand for storks." She slowly strides toward Hayden as she speaks, and Hayden moves away, trying to keep a healthy distance between them. "Can't you see he's igniting a stork revolution? Other storks who think they have no hope—who know they're second-class citizens—will rise up and demand fair treatment."

"And he'll do this by terrorist attacks?"

"Guerilla warfare!"

By now she has Hayden backed against the wall, and yet he appears at ease. Instead she feels like the one who's cornered.

"Every outlaw is eventually brought down, Bam."

Bam shakes her head, forcing the thought into submission. "Not if they win the war."

He slides away from her, to the other side of the room, and sits on the stack of chili cans. "Although it unsettles the stomach as much as this chili will, I have to give you at least some benefit of the doubt," he says. "It's true that history is full of self-important madmen who managed to claw their way to power and lead their people successfully. Offhand I can't think of any, but I'm sure they'll come to me."

"Alexander the Great," Bam suggests. "Napoléon Bonaparte."

Hayden tilts his head slightly and narrows his eyes, as if trying to visualize it. "So then, when you look at Mason Starkey, do you see any of the qualities of Alexander or Napoléon—aside from being short?"

Bam hardens her jaw and says, "I do."

And there's that slithery smirk from Hayden again. "I'm sorry, miss, but if you want the part, you'll have to do a much better job of acting than that."

Although Bam would like to knock out a few of Hayden's perfectly straightened teeth, she won't let her anger rule her now. Not after seeing how Starkey let his anger take control today. "We're done here," she tells Hayden, deciding not to wait until his guard returns.

Hayden's smirk broadens into a condescending smile, which is even more infuriating. Maybe she'll punch him after all. "But you haven't heard the best part yet," he says.

She should just leave now, before she becomes the butt of yet another one of his personal jokes, but she just can't do it. "And what might that be?"

Hayden stands and saunters toward her—which means that maybe he's going to say something that won't risk losing him some teeth. "I know you and Starkey are going to continue to liberate harvest camps, for better or for worse," he says. "That being the case, I'd like to help keep more of your storks alive. Remember, I was the head of tech at the Graveyard. I know a thing or two that could help."

Now it's Bam's turn to smirk. She knows Hayden too well. "And what do you want in return?"

"Like I said before, all I want is your ear—and not in an unwinding sense." Then he gets quiet. Serious. She's never seen Hayden serious. This is something new. "I want your promise that you'll listen to me—*really* listen to me—when I have something to say. You don't have to like it; you just have to hear it."

And although she had refused the same request five minutes ago, this time she agrees. Even though she feels like she's making a deal with the devil.

41 · Connor

Were Connor to come face-to-face with Camus Comprix under any other circumstances, he would hate the Rewind with every measure of his soul. Connor certainly has reason to despise him. For one, Cam is the darling of Proactive Citizenry. He's the shining star of all those who promote unwinding as a natural and acceptable consequence of civilization. Second—but even more important to Connor—is Cam's connection to Risa. Just imagining the two of them together—even if Risa was being blackmailed to be with him—draws his hand into a fist so tight his nails cut into his palm. It's Connor's jealousy and Roland's anger all rolled up into that powerful hand. No, there would be no hope that Connor and Cam could be anything but bitter enemies under any other circumstances.

However, the circumstance of their first encounter gives Connor some unexpected and unwanted pause for thought.

It begins with Una.

It's Connor, Lev, and Grace's eighth day holed up in her small apartment. With the announcement that Connor attacked a harvest camp in Nevada, word from Chal is that the Hopi are not too keen on giving him fictitious asylum. Even though the news recanted the accusation the next day, Chal is still having trouble making the deal, which means they're in a holding pattern here for who knows how long.

If the Tashi'ne home gave Connor cabin fever, being stuck in Una's place is like being packed in a shipping crate again. Even Grace, who can always find ways of entertaining herself, keeps asking with an "are we there yet" sort of persistence, if she can go out and *do* something.

"Just a walk. Maybe some shopping. Pleeeeeeeeeze?"

Only Lev seems unfazed by all of this, which Connor finds maddening.

"How can you just sit there and do nothing all day?"

"I'm not doing nothing," Lev responds, holding up a worn leather-bound tome he's been glued to. "I'm learning the Arápache language. It's actually very beautiful."

"Sometimes, Lev, I just want to smack you."

"You already hit him with a car," Grace tosses in from the other room. Connor's response is a growl that doesn't do much of anything but at least makes him feel a tiny bit better. He's sure Pivane would say he's connecting with his animal spirit.

"You forget that I was under house arrest for a year," Lev points out. "I got used to semi-incarceration."

Una spends most of her time down in the shop, either tending to customers or crafting new instruments in the workshop. The whine of drills and the gentle tapping of a hammer and chisel have become accustomed sounds. It's when those sounds stop that Connor wonders what's going on.

Two days ago, and then again yesterday, Connor heard Una locking up the shop, and he peeked through the blinds to see her leaving. He wouldn't have thought much of it, except for the fact that she was carrying a guitar in one hand and her leather rifle case in the other. Where she might be going with both a guitar and a rifle did not take Connor's imagination to happy places.

"Una has issues," was Lev's entire assessment of the situation.

Connor, however, suspects that it's more than that.

Later that afternoon, she leaves again, and Connor decides to follow, against Lev's warnings to just let her be. "We should be grateful she's letting us hide out here. Don't repay her by messing in her business."

But he doesn't have time to argue if he's going to effectively tail her. He pushes past Lev, down the stairs to the shop, then out into the street, where he sees her turning the corner. There are people in the streets, but Connor wears a woolen Arápache hat he found in Una's closet, so no one pays him much attention. Besides, it's not like Una is seeking out crowded places. Even though the rifle is in a carrying case, it's pretty obvious what it is. Wherever she's going, she probably doesn't want to be questioned about it, which, Connor reasons, is why she's taking only the quietest side streets to get wherever it is that she's going.

At the edge of town, Una lingers until there are neither cars nor pedestrians on the street; then she crosses to a narrow footpath that leads into the woods. Connor follows, giving her a long lead.

Although he can't see her in the dense woods, the ground is soft from an early-morning rain, and he can follow her footprints. There are several sets of them. She's been back and forth on this path many times over the past few days. About half a mile in, he comes to a building—if it can really be called a building. It's an odd-looking structure, the shape of an igloo, but made of mud and stone. He hears two voices inside. One is Una, and the other is male—but doesn't sound like anyone Connor's already met on the rez.

His first thought is that Una is meeting a lover here for a secret liaison and perhaps they should be left alone . . . but the argument inside doesn't sound like a lover's spat.

"No, I won't do it!" shouts the male voice. "Not now and not ever again!"

"Then you'll be left here to die," Una says.

"Better that than this!"

There's only one door, but the apex of the dome is in disrepair and full of holes. Carefully, quietly, Connor climbs the curving surface of the stone and mud structure until he can peer through a gap where the stones have given way.

His first impression hits a chord in him as resonant as any instrument Una could build. He sees a young man about his age with odd multitextured hair of different shades. He's tied to a pole, struggling to pull himself free. By the smell of the place and the look of him, he's been here for a while, in this helpless, hopeless situation, without even the freedom to relieve himself anywhere but in his clothes.

Connor's immediate gut reaction is identification. *This prisoner is me. Me being held in Argent's basement. Me desperately trying to escape. Me struggling to hold on to hope.* The sense of empathy is so strong it will flavor everything that transpires between them.

Una is not Argent, Connor must remind himself. Her motives, whatever they are, must be different. But why is she doing this? Connor waits and watches, hoping she'll give him a clue.

"Either you have to let me go, or you have to kill me," her captive says. "Please do one or the other, and let this end!"

To that, Una responds with a single, simple question. "What's my name?"

"I told you, I don't know! I didn't know yesterday, I don't know today, and I won't know tomorrow!"

"Then maybe today the music will remind you."

Then Una undoes his bonds. He doesn't even try to run—he must know it's no use. Instead he sobs, his arms going limp. And into those limp arms Una puts the guitar she brought.

"Do it," Una says. Now she speaks gently, and she caresses his hands, lifting them into position on the instrument. "Give it life. It's what you do. It's what you've always done."

"That wasn't me," he pleads.

Una moves away from him and sits down facing him.

Taking her rifle from its case, she lays it across her lap. "I said do it."

Her prisoner reluctantly begins to play. Sorrowful strains fill the space and echo, the entire building becoming like the tone chamber of the guitar. Connor feels it resonating in his chest.

This music is beautiful. This prisoner of Una's is a true master of the instrument. He's not sobbing anymore. Instead it's Una who sobs. She holds her gut as if there's great pain there. Her sobs grow into wails that resonate with the music like some great chanting of grief.

Then Connor shifts positions, and a pebble the size of a marble dislodges from the edge of the hole and drops to the ground inside.

In an instant Una leaps to her feet and swings her rifle into position, aiming it at him through the gap in the stones.

Connor pulls back reflexively, but loses his balance and falls over backward, tumbling down the outside shell of the building, bumping and bruising himself on the rough stone. He lands on his back, the wind knocked out of him, and when he tries to rise, Una is there with the rifle barrel just inches away from his nose.

"Don't you dare move!"

Connor freezes, half-convinced that she really is going to blow him away if he moves. Then, her prisoner, seeing his chance, bolts into the woods.

"*Hííko!*" she curses, and takes off after him. Connor gets to his feet in pursuit, to see where this little psychotic drama will end.

As she closes in on her escaping prisoner, Una drops her rifle and launches herself at him, landing on his back and bringing him down. She struggles with him, her long hair like a dark shroud covering both of them as they thrash on the ground, and Connor realizes that he is suddenly the one with a distinct advantage. He picks up Una's rifle and aims it at both of them.

"Up! Both of you! Now!"

And when they don't listen, he fires the rifle into the air.

That gets their attention. They stop struggling, and they both rise to their feet. Only now does Connor notice that there's something odd about this guy's face.

"What the hell is all this about?" Connor demands.

"None of your business!" Una snaps. "Give me back my rifle!"

"How about I just give you one of the bullets?" Connor keeps the rifle trained on her but shifts his gaze to her prisoner. The odd patchwork nature of his face—a starburst of flesh tones that seem to continue into the shades and textures of his hairline—is unnatural, yet familiar.

All at once it strikes Connor who this is. He's seen him enough in the media—imagined him enough in his nightmares. This is that abominable Rewind! The recognition must be mutual, because the Rewind's stolen eyes register recognition as well.

"It's you! You're the Akron AWOL!" And then, "Where is she? Is she here? Take me to her!"

The only thing Connor knows for sure at this moment is that there's too much flying at him to process. If he tries to sort it all out in his head right now, he'll make a crucial mistake, one of them will get ahold of this rifle, and someone else will end up dead—maybe him.

"This is what we're going to do," he says, forcing calm into his voice but keeping the rifle raised. "We're all going back to the igloo thing."

"Sweat lodge," snarls Una.

"Right. Whatever. We're going back there, we're going to

sit our asses down, and we're going to sweat this whole thing out until I'm satisfied. Got it?"

Una glares at him, then storms back toward the sweat lodge. The Rewind isn't as quick to move. Connor trains the rifle on him. "Move it," he says. "Or I'll turn you back into the pork and beans you were made from."

The Rewind gives him a condescending glare from his stolen eyes, then heads back toward the sweat lodge.

Connor knows his name, but calling him by a name implies too much humanity for Connor's liking. He'd much prefer to just call him "the Rewind." As the three of them sit in the sweat lodge, they are both reluctant to tell Connor anything—as if they resent him for cutting into this dark dance they've been doing.

"He has Wil's hands," Connor prompts, having already figured that much out. "Let's start there."

Una explains the details of Wil's abduction—or at least what she was told by Lev and Pivane. The Tashi'ne family never got any answers as to what happened to their son and never expected to. Kids who are taken by parts pirates rarely turn up at harvest camps; they're sold piece by piece on the black market. But apparently Wil Tashi'ne was a special case. Connor can't imagine the kind of pain Una must feel, knowing this creation before them has the hands of the boy she loved and has his talent literally woven right into its brain. His talent, his musical memory, and yet no memory of her. It could drive anyone mad—but to hold him prisoner like that?

"What were you thinking, Una?"

"Una!" The Rewind smiles triumphantly. "Her name is Una!"

"Quiet, Pork-n-beans," Connor says. "I'm not talking to you."

"I wasn't thinking clearly," Una admits quietly, looking down at the dirt floor of the sweat lodge. "I'm still not." Instead of talking about the Rewind, she talks about Wil again. How he would tune and test all of her guitars before they were sold. "He put his soul into his music. I always felt that a tiny bit of him was left resonating in the instrument after he played it. Once he was gone, the guitars never felt the same. Now when they play, it's only music."

"So you thought you'd make our friend here your little guitar slave."

She raises her eyes to burn him a glare—but she doesn't seem to have the strength for it anymore. She casts her eyes down again.

Connor turns to the Rewind, to find his eyes locked on Connor, practically drilling into him. Connor tightens the grip on the rifle in his lap.

"Why are you here?" Connor asks. "How did you even know to come here?"

"I have enough of Wil Tashi'ne's memory to know that this is where your friend the clapper would run to hide," he says. "And I think you know why I'm here. I'm here for Risa."

Hearing her name coming from his mouth brings Connor's blood toward a boil. *She hates you*, Connor wants to tell him. *She wants nothing to do with you. Ever.* But he sees and smells the Rewind's urine-stained pants and remembers the helplessness of the Rewind's captivity, so much like his own in Argent's basement. Sympathy is the last thing Connor wants to feel, but it's there all the same, undermining his hatred. Desperation just about oozes out of the Rewind's seams, and as much as Connor wants to add to this creature's pain, he can't find it in himself to do it.

"So, you're going to blackmail her into being with you, like before?"

"That wasn't me! That was Proactive Citizenry."

"And you want to bring her back to them."

"No! I'm here to help her, you idiot."

Connor finds himself mildly amused. "Careful, Pork-n-beans—I'm the one with the rifle."

"You're wasting your time," pipes in Una. "You can't reason with him. He's not human. He's not even alive."

"*Je pense, donc je suis*," the Rewind says.

Connor doesn't speak French, but he knows enough to decipher it.

"Just because you *think*, doesn't mean you *are*. Computers claim to think, but they're just mimicking the real thing. Garbage in/garbage out—and you're just a whole lot of garbage."

The Rewind looks down, his eyes glistening. "You don't know a thing."

Connor can tell he's struck a nerve in the Rewind—this whole subject of life. Of Existence with a capital *E*. Again, Connor feels that unwanted wave of sympathy.

"Of course, Unwinds aren't legally alive either," Connor says, making Cam's argument for him. "Once an unwind order is signed, as far as the law is concerned, they're nothing but a bunch of parts. Like you."

The Rewind lifts his eyes to him. A single tear falls, absorbed by the knee of his jeans. "Your point?"

"My point is, I get it. Whether you're a pile of parts, or a sack of garbage, or a full-fledged person has nothing to do with what I, or Una, or anyone else thinks—so do us all a favor and stop making it our problem."

He nods and looks down again. "Blue Fairy," he says.

"You see!" snaps Una. "He *is* like a computer—he spouts garbage that makes no sense."

But Connor finds himself making an unexpected leap of insight.

"Sorry, Pinocchio, but Risa's not your Blue Fairy. She can't turn you into a real boy."

Cam looks at him and grins. Connor finds the grin disarming, which makes him grip the rifle more tightly. He will not be disarmed in any way.

"How do you know she hasn't already?"

"She's pretty amazing, but not *that* amazing," Connor says. "You want magic, talk to Una. I'm sure the Arápache are more tuned in to magical stuff than the rest of us."

Una stiffens and frowns at him. "I don't have to take insults from a runaway Unwind."

"I was actually being sincere," Connor admits. "But I'm happy to insult you, if that's what you want."

Una holds her glare a moment more before returning her gaze to the ground.

"You said you want to help Risa," Connor asks the Rewind. "Help her how?"

"That's between me and her."

"Wrong," Connor tells him. "*I'm* between you and her. You talk to me, or you don't talk at all."

The Rewind seethes, breathing through his nose like a dragon about to flare. Then he backs down. "I can help her bring down Proactive Citizenry. I have all the evidence she needs. But I won't share it with anyone but her."

The Rewind seems sincere—but Connor knows he's not the best judge of character. He made a crucial mistake trusting Starkey. Connor won't make the same mistake again. "You expect me to believe that? Why would you bring down the people who made you?"

"I have my reasons."

"Are you going to tell him?" Una asks Connor, her patience failing. "Or do you intend to string him along all day?"

"Tell me what?" Cam looks back and forth between them.

Connor thought he'd relish giving him the news, but now it just feels empty. "Sorry to disappoint you, Pork-n-beans . . . but Risa's not here."

The despair in the Rewind's eyes is as soulful as any legitimate human being. Connor wonders if maybe the Blue Fairy paid him a visit after all.

"But . . . but . . . the news said she was traveling with you!"

"Yeah, the news also said I attacked a harvest camp in Nevada. You of all people should know not to trust the media."

"So, where is she?"

"I don't know," Connor tells him, then adds, "But if I did, I wouldn't tell you."

The Rewind stands in frustration. "You're lying!" Connor rises just as the Rewind lunges toward him. Connor levels the gun at his chest, and he stops in midlunge.

"Just give me a reason, Pork-n-beans!"

"Stop calling me that!"

"He's telling the truth," says Una. "It's just him, Lev, and some low-cortical girl. Risa Ward wasn't with them when they showed up."

It's more information than Connor wants him to know, but now he seems to accept the truth. He drops to the ground, putting his head in his hands.

"Sisyphus," he mumbles. Connor doesn't even try to figure that one out.

"You realize I can't let you go. I can't take the chance that you'll tell the authorities where we are."

"I'll tie him up again," says Una, advancing toward the Rewind. "No one comes out to this old sweat lodge anymore."

"No," Connor decides. "We're not doing that either. We'll take him back with us to your place."

"I don't want him there!"

"Too bad." Connor looks at both of them, judging their frame of mind as somewhat stable, and he clicks the safety back on the rifle. "Now, we're going to leave here and walk to Una's place like three old friends back from an afternoon of hunting. Are we clear?"

Both Cam and Una agree reluctantly.

Then he turns to the Rewind. "Whether you deserve dignity or not, I'm going to give you some." And although Connor finds this hard, he says, "Should I call you Camus?"

"Cam," he says.

"All right, Cam. I'm Connor—but you already know that. I'd say 'pleased to meet you,' but I don't like to lie."

Cam nods his acceptance. "I appreciate your honesty," he says. "The feeling is mutual."

Pivane is there when they get back to the shop. Connor hears his deep voice upstairs talking to Lev as they enter.

"He can't know about Cam," Una says. "The Tashi'nes must never know about Wil's hands. It will destroy them."

The way it destroyed you? Connor wants to say, but instead he just says, "Understood."

Una sends Cam down into the basement. He's too weary and spent to protest.

"I'll wait here and make sure he stays put," Una says. "Can I please have my rifle back?" And when Connor hesitates, she says, "Pivane will have a lot of questions if he sees you coming upstairs with that rifle."

Although the last thing Connor wants to do is put that rifle in her hands, he gives it to her—but only after taking out the shells.

Una takes it, leans it up against the wall, then reaches into her pocket, pulling out several more rifle shells, showing them to Connor in defiance. But rather than loading the weapon, she just puts the shells back into her pocket and sits herself down on a stool near the basement door. "Go upstairs and find out why Pivane's here."

Connor resents being given orders, but he recognizes Una's need to feel in control again—especially in her own domain. He heads upstairs, leaving her to guard Cam.

"Do I want to know why you were out?" Pivane asks as soon as Connor walks in.

"Probably not," Connor tells him, and leaves it at that. He glances at Lev, who clearly wants to know what happened but is wise enough not to ask in front of Pivane.

Grace is all smiles. "The Hopis got the Juvies' panties in a wad! Look at this!" She turns up the TV volume. It's a press conference in which a spokesman for the Hopi tribe "will neither confirm nor deny" rumors that they're giving sanctuary to the Akron AWOL. The reporters, however, seem to have plenty to go on. A shaky video of someone being moved in shadows into the Hopi council building. Media leaks from an "inside source," insisting that the Akron AWOL is there. It looks like Chal worked his magic after all.

"Leave it to my brother," Pivane says. "He could get milk from a stone."

"My idea!" Grace reminds them. "Send the Juvies on a detour, I said."

"Yes, you did, Grace," Connor says, and she gives him a hug for agreeing with her.

"With the authorities distracted," Pivane says, "now's the time to get on with your business. Elina's arranging for an unregistered car to be left at a rest stop just outside the north gate. I'll drive you there tomorrow. After that, you're on your own."

Connor never told anyone on the rez where they were

going—and he hoped Lev kept his mouth shut about it as well. Even if they're among friends, the fewer people who know, the easier it will be to disappear. But there's an added wrinkle now. What are they going to do about Cam?

42 · Nelson

Currently Nelson's biggest problem is not the inflamed, peeling burns on the right half of his face. Nor is it the infected bites on his arms and legs from various unidentified desert wildlife. It's the scrawny supermarket checker who's been riding shotgun beside him these past few weeks.

"How much farther do you think?" Argent asks. "Are we still a day out? Two days?"

"We'll be there by morning, if we drive through the night."

"Is that what we're doing? Driving through the night?"

"We'll see." The sun is behind them now, low in the sky. Argent has offered to drive since they left New Orleans, but Nelson will not surrender the wheel. He's tired. He's fighting a fever, but he won't let on.

After more than a week of searching, New Orleans turned out to be a bust. If Connor Lassiter had business at Mary LaVeau's, that business was done—and no one there could be persuaded to offer him information as to his whereabouts. Although New Orleans was a hot bed of illicit activity, none of it seemed to involve sheltering AWOLs. They wasted three more days heading north to Baton Rouge and searching there for signs of Lassiter or an Anti-Divisional underground that might be giving him sanctuary.

For more than a week they wandered, chasing hunches that Nelson had all over the deep South, until the damn checker said, "I don't know why we just don't go on to New York."

"Why would we go there?" Nelson had asked.

The checker had looked at him with the stupid blinking brainlessness of a rodent. "I told you the other night."

"You didn't tell me anything."

"Yeah, I did. Of course, you were storkfaced on whatever it was you were drinking. That and those pills of yours."

"You didn't tell me anything!"

"Okay, suit yourself," Argent said, way too smug. "I didn't tell you anything."

In the end Nelson had to play into it like a goddamn knock-knock joke. "What did you tell me?"

"It was that news report about the Statue of Liberty. How they're replacing her arm with an aluminum one on account of the copper one's too heavy."

Nelson didn't have much patience for this. "What about it?"

"So it made me remember that Connor talked about having a date with the lady in green. You really don't remember?"

Nelson had no memory of being told this, but to admit this to the rodent would give him way too much satisfaction. "Now I remember," Nelson had said.

It wasn't exactly the smoking gun Nelson wanted—"the lady in green" could mean a whole lot of things . . . but then again, wasn't the statue a favorite protest spot for AWOL sympathizers? What was Lassiter planning?

What finally propelled Nelson to head north was the news report that he knew would eventually come. Argent's picture with his hero, the Akron AWOL. Argent had been wandering out in the open for days. Someone will have recognized him; someone would turn him in.

Nelson knew he ought to cut his losses and take off alone, leaving Argent for the lions, but he found within himself the tiniest shred of pity and maybe even sentimentality. Argent

UnSouled

had actually captured two AWOLs for him. A useless gesture, but the thought did count for something—because seeing those two bottom-feeders bound and gagged and practically gift-wrapped for him had brought some cheer to an otherwise miserable day. In time Argent could even be useful as a mole, infiltrating packs of AWOLs for him. So he hadn't cut Argent loose. Instead he took him with him, following the threadbare lead to New York.

Now, as they cross from West Virginia into Pennsylvania, Nelson's doubts begin to feel like roadblocks before them, and Argent will not shut his mouth.

"We should stop in Hershey," Argent suggests. "They say the whole town smells like chocolate. There's roller coasters there too. You like roller coasters?"

A sign up ahead says, PITTSBURGH 45 MILES. Nelson feels his fever coming back. His joints are aching, and his face stings from his own sweat. He resolves to take the night in Pittsburgh. He's not up to driving through the night. He doesn't even have the strength to shut Argent up.

"Yeah, New Orleans was something. I could spend some real time there," Argent rambles. "I'll bet that voodoo shop was something too. Saw a thing about it on TV once. You shoulda got us a voodoo doll of the Akron AWOL. Make him feel some of our pain."

And now Nelson is glad he let Argent talk because it has turned out to be oh so informative. "Right. Make him feel our pain." Nelson resolves to treat himself well tonight and do a full reassessment of the current situation.

Mary LaVeau's House of Voodoo. Not something Argent heard out of Connor Lassiter's mouth, but something he saw on TV. The rodent has no idea how thoroughly he's just crucified himself.

43 · Argent

His mother always said, "When life gives you lemons, squirt 'em in someone's eyes." Argent knows that's not the actual expression, but she was right. Turning your misfortune into a weapon is much more useful than making lemonade. He's proud of the way he's effectively blinded the parts pirate.

"I'll bet there'll be plenty of AWOLs for us to catch in New York, huh?" Argent asks as rural Pennsylvania gives way to the suburbs of Pittsburgh.

"Like rats," Nelson tells him.

"Maybe you could catch a few," Argent suggests. "Show me how it's done. I mean, if I'm gonna be, like, your apprentice, I gotta know these things."

The thought of traveling the country with a bona-fide parts pirate and learning the tricks of the trade actually excites him. It's a career he could enjoy. He's got to keep stringing Nelson along, though. Making him believe that he needs Argent—until Argent can really show him what a good apprentice he can be. Make himself a valuable asset. That's what he has to do. But until then, he'll keep Nelson dangling.

The man's already given him some basic lessons, just in the course of conversation.

"Most AWOL Unwinds are smarter than the Juvenile Authority gives them credit for," Nelson had said. "You set a stupid trap, and all you'll get are stupid AWOLs. Worth a lot less on the black market. If the brain scan shows a high cortical score, you can double your money."

So much to know about the art of entrapment!

While last night was a cheap motel, tonight in Pittsburgh,

Nelson treats them to a two-bedroom suite in a fancy-schmancy place with doormen and half a dozen flags over the entrance.

"Tonight we indulge," Nelson tells him. "Because we owe it to ourselves."

If this is the life of a parts pirate, Argent's ready to go all in.

The suite is huge and smells of fresh flowers instead of mildew. Argent orders expensively from the room service menu, and Nelson doesn't bat an eye.

"Nothing's too good for my apprentice," he says, and raises his wineglass to emphasize the point. His own father was never so generous, either in wallet or in spirit. Nelson's breathing seems labored. The good side of his face is taking on a pale sheen. Argent doesn't think anything of it; right now Argent is all about his T-bone steak.

As their meal winds down, Argent drops his guard and Nelson begins to talk casually of the days ahead.

"New York's a great town," Nelson says. "Have you ever been?"

Argent shakes his head and swallows before he speaks, so as not to appear too uncultured for a room service meal. "Never. Always wanted to go, though. When our parents were alive, they used to say they'd take us to New York. See the Empire State Building. A Broadway show. Promised us the world, but we never went anywhere but Branson, Missouri." He takes another bite of steak, imagining the food will be even better in the Big Apple. "I swore to myself I'd go there someday. Swore I'd make it happen."

"And so you did." Nelson wipes his mouth with a silk napkin. "We'll have to make time for some sightseeing while we're there."

Argent grins. "That'd be sweet."

"Sure." Nelson smiles kindly. "Times Square, Central Park . . ."

"Heard about this club in an old factory," Argent says, nearly frothing at the mouth with excitement. "A different famous band plays there every night, but you never know who it's gonna be."

"Did you hear about that on TV?" Nelson asks. "Like the House of Voodoo?"

It takes a moment to settle, bouncing around Argent's mind like a pinball until it drops dead center. Game over.

When he looks up at Nelson, there is nothing kind about his smile. It's more predatory. Like a tiger anticipating its kill.

"Lassiter never said anything about Mary LaVeau or 'the green lady,' did he?"

"I . . . I was gonna tell you . . ."

"When? Before or after you got your all-expense-paid tour of New York?" Suddenly he flips the table. Dinnerware flies, a plate smashes against the mantel, and Nelson pounces, pinning Argent against the wall so hard Argent can feel the light switch digging into his back like a knife—but it's nowhere near as deadly as the steak knife Nelson now holds to his throat.

"Did you say anything that wasn't a lie?" He presses the knife harder against his neck. "I'll know if you're lying now."

Argent knows the truth won't help him, so he avoids the question. "If you kill me, there'll be a lot of blood," he says desperately. "And you wouldn't have fed me if you really meant to kill me!"

"Every man deserves a last meal." His presses the knife harder, drawing a bead of blood.

"Wait!" Argent hisses, pulling out the only ace he has to play. "There's a tracking chip!"

"What are you talking about?"

"My sister! When she was little she always used to wander off, so my parents had them put this tracking chip in her skin behind her ear. If she's still with Lassiter, we can find them. But I'm the only one who knows the chip's tracking code. Kill me and the code dies with me."

"You son of a bitch. You knew about that chip all along!"

"If I told you, you'd have no use for me!"

"I have no use for you now!" He drops the knife and uses his bare hand to close off Argent's windpipe. No blood. No mess. "Now that I know, I can find that code without you." Argent tries to fight him off, figuring he'll lose and that this is the end—but to Argent's surprise, he's stronger than Nelson. In fact, the man seems uncharacteristically weak. He pushes Nelson off, and Nelson stumbles, falling to one knee.

"Stay still and let me kill you!" Nelson says.

Argent grabs the knife from the ground, ready to defend himself. But Nelson doesn't come after him. His eyes roll. His lids flutter. He tries to stand, but falls again, this time on all fours.

"Damn it!"

Then his elbows give way, and he lands facedown on the carpet, as unconscious as if he'd been tranq'd.

Argent waits a moment. Then a moment more.

"Hey. You alive?"

Nothing. He reaches down to feel Nelson's neck. There's a pulse, rapid and strong—but he's hot. Really hot.

Argent can run. He can just take off and get the hell out of this situation . . . but he hesitates and stares at the unconscious parts pirate on the floor before him. He lets the pinball bounce around in his head a bit, then puts the knife gently down on the mantel. The ball is still in play, and there are plenty of points left to be scored.

44 · Nelson

When he regains consciousness, it takes him a few moments to realize where he is. The OmniWilliam Penn in Pittsburgh. The presidential suite. A detour on a wild-goose chase he should never have allowed himself to be on.

The TV in his bedroom plays an action movie at low volume. The waste-of-life grocery checker sits there watching it while eating room service French fries. He turns to Nelson and, seeing he's awake, pulls his chair over.

"Feeling better?"

Nelson doesn't dignify him with a response.

"This hotel's so fancy, they got a doctor on call," Argent says. "Had him come to check you out. Don't worry. I cleaned up the mess before he got here and put you all snug in the bed. You talked to him a little. You remember talking to him?"

Nelson still refuses to say a thing.

"Nah, didn't think you would. You mumbled crazy crap about a graveyard and a tornado. The doctor said those bites you got on your arms and legs—whatever they are—they're infected. He gave you a shot of antibiotics. Tried to convince me to take you to the emergency room, but I paid him cash and he shut up about it. I got it from your wallet. Hope you don't mind under the circumstances. Didn't cheat ya or anything. There's a receipt. From the pharmacy too, on accounta I filled the prescription for more antibiotics. Take three times a day, with meals."

Nelson is like a boulder in this stream of words. He gets some of it; the rest just flows past.

"What are you doing here?" Nelson finally asks.

"Couldn't just leave you on the floor to die, could I? We're a team. Right half, left half, and all."

"Get out of my sight."

When Argent doesn't move. Nelson turns his head to look the other way. Moving his head just the slightest bit makes him feel like he's on a carnival ride.

"I don't blame you for being pissed at me," Argent says. "And maybe you woulda killed me and maybe not. But if I'm gonna be your apprentice, I know I gotta put up with a lot."

Nelson forces himself to look at Argent again. "What universe do you think you're living in?"

"Same as you," Argent says. He looks at the label of the pill vial and puts it on the nightstand, pointedly out of Nelson's reach. "Whether you like it or not, you need me right now. As long as you need me, you won't get rid of me. You might even teach me a thing or two about being a parts pirate. One hand washes the other, as they say. And both our hands are kind of dirty. So I stay, and we both get what we need."

The fact that he is now entirely dependent on Argent Skinner makes Nelson want to laugh, if it didn't hurt so much to do so. "Are you my male nurse now?"

"I'm what you need, when you need it," Argent tells him. "Today you need a nurse, so that's what I'll be. Tomorrow maybe you'll need someone to help you set an Unwind trap again, so that's what I'll be tomorrow. And when you do track down Connor Lassiter and you need help bringing him down, you'll be real happy you kept me around." Then he opens the room service menu. "So, I'm thinking soup for you. And if you're good, maybe some ice cream after."

It's another day until Nelson feels strong enough to move around the suite. He's given up trying to fight Argent. The kid might be an idiot, but he's a shrewd idiot. He knows how to make himself indispensable to Nelson—at least for now.

"I know you'll kick me to the curb the moment you see fit," Argent tells him. "It's my job to make sure you never see fit."

They don't talk about their mission. Nelson doesn't ask him for the tracking code because he knows Argent won't surrender his one bargaining chip until he's good and ready. Besides, as much as Nelson wants to move forward, he knows he's in no condition. He has little choice but to convalesce in the presidential suite.

"Being a parts pirate must pay pretty good if you can afford a place like this," Argent comments more than once, baiting Nelson to talk about his profession. Although making conversation with Argent isn't exactly on his list of enjoyable activities, Nelson is a captive audience, so he endures it. He even tells Argent some of the things he wants to know, explaining the details of his best traps. The concrete tunnel lined with glue. The cigarette carton on a mattress perched over a pit. Argent hangs so fully on every word, Nelson begins to enjoy bragging about his best catches.

"I once had an AWOL swallow a miniature poison grenade, and I told him I'd set it off remotely if he didn't turn over his friends. He led five other kids right to me—each one of them a better specimen than him."

"Did you detonate the grenade?"

"It wasn't a grenade," Nelson tells Argent. "It was a cranberry."

It makes Argent laugh, and Nelson finds that his own laughter is genuine.

Nelson can't say that he's beginning to like Argent—there really isn't much about him to like. But he's coming to accept the necessity of Argent's presence. Like the AWOL who surrendered his friends, Argent Skinner has value to Nelson. For his services, Nelson had set the cranberry-eating AWOL free, because, after all, fair is fair, and Nelson has always seen himself as a man of integrity. In the end, Nelson will make sure Argent gets his just reward.

They set out the next day, Nelson feeling stronger, if not fully recovered. The bites are still red and swollen, the burned half of his face still raw and peeling, but at least his fever has broken. He endures the troubled gazes from other hotel guests as he checks out, just as he endured them when he had checked in.

"Are you gonna tell me where we're going?" Argent asks. Now that Nelson has regained his strength, Argent has gotten shifty and uncertain about his tenure.

"Not New York," is all Nelson is willing to offer, which sets Argent rambling on about other places he's never been, but would like to go, fishing for any hints that Nelson might give. "Doesn't make sense to be going unless we know where we're going."

"I know where we're going," Nelson tells him, taking great pleasure in Argent's discomfort.

"After all I done, least you could do is give me a clue."

Once they cross the Allegheny River and Pittsburgh falls behind them, Nelson reveals at least part of his hand. "We're going to Sarnia."

"Sarnia? Never heard of it."

"It's in Canada, across the border from Port Huron, Michigan. I'm going to introduce you to my contact in the black market, assuming he's not on one of his airborne jags. A gentleman by the name of Divan."

Argent twists his face like he's smelled something foul. "Funny name. We sold Chicken Divan at Publix."

"You'd be wise not to insult him. Divan runs the most successful harvest camp on the black market this side of Burma. State of the art. I bring him all the AWOLs I catch, and he's always treated me fairly and honorably. If you want to be a parts pirate, he's the man you need to know."

Argent shifts uncomfortably. "I heard stories about the black market. Rusty scalpels. No anesthesia."

"You're talking about the Burmese *Dah Zey*. Divan is the opposite. A gentleman, and an honorable one at that. He's always done right by me."

"Okay," says Argent. "Sounds good to me."

"And," adds Nelson, "in return for this show of good faith

on my part, I expect some good faith from you in return. I want the code for your sister's tracking chip."

Argent turns his eyes to the road ahead of them. "Maybe later."

"Maybe now."

Then Nelson calmly pulls the car to the shoulder of the highway. "If not, I'll be happy to leave you here, say good-bye, and let you live your miserable life with no interference from me."

Cars whiz past. Argent looks like he might be ill. "You'll never find Lassiter without that code."

"There's no guarantee your sister will still be with him anyway. If she's half as annoying as you, he probably ditched her an hour out of Heartsdale."

Argent considers it. He fidgets with his hands. He picks nervously at the stitches on his face.

"You promise you won't kill me?"

"I promise I won't kill you."

"Left half, right half, right? We're a team?"

"By necessity, if not by design."

Argent takes a deep breath. "We'll meet this Divan guy. And then I'll tell you."

Nelson pounds the steering wheel in fury. Then calms down. "Fine. If that's the way you want it." Then he pulls out his tranq gun, pulls the trigger, and tranqs Argent in the chest.

Argent's eyes are wide in shock at the betrayal.

"I can't tell you how good that felt," Nelson says.

Argent slumps in his seat, and Nelson is left supremely satisfied. If he must endure the presence of Argent Skinner on his way to finding Connor Lassiter and his stinking tithe friend, then Nelson will endure him. Although frequent unconsciousness on Argent's part may be required to make life bearable. Nelson smiles. In the end, perhaps he'll put Argent out of his misery the same way he plans to kill Lev Calder for leaving him tranq'd on an Arizona road. Or maybe he'll let Argent live. It's all within the realm of possibility and all within Nelson's power. He has to admit even when he was a Juvey-cop he enjoyed having power over life and death. As a parts pirate that feeling is so much more raw and visceral. He's come to love it. It all comes down to tracking Argent's sister. Then it's only a matter of time now until he achieves Lev Calder's death and earns Connor Lassiter's eyes. Plus the huge bounty Divan will pay for the rest of him, of course.

Nelson punches his destination into the GPS, and it plots the fastest route to Sarnia. Then, checking his rearview mirror, he pulls onto the freeway in blissful, satisfied silence.

45 · Hayden

Collaborating with the enemy. It's a crime that Hayden was convicted of in the court of public opinion without the benefit of a trial or the display of a single fact. In the eyes of the kids from Cold Springs Harvest Camp, he is 100 percent guilty, regardless of the fact that he's 100 percent innocent. He never even gave Menard, or anyone in the Juvenile Authority, a single stitch of information. His only consolation is that it's just the kids from Cold Springs who hate him. To the rest of the world he's still the same kid who delivered the Whollie's Manifesto—and called for a second teen uprising when he was taken into custody at the Graveyard. For once the media did him a favor.

Hayden can't say he's unhappy that Menard is dead. The man made Hayden's plush detention a living hell at Cold Springs, and there were many times Hayden might have killed the man himself if he'd had the means. However, the manner of his death—that cold-blooded execution on Starkey's dictatorial order—was far more wrong than it was right. It reeked of cruelty rather than justice. Hayden knows he's not the only one with such misgivings, but he can't voice it aloud—not when the survivors of Cold Springs Camp already think that he sold them out to the Juvies.

By the good grace of Starkey, Lord of Storks, Hayden has been allowed computer access in order to help Jeevan find their next target and a path to harvest camp liberation that doesn't leave a whole lot of dead kids behind.

Their "computer room" is a utility space near the entrance of the mine, still filled with rusty relics. A huge fan and ducts that, in theory, bring fresh air to the depths of the mine. Being so far from anything resembling civilization, Jeevan had jury-rigged a dish hidden in the brush outside the mine's entrance to tap into some poor unsuspecting satellite and provide them with full connectivity.

So now Hayden's working for Starkey. It's the first time he truly feels like he's collaborating with the enemy.

"If it means anything, sir, I don't believe what those kids are saying about you," says Jeevan, who sits behind him, watching over his shoulder as he chips away at various firewalls. "I don't believe you'd ever help the Juvenile Authority."

Hayden doesn't look up from the computer screen. "Does it mean anything to me? I suppose it means all it can mean coming from someone who betrayed Connor and led to hundreds of Whollies being captured."

Jeevan swallows with an audible click in his Adam's apple. "Starkey says it would have happened anyway. If we didn't get out, we'd have been caught too."

Although Hayden wants to argue the point, he knows his friends are few and far between here. He can't afford to alienate the ones he has. He forces himself to look at Jeevan and dredge up something resembling sincerity.

"I'm sorry, Jeeves. What happened, happened, and I know it wasn't your fault."

Jeevan is visibly relieved by Hayden's conciliation. Even now, he sees Hayden as some sort of superior officer. Hayden has to be careful not to lose that respect.

"They say he's alive," Jeevan says. "Connor, I mean. For a while they even thought he was with us."

"Yeah, well, I think this is the fifth of his nine lives, so he's got a few more left."

That just leaves Jeevan baffled, and Hayden has to laugh. "Don't think too hard on it, Jeeves. It's not worth it."

"Oh!" A lightbulb practically appears over Jeevan's head. "Like a cat. I get it!"

There are two guards assigned to Hayden now, plus Jeevan. One guard is there to make sure he's not attacked by angry AWOLs from Cold Springs seeking payback. The second guard is to make sure he doesn't bolt, since the computer room is so close to the mine's entrance. Jeevan's job is to spy on Hayden's online activities, to make sure he's not doing anything suspicious. Trust is not a part of Starkey's world.

"You keep coming back to this one harvest camp," Jeevan points out.

"So far it has the most potential."

Jeevan studies the satellite image and points to the screen. "But look at all those guard towers at the outer gate."

"Exactly. All their security is outwardly focused."

"Ahh."

Clearly Jeevan doesn't get it yet, but that's all right. He will.

"Tad's dead, by the way."

Hayden hadn't planned on saying it. He hadn't even been thinking about it. Perhaps the memory was tweaked by the heat of the computer room reminding him of that last awful day in the ComBom. The day that Hayden and his team of techies would have died had he not shot out the plane's windshield. There are still dark moments when he thinks he made a mistake. That he should have honored their wishes and let them die rather than be captured.

"Tad's dead?" The look of horror on Jeevan's face is both satisfying and troubling to Hayden.

"He fried to death in the ComBom. But don't worry. That's not Starkey's fault either." He doesn't know if Jeevan reads the sarcasm—he's about as literal as computer code. Maybe it's best if he doesn't.

"I haven't seen Trace here. He flew the plane, didn't he?"

Jeevan looks down. "Trace is dead too," he tells Hayden. "He didn't survive the crash."

"No," says Hayden. "I imagine he wouldn't have." Whether Trace's death was a result of the crash or secret human intervention is something Hayden supposes he'll never know. The truth most certainly died with Trace. Or without a trace, as the case may be.

Hayden hears footsteps coming up the steep slope from deeper in the mine. The way the guard steps aside so obediently telegraphs to Hayden who the visitor is even before he comes into view.

"Speak of the devil! We were just talking about you, Starkey. Jeevan and I were reminiscing about your magic tricks. Especially the one where you made a commercial jet disappear."

"It didn't disappear," says Starkey, refusing to be goaded. "It's at the bottom of the Salton Sea."

"He didn't actually call you the devil," Jeevan tells Starkey. Literal as code.

"We have a common enemy," Starkey points out. "The devils are all out there—and it's time they got their due."

Starkey dislodges Jeevan from his seat with the slightest

flick of his head. He takes his place, studying the image on the screen.

"Is that a harvest camp?"

"MoonCrater Harvest Camp, to be exact. Craters of the Moon, Idaho."

"What about it?" Starkey asks.

"All of its security is focused outward!" blurts Jeevan, as if he actually knows why that matters.

"Yes," says Hayden. "And they don't have eyes in the backs of their heads."

Starkey crosses his arms, making it clear that he doesn't have all day. "And why does that matter?"

"Here's why." Hayden drags up another window, showing schematics, and a third that shows a standard geological survey. "Craters of the Moon National Park is a lava field riddled with caves, and all the camp's utility conduits use the caves. Electricity, sewerage, ventilation, everything." Hayden zooms in on a schematic of the camp's main dormitory and starts pointing things out. "So, if we create a diversion at the main gate in the middle of the night—some smoke and mirrors, if you will—it will draw all their attention. Then, while the security forces are all focused on the gate, we go in through this utility hatch in the basement of the dormitory, bring all those kids down into the caves—and exit the caves here, almost a mile away."

Starkey is genuinely impressed. "And by the time they realize their Unwinds are gone, we'll be free and clear."

"That's the general idea. And no one gets hurt in the process."

He claps Hayden on the back hard enough that it stings. "That's genius, Hayden! Genius!"

"I thought you might appreciate a 'vanishing act,' approach." He touches the screen, changing the angle of the schematic to show the levels of the dormitory. "Boys are on the ground floor, girls on the second, and harvest camp staff on the third. There're only two stairwells, so if we man them and tranq any staff that tries to come down, we could theoretically be in and out before anyone figures out what's going on."

"How soon can we do this?"

There's a kind of greed in Starkey's eyes that makes Hayden close the computer's open windows so it doesn't prompt further scheming. "Well, after Cold Springs, I figured you'd want to lie low for a while."

"No way," Starkey says. "We should strike while the iron's hot. One-two punch. You plan the rescue. I'll take care of the diversion. I want this to go down in less than a week."

Hayden shudders at the thought of something so theoretical becoming real too quickly. "I really don't think—"

"Trust me. If you want to clean up your reputation around here, this is the way to do it, my friend." Starkey stands, his decision set in stone. "Make it happen, Hayden. I'm counting on you."

And Starkey leaves before Hayden can offer any more reservations.

Once Starkey is gone, Jeevan takes his seat next to Hayden again. "He called you his friend," Jeevan points out. "That's a really good thing!"

"Yes," says Hayden. "It thrills me no end." Jeevan takes that at face value, as Hayden knew he would.

Starkey had said they had a common enemy. *So then is my enemy's enemy my friend?* wonders Hayden. Somehow the old adage doesn't ring true if that friend is Mason Starkey.

The Stork Brigade hits MoonCrater Harvest Camp six days later. Hayden and a team consisting entirely of kids who knew Hayden from the Graveyard, map out the caves two days in advance. For the actual event, Starkey leads the way with his special-ops detail, but admits that it would be a good idea to have Hayden and his team there as well. Leaving a trail of flares in the jagged lava tunnels, they reach the camp's plumbing and conduit lines at 1:30 a.m. and follow them to the basement hatch, which is locked from the other side. They wait.

Then, at 2:00 a.m., a burning truck filled with ammunition crashes through the harvest camp's outer gate, and gunfire erupts from the volcanic wasteland beyond. Bam is in charge of the diversion, and Hayden does not envy her. She has her work cut out for her—she and her own team of storks must make this look like a real assault on the camp, and they must make it last for at least twenty minutes.

The moment the gunfire starts outside, the inside operation begins.

"Blow the hatch," Starkey orders his fairly psychotic demolitions kid. "Do it now!"

"No," says Hayden. "Not yet." Hayden knows that the building up above is going into lockdown mode—a security measure that will work to their advantage. Steel shutters are rolling down over the windows. Emergency doors are sealing. No one will be able to get in or out of the dormitory until the security system is reset.

Hayden counts to ten. "Okay, now!"

The hatch blows, and armed with only tranq weapons, they pile through the hole toward whatever awaits them.

The Unwinds in the dormitory, already awakened by the explosions and gunfire outside, are primed for death or rescue. Tonight, it will be the latter.

The rescue force tranqs a guard and a counselor on their way up the stairs to the main floor—a single huge communal room lined with row after row of beds. The space is dim. Only emergency lights shine now, hitting the beds at oblique angles, making the plywood headboards look like tombstones. The sounds of the battle outside are muted by the steel shutters. No one can see out, but that means no one on the outside can see in. With all the camp's attention on the fake assault on the outer gate, the rescue team is effectively invisible.

Starkey wastes no time. "You've just been liberated," he announces. The *PFFTT* of tranq pistols being fired herald several more staff members taken down by Starkey's special-ops team, all of whom are disturbingly good shots. "Everyone to the basement. Don't take anything but the clothes on your back and your shoes. Let's move it!"

Then he goes upstairs to announce the girls' liberation, leaving Hayden and his team to move the masses down and out.

In ten minutes, nearly three hundred kids are taken down into the caves and are on their way to freedom. Only the tithes, who are in a different building, and rescue-resistant by their very nature, must be left behind.

Hayden and his team lead the liberated Unwinds through the lava cave to the exit point, where four dark delivery trucks "borrowed" for the evening's festivities wait on a lonely road to spirit them all away.

Gunfire from the fake assault still rages as they emerge from the caves, but it's far away, like the sound of a distant battlefront. As the trucks are quickly packed with kids, Hayden dares to think that maybe, just maybe, he can turn Starkey's guerilla war into something meaningful, and even admirable. Perhaps the road ahead isn't all that bleak after all.

He has no idea that Starkey, who is still nowhere in sight, has just paved them a fresh road to hell.

46 · Starkey

Performing magic was never just about the tricks for Starkey. There must be style. There must be showmanship. There must be an audience. Making three hundred kids vanish is, admittedly, quite the trick, but liberating a harvest camp is about more than just freeing its Unwinds. Starkey sees a bigger, much more glorious picture.

Once the girls on the second floor are on the move toward the basement and Hayden is occupied getting everyone through the caves, Starkey takes a moment to study the high ceiling of the large dormitory, taking note of the ceiling fans. None of them are spinning, but that's fine. In fact, it's better that way.

"I need you to go upstairs and bring me six staff members," he tells his team. "Tranq anyone who gives you trouble, but make sure the ones you bring me are conscious."

"Why?" one of them asks. "What are we doing?"

"We're sending a message."

They return with three men and three women. Starkey has no idea what their positions are here. Administrators, surgeons, cooks—it doesn't matter. To Starkey they're all the same. They're all unwinders. He orders them bound and gagged with duct tape. He looks up to the ceiling fans once more. There are six fans, suspended about ten feet from the ground. And Starkey brought plenty of rope.

No one in his special-ops team knows much about tying knots. The nooses are crude and inelegant, but aesthetics don't matter as long as they hold. With the diversionary battle still raging outside like the shores of Normandy, Starkey and his team stand the six captives on chairs and lasso a blade of a ceiling fan above each of their heads with the other end of their respective ropes, pulling the ropes tight enough so that their captives can feel it, but not tight enough to actually hurt them. Once they're all in place, Starkey steps forward to address them.

"My name is Mason Michael Starkey, the leader of the Stork Brigade. You have been found guilty of crimes against humanity. You've unwound thousands of innocent kids—many of them storks—and there must be a reckoning." He pauses to let it sink in. Then he approaches the first captive—a woman who can't stop crying.

"I can see that you're frightened," he says.

The woman, unable to speak through the duct tape, nods and pleads with her tearful eyes.

"Don't worry," he tells her. "I'm not going to hurt you— but I need you to remember everything I've said. When they come to set you free, I want you to tell them. Can you do that for me?"

The woman nods.

"Tell them that this is only the beginning. We're coming for everyone who supports unwinding and mistreats storks. There's nowhere you people can hide from us. Make sure you tell them. Make sure they know."

The woman nods again, and Starkey pats her arm with his good hand, giving her a measure of comfort, and leaves her there on her chair, unharmed.

Then he goes to the five others, and one by one kicks the chair out from beneath them.

Part Five

A Murder of Storks

CHARLIE FUQUA, ARKANSAS LEGISLATIVE
CANDIDATE, ENDORSES DEATH PENALTY FOR
REBELLIOUS CHILDREN. . . .

The Huffington Post | By John Celock

Posted: 10/08/2012 1:29 p.m. Updated: 10/15/2012 8:08 a.m.

In . . . Fuqua's 2012 book, the candidate wrote that while parents
love their children, a process could be set up to allow for the insti-
tution of the death penalty for "rebellious children," according to
the *Arkansas Times*. Fuqua . . . points out that the course of action
involved in sentencing a child to death is described in the Bible
and would involve judicial approval. While it is unlikely that many
parents would seek to have their children killed by the government,
Fuqua wrote, such power would serve as a way to stop rebellious
children.

According to the *Arkansas Times*, Fuqua wrote:

The maintenance of civil order in society rests on the foundation
of family discipline. Therefore, a child who disrespects his parents
must be permanently removed from society in a way that gives an
example to all other children of the importance of respect for parents. The death penalty for rebellious children is not something to
be taken lightly. The guidelines for administering the death penalty
to rebellious children are given in Deut 21:18–21: This passage does
not give parents blanket authority to kill their children. They must
follow the proper procedure. . . . Even though this procedure would
rarely be used, if it were the law of the land, it would give parents
authority . . . and it would be a tremendous incentive for children to
give proper respect to their parents.

Full article: http://www.huffingtonpost.com/2012/10/08/

charlie-fuqua-arkansas-candidate-death-penalty-rebellious-children_n_1948490.
html

"I think my views are fairly well accepted by most people."
—Charlie Fuqua

The Rheinschilds

Janson and Sonia Rheinschild have been asked to resign from their positions at the university. The chancellor cites "unauthorized use of biological material" as the reason. They could either resign or be arrested and have their names—and their work—dragged through the mud.

BioDynix Medical Instruments has not returned Janson's calls for weeks. When he demands to know why, the receptionist, a bit flustered by his surliness, claims that they have no records of his previous calls, and in fact, they have no record of him in their system at all.

But the worst is yet to come.

Janson, unshaven and unshowered for maybe a week, shuffles to answer the doorbell. There's a kid there, eighteen or so. It takes a moment for Janson to recognize him as one of Austin's friends. Austin—Janson's research assistant, rehabilitated from the streets—has been living with them for the past year. Sonia's idea. They had converted their basement into an apartment for him. Of course, he has his own life, so the Rheinschilds don't follow his comings and goings, and he's been known to be away for days at a time when there's no work to be done. That being the case, his current absence hasn't been cause for alarm—especially now that Janson has neither an office nor research lab anymore.

"I don't know how to tell you this, so I'll just say it," the kid says. "Austin was taken away for unwinding last night."

Janson stammers for a moment in protective denial. "That can't be. There must be some mistake—he's too old to be unwound now! In fact, he celebrated his birthday just this past weekend."

"His actual birthday's tomorrow," the kid says.

"But . . . but . . . he's not a feral! He has a home! A job!"

The kid shakes his head. "Don't matter. His father signed an unwind order."

And in the stunned silence that follows, Sonia comes down the stairs. "Janson, what's wrong?"

But he finds he can't tell her. He can't even repeat the words aloud. She comes to his side, and the boy at the door, wringing a woolen hat in his hands, continues. "His dad, see—he's got a drug problem—that's the reason Austin was on the streets to begin with. From what I hear, someone offered him a lot of money to sign those papers."

Sonia gasps, covering her mouth as she realizes what has happened. Janson's face goes red with fury. "We'll stop it! We'll pay whatever we have to pay, bribe whomever we need to bribe—"

"It's too late," says the kid, looking to the welcome mat at his feet. "Austin was unwound this morning."

None of them can speak. The three stand in an impotent tableau of grief until the kid says, "I'm sorry," and hurries away.

Janson closes the door and then holds his wife close. They don't talk about it. They can't. He suspects they'll never speak of it to each other again. Janson knows this was intended as a warning—but a warning to do what? Stay quiet? Embrace unwinding? Cease to exist? And if he tries to rattle his saber at Proactive Citizenry, what good will it do? They haven't actually broken the law. They never do! Instead they mold the law to encompass whatever it is they wish to accomplish.

He lets go of Sonia and goes to the stairs, refusing to look at her. "I'm going to bed," he tells her.

"Janson, it's barely noon."

"Why should that make a difference?"

In the bedroom, he draws the shades, and as he buries him-

self in the covers, in the dark, he thinks back to the time Austin broke into their home and hit Janson in the head. Now Janson wishes that the blow would have killed him. Because then Austin might still be whole.

47 · Connor

Starkey. He should have known it was Starkey. The numbers of the dead reported from the crash in the Salton Sea didn't match with the numbers he knew escaped. He was foolish enough to think that either Starkey had been among the dead, or would lie low, content with his petty principality of storks. As Connor prepares to leave Una's apartment and continue the journey to Ohio, he can't help but be drawn in by the news reports coming in on every station about the attack on Moon-Crater Harvest Camp.

"You mean you know this guy?" Lev asks.

"He's the one who stole the escape plane," Connor explains. "You saw it take off from the Graveyard, didn't you? He took all the storks and left the rest of us for the Juvies."

"Nice guy."

"Yeah. I was an idiot for not seeing his psycho factor before it was too late."

The premeditated lynchings at MoonCrater is Starkey's line in the sand, and it's quickly deepening into a trench. Five staff members hung and a sixth one left alive to tell the tale. The media scrutiny is turning Mason Starkey into a swollen image much larger than his five-foot-six stature, and Connor realizes, as much as he hates to admit it, that they are in the same club now. They are both cult figures in hiding, hated by some, adored by others. Vilified and lionized. He wouldn't be surprised if someone starts making T-shirts featuring both of them side by side, as if their renegade status makes them in any way comrades in arms.

Starkey claims to speak for storks, but people don't differentiate when it comes to AWOLs. As far as the public is concerned, he's the maniacal voice of all Unwinds—and that's a big problem. As Starkey's trench in the sand fills with blood, the fear of AWOLs will grow, tearing apart everything Connor has fought for.

He used to impress upon the Whollies at the Graveyard the importance of keeping their wits about them and using their heads. "They think we're hopelessly violent and better off unwound," he would tell them. "We have to prove to the world that they're wrong."

All it might take to destroy everything that Connor has worked for is Starkey kicking out five chairs.

Connor turns off the TV, his eyes aching from all the coverage. "Starkey won't stop there," he tells Lev. "It's only going to get worse."

"Which means there are three sides in this war now," Lev points out, and Connor realizes that he's right.

"So, if the first side is driven by hate and the second by fear, what drives us?"

"Hope?" suggests Lev.

Connor shakes his head in frustration. "We're gonna need a lot more than that. Which is why we have to get to Akron and find out what Sonia knows."

Then from behind him he hears, "Sonia who?"

It's Cam, stepping out of the bathroom. He's been locked in the basement for safekeeping, but Una must have sent him up on one of his regular bathroom runs. Connor feels fury rise in him, not so much at Cam, but at himself—for having given away two crucial pieces of information. Their destination and a name.

"None of your goddamn business!" Connor snaps.

Cam raises his eyebrows, causing the pattern of multiracial seams in his forehead to compress. "Hot button," Cam says. "This Sonia must be important for you to react like that."

Their plan has been to leave Cam in Una's basement until Lev and Connor are too far away for him to pick up the trail. That way, although he knows where they've been, he won't know where they're going and can't bring the information back to his creators—because in spite of his claims to have turned on them, there's been no proof to back up the claim.

However, Cam now has a name as well as the city they're headed to. If he does go back to Proactive Citizenry, it won't take long for them to realize that this particular Sonia is the long-lost wife of their disavowed founder.

Connor realizes that everything has now changed, and their lives have become infinitely more complicated.

48 · Lev

More things have changed than Connor even realizes—but Lev is not about to hit him with his own big announcement just yet.

He watches as Connor grabs Cam's arm a little too hard, but then Lev realizes that he's using Roland's hand to do it, so that's understandable. He pulls him toward the stairs with troubling purpose.

"What are you going to do?" Lev asks.

Connor gives him a bitterly sardonic smile. "Have a meaningful discussion." Then Connor pulls Cam down the stairs, leaving Lev alone with Grace, who had eavesdropped on everything from the safety of Una's room. Grace, Lev knows, is another variable to be dealt with. Throughout all of this, she's kept her distance from Lev, and they've said very little to each other.

"So is Cam coming to Ohio?" she asks.

"Why on earth would Connor take him to Ohio?"

Grace shrugs. "Friends close, enemies closer kind of thing," she says. "Seems to me there's three choices. Leave him, take him, or kill him. Since he knows too much, that brings it down to the last two, and Connor don't seem the killing type. Even though he runned you down with a car."

"It was an accident," Lev reminds her.

"Yeah—anyways, best strategy is to bring him along. You watch. Connor's going to come back and tell you that you've gained a travel buddy." She hesitates for a moment, glances at him, then glances away. "When are you gonna tell him that you're not coming?"

Lev looks to her, a little shocked, a little angry. He had told no one of his decision yet. No one. How did she know?

"Don't look at me so funny. It's obvious to anyone with half a brain. You keep talking about *Connor* going to Ohio and *his* mission to find Sonia. You've already cut yourself out of that picture in your head. Which is why I gotta go with him. So there's two of us to keep Cam in line."

"You're relieved that I'm not coming, aren't you?"

Grace looks away from him. "I never said that." Then she adds, "It's because I know you don't like me!"

Lev grins. "No, actually, you're the one who doesn't like me."

"That's because I keep thinking you're gonna blow up! I know you say you can't, but what if you can? People step on mines that aren't supposed to work no more and blow themselves up, so what if you're like one of those mines?"

Lev responds by swinging his hands together. Grace flinches, but nothing comes from Lev's clap but a clap—and not even a loud one.

"Now you're just making fun of me."

"Actually," says Lev, "there are a lot of people I've come across that think 'once a clapper, always a clapper.' But I didn't blow us all sky-high when I got hit by the car, did I? If I was gonna blow, that would have done it."

Grace shakes her head. "You're still not safe. Maybe you won't blow up, but you're not safe in other ways. I can just tell."

Lev isn't exactly sure what she means, but he senses that she's right. He's not a clapper anymore, but neither is he the model of stability. He's not sure what he's capable of—good or bad. And it scares him.

"I'm glad you're going with Connor," Lev tells her. "And he'll take good care of you."

"I'll take care of him, you mean," Grace says, a bit offended. "He needs me, because you can't win a thing like this without the brains. I know they call me low-cortical and all, but even so, I got this one corner of my brain that's like Grand Central Station. Stuff that other people can't figure out comes easy to me. Argent always hated that and called me stupid, but only because it made him feel stupid."

Lev smiles. "Connor told me all about how you got him out during the raid at your house. You were the one who thought to send the Juvies looking elsewhere for us, and you also figured out the shooter wasn't trying to kill us."

"Right!" Grace says proudly. "And I even know who the shooter was—but like my mama always said, tellin' all you know just gets your head empty. Anyways, I thought on it and saw no need to tell."

Lev feels himself really warming to Grace for the first time. "I figured it out too. And I agree with you. No one needs to know." *But*, thinks Lev, *maybe there are things* Grace *needs to know*. He thinks about the situation with Starkey and realizes that if Grace is the strategist she appears to be, perhaps the challenge should be put to her. "I have a train for you to run through Grand Central Station," he says.

"Send it on through."

"The question is: How do you win a three-sided war?"

Grace frowns as she considers it. "That's a tough one. I'll think on it and give you an answer." Then she crosses her arms. "'Course I can't give you an answer if you don't come with us, can I?"

Lev offers her an apologetic smile. "Then don't give the answer to me. Give it to Connor."

49 · Connor

Holding tightly to Cam's arm, Connor escorts him down the stairs. Una is in the back room of her shop, building a new guitar, escaping into her work.

"You sent him up there without warning any of us!"

Una looks up from her work with only mild interest, as if, in her mind, they've already left. "I sent him to the bathroom. It's not like he was going to escape."

Connor doesn't bother to explain his anger. It's a waste of his breath. He continues down to the basement with Cam, who doesn't resist.

"So," says Cam, with irritating nonchalance. "Someone named Sonia in Akron."

Connor lets him loose. "We could have the Arápache lock you up as an enemy of the tribe, and you'll rot in a tribal jail for the rest of your miserable life."

"Maybe," says Cam, "but not without a trial—and everything I tell them will become a matter of public record."

Connor turns away from him, clenching his fists, growling in utter frustration—then turns back and finds Roland's hand swinging, connecting with Cam's jaw. Cam is knocked down, falling over a rickety wooden chair, and Connor prepares to hit him again. But then he looks at the arm. He holds eye contact with the shark. This might be satisfying, but it's not helping the situation. If he lets Roland's muscle memory rule that arm, then Connor loses more than just his temper. In a sense he loses a part of his soul.

"Stop," he tells the shark. Reluctantly, the muscles of Roland's fist relax. Cam is the prisoner here, not Connor. He has to remind himself that no matter how compromised he feels, he still has the upper hand in the situation. He reaches down, rights the chair, and backs away. "Take a seat," he tells Cam, folding his anger back in on itself.

Cam gets up off the dusty ground and pulls himself into the chair, rubbing his jaw. "That grafted arm of yours has its own set of talents, doesn't it? And is that someone else's eye, too? That puts you two steps closer to being just like me."

Connor knows Cam is trying to goad him into losing control again, but Connor won't let it happen. He brings the focus back to the matter at hand.

"You have nothing but a name and a city," Connor says, with relative calm. "It's more than I want you to know, but even if you bring it back to the people who made you, it won't make a difference. And Sonia's just a code name, anyway."

"A code name, huh?"

"Of course." Connor shrugs it off like it's nothing. "You don't think I'd be stupid enough to say a real name when anyone could hear."

Cam gives him a Cheshire smile. "Like a rug," he says. "I believe there's a brain bit in my right frontal lobe that's a BS detector, and it's pinging in the red."

"Believe what you want," Connor says with no choice but to stick to his story. "Una will keep you locked in this basement as long as she feels like it, and when she lets you go—*if* she lets you go—you can tell Proactive Citizenry whatever you want; they still won't find us."

"Why are you so convinced I'll crawl back to them? I already told you, I hate them just as much as you do."

"Do you expect me to believe you'd bite the hand that made you?" says Connor. "Yes, maybe you'd do it for Risa, but not for me. The way I see it, you'll go to them, and they'll take you back with open arms. The prodigal son returns."

And then Cam asks a question that will linger in Connor's mind for a long, long time. "Would you ever go back to the people who wanted to unwind you?"

The question throws Connor for a loop. "Wh—what has that got to do with anything?"

"Being rewound was a crime every bit as heinous as unwinding," Cam tells him. "I can't change the fact that I'm here, but I owe nothing to the people who rewound me. I would uncreate my creators if I could. I was hoping Risa would help me do that. But in her absence, it looks like I'll have to rely on you."

Although Connor doesn't trust him, there's a deep and indelible bruise to his words. His pain is real. His desire to bring down his creators is real.

"Prove it," Connor says. "Make me believe you want to tear them down as much as I do."

"If I do, will you take me with you?"

Connor has already realized they have little choice but to take him, but he plays this hand close. "I'll consider it."

Cam is silent for a moment, holding emotionless eye contact with Connor. Then he says "P, S, M, H, Y, A, R, E, H, N, L, R, A."

"What?"

"It's a thirteen-character ID on the public nimbus. As for the password, it's an anagram of Risa Ward. You'll have to figure it out for yourself."

"Why should I care what you have stored on the cloud?"

"You'll care when you see what it is."

Connor looks around the cluttered basement, finding a pen and a notepad among the debris on a table. He tosses them to Cam. "Write down the ID. Not all of us have photographic memories stitched into our heads. And I'm not guessing at passwords, so you'll write that down too."

Cam sneers at him, but obliges the request. When Cam is done, Connor takes the paper, putting it in his pocket for safekeeping, then locks Cam in the basement and returns to Una's apartment.

"I've decided to take Cam with us," he tells Lev and Grace, neither of whom seem surprised.

50 · Lev

He breaks the news to Connor in the morning—just a few hours before Pivane is due to take them to the car that's waiting for them outside the north gate. He thinks Connor will be furious, but that's not his reaction. Not at first. The look on Connor's face is one of pity—which Lev finds even worse than anger.

"They don't want you here, Lev. Whatever fantasy you've got in your head about staying here, you've gotta lose it. They don't want you."

It's only half-true, but it hurts to hear all the same. "It doesn't matter," he tells Connor. "It's what *I* want that matters, not what they want."

"So you're just going to disappear here? Pretend you're a ChanceFolk kid, living the simple life on the rez?"

"I think I can make a difference here."

"How? By going hunting with Pivane and reducing the rabbit population?" Now Connor's voice starts to rise as his anger comes to the surface. Good. Anger is something Lev can deal with.

"They need to start listening to outside voices. I can be that voice!" he tells Connor.

"Listen to yourself! After all you've been through, how can you still be so naive?"

Now it's Lev's turn to get angry. "*You're* the one who thinks talking to some old woman is going to change the world. If anyone is deluding themselves, it's you!"

That leaves Connor with nothing to say, maybe because he knows Lev is right.

"How can you walk away," Connor finally says, "when they're about to overthrow the Cap-17 law?"

"Do you really think anything you or I can do will change that?"

"Yes!" Connor yells. "I do. And I will. Or I'll die trying."

"Then you don't need my help. I'll just be an anchor around your neck. Let me do something useful here instead of just tagging along."

Connor's expression hardens. "Fine. Do whatever the hell you want. I don't care." Which he obviously does. Then he tosses a card at Lev, which he fumbles a bit before catching.

"What's this?"

"Read it. It was supposed to be your new identity once we left the rez."

It's a fake Arápache ID, with a bad picture of him he doesn't remember taking. The name on the ID is "Mahpee Kinkajou." It makes Lev smile. "I like it," Lev says. "I think I'll keep my new identity. What name did they give you?"

Connor looks at his own ID. "Bees-Neb Hebííte," Connor says. "Elina says it means 'stolen shark.'" He looks at the shark on his arm for a moment and opens his fingers, releasing his fist.

"Thank you for getting me out of the Graveyard," he tells

Lev, his anger resolving into a reluctant acceptance of the situation and maybe a begrudging respect for Lev's choice. "And thanks for saving me from the parts pirate. I'd probably be shipped around the world in pieces by now if it weren't for you."

Lev shrugs. "It's nothing. It wasn't so hard." Which they both know isn't true.

51 · Una

Una thought she'd be relieved that her obligation to Pivane was now over and her uninvited house guests would be leaving. However, the prospect of being alone with the knowledge of where Wil's hands have gone and where all his talent resides—a knowledge she can share with no one—is a difficult burden to bear. Things may go back to the way they were, but for Una, they will never be normal again.

She wishes her parents were here, or Elder Lenna, her mentor who left her the luthier shop—but they have all retired to Puerto Peñasco, a resort town on the Sea of Cortez that caters to ChanceFolk retirees. Perhaps Una could retire at nineteen—just pick up and move down there, spending her days like an old widow who never actually had the chance to marry.

The Tashi'nes are expected to come at nightfall, removing her guests and leaving her in ambivalent solitude. Now Cam will be going as well. She had thought she would be asked to sequester him a little while longer before flinging him back into the world, but he'll be gone with the others.

She busies herself that afternoon working on a new satinwood guitar, bending and bracing the sides by hand; then just before dark, she hears music coming from the basement.

She knows it must be Cam, and try as she might, she cannot bring herself to ignore it. She unlocks the door and slowly descends.

Cam sits in a chair, playing an old flamenco guitar he must have found in some forgotten corner and tuned on his own. The music coming from that old guitar seems to suck the oxygen out of the room. Una can't catch her breath. It's a powerful tune he plays, laden with rage and regret, but also with peaceful resolve. This is nothing Wil had ever played in his life, but is most definitely of Wil's unique composition.

Cam is too absorbed in the music to look up, but he knows Una is there. He must know. She doesn't want to speak, for words will break the spell woven by Wil's fingers on the strings. Cam crescendos, holds on the penultimate chord, then allows the song its conclusion, those final tones resonating in every hollow of the basement, including the hollow that Una knows resides within her. The silence that follows feels as important as the music that came before it, as if it's also a part of the piece. She finds she can't break that silence.

Finally Cam looks to her. "I wrote that for you," he says. The expression on his face is hard to read, for, like her, he is filled with the many emotions the song carried.

In some inexplicable way, Una feels violated. How dare he push so deeply into her with his music? *His* music, because Cam has layered his own soul upon Wil's. Something new, built upon the foundation laid down by the monsters who created him.

"Did you like it?" he asks.

How can she answer that question? That piece of music wasn't just *for* her; it *was* her. Somehow he distilled every ounce of her being into harmony and dissonance. He might as well ask if she likes herself—a question that has become just as complicated as the tonal qualities of the song.

Instead of answering, she says, with her voice catching in her throat, "Promise me you will never play that again."

Cam is surprised by her request. He considers it and says, "I promise that I will never play it for anyone but you." Then he puts down the guitar and stands. "Good-bye, Una. Knowing you has been"—he hesitates in search of the word—"necessary. For both of us, maybe."

Una finds herself drawn by his gravity, as she has been since he first appeared in her shop. Now she finds herself unable to resist it. She steps close to him. Looking to his left hand, she clasps it and caresses it. Then she looks to his right hand and takes it as well. Never looking up from those hands, she intertwines her fingers with his.

"You're not going to hit me with a rock again, are you?" he asks.

She closes her eyes, basking in the feel of those hands, which she loves still. She brings his right hand to her face, and he caresses her cheek. She feels that old shiver again, and this time she embraces the feeling, all the while hating herself for it.

Finally she looks into his eyes, unexpectedly shocked to see the eyes of a stranger. And as she kisses him, she knows she's kissing the lips of a stranger as well. How can his music be so in tune with her soul and the rest of him so disconnected? So out of joint? She should never have allowed this to happen, but she can't let go of his ill-gotten hands. And she finds it almost as hard to break away from the kiss.

"Once you leave here," she tells him, "never come back." And then she whispers desperately, passionately into his ear, "I despise you, Camus Comprix."

52 · Connor

They must travel by night, because a carload of young people is always suspect. At night it's easier to hide their identities, and the highway patrol will leave them alone as long as Connor doesn't speed or do anything to draw attention. Also, the car is a purple sedan. Not exactly low profile. Another reason why driving at night is called for.

"It was the best we could do," Elina told them as they saw them off. The Tashi'ne family had said their good-byes at Una's shop—and Una had volunteered to drive them to the car that was waiting just outside the northern gate of the reservation. It was the only way to keep Cam's presence a secret from them.

Lev's farewell to Connor was subdued and stilted, neither of them very good at saying good-bye.

"Do good. And stay whole," Lev had said to Connor.

Connor had thrown him the slightest of grins. "Get a haircut," he said, "by the next time I see you."

It's midnight when they cross from Colorado into Kansas. Cam and Grace are both in the back—Connor not trusting Cam enough to let him ride shotgun, but also not trusting him enough to leave him in the backseat by himself. With an unpleasant blast of déjà vu, Connor sees the sign for the Heartsdale exit and the approximate spot where he hit the ostrich. The bird is long gone, but Connor still grips the wheel, in case another one launches a suicide run into their path.

"Homesick, Grace?" he asks, as they near the town.

"Home *always* makes me sick," she says. "Drive on."

Connor finds himself holding his breath as they pass the exit, as if the place will reach out tentacles and drag them in.

Once they're past, the air in the car seems to lighten. Connor knows it's just his imagination, but he's grateful for the sense that their journey is back on track.

While Connor wants to drive through the night, drowsiness overtakes him a little after three in the morning.

"You can let me drive," Cam says. "There are a few excellent drivers in my internal community. I'm sure I can rally them to do the job."

"Thanks, but no thanks." Putting Cam in control of anything is still far beyond Connor's level of trust—and anyone who talks about an "internal community" really shouldn't be behind the wheel of an automobile anyway.

They pull off in the town of Russell, Kansas, in search of an inconspicuous place to spend the night. Most hotels require interaction with people, and any interaction will mean trouble, but like most interstate towns, there's an iMotel in Russell that dispenses its room keys via vending machine. All it requires is an ID and cash. As they stand before the vending kiosk, Cam grabs Connor's ID to look at it and is irritatingly amused.

"'Bees-Neb Hebííte.' There's a mouthful."

"He's the bees knees!" says Grace, and laughs.

Connor grabs the ID back and inserts it into the slot. "If it does the job, it's the best name in the world." Sure enough, the vending kiosk accepts the ID without a problem. Connor feeds in some of the money the Tashi'nes provided, and they have their room for the night. No worry, no hassle. They hunker down in a room with two beds that they'll have to share, but since only two of them will be asleep at any given time, the arrangement is just fine.

"You want me to keep an eye on Cam till dawn so's you can sleep?" Grace asks Connor, and although Cam protests that he doesn't need to be guarded, Grace sets herself up in a chair by the door, so even were she to doze, Cam would have to go through her to escape, and amuses herself by watching old war documentaries on the History Channel.

"I'd think you'd be more interested in the Game Show Network," Connor says innocently. "I mean, the way you like games."

Grace glares at him, insulted. "Those shows are all dumb luck and dumber people. I like watchin' wars. Strategy and tragedy all rolled up in one. Keeps your interest."

Connor falls asleep in minutes to the faint sounds of twentieth-century artillery barrages. He wakes a few hours later to the sun streaming in through a slit in the curtains and the TV playing old cartoons almost as violent as the war documentaries.

"Sorry," says Grace. "I couldn't close them tighter than that." Connor can hear activity in the rooms around them. Other muffled TVs, showers turning on and off, doors slamming as travelers leave to wherever it is they're going. Cam sleeps, without a care in the world it seems, and Connor relieves a grateful Grace, who takes Connor's space on the other bed and is snoring in a matter of minutes.

The room, which Connor had taken little notice of when they arrived, is the standard, unmemorable efficiency sleep space that dots highway off-ramps around the globe. Beige institutional furniture, dark carpet designed to hide stains. Comfortable beds to assure a return visit to the chain. There's also a computer interface built into the desk—also standard these days. Connor pulls out the slip of paper with the ID and password Cam had given him and logs in, to see if Cam's information is worth the trouble of having him along.

It turns out that Cam wasn't bluffing. Once logged in, he's given access to page after page of files Cam was hiding on the public nimbus. Files that had been digitally shredded but painstakingly reconstructed. These are communications within Proactive Citizenry that no one else was ever supposed to see. Much of it seems useless: Corporate e-mails that are mind-numbingly bland. Connor has to resist the urge to just skim through them. The more he reads however, the more key phrases begin to stand out. Things like "targeted demographic" and "placement in key markets." What's also curious are the domains where many of these e-mails are going to and coming from. These messages seem to be communications between the movers and shakers of Proactive Citizenry and media distributors, as well as production facilities. There are e-mails that discuss casting and expensive advertisements in all forms of media. It's pretty vague—intentionally so—but taken together it begins to point in some frightening directions.

Connor views some of the ads the communications seem to indicate. If Connor is piecing it all together correctly, then Proactive Citizenry, under different nonprofit names, is behind all the political adds in support of teenage unwinding. That's no surprise—in fact, Connor had already suspected that. What surprises him is that Proactive Citizenry is also behind the ads *against* the unwinding of teenagers but in favor of shelling prisoners and the voluntary unwinding of adults.

"Eye-opening, isn't it? Even if one of those eyes isn't yours."

Connor turns to see Cam sitting up in bed, watching him wade through the material. "And this is just the opening of the rabbit hole," Cam says. "I guarantee you there's darker, scarier stuff to find, the deeper we go."

"I don't get it." Connor points to the various windows of political ads on the desktop, ads that blast the Juvenile Authority and call the unwinding of kids unethical. "Why would Proactive Citizenry play both sides?"

"Two-headed coin," Cam says. Then he asks the strangest question. "Tell me, Connor, is this the first time you've been pregnant?"

"What?"

"Just answer the question, yes or no."

"Yes. I mean no! Shut up! What kind of stupid-ass question is that?"

Cam smiles. "You see? You're damned no matter how you answer. By playing both sides, Proactive Citizenry keeps people focused on choosing between two different kinds of unwinding, making people forget that the *real* question . . ."

"Is whether or not anyone should be unwound at all."

"Nail on the head," says Cam.

Now it makes perfect sense. Connor thinks back to all the things Trace Neuhauser had told him back in the Graveyard about the shrewd, insidious nature of Proactive Citizenry's dealings. Their subtle manipulation of the Juvenile Authority. The way they used the Admiral to warehouse Unwinds for them, all the while the Admiral—and then Connor—truly believing they were giving safe sanctuary to those kids.

"So whichever side wins, it keeps the status quo," Connor says. "People get unwound and the Unwinding Consortium still gets rich."

"The Unwinding Consortium?"

"It's what a friend once called all the people who make their money from unwinding. The companies who own the harvest camps, hospitals who do the transplants, the Juvenile Authority . . ."

Cam considers it with a single raised eyebrow that throws the symmetrical seams on his forehead out of balance and says. "All roads lead to Rome. Unwinding is the single most profitable industry in America—maybe even the world. An economic engine like that protects itself. We'll have to be smarter than they are to break it down." And then Cam smiles. "But they made one big mistake."

"What's that?"

"They built someone who's smarter than they are."

Cam and Connor pore over the information for another hour. But there's so much, it's hard to pull out what's important and what's not.

"There are financial records," Cam tells Connor. "They show huge amounts of money disappearing, as if into a black hole."

"Or a rabbit hole," suggests Connor.

"Exactly. If we can figure out where that money's going, I think we'll have the sword upon which Proactive Citizenry will impale itself." Then Cam gets quiet. "I think they're funding something very, very dark. I'm almost afraid to find out what it is."

And although Connor won't admit it, he is too.

53 · Bam

She carries out orders. She takes care of the new arrivals. She tries not to think about the MoonCrater five. That's what the media calls the harvest camp workers whom Starkey hung. They're martyrs now—evidence, according to some political pundits, of why certain incorrigible teens simply need to be unwound.

Two storks were killed and seven injured in the fake battle that Bam waged at the outer gate, for while Bam and her team weren't actually trying to kill anyone, the guards firing at them were. That they even made it out of there was a miracle. In the end, their assault served its purpose. It appeared to be a botched attempt to break into the camp—until the security force released the dormitory building from lockdown and found what they found.

Five people lynched in the MoonCrater dormitory.

The pictures are as disturbing as anything Bam has seen in history books.

Busy. She must keep herself busy. The storks were separated from the nonstorks right after they arrived back at the mine. This time rather than just leaving the unchosen to fend for themselves in the middle of nowhere, Bam arranged for them to be taken to Boise—the nearest major city. They'd be on their own, but at least they'd have the camouflage of concrete and crowds to keep them hidden. And who knows, maybe the ADR will find them and give them sanctuary. That is if the ADR even exists anymore.

Five people.

The boys' head counselor, a janitor, an office worker, a chop-shop nurse, and the chef's boyfriend, who was visiting the wrong place on the wrong weekend.

And now, thanks to the one woman whose life he spared, everyone knows the name Mason Michael Starkey.

"Congratulations," she told him when she had calmed down enough to speak to him without raging. "You're now Public Enemy Number One." To her disbelief, it actually made him smile.

"How could that possibly be a good thing?"

"I'm feared," he told her. "I'm a force to be reckoned with. They know that now."

And in the two days since the MoonCrater liberation, the fervent, ferocious, and almost viral support he gets from storks attests to his new larger-than-life status. It's not just from the Stork Brigade, either. Whole online communities have sprung up out of nowhere. "Storks unite!" they proclaim and "Ride, Starkey, ride," like he's some sort of Jesse James robbing stagecoaches. It seems everyone who's ever known him has tried to hop on his coattails to steal their own fifteen minutes of fame, posting stories and pictures of him, so the world knows every bit of his pre-AWOL life and every angle of his face.

It comes to light that he shot and killed one of the Juvey-rounders who picked him up from his home for unwinding, painting him in an even more dangerous light—and yet incredibly, the more vilified he is by polite society, the more support he gets from the disenfranchised.

Wrap it all together, and Starkey has achieved exactly what he wanted. His name has eclipsed the name of Connor Lassiter.

Because he hung five people in cold blood. Who knows how many it will be next time?

No! Bam can't let herself think that way. It's her job to shed light on the positive side. Hundreds of Unwinds saved. A rattling of the status quo. Bam reminds herself that she agreed to be a part of this. Back in the airplane graveyard, Starkey had put his faith in her when no one else would. He chose her to be his second in command in all things—if not his confidant, then at least his sounding board. She owes him allegiance in spite of everything. He's taken on this mission to be the Savior of Storks, to be a voice for the voiceless, and he's succeeding. Who is she to question his methods?

But Hayden has been questioning since the moment he arrived, if only to her and only when she will put up with it. He defied Starkey right to his face, though, when he found out about the hangings, refusing to return to the computer, wanting nothing to do with the next liberation. Starkey was furious, of course. He roared like a hurricane, but Hayden, who Bam never thought had much of a backbone, stood up to him.

"I won't work for a terrorist," Hayden had told him. "So behead me right here, or get the hell out of my face." Had it been in front of anyone other than Bam and Jeevan, Starkey might actually have obliged an old-fashioned head rolling, to set an example for the storks. Those of them who still believed Hayden had collaborated with the Juvies would have welcomed it. But then Starkey's anger suddenly broke and he began laughing, which somehow gave him more power in the moment than his anger had. If you can't win, then make a joke out of it. That had always been Hayden's MO, but Starkey had now stolen that from him.

"Never try to be serious, Hayden—it's too funny." Then he put Hayden back on food inventory, as if it had been his plan all along. "A menial job for a mediocre mind."

Well, apparently, Hayden's mind isn't as mediocre as Starkey would like to think, because a day and a half later, Starkey sends Bam on a mission to coax Hayden back to the computer room. As if she'll have any more sway than Starkey. Gentle persuasion is not one of Bam's gifts—and Hayden has already shown that he won't be bullied. It's a fool's errand, but lately, she's been feeling very much the fool.

She finds Hayden in the supply room, sitting against a support beam in that central patch of darkness. He's not doing much in terms of inventory and distribution, it seems. Although he's writing in the inventory notebook. When the guard on Hayden duty sees her, he stands and hefts his weapon, trying to pretend like he hadn't been dozing on a sack of rice.

Hayden doesn't even look up at her as she approaches.

"Why are you writing in the dark?"

"Because I'm such an awful writer, it's best no one sees it—not even me."

She steps into the pool of darkness to find it's not all that dark after all. It just seems that way when coming from the lighter edge. He doesn't stand up to greet her; he just continues writing.

"So what is it?"

"I'm keeping a journal of my time here. That way, when it's our turn to hang for the things we're doing, there'll be a record of what really happened. I'm calling it 'Starkey's Inferno,' although I'm not quite sure which level of hell this is."

"They don't hang people anymore," Bam points out. Then she thinks of Starkey's lynchings. "Or at least they don't hang people officially."

"True. I suppose they'll just shell us. Or at least they will if those shelling laws pass." He closes the notebook and looks up at her for the first time. "The Egyptians were the first to think of shelling. Did you know that? They mummified their leaders to preserve their bodies for the afterlife—but before they sent them on their unmerry way, they sucked their brains out of their heads." He pauses to consider it. "Geniuses, those Egyptians. They knew the last thing a pharaoh needs is a brain of his own, or he might do some real damage."

Finally he stands to face her. "So what are you doing here, Bam? What do you want?"

"We need you to show Jeevan how to break through firewalls. You don't have to do any of the breaking; you just need to show him."

"Jeevan knows how to defeat firewalls—he did it all the time at the Graveyard. If he's not doing it, it's because he doesn't want to but he's afraid to tell the Stork Lord."

"The Stork Lord—is that what the media's calling him now?"

"No. It's my own term of endearment," Hayden admits. "But if they did start calling him that, I'm sure Starkey would love it. I'll bet he'd build himself an altar so that the common folk may worship in song and sacrifice. Which reminds me—I've been toying with the idea of an appropriate Stork Lord salute. It's like a heil Hitler thing, but with just the middle finger. Like so." He demonstrates, and it makes Bam laugh.

"Hayden, you really are an asshole."

"Coming from you, I take that as a compliment." He gives

her a hint of his condescending smirk. She's actually glad to
see it.

He hesitates for a moment, takes a glance over at his guard,
who is dozing on the rice again; then he steps closer to her and
says quietly, "You'd be a better leader than Starkey, Bam."

There's silence between them. Bam finds she can't even
respond to that.

"You can't tell me you haven't thought of it," Hayden says.

He's right; she has thought about it. And she also dismissed
the idea before it could take root. "Starkey has a mission," she
tells him. "He has a goal. What do I have?"

Hayden shrugs. "Common sense? A survival instinct? Good
bone structure?"

Bam quickly decides this is not a conversation she's going to
have. "Put down the notebook and start doing your job. There
wasn't enough food yesterday—make sure there is tonight."

He gives her a middle-finger heil, and she leaves, chucking
a potato at the sleeping guard to wake him up.

It's that afternoon when Bam's world, already dangerously
off-kilter, turns upside down entirely. It's because of the Prissies. That's always been her special word for the kind of girls
she hates most. Dainty little things who have lived a carefree
life of privilege, whose troubles are limited to choice of nail
color and boyfriend woes and whose names sound normal but
are weirdly spelled. Even among the Stork Brigade there are
girls who qualify as Prissies, ever aloof and pretentious even
as their clothes tatter into rags. Somehow, in spite of all the
hardships they've endured, they manage to be pretty and petty
and as shallow as an oil slick.

There are three in particular who have formed their own
little click over the past few weeks. Two are sienna, one umber,
and all three are annoyingly beautiful. They didn't participate

in either harvest camp liberation—in fact, they never seem to do much of anything but talk among themselves and whisper derision of others. More than once Bam has heard them snarking behind her back about her height, her arguably mannish figure, and her general demeanor. She avoids them on principle, but today Bam's feeling belligerent. She wants to pick a fight, or at least to make others feel miserable—and who better to make miserable than girls who have a dainty figure instead of good bone structure?

She finds them in the area of the mine designated as "girls only." It's where they go to avoid unwanted advances from the hormonal male population when they've tired of flirting. Bam hasn't noticed them flirting lately. She doesn't think anything of it at first.

"Starkey needs munitions moved deeper into the mine," she tells them. "I've elected you three to do it. Try not to blow yourselves up."

"Why are you telling us?" Kate-Lynn asks. "Get some of the boys to do it."

"Nope. It's your turn today."

"But I'm not supposed to be lifting heavy things," whines Emmalee.

"Right," says Makayla. "None of us are."

"According to who?"

They look at one another like none of them wants to say. Finally Emmalee becomes the spokeswoman of the clique. "Well . . . according to Starkey."

That Starkey would give special privileges to the Prissies irritates Bam even further. Well, she's his workhorse around this place—she can take away any privileges she chooses.

"Every stork contributes," Bam tells them. "Get off your lazy butts and get to work."

Makayla whispers something into Kate-Lynn's ear, and

Kate-Lynn throws a telepathic sort of gaze at Emmalee, who shakes her head and turns back to Bam, offering an apologetic smile that's not apologetic at all.

"We really do have special permission directly from Starkey," she says.

"Permission to do nothing? I don't think so."

"Not to do nothing, but to take care of ourselves. And each other," Kate-Lynn says.

"Right," parrots Makayla. "Ourselves and each other."

Every word out of their mouths makes Bam want to just slap them silly. "What on earth are you talking about?"

They share that three-way telepathic gaze again; then Emmalee says, "We're really not supposed to talk about this with you."

"Really. Did Starkey tell you that?"

"Not exactly." Finally Emmalee rises to face Bam, holding her gaze and speaking slowly. "We have to take care of ourselves . . . because Starkey's made us unwind proof." Bam is not a stupid girl. She's not much when it comes to school smarts, because her attitude always got in the way—but she's always been a quick study in the school of life. This, however, is so far out of the realm of Bam's concept of reality, she just doesn't get it.

Now the other Prissies stand. Makayla puts a sympathetic hand on Bam's shoulder. "Unwind proof for nine months," she says. "Do you understand now?"

It hits her like a mortar blast. She actually stumbles back into the wall. "You're lying! You have to be!"

But now that it's out, their eyes take on a strange ecstatic look. *They're telling the truth! My God, they're telling the truth!*

"He's going to be a great man," Kate-Lynn says. "He already is."

"We might all be storks, but his children won't be," says another. Bam doesn't even know which one it is. They're all the same to her now. Three talking heads on a single body, like some horrible, beautiful hydra.

"He promises he'll take care of us."

"All of us."

"He swears he will."

"And you don't know what it's like."

"You *can't* know what it's like."

"To be chosen by him."

"To be touched by greatness."

"So we can't carry munitions today."

"Or tomorrow."

"Or ever."

"So sorry, Bam."

"Yes, so sorry."

"We hope you can understand."

Bam storms through the maze of the mine in search of Starkey, losing track of where she's been, her thoughts and emotions in such a tailspin, it's all she can do not to blow up like a clapper.

She finds him at the computer looking over Jeevan's shoulder at their next target, but right now, there's no room for that on Bam's radar. She's out of breath from running through the mine. She knows her emotions are on her sleeve, staining as brightly as blood. She knows she should have just run deeper into the mine and paced and stewed and broiled until her anger and disgust had faded. But she couldn't do it.

"When were you going to tell me?"

Starkey regards her for a moment, takes a sip from his canteen, and sends Jeevan away. He knows from the look on her face exactly what she's talking about. How could he not know?

"Why do you think it's your business?"

"I am your second in command. You don't keep secrets from me!"

"There a difference between a secret and discretion."

"Discretion? Don't you dare talk to me about discretion after scoring your little hat trick."

"This is a dangerous thing I'm doing out there. I'm not entirely blind to that. I know it might be messed up, but I want to leave something behind if I don't survive—and it's not like I forced them."

"You never force anyone, do you, Mason? You just hypnotize them. You dazzle them. And before you know it, people are willing to do anything for you."

Then Starkey slices through to the one thing hanging in the air between them—the one thing that shouldn't be said.

"You're just pissed off because you're not one of them."

Bam slaps him so hard he stumbles, nearly knocking over the computer. And when he comes back at her, anger in his eyes, she's ready. She grabs his ruined hand and squeezes it. Hard. The reaction is immediate. His legs buckle beneath him, and he falls to his knees. She squeezes harder.

"Let . . . go . . . ," he squeaks. "Please . . . let . . . go. . . ."

She grips his hand a moment longer, then releases it, prepared for whatever he does to her next. Let him throw her to the ground. Let him spit in her face. Let him hit her and hit her again. At least that would be something. At least there'd be some passion from him launched in her direction.

Instead of retaliating, he just grabs his ruined hand, rises, and closes his eyes until the pain passes.

"After all I've done for you," she says. "After all I've been for you, you go off with *them*?"

"Bambi, please—"

"Don't call me that! *Never* call me that!"

"If it were you instead of them, you couldn't be out there with me changing the world, could you? It would be too dangerous!"

"You could have given me the choice!"

"And then what? How could you be my second if *that's* between us?"

Bam finds she has no answer to that, and Starkey must know he's having an effect on her, because he takes a step closer. His voice becomes kinder. "Don't you know how much you mean to me, Bam? What we have is something I'll never have with those girls."

"And what they have, I'll never have."

He regards her. Gauging. Assessing. "Is that what you really want, Bam? Is that what would make you happy? Really?" Then he steps deep into her airspace. She's so tall that standing this close, he seems even shorter than he really is.

He cranes his neck to kiss her, but their lips are still an inch away, and instead of suffering the indignation of rising on his tiptoes, he reaches behind her head, pulling her down into the kiss. That kiss is like a conjurer's act. It's artful, it's worthy of applause, it is everything Bam ever dreamed it might be . . . but nothing will change the fact that it's only a trick, and today there is no audience to applaud it.

"I'm sorry I hurt you, Bam. And you're right; you deserve something real from me."

"That wasn't real, Mason."

He offers her something between a grin and a grimace. "It's as real as I get."

Bam wanders the mine, feeling spent in every possible way. Her fury at Starkey no longer knows where to go. Neither do any of her emotions. She feels the longing for something unnamable that's been lost. If she were more naive, she'd call it her innocence, but Bambi Ann Covalt has not been innocent for a very long time.

She bumps her head hard on a rock jutting from the low-slung ceiling. She doesn't even realize where she was going until her head smacks that rock.

"You again?" Hayden says when he sees her. This time, he's actually loading a cart with food for the evening meal.

Bam turns to his guard. "Go get me something to drink."

He looks confused. "But all the water and stuff is in here."

"Fine. Then go get me some sushi!"

"Huh?"

"Could you really be that stupid? Just get the hell out of here!"

"Yes, Miss Bam." He hurries out, practically tripping over his weapon.

Hayden is amused. "'Miss Bam.' Sounds like a good name for a kindergarten teacher. Have you ever considered the profession?"

"I don't like children."

"You don't like adults much either. Or, for that matter, anything in between."

For some reason, that makes tears rise like bile in her, but she bears down and holds them in, refusing to let Hayden see them.

"You're bleeding," Hayden says. Concerned, he takes a step toward her, but she waves him off.

"I'm fine." She touches her head. There's a small cut where she bumped it on the ceiling. The least of her problems. She'll make an appointment with the kid with the dental floss. "We need to talk."

"About?"

She checks to make sure the guard hasn't come back and they are truly alone. "I promised you'd have my ear. So bend it. Now."

54 · Force

The raid comes without warning, like a team of Juvie-rounders in the night. A *real* special-ops team—nothing like the playacting kids Starkey calls special ops. The invaders tranq the storks guarding the entrance to the mine before they can even raise their weapons and flood into the tunnels, tranq'ing anyone who comes into view. Their directive is simple: Get to Mason Starkey.

The commotion wakes kids deeper in the mine in time for them to scramble for weapons, which they've learned to use without hesitation and without fear. They bring several of the intruders down, but there are more behind them—and this force is armed with weapons the storks have never seen: squad machine guns that spray tiny tranq-tipped darts at such an alarming rate, they create an inescapable wall of unconsciousness before them. The layers of protection surrounding Starkey peel away until he's exposed and vulnerable before the invading force.

Starkey swings his own weapon up, but fumbles with it just long enough for his attackers to grab it and grab him.

The entire operation is over in less than five minutes.

55 · Starkey

It was madness to believe he was untouchable. He knows that now. The storks' hiding place was well concealed, but the Juvies are skilled at ferreting out the most resistant of AWOLs. Starkey struggles, but it's no use—and his ruined hand is in such pain from the iron grip of his assailants that the rest of his body drains of strength, just as it had when Bam had grabbed him.

All around him in the tunnels are the unconscious bodies of his precious storks with tiny spots of blood dotting their clothes where the tranq darts embedded in their skin. No one's fighting anymore. Anyone still conscious is on the run. The storks know they are outarmed and outclassed.

"Go deeper into the mine!" Starkey yells to them. "Deep as you can go. Don't let them take you alive."

Although he's terrified, he holds in his heart the anger that he's wielded so well and the knowledge that as a martyr he will live forever.

Wind whips the entrance of the mine, but it's not a natural wind. A helicopter darker than the night descends from above, tumbleweeds exploding out from its landing spot, as if racing to escape its crushing weight. This time Starkey has no trick up his sleeve to escape capture, so he embraces it. *I am important enough to be taken by helicopter*, he thinks.

The door is opened, and he's thrown inside, landing on all fours. His left hand feels like it will shatter all over again. *Why don't they tranq me? I can't bear this. I want it over.*

He feels the vertical acceleration of the helicopter lifting off, and when he looks up, he sees within this large industrial helicopter a sight he was not expecting. The space, rather than being filled with steel restraining chairs, is richly appointed. It's a lavish sanctuary of leather, brass, and polished wood, more like the cabin of a yacht than the inside of a helicopter.

A man in dress slacks and a comfortable sweater sits in one of several plush chairs facing a television screen. He pauses the TV with a remote, swivels to face Starkey—and Starkey wonders, as nausea and disorientation fill him, if maybe he was tranq'd after all, and this is a momentary hallucination before he passes out entirely. But his vision holds; the scene before him is real, and his dizziness is nothing more than the motion of the helicopter.

"Mason Michael Starkey," says the man. "I've been looking forward to meeting you."

He has dark hair, graying at the temples. He speaks crisp English with no hint of any regional accent and diction so perfect, it's unsettling.

"What's going on?" Starkey asks, knowing he must, even if he doesn't want to know the answer.

"Not what you think," the man tells him. "Come sit. We have things to discuss." He points a remote at the TV, starting a paused recording. It's a collection of news bytes, all featuring Starkey. "You're an overnight sensation," the man says.

Starkey rallies his fortitude and struggles to stand. The helicopter lists slightly starboard, and he has to hold the wall for balance. He moves no closer.

"Who are you?"

"A friend. That's all you really need to know, isn't it? As for my name, well, a name is a curious thing. Names can define us, and I do not wish to be defined. At least not in the current context."

Starkey, however, overheard a name mentioned while he was being captured. In the turmoil, he hadn't grasped it, but he does remember the first letter. "Your last name," says Starkey in defiance of the man, "starts with a 'D.'"

The man bristles, but only slightly. He pats the chair beside him. "Please sit, Mason. You never know when we'll hit some unexpected turbulence."

Reluctantly Starkey takes a seat. He figures this guy is going to try to offer him a deal—but what kind of deal could it possibly be? They've already captured him and the Stork Brigade. Perhaps they think he knows the whereabouts of Connor Lassiter—but even if he did, Starkey's now a bigger prize for the Juvenile Authority. Why would they even negotiate?

"You've created quite a lot of consternation and confusion out there," the man says. "People hate you; people love you—"

"I don't care what people think," Starkey snarls.

"Oh, you most certainly do," the man says with such condescension, Starkey wants to strike out at him but knows that wouldn't be wise. "We should all monitor our image in this world. Give it the proper spin to meet our best interests."

He knows this man is toying with him, but toward what end? Starkey hates this sense of not being in control.

Finally the man turns off the TV and swivels his chair so that he's fully facing Starkey. "I represent a movement that very much approves of your actions and the apparent madness of your methods because we know it's not madness at all."

Again, this is not what Starkey was expecting. "A movement?"

"I'd call it an organization, but just like a name, it would define us far more than would be prudent."

"You still haven't told me what you want."

He smiles broadly. It is neither warm nor comforting. "We want the liberation of harvest camps, and more to the point, the punishment of those who run them. That's something we'd very much like to see more of."

This still feels like it must be a trick. "Why?"

"Our movement thrives on chaos because disruption brings about change."

Starkey suspects he knows what the man is talking about, although he's almost afraid to say the word aloud. "Clappers?"

He offers that cool smile again. "You'd be amazed how deep the roots of the movement go and how committed people are. We'd like you to join us, if you're willing."

Starkey shakes his head. "I will not become a clapper."

The man actually laughs. "No, we're not asking you to.

What a waste that would be for everyone. We simply want to help you in your efforts in any way we can."

"And what do you want in return?"

The man turns on the video again. On the screen is a shot looking down the long room of the girls' dormitory at Moon-Crater and the five lifeless workers lynched from ceiling fans. "More iconic images such as you've created here," he says brightly. "Images that will haunt the souls of mankind for generations."

Starkey considers the scope of the undertaking. The power it will bring for the storks. The notoriety it will bring him. "I can do that."

"I hoped you would say that. We have a wealth of state-of-the-art weaponry and dedicated, if somewhat fanatical, followers willing to sacrifice themselves to create trigger points of mayhem." Then he holds out his hand for Starkey to shake—but it's his left hand held out, not his right. He's done that intentionally. "Consider us your partner, Mason." And although Starkey's left hand is still throbbing with pain, he extends it and lets the man grasp it. He bites back the searing sting, because Starkey knows, when it comes to alliances, it's the pain that seals the pact.

The helicopter flight is a journey to nowhere. It circles back when the conversation is over and the partnership has been struck, leaving Starkey off where he was picked up, near the entrance to the mine.

There is a heightened sense of reality to everything around Starkey now. A sense that he's not so much walking but levitating a fraction of an inch above the ground. As he steps into the cavelike entrance of the mine, everything around him seems to be moving differently—not so much in slow motion, but a sort of lateral peeling, as if the world is parting for his presence. Kids in the mine are beginning to regain consciousness. The fast-acting tranq darts were also short-lived, for the purpose was not to catch the storks but to incapacitate them long enough to pull Starkey out for his summit meeting.

Kids who managed to avoid the darts are doing their best to revive the others. When they see Starkey, they stand in awe. It must be what the kids at Happy Jack felt when they saw Connor Lassiter walking out of the Chop Shop alive.

"He escaped!" they yell, relaying the good news down into the deeper tunnels of the mine. "Starkey escaped!"

Jeevan comes up to him. "What happened?" he asks. "How did you get away? Why didn't they take us?"

"No one's taking us anywhere," Starkey tells him. "We've got a lot of work to do—but it can wait until morning." He orders the unconscious to be covered with blankets and moves through the mine, calming fears and telling everyone to get a good night's rest. "We have exciting days ahead."

"Where did they take you?" a wide-eyed stork asks.

"Into the sky," Starkey tells him. "And we have friends in very high places."

56 · Hayden

Supplies come like manna from the heavens. The food is far superior to anything they've been subsisting on. Vacuum-packed roasts that need no refrigeration. Vegetables in such quantities they don't need to ration. Hayden finds his inventory job becomes a full-time endeavor. But it's the other things that these new "partners" bring that is deeply disturbing to Hayden. There are weapons coming in that are like nothing Hayden's ever seen. Things like bazookas and what looks like hand-held missile launchers that are heavier than the kids who are supposed to wield them. Starkey has said nothing about who these new benefactors are, and Hayden wonders who would be insane enough to arm angry teenagers with weapons that were clearly meant for armies. More terrifying, though, is how Starkey might use them.

Starkey doesn't bother with Hayden anymore. As far as Starkey is concerned, Hayden's a nonentity, too small to be concerned with but too dangerous to let go.

"Why haven't you escaped yet?" Bam asks Hayden. "There were so many times you could have slipped away from that one inept guard."

"And leave all you fine people?" Hayden says. "I wouldn't dream of it."

The fact is, as much as he wants to bolt from this night-mare and save himself, he can't do it knowing that he's leav-ing all these kids to burn in the furnace of Starkey's ego. Yes, many of them worship the ground Starkey walks on, but only because they desperately need a hero. Hayden has no desire to be a hero. He just wants to survive and spread some of that survival around.

As Hayden feared, Starkey picks the Stork Brigade's next target quickly. Jeevan has broken down and used his skills to get through the firewalls. Now they have all the information they need for an attack. This time it won't be a subtle, secret attack, or even a mad dash at the gate. The storks will be going in with an iron fist. Hayden considers himself smart, crafty even, but he can't figure out a way to stop Starkey short of put-ting a bullet in his head, which Hayden just can't do.

Bam had asked Hayden to bend her ear and tell her what he thinks, as well as what he knows—and so as Starkey pre-pares his storks for the next attack, Hayden takes Bam to the computer room and shows her some of the things he's been finding out there in the world.

He begins to pull up one political advertisement after another. "There have been more and more of these online and on TV. They're blitzing the airwaves." He shows her impassioned calls to rescind the Cap-17 law and allow older teens to be unwound again.

There are advertisements about measures, propositions, and initiatives on the ballots calling for the mandatory unwinding of teenaged "undesirables," the further downsizing of state orphanages through unwinding, state bonds to build more harvest camps, and more.

Bam dismisses it. "So what? There are always a ton of those ads out there. There's nothing new about that."

"Yes, but look at this." He shows her a graph depicting the frequency the ads have been appearing. "Look how the ads started to flood the airwaves right after the Cold Springs liberation—and then they almost doubled after MoonCrater." Hayden takes a moment to look around to make sure they're unobserved but speaks in a whisper anyway. "Everything the Stork Brigade does might be freeing kids from harvest camps, but people out there are getting scared, Bam—and all of these laws that didn't have a hope in hell of passing a few months ago are now gaining more and more support. Starkey wants a war, right? But as soon as people see it as war, they'll have to choose sides, and the more fear there is, the more people lean toward the side of the Juvenile Authority. Which means that if it turns into a war . . . we lose."

Hayden can already imagine the results. Martial law would be declared against juveniles, just as it had during the teen uprising. Kids will be dragged from their homes and unwound for the slightest infractions, and the public will allow it to happen, out of fear.

"For every harvest camp we bring down, two more will pop up in its place." He leans close to her, trying to drive the point home. *"Starkey's not stopping unwinding, Bam. All he's doing is making sure it never, ever ends!"*

He can see by the pale look on Bam's face that she's finally getting it. He continues. "These people funding Starkey's war may want to mess with the system, but that kind of messing will only make the system stronger and give the Juvenile Authority more power."

Then Bam says something that Hayden hasn't even considered. "What if that's what they want? What if the people funding Starkey want the Juvies to have more power?"

And Hayden shivers, because he realizes Bam may have just found a vein in this old mine that leads right to the mother lode.

57 · Lev

All is peaceful. All is calm. The oasis of the Arápache Rez hides the reality of what's going on beyond its gates and walls. Calls to rescind Cap-17 and raise the legal age of unwinding back to eighteen and possibly beyond. Removing the brains of convicted criminals and unwinding the rest of their bodies. Allowing people to voluntarily submit themselves to unwinding for cash. It's all looming on the horizon, and any or all of it might come to pass, and worse, if it's not stopped. Like Connor, he knows he must do something.

"Throw a stone in a river, and it just sinks to the bottom," Elina tells him, "Put a boulder in its path and the river just flows around. What happens will happen, no matter what you do."

Elina has many fine qualities, but her passive, fatalistic view of the world is not one of them. Unfortunately, too many people on the rez share it.

"Enough boulders builds a dam," Lev counters.

Elina opens her mouth to deliver another metaphoric salvo—perhaps about how dams burst, causing floods worse than a river—but she thinks better of it and instead says, "Have some breakfast; you'll be less cranky."

Lev complies, munching down on yam cakes that, according to Elina, used to be served with agave syrup, but since the agave extinction, they've had to make due with maple. Lev can't deny that part of his choice to stay here was to be sheltered from the world, among people whom he genuinely cares for, and genuinely care for him, but there was a larger purpose for it.

There's an expression among ChanceFolk. "As go the Arápache, so go the nations." As the most financially successful, and arguably the most politically important ChanceFolk tribe, policy that's put in place here often spreads to other tribes. While the Arápache are still the most isolationist, instituting borders that require passports, many other tribes—particularly the ones that don't rely on tourism—have made their territory harder to access as well, taking their lead from the Arápache. On the outside, most people have no idea how many boulders are already in the river. If Lev can find a way to pull those boulders together, the course of history may very well change.

The problem is Wil Tashi'ne and what happened the first time Lev was here.

Like Una, the Arápache see Lev as a harbinger of doom. A victim of his own society perhaps, but like a bearer of the plague, he brings to them a taste of things they'd rather not know about. If he's going to have any sway here, he's going to have to win them over.

On Saturday he tells the Tashi'nes he's going into town.

"There's a band playing in Héétee Park," he tells them. "I'd like to hear them."

"Do you think it's wise to be so visible?" Chal asks him. "The council is happy to look the other way as long as you keep a low profile, but the more visible you are, the more likely they are to take issue with your presence."

"I can't hide forever," he tells him. He keeps to himself what he's really planning.

Although Kele begs to come, he's been grounded for cursing in Arápache—something he thought he could get away with, but didn't. A good thing too. The last thing Lev wants is to put Kele in the middle of this. He needs to go alone.

The concert has already started when Lev arrives. There are maybe two hundred people spread out on blankets and lawn chairs picnicking and enjoying the warm August day. The band is good. They play a curious mix of traditional native music, pop, and oldies. Something for everyone.

Lev lingers, trying to be as inconspicuous as possible, but he sees the occasional person spot him and whisper to the person beside them. Well, they'll have plenty more to gossip about in a few minutes.

Lev makes his way toward the front, and as soon as the band finishes their first set, he pulls two pieces of paper from his pocket and climbs to the stage. He pulls the lead singer's microphone down a few inches so he can speak without it blocking his face.

"Excuse me," he says. "Excuse me, can I have your attention!" He's startled by how loud and resonant his voice sounds. "My name is Levi Jedediah Garrity—but you probably know me as Lev Calder. I was a *Mahpee* taken in by the Tashi'ne family."

"We know who you are," someone shouts dismissively from the audience. "Now get off the stage."

A smattering of agreement—some derisive laughter. He

ignores it all. "I was there when Wil Tashi'ne offered himself to parts pirates in exchange for more than a dozen lives—including mine. Although one of the parts pirates died there, the two who lived took Wil, sold him to be unwound, and got away."

"Yeah, tells us something we don't know," yells another heckler.

"I plan to," Lev says. "Because I've found out their names, and I know where to find them."

Then he holds out the two pieces of paper—each one featuring an enlarged image of a parts pirate. One with a missing ear, the other with a face like a goat.

Suddenly the entire crowd is silent.

"Chandler Hennessey and Morton Fretwell. They hunted AWOLs for a while in Denver, but now they're trolling Minneapolis." Then he puts the pictures down and gets as close to the microphone as he can. "I'm going to track them down and bring them back here to face justice." And then, in perfect Arápache:

"Who will help me?"

The silence continues.

"I said, who will help me?"

For a long moment, Lev thinks no one will come forward, but then he hears a single voice—a woman's voice—from the back of the crowd.

"I will," she says in Arápache.

It's Una. Lev hadn't even seen her here. He's both grateful and troubled. He was hoping to put together a good old-fashioned posse. If it's just the two of them, what chance do they have of bringing in these pirates? What chance do they have of even surviving the attempt?

As Una moves through the crowd toward the stage, someone shouts, "C'mon! Clap for the clapper!"

People begin applauding. It starts slow, but it builds until the crowd is cheering by the time Una reaches the stage. Now any doubts he had are gone. His bid to win over the Arápache people has begun—and if he succeeds, he knows he'll be able to pull them into the battle against unwinding. He'll finally have his dam!

"Are you sure you know what you're doing, little brother?" Una asks him over the cheering crowd.

Lev smiles at her. "I've never been more sure of anything in my life."

Part Six

Akron

TERRORISTS PLAN ATTACK ON BRITAIN WITH BOMBS
INSIDE THEIR BODIES TO FOIL NEW AIRPORT
SCANNERS

By Christopher Leake, Mail On Sunday Home Affairs Editor

UPDATED: 17:01 EST, 30 January 2010

Until now, terrorists have attacked airlines, underground trains, and buses by secreting bombs in bags, shoes, or underwear to avoid detection. But an operation by MI5 has uncovered evidence that Al Qaeda is planning a new stage in its terror campaign by inserting "surgical bombs" inside people for the first time.

A leading source added that male bombers would have the explosive secreted near their appendix or in their buttocks, while females would have the material placed inside their breasts in the same way as figure-enhancing implants.

Experts said the explosive PETN (Pentaerythritol tetranitrate) would be placed in a plastic sachet inside the bomber's body before the wound was stitched up like a normal operation incision and allowed to heal.

Security sources fear the body bombers could pretend to be diabetics injecting themselves in order to prevent anyone stopping their suicide missions.

Patrick Mercer, chairman of the Commons Counterterrorism Sub-committee, said: "Our enemies are constantly evolving their techniques to try to defeat our methods of detection. This is one of the most savage forms that extremists could use, and while we are redeveloping travel security, we have got to take this new development into account."

Senior government security sources confirmed last night that they were aware of the new threat of body bombs, but were not prepared to make any official comment.

Published by permission of The Mail on Sunday.

See the full article here:

http://www.dailymail.co.uk/news/article-1247338/Terrorists-plan-attack-Britain-bombs-INSIDE-bodies-foil-new-airport-scanners.html

The Rheinschilds

Dr. Janson Rheinschild sits in a chair, in a room, in the dark, alone. His wife has gone to bed, but he cannot. After spending so many hours in bed, for so many weeks, he's plagued by crushing insomnia, an unyielding headache, and a hollowness in his soul that he cannot describe.

Were he more shallow, he could be a very happy man—after all, he's got millions in his bank account. He and Sonia could go anywhere they want and live out their lives in extravagant luxury. . . . But what would be the point? And where can they go that they won't be reminded of the darkness they leave behind?

Unwinding is spreading. China was the first to jump on the bandwagon, then Belgium and the Netherlands and the rest of the European Union. The Russians claimed to have come up with the idea themselves, as if it were something worth claiming, and in third-world nations, where laws change as quickly as governments, the black-market trade in human organs has grown into a major industry.

And what of his attempt to change all that? What of his "life's work that would end unwinding"? After one final attempt to get some answers out of BioDynix Medical Instruments, he was slapped with a cease-and-desist lawsuit and a restraining order that prevents him from coming within one hundred yards of any BioDynix employee.

Every day, the very existence of their basement reminds him that Austin—whom Janson and Sonia had come to care about like a son—is gone, and as if this cake needed any further icing, both he and Sonia have been virtually unwound themselves. Before Janson had been ousted from Proactive Citizenry for actually wanting to do some good in the world, they were working on digital footprint removal. It was supposed to be a way to protect one's privacy on the web by removing unwanted and unauthorized references and pictures of oneself.

But like everything else, Proactive Citizenry found a way to weaponize it.

Now any and all references to Janson or Sonia Rheinschild have been eliminated from the digital memory of the world. Not only don't they exist, but according to public records, they never existed. Those who know them will eventually forget them, and even if they don't, those people will eventually die. Janson's and Sonia's footprints on this earth will be washed as clean as a beach at high tide.

And so Janson Rheinschild sits alone in his chair, turning all of his anger, his disillusionment, and his disappointment inward, until finally he feels his heart seize in his chest, knotting in the lethal cramp of cardiac arrest.

And he's glad for it. He's grateful that at last the universe has chosen to show him some mercy.

58 · Connor

The sign on the highway reads WELCOME TO AKRON, THE RUBBER CAPITAL OF THE WORLD. The dark, threatening skies feel anything but welcoming. Connor finds himself white-knuckling the steering wheel and has to loosen his grip. *Calm down. Calm down. It's only a sign.*

"The scene of the crime," comments Cam from behind Connor, and then softens it by adding, "Of course, that depends on your definition of 'crime.'"

Grace, still beside Cam in the backseat, is content to decipher personalized license plates and analyze them. "SSADAB.

Dumbass spelled backward. '♥&SEOUL.' Some Korean guy who got an Unwind's heart." Grace seems immune to the heightened level of tension in the car until they approach a highway patrol car parked on the shoulder.

"Go slow! Go slow! Go slow!" she says.

"Don't worry, Grace," Connor tells her. "I'm right at the speed limit." How stupid if they get caught for speeding and captured at this point.

The woods are now broken by suburban subdevelopments, and as the road rolls by, Connor tries to find the spot where his, Risa's, and Lev's lives converged. He doesn't even know if this is the same freeway. It feels like something not just from another life, but from another world entirely. A world into which he's just initiated reentry. He feels like Frodo at the gates of Mordor. Who would have guessed that Ohio could hold such dark portent?

"Do you know what you're looking for?" asks Cam from the backseat. "Akron's a big town."

"Not so big," is Connor's only response.

Connor knows that Cam's presence on this journey is a necessary evil, but he wishes Cam were not sitting right behind him where Connor can't see him, except for suspicious glances in the rearview mirror. Cam's offerings of information have not won Connor over. There's something fundamentally underhanded and opaque about the Rewind, or at least about his intentions. Giving him the benefit of the doubt could damn them all.

"I imagine you must know Akron pretty well."

"Not at all," Connor tells him. "I've been here only once."

That makes Cam laugh. "And yet they call you the Akron AWOL."

"Yeah, funny how that works." Connor is actually from a suburb of Columbus, hours away, but Akron is where he turned the tranq on Nelson. Akron is where he became notorious. He didn't even know where he was at the time. He only knew it had been Akron once they gave him the irritating "Akron AWOL" label.

"Center-North!" Connor blurts.

"Center-north what?" Grace asks.

"That's the name of the school. Center-North High. I knew I'd remember it eventually."

"We're going to a school?"

"That's ground zero. We're looking for an antique shop near the school. I'll know it when I see it."

"You sure about that?" asks Cam. "Memory's a funny thing."

"Only yours," says Connor. He punches the name of the school into the GPS and a gentle voice directs them with confident, if somewhat soulless, purpose. In fifteen minutes, they're on the east side of town. They turn a corner and things look troublingly familiar to Connor.

The school looks exactly the same. Three stories of institutional redbrick that somehow looks as intimidating to him as the Texas School Book Depository had when Connor's family traveled to Dallas and took a tour of the infamous building where Oswald shot Kennedy. Connor takes a deep, shuddering breath.

It's midmorning on a Tuesday, so school is in session. It's just about the same time of day that the fire alarm went off and all hell broke loose. Connor rolls them slowly past. Across the street are homes, but up ahead is a main commercial street.

"Anything specific we should be looking for?" asks Cam. "Any defining characteristics of this antique shop?"

"Yeah," Connor says, "old stuff," which makes Grace laugh.

He wonders what Sonia will do when she sees him. Then

a horrible thought crosses Connor's mind: What if she's dead? Or what if she was caught and arrested for harboring Unwinds? He doesn't voice his concerns, because if he doesn't speak them aloud, maybe they won't be true.

Connor slams the brakes, nearly running a red light. A pedestrian crosses the street glaring at them.

"Not much of a driver, are ya?" says Grace, then turns to Cam. "Did you know he almost killed Lev?"

"My driving's fine," Connor insists, "but this place is eating my brain." He looks around, waiting for the light to change. "I don't recognize any of this, but I know the shop can't be more than a block or two away."

"So drive around the school in a spiral that gets bigger," suggests Grace. And then she adds, "Although since the streets ain't round, it's kinda a square spiral."

"That's called an Ulam spiral, by the way," Cam says. "A way of graphing prime numbers. Not that you would know that."

Connor gives him a disgusted look in the rearview mirror. "Is everyone in your internal community an ass?" Connor asks. It shuts Cam up.

They widen their search pattern until Connor hits the brakes suddenly again, but not because of a red light.

"There it is. It's still there."

The unprepossessing storefront of the corner shop has an understated sign that reads GOODYEAR HEIGHTS ANTIQUES. Being that it's two blocks off the main thoroughfare, it doesn't seem to be getting much business. Connor parks across the street, and they sit there in silence for about ten seconds. Then he unbuckles his seat belt.

"Well," he says, "let's go antiquing."

59 · Sonia

She's not surprised that the Lassiter boy has come here, but she is surprised by the company he's keeping. That blasted Rewind is the last travel companion she'd expect to see him with. She doesn't show her surprise though—and she doesn't show how happy she is to see Connor either. As far as Sonia is concerned, authentic emotions are a liability. They always come back to bite you. Her poker face has served her well over the years, and on many occasions it has saved her life.

"So you're back," she says to Connor, putting down a lamp she had just repaired. "And with friends, no less."

She makes no move to embrace him or even to shake his hand. Neither does Connor. He holds his distance—he too having learned the fine art of defensive dispassion. Still, he's not as good at it as Sonia. She can tell how relieved he is to be here and how happy he is to see her. Even if he doesn't wear it on his face, she can sense it in his general aura.

"Hello, Sonia," he says, then smirks. "Or should I say Dr. Rheinschild?"

This is a surprise. She hasn't heard the name spoken aloud in years. Her heart misses a beat, but she still doesn't let the emotion show on her face, and she chooses not to respond to his accusation—for an accusation is exactly what it is—although she knows a nonresponse is as good as an admission.

"Are you going to introduce me to your little posse?" she asks. "Or have you still not learned any manners?"

He starts with the chunky, vague-looking woman who seems

out of place in this trio—although to be honest, none of them really seem to fit together.

"This is Grace Skinner. She saved my life a few weeks ago."

"Hiya," Grace says. She's the only one who steps forward to force a handshake on Sonia. "I hear you saved his life too, so I guess we're in the same club."

Then Connor reluctantly introduces the Rewind. Sonia, however, stops him before he speaks the name.

"I know who he is." She steps closer to Cam, peering through glasses as antique as anything else in her shop—the wage of refusing new eyes. "Hmph," she says. "No scars at all—just seams. My compliments to your construction crew."

He appears uncomfortable at her scrutiny, although she imagines he's used to it. "They were surgeons, not construction workers," he says a bit bristly.

"And they say you speak nine languages."

"Plus I've been studying a few more."

"Hmph," she says again, irritated by the arrogant lilt in his voice. "I'm sure it's no surprise to you that your existence is disgusting to me."

"Understood," he says with a resigned sigh. "You're not the first to tell me that."

"I won't be the last, I'm sure—but as long as we understand each other, we'll be fine."

Outside a young couple walks by, engaged in conversation. Sonia watches them until she's sure they're not coming into the shop. They pass by and she's relieved. It makes her realize she's spent too much time in clear view with her visitors.

"Come in the back room," she tells them. "Unless you want to man the register."

"I have a lot of questions," Connor says as he leads the others through the curtain to the back room.

"Then you'll be disappointed, because I have no answers."

"You're lying," he says, point-blank. "Why are you lying?"

That makes Sonia grin. "A little wiser than when you left, I see. Or maybe just a little more jaded."

"Both, I guess."

"And a little taller too. Or is it just that I've shrunk?"

He gives her a wiseass smirk. "Both, I guess."

Then she catches sight of the shark on his arm. It makes her shiver, and she tries to look away, but it commands her attention. "I definitely don't want to know about *that*," she says, although she knows all about it already, from a different source.

"How are things in your basement?" Connor asks. "Still up to your old tricks?"

"I'm a creature of habit," she tells them. "And just because the ADR fell apart doesn't mean I have to." Then she glances to Cam, who seems to be taking mental snapshots of everything he sees, like a spy. "Can he be trusted?" she asks Connor.

Cam answers the question himself. "Similar objectives," he says. "Under any other circumstance, I would say no, you couldn't trust me—but I want to take down Proactive Citizenry as much as my AWOL friend does. So for all intents and purposes, *Ich bin ein* AWOL."

"Hmph." Sonia only half believes him, but she accepts Connor's judgment for the other half. "Necessity makes strange bedfellows, as they say."

"*The Tempest*," Cam responds as if chiming in on a game show. "Shakespeare. It's actually misery that makes strange bedfellows, but necessity works too."

"Fine." Sonia grabs her cane, which leans against her desk, and taps it on the old steamer trunk in the center of the cluttered back room. "Make yourself useful and push this aside."

Cam does so. Sonia notices Connor focused a bit deerlike on the trunk. He's the only one who knows its significance. What it contains and what it conceals.

Once the trunk is pushed aside, Connor takes it upon himself to roll away the dusty Persian rug beneath to reveal the trapdoor. Sonia, who is far less feeble than she lets on, reaches down, pulls on the iron ring, and lifts open the door. Somewhere downstairs whispers quickly give way to silence.

"I'll be right back," she says. "And don't touch anything." She wags a finger at Grace, who's been touching just about everything.

As Sonia stomps heavily but slowly down the steep wooden steps, she conceals a devious smile. She knows this is going to be complicated. She dreads it, but she also looks forward to it. An old woman needs some excitement in her life.

"It's only me," she says as she reaches the bottom step, and all her AWOLs come out of hiding. Or at least the ones who care.

"Lunch?" one of them asks.

"You just had breakfast. Don't be a pig."

She makes her way to a little alcove in the far corner of the cluttered maze of a basement, where a girl with stunning green eyes and gentle brown curls with amber highlights organizes a cache of first-aid supplies.

"You have visitors," Sonia tells her.

The look on the girl's face is too guarded to be hopeful. "What sort of visitors?"

Sonia smiles wickedly. "The angel and the devil on your shoulders, Risa. I hope you're wise enough to know which is which."

60 · Risa

It wasn't coincidence that brought Risa and Connor's lives converging once more on Akron. It was an absolute absence of other options.

In all of Risa's desperate wanderings since being loaded on the bus to be unwound, Sonia's basement was the only place that had any hope of being safe. The Graveyard had been purged, Audrey's shop was a nice respite, but had her on edge every day, and as for the safe houses she'd been shuttled to in the dark, Sonia's was the only one of which she knew the actual location.

She could backtrack and stay under the odd protection of CyFi's commune—but she knew she wasn't really welcomed by most of the Tyler-folk. For obvious reasons she could never feel part of that community. That left only a life on the streets, or a life in hiding alone. She'd had enough of looking over her shoulder, sleeping in Dumpsters like a fresh AWOL, just waiting to be recognized in spite of her makeover. It would only be a matter of time until someone reported her to the authorities, collected the reward, and handed her over to Proactive Citizenry, who would no doubt have many plans for her.

That left only one viable option. Sonia.

When Risa arrived a few weeks ago, there were customers in the antique shop, haggling with Sonia over an unremarkable end table. Risa strategically meandered down another aisle, marveling at how so many items could be precariously perched on one another and yet not fall— empirical evidence that Ohio is not prone to earthquakes.

Finally the couple had left, struggling with their table,

for which Sonia offered no help beyond, "Mind the step; it's crooked." Once the rusty hinges on the door squeaked closed, Risa stepped forward, presenting herself to be noticed.

Sonia pursed her lips when she saw here there, perhaps affronted that she had snuck in unobserved. "Something I can help you find?" Sonia asked.

Risa had been a bit tickled that Sonia didn't recognize her right away. And when she finally did, the old woman let out a howl of uncharacteristic joy and dropped her cane so she could wrap her arms around Risa.

And in that moment Risa realized it was the closest she might ever come to knowing what it felt like to be home.

Now, two weeks later, Risa finds herself playing Wendy to the Lost Boys, for lately, it seems the only AWOLs who are getting as far as Sonia's are boys, attesting to the sad fact that more female AWOLs are falling prey to parts pirates and other bottom-feeders.

When Sonia tells Risa she has "visitors," Risa starts up the stairs apprehensively, but she picks up her pace as that apprehension turns to excitement. There are very few people Sonia would send Risa upstairs for.

She doesn't dare hope which of those few people it might be, because she doesn't want disappointment to show on her face if it were someone like Hayden or Emby, both of whom she'd be happy to see, were she not hoping for something more.

She flies through the open trapdoor, almost banging her head on the edge of the floor panel, and she sees him right away. She says nothing because for an instant she's sure it's her imagination. That her mind has pasted Connor's face on top of someone else's, because she so much wants it to be him. But it's not her imagination. It is him, and his eyes reflect her own surprise.

"Risa?"

The voice isn't coming from Connor, and her eyes dart slightly to the right. It's Cam. His own astonishment has already turned into a broad grin.

Risa finds her head beginning to quiver. "Cuh . . . cuh . . ." She doesn't know which of their names to say first. The sight of the two of them in the same visual image hits her like a concussive shock and she takes a step backward, hitting the edge of the trapdoor. It slams shut an instant after Sonia cleared it. Had the woman not been faster up the stairs than she had been down, it would have crushed her skull.

Risa can't reconcile what she's seeing: These two separate parts of her life juxtaposed upon each other. It feels as if the universe itself has betrayed her. Exposed her, leaving her raw and vulnerable to all attacks. She didn't leave either Connor or Cam on the best of terms. Suddenly defensive, her surprise at seeing them decays into suspicion.

"Wh-what's going on here?"

Cam, still dazed by the sight of her, takes a step forward, only to be fully eclipsed by Connor stepping in front of him, not even aware that he had done it. "Aren't you even gonna say hello?" Connor asks cautiously.

"Hi," she says, with such weak impotence she's angry at herself. She clears her throat, and only now notices there's someone else here as well. A girl she doesn't know, who, for the moment, is content to observe.

With the prospects of this grand reunion fizzling like wet fireworks, Sonia raps her cane on the ground in frustration to get their attention. "Well, don't just stand there," she says. "Give us a love scene worthy of the ages, or at least a viral meme."

"Happy to oblige," says Cam, so arrogantly Risa wants to slap him.

"She wasn't talking to you," Connor says with such dismissive disdain, Risa wouldn't mind slapping him, too.

This isn't how this moment was supposed to be! Over these many months, she had pictured her reunion with Connor a dozen times in a dozen different ways. None of them were so rife with ice-cracking unease. As for Cam, she had thought she'd never see him again, so never entertained the idea of a reunion. Oddly, she finds herself more pleased to see him than she ever expected she would. It steals Connor's thunder, and a part of her resents both of them for it. They shouldn't be allowed to muddy each other's moments. The clouding of her emotions should not be permitted by a sane, compassionate universe. But then, when has life deigned to show her any compassion?

Cam has come out from behind Connor's eclipsing presence now. They stand there side by side as if waiting for Risa to choose. Suddenly Risa realizes that she has no idea how this is going to play out. She finds that as terrifying as being caught in a parts pirate's trap.

It's the girl—that unknown quantity in the room—who comes to her rescue.

"Hiya, I'm Grace," she says, pushing between Connor and Cam, grabbing Risa's hand and vigorously shaking it. "You can call me Grace or Gracie—I don't mind either way—or even Eleanor, 'cause that's my middle name. It's an honor to meet you, Miss Ward. Can I call you Risa? I know all about you from my brother, who kind of worshipped you—well, he worshipped Connor more, but you were there too, although you looked different then, but I guess that's on purpose. Smart to change your eye color. People think it's the hair, but it's the eyes that make a person look different."

"Yes—that's what the stylist who did it said," says Risa, a little flustered by Grace's barrage of enthusiasm.

"So is there stuff for us to eat in that basement down there, 'cause I'm starved?"

It's only later that Risa realizes how effectively Grace's rude intrusion completely defused an explosive situation. Almost as if she had planned it that way.

61 · Cam

This changes everything.

The fact that Risa is now smack in the middle of it all forces Cam to have to reevaluate his goal as well as his methods to achieve them. As a fugitive himself, he needed this shaky collaboration with Connor. Survival demanded it, and although in his heart he knows Connor is an enemy, he can only have one enemy at a time, and right now, it's Proactive Citizenry.

Cam has to admit that from the moment he met Connor, he was as fascinated by him as much as he despised him. The way he showed compassion—even empathy—when Una did not. Connor probably saved his life that day at the sweat lodge. Had the roles been reversed, Cam would not have done the same. It made Connor worthy of study.

The plan, from that moment on, was to get to know Connor—and to use him to help bring down Proactive Citizenry. Then, once Roberta and all of her high-and-mighty cronies have been hobbled, Cam would know Connor well enough to hobble him as well. He must clearly understand the pedestal that Risa has put the Akron AWOL on before he can engineer the pedestal's collapse, leaving Connor Lassiter as nothing in Risa's eyes.

But now that Risa is actually here, Cam feels like he's been reduced to being an ape having to pound his chest before her to win her affections. Is that all it comes down to, then?

Primitive mating rituals sublimated to appear civilized? Perhaps—but Cam knows he's a step forward in human evolution. A composite being. He has faith that his internal community will galvanize to outshine Connor at every turn. But why does it have to be now?

Sonia does not bring them down to the basement with the AWOLs-in-hiding.

"They'll tear this one apart the second they see him." She points her thumb at Cam like she's hitching a ride.

"Talking about someone in the third person is rude," Cam tells her coolly.

"Really?" says Connor. "When you're a hundred people, wouldn't third person be a compliment?"

Cam is fully prepared to snipe back at Connor, but he catches Risa's gaze and chooses not to. Let her see him as the model of restraint.

Sonia then takes a moment to look at Connor. "You don't want to be in that basement either with all those ogling eyes. You've probably had enough hero worship to last a lifetime."

"*I* haven't," chimes in Grace, who must feel like a mortal among gods.

"Consider yourself lucky, then," Sonia tells her. "In these times, the less noticed you are, the better your chances of living long enough to see things change."

"Well said!" Cam offers, but Sonia only scowls at him.

"Nobody asked you."

She takes them to the back alley where an old Suburban in need of major washing waits, and she ushers them all into it. Although Cam makes every effort to sit beside Risa, Grace barges her way in right after her in a "ladies first" sort of way and sits beside her. Risa makes eye contact with Cam and gives him a purse-lipped grin as if to say, "Better luck next time." He can't read her at all. He doesn't know whether she's relieved that Grace is there or disappointed. He glances at Connor, who appears not to care where he sits. *Appears*. That's the key word with Connor. He's extremely good at hiding what goes on in that perplexing space between his ears.

Being the last one in, Cam tries to sit shotgun, but Sonia won't allow it. "There's less of a chance you'll be seen in the back, since those windows are darker. And besides, your 'multicultural' face is too damn distracting for an old woman trying to drive a large vehicle." So the shotgun seat is left empty, and Cam ends up sitting in the back with Connor.

"So where are we going?" Connor asks.

Risa turns around to answer and offers him a grin. "You'll see."

Cam can't tell if it's the exact same grin she offered him a moment before, or if there's more warmth to it. He can't stand not knowing. The frustration of it makes his seams begin to itch. He knows it's all in his mind, but the crawling of his seams feels very real. The unspoken, undefined relationship between Risa and Connor is maddening.

Sonia drives with the practiced caution of the elderly, yet still manages to hit every bump and pothole in the road and issues forth curses that could make a longshoreman blush. Five minutes later, she pulls into the driveway of a modest two-story home.

"Did you warn her?" Risa asks as they come to a stop.

Sonia puts the car in park with a decisive thrust. "I don't warn," Sonia says. "I act, and people deal."

Cam idly wonders if Roberta will be like this if she lives long enough to be that old. It gives him an unexpected and unwanted shiver.

Once out of the Suburban, Sonia quickly leads them to a side gate, where a shih tzu has already begun barking and shows no sign of ceasing anytime soon. "We live in a backdoor world," Sonia tells them, "so move your collective asses before the neighbors get nosy." Sonia opens the gate, ignoring the dog, which tries to nip at everyone's heels at once, in futile defense of its territory.

"One of these days," says Sonia, as she leads them to the backyard, "I'll punt that fool dog into Central Time." And off of Grace's concerned look, Risa assures her that Sonia doesn't mean it.

With a high wooden fence around the perimeter of the yard, the back door is much less conspicuous than the front. Sonia raps loudly, and then raps again, not patient enough to wait for it to be answered. Finally a woman comes to the door. She seems to be in her midforties and is holding a toddler wearing a Minnie Mouse dress. A stork-job, Cam figures. Middle-aged people always seem to get babies dropped on their doorsteps these days.

"Oh good Lord. What now?" the beleaguered woman asks.

Then Connor gasps. "Didi?" he says, looking at the toddler.

Although the little girl regards him without a hint of recognition, the woman holding her appears both pleased and taken aback at the same time by the sight of Connor. "I changed her name to Dierdre."

"Well, I still call her Didi," says Risa. "You remember Hannah, don't you, Connor?" Risa says, clearly a prompt to save him the embarrassment of not remembering the woman's name.

When the woman looks at Cam, her face blanches, and Cam can't resist saying, "Trick or treat," although Halloween is months away.

Hannah puts Dierdre down and tells her to run inside and play, which she is more than happy to do, and the shih tzu, still unable to stop itself from barking, follows her just far enough to guard the threshold between the kitchen and the dining room.

"You're full of surprises, Sonia," Hannah says, her eyes still locked on Cam. Then she herds them all in before they draw unwanted neighborhood attention. Cam finds the house a little too warm, but maybe it's just in contrast to the chill of the overcast day.

"I spend my days helping Sonia," Risa says, "but Hannah's been kind enough to let me spend my nights here for the past few weeks." Now that they're safely inside, she introduces the rest of them to her, saving Cam for last, rather self-consciously calling him "the one and only Camus Comprix."

"Are you ADR?" Cam asks as he shakes Hannah's hand.

She eyes him with the same suspicion that everyone does. Everyone who isn't starstruck, that is. "No. I was never a part of the Anti-Divisional Resistance. I'm just a concerned citizen." Then she turns to Sonia. "We should talk. Alone."

Hannah pulls Sonia into another room. She spares a glance back at them and says, "Risa, keep an eye on Dierdre. The rest of you, make yourselves comfortable," then adds, "But not too comfortable."

Risa, now their temporary hostess, escorts them into a living room filled with the primary-colored detritus of preschool toys strewn haphazardly on the floor. Dierdre ignores the visitors, content to throw plastic blocks in the direction of the dog, who retrieves them, no longer interested in territorial defense.

The room has many clocks. Hannah must be a collector. They all show different times, as none of them are wound or plugged in. Well, almost none. There's one clock ticking, but Cam can't figure out where the sound is coming from. How appropriate, he thinks, that the house of an AWOL sympathizer is all about the importance of time, yet the timepieces are all at odds with one another.

Risa draws the curtains as they settle into their new holding pattern until Sonia and Hannah's summit meeting can bring about a decision as to what to do with them. "So," says

Risa with an absolute awkwardness that is completely unlike her, "here we are."

"And here be dragons," Cam says, he himself not even knowing exactly why he says it or what it means. All he knows is that in some odd way, it's true. He knows that Risa is still trying to process his and Connor's presence here. She doesn't even ask how they've come to be together, which tells Cam that she's so far from dealing with it, she doesn't even want to know.

They all sit spaced apart on a sectional sofa and the two chairs facing it, trying to keep this from feeling as awkward as it is. Grace is the only one who doesn't sit yet. She wanders around the room, seemingly immune to the tension, examining photographs and knickknacks and digging her hand into a jar of Jolly Ranchers on a shelf too high for Dierdre to get at.

Cam wishes he could dig into at least one part of himself that retains that much innocence. Not even the tithes he has residing within him are naive enough to feel safe in Hannah's comfortable living room. The memory bits of his tithes are more about feeling superior, so all he can dredge forth from them is aloofness. That's not going to endear him to Risa.

"Hannah's the teacher who saved Connor and me from the Juvey-cops when we were first on the run," Risa explains.

"Oh," says Cam impotently. "Good to know." All her explanation does is reinforce the history Risa has with Connor. Cam hates having to hear it.

Grace, happy to fly beneath the radar of conversation, lines up her cache of candies on the living room's coffee table. The bowl of Jolly Ranchers is still half-full, and the sight of it sparks absurd discord in Cam. Option Anxiety, he's come to call it. "One man's meat," he mumbles to himself, but realizes it's loud enough for the others to hear, so he explains. "It's not just taste buds that create a preference for flavors," he tells them. "My internal community is always at odds when it comes to things like those candies. A part of me loves the green apple and another the grape. Someone has a particular affinity for the peach ones—which they don't even make anymore—and someone else finds the whole concept of Jolly Ranchers nauseating." He sighs, trying to dismiss his pointless Option Anxiety. "Bowls of mixed things are the bane of my existence."

Connor looks at him with a blank zombie stare that must be well practiced. "You talk as if someone actually cares."

Risa offers that slim grin to Cam again. "How can people be interested in the inner workings of your mind, Cam, when they can't figure out the inner workings of their own?" It sounds like a sideways snipe against Connor, but then she gently pats Connor's hand, turning a perfectly good snipe into a playful barb.

"Why don't *you* choose a flavor for me?" Cam asks Risa, trying to be playful too, but Risa avoids the issue by saying, "After the trouble Roberta went through to find you such nice teeth, why rot them?"

"I got my favorites, but that don't matter," Grace announces. She indicates her well-spaced row of candies and puts a definitive end to the subject by saying, "I always eat them in alphabetical order."

Cam decides to obey the sense memory that doesn't like hard candy and doesn't take any.

"How are your friends at Proactive Citizenry?" Risa asks Cam tentatively.

"They're no more my friends than they are yours," he tells her. He's about to tell her that he's turned on them and has given up the shining spotlight to help her, but Connor steals the reveal from him.

"Camus showed me some damaging evidence we can use against them."

Cam regrets having shared it with Connor at all. Had he

known he'd come face-to-face with Risa here in Akron, he would have saved it all for her. Now he resents Connor for even knowing.

"And there's more," Cam adds. "You and I can talk later," he tells Risa.

Connor shifts uncomfortably and turns his attention to the pictures around the room. "My guess is that Hannah is divorced or recently widowed. There are pictures of a man with her in some photos, including one with Dierdre—but Hannah's not wearing a wedding ring."

"Definitely widowed," says Grace without looking up from her candy organization. "You don't keep pictures out of a guy you divorced."

Connor shrugs. "Anyway, it looks like she's really taken to raising this Dierdre as her own."

"She has," Risa admits. "It was a good choice for us to leave her with Hannah. Not that we had much of a choice."

The direction of the conversation makes Cam uncomfortable. "Exactly whose kid is it?"

Connor smirks at Cam and puts one arm around Risa. "Ours," he says. "Didn't you know?"

For a moment Cam believes him, for he knows Risa has many secrets yet to be discovered. Cam is disheartened until Risa slides deftly out of Connor's embrace.

"She was a storked baby that Connor picked up from a doorstep," Risa explains. "We took care of her for a brief time; then Hannah volunteered to take her off of our hands before we were shuttled to the next safe house."

"And did you find motherhood an interesting experience?" Cam asks, relieved enough to be amused at the thought.

"Yes," says Risa, "but I'm in no hurry to repeat it." Then she stands, moving away from both Cam and Connor. "I'll see what's in the refrigerator. You must be hungry."

After she's gone, Connor's demeanor changes a bit. He becomes dark. A brooding gray like the sky outside. "You'll keep your eyes and your hands off of her. Is that clear? You will not cause her any more grief than you already have."

"Ah! *The green-eyed monster which doth mock the meat it feeds on!*" Cam says. "She told me you were the jealous type, but you're a weak and pale Othello."

"I'll unwind you with my bare hands if you don't leave her alone."

That makes Cam genuinely laugh. "Your pointless bravado will be your downfall. All that arrogance with nothing to back it up."

"Arrogance? You're the one who's full of himself! Or full of others, I should say."

It's like a sword has finally been drawn in the duel. Grace looks up from her Jolly Ranchers, even Dierdre and the dog, way across the room, seem to tune in. How will Cam respond? Although the wild parts of himself want to lash out in anger, he reins them in. Anger is what Connor wants. It's what Connor knows how to deal with. Cam won't oblige.

"The fact that I'm physically, intellectually, and creatively better than you is not arrogance or conceit; it's a simple fact," Cam says with forced calm. "I'm the better man because I was made to be. I can't help what I *have* any more than you can help what you *don't*."

They hold hard gazes until Connor backs down. "If you want to joust over Risa, now's not the time. Right now we all need to be friends."

"Allies don't gotta be friends," Grace points out. "Take World War II. We couldn't a' won it without Russia, even though we hated each other's guts then."

"Point taken," says Cam, once more impressed by Grace's unexpected wisdom. "For now, let's agree that Risa is off-limits. A demilitarized zone."

"You're mixin' your wars," Grace says. "The Demilitarized Zone was Korea."

"She's a person, not a zone," says Connor. Then he goes over and plays with Dierdre, putting an end to all negotiations.

"You're forgetting," Cam says to Grace, who also noted the documentaries that so absorbed her at the motel, "that the United States and Russia almost nuked each other to smithereens after World War II."

"I'm not forgettin' nothin'," Grace says, returning to her candies. "When the two of you really go at it, I expect I'll build myself a bomb shelter."

62 · Connor

This changes everything.

Connor's initial thrill at seeing Risa is quickly crushed under the weight of the reality. Not the reality of Cam, but the reality of their situation. Now that Risa is with them, she's no longer out of harm's way. Connor had longed for her—there is no question about that. For all these months, he has ached to hear her voice and to be comforted by her words. He longed to massage her legs even though he knew she was no longer paralyzed. His feelings for her have not changed. Even when he thought she had betrayed the cause and had become a public voice in favor of unwinding, he knew deep down she could not be doing it of her own accord.

Then, when she came on live television to reveal it was a sham and thoroughly slapped down Proactive Citizenry, he loved her even more. After that, she vanished into hiding, just as completely as Connor had—and there was comfort in that. He could look out into the night and know she was out there somewhere, using her formidable wits to keep herself safe.

Connor, however, is anything but a safe harbor now. With what they mean to expose about Proactive Citizenry—and what he might potentially learn from Sonia—she is in much greater danger in his company than not. His journey is now into the flames, not away from them—and of course she'll want to go with him. And Cam's words still echo in his mind.

"I'm the better man because I was made to be."

For all of his handpicked intelligence, Cam is an imbecile to think jealousy is what this is all about. Yes, Connor admits that a certain amount of jealousy is there to cloud things, but competing for Risa's affections feels like a petty endeavor compared to Connor's need to protect her from both himself and from Cam.

As Connor plays with Dierdre on the living room floor, he tries to let his anger dissipate. It won't help the situation. Giving into his jealousy will only distract him.

Dierdre lies back and puts her feet in Connor's face.

"Tricker treat! Smell my feet!"

Her feet smell like the baby food she must have stepped in, orange globs of sweet potato marring the pattern of ducklings swimming all over her socks.

"Nice socks," Connor says, still amazed that this was the same baby he took from the doorstep of the fat, beady-eyed woman and her fat, beady-eyed son.

"Ducky socks!" says Dierdre happily. "Fishy arm!" She touches the shark on his arm with a sticky index finger. "Fishy arm. Army fish!" And she giggles. The giggle opens an escape valve in Connor; his frustration is soothed by Dierdre.

"It's a shark," he tells Dierdre.

"Shark!" repeats Dierdre. "Shark shark shark!" Dierdre snaps a woman's plastic head on a little plastic body of a firefighter. "Your mommy see the shark there? She mad at it?"

Connor sighs. Little kids, he's decided, are like cats. They always like to hop in the laps of people who are allergic. Connor wonders if Dierdre has any clue that the topic she just put in his lap is enough to make him break out in hives.

"No," he tells her. "My mommy doesn't know about the shark."

"You'll get in trouble?"

"No worries," Connor says.

"No worries," Dierdre repeats, and snaps a tire on top of the little plastic figure's head, making it look like an oversized Russian hat.

Dierdre doesn't know that there's a letter in a trunk in Sonia's back room. There are actually hundreds of letters. All written by AWOLs, all written to the parents who gave them over for unwinding. From the moment Connor saw the trunk earlier that day, he's been imagining what it would be like to hand deliver that letter and watch from a hidden location as his parents read it. Just thinking about it now causes Roland's arm to tighten into a fist. He imagines punching through a windowpane, grabbing the letter back from them before they can read it—but he chases the thought away, consciously releases his fingers and directs the hand to get back to the business of preschool play.

Roland's hand snaps together Legos just as efficiently as Connor's natural hand, proving it can create as well as it destroys.

Sonia's powers of persuasion must verge on superhuman, because Hannah consents to keeping them all under her protection.

"Grace can bunk with Risa. You boys can share my sewing room. There's a daybed in there—you'll have to either share it or slug it out," Hannah tells them. "I'll make this very clear. I am not a safe house. I am doing this just because it's the right

379

thing to do—but do *not* take advantage of my good nature." She goes on, instructing them to stay away from windows and hide if anyone comes to the door.

"We know the drill," Connor is quick to tell her. "It's not like we're new to this."

"Some of us are," Cam says, and indicates Grace. "From what I understand, *you* dragged her into this."

"I dragged myself," Grace tells him, keeping Connor from being drawn into a battle with Cam, "and I can hide as good as anyone."

Satisfied that the situation is under control, Sonia leaves. "Gotta feed the gremlins in my basement before they get restless," although Connor knows from experience that they're always restless.

A storm hits twenty minutes later—a steady stream of rain and distant lightning that threatens to draw closer but never does. Hannah orders in pizza for dinner—a bit of absurd normality in the midst of their situation.

The sewing room is upstairs with the rest of the bedrooms. A tiny space with a frilly daybed that insults the very concept of masculinity.

"I'll sleep on the floor," Cam offers, making sure Risa can see his selfless generosity. Risa's response is to grin at Connor. "He beat you to it."

"Yeah," says Connor. "I'll have to be quicker next time."

Cam, still locked in competition mode, is not amused. For the rest of the day Risa does her best to avoid being in the room with both of them at the same time, and since Cam won't let Connor out of his sight, their only interactions with Risa are her quick forays into their cramped room with blankets, towels, and toiletries. "We keep a collection of stuff for the kids in Sonia's basement," she says as she hands Connor toothpaste and Cam a toothbrush.

"So are we supposed to share it?" Cam asks with an annoyingly rakish grin.

Risa, flustered, apologizes. "I'll find another one."

Connor has never seen Risa flustered. He would dislike Cam all the more for making her so—but he knows it's not Cam, but the combination of the two of them. Connor wonders how Risa would be with him were the presence of Camus Comprix not a factor.

He finds out after dinner, while Cam's taking a shower.

Grace has taken to entertaining Dierdre. The giggles from the nursery attest to her success. Connor struggles to find a comfortable position on the dusty daybed. When Risa appears at the doorway, she just stands at the threshold. The sound of the shower down the hall makes it clear that Cam won't be back for at least a few minutes.

"Can I come in?" she asks tentatively.

Connor sits up on the bed, trying to be less fidgety than he feels. "Sure."

She sits on the room's only chair and smiles. "I've missed you, Connor."

This is a moment Connor has longed for. A moment that he's held in his mind to keep him going—but as much as Connor wants to return her affection, he knows he can't. They cannot be together. He cannot draw her back into this battle now that she's safe. But neither can he push her toward Cam.

So he clasps her hand, but doesn't hold it all that tightly. "Yeah," he says. "Same here." But he says it without the conviction he really feels.

She studies him, and he hopes she doesn't see through his cool facade. "All those things I said—the commercials, the public service announcements in favor of unwinding—you know I was being blackmailed, don't you? They were going to attack the Graveyard if I didn't do it."

"They attacked the Graveyard anyway," Connor points out.

Now she begins to get concerned. "Connor, you don't think—"

"No, I don't think you betrayed us," he tells her. He can't mislead her about his feelings that much. "But a lot of Whollies died that night." What he really wants to do is take her into his arms and hold her tightly. He wants to tell her that thinking of her is the only thing that kept him going. But instead he says, "They died. Let's just leave it at that."

"Next you'll be blaming me for Starkey."

"No," says Connor. "I blame myself for that."

Risa looks down. For a moment he sees tears building in her eyes, but when she looks up at him again, her expression is hard. Her vulnerability is once more protected by armor. "Well, I'm glad you're alive," she tells him, taking her hand back from him. "I'm glad you're safe."

"As safe as can be expected," says Connor, "considering I have a rogue parts pirate, Proactive Citizenry, and the Juvenile Authority after me."

Risa sighs. "I guess we'll never be safe."

"You're safe," Connor says before he can stop himself. "Do yourself a favor and stay that way."

Now she looks at him with suspicion. "What's that supposed to mean?"

"It means you've settled into this life with Hannah and Didi. Why throw it away?"

"Settled in? I've been here two weeks! That's hardly settled in—and now that you're here—"

Connor never considered himself much of an actor, but now he feigns irritation for all he's worth. "Now that I'm here, what? You think you're going to join me in raging against the machine? What makes you think I want that?"

Risa is speechless, as he hoped she would be. With the first emotional punch thrown, Connor follows up with "Things are different now, Risa. And what we had at the Graveyard . . ."

"We had nothing," Risa says, saving him the pain of yet another lie—replacing it with a different kind of pain. "We just got stuck smack in each other's way." Then she stands up just as Cam makes his appearance at the door. "But we're not in each other's way anymore."

Cam has a beach towel wrapped around his lower half, but his upper half is on display. The perfect package of six-pack abs and sculpted pecs. He came in here like that on purpose, Connor decides. Because he knows Risa is here.

"What did I miss?"

Risa puts her hand unabashedly on his chest, tracing the lines where his flesh tones meet. "They were right, Cam," she says gently. "Those seams healed perfectly. No scars at all." She smiles at him and gives him a peck on the cheek before she strides out of the room.

Conner hopes her sudden attention to Cam is merely a jab against him, but he can't be sure. Rather than thinking about it, Connor looks to his grafted arm, letting it draw his focus. He's conscious to keep the fingers from contracting into a fist. Some people wear their emotions on their sleeves. Connor wears his in the skin of his knuckles, pulled tight in a gesture both offensive and defensive. He concentrates on the shark on his wrist now. Its fiery unnatural eyes. Its oversized teeth. The muscular curve of its body. Such an ugly thing, yet disturbingly graceful. He hates it. In fact, he's come to love how much he hates it.

Cam closes the door and immodestly exposes the rest of himself as he dresses, as if Connor cares. He's all smiles the next time he looks at Connor, as if he knows more than he does.

"No surprise which way the wind is blowing when it comes to Risa," Cam says.

"The wind's gonna blow sand in your eyes if you're not careful," Connor responds.

"Is that a threat?"

"You know what? You're not half as smart as you think you are." Then he goes to take his own shower—a cold one that can hopefully numb the heat in his head.

63 · Grace

While playing with Dierdre is a treat, it's only to settle Grace's mind. Powerful forces are at work in this house, and those forces are a hairbreadth away from tearing each other apart. Cam and Connor had been so united in purpose until now, in spite of their rivalry. And although Grace considers herself just along for the ride, she knows she sees the things that the others don't.

For instance—she sees Connor: She knows he loves Risa and is intentionally pushing her away to save her. He will not save her. Risa will push back, acting out against his cold shoulder by throwing herself into the war against unwinding even more recklessly than before. By trying to save her, he may just get her killed.

And Risa: She would have stayed here had Connor not shown up, but now it's out of the question. Connor will never see that. He's convinced he knows her better than he truly does.

And Cam: He's the real loose cannon. He'll foolishly lap up any attention Risa gives him, whether that attention is real or calculated. In the end, whatever she gives will not be enough for him. He will feel betrayed and used—and even if Risa chooses him over Connor, he won't believe it. He won't trust it. His confused fury will fester. Grace knows that someday soon Cam will blow, and God help anyone near enough to get caught by the shrapnel.

So Grace plays with harmless Dierdre but hears every word, sees every move the others make, knowing nothing she can say will affect this doomed board of play.

Late that night Grace lies awake, staring at the ceiling. Shadow tree limbs crawl ominously across the ceiling with each passing headlight.

Risa gets up and quietly goes to the door.

"Don't," Grace says. "Please don't."

"I'm just going to the bathroom."

"No, you're not."

Risa hesitates, then stiffens a bit. "I have to." Then adds, "It's not your business anyway." But Grace knows she's wrong about that.

Risa leaves, and Grace closes her eyes, hearing the door to the boys' room creak open. She knows what will happen in there.

Risa will sit on Connor's bed, gently waking him up, if he's not already awake. Cam, who sleeps on the floor will not be asleep, but will pretend that he is. He'll hear everything.

Risa will whisper something to Connor along the lines of "We need to talk," and Connor will try to delay it. "In the morning," he'll say. But she'll touch his face, and that will make him look at her. They won't see each other's eyes but for a pinprick on their pupils of the reflected streetlight outside. It will be enough. Even in the darkness, Connor's facade will fall away, and Risa will know. They won't speak, because, after all, it was never about words, but about connection without words. A connection that can't be denied. They'll step just outside the door. Close it, but only partway, so that it doesn't make a sound.

Connor will initiate the kiss, but Risa will return the passion twofold. Any questions about their feelings for each other will be gone in a moment that they think only the two of them share. Just one kiss, and Risa will leave and sleep like a baby for the rest of the night, satisfied.

But Cam will know. And he will begin to make plans.

Grace has no idea what those plans will be, but she knows they won't help anybody. Not even himself.

She sees no hope for a winning outcome—until something drastic comes into play. It begins with a lack of shadow. A dark ceiling without the squirmy tree shadow . . . and yet there is the deep rumble of a car. No—two cars—but no headlights. Why would they be driving this time of night without headlights?

She looks out of the window to see a dark van and a dark sedan idling by the curb. The back doors of the van open, a team of armed men pile out, and without a sound they steal across the lawn toward the house.

Grace feels her heart kick into high gear. Her ears and cheeks grow hot from an adrenaline flush. They've been found!

She hears voices—whispers—and she locks onto them, hoping something they say can give her an advantage.

"You three around back," the team leader whispers. "Wait for the signal."

Then someone else whispers, "He's here. I can almost smell him."

Suddenly Grace knows all she needs to know.

She bursts out of the room to see Risa and Connor in the midst of that kiss she knew they'd take.

"Grace!" says Risa "What are you—"

But before she can finish, they all hear the double crash of both the back and front doors being kicked in. She pushes them into Cam and Connor's room, closing the door behind her. Cam leaps to his feet fully awake, as Grace knew he would be. She takes control, knowing they don't have much time. She knows this particular brand of salvation is only a fifty-fifty chance at best.

"Risa!" she whispers. "Get under the bed. Connor—facedown in your pillow. Now!" Then she turns to Cam. "And you—stay exactly where you are!"

Cam stares at her in disbelief "Are you nuts? They know we're here!"

Pounding footsteps on the stairs. Only seconds now.

"No," Grace tells him, just before she squeezes beneath the bed with Risa. "They know *you're* here."

64 · Cam

Two men in black armed with silenced tranq Magnums burst into the room. One aims his weapon at Cam, and Cam reflexively puts his hands up, furious to be caught so easily, but he knows that resisting will only get him tranq'd.

The second attacker doesn't hesitate, however, in tranq'ing the kid on the bed. Connor flinches from the shot and goes limp.

"You're a hard man to find, Mr. Comprix," says the guard with the weapon aimed squarely at Cam's chest. It almost makes him laugh.

"Me? Do you have any idea who you just tranq'd?"

"We don't care about the SlotMongers you've been slumming with," he says. "We're here for you."

Cam stares at him in amazement—and suddenly he realizes the awful and awesome power he's been handed. The power to save and to destroy. He instantly knows now that even in capture he will be a hero no matter what he does. The question is what kind of hero does he want to be? And to whom?

65 · Roberta

She does not enter the house until she's been given the all clear by the team leader. Inside, the men continue in high alert, even though their quarry has been caught. The shrill cries of a small child blare like a car alarm.

"We tranq'd the mother," the team leader tells her, "but we're worried about tranq'ing the kid. The dosage might kill it."

"Good call," says Roberta. "We lost neither our element of surprise, nor our humanity tonight." Still, the crying child is a nuisance. "Close its door. I'm sure it will cry itself back to sleep."

She follows the team leader upstairs, where two more of Proactive Citizenry's takedown force have Cam pushed up against a wall in a dark bedroom and are in the process of handcuffing him behind his back. She reaches over and flicks on the light.

"Must these things always be done in the dark?"

Once the handcuffs are snapped shut, she approaches him slowly. "Turn him to face me."

He's turned toward her, and she looks him over. He says nothing. "You don't look much worse for the wear," she says.

He glares at her. "The fugitive life suits me."

"That's a matter of opinion."

"So how did you find me?"

She runs her fingers through his hair, knowing he hates when she does that but also knowing he can't stop her while handcuffed. "You had already disappeared off the standard grid by the time I realized you were gone. I had thought you left the country, but you were far more clever than that. It never occurred to me that you'd take refuge on a ChanceFolk reservation—or that they'd even give you refuge. But People of Chance are an unpredictable lot, aren't they? In the end your thumbprint—or should I say Wil Tashi'ne's thumbprint—came up when the ID of someone named Bees-Neb Hebííte was scanned at an iMotel."

He grimaces, probably remembering the exact time and place he touched that ID, thereby leaving the incriminating print.

Roberta clicks her tongue at him. "Really, Cam, an iMotel? You were made for Fairmonts and Ritz-Carltons."

"Now what am I made for?"

"Undecided." She looks at the unconscious young man lying on the bed. "Can I assume I have the pleasure of meeting Mr. Hebííte?"

A pause, and then Cam says, "Yep. That's him."

She sits down on the bed, not even bothering to inspect the unconscious kid. "He must have been the star of the reservation parading you around there," Roberta says, mostly just to get a rise out of Cam. "If you stayed there, you might have evaded us for a good long time. Why didn't you?"

Cam shrugs and finally gives her his famous grin. "Phileas Fogg," he says. "I wanted to see the world."

"Well, you didn't quite make eighty days, but I hope it was sufficient." She turns to the team leader. "Time to wrap this up."

"Do we take the others?"

"Don't be ridiculous," Roberta chides. "We've gotten what we came for. I have no desire to complicate things with kidnapping."

"But taking me—that's not kidnapping?" Cam asks.

"No," Roberta says, happy to take the bait. "According to the law, it would be considered the retrieval of stolen property.

In fact, I could press charges against everyone in this house, but I won't. I've no need to be vindictive."

They haul him out to the car, but gently so, by Roberta's orders. Upstairs the child continues to cry, but the sound is greatly muffled when they pull the fractured front door closed. The mother, whoever she is, and the rest of this unseemly crew will eventually regain consciousness to take care of the irascible toddler. If not by morning, then a few hours later.

They drive off with Cam seated in the back of the sedan next to Roberta, handcuffs still on, although he's not struggling against them. Now that Cam has freed his grin, he won't stop. She has to admit it's a bit unnerving.

"I assume the senator and the general were fuming when I left."

"On the contrary," Roberta tells him happily. "They never knew that you left. I told them that you and I were going back to Hawaii for a few weeks before you reported to them. That you wished to spend some time at the clinic for a motivational makeover. And, of course, that's where we're now going. So that you can have some mild cortical retuning."

"Cortical retuning . . . ," he echoes.

"Only to be expected," Roberta tells him. "You've been prone to quite a lot of wrongful thinking ever since you were first rewound. But I'm happy to tell you that I have an effective way of taking what's wrong within that wonderful mind of yours . . . and making it right."

Roberta can't help but take pleasure in her victory as she watches the grin finally leave his face.

66 · Connor

Connor opens his eyes to the same room and the same bed he had been traq'd in. He knows this can't be right. They came for them, didn't they? *No,* he thinks. *Grace knew better. They came for Cam.*

"Welcome back from Tranqistan."

He turns his head to see Sonia sitting in a chair beside him. He tries to push himself up, but feels dizzy, so he lets his elbows slide out from under him, and his head hits the pillow, his brain clanging inside him like the clapper of a bell.

"Easy now. I'd think with all the times you've been traq'd, you know to take it slow."

He's about to ask where Risa is, but then she appears at the door. "Is he awake?"

"Barely." Sonia grabs her cane and rises with a grunt, vacating the seat for Risa. "It's almost noon. Time to open up shop, or the crowds may bust the door down." But before she leaves the room, she pats Connor comfortingly on the leg. "We'll talk later. I'll tell you everything you want to know about my husband. Or at least what this fool brain of mine still remembers."

Connor smiles at that. "I'm sure you remember things back to the Stone Age."

"Don't be a wiseass."

Then she waddles out, and Risa takes the seat. She also takes Connor's hand. He squeezes back, and unlike the day before, he does it wholeheartedly.

"I'm glad we let you sleep it off without waking you. You needed it."

"You don't get rest during tranq sleep. You just go away." He clears his throat, to remove a persistent frog. "So what happened?"

Risa explains how she and Grace were never even found under the bed and how Cam was collared, then taken away. Connor is amazed with their luck—but maybe he shouldn't be. If the mission of that task force was to simply capture Cam, they couldn't care less about his travel companions. Get in, get out. Their mission was accomplished, and they had no idea the forest they had missed for the tree.

"Cam could have turned us all in, but he didn't," Risa says. "He sacrificed himself for us."

"He was going down anyway," Connor points out. "It wasn't exactly a sacrifice."

"Give him some credit—by turning us in he would have bought himself some serious bargaining power." She thinks for a moment, her grip on Connor's hand loosening slightly. "He's not the monster you think he is."

She waits for Connor to respond to that, but he's still too tired and cranky from the tranquilizer to agree with her. And he might agree—after all, Cam had given them the information on Proactive Citizenry. Still, his motives seem to have too many layers to be anything but cloudy.

"Cam saved us, Connor—at least give him that."

He gives her something that could, from a certain angle, be considered a reluctant nod. "What do you think they'll do with him?"

"He's their golden child," Risa says. "They'll clean up the tarnish and make him shine again." Then she smiles, her thoughts drifting off to him. "Of course, Cam would point out that gold doesn't tarnish."

That smile is a little too warm, and although Connor knows he's playing with fire, he dares to say, "If I didn't know better, I'd think you were in love with him."

She holds his gaze, a little coolly. "Do you really want to go there?"

"No," Connor admits.

But Risa takes him there anyway. "I love what he did for us. I love that his heart is purer than anyone else believes. I love that he's far more innocent than he is jaded, but doesn't even know it."

"And you love that he's completely infatuated with you."

Risa smiles and tosses her hair like a shampoo model. "Well, that goes without saying." The move is so unlike her, it makes them both laugh.

Connor sits up, his head no longer spinning when he does. "I'm glad you chose me before they came for him."

"I didn't chose anything," Risa says, just the slightest bit annoyed.

"Well, I'm just glad," says Connor gently. "That's all." He touches her face with Roland's hand, the shark only inches away, but finally realizes that it will never be close enough to bite.

Sonia, still downstairs, decides that taking a tranq for the team is more than enough to ask of Hannah. She can't ask Hannah to keep fugitives in her home after last night's attack.

"I'm sorry—but I've got Dierdre to think about now," Hannah tells them with tears in her eyes. Holding the toddler in her arms, she wishes them all Godspeed. Connor finds he has a lump in his throat for the storked baby he saved and will never see again.

Sonia drives him, Risa, and Grace back to her shop in her dark-windowed Suburban. She decides to keep the shop closed today, and there in the back room, the five of them talk of issues weighty enough, it seems, to collapse the floor beneath them. Connor insists that Grace be included because, although she bounces her knees impatiently and appears to have little interest in the conversation, all of Grace's appearances are deceiving.

"A reliable source working with Proactive Citizenry told me a very interesting story," Connor begins. He has no idea if Trace Neuhauser even survived the crash in the Salton Sea. He thinks not, because Trace would never have allowed the massacres that Starkey is now orchestrating in the name of freedom. But at least Trace was able to pass what he knew on to Connor before he was forced to pilot that plane for Starkey. "My source talked about how the name of Janson Rheinschild still strikes fear into the hearts of Proactive Citizenry's inner circle."

Sonia gives a satisfied and somewhat sinister laugh. "Glad to hear it. I hope he's always the ghost in their lousy machine."

"So it's true that they"—Connor tries to choose his words carefully, but realizes there's no delicate way to say it—"that they took him out?"

"They didn't have to," Sonia says. "When you tear a man down to his roots, it doesn't leave much behind. Janson died a broken man. He willed himself to die along with his dreams, and I couldn't stop him."

Risa, who's hearing all this for the first time, asks, "Who was he?"

"My husband, dear." And then Sonia heaves a sorrowful sigh. "And my partner in crime."

That gets Grace's attention, although she doesn't say anything just yet.

"Proactive Citizenry wiped him from their history," Connor says.

"*Their* history? They wiped him from *world* history! Did you know we won the Nobel Prize?"

Risa just stares at her dumbfounded, and her expression makes Sonia laugh.

"Bioscience, dear. Back then antiquing was just my hobby."

"This was before the Heartland War?" she asks.

Sonia nods. "Wars have a way of reinventing people. And making too many things disappear."

Connor's chair scrapes on the wooden floor as he pulls it forward. "Lev and I looked for his name everywhere online. Totally gone. But there was one article that misspelled it—that was the only way we found him." Then Connor adds, "Your picture was in the photo. That's how we knew you were somehow involved."

Sonia turns to spit on the ground. "Deleting us from history was the ultimate insult. But it made it easier for me to disappear from them. From everyone."

"We know you started Proactive Citizenry," Connor says, noting Risa's jaw drop again.

"*That* was Janson. I was out of it by then. I saw the writing on the wall and knew it was in blood—but he was an idealist. His finest trait and his deepest flaw." Her eyes get moist and she points to a tissue box on the cluttered desk. Grace hands it to her. She blots her eyes once, then doesn't tear up again.

"We know Proactive Citizenry was supposed to be a watchdog organization," Connor says, "protecting the world against the abuse of biotech. What went wrong?"

"We let the genie out of the bottle," Sonia says sadly. "And a genie is loyal to no master."

From down below they can hear the grumbles of her hidden AWOLs arguing. Sonia bangs her cane on the trapdoor three times and they fall silent. Secrets below. Secrets above. Connor finds himself leaning closer as she begins to tell her tale.

"Janson and I pioneered the neurografting techniques that allowed every part of a donor body to be used in transplant. Every organ, every limb, every brain cell. The idea was to save lives. To better the world. But there's a road to hell for every good intention."

"The Unwind Accord?" says Connor.

Sonia nods. "It hadn't even been thought of when we perfected our techniques—but the Heartland War was raging, and with school systems failing all over the country, feral teens were filling the streets in massive numbers. People were scared, and people were desperate." Sonia's eyes seem to go far away as she drags back the memory. "The Unwind Accord took our lifesaving technology and weaponized it to use against all those kids that no one wanted to deal with. The board of Proactive Citizenry went along with it—pushing Janson out—because they saw more than just dollar signs: They saw an entire industry waiting to be born."

Connor finds himself taking a deep, shuddering breath at the suggestion of unwinding being "born."

"It happened so quickly," Sonia continues. "When no one was looking. The Juvenile Authority was established without public outcries and without much resistance. Everyone was so glad just to end the Heartland War and get the feral teens out of sight and out of mind. No one wanted to consider where they were going. Now there was a supply of anonymous parts for anyone who wanted them. And even if you didn't want younger hands or brighter eyes, there were advertisements everywhere to convince you that you did. 'A new you from the inside out!' the billboards said. 'Add fifty years to your life.'" Sonia shakes her head bitterly. "They created want . . . and want turned to need . . . and unwinding became woven into the fabric of everything."

No one says a word. It's like a moment of silence for the many kids lost to that great unwinding machine. The industry, as Sonia had called it. A mill of commerce trafficking in flesh, working outside the realm of ethics yet within the law and with the complete consent of society.

But then Connor realizes something. "There's more to the story, isn't there, Sonia? There has to be—or else why would Proactive Citizenry still be afraid of the man they defeated? Why would Janson Rheinschild's name still make them shake in their boots?"

Now Sonia smiles. "What word strikes fear into the heart of any industry?" And when no one answers, she whispers it like a dark mantra.

"Obsolescence . . ."

Out in the antique shop, in a dingy corner that generally doesn't see much traffic, is a stack of dusty old computers stacked one on top of another, daring gravity to topple it, which it never does. This is where Sonia leads them. "I keep these because every now and then a collector comes in looking for older machines—but not too often—and when they do, they never pay very much."

"So why are we here?" Connor asks.

She taps him more lightly than usual with her cane. "To illustrate a point. Technology doesn't age well—not like a fine piece of furniture." And she sits herself down on one of those fine pieces of furniture—a curvy wooden chair with a red velvet seat. The chair probably goes for more than all the computers combined.

"When they passed the Unwind Accord, I gave up. I was disgusted by my own unintentional role in making it happen. But Janson, he fought it down to the day he died. Now that people were hooked on parts, Janson knew the only way to end unwinding was to give them cheaper parts that you didn't have to harvest. Take away the need for harvesting, and suddenly people would rediscover their consciences. Unwinding would end."

"ChanceFolk use their spirit animals for transplant," Connor points out. "That's how they got around it."

"I'll do you one better," says Sonia. "What if you could grow an endless supply of cultured cells, put them into a machine, like—oh, say, a computer printer—and print yourself out an organ?"

Everyone looks to one another. Connor's not quite sure if she's being rhetorical, making a joke, or if she's just plain nuts.

"Like . . . an electronic nail builder?" Risa suggests.

"A variation on a theme," says Sonia. "Similar technology taken a huge leap forward."

"Uh . . . ," says Connor, "a picture of a liver isn't gonna help anyone much."

Then Sonia gets a funny look in her eye. A hint of the scientist she once was. "What if it's not just a picture?" she asks. "What if you could keep printing layer after layer of cells on top of one another, making it thicker and thicker? What if you were able to solve the blood flow problem by programming gaps in the printing sequence and lining those gaps with a semipermeable membrane that would mature into blood vessels?"

Now she moves her gaze, locking on each of them as she speaks. The passion behind her eyes is hypnotic. Suddenly she's no longer an old woman, but an impassioned scientist filled with a fire she's been holding within her for years.

"What if you invented a printer that could build *living human organs*?" Sonia rises from her chair. She's a short woman, but right now Connor could swear she's towering over them. "And what if you sold the patent to the nation's largest medical manufacturer . . . and what if they took all of that work . . . and *buried* it? And took the plans and *burned* them? And took every printer and *smashed* it, and prevented *anyone* from ever knowing that the technology existed?"

Sonia's whole body shakes, not out of weakness, but out of fury. "What if they made the solution to unwinding disappear because too many people have too much invested in keeping things *exactly . . . the way . . . they are.*"

Then in the shivering silence that follows, comes a single unpretentious, unassuming voice.

"And what if there's still one organ printer left," says Grace, "hiding in the corner of an antique shop?"

Sonia's rage resolves into the most perfect grandmotherly smile.

"And what if there is?"

Epilogue: The Widow Rheinschild

Years before Connor, or Risa, or Lev are even born, Sonia batters the bitter cold of a February day to carry a heavy cardboard box from her car to a storage unit—just one among many anonymous units in a large complex.

Her husband's funeral was only a week ago, but Sonia's not the kind of woman to wallow in self-pity for long.

Her storage unit is the largest one offered. Big enough to fit all the furniture, knickknacks, and objects of desire she and her late husband had collected over the years. Truth be told, it was mostly her collection. Janson was not a materialistic man. All he ever wanted was a comfortable chair and a place in history. Well, he was robbed of one and died in the other.

The lock on the unit is covered in frost. Only a week since the movers piled everything in, and already it has the semblance of something ancient. She tries to fit the key into the lock, but her gloves are too thick. In the end she must remove them and bear the cold on her fingers as she inserts the key, turns it, and tugs on the lock.

Everything has been moved to this storage unit. Her house is now empty—but it won't be for long. It's been sold to a lovely family, or so she was told by the Realtor. Sonia priced it way under market to make sure it would sell quickly.

As for all the money that was paid to Janson for the rights to the organ printer, she's chosen to give the bulk of it to Austin's friends. They say they're starting a secret organization to fight *unwinding. The Anti-Divisional Underground, or something like that. Well, if they can use that money to save as much as a single Unwind from going under the knife, it will be worth it.*

With a grunt, Sonia raises the rolling door and is faced with the trappings of her life, everything placed with puzzlelike precision so it all will fit. How odd that the objects of one's world can all be squeezed into such a compact space. The neutron star of life's tenure.

Looking on it brings her a moment of despair—but like the snow flurries outside, she doesn't let it stick. If there's one lesson she has learned from her late husband, it's that one cannot let the events of one's past murder one's future. And future is all that Sonia has now that her past has been so effectively erased. She actually had to purchase a counterfeit passport and driver's license, since her real ones were now invalid. She kept her first name, though, choosing to maintain a shred of her identity to spite those who would happily send her sailing into nameless oblivion.

While not bound for oblivion, Sonia is leaving, however. She doesn't care where—but when purchasing an airline ticket one must have a destination—so before the movers came, she had gone to the globe in Janson's study. She spun it, closed her eyes, and jabbed her finger at it. Her finger came down in the Mediterranean, on the island of Crete, so that is where she will go. She speaks no Greek, but she will learn, and the island will be the alpha and omega of her life for a good long while.

She searches the jam-packed storage space for a safe spot to leave the heavy box she carries. Its contents are too sensitive to have allowed the movers to handle. This is something she wanted to do for herself. Janson would be glad that she's doing it, too. She can feel him smiling at her the way he did on that wonderful night of giddy fantasy, when they ate the city's most expensive meal, drank champagne, and dared to dream that they were moving from the darkness back into the light.

Sonia is wise enough to know that she's moved through times of light and darkness all of her life. Now is a time of intense darkness—but she cannot let it consume her, as it consumed Janson. In time, perhaps she'll find herself in a place of light again with the courage and resolve enough to take a stand. To rise up and do something about the road to hell their good intentions have paved—or more accurately, the road that others had paved for them. But that's for a distant tomorrow. For now she's tired, and broken and just needs to run away.

At last she finds a suitable spot in the storage unit for the box and sets it down gently, making sure it's in a place where it can't fall and nothing will fall on it. Then she looks at the stacks of belongings around her.

"So much stuff," she says aloud. She could open up an antique shop with all the junk she's collected! If she ever does come back to the States someday, perhaps she will.

Satisfied, she wends her way to the entrance of the unit, pulls down the rolling door, and locks away her old life for ten, maybe twenty years.

As she drives away, she's surprised to find herself smiling in spite of everything. Yes, the very organization Janson founded ultimately turned on them to destroy their lives and tried to destroy every last glimmer of hope.

But that's where they failed.

Hope can be bruised and battered. It can be forced underground and even rendered unconscious, but hope cannot be killed. The blueprints to the organ printer are gone. So are all the large prototypes. Smashed and melted and buried in some unmarked grave of scuttled technology.

But no one knew about the smaller prototype. The one that gave Austin back his missing fingers—the one that Janson kept hidden in a cardboard box in his study.

Sonia gets on the highway, heading for the airport, and as she does, she turns on the radio, finds a station playing classic rock from her childhood, and she sings along, ignoring the icy winds that rattle the car.

There's no doubt about it; Janson's dream is dead . . . but when the time is right and the winds begin to change, even the deadest of dreams can be resurrected.

THE REAL LOLITA

ALSO BY SARAH WEINMAN

Women Crime Writers:
Eight Suspense Novels of the 1940s & 50s

Troubled Daughters, Twisted Wives:
Stories from the Trailblazers of Domestic Suspense

THE
REAL LOLITA

*The Kidnapping of Sally Horner
and the Novel That Scandalized the World*

SARAH WEINMAN

ecco

An Imprint of HarperCollins *Publishers*

FIRST EDITION

Designed by Suet Yee Chong

Library of Congress Cataloging-in-Publication Data

Names: Weinman, Sarah, author.
Title: The real Lolita : the kidnapping of Sally Horner and the novel that scandalized the world / [by Sarah Weinman].
Description: First edition. | New York, NY : HarperCollins Publishers, 2018. | Includes bibliographical references and index.
Identifiers: LCCN 2018006366 (print) | LCCN 2018021107 (ebook) | ISBN 9780062661944 (ebook) | ISBN 9780062861184 | ISBN 9780062661951 | ISBN 9780062661920 | ISBN 9780062661937
Subjects: LCSH: Horner, Sally. | Kidnapping—United States—Case studies. | Child abuse—United States—Case studies. | Captivity—United States—Case studies.
Classification: LCC HV6603.H67 (ebook) | LCC HV6603.H67 W45 2018 (print) | DDC 362.88092 [B] —dc23
LC record available at https://lccn.loc.gov/2018006366

ISBN 978-0-06-266192-0

18 19 20 21 22 LSC 10 9 8 7 6 5 4 3 2 1

For my mother

You have to be an artist and a madman, a creature of infinite melancholy, with a bubble of hot poison in your loins and a super-voluptuous flame permanently aglow in your subtle spine (oh, how you have to cringe and hide!), in order to discern at once, by ineffable signs—the slightly feline outline of a cheekbone, the slenderness of a downy limb, and other indices which despair and shame and tears of tenderness forbid me to tabulate—the little deadly demon among the wholesome children; *she* stands unrecognized by them and unconscious herself of her fantastic power.

—Vladimir Nabokov, *Lolita*

I want to go home as soon as I can.

—Sally Horner, March 21, 1950

CONTENTS

INTRODUCTION: *"Had I Done to Her . . . ?"*   I

ONE: *The Five-and-Dime*   15

TWO: *A Trip to the Beach*   21

THREE: *From Wellesley to Cornell*   27

FOUR: *Sally, at First*   33

FIVE: *The Search for Sally*   39

SIX: *Seeds of Compulsion*   45

SEVEN: *Frank, in Shadow*   57

EIGHT: *"A Lonely Mother Waits"*   67

NINE: *The Prosecutor*   73

TEN: *Baltimore*   83

ELEVEN: *Walks of Death*   93

TWELVE: *Across America by Oldsmobile*   101

THIRTEEN: *Dallas*   111

FOURTEEN: *The Neighbor*   117

FIFTEEN: *San Jose*   125

SIXTEEN: *After the Rescue*   135

SEVENTEEN: *A Guilty Plea*   143

EIGHTEEN: *When Nabokov (Really) Learned About Sally*   151

NINETEEN: *Rebuilding a Life*   157

TWENTY: Lolita *Progresses*   165

TWENTY-ONE: *Weekend in Wildwood*   169

TWENTY-TWO: *The Note Card*   177

TWENTY-THREE: *"A Darn Nice Girl"*   183

TWENTY-FOUR: *La Salle in Prison*   189

TWENTY-FIVE: *"Gee, Ed, That Was Bad Luck"*   199

TWENTY-SIX: *Writing and Publishing* Lolita   205

TWENTY-SEVEN: *Connecting Sally Horner to* Lolita   217

TWENTY-EIGHT: *"He Told Me Not to Tell"*   229

TWENTY-NINE: *Aftermaths*   235

EPILOGUE: *On Two Girls Named Lolita and Sally*   253

ACKNOWLEDGMENTS   261

NOTES   265

BIBLIOGRAPHY   287

PERMISSIONS   291

INDEX   295

THE REAL LOLITA

"Had I Done to Her . . . ?"

> "Had I done to Dolly, perhaps, what Frank Lasalle,
> a fifty-year-old mechanic, had done to eleven-year-old
> Sally Horner in 1948?"
>
> —Vladimir Nabokov, *Lolita*

A couple of years before her life changed course forever, Sally Horner posed for a photograph. Nine years old at the time, she stands in front of the back fence of her house, a thin, leafless tree disappearing into the top right-hand corner of the frame. Tendrils of Sally's hair brush her face and the top shoulder of her coat. She looks straight ahead at the photographer, her sister's husband, trust and love for him evident in her expression. The photo has a ghostly quality, enhanced by the sepia color and the blurred focus.

This wasn't the first photograph of Sally Horner that I saw, and I've seen a great many more since. But this is the one I think of the most. Because it's the only photo where Sally has

Florence "Sally" Horner, age nine.

a child's utter lack of guile, without any idea of what horrors lie ahead. Here was evidence of one future she might have had. Sally didn't have a chance to live that one out.

FLORENCE "SALLY" HORNER disappeared from Camden, New Jersey, in mid-June 1948, in the company of a man calling himself Frank La Salle. Twenty-one months later, in March 1950, with the help of a concerned neighbor, Sally telephoned her family from San Jose, California, begging for someone to send the FBI to rescue her. Sensational coverage and La Salle's hasty guilty plea ensued, and the man spent the remainder of his life in prison.

Sally Horner, however, had only two more years to live. And when she died, in mid-August 1952, news of her death reached Vladimir Nabokov at a critical time in the creation of his novel-in-progress—a book he had struggled with, in various forms, for more than a decade, and one that would transform his personal and professional life far beyond his imaginings.

Sally Horner's story buttressed the second half of *Lolita*. Instead of pitching the manuscript into the fire—Nabokov had come close twice, prevented only by the quick actions of his wife, Véra—he set to finish it, borrowing details from the real-life case as needed. Both Sally Horner and Nabokov's fictional creation Dolores Haze were brunette daughters of widowed mothers, fated to be captives of much older predators for nearly two years.

Lolita, when published, was infamous, then famous, always controversial, always a topic of discussion. It has sold more than sixty million copies worldwide in its sixty-plus years of life. Sally Horner, however, was largely forgotten, except by her immediate family members and close friends. They would not even learn of the connection to *Lolita* until just a few years ago. A curious reporter had drawn a line between the real girl and the fictional character in the early 1960s, only to be scoffed at by the Nabokovs. Then, around the novel's fiftieth anniversary, a well-versed Nabokov scholar explored the link between *Lolita* and Sally, showing just how deeply Nabokov embedded the true story into his fiction.

But neither of those men—the journalist or the academic—thought to look more closely at the brief life of Sally Horner. A life that at first resembled a hardscrabble American childhood, then became something extraordinary, then uplifting, and, last of all, tragic. A life that reverberated through the culture, and irrevocably changed the course of twentieth-century literature.

I TELL CRIME STORIES for a living. That means I read a great deal about, and immerse myself in, bad things happening to people, good or otherwise. Crime stories grapple with what causes people to topple over from sanity to madness, from decency to psychopathy, from love to rage. They ignite within me the twinned sense of obsession and compulsion. If these feelings persist, I know the story is mine to tell.

Some stories, I've learned over time, work best in short form. Others break loose from the artificial constraints of a magazine article. Without structure I cannot tell the story, but without a sense of emotional investment and mission, I cannot do justice to the people whose lives I attempt to re-create for readers.

Several years ago I stumbled upon what happened to Sally Horner while looking for a new story to tell. It was my habit then, and remains so now, to plumb obscure corners of the Internet for ideas. I gravitate toward the mid-twentieth century because that period is well documented by newspapers, radio, even early television, yet just outside the bounds of memory. Court records still exist, but require extra rounds of effort to uncover. There are people still alive who remember what happened, but few enough that their recollections are on the cusp of vanishing. Here, in that liminal space where the contemporary meets the past, are stories crying out for greater context and understanding.

Sally Horner caught my attention with particular urgency. Here was a young girl, victimized over a twenty-one-month odyssey from New Jersey to California, by an opportunistic child molester. Here was a girl who figured out a way to survive away from home against her will, who acted in ways that baffled her friends and relatives at the time. We better comprehend those means of survival now because of more recent accounts of girls and women in captivity. Here was a girl who survived her ordeal when so many others, snatched away from their lives, do not. Then for her to die so soon after her rescue, her story subsumed by a novel, one of the most iconic, important works of the twentieth century? Sally Horner got under my skin in a way that few stories ever have.

I dug for the details of Sally's life and its connections to *Lolita* throughout 2014 for a feature published that fall by the Canadian online magazine *Hazlitt*. Even after chasing down court documents, talking to family members, visiting some of the places she had lived—and some of the places where La Salle took her—and writing the piece, I knew I wasn't finished with Sally Horner. Or, more accurately, she was not finished with me.

What drove me then and galls me now is that Sally's abduction defined her entire short life. She never had a chance to grow up, pursue a career, marry, have children, grow old, be happy. She never got to build on the fierce intelligence so evident to her best friend that, nearly seven decades later, she spoke to me of Sally not as a peer, but as a mentor. After Sally died, her family rarely mentioned her or what had happened. They didn't speak of her with awe, or pity, or scorn. She was only an absence.

For decades Sally's claim to immortality was as an incidental reference in *Lolita,* one of the many utterances by the predatory narrator, Humbert Humbert, that allows him to control the narrative and, of course, to control Dolores Haze. Like Lolita, Sally Horner was no "little deadly demon among the wholesome children." Both girls, fictional and real, *were* wholesome children. Contrary to Humbert Humbert's assertions, Sally, like Lolita, was no seductress, "unconscious herself of her fantastic power."

The fantastic power both girls possessed was the capacity to haunt.

I FIRST READ *LOLITA* at sixteen, as a high school junior whose intellectual curiosity far exceeded her emotional maturity. It was something of a self-imposed dare. Only a few months earlier I'd breezed through *One Day in the Life of Ivan Denisovich* by Alexander Solzhenitsyn. Some months later I'd reckon with *Portnoy's Complaint* by Philip Roth. I thought I could handle what transpired between Dolores Haze and Humbert Humbert.

I thought I could appreciate the language and not be affected by the story. I pretended I was ready for *Lolita,* but I was nowhere close.

Those iconic opening lines, "Lolita, light of my life, fire of my loins. My sin, my soul. Lo-lee-ta," sent a frisson down my adolescent spine. I didn't like that feeling, but I wasn't supposed to. I was soon in thrall to Humbert Humbert's voice, the silken veneer barely concealing a loathsome predilection.

I kept reading, hoping there might be some salvation for Dolores, even though I should have known from the foreword, supplied by the fictional narrator John Ray, Jr., PhD, that it does not arrive for a long time. And when she finally escapes from Humbert's clutches to embrace her own life, her freedom is short-lived.

I realized, though I could not properly articulate it, that Vladimir Nabokov had pulled off something remarkable. *Lolita* was my first encounter with an unreliable narrator, one who must be regarded with suspicion. The whole book relies upon the mounting tension between what Humbert Humbert wants the reader to know and what the reader can discern. It is all too easy to be seduced by his sophisticated narration, his panoramic descriptions of America, circa 1947, and his observations of the girl he nicknames Lolita. Those who love language and literature are rewarded richly, but also duped. If you're not being careful, you lose sight of the fact that Humbert raped a twelve-year-old child repeatedly over the course of nearly two years, and got away with it.

It happened to the writer Mikita Brottman, who in *The Maximum Security Book Club* described her own cognitive dissonance discussing *Lolita* with the discussion group she led at a Maryland maximum-security prison. Brottman, reading the novel in advance, had "immediately fallen in love with the narrator," so much so that Humbert Humbert's "style, humor, and sophistication blind[ed] me to his faults." Brottman knew she shouldn't sympathize with a pedophile, but she couldn't help being mesmerized.

The prisoners in her book club were nowhere near so enchanted. An hour into the discussion, one of them looked up at Brottman and cried, "He's just an old pedo!" A second prisoner added: "It's all bullshit, all his long, fancy words. I can see through it. It's all a cover-up. I know what he wants to do with her." A third prisoner drove home the point that *Lolita* "isn't a *love story*. Get rid of all the fancy language, bring it down to the lower [*sic*] common denominator, and it's a grown man molesting a little girl."

Brottman, grappling with the prisoners' blunt responses, realized her foolishness. She wasn't the first, nor the last, to be seduced by style or manipulated by language. Millions of readers missed how *Lolita* folded in the story of a girl who experienced in real life what Dolores Haze suffered on the page. The appreciation of art can make a sucker out of those who forget the darkness of real life.

Knowing about Sally Horner does not diminish *Lolita*'s brilliance, or Nabokov's audacious inventiveness, but it does augment the horror he also captured in the novel.

WRITING ABOUT VLADIMIR NABOKOV daunted me, and still does. Reading his work and researching in his archives was like coming up against an electrified fence designed to keep me away from the truth. Clues would present themselves and then evaporate. Letters and diary entries would hint at larger meanings without supporting evidence. My central quest with respect to Nabokov was to figure out what he knew about Sally

Horner and when he knew it. Through a lifetime, and afterlife, of denials and omissions about the sources of his fiction, he made my pursuit as difficult as possible.

Nabokov loathed people scavenging for biographical details that would explain his work. "I hate tampering with the precious lives of great writers and I hate Tom-peeping over the fence of those lives," he once declared in a lecture about Russian literature to his students at Cornell University, where he taught from 1948 through 1959. "I hate the vulgarity of 'human interest,' I hate the rustle of skirts and giggles in the corridors of time—and no biographer will ever catch a glimpse of my private life."

He made his public distaste for the literal mapping of fiction to real life known as early as 1944, in his idiosyncratic, highly selective, and sharply critical biography of the Russian writer Nikolai Gogol. "It is strange, the morbid inclination we have to derive satisfaction from the fact (generally false and always irrelevant) that a work of art is traceable to a 'true story,'" Nabokov chided. "Is it because we begin to respect ourselves more when we learn that the writer, just like ourselves, was not clever enough to make up a story himself?"

The Gogol biography was more a window into Nabokov's own thinking than a treatise on the Russian master. With respect to his own work, Nabokov did not want critics, academics, students, and readers to look for literal meanings or real-life influences. Whatever source material he'd relied on was grist for his own literary mill, to be used as only he saw fit. His insistence on the utter command of his craft served Nabokov well as his reputation and fame grew after the American publication of Lolita in 1958. Scores of interviewers, whether they wrote him letters, interrogated him on television, or visited him at his house, abided by his rules of engagement. They handed over their questions in advance and accepted his answers, written at leisure, cobbling them together to mimic spontaneous conversation.

Nabokov erected roadblocks barring access to his private life for deeper, more complex reasons than to protect his inalienable right to tell stories. He kept family secrets, quotidian and gargantuan, that he did not wish anyone to air in public. And no wonder, when you consider what he lived through: the Russian Revolution, multiple emigrations, the rise of the Nazis, and the fruits of international bestselling success. After he immigrated to the United States in 1940, Nabokov also abandoned Russian, the language of the first half of his literary career, for English. He equated losing his mother tongue to losing a limb, even though, in terms of style and syntax, his English dazzled beyond the imagination of most native speakers.

Always by his side, aiding Nabokov with his lifelong quest to keep nosy people at bay, was his wife, Véra. She took on all of the tasks Nabokov wouldn't or couldn't do: assistant, chief letter writer, first reader, driver, subsidiary rights agent, and many other less-defined roles. She subsumed herself, willingly, for his art, and anyone who poked too deeply at her undying devotion looking for contrary feelings was rewarded with fierce denials, stonewalling, or outright untruths.

Yet this book exists in part because the Nabokovs' roadblocks eventually crumbled. Other people did gain access to his private life. There were three increasingly tendentious biographies by Andrew Field, whose relationship with his subject began in harmony but curdled into acrimony well before Nabokov died in 1977. A two-part definitive study by Brian Boyd is still the biographical standard, a quarter century after its publication, with which any Nabokov scholar must reckon. And

Stacy Schiff's 1999 portrayal of Véra Nabokov illuminated so much about their partnership and teased out the fragments of Véra's inner life.

We've also learned more about what made Nabokov tick since the Library of Congress lifted its fifty-year restriction upon his papers in 2009, opening the entire collection to the public. The more substantive trove at the New York Public Library's Berg Collection still has some restrictions, but I was able to immerse myself in Nabokov's work, his notes, his manuscripts, and also the ephemera—newspaper clippings, letters, photographs, diaries.

A strange thing happened as I looked for clues in his published work and his archives: Nabokov grew less knowable. Such is the paradox of a writer whose work is so filled with metaphor and allusion, so dissected by literary scholars and ordinary readers. Even Boyd claimed, more than a decade and a half after writing his biography of Nabokov, that he still did not fully understand *Lolita*.

What helped me grapple with the book was to reread it, again and again. Sometimes like a potboiler, in a single gulp, and other times slowing down to cross-check each sentence. No one could get every reference and recursion on the first try; the novel rewards repeated reading. Nabokov himself believed the only novels worth reading are the ones that demand to be read on multiple occasions. Once you grasp it, the contradictions of *Lolita*'s narrative and plot structure reveal a logic true to itself.

During one *Lolita* reread, I was reminded of the narrator of an earlier Nabokov story, "Spring in Fialta": "Personally, I never could understand the good of thinking up books, of penning things that had not really happened in some way or other . . .

were I a writer, I should allow only my heart to have imagination, and for the rest to rely upon memory, that long-drawn sunset shadow of one's personal truth."

Nabokov himself never openly admitted to such an attitude himself. But the clues are all there in his work. Particularly so in *Lolita*, with its careful attention to popular culture, the habits of preadolescent girls, and the banalities of then-modern American life. Searching out these signs of real-life happenings was no easy task. I found myself probing absence as much as presence, relying on inference and informed speculation as much as fact.

Some cases drop all the direct evidence into your lap. Some cases are more circumstantial. The case for what Vladimir Nabokov knew of Sally Horner and when he knew it falls squarely into the latter category. Investigating it, and how he incorporated Sally's story into *Lolita*, led me to uncover deeper ties between reality and fiction, and to the thematic compulsion Nabokov spent more than two decades exploring, in fits and starts, before finding full fruition in *Lolita*.

Lolita's narrative, it turns out, depended more on a real-life crime than Nabokov would ever admit.

OVER THE FOUR OR SO YEARS I spent working on this book project, I spoke with a great many people about *Lolita*. For some it was their favorite novel, or one of their favorites. Others had never read the book but ventured an opinion nonetheless. Some loathed it, or the idea of it. No one was neutral. Considering the subject matter, this was not a surprise. Not a single person, when I quoted the passage about Sally Horner, remembered it.

I can't say Nabokov designed the book to hide Sally from
the reader. Given that the story moves so quickly, perhaps an
homage to the highways Humbert and Dolores traverse over
many thousands of miles in their cross-country odyssey, it's
easy to miss a lot as you go. But I would argue that even casual
readers of *Lolita*, who number in the tens of millions, plus the
many more millions with some awareness of the novel, the two
film versions, or its place in the culture these past six decades,
should pay attention to the story of Sally Horner because it is
the story of so many girls and women, not just in America,
but everywhere. So many of these stories seem like everyday
injustices—young women denied opportunity to advance, tethered to marriage and motherhood. Others are more horrific,
girls and women abused, brutalized, kidnapped, or worse.

Yet Sally Horner's plight is also uniquely American, unfolding in the shadows of the Second World War, after victory
had created a solid, prosperous middle class that could not
compensate for terrible future decline. Her abduction is woven
into the fabric of her hometown of Camden, New Jersey, which
at the time believed itself to be at the apex of the American
Dream. Wandering its streets today, as I did on several occasions, was a stark reminder of how Camden has changed for
the worse. Sally should have been able to travel America of her
own volition, a culmination of the Dream. Instead she was
taken against her will, and the road trip became a nightmare.

Sally's life ended too soon. But her story helped inspire a
novel people are still discussing and debating more than sixty
years after its initial publication. Vladimir Nabokov, through
his use of language and formal invention, gave fictional authority to a pedophile and charmed and revolted millions of
readers in the process. By exploring the life of Sally Horner, I
reveal the truth behind the curtain of fiction. What Humbert

Humbert did to Dolores Haze is, in fact, what Frank La Salle did to Sally Horner in 1948.

With this book, Sally Horner takes precedence. Like the butterflies that Vladimir Nabokov so loved, she emerges from the cage of both fiction and fact, ready to fly free.

ONE

The Five-and-Dime

Sally Horner walked into the Woolworth's on Broadway and Federal in Camden, New Jersey, to steal a five-cent notebook. She'd been dared to by the clique of girls she desperately wanted to join. Sally had never stolen anything in her life; usually she went to that particular five-and-dime for school supplies and her favorite candy. The clique told her it would be easy. Nobody would suspect a girl like Sally, a fifth-grade honor pupil and president of the Junior Red Cross Club at Northeast School, to be a thief. Despite her mounting dread at breaking the law, she believed them. She had no idea a simple act of shoplifting on a March afternoon in 1948 would destroy her life.

Once inside Woolworth's, Sally reached for the first notebook she spied on the gleaming white nickel counter. She stuffed it into her bag and walked away, careful to look straight ahead to the exit door. Before she could cross the threshold to freedom, she felt a hand grab her arm.

Sally looked up. A slender, hawk-faced man loomed above her, iron-gray hair underneath a wide-brimmed fedora, eyes shifting between blue and gray. A scar sliced his cheek by the right side of his nose, while his shirt collar shrouded another mark on his throat. The hand gripping Sally's arm bore the traces of an even older, half-moon stamp forged by fire. Any adult would have sized him up as middle-aged, but to ten-year-old Sally, he looked positively ancient.

"I am an FBI agent," the man said to Sally. "And you are under arrest."

Sally did what many young girls would have done in a similar situation: She cried. She cowered. She felt immediately ashamed.

The man's low voice and steely gaze froze her in place. He pointed across the way to City Hall, the tallest building in Camden. That's where girls like her would be dealt with, he said. Sally didn't understand his meaning at first. Then he explained: to punish her for stealing, she would be sent to the reformatory.

Sally didn't know that much about reform school, but what she knew was not good. She kept crying.

Then his stern manner brightened. It was a lucky break for a little girl like her, he said, that he was the one who caught her and not some other FBI agent. If she agreed to report to him from time to time, he would let her go. Spare her the worst. Show some mercy.

Sally stopped crying. He was going to let her go. She wouldn't have to call her mother from jail—her poor, overworked mother, Ella, still struggling with the consequences of the suicide of her alcoholic husband, Sally's father, five years earlier; still tethered to her seamstress job, which meant that Sally, too often, went home to an empty house after school.

But she couldn't think about that. Not when she was about to escape real punishment. Any desire she felt about joining the girls' club fell away, overcome by relief she wouldn't face a much larger fear.

Sally did not know the reprieve had an expiration date. One that would come due at any time, without warning.

MONTHS PASSED WITHOUT further word from the FBI man. As the spring of 1948 inched its way to summer, Sally finished up fifth grade at Northeast School. She kept up her marks and remained on the honor roll. She also stuck with the Junior Red Cross and continued to volunteer at local hospitals. Her homeroom teacher, Sarah Hanlin, singled Sally out as "a perfectly lovely girl. . . . [A] better than average pupil, intelligent and well behaved." Sally had had a major escape. She must have been grateful for each successive day of freedom.

The Camden of Sally's girlhood was far removed from the Camden of today. Emma DiRenzo, one of Sally's classmates, remembered it as a "marvelous" place to grow up in. "Everything about Camden back then was wonderful," she said. "When you tell people now, they look at you with big eyes." There were pep rallies at City Hall and social events at the YMCA. Girls jumped rope on the sidewalks, near houses adorned with marble steps. Camden residents took pride in their neighborhoods and communities, whether they were among the Italians in South Camden, the Irish in the city's North Side, the Germans in the East Side neighborhood of

Cramer Hill, or the Polish living along Mt. Ephraim Avenue, lining up to buy homemade kielbasa at Jaskolski's or fresh bread at the Morton Bakery. They didn't dream of suburban flight because there was no reason to leave.

Sally lived at 944 Linden Street, between Ninth and Tenth Streets. Cornelius Martin Park lay a few blocks east, and the city's main downtown was within walking distance to the west, and the Ben Franklin Bridge connecting Camden to Philadelphia was minutes away. The neighborhood was quiet but within reach of Camden's bustling core. Now it isn't a neighborhood at all. The town house where Sally grew up was demolished decades ago. What houses remain across the street are decrepit, with boarded-up windows and doors.

Sally's life in Camden was not idyllic. Despite outward appearances, she was lonely. Sally knew how to take care of herself but she wished she didn't have to. She didn't want to come home to an empty house after school because her mother was working late. Sally couldn't help comparing her life with those of her classmates, who had both mother and father. She confided her frustrations to Hanlin, her teacher, who often walked home with her at the end of a school day.

It's not clear if Sally had close friends her age. Perhaps her desire to be accepted by the popular girls stemmed from a lack of companionship. Her father, Russell, had died three weeks before Sally's sixth birthday, and she'd hardly seen him much before then. Her mother, Ella, worked long hours, and was tired and distant when she was at home. Her sister, Susan, was pregnant with her first child. Sally looked forward to becoming an aunt, whatever being an aunt meant, but it made the eleven-year age gap between the sisters all the more unbridgeable. Sally was still a little girl. Susan was not only an adult, but about to be a mother.

SALLY HORNER WAS WALKING home from Northeast School by herself after the last bell on a mid-June day in 1948. The route from North Seventh and Vine to her house took ten minutes by foot. Somewhere along the way, Sally was intercepted by the man from Woolworth's. Sally had dared to think he'd forgotten about her. Seeing him again was a shock.

Keep in mind that Sally had just turned eleven. She believed he was an FBI agent. She felt his power and feared it, even though it was false. She was convinced if she didn't do what he said that she would be sent to the reformatory and be subject to its horrors, as well as worse ones conjured up in her imagination. No matter how he did it, the man convinced Sally that she must go with him to Atlantic City—the government insisted.

But how would she persuade her mother? This would be no easy task, despite Ella's general state of apathy and exhaustion. The man had an answer for that, too. Sally was to tell her mother that he was the father of two school friends who had invited her to a seashore vacation after school ended for the year. He would take care of the rest with a phone call to her mother. Sally wasn't to worry—he would never let on that she was in trouble with the law. He sent the girl on her way.

At home, Sally waited for her mother to return from work, then parroted the FBI man's story. Ella was uneasy, and let it show. Sally sounded sincere in her desire to go to the Jersey Shore for a week's vacation with friends, but who were these people? Ella had never heard Sally mention the names of these two girls before, nor that of their father, Frank Warner. Or if she had, Ella didn't recall.

The telephone rang. The man on the other end of the line told Ella he was Mr. Warner, father to Sally's school friends. His manner was affable, polite. He seemed courteous, even

charming. Sally stayed by her mother as the conversation unfolded. "Warner" told Ella that he and his wife had "plenty of
room" in their five-room apartment in Atlantic City to put Sally
up for the week.

Under the force of his persuasion, Ella let her concerns
slide. "It was a chance for Sally to get a little vacation," she said
weeks later. "I couldn't afford to give her one." She did wonder
why Sally didn't seem to be all that excited about the vacation.
It was out of character. Normally her bright little girl loved to
go places.

On June 14, 1948, Ella took Sally to the Camden bus depot. She kissed her daughter goodbye and watched her climb
aboard an express bus to Atlantic City. She spied the outlines
of a middle-aged man, the one she took to be "Warner," next
to Sally, but he did not come out to greet her. Ella also did not
see anyone else with the man, neither wife nor children. Still,
she tamped down her suspicions. She wanted so badly for her
daughter to enjoy herself. And it seemed, from the first few letters Sally sent her from Atlantic City, that the girl was having
a good time.

Ella Horner never dreamed that, within weeks, her girl
would become a ghost. By sending Sally off on that bus to
Atlantic City, she had consigned her daughter to the stuff of
nightmares that would rip any mother apart.

A Trip to the Beach

R obert and Jean Pfeffer were newlyweds who couldn't afford a honeymoon. So the couple, both twenty-two, settled on a day trip with their family, which included Robert's mother, Emily, his seventeen-year-old sister, also named Emily, his nine-year-old younger sister, Barbara, and four other relatives whose names have been lost to time. The sea-cooled Brigantine Beach, a small town east of Atlantic City, was far enough away from their North Philadelphia neighborhood of Nicetown to feel like a treat, but close enough to get back home by nightfall.

Robert, Jean, Emily senior and junior, and Barbara piled into Robert's car on a weekend morning in July 1948 and set out for the beach. (The other four relatives had their own car.) Somewhere along Route 40, a tire blew out. Robert's car went off the road and landed on its side.

The Pfeffers climbed out, shaken and in shock. No one was hurt, thank goodness, but the car was far too damaged to continue. As Robert stood there, wondering how much it would cost to get the car towed and fixed, a station wagon pulled up. A middle-aged man got out of the front seat, and a girl he introduced as his daughter stepped out from the passenger side.

From there the story Robert Pfeffer told both the *Philadelphia Inquirer* and the Camden *Courier-Post* turns strange, riddled with unsolvable inconsistencies. People turn up where they shouldn't. Chronologies bend out of shape. What's clear is that he was so disturbed by what happened that July morning that he alerted law enforcement and, when they didn't listen, the newspapers.

The man told the Pfeffers his name was Frank and that his daughter's name was Sally. (Robert later recalled the man used La Salle as a last name, but it's unclear if that was really the case.) La Salle offered to take the young couple to get help. Robert and Jean agreed. They got into the back of La Salle's station wagon, and La Salle, with Sally beside him, drove them to the nearest roadside phone. Robert called his father and told him about the accident and the Good Samaritan who had come to their aid. He also asked his father to come pick up his wife and daughters.

There was a hamburger joint at the rest stop, and La Salle, Sally, Robert, and Jean stopped for a quick bite to eat. The waitress seemed to be familiar with Frank and Sally, addressing them by name. Robert figured they must be regulars. After the meal, everyone returned to the wreck and La Salle offered to drive the entire family to Brigantine Beach so their day trip wouldn't be spoiled. He also said he would take care of towing and fixing the car. The Pfeffers accepted.

Sally and Barbara, only two years apart in age, hit it off right away. They went swimming together and played on the beach. La Salle told the Pfeffers that he operated a gas station and garage in Atlantic City, that he was divorced, and that Sally lived with him on summer vacations. Sally behaved as if nothing was amiss. She referred to Frank as "Daddy" and treated him with affection. "She told us how good he had been to her," Pfeffer said.

Later that day, Sally suggested that her "dad" could drive her and Barbara back to their place to clean themselves up. They lived on Pacific Avenue in Atlantic City, just ten minutes away by car.

The minutes passed, then became an hour, then an hour and a half. The Pfeffers, waiting at the beach, started to worry. What was taking so long? Robert's father had arrived, and he offered to squeeze everyone into his car and drive into Atlantic City to see what was going on. Why had they let Barbara go off with strangers, even if one of those strangers was a friendly, blue-eyed little girl? Minutes into the drive, they saw La Salle's station wagon coming toward them, with Sally and Barbara sitting together in the backseat.

They headed back to the wrecked car, which La Salle attached to the back of his station wagon. The group, divided between La Salle's vehicle and Robert's father's car, drove to the Atlantic City garage where La Salle claimed he worked and dropped off the damaged vehicle to be fixed. The body shop, Robert noted, was across the street from a New Jersey State Police station.

Before the Pfeffers went back to Philadelphia, Sally invited Barbara to come stay with her for a weekend. La Salle said they'd love to have the girl visit. The family did not take them up on the invite.

Several days later, the Pfeffers would have even more reason to remember their extended encounter with the middle-
aged man and the girl he claimed was his daughter.

EVERY TIME ELLA HORNER began to wonder if she had done
the right thing in sending Sally off to Atlantic City, a letter
or a call—always from a pay phone—arrived to assuage her
guilt and soothe her mind. Sally seemed to be having a swell
time, or so Ella convinced herself. Perhaps she felt some relief, too, at having a reprieve from the expense of feeding and
entertaining her little girl, which stretched her puny paycheck
beyond its limits.

At the end of her first week away, Sally told her mother she
wanted to stay longer so she could see the Ice Follies. Ella reluctantly gave permission. After two weeks, Sally's excuses for
staying in Atlantic City grew more vague, but Ella thought her
daughter still sounded well. Then, at the three-week mark, the
phone calls stopped. Ella's letters to her daughter came back
with "return to sender" stamped on the front.

On July 31, 1948, Ella was relieved to receive another letter.
Sally wrote to say she was leaving Atlantic City and going on
to Baltimore with Mr. Warner. Though she promised to return
home to Camden by the end of the week, she added, "I don't
want to write anymore."

At last, something woke up inside Ella's mind. "I don't
think my little girl has stayed with that man all this time of
her own accord." Her sister, Susan, was days away from giving birth. Would Sally really choose to stay away when she was
about to become an aunt? Ella finally understood the horrible
truth. She called the police.

After Detective Joseph Schultz spoke with Ella, he sent

two other Camden detectives, William Marter and Marshall Thompson, to look for Sally in Atlantic City. On August 4, they arrived at the lodging house on 203 Pacific Avenue that Sally gave as the return address on her letters. There they learned from the landlady, Mrs. McCord, that Warner had been living there, and he'd been posing as Sally's father. There were no other daughters, nor was there a wife. Just one little girl, Sally.

The police also learned the man Ella knew as "Mr. Warner" worked at a gas station, and adopted the alias of "Frank Robinson." When the cops went to the gas station, he wasn't there. He'd failed to show up for work and hadn't even bothered to pick up his final paycheck. "Robinson" had disappeared, and so had Sally. Two suitcases remained in their room, as did several unsent postcards from Sally to her mother. "He didn't take any of his or the girl's clothes, either," Thompson told the *Philadelphia Inquirer.* "He didn't even stop long enough to get his hat."

Among the items left behind in the rooming house was a photograph, one that Ella had never seen before. In it, Sally sat on a swing, feet dangling just above the ground, staring directly at the camera. She wore a cream-colored dress, white socks, and black patent

Photograph of Sally discovered at the Atlantic City boardinghouse in August 1948, six weeks after her disappearance.

shoes, and her honey-streaked light brown hair was pulled away from her face. Her eyes conveyed a mixture of fear and a bottomless desire to please. She looked like she wanted to get this moment right, but didn't know what "right" was supposed to be, when everything was so wrong.

It seemed likely that Sally's kidnapper was the photographer. She was only three months past her eleventh birthday.

Marshall Thompson led the search for Sally in Atlantic City. When that search turned up empty, he took the photo of her back to Camden police headquarters to be sent out on the teletypes. He had to find Sally, the sooner, the better, because police now knew who they were dealing with.

For Sally's mother, it was awful enough that the Camden police had failed to bring her daughter home. Far worse was the news they broke to Ella: the man who had called himself "Warner" was well-known to local law enforcement. They knew him as Frank La Salle. And only six months before he'd abducted Sally, he had been released from prison after serving a sentence for the statutory rape of five girls between the ages of twelve and fourteen.

THREE

From Wellesley to Cornell

The year 1948 was a pivotal one for Vladimir Nabokov. He had spent six years in Cambridge, Massachusetts, teaching literature to Wellesley College undergraduates and, in his spare time, indulging his passion for studying butterflies at Harvard's Museum of Comparative Zoology. After eight years in the United States, the tumult and trauma of emigration had receded. English, Nabokov said many times, was the first language he remembered learning, and the lure of America had sustained him as he fled the Russian Revolution for Germany, and then from the Nazis to Paris—a necessary step when married to a woman who was proud and unafraid to be Jewish.

The United States, and particularly the Boston area, proved a generally happy environment for Nabokov, Véra, and their son, Dmitri, who was fourteen years old in 1948. Since they'd found a haven there, Nabokov had worked on a book about Nikolai Gogol, about whom he had decidedly mixed feelings; published a novel, *Bend Sinister;* and begun the version of his autobiography that would appear as *Conclusive Evidence* a couple of years later. (He would later rewrite it and publish it under the title *Speak, Memory.*)

Nabokov had also traveled across America three times, in the summers of 1941, 1943, and 1947. (He would repeat the cross-country trip four more times.) He never drove, entrusting the task to his wife, Véra, or a graduate student. The first time, Dorothy Leuthold, a middle-aged student in his language class, had spirited the Nabokovs from New York City in a brand-new Pontiac (dubbed Pon'ka, the Russian word for "pony") all the way to Palo Alto, California.

The trio stayed in motor courts and budget hotels and other cheap lodgings that wouldn't break the bank. The America Nabokov witnessed on these trips was eventually immortalized as the "lovely, trustful, dreamy, enormous country" that Humbert Humbert comments on in *Lolita:* "Beyond the tilled plain . . . there would be a slow suffusion of inutile loveliness, a low sun in a platinum haze with a warm, peeled-peach tinge pervading the upper edge of a two-dimensional, dove-gray cloud." Though his marriage to Véra was once again stable, an affair had nearly derailed it a decade earlier, when she had gone on to Paris before him. Perhaps news of his romantic attentions to at least one Wellesley student had not reached Véra—or if it had, she did not view the dalliance as anything serious.

Nabokov had been ill for much of the first half of 1948. He suffered a litany of lung troubles during the spring that no doctor could adequately diagnose. They thought it might be tuberculosis because of the alarming quantities of blood Nabokov coughed up. It wasn't. The next guess was cancer. That, too, proved untrue. When doctors put a vulcanized rubber tube down his windpipe under local anesthetic to inspect his ailing lungs, all they found was a single ruptured blood vessel. Nabokov himself figured his body was "ridding itself of the damage caused by thirty years of heavy smoking." Bedridden, he had enough energy to write, but not to teach, so Véra stood in for him as lecturer.

After these summer trips, Nabokov was always glad to return to Cambridge. Wellesley, his academic and personal refuge, had turned down his multiple entreaties for a full-time professorship. Nor could he find full-time work at Harvard, where he'd made a quixotic bid to turn his butterfly-hunting hobby into a proper profession. But the Nabokovs' fortunes were about to change thanks to Morris Bishop, a romance literature professor at Cornell who would remain a close friend to both Vladimir and Véra. Bishop lobbied Cornell to appoint Nabokov a professor of Russian literature, and it worked. On July 1, the Nabokovs moved to Ithaca, New York, finding solace in a "quiet summer in green surroundings." By August, they had rented a large house on 802 East Seneca Street, one far bigger than their "wrinkled-dwarf Cambridge flatlet"—and future inspiration for the house where a man named Humbert Humbert would discover the object of his obsession.

The summer also brought Nabokov a formative book, thanks to the literary critic Edmund Wilson, who sent Nabokov a copy of Havelock Ellis's *Studies in the Psychology of Sex*. He drew attention to one appendix that contained the late-nineteenth-century confession of an unnamed engineer of Ukrainian descent. The man had first had sex at age twelve with another child, found the experience so intoxicating he repeated it, and eventually destroyed his marriage by sleeping with child prostitutes. From there the man went further downhill, to the point where he

flashed young girls in public. The confession, as Nabokov related in a later interview, "ends with a feeling of hopelessness,
of a life ruined by hunger beyond control."

Nabokov appreciated Wilson's gift and wrote him after
reading the case histories. "I enjoyed the Russian's love-life
hugely. It is wonderfully funny. As a boy, he seems to have
been quite extraordinarily lucky in coming across [willing
girls]. . . . The end is rather bathetic." Nabokov also directly
acknowledged the impact of Ellis to his first biographer. "I was
always interested in psychology," he told Andrew Field. "I knew
my Havelock Ellis rather well. . . ."

He was, by this point, five years from finishing the manuscript for *Lolita*, and a decade from its triumphant American
publication. But Nabokov was also nearly twenty years into his
efforts to wrestle a thematic compulsion into its final form: the
character who became Humbert Humbert.

SKIP PAST THE OFT-QUOTED opening paragraph of *Lolita*'s
first chapter. Chances are, even if you've never read the novel,
you probably know it by heart, or some version of it. Move
directly to paragraph two: "She was Lo, plain Lo, in the morning, standing four feet ten in one sock. She was Lola in slacks.
She was Dolly at school. She was Dolores on the dotted line."

In Humbert Humbert's eyes, the girl named Dolores Haze
is a canvas blank enough to project whatever he, and by virtue
of his narration, the reader, sees or desires—"But in my arms
she was always Lolita." She is never allowed to be herself. Not
in Humbert's telling.

When the reader meets her, Dolores Haze is just shy of
twelve years old, born around the first of the year in 1935, making her two years and three months older than Sally Horner.

She is an inch shorter than Sally and, at seventy-eight pounds, a good twenty pounds lighter than her real-life counterpart. There aren't other facts and figures available for Sally, but Humbert measures every physical aspect of Dolores: twenty-seven-inch chest, twenty-three-inch waist, twenty-nine-inch hips, while her thigh, calf, and neck circumferences were seventeen, eleven, and eleven, respectively.

Dolores's mother, the former Charlotte Becker, and her father, Harold Haze, were living in Pisky, a town somewhere in the Midwest best known for producing hogs, corn, and coal, when their daughter was born. Conception, however, took place in Veracruz, Mexico, during the Hazes' honeymoon. Another child followed in 1937, the year of Sally's birth, but that offspring, a blond-haired boy, died at two. Sometime thereafter—Humbert is vague on details—Harold also perished, leaving Charlotte a widowed single mother. She and Dolores move east to Ramsdale, and set up house at 342 Lawn Street, where both mother and daughter will encounter a man who will alter their lives irrevocably and with monumental consequences.

When he first sees her, Humbert Humbert describes Dolores in poetic terms: "frail, honey-hued shoulders . . . silky supple bare back . . . chestnut head of hair" and wearing "a polka-dotted black kerchief tied around her chest" that shields her breasts from Humbert's "aging ape eyes."

Humbert confides to the reader that when he was nine, he met a girl named Annabel Leigh, also nine. They embarked on a friendship with strong romantic overtones and multiple rendezvous by the beach. Then Annabel fell ill and died prematurely, the idyll forever cut short. Her death imprinted a type, and a predilection, upon Humbert for the rest of his days. Girls who fall between the ages of nine and fourteen. Girls whose "true nature," according to Humbert, bore little resemblance to real life. Girls he characterized as "little deadly demons." Girls immortalized, forevermore, by him as well as his creator, as nymphets.

Humbert Humbert was describing a compulsion. Vladimir Nabokov set out to create an archetype. But the real little girls who fit this idea of the mythical nymphet end up getting lost in the need for artistic license. The abuse that Sally Horner, and other girls like her, endured should not be subsumed by dazzling prose, no matter how brilliant.

FOUR

Sally, at First

The seeds of Sally Horner's kidnapping grew out of choices made by her mother. Ella kept secrets about the circumstances of her daughters' births and the death of Sally's father. Sally never knew of them. Susan may have, but if so she never spoke of them to her family. Digging up these secrets transformed me into an accidental forensic genealogical detective. I spent so many months stuck on Sally's origin story and the clash between what was reported and what really happened because I thought it would help me better understand Ella's behavior.

Her decisions, with respect to Sally's disappearance, hold her up to severe scrutiny by the modern world. She let her daughter go off with a stranger she'd only spoken to by telephone. She grew more distant, perhaps more baffling, to her family, let alone to neighbors. She fit the pejorative "difficult" bill so often affixed to women who don't fit within neat little boxes. But in 1948, with little money and fewer resources available to Ella as a single mother, she functioned within her own limited framework. Her best was not good enough for Sally, but it was all she knew based on the life she'd lived up until she saw her daughter off at the Camden bus depot.

SALLY WAS HER NICKNAME. No one is alive to remember why, or who used it first, or how it stuck. Her legal name, listed on the certificate announcing her birth at Trenton Hospital on April 18, 1937, was Florence, no middle name, Horner. Her mother, the former Ella Katherine Goff, took the baby back to the home she shared with Russell Horner in Roebling, New Jersey. The house at 238 Fourth Avenue is long gone, replaced by a more modern town house a stone's throw from the River Line train station to the east, and several blocks south of the Delaware River.

Ella's older daughter, Susan, also lived with the Horners, though Russell was not her father. Eleven years earlier, at the age of nineteen, Ella had had some sort of relationship with an older man of about thirty. When the subject came up, Ella told her family that she and Susan's birth father, whom she never named, were married, but that he passed away. Susan knew her father's real name, William Ralph Swain, because she listed it on her marriage license. She likely knew little else.

Ella had good reason to keep Swain's existence a secret, and never mention him by name. Records indicate he was married to someone else when Susan was born, contrary to the "yes" ticked off on Susan's birth certificate, indicating her legitimate status. Nor could I find any existing marriage record between Swain and Ella, though one may turn up in the future—vital records are irregularly stored from city to city, state by state. To confuse matters further, the 1930 census listed Ella's last name as Albara, which she used for at least a half dozen more years. The census record also listed her as being married, but I could not track down any marriage record between Ella and a man named Albara.

Ella raised Susan on her own, with occasional help from her parents, Job and Susannah Goff. One subject they all fretted about was how long it took Susan to learn to speak. She'd had some sort of head injury as a baby, and did not begin talking in earnest until she was five, by which time she and her mother had moved to Prospertown to be closer to Ella's parents, who were growing older and more infirm.

That's where Ella met Russell Horner, a widower with a son, also named Russell. Horner began to court her, and some of their meetings were recorded by the local papers, as was the custom of the day. On December 9, 1935, the *Asbury Park Press* noted that Ella and Russell were "recent visitors to friends in Lakehurst." The paper also reported on June 8, 1936, that Ella and Susan visited Russell and his son (both names were spelled as "Russel") in New Egypt, and noted a solo visit by Ella to the town on August 8. Ella and Russell were not husband and wife, though. It seems Ella had repeated the pattern begun with Swain. While Russell's first wife, the mother of his son, had died, he had married a second time and never bothered to divorce the woman. By the end of 1937, Russell and Ella were living as husband and wife at the Fourth Avenue house in Roebling.

As for Russell Junior, he married two months before Sally Horner's birth. Sally never knew of her half brother's existence. Neither her mother nor Susan mentioned him.

Ella and Russell's domestic arrangement was as short-lived

as their earlier relationships. By the time Sally was about three, the situation had grown volatile. Russell had a drinking problem, which did not mix well with his job as a crane operator, and he could be abusive to his wife and her daughters. Susan remembered the beatings her stepfather gave her mother, memories she did not allow herself to think about until close to the end of her own life. Sally, much younger when her parents split up, may have been spared the worst of these memories.

Eventually, Ella fled her relationship. She took Susan and Sally to Camden, where they moved into the town house at 944 Linden Street. Russell became itinerant, drifting from town to town around southern New Jersey, looking for and not finding work. He lost his driver's license when caught taking a shortcut along some railroad tracks. By the beginning of 1943, he was living at his parents' farm in Cassville. On March 24, he hanged himself from the rafters of the garage. Horner left a note for his mother in the kitchen, directing her where to find his body. According to the state police, he "had been despondent over ill health for some time."

Police told the *Asbury Park Press* that Russell had been married twice and was "estranged from his current wife," though they did not say whether the wife in question was Ella. But the address listed on Russell's death certificate was the address where he'd lived with Ella and the girls in Roebling. And the name of his daughter, "Florence," is handwritten just below the address line.

Sally was not quite six years old when her father committed suicide. It isn't clear how much she knew of her father's history and manner of death. Later, when it became necessary to clarify her parentage, she said, "My real daddy died when I was six and I remember what he looks like."

After Russell killed himself, Ella, already living as a single mother, was truly on her own. Her mother, Susannah, had passed away in 1939, while her father, Job, died in January 1943, just two months before Russell killed himself. Ella had to go to work as a seamstress.

Susan, by now sixteen, had left school and was working a factory job. That summer, Susan met Alvin Panaro, a sailor on leave, at a friend's party. Though Al was three years older, he was immediately smitten, but the Second World War was on and they were too young to marry. Al hailed from Florence, near the same part of town where Susan and Sally had once lived. His parents owned a greenhouse, and planned for Al to take over responsibility running it once he was finished with the navy, once he was home for good. It was also understood he might not get that chance; even the navy carried a high casualty risk.

When Susan turned eighteen, they decided not to wait any longer. On his next furlough, she and Al wed in Florence on February 17, 1945. When the war ended, Al received his honorable discharge and he and Susan began married life in earnest, running the greenhouse together. They wanted children, but Susan's initial pregnancies ended in early miscarriages. Then their luck turned.

In June 1948, Susan and Al Panaro were two months away from the birth of their daughter, Diana, Ella's first grandchild. But when the baby girl arrived that August, celebration was the furthest thing from the minds of her parents and grandmother. Sally had disappeared and they knew who had taken her. They also now knew what sort of man he was.

FIVE

The Search for Sally

A n eight-state police search for Sally Horner began on August 5, 1948. By then she had been gone from Camden for six weeks. The news wires picked up the story of her abduction, as well as Ella's delay in reporting her daughter missing. The picture of Sally on the swing went out across the country, appearing in wire reports published from Salt Lake City, Utah, to Rochester, New York, and in local papers like the Camden *Courier-Post* and the *Philadelphia Inquirer*.

Robert and Jean Pfeffer were among those who read the news about Sally Horner's disappearance. How strange, the couple thought. "If [Sally] had wanted to warn us about anything she had every opportunity, but never did so." Robert picked up the phone, called the Camden police, and told the officer who answered about their encounter in Brigantine Beach. Robert also mentioned his little sister Barbara's visit to

La Salle's apartment, which had stretched to ninety agonizing minutes of waiting. Perhaps reading about La Salle's prior incarceration made him wonder what, exactly, might have happened to Barbara during those ninety minutes. He never heard a word back from the police.

The shock of the news about Sally, combined with mundane family matters, delayed Pfeffer from making the two-and-a-half-hour round trip back to Atlantic City to pick up their car for several weeks. He never learned whether La Salle himself or some other mechanic restored it to good working order.

Sally and La Salle, however, were long gone from Atlantic City. Camden police now knew, with queasy certainty, why Sally's family had ample reason to be fearful of what Frank La Salle might do to their little girl.

AT FIRST MARSHALL THOMPSON worked the Sally Horner case with other Camden police officers. But when the summer of 1948 gave way to fall, he took on the investigation full-time and never stopped. As the months wore on, his colleagues weren't shy about voicing their opinions. The girl had to be dead. She couldn't up and vanish like this, no trace, no word, when they knew who had her, what they both looked like, and that they were posing as father and daughter.

Thompson felt otherwise. Sally must be alive. He figured it was likely she was still near enough to Camden. And even if she wasn't, he would find her. It was his job as detective to care about every case, but the plight of a missing girl really got to him.

He had been promoted to detective only the year before, nearly two decades into his time on the force. Thompson's appointment in March 1928 happened the same year his only daughter, Caroline, was born, and not long after he and his wife, Emma, moved to the Cramer Hill neighborhood in Northeast Camden. The young couple had long-standing Camden roots, Thompson in particular. His father, George, had served as justice of the peace, and his grandfather John Reeve Thompson was a member of Camden's first city council.

Tangles with "local pugilists," raids on illegal speakeasies, breaking up home gambling dens, and other minor crimes littered Thompson's stretch as a Camden cop. Most of the time he worked with Sergeant Nathan Petit; their names often appeared together in the local papers' accounts of various notable arrests.

Off duty, Thompson entertained family and friends by playing classical piano, which his mother, Harriette, taught him as a child. His musical ability was called out with hyperbolic flourish by a *Courier-Post* columnist in 1939: "Marshall Thompson, one of Camden's finest, is a talented pianist. He never took a music lesson."

Thompson's innate tenacity made him the perfect choice to look for Sally Horner and Frank La Salle. Over the course of his investigation Thompson learned much about Sally's abductor, from his choice of haircut to the "quantity of sugar and cream he desired when drinking coffee." He chased every lead and followed up on every tip. One phone call came in to say La Salle was holed up in a house on Trenton Avenue and Washington Street in downtown Camden. A state police teletype arrived placing La Salle at a residence on Third and Sumner Avenue in Florence, the same town where Sally lived as a little girl. Neither tip panned out.

Once Thompson was on the case full-time, he let it dictate his entire waking life. He got in touch, in person and by telephone, with the FBI; state and city police at Columbus,

Newton, Riverton, and Langhorne, Pennsylvania; state parole offices at Trenton and Camden; detective divisions in Philadelphia; and the Trenton post office. Several months into Sally's disappearance, Thompson received reports of La Salle being spotted in Philadelphia, northern New Jersey, South Jersey Shore resorts, and at a restaurant in Haddonfield, observed by a waitress working there. He followed each lead to no avail.

Thompson also cast his net farther and deeper in the surrounding states. He checked in regularly with state and city police in Absecon, Pleasantville, Maple Shade, Newark, Orange, and Paterson, New Jersey; parole offices in Atlantic City and the state prison farm in Leesburg; and the Compensation Bureau in Trenton, in case La Salle drew or cashed a paycheck in the state.

There were periods where he worked twenty-four hours or more without taking a break. Finding Sally Horner was more important than sleep. Thompson tracked down La Salle's first wife in Portland, Maine, but she knew nothing of his whereabouts. The detective also contacted La Salle's second wife, now living in Delaware Township with her daughter, her new husband, and their baby son. The woman gave Thompson an earful about her wayward, criminal ex-husband's habits and history, including the dramatic beginning of their marriage and its equally explosive end.

Thompson used his holidays to travel for the case. On one six-day "vacation," Thompson went to the Trenton State Fair. Each morning, he stood outside the entrance to the grounds, hoping that La Salle might turn up to apply for a job. Or perhaps he would bring Sally with him.

None of the leads amounted to anything. Nor did tips from numerous anonymous phone calls and letters. All had to be followed up on, but none yielded the answer Detective Marshall Thompson craved: the whereabouts of Sally Horner.

It was the nature of a detective's job to get hopes up and have them crushed. So many of his colleagues believed the girl was dead. But not Thompson. He could not give up. He knew in his bones that he would, someday, find Sally alive and bring her back to Camden, to her mother, her family.

And that he would find Frank La Salle and see justice done.

SIX

Seeds of Compulsion

Vladimir Nabokov holding a butterfly, 1947, at Harvard's Museum of Comparative Zoology, where he was a fellow.

As Marshall Thompson continued to track Frank La Salle's whereabouts without results, Vladimir Nabokov remained on a quest to plumb the fictional mind of a man with a similar appetite for young girls. So far, he had not been successful. He could have, and tried to, abandon it altogether—there were plenty of other literary projects for

Nabokov to pursue. But the drive to get this story right went beyond formal exercise. Otherwise, why did Nabokov explore this same topic, over and over, for more than twenty years? At almost every stage of his literary career, Nabokov was preoccupied with the idea of the middle-aged man's obsession with a young girl.

As Martin Amis wrote in a 2011 essay for the *Times Literary Supplement,* "Of the nineteen fictions, no fewer than six wholly or partly concern themselves with the sexuality of prepubescent girls. . . . [T]o be clear as one can be: the unignorable infestation of nymphets . . . is not a matter of morality; it is a matter of aesthetics. There are just too many of them."

"Aesthetics" is one way to phrase it. Robert Roper, in his 2015 book *Nabokov in America,* suggested a more likely culprit: compulsion—"a literary equivalent of the persistent impulse of a pedophile." Over and over, scholars and biographers have searched for direct connections between Nabokov and young children, and failed to find them. What impulses he possessed were literary, not literal, in the manner of the "well-adjusted" writer who persists in writing about the worst sort of crimes. We generally don't bear the same suspicions of writers who turn serial killers into folk heroes. No one, for example, thinks Thomas Harris capable of the terrible deeds of Hannibal Lecter, even though he invented them with chilling psychological insight.

Nabokov likely realized how often this theme persisted in his work. That would explain why he was quick to deny connections between *Lolita* and real-life figures, or to later claim the novel's inspiration emerged from, of all things, a brief article in a French newspaper about "an ape in the Jardin des Plantes who, after months of coaxing by a scientist, produced the first drawing ever charcoaled by an animal: this sketch showed the bars of the poor creature's cage."

But there is no getting around the deep-seated compulsion that recurs again and again in Nabokov's work. I read through his earlier Russian-language novels, as well as more contemporary accounts by literary critics, to figure out why this awful subject held such allure for him.

NABOKOV'S INITIAL EXPLORATION of an older man's unnatural desire for a preteen girl was published in 1926, within the first year of his career as a prose writer. Before then, he devoted himself exclusively to poetry. Did prose free Nabokov up to wrestle with the darkness and tumult that already surrounded him? His father, the jurist and journalist Vladimir D. Nabokov, had been assassinated four years earlier, and he was a year into his marriage to Véra Slonim, a fellow émigré he met while both lived in Berlin among the community of other Russians who'd fled the Revolution. Neither particularly cared for the city, but they stayed in Berlin for fifteen years, Nabokov supplementing his writing income and growing literary reputation by teaching tennis, boxing, and foreign languages to students.

Nabokov published his first novel, *Mashen'ka* (*Mary*), in 1926, under the pseudonym of V. Sirin, which he would use for all of his poetry and prose published before he moved to America. That same year Nabokov, as Sirin, published "A Nursery Tale." The short story includes a section on a fourteen-year-old girl clad in a grown-up cocktail dress designed to show off her cleavage, though it isn't clear that the narrator, Erwin, immediately notices that aspect:

"There was something odd about that face, odd was the flitting glance of her much too shiny eyes, and if she were not just a little girl—the old man's granddaughter, no doubt—one might suspect her lips were touched up with rouge. She walked

swinging her hips very, very slightly, her legs moved closer together, she was asking her companion something in a ringing
voice—and although Erwin gave no command mentally, he
knew that his swift secret wish had been fulfilled."

Erwin's "swift secret wish" is his inappropriate desire for
the girl.

Two years later, in 1928, Nabokov tackled the subject in poetry. "Lilith" also strongly features the so-called demonic effect
of a little girl, of her "russet armpit" and a "green eye over her
shoulder" upon an older man: "She had a water lily in her curls
and was as graceful as a woman." The poem continues:

> And how enticing, and how merry,
> her upturned face! And with a wild
> lunge of my loins I penetrated
> into an unforgotten child.
> Snake within snake, vessel in vessel
> smooth-fitting part, I moved in her,
> through the ascending itch forefeeling
> unutterable pleasure stir.

But this illicit coupling is the man's ruin. Lilith closed herself off to him and forced him out, and as he shouts, "let me
in!" his fate is sealed: "The door stayed silent, and for all to see /
writhing with agony I spilled my seed / and knew abruptly that
I was in Hell." Two and a half decades before *Lolita*, Nabokov
anticipated Humbert Humbert's remark that he was "perfectly
capable of intercourse with Eve, but it was Lilith he longed for."

Another proto-nymphet appears in *Laughter in the Dark*,
though this one, Margot, is a little older: eighteen in the original version published in Russian, *Camera Obscura* (1932), and
sixteen in the heavily revised and retitled edition Nabokov re-

leased six years later. (Nabokov rewrote the novel a third time in the 1960s.) Margot attracts the attention of the much-older, wealthy art critic Albert Albinus,* whose name foreshadows Humbert Humbert.

We only see Margot's actions and personality filtered through Albinus's eyes. He depicts her as capricious, whimsical, and full of manipulation. Just as in *Lolita*, when Humbert's plans are upended by the arrival of Clare Quilty, an interloper foils the relationship between Albinus and Margot. Axel Rex's affair with Margot in *Laughter in the Dark* serves a more mercenary purpose—gaining access to Albinus's status and fortune—while Quilty is after Dolores for the same illicit reasons as Humbert Humbert.

Except for Margot, who is a proper character, the early precursors to Dolores Haze are merely images that tempt and torment Nabokov's male protagonists. The image grows in substance in tandem with Nabokov's artistic growth. A paragraph in *Dar*, written between 1935 and 1937 but not published until 1952 (the English translation, published as *The Gift*, appeared a decade later), all but summarizes the future plot of *Lolita*. "What a novel I would whip off!" declares a secondary character, contemplating his much, much younger stepdaughter:

> Imagine this kind of thing: an old dog—but still in his prime, fiery, thirsting for happiness—gets to know a widow, and she has a daughter, still quite a little girl—you know what I mean—when nothing is formed yet but she has a way of walking that drives you out of

---

* In the original Russian, Albinus was called Bruno Kretchmar, while Margot's name was Magda.

your mind—A slip of a girl, very fair, pale with blue under the eyes—and of course she doesn't even look at the old goat. What to do? Well, not long [after] he ups and marries the widow. Okay. They settle down, the three of them. Here you can go on indefinitely—the temptation, the torment, the itch, the mad hopes . . .

Nabokov did not exactly "whip off" the novel that became *Lolita.* There was one more abortive attempt written in his mother tongue, *Volshebnik,* which was the last piece of fiction he wrote in Russian. He worked on it at a critical point in his life, while waiting to see if he and his family would be able to flee Europe and immigrate to America. But *Volshebnik* would not see publication until almost a decade after his death.

WHEN GERMANY DECLARED WAR on Poland in September 1939, plunging the rest of the world into global battle, Vladimir Nabokov was under considerable stress. He had reunited with his wife, Véra, and their son, Dmitri, in Paris, after an extended separation stranded them in Germany. He had broken off his affair with fellow émigré Irina Guadanini to join his family, but Paris was no safe haven anymore, as the Vichy regime became increasingly close with the Nazis. Véra was Jewish, and so was Dmitri, and if they could not get out of France, they might be bound for concentration camps.

The personal stakes were never higher, and Nabokov's health suffered. That fall, or perhaps in the early winter of 1940, he was "laid up with a severe attack of intercostal neuralgia," a mysterious ailment of damage to nerves running between the ribs that would plague him off and on for the rest of his life. He could not do much more than read and write, and he retreated into the refuge of his imagination. What emerged was *Volshebnik*, the fifty-five-page novella that most closely mirrored the future novel.

Unlike Humbert Humbert, the narrator of *Volshebnik* is nameless (though Nabokov once referred to him as "Arthur"). He does not have Humbert's artful insolence. Instead he is in torment from the first sentence, "How can I come to terms with myself?" A jeweler by trade, he moves back and forth between being open about his attraction to underage girls and his resolve to do nothing about it, coupling his inner torment to overweening self-justification. "I'm no ravisher," he declares. "I am a pickpocket, not a burglar." Humbert would sneer at the hypocrisy of this declaration.

Nabokov was not the artist he would later become, and it shows in the prose: "I'm not attracted to every schoolgirl that comes along, far from it—how many one sees, on a gray morning street that are husky, or skinny, or have a necklace of pimples or wear spectacles—*those* kinds interest me as little, in the amorous sense, as a lumpy female acquaintance might interest someone else." He doesn't have the wherewithal to describe his chosen prey, whom he first sees roller-skating in a park, as a nymphet. Such a word isn't in his vocabulary because it wasn't yet in Nabokov's.

Still there are glimpses of *Lolita*'s formidable style, as when *Volshebnik*'s narrator comments on "the radiance of [one girl's] large, slightly vacuous eyes, somehow suggesting translucent gooseberries" or "the summery tint of her bare arms with the sleek little foxlike hairs running along the forearms." Not quite up to the level and the hypnotic rhythm of Humbert's rhapsodizing about Dolores Haze ("The soot-black lashes of her pale-gray vacant eyes . . . I might say her hair is auburn, and her lips as red as licked candy"), but the disquiet is present, waiting to spring like a trapdoor.

As in the later novel, Nabokov's narrator preys upon his underage quarry through her mother. She is more broadly cast than Charlotte Haze, whose rages against and aspirations for her daughter make her an interesting figure. The mother here is little more than a cipher, a plot device to engineer the man and girl toward their fates.

Volshebnik's narrator may be tormented by his unnatural tastes, but he knows he is about to entice his chosen girl to cross a chasm that cannot be uncrossed. Namely, she is innocent now, but she won't be after he has his way with her. Humbert Humbert would never be so obvious. He has the "fancy prose style" at his disposal to couch or deflect his intentions. So when he does state the obvious—as he will, again and again— the reader is essentially magicked into believing Dolores is as much the pursuer as the pursuee.

Both men's plans are the same: "He knew he would make no attempt on her virginity in the tightest and pinkest sense of the term until the evolution of their caresses had ascended a certain invisible step," says *Volshebnik*'s narrator. He also sets the same stage for his seduction, in a faraway hotel, away from knowing, prying eyes, or so he thinks. The hotel, in Europe, is less shabby than Humbert's choice of The Enchanted Hunters, but serves the same purpose: allowing the narrator to watch over the sleeping girl and make his move against her will.

The outcome differs from *Lolita*. The narrator is consumed by the girl lying supine on the bed, robe half-open, and begins "little by little to cast his spell . . . passing his magic wand above her body," measuring her "with an enchanted yardstick." Here, again, Humbert Humbert would sneer. But then he did not have the girl look "wild-eyed at his rearing nudity," caught out like the pedophile he is. Nor does Humbert become "deafened by his own horror" when the girl begins to scream at his rejected advances. Humbert is all about self-justification; *Volshebnik*'s narrator suffers no such delusion about his quarry.

He tries to soothe the girl—"be quiet, it's nothing bad, it's just a kind of game, it happens sometimes, just be quiet"—but she will not be placated. And when two old women burst into the room, he flees, only to be hit by a truck, the ensuing gory mess described as "an instantaneous cinema of dismemberment." The narrator's fate is awful and inevitable. He is the predator hunted, captured, taken down. The girl's big bad wolf is punished by a passing truck.

Nabokov did not publish *Volshebnik* during his lifetime because he knew, as was clear to me upon reading it, that the story was not a stand-alone work but source material. It is more straightforward and less sophisticated than *Lolita*. As the scholar Simon Karlinsky wrote when *Volshebnik* was finally published in English as *The Enchanter* in 1986, the novella's pleasure is "comparable to the one afforded by studying Beethoven's published sketchbooks: seeing the murky and unpromising material out of which the writer and the composer were later able to fashion an incandescent masterpiece."

In other words, the story carries equal value to the creation of *Lolita* as did the story of Sally Horner. One was fiction; the other was truth. But art is fickle and merciless, as Nabokov explained repeatedly throughout his life. *Volshebnik* possesses a powerful engine of its own. It does not possess *Lolita*'s literary trickery and mastery of obfuscation, which continue to make moral mincemeat out of the novel's wider readership. Here, instead, is a more prosaic depiction of deviant compulsion and tragic consequences.

TWO OTHER WORKS are notable influences upon *Lolita*. Annabel Leigh, Humbert Humbert's first love, is named in homage to Edgar Allan Poe's poem "Annabel Lee." The novel's working title, *The Kingdom by the Sea*, is a quote from that poem, and Humbert's memories of his Annabel, dead of typhus four months after their seaside near-consummation, echo many more of Poe's lines. (Nabokov: "I was a child and she was a child." Poe: "I was a child and she was a child.")

Lolita also owes a great deal to an influence never explicitly referenced in the text, but one Nabokov knew well from translating into Russian in his early twenties: *Alice's Adventures in Wonderland*, by Lewis Carroll. As he later explained to the literary critic Alfred Appel:

"[Carroll] has a pathetic affinity with Humbert Humbert but some odd scruple prevented me from alluding in *Lolita* to his wretched perversion and to those ambiguous photographs he took in dim rooms. He got away with it, as so many Victorians got away with pederasty and nympholepsy. His were sad scrawny little nymphets, bedraggled and half-undressed, or rather semi-undraped, as if participating in some dusty and dreadful charade."

Perhaps a similar "odd scruple" may explain why Nabokov was quick to deny any connection between *Lolita* and a real-life figure he knew early on in his American tenure. Henry Lanz was a Stanford professor of motley European stock, "of Finnish descent, son of a naturalized American father, born in Moscow and educated there and in Germany." He was fluent in many languages, an avid chess player. By World War I Lanz was in London, married, at the age of thirty, to a fourteen-year-old.

Not long after the Nabokovs immigrated to America in May 1940, arriving in New York on the SS *Champlain,* Lanz arranged for Nabokov to teach at Stanford. Their friendship grew over regular chess games; Nabokov beat Lanz more than two hundred times. Over these jousts Lanz revealed his predilections—specifically, that he most enjoyed seducing young girls and he loved to watch them urinate. Four years later, Lanz was dead of a heart attack at the age of fifty-nine.

Nabokov's first biographer, Andrew Field, suggested that Lanz was a prototype for Humbert Humbert. Nabokov, however, denied it: "No, no, no. I may have had [Lanz] in the back of my mind. He himself was what is called a fountainist, like Bloom in *Ulysses*. First of all, this is the commonest thing. In Swiss papers they always call them un triste individuel."

Such a denial makes sense, in light of other future denials of real-life influence. Yet the months Nabokov spent being peppered with stories from a known pederast could not help but inform his fiction—and further bolster his involuntary, unconscious need to unspool *this* particular, horrible narrative.

SEVEN

Frank, in Shadow

Unlike Humbert Humbert, there was nothing erudite about Frank La Salle. His prison writings are unreliable, lacking the silky sheen that is *Lolita*'s narrative hallmark; grammatical mistakes pepper La Salle's rambling and incoherent oral and typewritten declamations. When he was employed, irregularly at best, he worked blue-collar jobs, a far cry from teaching foreign languages.

La Salle was a crude, slippery figure, who lied so much in middle age that it was impossible for me to verify the facts of the first four decades of his life. One pseudonym dead-ended into another. Calls and emails to helpful, friendly archivists around the country bore no fruit, save for commiseration over my extended, failed, quest.

Without knowing the substance of his childhood and upbringing, and whether or not his predilections asserted themselves early on, it was difficult for me to determine where he came by his long-running desire for young girls. La Salle behaved as a pedophile, but it's hard to say whether that was his orientation—compulsion spurring opportunity—or he impulsively seized on opportunity as a means of asserting power. Whatever he was is dwarfed by what he did.

A likely birth date is May 27, 1895, give or take a year, somewhere in the Midwest. Frank La Salle was probably not his birth name. Once, he said that his parents were Frank Patterson and Nora LaPlante. Another time he wrote down their names as Frank La Salle and Nora Johnson. He hailed from Indianapolis, or perhaps Chicago. He said he served four years at the Leavenworth, Kansas, federal prison between 1924 and 1928 on a bootlegging charge, but the prison has no record of him being there during those years. He needed a new origin story every time he changed aliases, among them Patterson, Johnson, LaPlante, and O'Keefe. As far as I could find out, the first name almost never varied.

For someone who shrouded his life in secrecy, it seems fitting that one of his most notorious aliases was that of Frank Fogg.

It is as Fogg that a sharper picture forms of the man later known as La Salle. In the summer of 1937, Fogg had a wife and a nine-year-old son. They lived in a trailer in Maple Shade, New Jersey. He claimed that his wife took their son and ran away with a mechanic. It's possible that might be true. By July 14 they were gone, and just over a week later Fogg himself would become a fugitive, with a new wife in tow.

He met her at a carnival: Dorothy Dare, not quite eighteen, with brown curly hair that framed an openhearted, bespectacled face. Born in Philadelphia, the oldest of six, Dorothy lived with her family in Merchantville, a ten-minute car trip from

Maple Shade, and had graduated high school just the month before. Fights with her father over his strict parenting had grown so tense that Dorothy looked for every chance to escape. At the carnival, she found it in the man calling himself Frank Fogg.

He was more than twice as old as Dorothy, but she didn't mind the age difference. He wanted to marry her and she thought it was a terrific idea to elope. Which they did, only a few days after meeting, to Elkton, Maryland, the "Gretna Green of the United States," where weddings happened fast with few questions asked.

Dorothy's father, David Dare, was livid. Though they fought, he knew Dorothy was fundamentally a good girl. Even if she was not, technically, a minor, she was young, and this Fogg fellow was clearly not. When Dare discovered that Fogg was using a fake name, and was actually married, he got local police to swear out an eight-state warrant for the man's arrest on kidnapping and statutory rape charges on July 22, 1937. He claimed that Dorothy was fifteen, and thus a minor. The law caught up with the couple ten days later.

Cops arrested La Salle, still using the Fogg alias, in Roxborough, Pennsylvania, where he'd found a job, and took him to jail in Haddonfield, New Jersey. The charge: enticing a minor. Bail: withheld. Police simultaneously picked up Dorothy in the Philadelphia neighborhood of Wissahickon, where the couple had rented a room, and also brought her to jail. The two had a surprise for the arresting officers: Dorothy was not a minor, their Elkton marriage was legit, and Frank had the certificate, dated July 31, to prove it.

"He told me the truth," Dorothy cried, nervously fingering the shiny gold ring on her left hand. "I know he did. He couldn't have been married before. But if he did—oh, I'd just want to die!" Not long after uttering those words, Dorothy was released from jail, and slipped away from her parents, not yet ready to give up on her new husband, Frank.

The next morning, La Salle appeared in Delaware Township court. Dorothy was not there; nor did anyone know her where-abouts. Her father, however, was very much present. When he spotted La Salle, he punched the other man in the jaw. Dare grew even more furious when the presiding judge, Ralph King, dismissed the charges against La Salle, after the man testified that Dorothy had gone with him of her own will, and that they were lawfully married.

"I'll lock you up if you aren't careful," King warned Dare after he raised his voice in court one too many times demand-ing La Salle be held. But in the end, Dare got his wish, because the court wasn't done with Frank.

A day after the eight-state warrant had gone out on the wire, there was a hit-and-run accident near Marlton. A car re-sembling the one La Salle drove collided with a car owned by a man named Curt Scheffler. The driver of the first car fled the scene. La Salle, in court, denied he had been the driver. Justice of the Peace Oliver Bowen disagreed. On August 11, 1937, La Salle was fined fifty dollars and sentenced to fifteen days in jail. He also received an additional thirty days' sentence after failing to pay a two-hundred-dollar fine for giving false infor-mation. When he got out of jail, Dorothy was waiting. They picked up their marriage where it had been interrupted, and, apparently, the next few years were happy ones.

Dorothy and Frank, who cast off the Fogg alias and was La Salle once more, moved to Atlantic City. Their daughter, Made-line (not her real name), was born in 1939, and the young fam-ily were living at 203 Pacific Avenue when the Census came knocking a year later. So, too, did police, who this time arrested

La Salle on bigamy charges. Few details are available—was it the earlier wife or a different woman?—save that La Salle wriggled out of it with an acquittal.

Two years later, when Madeline was three, Dorothy sued Frank for desertion and nonpayment of child support. Dare family lore had it that Dorothy discovered her husband in a car with another woman, and grew so enraged she hit the other woman over the head with her shoe.

What was passed down as a dark but amusing family story turned out to hide a more sinister truth. What Dorothy Dare discovered about her husband first came to light in the wee hours of March 10, 1942.

THREE CAMDEN POLICE OFFICERS walked into a restaurant on Broadway near the corner of Penn and spotted a girl sitting alone in a booth. Women sitting by themselves in public at three in the morning still stand out. Imagine what the cops thought in the early 1940s when they stumbled across a twelve-year-old girl all on her own so late in the night.

When acting sergeant Edward Shapiro and patrolmen Thomas Carroll and Donald Watson asked the girl what she was up to, "being out alone at such an hour," she evaded their questioning. So the policemen took her back to headquarters, where a city detective would ask the questions.

Under gentle coaxing by police sergeant John V. Wilkie, the girl opened up. She admitted she'd been out that night because she "had a date with a man about 40 years old." The man's name, she said, was Frank La Salle. He'd given her a card with the phone number and address of the Philadelphia auto body shop where he worked.

In his report, Wilkie wrote that the girl said La Salle had

"forced her into intimacies." The girl almost certainly used plainer language. She also told Wilkie that La Salle made her introduce him to four of her friends by threatening to tell her mother what she had done with him.

The five girls were Loretta, Margaret, Sarah, Erma, and Virginia.* From the available records, it's not clear which of them was the one in the diner, but based on their birth dates, it was likely Loretta or Margaret. (Sarah, the oldest, had just turned fifteen.) All of them lived in Camden County, either in the city or in nearby Pennsauken. All of them were named in a 1944 divorce petition by Dorothy Dare as having "committed adultery" with her husband.

When police brought the other girls in to be questioned, Wilkie reported, each of them also told of "how they had been raped by La Salle."

SERGEANT WILKIE SWORE OUT a warrant for Frank La Salle's arrest, alerting police in Philadelphia of the twelve-year-old girl's sickening allegation. But when police showed up at La Salle's workplace, he wasn't there. They didn't find him at his last known address, either. Who knows how La Salle learned the police were coming for him, but he had fled. What's more, police learned, he'd gone back to his earlier alias of Fogg. They dug up an address in Maple Shade, then received word that he, Dorothy, and Madeline had moved back to Camden.

Police got a tip La Salle and his family now lived at a house on the 1000 block on Cooper Street. They kept the place under

---

* I am withholding their last names to protect the privacy of their families, and because of the difficulty in locating descendants to verify the details.

constant surveillance, hoping he might turn up. On the evening of March 15, a car pulled up in front of the house. The car had a license number linked to La Salle.

Detectives rushed into the house. They found and arrested a nineteen-year-old man who claimed he was La Salle's brother-in-law. But no La Salle. "We found out later," Wilkie said, "that as detectives walked up the front steps, La Salle made his escape out the back door."

For nearly a year, La Salle eluded the law. An official indictment for the statutory rape of the five girls came down on September 4, 1942. Tips streamed into Camden and Philadelphia police placing him in New Jersey, and sometimes in Pennsylvania, but nothing panned out—not until the beginning of February 1943, when cops got a tip that La Salle now lived at 1414 Euclid Avenue in Philadelphia, in the heart of where Temple University stands today.

On February 2, police descended upon the house and found La Salle, alone. They arrested him, taking him back to Camden to be arraigned. The Camden city court judge who signed the indictment and oversaw the February 10 hearing was a man named Mitchell Cohen. The two men would meet again, seven years later, in even more explosive circumstances.

La Salle pleaded not guilty to the multiple rape indictments from the Camden grand jury, but on March 22, 1943, he changed his plea to *non vult*, or no contest. The presiding judge, Bartholomew Sheehan, sentenced La Salle to two and a half years on each rape charge, to be served concurrently at Trenton State Prison.

WHILE LA SALLE was incarcerated, Dorothy and Madeline had moved back to Merchantville to be closer to Dorothy's parents.

Mug shot of Frank La Salle taken upon the start of his prison sentence for the statutory rape of five girls, 1943.

She moved quickly to divorce him, filing a petition on January 11, 1944, stating that La Salle had "committed adultery" with the five girls beginning on March 9, 1942—the night the first girl reported her rape to police—and "at various times" between that date and February 1943, when La Salle was finally arrested. Frank wrote her frequently from prison—a habit he would repeat later in life—but if he meant to persuade Dorothy to stay married to him, he was not successful.

La Salle was paroled on June 18, 1944, after fourteen months in prison. He took a room at the YMCA on Broadway and Federal, registered for the draft, and got his Social Security card. He also had to register with the city as a convicted criminal; a blurry photo from June 29, 1944, shows a middle-aged man with gray hair, blue eyes, high cheekbones, and a squint. He wore a more subdued expression than in the prison intake photo from March 1943, where he'd smirked at the camera, seemingly free from worry or care.

La Salle found work as a car mechanic in Philadelphia, but found himself in repeated trouble with the law. An indecent assault charge was dropped on Halloween, but the following August, he got caught at Camden's Third National Bank trying to pass off a forged $110 check. He was indicted the following month and swiftly convicted for "obtaining money under false pretenses." His divorce from Dorothy also moved toward completion that same month. The family court judge awarded full custody of Madeline to her mother on August 21. The divorce was final on November 23.

La Salle returned to Trenton State Prison on March 18, 1946, to serve eighteen months to five years on the new charges. The clock also began again on the balance of the statutory rape sentence. La Salle finished up both those sentences in January 1948, and was paroled again on the fifteenth of that month.

Now that he was back on the streets, it seems likely La Salle went to the downtown Camden YMCA for a cheap place to stay. It was across the street from Woolworth's, where weeks later, on a crisp March afternoon, he would spy a ten-year-old girl attempting to steal a five-cent notebook.

EIGHT

"A Lonely Mother Waits"

The more months that slipped by without answers, the greater the existential toll on Sally Horner's family. Ella bore the brunt of it. Sally was her daughter. She'd let the girl go off with a stranger because he'd said he was the father of school friends, who were waiting for her down by the Jersey Shore. She believed the lies the man forced her daughter to tell, and now the girl was gone.

Perhaps Ella entertained fleeting thoughts that Sally was dead, but she never admitted it in public. She'd found work as a seamstress for Quartermaster Depot, so at least there was enough money coming in to keep the lights on in the house, as well as the telephone in operation. Sally hadn't called home again, but if she ever chose to, it would be a disaster if the line was disconnected.

Ella aired her anguish in a December 10, 1948, article pub-

lished by the *Philadelphia Inquirer,* headlined "A Christmas
Tree Glows, a Lonely Mother Waits." Sally had been missing
for nearly half a year by that point. Ella kept a figurative candle
burning for the time when her daughter would return home
safe. And with Christmas a little more than two weeks away,
the tree Ella set up was, according to the unbylined reporter,
"freighted with memories of other and happier Christmases," a
means of multiplying the "candle's tiny gleam." Ella could think
of no better way to express her faith that Sally would come back
to her.

When that happened—Ella could not allow herself to think
"if," only "when"—Sally would have to contend with one very
big change to the family. Her niece, Diana, was five months old
when the article appeared in the *Inquirer.* But Diana's arrival
couldn't help but be bittersweet for her grandmother, Susan,
and her husband, as long as they had no clue to Sally's whereabouts. Sally had so looked forward to being an aunt.

The young couple buried their uncertainty and despair in
the daily care of their new baby. Changing diapers, rocking her
to sleep, trying to get much-needed rest in small bursts. They
also had the family greenhouse to look after—the flowers and
plants wouldn't grow themselves.

Ella was thrilled to be a grandmother. But her joy was always tempered so long as Sally wasn't here with her. And as
she told the *Inquirer,* the moment Sally walked back through
the front door at 944 Linden Street, she would not be punished
in any way. "Whatever she has done, I can forgive her for it. If I
can just have her back again."

SALLY HORNER'S TWELFTH BIRTHDAY, on April 18, 1949,
came and went with no news. Had she vanished into the ether?

Would her body turn up? Or was Sally out there, ready to be found, hoping that she would come home again? Camden police kept the case open, and Marshall Thompson tracked every lead.

The case had taken on added urgency a month earlier, on March 17, when the Camden County prosecutor's office added a second, more serious, indictment of kidnapping to the existing charge against La Salle. Where abduction carried a maximum prison sentence of only a few years, a kidnapping conviction upped the ante to between thirty and thirty-five years—effectively, for someone of Frank La Salle's age, a life sentence.

No documents have survived to explain the more serious charge. Perhaps the prosecutor, or the Camden Police Department, had received a credible tip to La Salle's whereabouts and hoped that news of the new indictment might flush him out. Or perhaps there were concerns about the statute of limitations on the original abduction charge if Sally stayed missing for a long time, or even forever.

The media moved on from covering the story. No one marked the first anniversary of her disappearance. At Christmas 1949, they did not publicize appeals for Sally's safe return. Other sensational local crimes pushed her out of the papers, including a mass shooting on Camden's East Side and another mysterious disappearance: that of the wife of Jules Forstein, a Philadelphia magistrate.

Dorothy Forstein's disappearance baffled investigators. She had spent the previous four years in a state of anxiety after an unknown assailant nearly killed her just outside her front door. On the evening of October 18, 1949, Dorothy's husband, Jules, attended a party on his own. He said he asked Dorothy to come with him, but she insisted she'd rather stay home with the children, stepdaughter Marcy, nine, and their seven-year-old, Edward.

When Jules got home at 11:30 P.M. Dorothy was gone and the children were frantic. They claimed a stranger had come into the house, knocked their mother unconscious, and then hefted the five-foot-two, 125-pound woman, clad in pajamas and red slippers, over his shoulder, carrying her out and locking the door behind them. Before he left, he patted Marcy on the head and told her, "Go back to sleep." Marcy recalled that he was wearing a brown cap and "something brown in his shirt."

Jules said he did not report Dorothy missing right away because he thought Marcy was telling a fib, and believed—oddly, considering her near-agoraphobia—that his wife must still be in the neighborhood. He called police four and a half hours later, just before 4:00 A.M. The police also brushed off Marcy's story as fantasy. Then a female psychiatrist was called in to question the little girl, and after several lengthy conversations, the psychiatrist concluded Marcy was telling the truth about what happened that night.

Over the next few days, people reported sightings of the missing woman all over the Philadelphia area. Camden also figured in the initial investigation. The Friday night after Dorothy vanished, Camden patrolman Edward Shapiro noticed a blond woman hovering around the corner of Broadway and Fourth Street. Shapiro told Philadelphia detectives he first saw the woman coming out of a telephone booth next to a candy store. She seemed startled to see him, and he was himself startled by how much she resembled Dorothy Forstein. Shapiro followed her to a tavern, where she ordered a beer, but when the woman noticed him again, she split.

The following night, Shapiro saw the woman again on the same corner, and overheard her speaking with a male companion. "I've only got one arm," he heard the woman say. This statement caused detectives to perk up. One of Dorothy's lingering injuries from her earlier attack was a recurrent dislocated shoulder that landed her in the hospital for treatment several times a year. Detectives were certain Dorothy, even under a false name, might turn up at a hospital to have her shoulder reset again. She did not. A thousand-dollar reward offered by Jules Forstein yielded no new leads. Dorothy was declared legally dead eight years later, in 1957, a year after her husband had died of a heart attack at home.

SALLY'S FAMILY took the waning public interest as a sign that it was better not to speak of her disappearance, even among themselves. Her absence was a low thrum, ever-present but unacknowledged. Of course they worried. Of course they feared for her safety. But no news meant no answers, and her fate was beyond their control. It was better to carry on with life.

Baby Diana turned one in August 1949. She was, by her parents' account and her own later recollection, a happy little girl, eager and talkative, who loved eating Grape-Nuts and drinking apple juice. Al ran the greenhouse, and Susan stopped in when she was up to it. Ella remained at 944 Linden Street, but living there was like a nightmare. "It was so different when Sally was here," she later recalled. "She was so cheerful and full of life."

Ella had difficulty sleeping. Many times in the night she would leave her room and go to Sally's. She would take out her daughter's toys and games and "just sit there and look at them." Ella washed and rewashed Sally's clothes "so they would be ready for her when she came back."

As the months wore on, she lost jobs and found others.

Sometimes she couldn't pay her bills for weeks. Sometimes the phone got disconnected, or the electricity was shut off. Periodically, Ella would go to Florence to stay with Susan and look after her granddaughter. Otherwise, Ella was alone. Alone to contemplate again and again the ways in which she held herself responsible for Sally's disappearance.

NINE

The Prosecutor

S ally Horner disappeared a few months after Mitchell Cohen was appointed as prosecutor for Camden County, a ten-year term that would last until 1958. He was already on the way to becoming the pivotal law enforcement figure in the city, a status that saw his name emblazoned, decades later, on the downtown federal courthouse. Taking on the prosecutor gig only bolstered his reputation. In the late 1940s, Camden County did not have enough major crime to justify a full-time prosecutor. So Cohen worked in spurts, spending the rest of his time on Republican party politics. He was so successful at it that he became the state party's de facto leader, allied closely with the New Jersey governor of the day, Alfred Driscoll.

Cohen's term as prosecutor was one of many jobs he held in law enforcement over a long legal career that stretched from early private practice with local law firms all the way to chief judge for the federal district court of New Jersey. He moved smoothly between prosecuting criminals and delivering judgments. Cohen wasn't one to bask in career glories, though. He was far too busy working to spend much time reflecting on the past.

Cohen did, however, take the time to dress the part of a big-shot lawyer. In his bespoke suits, he cut a figure that landed somewhere between David Niven and Fred Astaire. One lawyer told Cohen's son, Fred, "Whenever I appeared in front of your father, I felt I wanted to wear a white tie and tails and be at the top of my game because he was a classy guy."

Any resemblance Cohen bore to famous actors was, perhaps, intentional. He caught the bug for theater early in life, making trips up to New York to see Broadway shows a priority. In his younger years, Cohen spent his Saturday nights in line for concerts and stage performances at Philadelphia's Academy of Music, angling for a twenty-five-cent seat in the gallery. Once established in his legal career, he could afford to split a box seat with a friend.

He'd met Herman Levin at South Philadelphia High; they remained pals even after Cohen's family moved to Camden just before his senior year. The boys made a point of seeing every play in Philadelphia—long a city where Broadway-bound shows worked out problems and test-ran productions on audiences—on opening night. Levin ended up producing musicals like *Gentlemen Prefer Blondes, Destry Rides Again,* and *My Fair Lady.* Before the latter show opened in 1956, Levin told Cohen to "hock everything he had in the world" to invest in the production. Cohen did, and reaped the benefits as *My Fair Lady* smashed box-office records. Cohen also became a theatrical producer himself, cochairing the short-lived Camden County Music Circus during the summers of 1956 and 1957.

But Cohen's fashion sense, his theatrical interests, and even his political machinations did not overshadow his commitment to jurisprudence. Cohen cared about the law and about being fair. He believed it was as important to know when *not* to prosecute a case as when to prosecute. In 1938, early in his tenure as acting judge for the city of Camden, a husband and wife appeared together in his courtroom after she had attempted suicide by poison—back then a punishable crime.

"We had a quarrel, and I thought he didn't love me anymore," the twenty-eight-year-old woman told Cohen.

"Do you?" Cohen asked her husband, who was twenty-nine.

"I sure do."

"Then go home and forget about it."

Cohen didn't seek out notorious cases. They found him. When he won a trial, he didn't dwell upon the details. Those cases, and how Cohen approached them, are an important window into 1940s Camden, as well as the forces that set the city up for great societal changes.

WHEN MITCHELL COHEN set out to prosecute the men responsible for the murder of Wanda Dworecki in the fall of 1939, he had never worked on a capital case before, even though he'd been appointed city prosecutor for Camden three years earlier. Murders were rare then, a far cry from the statistics that designated the city as America's murder capital as recently as 2012. The strangulation of a girl a month shy of her eighteenth birthday stood out in its singular brutality.

Wanda's body was discovered on the morning of August 8, 1939, in an area near Camden High School frequently used as a lovers' lane. A corsage of red and white roses adorned her neck. The killer strangled her so forcefully that he broke her collarbone and breastbone. Then he dropped a rock onto her head, fracturing her skull.

Police working on the case weren't all that surprised Wanda had died so violently. Four months before her murder, in April 1939, two men had accosted Wanda on the street and thrown her into their car. They beat her up—a near-fatal assault—and tossed her out into a field in a desolate part of Salem County, just south of Camden. She spent weeks recovering in the hospital.

That beating wasn't Wanda's first brush with violence. In late 1938, she and a friend had been out walking in the neighborhood when several men tried to kidnap them. Police were convinced—or at least, this is what they said—that Wanda was "destined to be murdered." What they would soon learn is how much one man manipulated things so that destiny would become reality.

Wanda's father, Walter Dworecki, who had emigrated from Poland in 1913, appeared to be an upstanding figure. He preached at the First Polish Baptist Church, a congregation he'd founded when the family moved to Camden from rural Pennsylvania. His teenage daughter troubled him, especially after her mother, Theresa, collapsed at the breakfast table and died in 1938. He brooded over Wanda's fondness for the opposite sex, lecturing her about preserving her virtue, verbally abusing her in such a way to make an example of her to her younger siblings, Mildred and Alfred.

Respectable appearances can hide awful secrets, and Dworecki had plenty. Like being out on bail for setting fire to a house in Chester, Pennsylvania, in a scheme to collect insurance. Or having been sentenced to five years' probation for passing counterfeit money. Like getting so angry at a neighborhood boy that he allegedly fractured the teen's jaw with a broomstick. Or taking out a $2,500 life insurance policy (nearly

$45,000 in 2018 dollars) on his wife, Theresa, whose cause of death was officially "lobar pneumonia"—the same cause of death listed for a number of victims of a murder-for-insurance scheme in Philadelphia whose culprits had some connections to the preacher.

The secret Walter Dworecki should have tried harder to keep was his fondness for hanging around Philadelphia dives, looking for men who might be willing and able to kill his daughter.

Immediately after Wanda's murder, Dworecki slipped into the role of grieving father. He cried, "My poor Wanda!" when he saw his daughter's body at the morgue, and then fainted. He had an alibi for the time of her death, but his grief-stricken act cracked quickly once police started to investigate.

A witness had seen Wanda with a "large blond gentleman" the night before she was murdered, who turned out to be twenty-year-old Peter Shewchuk, who boarded at the Dworeckis' and romanced Wanda every now and then. When Shewchuk learned he was wanted for questioning, he fled Camden for his boyhood home in rural Pennsylvania. Police caught up to him on August 27, after his father turned him in.

In the interview room, all it took was the offer of a single cigarette for Shewchuk to open up. He told the detectives that he and Dworecki had met up in Philadelphia earlier in the evening of August 7. "He gave me 50 cents to cover my expenses and then went to conduct his religious services. I met Wanda and we strolled down the street." Walking past the lovers' lane, Shewchuk said he "suddenly felt the urge to kill" Wanda the way her father had told him to: "Choke her, hit her with a rock, twist her neck." Dworecki was supposed to pay Shewchuk a hundred dollars for the murder, but after Wanda was dead, he reneged on the deal.

Armed with Shewchuk's confession, Camden police brought in the preacher. It turned out Dworecki had taken out a life insurance policy on Wanda around the same time as he had taken one out on her mother. He had hired three men, including Shewchuk, to kidnap and kill Wanda back in April. When she survived the failed attempt, Dworecki upped the policy on his daughter to nearly $2,700, with a double indemnity clause should she die in an accident, and got ready to try again.

Dworecki eventually confessed in a statement that ran to nearly thirty pages. The preacher admitted to being aggrieved by Wanda's behavior, but he claimed the idea to kill Wanda originated with two men, Joe Rock and John Popolo, whom he'd met in Philadelphia. Dworecki said they urged him to kill his daughter to collect the insurance money and pressed him again as time went on. He roped Shewchuk into the murder plot after learning the younger man had bragged about sleeping with Wanda. Shewchuk denied it, but Dworecki sensed an opportunity to manipulate the boy into carrying out his murderous scheme.

Both men entered guilty pleas in Camden County Court on August 29, 1939. Dworecki refused to look at anyone. Shewchuk chose the opposite tack, smiling whenever someone caught his eye. Then Mitchell Cohen, the city prosecutor, explained to the assembled crowd, including the surprised defendants and their lawyers, why the guilty pleas had to be thrown out. New Jersey state law at the time stipulated that one was not allowed to be sentenced to death if he pleaded guilty. Capital cases, and murder certainly counted, required that the defendants face a full trial, verdict, and sentencing.

Cohen voided the pleas, then bound the cases over to the county court, where Samuel Orlando (whom Cohen would succeed a few years later) would prosecute them. Cohen's work was done, but he paid attention to what happened in the county courtroom. Orlando cross-examined both Shewchuk and Dworecki with extra vigor. Shewchuk received a life sentence in exchange for being the primary witness against Dworecki. The preacher's confession was admitted into evidence, despite his lawyer protesting it should be kept out. The jury found him guilty after swift deliberations.

Shewchuk was paroled in 1959 after surviving his own near-fatal beating in prison; he died in the late 1980s. Dworecki was put to death by electric chair on March 28, 1940. Before his execution, he implored his surviving children, Mildred and Alfred, to lead pious lives and asked that "God have mercy on their souls." Dworecki's grave lies next to that of the daughter he murdered.

UNLIKE THE DWORECKI CASE, where Cohen did not have to work to establish the defendants' guilt, he played a larger role in a subsequent murder trial that garnered a great deal of media attention. This case concerned the death of twenty-three-year-old Margaret McDade (Rita to her friends) on August 14, 1945, as Philadelphia, Camden, and the entire country celebrated V-J Day. That night, Rita's best friend and fellow waitress Ann Rust saw her in the arms of a stranger, dancing to a Johnny Mercer tune. Five days later, Rita was found naked and dead at the bottom of a cistern near a sewage disposal plant. An autopsy determined that she had been raped, beaten bloody, and tossed into the cistern alive. She died of suffocation.

Not long after, police arrested the stranger Rita had danced with on the last night she was seen alive. Howard Auld was a former army paratrooper, recently discharged. When police found him, Auld gave them a fake name ("George Jackson") and claimed to be innocent. Discharge papers he carried caught him out on the first lie. Careful interrogation spurred Auld to confess to McDade's murder.

Auld recounted an all-too-familiar, all-too-horrible story: after the dance, he had made a move on Rita that she turned down. He got angry, punched her in the face, and choked her until she passed out. Auld claimed he felt for a pulse and, when he found none, dumped her into the cistern. (Never mind that she was still alive and he omitted mention of the rape.) Auld's time in the army also included repeated stints in a mental hospital and various bouts of violent behavior, which his lawyer, a court-appointed defense attorney named Rocco Palese, would use as a mitigating circumstance in the trial.

Auld was sentenced to death for Rita McDade's murder in 1946, but the conviction was tossed out on appeal several months later. The presiding judge, Bartholomew Sheehan, had failed to tell the jury that they could recommend mercy—meaning, a verdict other than death—in finding Auld guilty of first-degree murder. The Camden County prosecutor's office moved quickly to try Auld again, but proceedings did not begin until 1948, after Mitchell Cohen's appointment as top prosecutor.

Sheehan was also the judge for the second trial. Cohen asked for the death penalty, in accordance with New Jersey state law. Auld's new court-appointed attorney, John Morrissey—Palese had since been appointed as a judge—implored the jury to be lenient toward his client, "a feeble-minded boy," and deliver a not-guilty verdict by reason of insanity. But Cohen prevailed with the jury. Morrissey indicated he would appeal, and did, several times over, delaying the execution date a half dozen times. Howard Auld did not die in New Jersey's "Old Smokey" until March 27, 1951. His final words were "Jesus, have mercy on me."

BY THE END OF 1949, Mitchell Cohen had established his bona fides as Camden County prosecutor. He had tried one capital case directly and worked on another, even though he was deeply conflicted about the death penalty. Decades later his son, Fred, recalled Cohen becoming "very emotional" when the subject came up, so much so that they did not discuss it again. Cohen did his duty, whether asking for the harshest sentence as a prosecutor or delivering the sentence as a judge. But he did not have to like it and, with that single exception, took care not to bring his feelings home to the Rittenhouse Square town house he shared with his family.

He would also vault onto the national stage with his handling of a case that would shake the city to its foundation, and foreshadow similar massacres in the decades to come. But he did not close the books on Sally Horner's abduction. To his knowledge, the new kidnapping charge had not flushed out Frank La Salle. Sally was still missing. And the more time passed, the less likely the outcome would be a good one.

TEN

Baltimore

Here's the point in the narrative where I would like to tell you everything that happened to Sally Horner after Frank La Salle spirited her away from Atlantic City to Baltimore, and the eight months they lived in the city, from August 1948 through April 1949. The trouble is, I didn't find out all that much. A scattershot list of addresses and court documents can't bring to life what a little girl thought or felt. Visiting the neighborhood where Sally lived, and walking by the school she attended, can't adequately bridge the decades. The neighborhood has changed, demographically and socio-economically. Sally, were she still alive today, would barely recognize it.

The meager paper trail frustrated me. My patience frayed as I ran up against dead end after dead end, record search after fruitless record search, to try to build up a picture of the months Sally lived in Baltimore. If she made friends, or had someone she felt she could trust, I couldn't find them. If there are people still living who knew her at the time, I could not track them down. If she kept a journal during her captivity, it did not survive. She did go to school in Baltimore—a Catholic school—but if any of its records remain, they are buried under decades of detritus no one has the inclination to sift through.

But I needed to understand what Sally was thinking and feeling—or at least approximate an understanding—so I read as many accounts as I could find by girls, born one or two generations after her, who survived years or decades of abuse by their kidnappers. I also examined kidnappings from the decade or so before Sally was taken.

Stranger abductions are rare now and were, perhaps, even rarer when Sally vanished. That's why the kidnapping of Charles Lindbergh, Jr., in 1932 caught America's attention and held it for weeks. The celebrity of the boy's parents, superstar pilot Charles Lindbergh and his wife, Anne Morrow Lindbergh, certainly helped, but the boy's snatching felt like the manifestation of every parent's worst fear—that their child might be stolen in the middle of the night from his bedroom by strangers—and kept the country gripped until the baby's body was discovered weeks later.

Abductions where the child is held for a significant period of time before being rescued alive occur with even lesser frequency. That's why, fourteen years before Sally Horner's abduction, the kidnapping of six-year-old June Robles, the daughter of a well-to-do Tucson, Arizona, family, stood out. A man driving a Ford sedan waited for June after school on April 25, 1934, and enticed her to get into his car. Several ransom notes arrived at the Robles household. The first demanded fifteen thousand dollars; the second, ten thousand. Days passed with false sightings and near-arrests, until a Chicago-postmarked letter delivered to Arizona governor B. B. Moeur's residence described where June was being held. A search in the Tucson desert turned up a metal box buried three feet underground. June, chained, malnourished, and covered in ant bites, was found alive inside.

For someone held captive in a tiny box for nineteen days, the girl was in remarkably good spirits. Several days after her rescue, June appeared at a press conference filmed by Pathé studios. (Reporters did not ask her questions, though, allowing her father, Fernando, to steer June through the session.) The little girl seemed poised, her answers sounding rehearsed. She said she was looking forward to going back to school that Friday. It was the last interview Robles ever gave. She never spoke to the media again.

As June's public silence stretched, so did the investigation. Leads proved false, no arrests were made, a grand jury failed to indict anyone, and the FBI eventually gave up, privately agreeing with the grand jury's conclusion of "alleged kidnapping." June stayed in Tucson, where she married and had children and grandchildren. By the time she died in 2014, in such obscurity that it took the press three years to connect her to her childhood ordeal, authorities still had no proper answer about who kidnapped her. It remains a mystery, as does the effect the kidnapping had upon June and her family.

Captivity narratives, such as the recent "found alive" stories of young women including Elizabeth Smart, Jaycee Dugard, Natascha Kampusch, and the trio Ariel Castro held prisoner in Cleveland, opened up a psychological trapdoor into Sally's probable state of mind. They also allowed me to understand how kidnappers were able to subject these girls and women to years of sexual, physical, and psychological abuse.

Smart, Dugard, and Colleen Stan—the "Girl in the Box" under her tormentors' sway for seven years—left their abductors' homes, shopped at supermarkets, and even traveled (Stan visited her parents while she was a captive) without asking anyone for help. They survived by adjusting their mental maps so that brutality could be endured, but never entirely accepted as normal. Every day, every hour, their kidnappers told these women that their families had forgotten all about them. Year after year, their only experience of "love" came from those who abused, raped, and tortured them, creating a cognitive dissonance impossible to escape.

Dugard's eighteen-year bond with her abductor resulted in her bearing two children by him. The fear of losing her daughters, no matter how squalid her situation, caused her to deny her real identity to the police at first, revealing the truth only when she felt secure that she was safe from her kidnappers. Smart, too, needed the same foundation of trust to tell law enforcement who she really was.

We know how these girls coped and felt because several of them published books about their extended ordeals. Smart, Dugard, and the Cleveland three—Amanda Berry and Gina DeJesus together, and Michelle Knight on her own—were able to tell their stories the way they wished and when they chose. In doing so they sought to make something meaningful of their lives.

Sally Horner did not have the chance to tell her story to the world, unlike the women and girls of later generations. She also didn't have the choice of keeping her account wholly private, unlike June Robles. What remains of her time on the road with Frank La Salle are bits and pieces cobbled together from court documents and corroborated by city records. Absence is as telling as substance. Inference will have to stand in for confidence. Imagination will have to fill in the rest.

THE SUMMER'S GREAT HEAT WAVE was some weeks away, but it still sweltered plenty on the Baltimore-bound bus. Frank La Salle and Sally Horner had taken a taxicab to the bus depot in Philadelphia. Perhaps Sally wondered why they were going so far out of the way if they were headed south. Maybe she asked why they had to leave Atlantic City so quickly, or where the station wagon had gone, or why they had to leave their clothes and photos behind. Most likely, she kept any complaints or questions to herself.

She had to keep remembering the script, that La Salle was her father. His word was law. She had to stick to the story to avoid punishment. She had to endure his daily torments. She had to retreat to her own mind to escape the void of her current situation.

The cab pulled up in front of the Philadelphia station. Frank and Sally made their way to the Greyhound bus bound for Baltimore before it pulled away at 11:00 A.M. He bought their tickets, Sally squeaking under the wire for the half-price fare. They settled in their seats for the three-hour trip. They may not have been alone. Sally later said that a woman she knew as "Miss Robinson" had joined them. La Salle had told her the woman was some sort of assistant or secretary. She was perhaps twenty-five, though an eleven-year-old girl's sense of how old people are can be skewed.

The Philadelphia Greyhound made one stop along the way, either in Wilmington or in Oxford, Delaware. After the short break, the bus moved over to Route 40, which turned into the

Pulaski Highway. Was Sally impressed by the wider lanes and speeding cars on the still-new highway? What did she allow herself to dream over the three-hour trip before the bus pulled into the downtown depot in Baltimore? Did she hope for a chance of escape, or had she resigned herself to being trapped by La Salle's new vision of her life?

They arrived in Baltimore just after 2:15 in the afternoon. "Miss Robinson," if she existed, vanished from the picture, perhaps as soon as they got off the bus, collected their luggage, and looked for a cab or local transit to take them to their lodgings. Most likely they ended up staying downtown that first evening and for the next few days, around West Franklin Street in the neighborhood of Mount Vernon. Blocks away lay the city's most prized landmarks, including City Hall, the Museum of Art, and the original Washington Monument. Testaments to Baltimore's beauty and power, but also a refuge out of Sally's grasp.

La Salle needed to find work right away. The Belvedere Hotel, a place so swanky that Woodrow Wilson, Theodore Roosevelt, and King Edward VIII and Wallis Simpson stayed there, may have hired him. It was less than a mile's walk from West Franklin Street. It would explain why La Salle listed a hotel bellman named Anthony Janney as a reference in later court documents. And what better place for a fugitive to hide than among hotel staff serving the toniest, richest guests in a Beaux Arts building nestled within Baltimore's most prominent neighborhood?

I was also struck, while walking around the district, by how close Sally was to the Enoch Pratt Free Library. It's a wonderful place for researchers, and a safe harbor for bookish types of all kinds. Sally loved to read; were books a way for her to imagine herself in different worlds she could control, or was the library yet another place she couldn't go, somewhere she fantasized about as a refuge from Frank La Salle's relentless assaults?

Because in Baltimore, something changed in their relationship. Publicly, they kept up the pose of father and daughter. In private, the power imbalance between them grew more noxious. It was in Baltimore, according to Sally, that rape became a regular occurrence. It was the place where Frank La Salle subjugated her totally to his will psychologically and physically. The outside world never had a clue, even after La Salle sent his "daughter" to school.

There was no way he could have kept her home if he wanted to maintain the illusion of normalcy. The summer was over and an eleven-year-old girl, shut away at home or loose on the streets while he was at work, would draw attention—and questions. La Salle couldn't control her every thought and move while she was at school, true. But by this point he'd broken her down enough, between the threats and the rapes, and the apologies and the treats, that he must have felt a measure of confidence that Sally would do exactly what he said, at all times.

To enroll Sally at Saint Ann's Catholic School, they had to leave West Franklin Street. So in September 1948, they moved to Barclay, a neighborhood on Baltimore's east side. There La Salle and Sally settled in an apartment around East Twentieth Street between Barclay and Greenmount Avenues, a block up from the local cemetery. At the time, the neighborhood was a middle-class enclave of brick town houses, where neighbors mingled freely if they wished, or kept to themselves if they did not. Over the next eight months, Sally got used to the new name Frank had given her: Madeline LaPlante.

Here's how I imagine Sally Horner's days during the 1948–1949 school year. She'd wake up, get dressed, act the part of daughter to her "daddy," and shove from her mind the fact that her current life was the opposite of normal. He probably took Sally to school for the first week, just to be sure she wouldn't do anything rash like speak out or run away. Afterward, he trusted Sally to go by herself. She knew he had to be at work early in a different part of town. She did not want to disappoint him. She resolved she never would.

She'd smile and nod to their landlady—Mary or Ann Troy; she got the two confused even though she'd been told over and over that they weren't related—and other neighbors as they headed off to work. Then, she'd walk west along East Twentieth Street. At the end of the block was the Diamond, the diner where she and La Salle took many of their meals, since he didn't have the time or the patience to cook, and she was still learning how. Sally usually skipped breakfast, waiting to eat until after morning prayers. Perhaps on some days, the waitress, Marie Farrell, packed up a piping-hot fried egg sandwich for her and put it on Frank's tab.

Breakfast in hand, Sally would turn right at the end of the block, walking up Greenmount Avenue until she reached the corner of Twenty-Second Street. There was Saint Ann's, an extension of a Roman Catholic church that had been in Barclay for more than a century. The schedule was strict. All students had to attend mass first thing in the morning. Sally sat with her classmates on uncomfortable pews as Monsignor Quinn, Saint Ann's pastor and principal, intoned the daily prayers in Latin and English. She kept an eagle eye out for Mother Superior Cornellous—the older woman did not tolerate her students fidgeting or misbehaving.

Then, if she had remembered to fast, Sally took Communion. The priest placed the host on her tongue. As it melted, Sally knelt and prayed for her eternal soul. Was the possibility

of escape part of her prayers? Did she pray that someone would
see behind the calm facade of Madeline LaPlante to the captive
Sally Horner? Did she wonder if the things Frank asked her to
do, which he said were "perfectly natural," were, in fact, a mortal sin? Or did she pray for things to stay as they were because
they might get even worse?

When Communion ended, Sally went back to her pew.
Mass was over, so it was time for the fried egg sandwich, now
cool enough to eat, and then for her classes. So many hours
in the day stretched ahead where all she had to think about
was her studies. She had to do well and keep up her grades
or else there would be more punishment at home, and so she
likely did. But Sally also didn't want to draw undue attention
to herself, in case someone—especially the Monsignor or the
Mother Superior—grew suspicious and started asking too
many questions. Better to embrace the invisibility. Better not
to stand out.

When the last school bell rang and it was time to go home,
Sally reversed her morning walk. But if there was time, or if
she felt a smidgen bolder, perhaps she ventured up a block to
Mund Park. The park was a place where the mind could roam
and think of freedom. Where the green grass grew just like it
did in Camden. Where she could think of her real home, and
wonder if she would ever see it again.

I DON'T KNOW WHY La Salle chose to enroll Sally in Catholic
schools, both in Baltimore and elsewhere. No one remembered
him being a churchgoer or having any religious leanings. Before her abduction, Sally likely attended a Protestant church.
One possible reason is that a parochial school did not have to
conform to the same rules and regulations as public schools.

Catholic institutions were less likely to ask questions of a new student arriving later in the school year, under a false name, with dubious documentation at best. Instead of viewing a girl like Sally with suspicion, some opposite effect, like sympathy, may have prevailed.

But I suspect La Salle gravitated toward Catholic institutions because they were a good place to hide in plain sight. The Church, as we now know from decades' worth of scandal, hid generations of abused victims, and moved pedophile priests from parish to parish because covering up their crimes protected the Church's carefully crafted image. Perhaps La Salle saw parochial schools for what they were: a place for complicity and enabling to flourish. A place where no one would ask Sally Horner if something terrible was happening to her.

ELEVEN

Walks of Death

Back in Camden, Sally Horner's plight had been consigned to the same purgatory that befalls every long-term missing child investigation. The city hadn't moved on, but her fate was no longer the highest priority. Camden residents wanted to embrace progress, to bask in fortunes they believed would last forever. There was little warning of the outsized event that would bewilder them and foreshadow the precipitous decline in the city's near-future.

In the fall of 1949, Camden believed in its own prosperity. It had weathered the Great Depression and near-bankruptcy in 1936, the result of financial mismanagement by the local government. Private industry still thrived. The New York Shipbuilding Corporation still had contracts from the navy and the Maritime Administration. Smaller shipbuilding companies, like John Mathis & Company, had doubled their workforce during the Second World War and seemed primed to expand. Manufacturing jobs in the region were a year away from an all-time peak of 43,267. Campbell's Soup still employed thousands of workers at its local headquarters.

No company represented Camden's sense that the future was theirs for the taking more than RCA Victor, the phonograph company. In June 1949, it had introduced the "45," a smaller, faster alternative to Columbia's "LP" record format. RCA Victor also began producing technology for television, making equipment required by broadcast studios as well as for television sets regular home-buyers could acquire.

A great many forces underlay Camden's eventual negative transformation. But Sally Horner's abduction wasn't the spark. Rather, the morning of September 6, 1949, seems to me like the inflection point between progress and backlash, hope and despair, promise and decline. The scope of the crime seemed an unfathomable one-off, but its grotesque repetition in the decades to come demonstrates how a singular evil can become all too mundane.

AT EIGHT O'CLOCK that morning, a mother woke up her son for breakfast. He'd been out late the night before, sitting and stewing in a movie theater on Market Street in Philadelphia, waiting for a date who never showed. The son's homosexuality wasn't quite a secret, but nor could he flaunt it when sex between men was still very much against the law.

That his date, a man with whom he'd been in the midst of a weeks-long affair, stood him up was indignity enough. Then he'd returned to his home in Cramer Hill to find the fence he built to separate his house from his neighbors' home had been torn down.

The man drank a glass of milk and ate the fried eggs his mother, Freda, prepared. Then he went into the basement, whose walls were covered in memorabilia from the war he'd fought in, and where he had written down meticulous notes on each enemy soldier he'd killed. He regarded his nine-millimeter pistol, a Luger Po8, for which he had two full clips and thirty-three loose cartridges, and thought about the list of people—neighbors, shopkeepers, even his mother—he wanted to wipe off the face of the earth.

He grabbed a wrench and went back to the kitchen. He raised it, threatening Freda. "What do you want to do that for, Howard?" she cried. When he didn't answer, she repeated the question as she backed away from him, then ran out of the house to a neighbor's. He retrieved his Luger and ammunition from the basement, as well as a six-inch knife and a five-inch pen-like weapon tricked up to hold six shells. Then he cut through the backyard and shot at the first person he saw: a bread deliveryman sitting in his truck.

Howard Unruh missed his first target, but he wouldn't miss many more. Twenty minutes. Thirteen dead. And a neighborhood, a city, and a nation forever marked by his "Walk of Death."

FOR MARSHALL THOMPSON, Unruh's murderous spree hit too close for comfort. He and his family lived around the corner from Unruh and his mother, at 943 North Thirty-Second Street. Most of those who died or were injured on the morning of September 6 were Unruh's neighbors on River Road, which was the main thoroughfare of East Camden.

Thompson might have gotten his hair cut at Clark Hoover's barbershop a few feet down River Road. That awful morning, the barber took a fatal shot, as did six-year-old Orris Smith, perched on a hobbyhorse inside the shop. If Thompson needed his shoes repaired and shined, he likely got it done at the repair shop next door, where Unruh killed the cobbler, John Pilarchik. Down the street was the tailor shop, owned by Thomas Zegrino. He was out when Unruh arrived, but Zegrino's new wife, Helen, was not, and she paid the price.

Unruh then shot Alvin Day, the television repairman. James Hutton, the insurance agent, made the dreadful mistake of running out of the drugstore to see what the commotion was all about, and also died. So, too, did a mother and daughter, Emma Matlack, sixty-six, and Helen Matlack Wilson, who'd driven in from Pennsauken for the day and failed to comprehend the massacre unfolding. Unruh shot them dead, and Helen's twelve-year-old son, John, took a bullet in the neck. He died the next day in the hospital.

Others were injured. Like Madeline Harrie, caught in the arm by a bullet after Unruh's first two missed, and her son, Armand, who tried vainly to tackle Unruh when he invaded their home.

Unruh moved on to his worst grudge late in the rampage, hunting down his next-door neighbor, Maurice Cohen, owner of the drugstore, to make him pay for the business with the fence as well as other perceived grievances. Not spotting him in the store, Unruh went upstairs to the family apartment. As Maurice climbed onto the roof, his wife, Rose, shoved their son, twelve-year-old Charles, into a closet, and then hid in a separate one. Unruh searched the apartment and then went out on the roof, where he caught a glimpse of Maurice running away. Unruh fired into the druggist's back. The shot jerked Maurice off the roof and he was dead before hitting the street.

Unruh went back inside and fired his Luger several times into the closet where Rose was hiding. She died instantly. Maurice's mother, Minnie, was in the bedroom, in a frantic state as she tried to get police on the phone, when Unruh caught up to her. He shot her in the head and body. She fell back on the bed and died there.

Charles stayed hidden until it was utterly quiet. When officers finally found him, he would not be comforted—he'd heard everything. Charles leaned halfway out his apartment window and screamed, "He's going to kill me. He's killing everybody."

Howard Unruh had walked down the stairs and made his way to the Harries' place. There he discovered he was out of ammunition. Hearing the police sirens, he doubled back to his mother's house to await his fate.

IN A LARGER CITY, where officers didn't walk the beats where they lived, Marshall Thompson might not have taken part in police efforts to apprehend Howard Unruh. But it's unlikely Thompson could have begged off even if he wished. One of Thompson's colleagues on the Camden detective squad, John Ferry, also lived in Unruh's Cramer Hill neighborhood. The summer before, Ferry had tried to help Unruh find a job as a favor to the man's uncle, a deputy fire chief.

Ferry had just finished up a midnight-to-eight shift. He was on his way home when he saw his insurance man dead in the street, as well as other victims. "When the other cops started arriving I went home and came back with my shotgun," Ferry recalled in 1974, the twenty-fifth anniversary of the massacre. With the body count rising and ambulances blaring to and from Cooper Hospital, Thompson was one of more than four dozen cops who descended upon Cramer Hill that morning.

Howard Unruh had barricaded himself in his home. It was up to a group of policemen led by Detective Russ Maurer to figure out how to coax him out. Maurer sidled up to the front of the house. A throng of cops, including Thompson, covered Maurer, poised to throw tear gas through the window if Unruh acted rashly. As *Courier-Post* columnist Charley Humes observed, "Russ [Maurer] could have paid with his life, because the killer seldom missed. That was a brave act."

John Ferry was crouched with several other policemen in Unruh's backyard, awaiting any sign of the man. When Unruh appeared in the window, Ferry turned to James Mulligan, his supervisor on the detective unit, and asked, "Jim, should I take his head off?"

"No," replied Mulligan. "There has been plenty of killing."

Unruh later told police he "could have killed Johnny Ferry . . . any time I wanted." Ferry's past attempt to find Unruh a job may well have saved his life, and perhaps the others. Unruh made his decision. "Okay. I give up, I'm coming down," he shouted to the cops down below.

"Where's that gun?" a sergeant yelled.

"It's on my desk, up here in the room," Unruh said, then repeated: "I'm coming down."

Unruh opened the back door and came out with his hands up. More than two dozen officers trained their guns upon him. One yelled, "What's the matter with you? You a psycho?"

"I'm no psycho," said Unruh. "I've got a good mind."

MITCHELL COHEN, THE Camden County prosecutor, had just returned from a summer vacation at the Jersey Shore. He expected his office would be its usual bustling self the morning after Labor Day, and that he would be faced with a fresh round

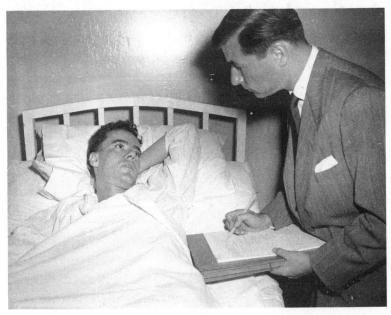

Mitchell Cohen questions Howard Unruh in a hospital bed,
September 7, 1949.

of indictable crimes, from gambling rackets, to robberies, to teens illegally buying beer.

The office was the opposite of bustling. None of the detectives were around, and the quiet cast a strange pall over the place. Then the phone rang. Larry Doran, chief of detectives, was on the line. He told Cohen that a local man had gone "berserk on River Road and was shooting people," which was why every police officer was out of the office. He also told Cohen that Unruh was alive and in custody after his twenty-minute rampage.

Cohen walked over to the police station to interview the mass shooter and found him cooperative. "It was a horrible, revolting narrative," Cohen recalled in a 1974 interview. "He really gave it cold, cut-and-dry. There was no attempt to conceal or be furtive. He didn't seem to experience the normal relief of getting it off his chest. There was no remorse, no tears. There was a lack of all emotion."

Over the two or so hours he spoke with Cohen, Unruh was concealing something. When Cohen realized what it was, he was stunned. "What really convinced me that [Unruh] was terribly insane was when he got up after two hours and his chair was covered with blood. . . . He had been shot and wasn't even aware of it." Unruh was sent to a nearby hospital to recuperate, and Cohen interrogated him further upon his recovery from the bullet wound.

One month after the massacre, Cohen released the psychiatric reports he'd ordered on Unruh to the public. Unruh had been ruled clinically insane, and therefore not competent to stand trial. And so the deaths of thirteen people and the injuries of many more were never properly accounted for in court. Unruh didn't go free. He would spend the rest of his life in mental institutions in and around Trenton. But for those who survived the massacre, who attended hearing after hearing to ensure Unruh was never released, it did not seem like proper justice. He died in 2009 at the age of eighty-eight, just one month after Charles Cohen, the last survivor of the massacre, died.

Unruh's "Walk of Death" also seemed to foreshadow Camden's deeper decline. "It's something you never really forget. . . . You take extra precautions to protect your family and your property," Paul Schopp, a former director of the Camden County Historical Society, said in an interview to mark the sixtieth anniversary of the mass shooting. "He didn't just rob them of their lives. He robbed them of their essence." The trauma of a mass shooting, and a collective desire to forget, seems like the true beginning of Camden's downward slope.

TWELVE

Across America by Oldsmobile

Vladimir Nabokov finished the 1948–1949 academic year at Cornell University in a state of irritation. He hadn't found much time to write. He fumed over cuts and changes made without his permission by the *New York Times Book Review* to his review of Jean-Paul Sartre's *La Nausée,* which he had submitted in March. His finances were depleted: Nabokov hadn't budgeted for unexpected housing costs and the added expense of Social Security (what he termed "old-age insurance") taken out of his monthly salary. And he was exhausted from teaching a full load of English and Russian literature undergraduate classes, exacerbated by the extra work he'd inflicted upon himself by translating a pivotal Russian poetic masterpiece, "The Song of Igor's Campaign," for one of those classes.

Nabokov had, at least, completed another two chapters

of his memoir, *Conclusive Evidence*, both of which were published later that year in the *New Yorker*. He did love teaching, and Cornell proved to be more amenable to his idiosyncrasies than Wellesley. But he couldn't resist complaining: "I have always more to do than I can fit into the most elastic time, even with the most careful packing," he wrote his friend Mstislav Dobuzhinsky in the spring of 1949. "At the moment I am surrounded by the scaffoldings of several large structures on which I have to work by fits and starts and very slowly."

Lolita, which he still thought of as *The Kingdom by the Sea*, was less a work in progress than a seed in Nabokov's mind, one that wasn't quite ready to germinate. Perhaps he would make a beautiful work on his summer trip—another cross-country jaunt with Véra and Dmitri. They said goodbye to the Plymouth that had carried them all the way to Palo Alto, California, in 1941, and hello to a used black 1946 Oldsmobile. Dorothy Leuthold, who had shared the driving with Véra eight years earlier, wasn't available, and neither were two other friends, Andree Bruel and Vladimir Zenzinov. But one of Nabokov's Russian literature students, Richard Buxbaum, volunteered, and the Nabokovs picked him up at Canandaigua on June 22.

Their first destination was Salt Lake City, where Nabokov was to take part in a ten-day writers' conference at the University of Utah starting on July 5. But their westward journey almost ended a few miles from Canandaigua, when Véra changed lanes on the highway and narrowly missed plowing into an oncoming truck. Pulling over, she turned to Buxbaum and said: "Perhaps you'd better drive."

With Buxbaum now behind the wheel, the group traveled south of the Great Lakes and across Iowa and Nebraska. The Nabokovs spoke Russian and encouraged Buxbaum to do the same, chiding him when he lapsed into English. Vladimir was never without his notebook, ready to record all observations, however minuscule, of quotidian American life on the road, be it overheard conversation at a restaurant or vivid impressions of the landscape. They arrived in Salt Lake City on July 3, two days before the conference's start, and were lodged at a sorority house, Alpha Delta Phi, where the Nabokovs had a room with a private bath—a pivotal part of his participation agreement.

The conference introduced Nabokov to writers he might not have otherwise met, including John Crowe Ransom, the poet and critic who founded and edited the *Kenyon Review;* and Ted Geisel, a few years away from children's book superstardom as Dr. Seuss, whom Nabokov recalled as "a charming man, one of the most gifted people on this list." He also got reacquainted with Wallace Stegner, whom he'd first met at Stanford. Nabokov and Stegner spent the conference debating each other in the novel workshops and in the off-hours playing doubles on the tennis courts, with their sons as partners.

Nabokov did not have much time to idle, though. He taught three workshops on the novel, one on the short story, and another on biography. He took part in a reading with several poets, and repurposed an old lecture on Russian literature under a new title, "The Government, the Critic, and the Reader." When the conference ended on July 16, he, Véra, Dmitri, and Richard Buxbaum headed north to the Grand Tetons in Wyoming.

Nabokov, once more, was game to hunt more butterflies. But Véra was worried. The Teton Range, she had heard, was a haven for grizzly bears. How would Vladimir protect himself against them carrying a mere butterfly net? Nabokov wrote to the lepidopterist Alexander Klots for advice; Klots assured him that Grand Teton was "just another damned touristed-out National Park." Any danger would come from clueless visitors, not ravenous bears.

Nabokov re-creating the process of writing Lolita *on note cards.*

From there the quartet headed to Jackson Hole, where Nabokov wanted to look for a particularly elusive subspecies of butterfly, *Lycaeides argyrognomon longinus.* On the way the Oldsmobile blew a tire. As Dmitri and Richard started changing it, Nabokov said, "I'm no use to you," and spent the next hour catching butterflies. They arrived the following day, around July 19. For the next month and a half, the Nabokovs' home base was the Teton Pass Ranch, at the foot of the mountain range. Nabokov's hunt for his coveted butterfly subspecies proved successful.

The six-week stay was not without rough moments, though. Dmitri and Richard Buxbaum decided to try climbing Disappointment Peak, next to the Grand Tetons' East Ridge. The climb to the top, seven thousand feet above base level, was straightforward at first. Then Dmitri, with the overconfidence befitting a fifteen-year-old boy, decided they should switch to a more difficult path, one that required extra equipment they lacked. Realizing they would get stuck up there if they carried on, they turned around, but hours passed—and the sun nearly set—by the time they made it back to Vladimir and Véra, who were understandably frantic.

Buxbaum hitchhiked home at the end of August. The Nabokovs, with Véra now driving, ventured northeast to Minnesota, then up to northern Ontario, for more butterfly collecting, before they finally arrived in Ithaca on September 4. Nabokov had three courses to teach that fall, but had attracted only twenty-one students, combined, a workload greeted with suspicion by his fellow professors. Even so, Nabokov wanted more money.

Cornell's head of the Literature Department, David Daiches, received Nabokov's request and offered a deal: he would approve a salary raise if Nabokov took over teaching the European fiction course, Literature 311-12. Nabokov could shape the curriculum as he saw fit and pick the authors he liked most. Nabokov said yes. He began right away, scribbling notes on the back of Daiches's letter for the course that would define his Cornell career for the next decade.

And in spare moments, Nabokov began at last to shape the novel that had lived in his head for so long.

NABOKOV'S RAMSDALE IS not Camden. The made-up town where Humbert Humbert insinuates himself into the lives of Charlotte and Dolores Haze is most likely located in New England, which is why Dolores is deposited in a school in the Berkshires, and why both older man and younger girl seem to know the area well. Nabokov gleaned this knowledge during his years living in Cambridge, Massachusetts. But the names of the towns are similar, as is the Linden Street of Sally Horner's childhood home and the Lawn Street where the Haze women live. Both towns shared a white, middle-class bucolic atmosphere. As would happen again and again, the Sally Horner story parallels *Lolita* in all sorts of surprising ways.

Humbert Humbert came to Ramsdale by design, but moved into the Haze home at 342 Lawn Street by accident. He meant to stay nearby with the McCoos, parents to "two little daughters, one a baby the other a girl of twelve." Lodging there, he assumed, would allow him to "coach in French and fondle in Humbertish." But when Humbert gets there, he finds out that the McCoos' house has burned down, and he must find someplace else to live.

He is not pleased to be shuffled off to a "white-frame horror . . . looking dingy and old, more gray than white—the kind of place you know will have a rubber tube affixable to the tub faucet in lieu of a shower." Humbert is further irked upon overhearing Charlotte Haze's contralto voice ask a friend if "Monsieur Humbert" has arrived.

Then she comes down the steps—"sandals, maroon slacks, yellow silk blouse, squarish face, in that order"—tapping her cigarette with her index finger. In Humbert's estimation, Charlotte isn't much: "the poor lady was in her middle thirties, she had a shiny forehead, plucked eyebrows and quite simple but not unattractive features of a type that may be defined as a weak solution of Marlene Dietrich." Then he spies Dolores, and it is as if he saw his "Riviera love peering at me over dark glasses," two and a half decades after his prepubescent romance with Annabel, as if the years "tapered to a palpitating point, and vanished." Now that the true object of Humbert's obsession has revealed herself, Charlotte becomes a nuisance to be manipulated and endured.

When Charlotte sends Humbert a letter, confessing she is "a passionate and lonely woman and you are the love of my life," he senses opportunity: marry Charlotte to gain access to Dolores. Another line in Charlotte's letter stands out: that if Humbert were to take advantage of her, "then you would be a criminal—worse than a kidnapper who rapes a child." Charlotte, bafflingly, concludes that if he showed no sign of romantic interest in her, and remained in her home, then she would take it that he was "ready to link up your life with mine forever and ever and be a father to my little girl." (Since we're always in Humbert's head, we only have his word that Charlotte wrote this.)

The American widow and the European widower marry in haste while Dolores is away at summer camp. It is, suffice to say, a bad match. What galls Humbert the most is what he describes as Charlotte's vituperative attitude toward her daughter. The words Charlotte underlined in her copy of *A Guide to Your Child's Development* to mark her daughter's twelfth birthday: "aggressive, boisterous, critical, distrustful, impatient, irritable, inquisitive, listless, negativistic (underlined twice) and obstinate."

Humbert has already decided to murder Charlotte and stage it as an accident, perhaps at a thinly populated beach they visited ("The setting was really perfect for a brisk bubbling murder"). His simmering rage boils over when Charlotte informs him that she intends to send Dolores to boarding school at Beardsley, so that the two of them can take a trip to England. He resists. They argue. Then she reveals to him that she has read his notes, and knows the truth about him: "You're a monster. You're a detestable, abominable, criminal fraud. If you come near—I'll scream out the window. Get back!"

Humbert exits the house. He notes that Charlotte's face is "disfigured by her emotion" and remains calm. He goes back into the house. He opens a bottle of Scotch. Then, quietly, he begins to gaslight her. "You are ruining my life and yours. Let us be civilized people. It is all your hallucination. You are crazy, Charlotte. The notes you found were fragments of a novel."

Charlotte runs back to her room, claiming she has a letter to write. Humbert makes her a drink—or so he says—while she is gone. He realizes she is not, in fact, in her room. The telephone rings. "Mrs. Humbert, sir, has been run over and you'd better come quick." Fate has played a trick. Instead of becoming the potential savior of her daughter's virtue, Charlotte ends up dead. It's also played a fast one upon Humbert: he was all set to become a murderer.

THE DESCRIPTION OF CHARLOTTE HAZE as Dietrich-lite sounds a jarringly familiar bell when I look at pictures of Ella Horner from when her daughter disappeared in 1948. She was forty-one and often wore her hair pulled back, sometimes in a bun (a "bronze-brown bun"), and plucked her eyebrows over eyes that tended to disappear into their creases. Her other facial features—strong jawline, prominent nose, pronounced cheekbones—were reminiscent of Marlene Dietrich before she emigrated from Germany and became a Hollywood star. Based on the photographs of her that I've seen from before and after Sally's kidnapping, I imagine when Ella smiled, it didn't often reach her eyes. (Humbert on Charlotte: "Her smile was but a quizzical jerk of one eyebrow.")

There is another similarity, coincidence or otherwise, that

ties Charlotte Haze to Ella Horner: the device of marriage to gain access to their daughter. For the fictional Humbert Humbert it was a real gambit. For Frank La Salle, it was a delusion he created to explain why he took Sally away from her mother. It was a ruse Sally had to live by in order to survive being with him in Atlantic City and Baltimore, and she would have to endure it for quite a while longer.

THIRTEEN

Dallas

Frank La Salle took Sally Horner aside one day in March 1949 and broke the news that they were leaving Baltimore. He told her that the FBI had assigned him a new case, one that required him to move southwest to investigate. By then she'd been with him for nine months. Sally did not know, and could not know, that the real reason they were leaving Baltimore was that Camden County prosecutor Mitchell Cohen had indicted La Salle on the more serious charge of kidnapping on March 17. The new indictment meant La Salle could face between thirty and thirty-five years for taking Sally. Police had not located the pair, but this charge, on top of the original indictment, promised greater scrutiny, more resources for the hunt, and a better probability of arrest. Baltimore was no longer safe, nor was the entire East Coast. Instead of flushing La Salle out, the new charge caused him to run.

The journey from Baltimore to Dallas is approximately 1,366 miles. Today, by car, it would take about twenty hours to drive, on I-81 and I-40. Neither of those highways existed in 1949. La Salle and Sally likely drove south on U.S. 11, traveling all the way to the highway's end in New Orleans, Louisiana, before switching over to U.S. 80, arriving in Dallas less than two hundred miles later. However they traveled, Sally and La Salle got to Dallas around April 22, 1949. For the next eleven months, she and Frank continued to play father and daughter, sticking to the cover story that he had taken Sally away from her wayward mother to provide her with a more stable upbringing. None of their new neighbors seemed to question this. At least, not right away.

They moved into a quiet, well-kept trailer park on West Commerce Street, about four hundred feet from Dallas's bustling downtown core. The park was designed like a horseshoe, with trailers—including one that La Salle bought on the premises—dotted all along the curve. The park could hold as many as a hundred motor homes. The mothers mostly stayed home and the fathers worked as farmhands, for steel companies, or at gas stations. Neighbors were closer in the trailer park than they had been in Baltimore. They could pay more attention to the pair, and get to know Sally—or think they did.

La Salle had changed their names again. Sally was no longer known as Madeline LaPlante, but as Florence Planette. Oddly, it isn't clear whether La Salle also used the "Planette" alias. One of their new neighbors, Dale Kagamaster, who ended up working with La Salle, knew him as LaPlante. Frank also told people that he was widowed, a change from the divorced father cover story he used in Atlantic City and Baltimore.

The trailer park was owned by Nelrose and Charles Pfeil, who'd bought it a year earlier, after moving to Dallas from Akron, Ohio, with their three sons. Tom, the eldest, was nine years old when Frank and Sally arrived at the trailer park. He did not recall the name "LaPlante," but thought "La Salle" seemed familiar. He also remembered "Florence's" father as aloof, cold, standoffish. "I understand why, now," Pfeil told me. "He had to be suspicious of everyone around him." Tom had dim memories of Sally. "I don't know if I could tell you I remember much of her except for talking a time or two. I was nine. I just wanted to play ball."

As in Baltimore, La Salle got a job as a mechanic, but kept Sally in the dark about what he was really doing all day. He also enrolled Sally in another Catholic school. This time it was Our Lady of Good Counsel Academy at 210 Marsalis Avenue in the neighborhood of Oak Cliff, about a seven-minute drive away from West Commerce Street. Like Saint Ann's in Baltimore, Our Lady of Good Counsel no longer exists, having been absorbed into Bishop Dunne Catholic School in 1961. None of its records have survived. And also like Saint Ann's, the school was in a predominantly white, middle-class neighborhood that is no longer so, thanks to suburban migration, systemic inequality, and poverty.

Sally likely kept to a routine similar to the one she had in Baltimore. A bus ride to Our Lady of Good Counsel, where she began the day with morning prayers. Schoolwork wasn't a breeze, but her grades were generally good: a copy of Sally's report card from between September 1949 and February 1950, which La Salle kept after she brought it home, showed she received primarily As and A-minuses, with the occasional B, in geography and writing. The only time she received a lower grade—a C-plus, in languages—was in her final month at the school.

At first their Commerce Street neighbors didn't see anything amiss. Sally appeared to be a typical twelve-year-old living with her widowed father, albeit one he never let out of his sight except to go to school. Sally never displayed despair or asked for help. La Salle wouldn't let her.

Her neighbors thought Sally seemed to enjoy taking care of her home. She would bake every once in a while. She had a dog, one she apparently spoiled. La Salle provided her with a generous allowance for clothes and sweets. She would go shopping, swimming, and to her neighbors' trailers for dinner—sometimes with La Salle, and other times by herself, when he told her he was working the case for the FBI.

Dale Kagamaster's wife, Josephine, thought Sally was a well-adjusted girl. "There were several times we noticed the need for the love and care of a mother but we both felt that the father was doing a good job of providing better living conditions for [her]." The consensus about Sally and her "father" was that they "seemed happy and entirely devoted to each other." Maude Smillie, who was living in a nearby trailer, seemed bewildered by the idea that Sally had been a virtual prisoner: "[Sally] spent one day at the beauty parlor with me. I gave her a permanent and she never mentioned a thing. She should have known she could have confided in me."

Nelrose Pfeil was quoted in a court document several years later saying something similar: "Sally was in my home many times a day and she had access to several phones should she choose to use one. Sally had plenty of time to talk to me about being kidnaped [sic] if she had wanted to and I am sure she knew me well enough to know if she had said anything like that I would have helped her." The only time La Salle kept Sally from playing with other children, according to Pfeil's statement, "was when the person's character was in question."

It appears the Pfeils, the Kagamasters, and other neighbors

bought La Salle's cover story about Sally. They did not notice anything amiss, even for the ten-day period when Sally dropped off the radar and didn't attend school. She'd suffered an appendicitis attack, one that required her to undergo an operation and spend three nights at the Texas Crippled Children's Hospital (now the Texas Scottish Rite Hospital for Children). The other seven days, presumably, she spent at home, recuperating.

Something did change in Sally, though, after the operation. She grew more pensive. Josephine Kagamaster observed that the girl did not move like a "healthy, light-hearted youngster." She'd heard La Salle say the girl "walks like an old woman."

ON THE SURFACE, Sally acted as free as she had been in Camden, before Frank La Salle took her away from everyone she loved. She might have been left alone for long stretches at a time, stayed late at a neighbor's house watching television, and been on her own in the hospital for several nights. But if she told the truth, who would believe her story? Who would believe she had been abducted when, to all appearances, Frank La Salle was her father, and a loving one at that? And even if someone *did* believe her, could they help, or would they put Sally in greater peril?

Later, Josephine Kagamaster, Nelrose Pfeil, Maude Smillie, and others said they would have helped Sally had she chosen to confide in them. But they made such declarations with the benefit of hindsight, months or years after Frank La Salle's diabolical crimes were exposed to the public. At the time, they were living ordinary and happy lives. The idea that a young girl and an older man would be in a cruel parody of a father-daughter relationship seemed inconceivable, unimaginable. And no matter what they believed about what they would have done, Sally did not confide in these neighbors. She did not feel she could trust them.

But Sally did talk to someone, a woman named Ruth Janisch, and she believed what the girl had to say. Though Ruth's motivations were more complex than anyone knew, her belief in the girl eventually emboldened Sally to make the most important decision of her life.

FOURTEEN

The Neighbor

Ruth Janisch and her family arrived at the Commerce Street trailer park around December 1948. They had spent most of the 1940s traveling a particular geographic loop, following the employment her husband, George, found repairing televisions or working in bowling alleys. It began in San Jose, where Ruth and George met and married, then moved up to Washington, where she'd grown up, tracked east to Minnesota, the home of George's parents, and finally on to Texas, situated more or less in between. The Janisches bought a caravan somewhere along the way and made it the family home.

Periodically, the trailer ran into trouble. On Thanksgiving 1948, it broke down on the way to Dallas, somewhere in the desert. New Mexico, perhaps, or Arizona. George and his elder stepson, Pat, went looking for help, leaving the rest of the family stranded by the road. Ruth and her other children—another boy from an earlier marriage, and two girls sired by George—figured that if they were stuck by the road, they might as well have Thanksgiving dinner while they waited.

They fetched chairs from a closet in the trailer and set up outside. Ruth cooked up an impromptu meal of pancakes and beans, which she served inside the broken-down trailer. The children lined up to get their meal and then ate outside in the baking desert sun. Ruth warned the children not to stay outside for too long. She was nervous that rattlesnakes might bite them if the kids lingered.

Eventually George and Pat returned with the part they needed to fix the trailer, and they drove on to Dallas, setting up camp at the Commerce Street site. A few months later, in April 1949, a man in his fifties and a girl he said was his daughter moved into the trailer next door. The Janisch girls immediately took to the girl, who introduced herself as Florence Planette. She was twelve, practically grown up, but she was willing to give them her attention. The little girls were five, six, and seven, and regarded her with a mixture of awe and envy.

Ruth may well have regarded the girl's father with extramarital interest. That's her children's theory now. Whatever her motives, Ruth noticed something askew in the relationship between Sally Horner and Frank La Salle that had eluded everyone else who interacted with them. What Ruth saw between the older man and the young girl spurred her to the single gesture that defined her as a decent human being, an act she would relive for the rest of her days and memorialize in scrapbooks. That act did not make her a heroine in the eyes of her children. But it would bring her a level of attention she spent the rest of her life trying to find again.

Ruth Janisch may have been suspicious of Frank La Salle

because she wasn't in the habit of trusting people. She craved love she never found. She got pregnant so often she was in a perpetual state of exhaustion, dealing with babies and children. George always found work, but the money he brought in was hardly enough for an ever-expanding family. When her children misbehaved, it was all too easy for Ruth to fall back into the patterns she learned as a child, berating them the way her mother had berated her, telling them they were worthless, useless, or worse.

Ruth Janisch, ca. 1940s.

Her bitter outlook took hold upon leaving Washington State to marry her second husband, Everett Findley. (Ruth later said her first marriage, at sixteen to a man whose name she failed to remember, didn't count.) The former Ruth Douglass was eager to flee her mother, Myrtle, whose cuts were always unkind, and her father, Frank, whom her children later grew fond of but whom Ruth, in her cups, recalled as being "not so innocent." The children were never sure if Ruth was referring to her father's penchant for drink or something uglier.

After their marriage, Ruth had followed Findley, a man more than twice her age, to San Jose, and bore him two sons. She met husband number three, George Janisch, sometime after the dissolution of her marriage to Findley. George hailed from Minneapolis; he was short and slight, and his blond hair and fair appearance befitted his Scandinavian heritage.

He'd moved west for work and to escape the harsh Minnesota winter.

George and Ruth ran off to Carson City, Nevada, to wed on October 24, 1940. Perhaps they married for love. Not long before he died, George confided in one of his daughters that before their wedding, Ruth was a "good girl." But afterward, according to George, she changed, and he admitted that it was his fault.

It wasn't enough for George to sleep with his wife. He had to sleep with other men's wives, too. Ruth herself had taken up with him while he was married. Since George was fine if Ruth slept with the leftover husbands, she wasn't about to say no. The fact was that Ruth had a craving for men that would persist for the rest of her life.

The extramarital doings damaged the already tenuous bond between the Janisches, which had been frayed by having three daughters in quick succession. The couple seemed to bring out the worst in each other. One particularly clever, or insidious, way Ruth and George tested each other was with the naming of every new child. Each baby received a first name either spouse liked. The middle names, however, were those of former lovers. Nine children later, Ruth and George split up. He would marry twice more; she married ten times in total, with lovers scattered in between.

By 1949, Ruth was thirty-three (though would only admit to thirty-one) with a husband she couldn't help needling and at the mercy of that perpetual pregnancy-birth cycle. She still had most of her looks, with dark hair curling about her face, full, pointed breasts, a strong nose and wide-lipped mouth. Every new child added another dose of bitterness at her lot in life, and the family's poverty.

But there was something about Sally Horner that Ruth

could see clearly. The way the girl shuffled after coming home from an extended hospital stay after an appendectomy. The way Sally's smile didn't reach her eyes. The closeness between Sally and Frank that did not strike the right note. "He never let Sally out of his sight, except when she was at school," Ruth later recounted. "She never had any friends her own age. She never went any place, just stayed with La Salle in the trailer." She thought La Salle seemed "abnormally possessive" of the girl he said was his daughter. Ruth tried to cajole Sally, still recovering from her appendectomy, to tell her the "true story" of her relationship with La Salle. Sally wouldn't open up.

In early 1950, the Janisches packed up their trailer and drove west. Work had dried up for George in Dallas, and he figured he might have better luck in San Jose, which had proven lucky in the past. Once the family, larger by two more children, landed at the El Cortez Motor Inn—perhaps at their exact prior parking space—Ruth wrote to Frank saying that he and Sally should follow them to California. There's work to be had here, she said. He and Sally could be their neighbors again.

La Salle agreed. Perhaps he had some other pressing reason to abandon Dallas. Maybe he sensed that Sally was distancing herself from him and another move might keep her closer. Whatever the reason, La Salle pulled Sally out of school in February 1950 and they drove the house trailer attached to his car from Dallas to San Jose. Just as in Baltimore, and Atlantic City before it, La Salle had decided he and Sally needed to be on the move. And just as before, Sally had no say in the decision. She did what Frank La Salle told her to do. But his mood was different on the day they headed west. This time they were running toward opportunity, not running from the law.

Sally and La Salle's journey to San Jose took at least a week, if not more. He drove the trailer through Texas, going around the border of Oklahoma, then through New Mexico, Arizona, and Southern California, before moving up the South Bay to their final destination, the farthest Sally had ever been from Camden. She would never venture this far again. Sally had been La Salle's captive for nearly two years, since she was just eleven. She felt his presence at every turn, even when she was alone and seemingly free to do what she pleased. How trapped she must have felt to be in such close quarters to him as they spent that week or ten days on the road.

If Sally had allowed herself to let her mind roam, she might have given in to feelings of despair, or to anger over what La Salle had taken away from her. Or perhaps she was focused on how vital it was for her to survive. After days in the car and nights in the trailer parked at a rest stop, eating at diners, one after another, the emotional toll on her must have been considerable.

On the West Coast, Northern California in particular, palm trees lined broad boulevards where cars had room to move instead of getting jammed up like they did back home. Police in uniform shorts patrolled the streets on motorcycles. The air was far less humid than in Dallas, or even on the East Coast. But the prospects of betterment that had enticed La Salle, and so many others before him, were not on Sally's mind. She had a great many other things to think about.

By the time Frank La Salle pulled the house trailer into the El Cortez Motor Inn on Saturday, March 18, Sally Horner felt able to reckon with the changes roiling inside her. She'd already made a significant first step. Before leaving Dallas, she'd mustered up the courage to tell a friend at school that her relationship with her "father" involved sexual intercourse. The friend told Sally her behavior was "wrong" and that "she ought to stop," as Sally later explained. As her friend's admonishment sank in, Sally began refusing La Salle's advances, but kept up the illusion he was her dad.

For so long she felt she had to stay silent, or to accept what the man posing as her father said was the natural thing to do between them. All this time she opted to give in because it seemed the surest path to survival. Now Sally felt freer in a small way. Not free—she was still in La Salle's clutches, and could not see a way to escape. But she could say no now, and he didn't punish her like he had in the old days. Perhaps he looked at Sally, a month shy of her thirteenth birthday, and saw a girl aging out of his tastes. Or perhaps he trusted that Sally belonged to him so completely he no longer needed to use rape as a means of physical and psychological control.

What she knew now was that her relationship with Frank La Salle was the opposite of natural. It was against nature. It was wrong.

FRANK LA SALLE needed to find work. Several days after landing at the trailer park, La Salle abandoned his car—perhaps it needed repairs after so many days on bumpy, unevenly paved highway roads—and took the bus two miles into town to look for a job. Sally was already enrolled in school, and may have attended as many as four days of classes. She did not attend class that morning, though. By staying away, Sally changed the course her life had traveled on for the past twenty-one months.

FIFTEEN

San Jose

On the morning of March 21, 1950, Ruth Janisch invited Sally Horner over to her trailer. She knew Frank La Salle wouldn't return from his job search for several more hours, and sensed the girl might open up to her. All it would take was the right push at the right time. If Ruth didn't seize the opportunity now, she never would. Gently, she coaxed more honesty out of the young girl. Before, in Dallas, Sally wouldn't budge. This time, in San Jose, she did.

Sally confirmed Ruth's suspicion that Frank La Salle was not, in fact, her father, and that he'd forced her to stay with him for nearly two years. She said she missed her mother, Ella, and her older sister, Susan. Sally told Ruth she wanted to go home.

Ruth absorbed what the girl told her. Though she had been suspicious of the relationship, she never imagined that La Salle had kidnapped Sally. Then she sprang into action. She beckoned Sally over to the telephone and showed her how to make a long-distance phone call. Sally had never done so before.

Sally dialed her mother's number first, but the line was disconnected; Ella had lost her seamstress job in January and, while unemployed, could not afford to pay the bill. Next, she tried her sister, Susan, in Florence. No one answered the house phone, so Sally tried the greenhouse next.

Her brother-in-law, Al Panaro, picked up.

"Will you accept a collect call from Sally Horner in San Jose, California?" the operator asked.

"You bet I will," Panaro replied.

"Hello, Al, this is Sally. May I speak to Susan?"

He could barely contain his excitement. "Where are you at? Give me your exact location."

"I'm with a lady friend in California. Send the FBI after me, please! Tell Mother I'm okay, and don't worry. I want to come home. I've been afraid to call before."

The connection was poor, and Al had a hard time hearing his sister-in-law. But he heard enough to get the trailer park address down on paper, and to assure Sally he would call the FBI. She just had to stay exactly where she was.

Then Panaro passed the phone over to Susan, who was with him in the greenhouse. She was flabbergasted that her younger sister was alive, and on the telephone line. She also urged Sally to stay put and wait for the police.

After Sally hung up, she turned to Ruth, her face drained of color. She looked ready to collapse. She kept saying, over and over, "What will Frank do when he finds out what I have done?"

Ruth spent the next little while keeping Sally calm, hoping the FBI, or even the local police, would show up soon and arrest Frank. Sally, anxious, thought she should go back to her own trailer to wait for the police. Ruth let her go, hoping it would not be for too long.

AFTER SPEAKING with his sister-in-law for the first time in nearly two years, Al Panaro immediately called the Camden County Police Department. He asked for Detective Marshall Thompson, the man who'd been investigating Sally's disappearance exclusively for more than a year. But Thompson worked the night shift and was home in bed when Panaro's call came in. William Marter, another detective, answered.

Marter was the one who relayed Sally's whereabouts to the New York FBI office. He warned them to proceed with caution around La Salle. He had eluded capture before, and they needed to be certain he would not escape again. Then the FBI rang the sheriff's office in Santa Clara County. Sheriff Howard Hornbuckle picked up, and soon learned that a girl abducted almost two years earlier was alive and well and in his jurisdiction.

Hornbuckle had been elected sheriff three years earlier. He was a local boy, a graduate of San Jose High School, and had attended the state college before he joined the police department in 1931. He had spent fourteen years on the force, as a detective and later a captain. He'd also moonlighted as a traffic safety instructor in his spare time, where he stressed the danger of cars and how too many young people died while at the wheel. A cautionary slogan he coined—"Death Begins at 40"—even got picked up by the wire services and circulated nationally for a while.

Santa Clara County had its fair share of crime. Hornbuckle's own predecessor was indicted on gambling and bribery charges, and more recently the brutal murder of a high school girl had garnered headlines. But this situation was extraordinary. While many in local law enforcement got their hackles up when the FBI called, Hornbuckle did not. The case of a young girl so far from home was no time to get your nose out of joint. The FBI and the sheriff's office would work together on this.

When Hornbuckle sent his deputies to the trailer park on Monterey Road, federal agents were already on their way. The fleet of cops, local and national, sped to the El Cortez Motor Inn. Three men from the sheriff's office, Lieutenant John Gibbons and Officers Frank Leva and Douglas Logan, found Sally, alone, in La Salle's trailer.

"Please get me away from here before he gets back from town," she said, terror winning out over relief for the moment. What if he returned before she could get away from the trailer park? What if he tried to take her again? And if he did, what if he did things to her she didn't want to think about?

But this time she was in the hands of the real police and the real FBI, not the pretend agent, Frank La Salle. These cops promised Sally she was safe. La Salle would not be able to take her or touch her again. Three deputies whisked her to a detention center in the city, run by Matron Lillian Nelson. Once she was settled there, the remaining local and federal police waited for La Salle to return.

Lieutenant Gibbons at first held back from questioning Sally. "She's too shaken up," he told reporters a few hours later when they pressed him for details. But when Sally calmed down, Sheriff Hornbuckle led her into an interview room where she told him what had happened, and where she had been all this time. Hornbuckle listened, with patience, as Sally told him the whole terrible story. At first she gasped, sobbed, and cried. The hysterics were understandable, and the sheriff did not hurry her.

Then, at last, Sally found her voice. She started at the beginning, describing how La Salle caught her trying to steal a notebook on a dare at the five-and-dime. How he said he was an FBI agent and that she was "under arrest." How scared she was, and then how relieved when he let her go. How he found her again several months later, coming home from school. And how he told her she could avoid reform school only if she went away to Atlantic City with him, telling her mother he was the father to her friends, "because the government insisted I go there."

Sally confirmed that she and La Salle had lived in Baltimore for eight months before moving on to Dallas, and had only just arrived in San Jose. The entire time he held on to her, La Salle told Sally "that if I went back home, or they sent for me, or I ran away, I'd go to prison. The government ordered him to keep me and take care of me, that's what he said."

Hornbuckle then had to ask Sally the toughest question: whether La Salle had forced her to have sex with him during their nearly two years on the road. He phrased it delicately, asking if Sally had "been intimate" with La Salle. She denied it. But later, after a doctor's examination, she confessed the truth. "The first time was in Baltimore right after we got there. And ever since, too." And then in Dallas, she said a "school chum of mine" told her that what she was doing with Frank was "wrong, and I ought to stop. I did stop, too."

She said La Salle was "mean and scolded me a little, but the rest of the time he treated me like a father." Sally also said he had carried a gun for a time, in keeping with his pose as an FBI agent, but she thought La Salle had left it behind in Baltimore.

Sally was emphatic that La Salle was not her father. "My real daddy died when I was six and I remember what he looks like. I never saw [La Salle] before that day in the dime store."

Once she began to talk, she could not stop. Until finally, pausing for breath, she said, "I want to go home as soon as I can."

IT'S NOT CLEAR if Frank La Salle found gainful employment that morning in San Jose. When he stepped off the bus and walked back to the trailer just after one o'clock in the afternoon, dozens of police officers surrounded him before he could reach his front door. They'd been hiding behind other trailers. Deputies from the sheriff's office. FBI agents. Local San Jose cops. All present because of a chain of events that began as soon as Sally Horner hung up the phone. La Salle did not fight, but instead surrendered quietly.

At the San Jose jail, La Salle grew more animated. He denied abducting Sally. He insisted he was her father and that her mother "has known where I am and where the girl is every day since I've been gone." La Salle elaborated his alternate reality. "I took her when she was a little thing. . . . I am the father of six kids, three by this wife (Mrs. Horner) and three by another wife. I didn't take [Sally] from Camden but from New York. It was four years ago, not two. She kept house for me and she had money and freedom." The authorities, La Salle claimed, could have found him "at any time." He had a business in Dallas, after all, and "always had cars registered in my name." When he was done protesting his innocence, La Salle refused to speak further.

"He's a tough, vicious character," said Lieutenant Gibbons.

ELLA HORNER WAS OVERJOYED and overcome by the news that her daughter was alive and had been found. So much so that at first, she could hardly speak. When she composed herself, she told the large crowd of reporters and photographers who had descended upon 944 Linden Street that she was chiefly concerned with Sally's safety. "I just want her back and to see her again. I am very thankful, and I will be a whole lot more thankful when I really see Sally."

She also repeated the sentiment she'd expressed to the press—and, perhaps, countless other times in private—back in December 1948, while Sally was still missing. "Whatever she has done, I can forgive her."

Later that day, a Camden *Courier-Post* reporter, Jacob Weiner, found Ella clutching a photo of Sally, the one that had been recovered from the Atlantic City boardinghouse in August 1948. "It seems so long ago, Sally, so long ago," Ella murmured, gazing at the picture of her daughter. In a stronger tone, but with her voice still shaking, Ella said: "I'm so relieved."

Ella repeated that Sally had been gone for nearly two years. "That's a long time," she said. "During that time, I didn't hear from her. No word. No postcard. No news of any kind."

About that June day when she allowed Sally to accompany Frank La Salle for a seashore vacation, she said, "I must have been very foolish . . . at least I know it now." She picked up the picture of Sally again. "Anyway, I let her go. I haven't seen her since. . . ."

Weiner asked Ella if she ever gave up hope that Sally would be found alive. There were times, Ella said, where she felt "pretty hopeless" because "I always knew she had enough sense to call me or drop me a line." And yet Sally hadn't.

What did Ella think about Frank La Salle? "That man . . . ," she began, but her voice broke.

Susan was sitting with her mother during Weiner's interview, and picked up the thread. "I hope that man La Salle is properly punished. He should receive life imprisonment . . . or the electric chair."

Then Susan turned her thoughts to a second telephone conversation she'd just had with her younger sister. "I couldn't believe it was Sally I was talking to. It was wonderful." Her eyes filled with tears. "I can't wait to see her."

Sally had asked Susan how their mother was faring. She also asked after Susan's daughter, Diana, now nineteen months old.

"She looks just like you," Susan said, and Sally burst into tears.

TELEPHONES ARE A recurring motif in *Lolita*. The incessant ringing of the "machina telephonica and its sudden god" in-

Sally on the telephone to her family in the hours after her rescue.

terrupts the narrative, as Humbert Humbert's psyche begins to fissure—the monster underneath waging war with the amiable surface personality he presents to the world. Telephones are also the means through which Humbert discovers Charlotte's accidental death, since he is too preoccupied with fixing her a drink to notice that she has left the house.

With Charlotte permanently out of the picture, he

goes to pick up Dolores at Camp Q to break the news of her mother's death in his own special way—"all a-jitter lest delay might give her the opportunity of some idle telephone call to Ramsdale." After he picks her up, he takes Dolores to the Enchanted Hunters hotel, where he rapes her for the first time. The following morning, the telephone plays a pivotal role in binding the older man and girl together. Humbert had told Dolores that he was taking her to Charlotte, who he said was in the hospital in Lepingville. At a rest stop, Dolores asks: "Give me some dimes and nickels. I want to call mother in the hospital. What's the number?"

Humbert says, "You can't call that number."

"Why?" cries Dolores. "Why can't I call my mother if I want to?"

"Because," he says, "your mother is dead."

It is the news that totally breaks Lolita and puts her in Humbert Humbert's power. He knows it, too: "At the hotel we had separate rooms, but in the middle of the night she came sobbing into mine, and we made it up very gently. You see, she had absolutely nowhere else to go."

From there Humbert and Dolores begin their road trip, a journey that would take them thousands of miles across the United States. Deep into their trip, Humbert's paranoia grows as he suspects Dolores has confided the truth about him to Mona, a school friend suspicious of the relationship between the so-called father and daughter: "the stealthy thought . . . that perhaps after all Mona was right, and she, orphan Lo, could expose [Humbert] without getting penalized herself."

Dolores's first escape, after she yells "unprintable things" and accuses Humbert of murdering her mother and violating her, occurs as the phone rings and she breaks free of his grip on her wrist (in part echoing La Salle's grip upon Sally's arm at the Camden five-and-dime). That escape lasts only a few hours, and Humbert finds her "some ten paces away, through the glass of a telephone booth (membranous god still with us)."

After that, Dolores asserts her will as to where they should go next. And then, though the reader is not privy to it, she makes a final, mysterious call, presumably to Clare Quilty, to help her escape. Telephones, Humbert concludes, "happened to be, for reasons unfathomable, the points where my destiny was liable to catch." For Dolores, telephones are the means for her to find freedom from the abuser who has engulfed her life—just as a telephone call was for Sally Horner.

SIXTEEN

After the Rescue

Though Frank La Salle was in jail, it wasn't clear which law enforcement agency would have jurisdiction over him. There were the outstanding warrants for kidnapping and abduction from Camden County. But because La Salle had transported Sally across several states, it became a federal case. La Salle was charged with violating the Mann Act, for "allegedly taking the girl across state lines for immoral purposes."

On the morning of March 22, Camden County prosecutor Mitchell Cohen spoke with the San Jose police, including Sheriff Hornbuckle. After the thirty-minute call, he told reporters in Camden that he would convene a grand jury to indict La Salle on the outstanding warrants, and start extradition proceedings immediately.

La Salle seemed ready to fight his extradition to Camden,

but Cohen was undeterred. "Regardless of what La Salle says he will do about returning here, I am taking no chances," Cohen said. "I will start formal proceedings at once and get him back here as soon as possible." But the prosecutor had to wait on New Jersey governor Alfred Driscoll's approval, and there was a delay because Driscoll was out of town on a business trip.

That afternoon, in California, Commissioner Marshall Hall presided over La Salle's arraignment on the Mann Act charges. He set a $10,000 bond and scheduled a hearing for the following morning. La Salle retained Manny Gomez as his attorney, while Frank Hennessy was the federal prosecutor.

The hearing began at 10:30 A.M. on March 23. There Hennessy revealed that La Salle's birth name was Frank La Plante; if true, then at various points during Sally's captivity, she'd attended school using the first name of La Salle's biological daughter and his own real last name.

When police officers attempted to lead Sally into the courtroom, she resisted at first, frantic at the thought of seeing La Salle: "I'm afraid, I'm afraid," she cried.

May Smothers, a juvenile court matron, had accompanied the girl to court, and calmed her down. Sally finally entered the courtroom clutching Smothers's hand. She took a seat only four feet away from La Salle and stole furtive glances at him throughout the proceedings, looking away whenever she came close to breaking down. La Salle stared at her, impassive, saying nothing.

When Sally began her testimony, Commissioner Hall asked, "Are you afraid of anything? Is there anything you want?"

"I want to go home!"

"He can't hurt you," said Hall.

And so, once more, Sally described her ordeal, starting with the Camden five-and-dime and ending with the San Jose trailer park. She told the court how La Salle had forced her to have sex with him, the abuse only ending in Dallas. La Salle told his story again, too, continuing to insist that he was Sally's real father.

Commissioner Hall affirmed the $10,000 bond, and ordered La Salle transferred to the county jail in San Francisco.

The hearing also decided La Salle's jurisdictional fate. Hennessy told the court that the federal charges would eventually be dropped because the New Jersey state kidnapping charges took precedence. But for the time being, La Salle would sit tight. Even if he raised the full $10,000 bond, federal authorities "were confident they could hold [La Salle] on other charges until he could be extradited," reported the *Courier-Post*.

Sally returned to the San Jose detention center. At first, she was so anxious about La Salle possibly going free that she could hardly eat. Matron Smothers told the papers that Sally also "fretted a lot about whether her folks would want her after what happened." Sally was kept apart from the other detained juveniles because, an unnamed sheriff's official told the *Courier-Post*, "We have some pretty hardened kids here and we don't want Sally to come in contact with them."

Over the next few days, Sally grew more secure in the detention center. Matron Smothers took her shopping for new clothes, because in her estimation, Sally's old ones did not measure up: "The clothes she had at the [trailer park] were neat but shabby and very inadequate." Smothers said that Sally had also stopped worrying about whether her family would welcome her back. "All she's thinking about is getting home and what she'll do when she gets there."

The detention center felt "responsible for Sally's well-being until New Jersey's authorities arrive to take her home," said an unnamed sheriff's official. "We've had a number of offers from people in San Jose to take care of Sally until she's ready to go home, but we are positive no harm can come to her where she is now."

BACK IN CAMDEN, police continued to investigate another dangling thread: the mysterious "Miss Robinson" Sally said had accompanied her and Frank La Salle on the bus to Baltimore, after which she disappeared. Camden police tried to reconcile Sally's statement to Sheriff Hornbuckle with what they found in their own initial investigations. They had proof, after all, that Sally and La Salle had spent time in Atlantic City, in the form of unsent letters, photographs, clothing, and other material abandoned at 203 Pacific Avenue. Proof bolstered by the recollections of Robert and Jean Pfeffer, the young Philadelphia couple who had reported spending a summer day with Sally and La Salle.

No trace of the woman known as "Miss Robinson" was ever discovered by law enforcement. It remains another of the unresolved mysteries of Sally's captivity. I believe the woman existed, because I believe Sally. Just because police did not track the woman down, and that decades later I also could not find her, does not mean Sally made her up.

A CAMDEN GRAND JURY indicted La Salle for kidnapping and abduction at 2:20 P.M. on March 23, the same day as the hearing in San Francisco. Ella Horner testified in front of the grand jury. There's no record of what she said, but she was likely asked about why she put Sally on the bus to Atlantic City and whether La Salle was her daughter's biological father, as he claimed.

Mitchell Cohen sent a copy of the grand jury indictment

to the New Jersey governor to start the extradition process. A second copy of the proceedings, signed by Judge Rocco Palese, was airmailed to California to reinforce La Salle's detention. Cohen also received permission to bring both Sally and La Salle—separately—back to Camden, and to cover their travel expenses, as well as those of Camden city detective Marshall Thompson and county detective Wilfred Dube.

Cohen, Dube, and Thompson flew into San Francisco on Sunday, March 26. Over the next few days, Cohen received approval to extradite La Salle from Governor Driscoll in New Jersey as well as his California counterpart (and future chief justice of the Supreme Court) Earl Warren. Cohen also interviewed various residents of the trailer park. One was Ruth Janisch, who told Cohen she was willing to testify at La Salle's trial.

On Thursday, Sally was released from the San Jose detention center into Cohen's custody. Just after 8:40 A.M. Pacific time on Friday, March 31, Sally and Cohen boarded a United Airlines flight headed for Philadelphia. Sally wore a navy-blue suit, polka-dot blouse, black shoes, a red coat, and a straw Easter bonnet for her first-ever plane trip. She told Cohen how much she looked forward to seeing her family. She threw up only once, when the plane ran into turbulence just outside of Chicago.

Ella waited at the airport in the backseat of Assistant

Sally Horner and Mitchell Cohen board a Philadelphia-bound United Airlines flight, March 31, 1950.

Camden County Prosecutor (and future New Jersey governor) William Cahill's car. The rest of Sally's family, including Susan, Al, and their baby, Diana, arrived separately. Several other planes landed first, each one lifting Ella's spirits before crushing them again. "Why doesn't it come," Ella said, her face pressed against the car window. Sally's plane finally landed just after midnight, just over an hour late.

From the plane, Sally spotted her brother-in-law in the crowd. Sally wanted to get out right away, but Cohen told her to wait for the other passengers to leave first. Then she spotted her mother. "I want to see Mama!" she cried.

"All right, Sally," said Cohen. "Let's go."

Sally stood at the doorway for a moment, looking around. Then she spotted her mother running toward her, holding out her arms. Sally raced down the steps, her face lit up with joy and washed in tears.

Sally sees her mother, Ella Horner, for the first time in twenty-one months.

She and her mother clung to each other for several minutes, oblivious to the myriad flash-bulbs popping at them. At first, they were weeping too hard to speak. Then Sally said: "I want to go home. I just want to go home."

When they were safely in Assistant Prosecutor Cahill's car, Ella explained to Sally that she couldn't go home just yet. Instead, the authorities would take her to the Camden County Children's Shelter in nearby Pennsauken, New Jersey, where she had to stay "until the trial is over."

Sally leans on her mother's shoulder minutes after they are reunited.

After a short drive, their car arrived at the center, the Panaros following closely behind in a separate vehicle. Susan got out of the car at the same time as Sally.

"Susan!" Sally cried upon spotting her older sibling. Sally had been so overwhelmed by the sight of her mother, the photographers, and so many well-wishers that she hadn't realized her sister was part of the crowd.

"I kissed you at the airport but you didn't recognize me!" Susan said.

Then Sally realized her sister was holding a little girl in her arms. Sally reached for Diana, the niece she'd never met, and hugged her tightly. "Gee, she looks like pictures of me taken when I was a baby!"

Cohen, exhausted from the trip, gently informed the family that Sally needed to get some sleep.

In the days that followed, Ella was the only family member allowed to visit Sally at the Children's Shelter, to ensure the girl stayed in a calm frame of mind before and during the trial. Fortunately, Sally got along well with the matron. She also attended Palm Sunday mass with six other children from the shelter the day before her first scheduled court appearance, and that offered some solace. No one knew how long La Salle's trial would last, and they tried not to bring the subject up with Sally, lest she get upset. The place she really wanted to be, after all, was home.

Thanks to an unexpected development, Sally's stay at the center didn't last long at all.

SEVENTEEN

A Guilty Plea

Frank La Salle wasn't allowed to travel from California to Camden by plane. Airline regulations at the time did not allow for passengers to be shackled, and Mitchell Cohen wasn't about to take any chances that the man would escape. "It is possible he could be a docile prisoner," Cohen remarked. "On the other hand, he could cause trouble."

The solution was to transport La Salle by train. Doing so would increase the travel time from hours to days, but on the train he could stay handcuffed to an officer for the entire duration. Marshall Thompson got stuck with being shackled to the prisoner for the cross-country trip, hardly a reward for all of his dogged investigative efforts. Wilfred Dube took the berth next door to Thompson and La Salle, staying as close as possible to the two men. (While it would have made sense for the two

detectives to trade off being handcuffed to La Salle, I couldn't
find any evidence that they did.)

Mitchell Cohen was at the train station to see La Salle and
the detectives off. Before La Salle boarded, he asked Cohen why
he and Sally Horner weren't getting on the same train. Cohen
explained the two were due to fly later on in the day.

"Well, take good care of Sally," said La Salle.

"I'll take better care of her than you did," Cohen replied.

The train trip took two nights and two days. La Salle, Detective Thompson, and Detective Dube left San Francisco at 5:00
P.M. Pacific time on the *City of San Francisco*. Overnight the
train passed through Sacramento, Salt Lake City, Cheyenne,
Omaha, and Council Bluffs and reached Chicago early Saturday morning, where the trio changed trains to the New York–
bound *General*. Thompson had no relief or privacy, shackled to
the man he'd been chasing for nearly two years. Just as La Salle
could not escape the law, so could the law not escape La Salle.

The *General* pulled into North Philadelphia Station at six
minutes before seven in the morning on April 1. To the surprise of waiting reporters and photographers, the trio of men
were not on board. To avoid the scrum, they'd gotten off at an
earlier stop in Paoli, met there at 6:30 A.M. by Assistant Prosecutor William Cahill and Camden County Police Captain
James Mulligan.

They took La Salle directly to the prosecutor's office. Then
Thompson went home, no doubt relieved to be free of the man.
Dube, Mulligan, and Cahill stuck around for Cohen's interroga-
tion of La Salle, which lasted about four hours. At 1:00 P.M., La
Salle was taken to the Camden County jail.

Mitchell Cohen told the press later on Sunday that he expected the case to go before the jury no earlier than June. Early
on the morning of April 3, 1950, the day La Salle was due to

be arraigned on the abduction and kidnapping charges, Cohen received a phone call from the county jail. The accused wanted to talk.

Cohen arrived at the jail at 9:45 A.M. and discovered La Salle by himself in a waiting room. He still lacked a lawyer—he hadn't been able to keep on Manuel Gomez because Gomez was not licensed to practice outside of California.

Cohen reminded La Salle of his right to an attorney. If he couldn't afford one, the court would appoint a lawyer for him.

"I don't need any counsel," La Salle replied. "I am guilty, and I am willing to go in and plead guilty. The sooner the better. I want to get it off my chest, and I want my time to commence to run."

When Cohen asked him why he wanted to plead guilty, La Salle said, "I want to avoid this girl [receiving] any further unfavorable publicity."

Cohen told him that court was already in session, and he could immediately enter his plea.

"Then I want to get it over with now," said La Salle.

Cohen left the Camden County jail and went straight to the courthouse for the arraignment. The courtroom was packed with onlookers. Sally Horner took her seat at the back next to a detective assigned to guard her. She wore a blue suit, pink blouse, straw hat, and patent leather Mary Jane shoes.

At ten minutes to noon, La Salle filed in, wearing a navy-blue suit, white collared shirt, and tie.

As Judge Rocco Palese entered, the room rose to attention. Like Mitchell Cohen, the judge had tangled with La Salle before. Palese, then a lawyer, had worked on Dorothy Dare's divorce petition against La Salle in 1944, even filling in for Dorothy's main lawyer, Bruce Wallace, at one of the hearings while La Salle was still serving time for statutory rape.

Palese, to the best of anyone's knowledge, never disclosed this prior association with the defendant. Perhaps he did not remember. Perhaps he didn't see a conflict because he had never engaged La Salle directly in court. Camden County's legal world was so small that defense attorneys became prosecutors who then became judges, everyone working with everyone else. What mattered was that, right now, Frank La Salle was in Judge Palese's courtroom.

When the gallery took their seats again, Palese called on Cohen to begin.

The prosecutor first outlined the story of Sally's kidnapping and confinement. How La Salle "persuaded and enticed her" to leave her mother in mid-June 1948, and told her that his repeated rapes of her were "natural." How Ruth Janisch "broke La Salle's spell" in San Jose, and Sally made the fateful phone call to the Panaros. How La Salle's long criminal record and his deviant behavior toward Sally made him, in Cohen's estimation, "a menace to society—a depraved man and a moral leper."

Cohen addressed both the judge and the crowd with his final words: "Mothers throughout the country will give a sigh of relief to know that a man of this type is safely in prison. That La Salle is somewhere safe, unable to harm anyone else."

Judge Palese asked Cohen if he had anything further. He did.

"If the Court please, at this time I propose to take pleas from this defendant, Frank La Salle, but before doing so I want the Court to know that I have discussed this case quite at length with this defendant, I have advised him of his right to be represented by counsel, and to have the benefit of the advice of counsel. I have warned him of the seriousness of these charges, and the length of the sentences which these charges impose.

"Being in Court is not an unfamiliar subject to this defendant and he understands, and he has told me so, the contents of both indictments. He understands the seriousness of them and the sentences, the minimum sentences, which the Court can impose, and he has advised me he does not desire to obtain counsel either on his own or appointed by the Court. I do, however, feel, in order that this defendant may properly understand the situation that it may be best for the Court to repeat to him his rights before I take the pleas."

Judge Palese then addressed Frank La Salle. "Mr. La Salle, you have just heard the prosecutor advise the Court that he has talked to you and explained to you the two indictments that have been returned against you by the Grand Jury of our County, and he has indicated to the Court that you do not desire to be represented by counsel and you desire to proceed in the matter without representation, is that correct?"

La Salle replied, "Yes."

"You understand the seriousness of the two indictments that have been returned against you by our Grand Jury?" Palese asked.

"Yes, sir."

"And that they carry with them rather serious sentences?"

Again, La Salle replied, "Yes, sir."

Judge Palese asked how La Salle would plead.

"Guilty," he said, in a voice barely audible.

The judge asked if there was anything more La Salle wished to say before he handed down the sentence.

La Salle said, his voice still weak: "I don't want any more publicity for the children." (Cohen later explained to reporters that La Salle was likely nervous and meant to say "child.")

Just like that, the proceeding was over. The whole matter took perhaps twenty minutes, ending just after noon. But not before Palese decided upon a sentence for Frank La Salle. The judge ordered Sally's abductor to spend no less than thirty and no more than thirty-five years in prison for the kidnapping charge. He would have to serve at least three-quarters of the full sentence before being eligible for parole. Palese also added a two- to three-year sentence for the original abduction charge, as well as an additional two to three years for violating his parole.

Frank La Salle, after pleading guilty.

Two days later, just after noon on April 5, La Salle began his sentence at Trenton State Prison.

BECAUSE FRANK LA SALLE pleaded guilty, Sally did not get to testify against him. In Mitchell Cohen's office after the hearing, she asked, once more, letting go of the earlier courtroom stoicism and blinking back tears, when she could go home. With the case finished, and Frank La Salle going to prison, surely she could return to her mother right away?

Cohen sympathized with Sally, and told her so. There seemed no reason to keep her in the state's custody when the case was finished and La Salle incarcerated, but the wheels of bureaucracy turned at their own pace, not his. Judge Palese was the one who would have to decide when she could be released into Ella's custody again. Palese did so the very next day.

At noon on April 4, 1950, Cohen summoned Sally and Ella to his office for what he later told the press was a "lengthy conference" in which he delivered the news both of them wanted to hear the most. He also offered mother and daughter some advice. They were free, of course, to return to 944 Linden Street, but he thought it best they "went away from this area, changed their names and began life anew."

The extensive media coverage meant all of Camden, and much of Philadelphia and the surrounding towns, knew what had happened to Sally. Cohen worried the girl might be judged harshly for the forcible loss of her virtue, even if that reaction was in no way warranted. Cohen also urged Ella to seek the advice of the Reverend Alfred Jass, director of the Bureau of Catholic Charities, "in directing Sally's return to a normal life." Ella was a Protestant, but clergy was still clergy, and Sally's recent attendance at Catholic schools may have influenced Cohen's choice of religious advisor.

Sally and Ella got home at 1:45 P.M. Waiting reporters and photographers shouted questions and snapped pictures as they walked through the front door, Ella shielding her daughter. Ignoring the shouts, she shut the door firmly behind them.

From that afternoon on, the Horner women were private citizens. They were no longer at the mercy of the legal system, or the national press. The rest of the world could leave them alone.

In some fashion, it worked out that way, but their new-found calm did not last for long.

EIGHTEEN

When Nabokov (Really)
Learned About Sally

Vladimir Nabokov spent the morning of March 22, 1950, much as he would every morning for the next month: bedridden and pain-plagued from the same neurological malady that had afflicted him a decade earlier, in the months leading up to his arrival in America. "I have followed your example and am in bed with a temperature above 102 degrees," Nabokov wrote Katharine White, his editor at the *New Yorker,* on March 24. "No bronchitis but grippe with me is invariably accompanied by the hideous pain of intercostal neuralgia."

White had also been ill and advised Nabokov to prize rest above work. Nabokov rested, but did not stop working. Just as he had written *The Enchanter* while bedridden a decade earlier, so now did he complete two late chapters of *Conclusive*

Evidence, the first version of the autobiography that became *Speak, Memory.* But as Nabokov told James Laughlin, his editor at New Directions, a month later, he did not "get back to normal conditions" for weeks. That summer, he and Véra did not travel across America to hunt butterflies, as they had done the previous year and on three earlier occasions. Not enough time, not nearly enough money, and too many deadlines loomed as his health slowly mended.

It's easy to imagine that, as he was laid up in bed at home in Ithaca with limited capacity to work, Nabokov picked up a copy of the local newspaper and came across the news of a kidnapped girl rescued in California after almost two years of cross-country captivity. It is not difficult to believe Nabokov, whom Véra described in their diary as being fascinated by true crime, paid avid attention from his sickbed as each day brought fresh news about Sally's rescue and Frank La Salle's crimes.

Here, in newspaper accounts of Sally Horner's plight, was a possible solution to a long-standing problem with the manuscript that would become *Lolita:* how to create the necessary scaffolding for all of the ideas rattling around in his mind, the decades of compulsion, and the games he wished to play with the reader.

Robert Roper, the author of *Nabokov in America,* was certainly convinced that Nabokov "read newspaper reports of a sensational crime" around the time of Sally's rescue. He told me, "I think reading about Sally was momentous for [Nabokov]. He was on the verge of abandoning his project when the March 1950 stories appeared, and it was as if the world were providing him with justification and template for writing his daring little sex novel. He cribbed so much from the story."

Yet there is no direct proof that Vladimir Nabokov learned of Sally Horner's abduction and rescue in March 1950. There was no story in the papers he was most likely to read—the *Cornell Daily Sun,* the college newspaper, or the *New York Times.* Similarly, there's no direct proof he glanced at the Camden or Philadelphia papers, the ones that carried the best details and the most vivid photos. Neither his archives at the New York Public Library nor those at the Library of Congress contain newspaper clippings about Sally. Any connection dances just outside the frame.

However, there is plenty of indirect proof that Nabokov knew about Sally Horner and her rescue. The circumstantial evidence is there in *Lolita.* And I believe he would never have fully realized the character of Dolores Haze without knowing of Sally's real-life plight.

LET'S FIRST CONSIDER HOW, roughly at the halfway point of *Lolita,* Humbert Humbert threatens Dolores into complying with him. He tells her that if he is arrested or if she reveals the true nature of their relationship, she "will be given a choice of varying dwelling places, all more or less the same, the correctional school, the reformatory, the juvenile detention home. . . ." Humbert's ultimatum echoes La Salle's repeated threats to Sally Horner, reported in the newspapers in March 1950, that if she did not do what he said, she would be bound for juvenile hall.

But earlier in the same scene, the comparison between Humbert and Frank La Salle is even more explicit: "Only the other day we read in the newspapers some bunkum about a middle-aged morals offender who pleaded guilty to the violation of the Mann Act and to transporting a nine-year-old girl across state lines for immoral purposes, whatever they are. Dolores darling! You are not nine but almost thirteen, and I would not advise you to consider yourself my cross-country slave. . . . I am your father, and I am speaking English, and I love you."

As Nabokov scholar Alexander Dolinin pointed out in his 2005 essay linking Sally Horner to *Lolita,* Nabokov fiddled with the case chronology. The cross-country journey in *Lolita* begins in 1947, an entire year before Sally Horner's abduction. At that time, Sally would have been nine going on ten, matching the age Humbert cites to his Lolita instead of the age she was when Frank La Salle abducted her. It is clear to Dolinin that "the legal formulae used by [Humbert Humbert] as well as his implying that he, in contrast to La Salle, is really Lolita's father, leave no doubt that the passage refers to the newspaper reports of 1950. . . ." In other words, the circumstantial evidence is right there in the text that Nabokov did, in fact, read about Sally Horner in March 1950, rather than retroactively inserting her story into *Lolita* several years after the fact.

To throw off the scent, or perhaps to amuse himself, Nabokov assigned details of La Salle to other characters. Dolores's eventual husband and the father of her child, Dick Schiller, is a mechanic. Meanwhile, Vivian Darkbloom—an anagram for Vladimir Nabokov—has a "hawk face," a phrase akin to the description of La Salle as a "hawk-faced man" in the March 1950 coverage of Sally's rescue. And as Dolinin underscored, references to Dolores's "Florentine hands" and "Florentine breasts" seem to point as much to Sally Horner's legal first name of Florence as they do to Botticelli.

Sally's captivity lasted twenty-one months, from June 1948 to March 1950. At the twenty-first month mark of their connection, Lolita and Humbert land at Beardsley, where Humbert realizes that he no longer has the same hold on the girl he once possessed. He worries Dolores has confided the true nature of her relationship with her "stepfather" to her school friend, Mona. And that in doing so, she might be cherishing "the stealthy thought . . . that perhaps after all Mona was right, and she, orphan Lo, could expose [Humbert] without getting penalized herself."

Dolores's potential confession to Mona echoes Sally's actual confession of her abuse at Frank La Salle's hands, first to the unnamed school friend, and later to Ruth Janisch. And just as Sally's escape comes about because of her long-distance phone call to her family, so, too, does Dolores make a mysterious phone call—immediately after fighting with Humbert—and then announces, "A great decision has been made." She doesn't flee him for another month, but the setup is already in place.

Then there is Humbert's aside in *Lolita*'s final chapter. He states that he would have given himself "at least thirty-five years for rape, and dismissed the rest of the charges." The exact sentence Frank La Salle received.

NINETEEN

Rebuilding a Life

Sally Horner was only two months past her eleventh birthday when Frank La Salle spirited her away from Camden. She returned home less than two weeks before turning thirteen on April 18. "When she went away she was a little girl," Ella murmured on the day she was finally reunited with her daughter. "Now she is practically a young lady." Sally had seen the country and how different so many other places were from Camden. She had been forced to grow up in the cruelest way possible, knowledge foisted upon her that could not be suppressed.

How the family marked her birthday isn't known, since no one, aside from Sally's niece, Diana, is alive to recall—and Diana was only twenty months old at the time. But a family outing to the Philadelphia Zoo, captured on a minute-long film clip shot by Sally's brother-in-law, Al Panaro, appears to provide a possible answer. It is the only known surviving footage of Sally.

In it, Sally seems dressed for spring, wearing the same outfit that she had on the plane from California, as well as to court the day that Frank La Salle pleaded guilty to her kidnapping. Her sister, Susan, has on a cream or white coat covering a pale blouse and dark skirt, while Diana is dressed in a pink two-piece suit.

Sally walks, shoulders hunched, beside Susan. At one point she pushes her niece in a white-handled stroller. She moves slowly, with hesitation, but it's not clear whether that's how she really moved or if the film clip was preserved at a slower speed.

In a close-up, Sally's face is angled to the left. Her expression is tentative, suggesting she still feels vulnerable out in public. That even though she is among her family, among those she loves, she isn't ready to let down her guard.

She does not look at the camera once.

THERE WERE OTHER PRESSING MATTERS as Sally Horner readjusted to life with her family, in Camden and elsewhere. She had been taken at the tail end of sixth grade; in the fall she would start eighth grade at Clara S. Burrough Junior High School, and was eager for what promised to be a fresh start. When she had gone to school during her captivity period, her energy was focused on surviving each day with Frank La Salle instead of dreaming about what she might want to be when she grew up. Now that Sally was free, she could think of what she wanted, for her own future. "She has a definite ambition," the San Jose detention center matron had said a few days after Sally's dramatic rescue. "She wants to be a doctor."

Ella, who had been out of work, needed to find a new job to support not only herself, but also a daughter who, through no fault of her own, was far closer to womanhood than any thirteen-year-old was supposed to be. Ella's repetition to the press of the phrase "whatever Sally has done, I can forgive her" points to her discomfort about the abuse Sally suffered, or even her lack of comprehension.

There was no vocabulary, in 1950, to describe the mechanism or the impact of Sally's victimization, where the violence was psychological manipulation, not necessarily brute force. Where the innocent-seeming facade of the father-daughter dynamic masked repeated rapes, unbeknownst to almost everyone around her. For Ella, who was struggling to pay the bills, put food on the table, and keep the lights on in the house, the details of Sally's captivity may have been too much to bear. As was the idea of starting over where no one knew what had happened to her. The stigma they knew must have seemed a better choice than the uncertainty of what they didn't know.

Taking Cohen's advice under consideration, Ella opted for a compromise: Sally would spend the summer of 1950 with the Panaros in Florence, while Ella remained in Camden. No one changed their names, and no one would discuss what happened to Sally for decades.

Over the summer of 1950, Sally Horner allowed herself to feel safe. She looked after Diana when Susan and Al Panaro had to work in the greenhouse, and sometimes Sally tended to the flowers and herbs as well. One family photo shows Sally in the greenhouse next to Susan, wearing dungarees, a white shirt, and a dark cardigan, her curly hair tousled around her face and chin, her mouth open as she is caught in mid-conversation with her sister.

Sally Horner and her older sister, Susan Panaro,
in the family greenhouse.

Other photographs from the same time suggest that living at the Panaros did Sally some good. One shows Sally standing by herself, clad in an elaborate pale-hued frock suitable for going to church or an afternoon social event. She's smiling at the camera, though her eyes carry remnants of the shyness she displayed while being filmed at the Philadelphia Zoo.

Sally's smile is wider in a second photo of her in a different fancy dress. Here she poses with a dark-haired young man wearing a suit at least two sizes too large. The boy is her apparent date, for a school dance or a church social. His name, and how the evening went, is lost to time—as is whether he was aware of what had happened to Sally.

By Sally's fourteenth birthday in April 1951, she looked like the typical American teenager of that period, the type to be wowed by Perry Como or Tony Bennett or Doris Day or other popular singers of the time. (In *Lolita*, Nabokov dutifully listed the soundtrack of Dolores and Humbert's road trip, including Eddie Fisher's "Wish You Were Here," Peggy Lee's "Forgive Me," and Tony Bennett's "Sleepless" and "Here in My Heart.")

One candid photo, likely taken by Al Panaro, hints at more complicated undercurrents in her than in a "bobby-soxer," as Sally was sometimes referred to in the press coverage of her rescue. She wears jeans again, as she did in the greenhouse photo with Susan, but now her shirt is dark, and her curly hair is pulled back. Her lipstick looks near-black in the black-and-white photo, which suggests she is wearing a ruby-red shade. The camera has captured Sally as she emerged from her bedroom, newspaper in her right hand, expression quizzical, as if she'd been interrupted while reading the funnies. She seems to be in need of sleep, caffeine, or a combination of the two.

A candid shot of Sally holding a newspaper.

Though Sally adopted a mask of good-natured resilience, Al recalled his sister-in-law drifting into melancholic moods. She would be in the moment, then gone. A light would shine, and then flicker out. "She never said she was sad and depressed," Al told me in 2014, "but you knew something was wrong." The family discouraged discussion about her ordeal, and she almost never spoke of what happened with anyone. There were no heart-to-hearts. She underwent no psychological examinations; nor did she see a therapist. There was only Before, and After.

At Burrough Junior High, located on the corner of Haddon and Newton Avenues, Sally, once more, excelled on the academic side. Al recalled his sister-in-law being "very smart, an A student," and said that "it seemed like she knew a subject before it was taught." She graduated in June 1952 with honors.

Despite the photo of Sally with a date, her social life did not open up. She'd had trouble making friends before her abduction; afterward it became even more difficult. Classmates whispered and gossiped about her time with La Salle. Boys, emboldened and entitled, peppered her with unwanted remarks and propositions. As her classmate Carol Taylor—née Carol Starts—remembered, "they looked at her as a total whore." Emma DiRenzo, whom Sally knew as Emma Annibale, agreed. "She had a little bit of a rough time at first. Not everyone was very nice. I think some people didn't believe her."

It didn't matter to Sally's classmates that she had been abducted and raped. That she was not a virgin was enough to taint her. Nice girls were supposed to be pure until marriage. "No matter how you looked at it, she was a slut," Carol said. "That's the way it was in those days."

Carol met Sally in eighth-grade homeroom. Carol had street smarts; Sally did, too, but she wanted to close the door on how she got them, and escaped into the land of books. Carol lived two blocks away from the junior high while Sally had a longer daily walk of four to five blocks. Carol came from a large family—she was one of ten siblings, a far cry from Sally's smaller pool of immediate relatives. Carol had some other friends. Sally had no one but Carol, who didn't care a whit what anyone else thought of Sally. Carol said she was oblivious about Sally's supposedly sullied reputation, but it's as likely Carol chose not to behave the same way as her classmates, and not to judge Sally so harshly. Carol admired Sally's manners, her love of books, and sophisticated outlook. Sally admired Carol's freedom. She was as eager to be Carol's friend as Carol was to be hers.

Sally found refuge in the outdoors. She loved everything about being outside: the sun, swimming, and especially the Jersey Shore. As a little girl, before Frank La Salle kidnapped her, she'd spent many summer weekends at various seaside towns, like Wildwood and Cape May. After her rescue, the beach was a place where she could forget about cruel taunts and pervading despair. The Shore couldn't solve all of her problems, but at least it provided space for her to feel happiness.

In the summer of 1952, Sally was looking forward to starting Woodrow Wilson High School. At fifteen, she looked far older than her years. She wanted to make more friends and find a boyfriend.

Then, one weekend in the middle of August, she took another trip to Wildwood.

TWENTY

Lolita Progresses

The Nabokovs couldn't afford to road-trip across America during the summer of 1950, but the next summer Vladimir and Véra left Ithaca in June, at the end of Cornell's spring semester. Vladimir had turned in his grades for his European fiction class, and they gave up the lease on the house on East Seneca Street, their home the last three years, having found cheaper accommodations for the fall.

By the time Véra turned their aging Oldsmobile off U.S. Highway 36 at St. Francis, Kansas, on June 30, the pattern was set: hunt for butterflies for as many hours as a given day allowed, depending on their stamina and the weather. On rainier days—which dominated the trip—or when fatigue set in, usually in afternoons, Nabokov worked on the manuscript he was still calling *The Kingdom by the Sea*.

Véra and Nabokov chasing butterflies.

Nabokov worked in the passenger seat of the Oldsmobile, away from the noise coming through the motel room walls and insulated from the floods and storms that curtailed his exercises in lepidoptery. Dmitri, now seventeen, joined his parents in Telluride, Colorado—he was coming from Harvard, where he'd finished up his first year—and took over the driving duties, too. The family wended their way through the Rockies, Wyoming, and West Yellowstone, Montana, before returning to Ithaca at the end of August.

Weeks of butterfly-hunting in the Rockies, often shirtless with his chest exposed to the sun, had little immediate effect upon Nabokov's health. The accumulated exposure didn't cause any issue until he returned to Cornell, when a nasty case of sunstroke finally hit, confining him to bed for two solid weeks. "Silly situation . . . to be smitten by the insipid N.Y. sun on a dapper lawn," Nabokov noted in his diary. "High temperature, pain in the temples, insomnia and an incessant, brilliant but sterile turmoil of thoughts and fancies."

The Nabokovs changed their itinerary for the summer of 1952. They began their journey in Cambridge, Massachusetts, rather than Ithaca, because Vladimir had taken up a teaching post at Harvard for the spring semester (he was on sabbatical from Cornell). A mitigating factor in moving back to the Cambridge area was to be closer to Dmitri, continuing his studies at Harvard.

Vladimir, Véra, and Dmitri, driving the same Oldsmobile as in earlier years, landed in Laramie, Wyoming, at the end of June, about ten days after departing Cambridge. They stayed in the state hunting butterflies all along the Continental Divide. They traveled through Medicine Bow National Forest ("using the abominable local road") to Riverside in time for the Fourth of July (where "some noisy festival is underway") and, by early August, arrived in Afton.

All the while Nabokov continued to scribble down notes on index card after index card, adding to the novel that had bedeviled him for so long. He had spent the previous year sharpening his observations of quotidian matters. He noted down all sorts of minutiae, the better to portray the American prepubescent girl at the heart of his novel with greater accuracy. Nabokov recorded heights and weights, average age of first menstruation, attitude changes, even the "proper method of inserting an enema tip into a rectum."

He also jotted down teen magazine slang—which is why phrases like "It's a sketch" or "She was loads of fun" appear in *Lolita* and sound right, not tin-eared. To create the character of Miss Pratt, the Beardsley school head, Nabokov interviewed a real school principal under the guise of having a (fictional) daughter who wanted to enroll.

But he did not make as much progress on *Lolita* as he wished while wandering along the Continental Divide. The academic year had exhausted Nabokov more than he realized. He saved most of his energy to scour for blues, including a successful sighting of *Vanessa cardui*. In due course it was time for the Nabokovs to return east. Dmitri had gone back to Cambridge earlier, leaving his parents to travel by themselves along two-lane highways. The couple likely needed two weeks to make the 1,850-plus-mile trip back to Ithaca. They reached the town, and another new rental home, on September 1, 1952.

By that time, Nabokov had read a new story about Sally Horner, one that would change the direction of *Lolita* so much it's surprising to think the novel could have existed without it.

TWENTY ONE

Weekend in Wildwood

Carol Starts, Sally Horner's best friend, summer of 1952.

C arol Taylor no longer remembers why she and Sally decided to go down to Wildwood that summer weekend in 1952. It was mid-August in Camden, a time of relentless heat and humidity. Nobody had air-conditioning, and heading to the Jersey Shore was an easy way to find some relief.

Carol and Sally were both working summer jobs as waitresses at the Sun Ray drugstore in nearby Haddonfield. They were best friends. They were fifteen. They were just a few weeks away from their first freshman class at Woodrow Wilson High. Why not head down to Wildwood for a quick getaway?

The girls saved up their pennies for bus fare and headed south on Friday, August 15, an hour-and-a-half-long ride covering just over eighty-six miles. They got there in the late afternoon. Wildwood bustled with the energy of all the young people making similar weekend pilgrimages for sun, sand, beach, and nightlife. Carol and Sally also carried fake identification cards saying they were twenty-one years old. This would lead to confusion later on.

Sally and Carol weren't drinkers. Sally did not touch alcohol at all, while Carol only occasionally sipped some beer or wine. The fake IDs weren't about boozing. If you wanted to dance, you had to go to clubs like the Bamboo Room, the Riptide, or the Bolero, and you needed to be over the age of twenty-one to get in. Every other Camden high school kid had a fake ID. Plus it was so easy: go to City Hall, get a card-sized version of your birth certificate, adjust the birth date, bleach it out then dye it green with vegetable food coloring, get it laminated, and voilà, a genuine-looking false identification card.

Sally and Carol hit the beach, and after that danced the night away. Then, on Saturday, the friends' plans split apart. For that was when Eddie met Sally.

EDWARD JOHN BAKER drove down to Wildwood nearly every summer weekend in 1952. When Sally Horner met him, he must have seemed like a boy for whom fun was something not just to be had, but to be lived.

In photographs from his high school yearbooks and local newspapers, Baker's eyes dance with merriment. It's there even in the classic high school graduation head shot: while other classmates try for seriousness belying their years, Baker, his dark hair tousled and his eyebrows raised, makes the thought of putting away childish things seem eminently unreasonable. The sparkle in his eye lurks in group photos of the many school musical groups he played with, from the senior jazz band to the string orchestra to the treble clef quartet. In

Edward Baker's high school graduation photo, 1950.

all those shots, Baker holds his trusty soprano saxophone like the proverbial piper ready to entice those eager to follow him wherever he may go.

Photographs lie, of course. They are but millisecond-long glimpses of a more complicated set of feelings, emotions, interactions. One should be careful of reading too much into them. But photos are all that remain, since Baker—Eddie in his youth—isn't around anymore to say what was in his mind at the time. He died in 2014, age eighty-two, still living in his hometown of Vineland, New Jersey.

What is clear from those photos of Baker is why Sally found him attractive at a time when she was finally ready to feel such things. Edward Baker was tall, dark, and twenty to Sally's mature-not-by-choice fifteen. She didn't tell Baker her real age; she said she was seventeen, and Baker said later he "thought she probably was. She looked it." Carol said that Sally was "bananas" for him as soon as she saw him.

Sally had confided in Carol throughout their yearlong friendship, and especially over that summer, about her loneliness and longing for a boyfriend. How that seemed impossible in Camden, where too many people knew about her kidnapping. Where she was viciously mocked by boys and girls alike. Branded a slut. Shunned.

Baker was a tonic to all that. Just the right amount of older, taller, handsomer. She wasn't about to correct him if he believed she was seventeen, or tell him that the new school she was about to start in the fall was Woodrow Wilson High. Perhaps she hoped Baker could pry her away from the darkness. Or perhaps Sally merely wanted a weekend diversion.

After meeting at the beach on Saturday, they spent the afternoon and evening together, and on Sunday morning they went to church. "She impressed me as a darn nice girl," said Baker. "She was good-looking, reserved . . . and was apparently a church-goer."

If something more happened between Saturday night and Sunday morning, Sally did not confide in Carol. Sally did, however, ask a gigantic favor from her best friend after she and Eddie returned from church: Would Carol be okay heading back to Camden on her own? If she was, Sally would go with Baker in his glossy black Ford sedan to his hometown of Vineland and catch a bus from there.

"She really, really, wanted to go home with him," recalled Carol. "She thought he was so nice."

Carol said sure, she didn't mind. She had no reason to get in the way of her best friend's infatuation. Baker seemed all right, not someone who would do Sally harm. Besides, other friends of Carol's were in Wildwood that weekend, too, and they had room for Carol in their car.

The ride home to Camden was tranquil for Carol. The following morning would be nothing of the sort.

ED BAKER PULLED onto the highway with Sally Horner in the passenger seat. Her spirits must have been high as they began the trip to Vineland. They'd spent all of Sunday together, just like they had on Saturday. She was dead gone on him, and he seemed to feel the same way about her. That evening, she'd met Eddie for supper, after which they walked along Wildwood's bustling boardwalk. Away from the carnival barkers and the screaming children, they spied a free bench and sat down. They talked and talked, and perhaps even kissed, and then headed for his car well after dark. She didn't want to say goodbye just yet.

The trip from Wildwood to Vineland normally took about forty minutes. Perhaps, given that it was after eleven o'clock at night, Ed Baker wanted to drive a little faster. Perhaps they were rushing to get Sally to the station before the last bus left for Camden. Or maybe their plans were not so innocent, and they didn't want anyone else to know.

As the clock neared midnight, Ed Baker and Sally Horner were seventeen miles north of Wildwood. A car approached from the opposite direction of the two-lane highway, and Baker shifted his headlights to low beam. He kept both hands on the steering wheel to hold the car in the center of the road. Through the glare, Baker caught a glimpse of something off to the side, but not fast enough to avoid a collision.

Sally never felt a thing.

JUST AFTER MIDNIGHT on Monday, August 18, 1952, the New Jersey State Police arrived on the scene of a four-vehicle highway accident on lower Woodbine Road where the county line divided North Dennis from Woodbine. (The entire stretch is now part of Highway 78.) Baker had barreled into the back of a parked truck, owned by Jacob Benson, which proceeded to crash into another parked truck, owned by John Rifkin. The impact caused Rifkin's truck to be thrown into the highway, where it was hit again by the car directly behind Baker's Ford.

State Trooper Paul Heilfurth told the *Wildwood Leader* that if the multi-car crash had happened three minutes later, it "would probably have been more serious." That's because Benson's truck was about to be towed by Rifkin's truck, and both men were safely away from the vehicles when Baker plowed into them.

Those three extra minutes saved the men's lives. Baker broke his left knee, needed fifteen stitches to close a gash on his right arm, and was cut up and bruised.

The car crash killed Sally Horner instantly.

Rescue crews took more than two hours to free Sally's body from the wreckage. Her head had been crushed by the truck's tailgate, which had come through the windshield when the vehicles collided. Police discovered the fake ID that claimed Sally was twenty-one. Initial news reports misreported her age as a result. Once they realized who she was and that she had been in the news before, Sally's true age emerged.

The death certificate, issued by Cape May County three days later, listed the cause of Sally's death as a fractured skull from a blow to the right side of her head. She'd broken her neck; other mortal injuries included a crushed chest and internal injuries, as well as a right leg fracture above the knee. The coroner didn't bother with an autopsy.

The damage to her face was so severe that the state police felt Ella would be too traumatized to identify her daughter. Instead, Al Panaro went to the morgue. "The only way I knew it was Sally," he said, "was because she had a scar on her leg. I couldn't tell from her face."

CAROL STARTS WAS WOKEN UP on the morning of August 18 by the sound of her mother yelling, "There's someone on the phone for you!" There was only one phone, located in the living room. Carol got herself up and rushed out to take the call. The person on the line sounded official, like a policeman or a detective.

The caller wanted to know if Carol had been with Sally Horner the previous night.

"Yes, I was," Carol replied.

"And you're aware who she was with?"

"Yes I am. Why are you asking me this?"

Carol could not grasp what the caller wanted. Without waiting for an answer, she hung up the phone, then picked it up again and dialed Sally's number. Ella answered.

"Hi, Mrs. Horner. Where's Sally? Is she up yet?"

Ella began to sob. Then she told Carol that Sally had died in a car accident the night before.

Things grew strange for Carol. She did not react right away to the death of her best friend. She got dressed, left the house, and went straight to the movie theater. "I don't know what I saw. I don't know what outfit I wore. But when people wanted to talk to me, I went to the movies." Later she understood she had gone into shock.

When Carol returned home, Ella called again. She explained in greater detail what had happened to Sally, describing the injuries she'd sustained, or at least what Ella knew of them. Only after hanging up did Carol feel the loss of her friend. "I cried and cried and cried."

Carol also couldn't bring herself to ask Ella about a more mundane matter. She and Sally had borrowed each other's favorite dresses in Wildwood—and Carol's blue frock was packed in Sally's bag. It wouldn't have been right to ask Ella about what happened to her dress, so Carol didn't.

But Carol told Ella she'd met the boy who'd taken Sally on her final, fatal journey.

TWENTY-TWO

The Note Card

On the morning of August 19, 1952, as he and Véra were about to begin the long drive back to Ithaca, Vladimir Nabokov opened up a newspaper somewhere near Afton, Wyoming, and chanced upon an Associated Press story. Perhaps the newspaper Nabokov read was the *New York Times*, which carried the wire report of Sally Horner's death on page twelve of their early edition. Maybe it was a local daily, which splashed the sensational news on or near the front page. Wherever Nabokov read the report, he took notes on one of his ninety-four surviving *Lolita* index cards.

The handwritten card reads as follows:

20.viii.52

Woodbine, N.J. –

> Sally Horner, 15-year-old Camden, N.J. Girl who spent
> 21 months as the captive of a middle-aged morals offender
> a few years ago, was killed in a highway mishap early
> Monday . . . Sally vanished from her Camden home in
> 1948 and wasn't heard from again until 1950 when she
> told a hararing [sic] story of spending 21 months as the
> cross-country slave of Frank La Salle, 52.
>
> LaSalle [sic], a mechanic, was arrested in San Jose,
> Cal . . . he pleaded guilty to (two) charges of kidnaping
> and was sentenced to 30 to 35 years in prison. He was
> branded a "moral leper" by the sentencing judge.

Here, in this note card, is proof that Nabokov knew of the Sally Horner case. It is proof that her story captured his attention and that her real-life ordeal was inspiration for Dolores Haze's fictional plight. Less clear is whether the wire report Nabokov read in August 1952 was the first time he had heard of the girl, or if he was, like all who had read the news stories in March and April 1950, stunned to realize that she'd only lived two more years after her rescue.

The note card, written on front and back, included a number of strikethroughs that ended up in the text of *Lolita* itself. Nabokov crossed out "middle-aged morals offender" and "cross-country slave," both phrases that serve as Humbert Humbert's justification to Lolita that the "bunkum" they read in the newspapers has no relation to their "father-daughter" relationship. Misspellings dotted the note card. The most notable is "harrowing," which Nabokov tortured into some alternate, Russified version of the word.

At the top of the note card Nabokov wrote: "in Ench. H. revisited? . . . . in the newspaper?" As Alexander Dolinin explained, Nabokov was referring to "a scene (Chapter 26, Part II) in

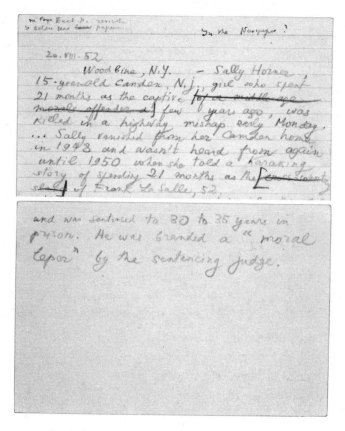

*AP story of Sally Horner's death transcribed onto
a note card by Vladimir Nabokov.*

which Humbert revisits Briceland and in a library browses
through a 'coffin-black volume' with old files of the local *Gazette* for August 1947. Humbert is looking for a printed picture of himself 'as a younger brute' on his 'dark way to Lolita's
bed' in the Enchanted Hunters hotel, and Nabokov evidently
thought of making him come across a report of Sally Horner's
death in what the narrator aptly calls the 'book of doom.'"

Nabokov decided against this approach. Instead, he seeded

Sally Horner's abduction story throughout the entire *Lolita* narrative, making it a tantalizing thread for readers to discover on their own—though the vast majority never did.

AN ALTERNATE THEORY of the ending of *Lolita* pops up in Nabokovian circles from time to time. It contends that Dolores Haze, rather than meeting and marrying Dick Schiller, becoming pregnant, and then dying in childbirth before she is eighteen, actually died at the age of fourteen and a half. Her short, tragic adult life is in fact Humbert Humbert's delusion, a projected fantasy in order to create some sort of romanticized ending for the girl he defiled.

In this version, rather than bearing responsibility for her death, Humbert can indulge in the illusion that—at least for a short time—Dolores found her way to a kind of happiness. By extension, he can remold their rapist-victim power dynamic into real love. Humbert can convince himself he did not want Dolores because she fit the nymphet type born out of his childhood obsession with Annabel Leigh, but that he pursued the girl out of some special regard for her as a human being.

If that theory is true—Nabokov certainly never confirmed or denied—Humbert's final visit to Ramsdale carries an extra sharpness. Just before Nabokov invokes Sally Horner and Frank La Salle in a parenthetical aside, the reliable means through which he conveys true meaning to the reader, he has Humbert Humbert walking through Ramsdale, reminiscing about his first, fateful glimpse of Dolores Haze. Humbert strolls by his old house and spies a "For Sale" sign with a black velvet hair ribbon attached. Just then, "a golden-skinned, brown-haired nymphet of nine or ten" passes him, looking at him with "wild fascination in her large blue-black eyes."

She could be a composite of Lolita and Sally, her eyes the same color as Sally's, more or less. Humbert says, "I said something pleasant to her, meaning no harm, an old-world compliment, what nice eyes you have, but she retreated in haste and the music stopped abruptly, and a violent-looking dark man, glistening with sweat, came out and glared at me. I was on the point of identifying myself when, with a pang of dream-embarrassment, I became aware of my mud-caked dungarees, my filthy and torn sweater, my bristly chin, my bum's bloodshot eyes."

Here, so late in *Lolita*, Humbert has his moment of reckoning. He understands, briefly, "what he might really look like in the eyes of his eternal jury: children and their protectors." The glib charm, all of the smooth veneer, is stripped away in an instant. Humbert reveals himself as the monster he knows he is. And by killing Clare Quilty for taking Dolores away from him—in his mind, taking away what was rightfully his—Humbert Humbert loses his last vestige of morality.

Dolinin takes a charitable view of Nabokov's treatment of Sally Horner in *Lolita*, claiming that the number of references, including the architecture of the novel's second half, does not obscure the real girl. Rather, he writes, "[Nabokov] wanted us to remember and pity the poor girl whose stolen childhood and untimely death helped to give birth to his (not Humbert Humbert's) Lolita—the genuine heroine of the novel hidden behind the narrator's self-indulgent verbosity."

This sense of pity Dolinin speaks of emerges in Humbert's final meeting with Dolores. She is married, pregnant, and seventeen, with "adult, rope-veined narrow hands." She has aged out of his perverse desires, and he finally understands, through the use of the parenthetical, how much he defiled and violated her, how much damage he has caused:

". . . in the infinite run it does not matter a jot that a North American girl-child named Dolores Haze had been deprived of her childhood by a maniac, unless this can be proven (and if it can, then life is a joke), I see nothing for the treatment of my misery but the melancholy . . . palliative of articulate art."

Humbert's epiphany is in keeping with Véra's diary note only days after the American publication of *Lolita* in 1958. She was ecstatic about the largely positive press and fast sales of the novel, but was unnerved by what critics weren't saying. "I wish, though, somebody would notice the tender description of the child's helplessness, her pathetic dependence on monstrous HH, and her heartrending courage all along."

It is to Nabokov's credit that something of the true character of Dolores—her messy, complicated, childish self—emerges out of the haze of his narrator's perverse pedestal-placing. She is no "charming brat lifted from an ordinary existence only by the special brand of love." She excels at tennis; she is free with sharp comebacks ("You talk like a book, *Dad*"); and when she seizes the opportunity to break away from Humbert and run off with Clare Quilty, she does so in order to survive. Any fate is better than staying with her stepfather.

Never mind that she will, later, run from Quilty's desire to embroil her in pornography with multiple people. Never mind that Dolores will "settle" for Dick Schiller and a life of domesticity and motherhood that is, sadly, cut short. She still has the freedom and the autonomy to make these choices for herself, a freedom she never had while under Humbert Humbert's power.

These choices are likely why Véra rated Dolores so highly in the diary entry, and why Nabokov himself ranked Lolita second (after Pnin) of all the characters he ever created that he admired most as a person.

TWENTY-THREE

"A Darn Nice Girl"

On August 21, 1952, three days after the car accident that killed Sally Horner, the *Vineland Daily Journal* published a front-page interview with Edward Baker. He said he was "bewildered by publicity" over Sally's death. "I'd never met Sally before. She didn't tell me if she had ever been to Wildwood before, but I got the impression this was probably the first time she'd ever visited the place." Baker said he frequented the resort town "just about every weekend." On Friday, August 15, he left early from Kimble's, the glass plant where he worked as an apprentice machinist. He met Sally the next day, as well as "a whole bunch of other fellows and girls I met down there . . . Sally and I hung around with them most of the time."

He insisted news accounts of the car accident were wrong. "The fellow who owned the truck I hit [Benson] said he was on the shoulder of the road. But I certainly wasn't on the shoulder, and my skidmarks will prove it. The fellow behind me, even with the benefit of my lights, didn't see the truck, and he crashed into it also." Baker said that what saved his life was the fact that he had both of his hands on the steering wheel, which broke in the collision.

Three days of coast-to-coast news stories had rattled Baker's nerves, and he wanted to set the record straight about what happened between him and Sally. "She seemed like a nice girl. Some of the stories that followed the accident sounded as though we were making a sinful weekend of it. We didn't do anything wrong. . . . We weren't 'fooling around' in the car, or anything. If we had been, she probably wouldn't have been killed and I might have been."

Baker was even more flabbergasted by the revelations of Sally's past ordeal. "Nobody had any idea this girl was the one who had been kidnapped four years ago. How should we remember?" Never mind that Sally's rescue was reported nationwide, as well as on the front page of the *Daily Journal*.

He was still grappling with how young Sally really was. "She told me she was 17 years old. She may have had a birth certificate with her saying she was 21, but I never saw it. Who asks to see birth certificates when you go out with a girl?"

The *Daily Journal* also spoke to Baker's mother, Marie Young. She'd received a call from her son not long after the accident. "He said he wished it was him that was killed instead of that innocent girl. He was pretty broken up." He'd told his mother how nice a girl she was, and how he admired her commitment to going to church on Sundays, even down in Wildwood. He would never get past that "she got killed because she wanted him to take her into Vineland."

Both Baker and his mother had added reasons to defend

themselves. After he was treated at Burdette Tomlin Hospital in Cape May for the injuries he sustained in the car accident, police arrested and charged him with reckless homicide. Baker was freed on a thousand dollars' bail—his stepfather, James Young, put up the money—on August 20. A news account sympathetic to Baker, stressing his lack of culpability in the accident, might help his case.

But a strike against him was that the crash leading to Sally's death was not Baker's first car accident. Only the year before, Baker was driving the car, which belonged to his mother, Marie Young, in Newfield, four miles north of Vineland. He hit another car while running a red light. Then, too, Baker's injuries were not life-threatening. Neither were those of Marie, sitting in the passenger seat.

SALLY HORNER'S FUNERAL was held on August 22, four days after her death. More than three hundred people crowded into the Frank J. Leonard Funeral Home at 1451 Broadway to pay their respects. Many floral arrangements sent by well-wishers flanked Sally's casket.

The burial was a more private affair. Only a handful of family members, including Ella, Susan, Al, and some aunts and cousins, drove out to Emleys Hill Cemetery in Cream Ridge, where Sally's remains were interred in the Goff family plot.

For Carol Starts, the funeral was awful. She sat by herself in a corner pew. Ella and Susan requested the casket be open at first, for those who wished to pay their last respects to Sally. "I wanted to see her so badly. Then I did, and it nearly broke me in half," Carol recalled. When she could no longer stand the proceedings, Carol fled the service and went home.

Carol stayed away from school for an entire week after

Sally's death. "I couldn't handle it. This was the most heavy-duty thing I had ever gone through." Carol's first experience of deep loss would mark her for the rest of her life. As she grew older and friends began to die, Carol tended to grieve in an open and wild manner that puzzled those around her. "I would hear, 'but they were just a friend.' I would hear that about Sally. That we should be moving right along. I wasn't willing to move right along. I wanted to grieve. And when I finally came out of shock, I did."

FRANK LA SALLE made his presence known to Sally Horner's family one final time. On the morning of her funeral, they discovered he had sent a spray of flowers. The Panaros insisted they not be displayed.

THE FIRST COURT HEARING stemming from the accident that killed Sally Horner took place on Tuesday, August 26. It lasted more than two and a half hours. A full record of the proceeding does not exist, but the surviving court docket reported that Baker pleaded not guilty to a count of careless driving and that Judge Thomas Sears found him not guilty of the charge.

New Jersey state law enforcement was not about to let Baker go so easily, and what followed was a complicated series of charges, court hearings, and verdicts. Prosecutors even charged Baker for "operating a car with illegal equipment"—specifically, unapproved headlight shields. Police told the *Vineland Daily Journal* that Baker's headlights "were partially obscured by a device he had purchased and attached to other lights."

The most serious charge came from the Cape May grand jury. On September 3, 1952, they indicted Baker for the "reckless killing by auto" of Sally Horner, stating that he had acted "carelessly and heedlessly, in wilful and wanton disregard of the rights and safety of others . . . and against the peace of this State, the Government, and dignity of the same."

The following week, on September 10, Baker pleaded not guilty to that charge in front of Judge Harry Tanenbaum. Carol was called to testify to her friendship with Sally, as well as the whole business with the fake identification cards. Her memory of the experience was hazy, but she had vivid recall of Baker's attitude.

"He was very arrogant," Carol told me. "He would make these weird remarks, like how the courtroom was only thirty feet long instead of being a hundred feet as it was supposed to. I didn't understand what he meant and still don't." She was still so worked up about his comment about the courtroom size that she mentioned it to me three times in one conversation. It demonstrated, to her, Baker's inability to take the hearing seriously: "He snickered a great deal. Acting stupid." Her reaction to him was visceral: "I hated him because he was driving and had the accident that killed my best friend."

Perhaps Carol was also upset by the court's decision, delayed until January 15, 1953. Judge Tenenbaum threw out the charge against Baker for reckless killing by auto—the sketchy court records did not give a reason—and also found Baker not guilty of the unapproved headlight shields count.

But Baker's legal troubles were not done. He faced a cluster of civil actions, too. As with the criminal court proceedings, the surviving civil court documents are light on detail and full of unresolved gaps. But both the *Cape May County Gazette* and the Camden *Courier-Post* reported important details on the complicated joint lawsuits.

All five complaints were heard together the week of May 21,

1953. Dominick Caprioni, who owned the car right behind Baker's on the night Sally Horner died, sued Jacob Benson, owner of the parked truck that both Baker and Caprioni crashed into. Caprioni also sued Baker and his mother, Marie Young, since she owned the Ford Baker was driving, seeking $13,300 in damages in his lawsuits. Benson sued Baker and Caprioni without asking for any money, while Baker and Young in turn sued Benson for $52,500. Lastly—and the civil action that matters most—Ella Horner sued Baker, Young, and Benson for $50,000.

The byzantine nature of the lawsuits, heard by Superior Court judge Elmer B. Woods, may explain why there was a mistrial on the first day, after someone observed a juror talking to one of the witnesses during the noon recess. A new hearing lasted two days before ending in an abrupt settlement on May 28, 1953. It's not clear how much each of the plaintiffs (some of whom were also doubling as defendants) received.

The cases against Baker were over, but Cape May County did not officially close the books until June 30, 1954. Written beside his name on the ledger for that day was "nolle pros"—they declined to prosecute. At last the car crash that killed Sally Horner, in the eyes of the criminal justice system, had been ruled a tragic accident.

TWENTY-FOUR

La Salle in Prison

Frank La Salle's lengthy prison sentence meant Sally Horner's family could push her abductor to the back of their minds. The New Jersey court systems, however, weren't so lucky. La Salle may have pleaded guilty and shrugged off his right to an attorney, but he still thought he could find a way out of prison, banking on an outlandish fantasy about the life he'd led with Sally. Unlike Humbert Humbert, who tried to attach some grander meaning to his delusions of exemplary parenthood, La Salle came up with a rationale that was crude, obvious, and disappointingly banal.

He applied for, and received, a writ of habeas corpus from the Mercer County Court (Trenton State Prison fell under their jurisdiction). The gist of La Salle's first appeal was that he'd never waived his right to extradition from California and was thus brought to Camden against his will. In lengthy testimony at the Mercer County Courthouse on September 24, 1951, La Salle also claimed he "did not plead guilty before Judge Palese in Camden" and was thus "deprived of his liberty without due process of law."

While the transcript of the proceeding is lost, I discovered the outcome of La Salle's habeas hearing in a motion filed after the fact by Camden County prosecutor Mitchell Cohen: La Salle perjured himself on the stand by denying he had pleaded guilty to the abduction and kidnapping charges when, in fact, he made that plea in open court in April 1950.

Future New Jersey governor and chief justice of the State Supreme Court Richard Hughes presided over the case as a county court judge. Hughes was so incensed by La Salle's lies on the stand that he told the prisoner: "I hardly think you should be able to finish your first [prison] sentence, but in case you should, I am imposing another. You have attempted to subvert and obstruct the proper administration of law by an application for a writ [of habeas corpus] with absolutely no foundation." Hughes ordered La Salle to serve an additional thirty days in the Mercer County Jail.

Judge Hughes's ire toward La Salle was compounded by the recent uptick of prisoners acting as their own jailhouse lawyers who showed no compunction about lying in their filings. "The courts always lend a willing ear where the deprivation of rights are concerned," Hughes wrote, "but of late there has been a great abuse of this privilege by prisoners who lie when they file sworn statements. It must be broken up."

The contempt of court finding did not deter La Salle from his appeals. He kept on, in a lengthy series of motions and affidavits filed in waves between 1952 and 1955. They are the only surviving evidence of La Salle's state of mind during and after Sally's abduction, and they are remarkable proof of a false narrative. The authority and control he radiated when he had Sally in his power, his ability to manipulate others into believing in his act, vanished upon his arrest in March 1950. Now he exuded desperation and falsity.

In his appeals, La Salle refused to acknowledge that Sally was not, and had never been, his daughter. He referred to her repeatedly as "Natural Daughter Florence Horner La Salle," apparently having convinced himself, through the selective reading of legal precedents, that "a father cannot be convicted of kidnaping his own child."

He spun a shambling yarn about living in Camden, but "not with his family," in January 1948, "doing what he thought right by giving money in sufficient sums to his former common-law wife for the care and maintenance of his [daughter]" and seeing Sally "on the streets by herself as late as 12 AM midnight," at which point he would "make her go home and give her money." La Salle neglected to mention his January 15, 1948, parole on the statutory rape charges, or that he never knew, let alone had any domestic relationship with, Ella Horner. And he most certainly never saw Sally out at midnight; nor did he give her money and tell her to go home.

La Salle justified his kidnapping of Sally, both in his appeals and, later, in person, to his actual daughter, Madeline, on the grounds that he was saving Sally from a mother who was "always out with some man or [was home] in bed," or by falsely quoting Sally saying that her mother "does not care what becomes of me. She seems to hate me, and never buys any clothing or take [sic] care of me and is never at home."

He embellished these poorly written fantasies of devoted fatherhood to Madeline, a daughter he never saw grow up, by describing trips to Philadelphia "to see his other daughter by his legal wife who he was at the time separated from, but there was nobody at home." (Dorothy Dare, of course, had filed for divorce from La Salle in 1943 after he was arrested on the statutory rape charges.)

La Salle attested, time and again, to having "sworn proof" that Sally was his daughter, but of course he could never deliver the goods. He even reproved the media for publishing Sally's name after she was rescued in San Jose on the grounds of "a statute against such publicity for a child." He claimed his quick guilty plea resulted from being afraid of "MOB VIOLENCE" (the capitalization is La Salle's) and also claimed that the prosecutor, Cohen, "told the defendant there was no use of his trying to get an attorney as no attorney could do any good."

La Salle's appeal documents include purported affidavits that bolstered his claims of loving fatherhood. If the documents are real, they show how many missed opportunities there were for one of Sally's neighbors to see past the facade of amiable father-daughter interaction to the horrifying reality. If the documents are forgeries, they amplify the grimy, sordid truth of Sally's abuse: she was under the power of a man so determined to present himself as a well-adjusted human and bury the depth of his crimes that he lied, above all, to himself.

MOST OF THE STATEMENTS attributed to Sally Horner and Frank La Salle's neighbors in Dallas come from affidavits included with La Salle's appellate brief in 1954. After reading a copy of the statement his mother, Nelrose Pfeil, purportedly gave about Sally, Tom Pfeil denied she'd ever said anything of the sort. "It was definitely not the way my mother talked. Not her wording or verbiage, anyhow," he told me. Frequent misspellings in the alleged affidavit also gave Tom pause: "My mother was a good speller," he said. "She was a secretary for three attorneys just out of college. She may not have had a legal mind, but she was precise."

Tom Pfeil scoffed at his mother's supposed statement that Sally spent "many hours a day" at the family home. For one thing, none of the Pfeils were home much. Charles and Nelrose also owned and operated a lumberyard along with the trailer park. They worked sixteen- to eighteen-hour days during the week, and the boys started working at the yard in their teens, considering it a victory when they negotiated a weekly half day off. When Tom joined the marines out of high school and began boot camp, he told me he thought, "Man, I've been down this road already."

"My mother was a very strong woman," said Tom. "She wasn't but five foot one but she could thread iron into a water pipe. If a water line froze or broke, [Nelrose] would put it back in the drain. She wasn't mean, but running a trailer park wasn't running a bridal store." She had such a solid work ethic that she worked at the yard most every day until four months before she died in 2001, at the age of eighty-four. She and Charles had an ironclad rule at the trailer park: no socializing with the tenants. "She collected the rent, and not much other than that," said Tom. "That was one of the things they decided because they got hurt. A couple of times, I befriended some people I shouldn't have and, unfortunately, they took my parents to the cleaners. As soon as you become a friend, it becomes, 'Oh, I can't pay this week.'" As a result, the Pfeils kept their interactions with the trailer park residents to the bare minimum. "Sally would *not* be in the house several times a day," Tom emphasized.

His recollections, however, jibe with what his mother's supposed affidavit said about La Salle spoiling Sally. "She wasn't laying [sic] on the ground kicking. . . . When she asked [La Salle] for something, she got it," said Tom. "She had nice clothes. She wasn't running around in rags. Certainly she was not mistreated. That's why everybody was surprised. We thought it was a dad's adoration of a daughter and how nice that was."

One curious anomaly with Nelrose Pfeil's alleged affidavit was that it included the family's new address, 2240 Lawndale Avenue. If the affidavit was a fabrication, as her son insisted, how would Frank La Salle have known where the Pfeils had moved after they stopped living at the Commerce Street trailer park?

Tom Pfeil was adamant that his mother was never in touch with La Salle while he was in prison. "For my mother to have anything to do with an affidavit or anything . . . is about as far-fetched as if she came back from Mars."

FRANK LA SALLE also wrote letters while incarcerated at Trenton State Prison, just as he had during earlier prison stints. According to some of Ruth Janisch's children, he wrote their mother on a number of occasions. Both Vanessa Janisch, who was not born until after Sally was rescued, and her older sister Rachel* remembered seeing La Salle's letters bundled up and tucked in one of the many scrapbooks—at least one chiefly devoted to media coverage of Sally's rescue—that Ruth kept of her life.

As of this writing, I have not been able to see Ruth's scrapbooks for myself. They have been passed on from family member to family member, down generational lines. Ruth clung to

---

* Not their real names.

her role in Sally's rescue for the rest of her life, and brought it up again and again to her children. She wanted them to believe in her as a heroine. She wanted them to know she was capable of a decent act. Some of her sons and daughters never reconciled Ruth's contradictions. Rachel, however, finally came to believe that her mother "did the best she knew how," no matter how many grievous mistakes she made as a mother and a human being.

SALLY HORNER'S FAMILY had to grapple with her sudden loss for the rest of their lives. Dolores Haze's husband, Dick Schiller, had to raise their child without her. But another woman had to reckon with the collateral damage of a father's abuse. That woman was Frank La Salle's daughter, known as Madeline.

Her mother, Dorothy, spent the Second World War working at the Brooklyn Navy Yard and rebuilding her life while her former husband was in prison. The choices she made as a newly divorced wife and single mother bear some resemblance to what was in store for Dolores Haze as Dick Schiller's wife. Madeline stayed with her mother during the summer months, and spent winters at her grandfather's house in Merchantville. After the war, when Madeline was ten, Dorothy met and married an army veteran several years her senior. He adopted Madeline and he and Dorothy had another child. Their marriage lasted until his death in 1986, almost four decades.

When her children were grown, Dorothy got a job with a small advertising firm, and then with Campbell's Soup, whose headquarters are still in Camden. She worked for the company for thirty years, retiring in 1991. Dorothy was also active in her local Baptist church for more than half a century, serving several years on the Board of Deaconesses.

When Dorothy died at ninety-two in 2011, her survivors included her children and almost a dozen grandchildren and great-grandchildren. The longer Dorothy lived, the more distance she put between her more settled, family-oriented existence and her turbulent early life with Frank La Salle. Madeline did not learn any details of her father's imprisonment until she was in her early twenties, newly married with children of her own. "There was an article in the newspaper, and my mother felt she had to tell me," she said in 2014. Knowing that her father was in prison did not repel Madeline. It made her curious. "I wanted to see him. I wanted to talk to him."

She reestablished relations with La Salle in the final year of his life, visiting him in Trenton State Prison along with her children, preschoolers at the time. He made model boats for the kids and leather pocket books for Madeline and her husband. When he was up for parole, sick with lung and heart problems, Madeline volunteered to have him live at her house should he be released early. That did not happen.

"When I looked at him, I could see a lot of myself in his face," Madeline said. "My husband picked it up right away." For those last months, Madeline did not clutter her relationship with questions of what La Salle had done to land him in prison. "We talked as father and daughter would talk," Madeline told me. "There wasn't a strain. He was just Dad. Truth be told, I never thought about whether he was guilty or not guilty."

Just as John Ray, Jr., became the conduit for Humbert Humbert's so-called confession, Madeline, unwittingly, became the keeper of Frank La Salle's version of the story. When I mentioned the word "abduction" to Madeline, she interrupted me with some force. "That's not the way he described it to me," she said. She then proceeded to parrot the version La Salle had presented in his appeals—a version the court had soundly rejected as fantasy.

FRANK LA SALLE never saw the outside world again. He appealed his sentence one final time, in 1962, and was again denied. He died of arteriosclerosis in Trenton State Prison on March 22, 1966, sixteen years into his sentence. He was, according to his death certificate, two months shy of turning seventy. The certificate listed him as "Frank La Salle III," the first time he ever used this sobriquet. That he died with his age shrouded in mystery and under a false name fits with the entire life of a man determined to conceal terrible truths.

TWENTY-FIVE

"Gee, Ed, That Was Bad Luck"

T wo weeks after Sally Horner's death, on September 2, 1952, another sensational crime reported by the Associated Press caught Vladimir Nabokov's attention, and he filled another of his note cards. Unlike Sally's story, which merited a single parenthetical in *Lolita* but was seeded throughout the novel, this case got an entire paragraph at the beginning of chapter thirty-three. Humbert Humbert has returned to Ramsdale. Before making himself known in his former haunt, he stops off at the local cemetery, where he wanders as he ruminates upon his past. During his peregrinations, he stumbles across a particular sight:

> On some of the graves there were pale, transparent little national flags slumped in the windless air under the evergreens. Gee, Ed, that was bad luck—referring

to G. Edward Grammar, a thirty-five-year old New
York office manager who had just been arrayed on a
charge of murdering his thirty-three-year-old wife,
Dorothy. Bidding for the perfect crime, Ed had blud-
geoned his wife and put her into a car. The case came
to light when two county policemen on patrol saw
Mrs. Grammar's new big blue Chrysler, an anniversary present from her husband, speeding crazily down
a hill, just inside their jurisdiction (God bless our good
cops!). The car sideswiped a pole, ran up an embank-
ment covered with beard grass, wild strawberry and
cinquefoil, and overturned. The wheels were still gently
spinning in the mellow sunlight when the officers
removed Mrs. G's body. It appeared to be a routine
highway accident at first. Alas, the woman's battered
body did not match up with only minor damage suffered by the car. I did better.

Nabokov cleverly phrased it so that the reader isn't clear if
Humbert actually stumbles across the murderer's grave or if
he is merely thinking about the case as he looks at the graves.
It has to be the latter, because Ramsdale is supposed to be
somewhere in New England, an area Nabokov knew very well.
The G. Edward Grammer case happened in Baltimore, a city
Nabokov did not know at all. Nabokov's misspelling of Grammer's last name was deliberate, an opportunity for the noted
literary prankster to sneak in another joke. It was also a sly
reference to Humbert's professed intention, earlier in *Lolita,* to
teach French grammar to Ramsdale's local children.

The text of Nabokov's surviving note card about the G. Edward Grammer case is close to, but not exactly, the final version. It includes the phrases "Gee Ed, that was bad luck" as

well as "god bless our good cops!" But another wry aside about "Mrs. Grammar's new automobile" and Grammer's murderous actions did not make it into the final text: "ought to have doctored it first, Ed!"

One could see how this story, in tandem with Sally Horner's death, served as important inspiration for Nabokov. The Grammer case was a media sensation, capturing public attention for being an almost perfect murder. Grammer very nearly got away with it—except the Baltimore police noticed some details that did not add up, like a pebble jammed underneath the accelerator pedal.

The crime unfolded much as Nabokov described in *Lolita*. On the evening of August 19, 1952, Ed Grammer was getting ready to go back to New York City after a weekend with his wife and both of their daughters. Dorothy and the kids had moved to Parkville, a suburb of Baltimore, to care for her bereaved mother, while Ed remained in their Bronx apartment. The Sunday night routine was for Dorothy to drive Ed in their big blue Chrysler to Baltimore Penn Station, where he would give his wife some money for the week and catch the 11:28 P.M. train. For a few days after the "accident," Grammer insisted that Dorothy had dropped him off as usual, and that the last he'd seen her alive was at the train station.

But the facts didn't add up. The witnesses who saw the Chrysler speed down the hill along Taylor Avenue and sideswipe a telephone pole turned out to be patrolmen. For the victim of a car accident, Dorothy was astonishingly little-bruised in the areas they expected to be bruised, whereas her head had clearly been bashed in. There was blood in the driver's seat but the spatter wasn't substantial enough to suggest she had been killed on impact. More curious: Dorothy's purse and glasses were missing. When the pebble was discovered, pushing the accelerator forward, what seemed an accident transformed into murder, confirmed when Grammer confessed, at last, to Balti- more County police.

The fishbowl atmosphere intensified when reporters sniffed out the prospect of a mistress, which provided a mo- tive for Dorothy Grammer's murder. But when they found her, she turned out to be a United Nations communications officer named Matilda Mizibrocky who swore she didn't know her beau was married, and they didn't print her name right away. Even the court hid her under the pseudonym of "Mary Matthews" so that she wouldn't be hounded further, and her testimony pos- sibly tainted. It didn't work. Grammer's defense team was livid that the court tried to shield Mizibrocky from them, too, and hinder their ability to prepare their case.

It isn't clear if Nabokov followed the news after Grammer's arrest. The trial showcased further lurid details, and Gram- mer's execution by hanging in 1954 became an added spectacle because it was initially botched. But the main affair—husband murders wife, passes it off as car accident—was enough inspi- ration for him. The Grammer case clearly echoed the untimely death of Charlotte Haze, struck by a car after running away from the argument with Humbert where she learns of his true designs on her daughter.

The final line of the Grammer paragraph in *Lolita* reads with further chilling force. Grammer could not conceal his crime from the world after all. Humbert Humbert, system- atically raping Dolores Haze for nearly two years on a cross- country odyssey, could, and did. No wonder he concluded: "I did better."

I bring up the Grammer case because it is another concrete example of Vladimir Nabokov drawing upon real-life crimes to help him with his novel. As with Sally Horner's kidnapping, the note card's survival indicates that Nabokov attached enough importance to the case that he wished people to know he did at some future point.

But the case also demonstrates Nabokov's extended interest in crime stories. This, too, he sought to deny in public; he was also openly critical of mystery novels despite his boyhood love of Edgar Allan Poe and Arthur Conan Doyle's Sherlock Holmes tales, and he called out Dostoevsky as a hack, though he taught *Crime and Punishment* to his Cornell students. He disdained those who would reduce *Lolita* to genre, yet a great deal of Nabokov's fiction relies on the tropes of crime and suspense: *Invitation to a Beheading* centers around a man waiting to be executed; *Despair* hinges upon a man ready to murder his double; and *Lolita*, of course, is about kidnapping and rape, and culminates in murder.

Which is also why Nabokov's interest, just over a month after *Lolita*'s American publication, in a third crime jumped out at me. As Véra told their close friend Morris Bishop when he telephoned with congratulations on the novel's success, in the week of September 12, 1958, Vladimir had become obsessed with reading up on the stabbing murders of Dr. Melvin Nimer and his wife, Louise Jean, in their Staten Island home. What fascinated Nabokov was that police initially treated their eight-year-old son, Melvin Jr., as a suspect. Even though strips of cloth found on the boy's bed suggested he had been restrained while his parents were murdered, Melvin's "unnaturally calm demeanor" raised red flags in investigators' minds, as did an apparent confession elicited during a mental health evaluation, and the lack of forced entry into the Nimer home.

But the presumed case against the little boy soon fell apart. No physical evidence linked Melvin to his parents' murders. And police learned that Dr. Nimer had left a set of spare keys at

the hospital where he worked, which had vanished—thus answering the "lack of forced entry" question. The case remains
unsolved to this day, but there were police detectives still claiming as recently as 2007 that Melvin Nimer was the best suspect
in the case.

THE NABOKOVS WOULD VENTURE WEST one more time before
Vladimir finished the *Lolita* manuscript. After so many years
of work—five or six, depending on who was counting and who
was listening—*Lolita* was nearly done, despite not being anywhere close to publication. This road trip also proved to be the
longest Vladimir and Véra stayed away from the East Coast.

They left Ithaca in that still-reliable Oldsmobile in early
April 1953. From there they headed toward Birmingham, Ala-
bama, a pit stop en route to the Chiricahua Mountains in Arizona, where butterflies were supposed to be plentiful. What
Nabokov discovered upon arrival in May was that the weather
was too cold, the wind gusts too strong, for decent butterfly-
catching. By the end of the month he and Véra had moved farther west, passing by several California lakes and ending up in
Ashland, Oregon.

There the couple stayed from the first of June through the
end of August, living at 163 Mead Street. When there were no
butterflies to catalog, Nabokov was on a mad sprint to finish
Lolita, burning his handwritten pages as soon as Véra typed
them up. When their Oregon summer idyll ended, the Nabokovs wended their way back east via Jenny Lake and the Grand
Tetons.

Once more, they were back in Ithaca at the start of September, and this time, the end of *Lolita* was in sight.

TWENTY-SIX

Writing and Publishing Lolita

On December 6, 1953, Vladimir Nabokov wrote a note in his diary, at the bottom of a page largely filled with numerical grades for the final assignment of his literature class. "Finished *Lolita* which was begun exactly 5 years ago." It was a finish line he'd spent many of those years never expecting to reach.

There were classes to teach at Cornell to pay the bills and to fund his summer trips to hunt butterflies. Other projects had also interrupted Nabokov's progress on *Lolita,* from translation work (*The Song of Igor's Campaign*) to the first version of his autobiography, which was published in 1951. *Lolita* ought to have been "a novel I would be able to finish in a year if I could completely concentrate upon it." Instead it emerged piecemeal, with him writing on index cards in the passenger seat of a car or lying in bed at night.

Nabokov had spent the summer of 1953 trip writing steadily, almost maniacally, dictating his prose to Véra, then "crumpling each old manuscript sheet once it had served its turn and discarding the pages out the car window or into a hotel fireplace." Nabokov put in sixteen-hour writing days over the course of the fall of 1953—on Cornell's dime—delegating the teaching and exam-marking to Véra.

He grew anxious about the manuscript as the pages piled up. In a September 29, 1953, letter to Katharine White at the *New Yorker,* Nabokov called the book an "enormous, mysterious, heartbreaking novel that, after five years of monstrous misgivings and diabolical labors, I have more or less completed." He was certain the *New Yorker* wouldn't want to publish an excerpt, but the magazine had a first-look agreement on anything Nabokov wrote, and he always listened to White's feedback, whatever the outcome. She liked it, but confirmed Nabokov's suspicions that the magazine wasn't the right home for an excerpt.

Now, the book was finished. An odyssey that did not, in fact, begin on December 6, 1948, but at least a decade earlier, as *Volshebnik,* or in 1947, when Nabokov wrote to Edmund Wilson: "I am writing . . . a short novel about a man who liked little girls—and it's going to be called *The Kingdom by the Sea.*" Nabokov knew he was writing a novel that could cause outrage and controversy. No wonder he attempted to destroy the manuscript at least twice that we know of.

The first time was in the fall of 1948. As Stacy Schiff recounted in her biography of Véra, Nabokov carried his manuscript to the trash cans behind his house on Seneca Street in Ithaca. When Véra realized what Vladimir was set upon doing, she raced out to stop him. Just before she got there, one of Nabokov's students at Cornell, Dick Keegan, chanced upon the scene. He saw Nabokov beginning to feed his manuscript sheets into a fire set near the trash cans. "Appalled, [Véra] fished the few sheets she could from the flames. Her husband began to protest. 'Get away from there!' Véra commanded, an order Vladimir obeyed as she stomped on the pages she had retrieved. 'We are keeping this,' she announced."

On at least one other occasion, when Nabokov wished to destroy the *Lolita* manuscript, Véra also stepped in as savior. It may well be that Nabokov's attempts to get rid of *Lolita* were more about performance than intent. As Robert Roper pointed out, "Véra came to the rescue because she was nearby; he did not start fires when his wife was out of the house." These acts made Véra a veritable Saint Joan* figure with respect to *Lolita,* sacrificing herself—if risking her husband's ire was a sacrifice—to step in and save what would be one of the most important works of literature in the twentieth century.

Nabokov later told the *Paris Review* of yet another instance of near-destruction, "one day in 1950." Once more, Véra "was responsible for stopping me and urging delay and second thoughts as, beset with technical difficulties and doubts, I was carrying the first chapters of *Lolita* to the garden incinerator." He may have mixed up the dates and this was the incident that Dick Keegan witnessed. Or there might have been an unrecorded instance where Véra saved the day.

Lolita was ready to be submitted to publishers, but there was a catch: Nabokov refused to put his own name to the novel. He asked Katharine White, in the same letter in which he solicited her feedback, whether book publishers would go

---

* Nabokov settled upon the "Lolita" sobriquet for his heroine very late in the writing process. Before then her name was "Juanita Dark"—a sly, Spanishized reworking of Jeanne d'Arc, or Saint Joan.

along with his request. She replied that "from her experience, an author's identity sooner or later leaked out." Still, Nabokov wanted to keep his identity secret, for the same reasons that spurred him to burn the manuscript pages of *Lolita* as he finished them. He believed being publicly associated with such an incendiary book might imperil both his literary and his teaching careers.

As the manuscript for *Lolita* made its way around New York publishing houses, Nabokov continued to insist that he publish under a pseudonym. His stubborn desire for anonymity may be one of the reasons why that first round of publishers decided against acquiring *Lolita*.

Nabokov's editor at Viking, Pascal Covici, rejected the manuscript. So, too, did James Laughlin, the New Directions publisher whom Nabokov worked with on *The Real Life of Sebastian Knight, Laughter in the Dark,* and *Nikolai Gogol.* Farrar, Straus and Simon & Schuster also came back with the same verdict: they didn't believe they could publish because it would be too expensive to defend in court on possible obscenity charges. Jason Epstein at Doubleday *did* want to publish, but the company president, once he got wind of what *Lolita* was about, overruled him.

The manuscript also detoured away from publishing offices, making its way into the literary world. The critic Edmund Wilson read half and expressed complicated feelings about the book in a letter to Nabokov ("I like it less than anything else of yours I have read"), perhaps because it reminded him too much of his own censorship battles after the publication of his novel *Memoirs of Hecate County,* which was banned and then pulped. Wilson's former wife, the novelist and literary critic Mary McCarthy, grew "negative and perplexed" by *Lolita,* but Wilson's present wife, Elena, liked the book. Dorothy Parker almost certainly read it, too, if a parody piece in the *New Yorker* featuring a character named "Lolita" is enough to go by.

Influential literary readers were all well and good, but their verdicts did not matter if the book never found a publisher. The last of the rejections by American book firms arrived in February 1955. To publish *Lolita,* Nabokov had to look outside of America, and beyond highbrow intellectual circles. Nabokov joked to Edmund Wilson several weeks later: "I suppose it will be finally published by some shady firm with a Viennese-Dream name." The joke became truth before the summer of 1955 was over.

MAURICE GIRODIAS was the founder and publisher of Olympia Press, best known for publishing books others wouldn't touch. Most of those books were, in fact, smut—badly written, hastily produced. Others got that label affixed to them, like Henry Miller's *Tropic of Capricorn* and *Tropic of Cancer,* J. P. Donleavy's *The Ginger Man,* and the pseudonymous *The Story of O* (revealed, decades later, to be the work of Anne Desclos).

Nabokov's Europe-based agent, Doussia Ergaz, submitted *Lolita* to Girodias because of his work as an art-book publisher. She didn't seem to know much about the seedier side of Olympia Press. Girodias was fully aware of the literary value of Nabokov's work, and what a boon it would be for Olympia's list. Girodias offered on the book in mid-May 1955. Ergaz then wrote Nabokov: "He finds the book not only admirable from the literary point of view, but he thinks that it might lead to a change in social attitudes toward the kind of love described in *Lolita,* provided of course that it has this authenticity, this burning and irrepressible ardor."

Nabokov went along with Girodias's misapprehension

about there being a social aim to the novel because he was relieved *Lolita* had at last found a publisher. That relief dissipated quickly, once he realized the contract he'd signed on June 6, 1955, better resembled a devil's bargain. Nabokov's new publisher had mistaken the author for his creation, thinking Nabokov drew upon some perverse experience. Girodias also insisted the novel be published under Nabokov's name, and Nabokov did not feel he had the leverage to object, when the alternate option was no publication at all. Nabokov also did not see galley proofs until it was too late to make changes, which vexed a man known for his fastidiousness to no end. Olympia Press published *Lolita* on September 16, 1955, but Nabokov did not discover that it was out for several weeks. And the published version, as Nabokov feared, was riddled with errors.

What most infuriated Nabokov, however, was Girodias's blithe attitude about copyright and about paying him what he was owed. The publisher had registered *Lolita*'s copyright in Nabokov's name as well as to Olympia Press. Nabokov did not discover the joint copyright registration until early 1956, and because of American copyright laws at the time, he had just five years to republish *Lolita* in America or else the novel would fall into the public domain.

The Copyright Office in Washington advised Nabokov to get a "quit-claim"—a formal renunciation of copyright. The publisher did not reply at first, then dragged his feet throughout 1956 and 1957. As Nabokov later recalled, "From the very start I was confronted with the peculiar aura surrounding [Girodias's] business transactions with me, an aura of negligence, evasiveness, procrastination, and falsity."

Girodias also had a pesky habit of failing to pay royalties or to send statements. Thus, Nabokov saw no money from *Lolita* over the first two years of publication, despite strong sales in

France. In October 1957, he had finally had enough of Girodias's prevarications and shady dealings, telling him the deal was off and that as a result, all rights reverted back to him. Girodias paid what was owed (44,220 *"anciens* francs"), and Nabokov let the matter go. Girodias, however, soon reverted back to his nonpayment ways, and Nabokov's irritation increased. He needed the money, but above all, he needed to be free of Olympia in order to publish *Lolita* the way he had always wished.

Fortunately for Nabokov, his mood was about to lighten. *Lolita* was about to find, at long last, a home in America.

ON AUGUST 30, 1957, Nabokov received a letter from Walter Minton, president and publisher of G. P. Putnam's Sons. "Being a rather backward example of that rather backward species, the American publisher, it was only recently that I began to hear about a book called *Lolita*," Minton wrote. After some more preamble, he got to the point: "I am wondering if the book is available for publication."

Minton, in his early thirties, had succeeded his father, Melville, as publisher two years earlier, and within months established his taste for novels too controversial for other publishers. Putnam published Norman Mailer's second novel, *The Deer Park*, which had been turned down by his option publisher, and several others, for a graphic description of oral sex that each publisher feared would run afoul of obscenity laws. This passage did not deter Minton, who authorized Putnam to run newspaper ads declaring *The Deer Park* was "The Book Six Publishers Refused to Bring You!"

Minton enjoyed being part of the cultural conversation, especially when there was a chance that the conversation would offend people. In hindsight, it made sense he ended up publishing *Lolita*. The delicious thing is that he learned of the novel from an unlikely source: his then-mistress Rosemary Ridgewell, a showgirl at a Midtown Manhattan nightclub called the Latin Quarter. Ridgewell had read excerpts of *Lolita* in the *Anchor Review*. "I thought Nabokov had a very interesting way of writing, very, you know—crystalline?" said Ridgewell in 1958.

Minton, in turn, discovered the pages at her Upper East Side apartment. "I woke in the middle of the night and there was this story on the table. I started reading," he recalled in early 2018, sixty years later. "By morning, I knew I had to publish it." (Ridgewell was in line for a tidy payday for her literary scouting efforts, per a standing Putnam policy: the equivalent of 10 percent of an author's royalties for the first year, plus 10 percent of the publisher's share of subsidiary rights for two years.)

When Nabokov received Minton's letter, he had all but given up on *Lolita*'s publishing prospects in America. For more than three years, multiple publishers had expressed interest, only to back off. Now it irked him that Girodias might be in line for a significant payout when he had been so slow with the initial *Lolita* royalties, and then did not bother to pay further monies Nabokov was owed. In the two years since *Lolita* first appeared in book form, he was desperate to reap the financial rewards—as well as to get the critical attention he deserved.

Lolita had been banned in France, excerpted in the *Anchor Review*, praised by the novelist Graham Greene, excoriated by the literary editor and critic John Gordon, and bought in droves by those willing to smuggle copies back into America. All manner of people benefited from *Lolita*, whether to praise or denounce it, but Vladimir Nabokov had hardly earned a dime for his years of creative labor.

Minton's letter augured a change in fortune. Nabokov

wrote back on September 7 to say Minton was free to negotiate with Olympia Press, though "I would have to give my approval to the final arrangements." Nabokov added a warning: "Mr. Girodias, the owner of Olympia, is a rather difficult person. I shall be delighted if you come to terms with him." Minton did not seem fazed by Girodias's unsavory reputation. Nor was the Putnam publisher perturbed by the prospect of defending *Lolita* all the way to the Supreme Court, if necessary, though he cautioned Nabokov that he could not make such a "blanket guarantee"—rather, he wrote that it was more prudent to "present the book in such a way as to minimize its chance of prosecution."

Minton also wondered whether *Lolita* could, in fact, fall into the public domain. He said as much when he met the author in Ithaca, braving a snowstorm to do so. Nabokov told Minton that he knew "at least three or four thousand copies" of the Olympia Press edition of *Lolita* had been sold in the United States. Minton explained, "I said to him, 'Don't ever open your mouth about that to anybody because if it ever became established your copyright wouldn't be worth *beans*.'"

Nabokov kept his mouth shut about these extra sales. He took more time to swallow his pride with respect to Girodias. Much as he wanted to be financially free of his former publisher—going so far as to declare the original contract null and void in light of Girodias's inability to abide by the terms—he agreed, grudgingly, with Minton that it was better to allow Girodias a stake in *Lolita*'s American publication so they could be sure to get the book out as soon as possible.

As Minton explained to him over the winter of 1958, publishing *Lolita* when interest was high would make it more likely that the courts would rule in Nabokov's favor: the many articles, vociferous discussion, and chatter would demonstrate this was a book of high literary merit, not low smut. Should Nabokov delay in publishing *Lolita* in America to resolve his dispute with Girodias, the favorable publicity could evaporate—and so would the potential for a great financial windfall, whatever a court of law might decide.

Nabokov saw Minton's logic. He wrote the publisher back in early February 1958 to agree to terms (including the 50/50 royalty split with Girodias, with each receiving 7.5 percent of the hardcover proceeds). Minton cabled Girodias on February 11 and received Nabokov's signed contract on March 1.

By the time of the novel's American publication date on August 18, 1958, it was clear to all, but most especially to Nabokov, that he was about to be vaulted from literary obscurity, and that *Lolita* was about to arrive with hurricane-level force.

VLADIMIR AND VÉRA NABOKOV left Ithaca on another road trip in the summer of 1958. Whether to fend off nerves or steel themselves for what was to come, the couple traveled more than eight thousand miles in search of butterflies. Nabokov had also decided to take a leave of absence from Cornell beginning in the fall because of all of the prepublication demands for *Lolita*. They returned to New York in early August, in time for a press reception at the Harvard Club. Véra recorded her impressions of the evening, and of her husband, in their shared Page-a-Day diary: "Vladimir was a tremendous success . . . amusing, brilliant, and—thank God—did not say what he thinks of some famous contemporaries."

On publication day, Minton sent the following telegram to the Nabokovs: "EVERYBODY TALKING OF LOLITA ON PUBLICATION DAY YESTERDAYS REVIEWS MAGNIFICENT AND NEW YORK TIMES BLAST THIS MORNING PROVIDED NECESSARY FUEL TO FLAME 300 REORDERS THIS

MORNING AND BOOK STORES REPORT EXCELLENT DEMAND CONGRATU-LATIONS."

Minton was referring to Elizabeth Janeway's rave review, which ran on Sunday, August 17, in the *New York Times Book Review*. She described the novel as "one of the funniest and one of the saddest books of the year" and declared that it was anything but pornographic: "I can think of few volumes more likely to quench the flames of lust than this exact and immediate description of its consequences." Janeway's positive reaction, plus the increased demand, would compensate for Orville Prescott's pan in the daily paper on publication day proper, August 18.

The reorder number from retailers zoomed up to 6,777 in the first four days after its publication. By the end of September, *Lolita* was atop the *New York Times* bestseller list, having sold more than eighty thousand copies. It remained at number one for the next seven weeks. Six months after ensuring *Lolita* would be published in America without legal hassle or copyright consequence, Nabokov and Minton's mutual investment was paying clear and major dividends. There were more riches in store for the Nabokovs. On Minton's recommendation, they retained Irving "Swifty" Lazar to sell film rights to *Lolita* to Stanley Kubrick for $150,000.

Véra was the one who kept track of it all, recording every bit of *Lolita*-related news in the months immediately preceding and following the novel's publication in the Page-a-Day diary. Nabokov, on the other hand, seemed "supremely indifferent—occupied with a new story" and with cataloging his summertime butterfly-hunting bounty. Or at least that was the guise he adopted, as described by his wife. As the deluge of letters, interview requests, and subsidiary rights inquiries streamed in, Nabokov wrote his sister: "[All this] ought to have happened thirty years ago. . . . I don't think I shall need to teach any more."

Nabokov proved correct. The indefinite leave of 1958 became permanent retirement from Cornell at the end of 1959, when he was sixty. *Lolita*'s success enabled his permanent break with the United States, though he would continue to insist, years after moving to the Montreux Palace hotel in Switzerland, that he might return. But Switzerland's advantageous tax laws were too much of a boon—as was a greater sense of control and privacy, as "Hurricane *Lolita*" grew stronger and louder. Now that Nabokov could afford to write full-time, thanks to his most American book, he could embark upon his next phase: as a literary celebrity in voluntary exile, as opposed to the peripatetic refugee. He would see the country that gave him shelter, sanctuary, and the source material for his most famous novel again only a handful of times.

Lolita moved far beyond the bestseller list to become a cultural and global phenomenon. The template was in place for generations of readers to be taken in by Humbert Humbert, forgetting that Dolores Haze was his victim, not his seducer.

At the time, no one noticed that *Lolita* was published in the United States on the sixth anniversary, to the day, of Sally's death. And no one made the connection between fictional nymphet and real girl for several more years.

TWENTY-SEVEN

Connecting Sally Horner
to Lolita

eter Welding was a young freelance reporter in 1963, still a few years shy of thirty. A Philadelphia native, he had already built up a solid series of bylines, mostly for music magazines like *Downbeat*. He was also a fledgling music producer, founding Testament Records that same year to issue old and new jazz, gospel, and blues recordings. Welding had moved to Chicago to further his producing career, but not before setting out to tell a story that unfolded across the river from his hometown.

Welding was born in 1935, two years earlier than Sally Horner; no doubt her kidnapping and rescue made a large impression on him as a teenager. Welding remembered reading of Sally's plight in his local newspapers, the *Philadelphia Inquirer* and the *Evening Bulletin*, and decided to examine the

Image accompanying Peter Welding's November 1963 article for Nugget.

parallels between Sally's story and *Lolita*. He zeroed in on the same parenthetical phrase that, decades later, first caught the attention of Nabokov scholar Alexander Dolinin and, then, me. He compared specific events that occurred in *Lolita* to what happened to Sally. The results were published in an unusual venue: the men's magazine *Nugget,* racier than *Esquire* or *GQ* but more prudent than *Playboy.*

Nugget had a knack for publishing stories with literary connections. It helped that its editor at the time was Seymour Krim, who was affiliated with the Beat Generation, hanging around with Jack Kerouac, Allen Ginsberg, and Neal Cassady, though unlike them, he never wrote poetry or fiction. Krim also embraced the New Journalism ethos while working at the *New York Herald Tribune* with future stars Tom Wolfe, Jimmy Breslin, and Dick Schaap. *Nugget,* under Krim's editorial guidance, featured stories and articles by Norman Mailer, James Baldwin, Otto Preminger, William Saroyan, Chester Himes, and Paddy Chayefsky—and that was just in 1963.

Despite shooting for high literary quality, *Nugget* wanted to reach a mass audience—though Krim and his staffers sabotaged their own efforts by failing to stick to a regular publishing schedule. Just five issues of *Nugget* appeared in 1963;

Nugget's frequency during Krim's editorial tenure might be best described as "bimonthly-ish." Welding's story, *"Lolita* Has a Secret—Shhh!" ran in the November issue.

The piece opened with a summary of both *Lolita* and Sally's abduction, which Welding had gleaned entirely from news reports in his hometown papers, the *Inquirer* and *Evening Bulletin*. He recounted the five-and-dime meet-up, La Salle's threat of juvenile incarceration if Sally didn't go along with his plan, the basic outlines of the twenty-one-month-long cross-country trip, Ruth Janisch's role as rescuer, and Sally's eventual recovery.*

After Welding finished with his summary, he declared that the Horner case and *Lolita* "parallel each other much too closely to be coincidental." Welding took particular note of Sally's fear of being sent to reform school, which he compared to Humbert's declaration, roughly halfway into the novel, that "the reformatory threat is the one I recall with the deepest moan of shame." And further:

". . . What happens if you complain to the police of my having kidnapped and raped you? . . . So I go to jail. Okay. I go to jail. But what happens to you, my orphan? . . . While I stand gripping the bars, you happy neglected child, will be given a choice of various dwelling places, all more or less the same, the correctional school, the reformatory, the juvenile detention home. . . ."

Welding also drew a comparison between Humbert marrying Charlotte Haze to gain access to Dolores and La Salle claiming

---

* Oddly, Welding referred to the girl as "Florence 'Sally' Ann Horner." It is a mystery why he gave her a middle name that was never reported and did not exist. The error continued to propagate, also cited by Alfred Appel, Jr., in *The Annotated Lolita*.

to be married to Sally's mother. Welding further speculated that the actions of Humbert's housekeeper at Beardsley, Mrs. Holigan, might be based on the actions of Ruth Janisch ("on the rare occasions where Holigan's presence happened to coincide with Lo's, simple Lo might succumb to buxom sympathy in the course of a cozy kitchen chat").

Finally, Welding arrived at his own smoking gun: that neon-light parenthetical late in *Lolita*: "in this single reference [Nabokov] has all the essentials—the full names, the ages of the pair, La Salle's occupation, the date of the abduction— neatly packaged in one sentence," which suggests thorough familiarity rather than casual knowledge.

Eventually Welding seemed to tire of the compare/ contrast—"More parallels could easily be shown, but to what further purpose?"—but he felt confident enough to conclude: "The plot line of *Lolita* derives in large measure from the case and is solidly based on actual fact. . . . The conclusion is almost inescapable: Nabokov has inserted the reference to the LaSalle-Horner story either as a conscious (or unconscious) acknowledgment of a primary source material, or as a shrewd maneuver to provide himself legal protection."

I'm not certain what Welding meant here. He didn't elaborate further in the piece, so I can't know for sure, but perhaps he believed, based on this statement, that lawyers, already made nervous by *Lolita*'s worldwide controversy, legal challenges, and publication bans, insisted Nabokov insert the reference to avoid an additional legal issue, such as a plagiarism charge.

Welding made several mistakes in his piece. First, he got Humbert's parenthetical comment wrong, suggesting that it was from the vantage point of Mrs. Chatfield, the mother of one of Lolita's classmates whom Humbert meets in a hotel lobby upon his return, after more than five years away, to Ramsdale. Still, Welding understood the importance of the Sally Horner aside decades before anyone else.

More baffling to me was his omission of Sally Horner's fate from the article. Was Welding unaware that Sally died in a car accident a decade earlier? Could the "shrewd maneuver" line have referred to possible grounds for Sally to sue, had she been alive? In omitting Sally's death, he missed an opportunity to compare her fate to Charlotte Haze's death by car accident. What was beyond Welding's grasp, though, was the direct proof Nabokov knew all about Sally Horner, since the transcribed and reworked wire report that is part of his archives at the Library of Congress was not available to the public in 1963.

Lastly, Welding theorized, with the careful, awkwardly worded hedge, that "it is not unlikely to suppose" that Nabokov did not begin to work on *Lolita* "until 1950, under the stimulus of the stories of the LaSalle-Horner case. All evidence, in fact, would seem to support this position." This is false, since Nabokov's own December 1953 diary entry, celebrating the completion of the manuscript after five years of work, refutes Welding. We also know this supposition is false thanks to the existence of *The Enchanter*.

However, 1950 was around the time Nabokov came close to junking what was still then called *The Kingdom by the Sea*. Welding was off base but his suppositions make sense: whenever Nabokov first learned of what happened to Sally Horner, that knowledge helped him to transform a partial manuscript primed for failure into the eventual, unlikely, staggering success of *Lolita*. If such knowledge was publicized, it would not look good for Nabokov—rightly or wrongly—to be seen as pilfering from a real girl's plight for his fictional masterpiece.

THE NOVEMBER 1963 ISSUE of *Nugget* came and went without much notice. It attracted nowhere near the attention of the release of the film version of *Lolita* a month later, or the millions of sales garnered by the novel to date. But one person did pay attention: a *New York Post* reporter named Alan Levin.

Levin eventually became an award-winning documentary filmmaker, working with his son, Marc, and with Bill Moyers, on films shown by PBS and HBO. But he cut his journalistic teeth for the Associated Press and then joined the *Post* in the late 1950s, where his reporting on organized crime garnered him a Pulitzer Prize nomination.

It's not clear whether Levin, thirty-seven at the time, found an advance copy of the November issue of *Nugget* on his own or if someone tipped him off. However he got ahold of Welding's story, Levin knew there was one of his own to write—could it be true that *Lolita* owed its plot to a sensational kidnapping? And if it was true, what would the great Vladimir Nabokov have to say on the matter?

Levin posted a letter to Nabokov on September 9, 1963, which arrived in Montreux, Switzerland, just four days later. The official Nabokov response, written and signed by Véra, reached Levin soon thereafter. Levin's story for the *Post*—"Nabokov Says 'Lolita' Is More Art Than Life"—ran on September 18, 1963, a day after Levin received Véra's letter.

The article began with a provocative lede: "Is it possible that Humbert Humbert was a 50-year-old Philadelphia auto mechanic and his nymphet, Lolita, an 11-year-old from Camden, NJ?" Levin quoted just enough of Véra's letter to make the Nabokov case plain, and enough of Welding's *Nugget* piece to answer the question. But it's helpful to read Véra's letter to Levin in full, as it offers a fascinating window into her (and

Nabokov's) thought process. Her response also carries an air of protesting too much:

> Montreux, September 13, 1963
> Palace Hotel
>
> Dear Mr. Levin,
>   My husband asks me to thank you for your letter of September 9. He has not seen the article in Nugget, which makes it difficult for him to answer your letter. At the time he was writing LOLITA he studied a considerable number of case histories ("real" stories) many of which have more affinities with the LOLITA plot than the one mentioned by Mr. Welding. The latter is mentioned also in the book LOLITA. It did not inspire the book. My husband wonders what importance could possibly be attached to the existence in "real" life of "actual rape abductions" when explaining the existence of an "invented" book. He is particularly curious as regards the meaning of Mr. Welding's statement about "a shrewd maneuver to provide himself legal protection." Legal protection against what?
>   Had he read Mr. Welding's article, my husband might have been able to give you more pertinent comment although he fails to see what importance that article could possibly have.
>   Sincerely yours,
>   (Mrs. Vladimir Nabokov)

Véra's letter showcases the many roles she played as "Mrs. Vladimir Nabokov": defender of her husband, curator of a singular line of vision about Nabokov's work that put his creative genius above everything else, and master obfuscator when presented with anything that dented the Nabokov myth. Véra, again, showed herself to be the consummate brand manager for Vladimir. Any speculation that *Lolita* could be inspired by a real-life case went against the single-minded Nabokovian belief that art supersedes influence, and so influence must be brushed off.

How the Nabokovs handled Levin's letter, and by extension Welding's article for *Nugget,* is a window into their maddening, contradictory behavior when anyone probed *Lolita*'s possible influences. They denied the importance of Sally Horner but acknowledged the parenthetical. They mentioned a "considerable number" of case histories, but only Sally's is described in the novel.

Véra's stubborn insistence that the Sally Horner story "did not inspire the book" is akin to trying to drown out a troublesome argument with the braying of one's own voice. Though it worked, since Levin did not push back—at least, not that we know of.

That Véra claimed the Nabokovs had not seen the *Nugget* piece is odd on several counts. First, the author's main archive at the New York Public Library contains over half a dozen boxes' worth of newspaper clippings about *Lolita,* starting from its original 1955 publication by Olympia Press through its American publication by Putnam in 1958, well into the 1960s and early 1970s. The Nabokovs subscribed to several clipping services based in New York and Paris. They seemed to have kept every review in every possible language they spoke or read—English, French, German, Italian, Russian—whether good or bad, critical or full of praise, defending its content or wishing the book banned from the earth.

There is also an entire box of clippings related to the *Lolita* film, beginning with who would be cast to play Dolores Haze. The Nabokovs even kept a copy of the August 1960 issue of *Cosmopolitan,* featuring Zsa Zsa Gabor, at the ripe old age of forty-three, dressed up as twelve-year-old Lolita in a straining baby-doll nightgown, an apple in her hands, licking her lips in equal parts faux-innocence and come-hither enticement. And other fashion and girlie mags from France and Italy, each with photo shoots of starlets garbed in Lolita-like frocks as a pictorial audition for a film part they desperately wanted to play.

It staggered me, this voluminous collection of *Lolita* ephemera. And yet, there was no sign of the relevant issue of *Nugget*. Compared to other periodicals collected and kept by the Nabokovs, *Nugget* was not so obscure. Its absence is telling because it is part of a larger absence in Nabokov's archives: any reference whatsoever to Sally Horner.

Véra Nabokov, in her letter to Al Levin, emphasized that Sally's abduction "did not inspire the book." Moreover, she insisted Nabokov "studied a considerable number of case histories . . . many of which have more affinities with the *Lolita* plot than the one mentioned by Mr. Welding." Even if that was true, the statement was disingenuous. For only two of the "considerable number of case histories" were explicitly mentioned in *Lolita:* the story of G. Edward Grammer, and the story of Sally Horner.

Nabokov must have had a reason to hold on to those two index cards and not burn them, as he had burned handwritten pages of the manuscript. He had been compelled to write notes on both cases, and in particular the death of Sally Horner. He included the parenthetical reference in the novel when he could have left out any mention altogether. Sally's story mattered to Nabokov because *Lolita* would not have been finished if he hadn't read of Sally's kidnapping.

The Nabokovs' behavior could, I suppose, be attributed as much to carelessness as willful obfuscation. Stacy Schiff, Véra's biographer, strongly advised against reading anything specific into Véra's blanket denial to Levin. Schiff told me that Véra's letter "reads like everything else [the Nabokovs said] about the primacy of art. It's a realm unto itself, and everything else is on some pedestrian or insignificant level." Véra, Schiff said, dismissed anything that could be perceived as a "mandarin influence on high art." The everyday needed to be discarded at the altar of creative imagination.

Except Vladimir and Véra were not careless people. His art, and her management and protection of his art, was all about command and control, about rejecting interpretations that did not fit with their vision. If art was to prevail—and for the Nabokovs, it always did—then explicitly revealing what lay behind the curtain of fiction in the form of a real-life case could shatter the illusion of total creative control.

Véra's denial by letter had to be definitive to make pesky tabloid reporters slink away without investigating the matter more deeply. Levin published his piece in the *Post,* but it was soon forgotten, setting the template for further neglect of the Sally Horner case. Andrew Field, in his 1967 critical biography *Nabokov: His Life in Art,* merely cited the parenthetical as "an actual case of a Philadelphia mechanic who took an eleven-year-old Camden girl to Atlantic City."

Alfred Appel, in his annotated *Lolita* published in 1970 (as well as in the revised 1991 version), dutifully footnoted the reference to her, but failed to mention Sally by name. Brian Boyd's definitive biography of Nabokov was better, noting "'a middle-aged morals offender' who abducted fifteen-year-old Sally Horner from New Jersey and kept her for twenty-one months as his 'cross-country slave'"—but misstated Sally's age at her abduction by four years.

Vladimir Nabokov's otherwise scrupulous archive of *Lolita*-related clippings failed to include anything about Sally Horner because if it had, then the dots would connect with more force, which would upset the carefully constructed myth of Nabokov, the sui generis artist, whose imagination and gifts were far superior to others'. It's as if he didn't trust *Lolita* to stand on its own against the real story of Sally Horner. As a result, Sally's plight was sanded over, all but forgotten.

TWENTY-EIGHT

"He Told Me Not to Tell"

Decades after Ruth Janisch gently coaxed Sally Horner to make the long-distance telephone call that freed her from Frank La Salle, Ruth was having tea with her daughter Rachel. After years of estrangement, Rachel had decided she wanted a closer relationship to her mother.

In Sally's story, Ruth was a heroine whose actions changed the course of a girl's life forever. But to her children, Ruth was a more complicated, infuriating, mercurial, manipulative creature, whose actions led to long estrangements. That troubling Ruth was not yet in full bloom in 1949 and 1950. Much of her aberrant behavior was still in the future. Rachel described her mother's life philosophy to me: Ruth would meet someone and say something along the lines of "Hello, my name is Ruth. What can you do for me?"

Years into adulthood, some of Ruth's children would make

peace with the woman she was. Yes, Ruth had done terrible things in the past. She had looked the other way when her children were abused, physically, emotionally, and sexually, by the men in her life, be they husbands or short-lived romantic partners. Ruth had, at times, enabled that abuse by not believing her children and choosing, instead, to believe the men. One of them ended up as Rachel's first and only husband.

Ruth was working at a bus station in the Bay Area at that time, around the early 1960s. One of her coworkers had two sons, whom Ruth decided must meet her daughters. Ruth wanted the older boy for herself, but she thought the younger one, still a teenager, would be perfect for Rachel. Instead, the younger boy expressed no interest, and the older one gravitated toward Rachel in a way that made her wonder, much later, if there was something more calculated at play.

Rachel grew certain that her mother had made some sordid arrangement with the older boy. That in order for him to have access to Rachel, he had to have some romantic involvement with her mother. Ruth also goaded her daughter about him at the time, saying she couldn't possibly land a man like him. Rachel would not grasp the impact of her mother's verbal abuse for years. Then, she thought Ruth's behavior was normal.

Rachel did "land" the boy, became pregnant, and she then married him in haste and moved away from home. Seventeen years, three children, numerous moves, and countless beatings, rapes, and threats to her life later, Rachel managed to break free. "It was less a marriage than extended captivity," she said. When she dared to speak up for herself, her husband punished her. He repeated the pattern she knew too well from childhood, when confessing that something hurt her caused more hurt, psychologically from Ruth and physically from her husbands or partners.

Once Rachel's divorce was final, in the late 1970s, she

found a job near where her mother lived. She also thought about what kind of relationship she wanted with Ruth. Because Rachel, despite the past, *liked* her mother. They shared a love of gardening and of books. As adult women, they could converse, if not as equals then at least on a similar plane. Rachel decided she could handle visiting Ruth at least once a week for tea. The visits were calm at first. She felt herself understanding her mother better. She felt she had enough emotional distance to appreciate Ruth, the woman, and leave the baggage of neglect and abuse behind.

What Rachel created in this new relationship with her mother was a cocoon where old wounds could be erased. But the cocoon turned out to be an illusion. That it broke apart, Rachel realized, should not have surprised her as it did.

One afternoon, Rachel turned up at Ruth's house and found her mother immersed in her scrapbooks. They were a living testament to Ruth's belief that she mattered. Subsequent visits by Rachel and other daughters led to them discovering that the scrapbooks contained items Ruth had no business possessing, items she had pilfered from her children without their immediate knowledge, but Rachel wasn't aware of that yet. As mother and daughter sat for tea, one scrapbook lay between them. The one Ruth had been working on earlier that morning.

Lying next to the scrapbook was an old paperback novel that Rachel didn't recognize.

Ruth pointed to a newspaper clipping in the scrapbook. "Do you remember this little girl?" Ruth moved her finger to the headline. "Do you remember that girl, Sally Horner?"

"I do remember," said Rachel.

"And do you remember Frank La Salle, the man who kidnapped her?"

"I do remember," Rachel said again.

Rachel told me that she felt herself grow cold. But Ruth did not notice, or even understand, her daughter's reaction.

"Wasn't that quite the story?" Ruth carried on. "They're mentioned in this novel, *Lolita*!"

Rachel hadn't heard this story before. She would hear a different version of it years later from her sister Vanessa, who had read the novel—that same tattered paperback—at Ruth's insistence. Vanessa, sixteen at the time, was puzzled at first at her mother's insistence she read the novel. Then Ruth explained: "*Lolita* tells the story of a girl named Sally Horner. A girl who died just before you were born. A girl I helped rescue from a man named Frank La Salle." This was no mere novel, but literary validation of Ruth's sense of self, that her single act of decency had larger heroic meaning. Vanessa couldn't help but read *Lolita* with her mother's words echoing in her head. But she also couldn't read it without thinking of the ways in which Ruth had wronged the family.

Staring at the scrapbook, Rachel knew she had to speak up now or she would never be able to say the words again.

"Mom, there's something I need to tell you. Something I never told you. Frank La Salle didn't only molest Sally. He also molested me."

ONE AFTERNOON while Sally Horner was at school, Frank La Salle invited Rachel over to his trailer. At age five, Rachel wore her white-blond hair in pigtails, a ribbon adorning the left plait. She put on her favorite striped black-and-white dress every chance she got. One portrait of Rachel from that time depicts her as the ideal of innocence. Her smile is trusting, guileless. Her expression is pliant, hinting at a gullible streak that would plague her repeatedly in adulthood.

She might have been by herself, or with one of her sisters. What she most recalled was that Frank was nice to her. He seemed to understand what Rachel wanted. That she saw what Sally had—toys, games, a father's love—and didn't have them. Not the toys. Not the games. And her father, George, was a remote presence, more comfortable with adults than with his children.

Of all the things Sally possessed, what interested Rachel most were her crayons and coloring books. They reminded Rachel of an earlier stay at a Minnesota hospital when she was three, quarantined for months with rheumatic fever. She went to school at the hospital because she wasn't allowed to go home. There were troubles, both at home and in the hospital, the kind so traumatizing Rachel would not remember them for decades without the trigger of unexpected smells and brief image flashes. But what came back to her now was the memory of her parents visiting with big smiles and good cheer, and of learning how to draw with crayons.

Frank made Rachel a deal: She could play with anything of Sally's. Anything at all. But she had to do favors for him first.

"Essentially, what he wanted from me was to give him a blow job," Rachel said. "So I did."

Rachel remembered a single incident. There may have been others that she blocked out. She didn't remember it until after she was married, and her husband wanted the same thing. The sexual act seemed disgusting to the newly married Rachel, and it would take her years to learn it flowed from normal, healthy desire.

She only realized the enormity of what Frank had done to her when she stumbled across a pamphlet at the local library, long after the end of her marriage. The pamphlet was about child molestation. Its title: "He Told Me Not to Tell."

Frank La Salle had told Rachel not to tell. But Rachel would have stayed silent regardless. The girl's earlier hospital experience taught her not to trust adults. They could abandon you for months. They could leave you alone and never tell you when you might come home. And when you did come home, you didn't know what awaited. Whether it was a safe haven or a recurring nightmare.

While telling the story to me nearly forty years after the fact, Rachel would recall that when she told her mother what La Salle had done, a barrier went up right away between herself and Ruth. Like an electrified fence where venturing too close might lead to a surprise shock. She felt her mother shut down. Rachel decided to change the subject to safer territory. She had taken a risk and it did not work. When that happened, as it had so many times in her past, the best thing to do was to be like a turtle. Retreat within the shell and never reveal your vulnerable self again.

Afterwards, she and Ruth would never be as close. (There would be other visits, including a reunion of all but one of Ruth's children in 1998, six years before Ruth died.) Rachel sensed her mother must have known, on some level, why there was a new breach between them. Perhaps, Rachel theorized, her mother had helped Sally Horner because she knew she could not save her own children from nearby monsters. But letting her thoughts run in this direction was too much for Rachel. She suspected Ruth never allowed herself to contemplate her complicity in the damage done to her own children.

No wonder Ruth acted as if the conversation never happened. The subject never came up between them again. Neither did *Lolita*.

TWENTY-NINE

Aftermaths

S ally Horner's premature death cast a pall on the lives of those who knew her best and loved her most. Ella, who did not display much of her inner turmoil while Sally lived, buried it completely after her daughter's death. She could not think of another way to handle it besides burying her emotions, but at least she did not have to bear her grief alone. The Panaros remained nearby. Ella could watch her granddaughter, Diana, grow up.

A year before Sally died, Ella had connected with a new partner: Arthur Burkett, a Camden native five years her junior, who moved into 944 Linden Street. They decamped for Pennsauken, five miles away, within a year of the car accident that killed Sally, and in the early 1960s migrated west to Palo Alto, California—less than an hour's drive away from the San Jose trailer park where Sally had been rescued. Burkett found work as a groundsman for a local college, and Ella and Ott, as he was called, made their union legal in January 1965.

Five years later, Burkett was dead. His tractor had overturned on him as he cut grass on a steep hill on the college grounds. While he was recuperating from the accident, doctors discovered he had gastric cancer, which had already spread to his liver. Without any other ties to Palo Alto, after he died Ella returned to New Jersey to be closer to her family.

When she visited her family, she never spoke of what happened to Sally. She didn't speak much of the past at all. There didn't seem to be much purpose in revisiting painful memories with a generation that hadn't been born when the worst had happened. Ella preferred to play cards—gin rummy was a favorite—or talk about what books she liked to read. Mystery novels, in particular.

Ella's silence about what happened to her younger daughter carried over to the next generation. Diana didn't learn the truth that her dead aunt Sally had been kidnapped until she was in her teens. She didn't remember the exact details of the conversation she had with her father about Sally, but she recalled it didn't last long. A mere recounting of the basic facts: that before her aunt died, she had been taken by a stranger posing as her father. The rest was left up to Diana's imagination.

Diana was only four years old when Sally died. Her parents were chiefly concerned with making sure their daughter had a happy childhood, and hiding their hurt, however deep the wounds ran. Just as Susan didn't speak much about her younger sister, neither did Al speak of his experiences in World War II. It seemed easier to keep the past behind a locked door and to keep silent on family tragedy.

"I still can't believe something like this happened in my family," Diana told me. "I never got to know my aunt Sally. I also wish I could have been able to support my mom during that awful period."

By this point, the Panaros had had a son, Brian, born in 1968, twenty years after Diana. Susan and Al had given up on the greenhouse well before Brian's birth (a surprise pregnancy after several additional miscarriages made the likelihood of another child seem all the more remote). They had also left New Jersey for South Carolina, with Ella joining them for a time, though they would return to their home state in the mid-1970s. Susan became a full-time homemaker. She spent ample time gardening—for pleasure, not for income—volunteering with her church, and with her family.

When the Panaros returned to New Jersey, Ella settled back in New Egypt, where she had spent much of her childhood and early motherhood. She then moved to a nursing home in Pemberton, where she died in 1998 at the age of ninety-one. Susan died in 2012, and Al passed away in February 2016.

"DID YOU SAY THAT SALLY HORNER was the inspiration for *Lolita?*" Carol Starts said at the beginning of our first conversation in December 2016, once I'd explained why I was calling her out of the blue. Her incredulity was palpable. So, too, was her admiration for her long-deceased best friend.

"I was so unbelievably impressed by her. Sally taught me a great deal. After she was gone, I went through modeling classes to be a 'lady.' Because that's the way Sally was. I wanted to be like her. So I was. I went through those classes, how to walk and sit and stand and so forth. I paid attention to actions, movements, how to dress, and thoroughly enjoyed it because I could be just like Sally. I was on the wrong side of the tracks. I didn't have much mentorship prior to her."

The strong impression Sally made endured for Carol's entire life. She left Camden for California at eighteen to marry her first husband. She kept his last name of Taylor—she was glad to shed her maiden name, which had caused her no end of teasing at school—married and divorced three more times, and had four children. Carol died on October 30, 2017, in Melbourne, Florida, where she lived with one of her daughters. She was eighty years old.

EDWARD BAKER GOT ON with his life after the accident that killed Sally. He was drafted into the army in the summer of 1954 and spent more than eight months at Schweinfurt, Germany, where he celebrated his twenty-third birthday. Upon returning to Vineland, he married, had a son he named Edward Jr., and worked as a machinist, with side interests in riding and fixing motorcycles and watching NASCAR. Both father and son volunteered substantial amounts of time with the local YMCA. But several years before Edward Baker's death in 2014, fate had another twist in store for him.

On the afternoon of Wednesday, May 17, 2007, his son fell asleep in his Mercury Grand Marquis. The car crossed the middle lane and into the median, then careened along the shoulder of Route 55, slamming into a tree. Just as Sally Horner had, fifty-five years earlier, Edward Baker, Jr., died instantly.

THE TWO CAMDEN POLICE DETECTIVES involved with Sally Horner's rescue, Marshall Thompson and Wilfred Dube, both retired in the mid-1960s. Dube had risen to become chief of detectives; Thompson remained a detective until his sixtieth birthday. Dube died in 1980; Thompson in 1982. Howard Hornbuckle served one more term as Santa Clara County sheriff, and retired to work as a dairy farm sales representative. He died in 1962.

MITCHELL COHEN'S HEALTH suffered after the Sally Horner case concluded. Her rescue, and Frank La Salle's imprisonment, took place only a few months after Howard Unruh's massacre, an exhausting one-two combination for the Camden County prosecutor. Cohen spent three days in the hospital at the end of August 1950. Doctors ordered him to take a rest from his work; he took their advice and left Camden for a week in the White Mountains of New Hampshire.

Upon his return, and over the next eight years, there were more major crimes for Cohen to prosecute, including the ones resulting in the 1955 execution of three men for murdering a luncheonette owner during a botched robbery. Then came his next career move, when the new New Jersey governor at the time, Robert B. Meyner, appointed Cohen as Camden County Court judge. In doing so the governor displaced Rocco Palese, the judge who had sentenced Frank La Salle to prison. Controversy ensued in the form of a letter-writing campaign and newspaper editorials, but Palese eventually acquiesced and moved into private practice. (He died in 1987 at the age of ninety-three.)

Cohen served three years on the county court bench before moving over to the appeals court for a year. He was then appointed a federal court judge by President Kennedy in 1962, and he stayed on the bench for the rest of his life. Cohen died in 1991, at eighty-six.

AS *LOLITA* BEGAN its climb up the bestseller charts, Véra Nabokov continued what had become a custom for her since May 20, 1958: jotting down her private thoughts in the diary that had previously been the sole property of her husband. Véra's notes largely indicate delight at *Lolita*'s success, but one subject bothered her above all: the way that public reception, and critical assessments, seemed to forget that there was a little girl at the center of the novel, and that she deserved more attention and care:

> I wish someone would notice the tender description of the child's helplessness, her pathetic dependence upon the monstrous HH, and her heartrending courage all along, culminating in that squalid but essentially pure and healthy marriage, and her letter, and her dog. And that terrible expression on her face when she had been cheated by HH out of some little pleasure that had been promised. They all miss the fact that the "horrid little brat" Lolita is essentially very good indeed—or she would not have straightened out after being crushed so terribly, and found a decent life with poor Dick more to her liking than the other kind.

Véra, of course, did not intend her thoughts for publication, and Vladimir Nabokov did not express these thoughts in public, either. *Lolita*'s success almost seemed designed so people missed the point. Its original publication by Olympia Press established its bona fides as a book too controversial for American consumption. And then, once it was finally published in the United States, the conversation centered around Humbert Humbert's desires and his "love story" with Dolores

Haze, with few acknowledging, or even comprehending, that their relationship was an abuse of power.

As a result, that left a vacuum for decades of readers to misinterpret *Lolita*. It allowed for a culture of teen-temptress vamping that did not account for the victimization at the novel's core. Sixty years on, many readers still don't see through Humbert Humbert's vile perversions, and still blame Dolores Haze for her behavior, as if she had the will to resist, and chose not to.

LATER IN THE YEAR, Véra wrote in her diary about a strange evening that foreshadowed all the ways in which *Lolita* would be viewed as grim comedy instead of the moral indictment she'd hoped for. On November 26, 1958, Vladimir and Véra Nabokov went out to dinner at Cafe Chambord on Third Avenue and Forty-Ninth Street. The other dinner guests included Walter Minton and his wife, Polly, as well as Victor Schaller, Putnam's head of finance, and his wife. The mood should have been celebratory in light of *Lolita*'s increasing success. It was not, as Véra later wrote in great detail, because the Mintons were unduly preoccupied with a *Time* magazine article published the previous week.

The article, unbylined but written by staff writer and future *Los Angeles Times* gossip columnist Joyce Haber, was ostensibly about the public reception of *Lolita*. Haber opened with an account of Nabokov at a Putnam-sponsored reception for the novel, where he, according to Haber, "faced a formidable force of 1,000 literature-loving women." After quickly dispensing with the positive and negative critical reception for *Lolita*, Haber let loose on Rosemary Ridgewell, the showgirl-turned-literary-scout, with carefully calibrated bile.

Haber described Ridgewell as "a superannuated (27)

nymphet . . . a tall (5 ft. 8 in.) slithery-blithery onetime Latin Quarter showgirl who wears a gold swizzle stick around her neck and a bubbly smile on her face. Well may she bubble." Ridgewell merited Haber's attention for tipping off Minton to *Lolita*'s existence after reading excerpts in the *Anchor Review*. But the cause of Haber's ire was that she and Ridgewell were Walter Minton's mistresses at the same time. No wonder she felt compelled to douse her rival in the prose equivalent of hydrochloric acid.

Véra Nabokov would learn some of these details at the Cafe Chambord dinner, where she sat next to Walter Minton's wife, Polly. The younger woman—"a pretty girl, rather unhappy"— immediately began to unburden herself to Véra, whom she'd never met. The "frightened, bewildered" Polly looked upon *Lolita* as a source of pain and problems in her marriage to Walter. Where once the couple was happy, Polly confided, since the novel's arrival in their lives her husband "began to see a lot of people and get mixed up."

Polly let slip to Véra that she first learned of her husband's involvement with Ridgewell through the "horrid" *Time* article. Véra was, apparently, unnerved by Polly's confession, but had the wherewithal to observe in her diary: "Poor Polly, small-town little girl, craving for so many pounds of 'culture' gift-boxed and tied with a nice pink bow!" Véra did not know Rosemary, but based on what Polly told her and the *Time* article, she judged her as "a pretty awful, vulgar but flashy young female."

Odd as this encounter was for Véra, the evening devolved further. After Victor Schaller and his wife bid the Nabokovs and the Mintons adieu, Dmitri turned up, driving his 1957 MG sports car. Polly, enthralled, requested a ride, and Dmitri obliged. Vladimir and Véra took a cab to their hotel, accompanied by Minton, who proceeded—within earshot of the driver, and perhaps unprompted—to admit his affairs with both Ridgewell and Haber.

"Between his two little harlots," Véra wrote, "M[inton] ruined his family life." Minton swore both affairs were over, that he had "made it up to Polly," and presented Rosemary "in a very unsavory light, a little courtesan, almost a 'call girl,' trying to collect as much money as she could from Walter and spouting nonsense about *Lolita*."

When the trio arrived at the hotel, Polly and Dmitri were still MIA. The Nabokovs and Minton "waited and waited," Véra recording this phrase and then crossing it out. When the duo finally appeared in the hotel lobby, Dmitri informed his parents "with a sly smile" that he and Polly had driven to his apartment, because she had wished to see it. The next day, Véra wrote, "Minton told V., 'I hear Dmitri gave Polly a good time last night.'" Véra did not know what to make of Minton's comment. "I wonder if this sort of thing is normal or typical of today's America? A bad novel by some O'Hara or Cozens [*sic*] suddenly come to life."

The dark comedy of the evening did indeed resemble a John O'Hara story or James Gould Cozzens's *By Love Possessed*, which had been a bestseller the year before. What Véra Nabokov witnessed, and grew so disturbed by that she was compelled to write about it in her diary, seemed like a harbinger of all the ways in which American culture would corrupt *Lolita* and misunderstand Nabokov's meaning. If those closest to the Nabokovs were behaving strangely, who else might this novel have the power to corrupt?

LOLITA WAS A PROPER HIT. The more the novel sold, the more people ventured an opinion, whether they had read it or not.

Comedians turned *Lolita* into late-night fodder (Groucho Marx: "I'll put off reading *Lolita* for six more years until she turns eighteen"; Milton Berle: "First of all, let me congratulate Lolita now. She is thirteen"), another signal of *Lolita* reaching a level of success far beyond literary spheres.

Nabokov enjoyed the attention. He gave interviews to journalists and appeared on talk shows on both sides of the Atlantic. A cartoon featuring *Lolita* in the July 1959 issue of *Playboy* amused him enough that he mentioned it to his American publisher, and Véra noted in her diary how she and Vladimir delighted in the jokes broadcast on television.

Lolita's appeal extended to fashion magazines and film, with dissonant, even bizarre results. These depictions were largely knowing, winking parodies, playing up the overt sexuality of certain blond bombshell personas in the guise of younger girls. The most blatant reference to Nabokov's creation, equal parts amusing and disturbing, appeared in the film *Let's Make Love*, which features Marilyn Monroe singing a version of Cole Porter's "My Heart Belongs to Daddy" after announcing: "My name . . . is Lolita. And I'm . . . not supposed to . . . play . . . with boys!"

Another bizarre stunt affected the Nabokovs more personally. Their son, Dmitri, had moved to Milan to pursue an opera-singing career. But it was getting access to his famous father that left Dmitri open to strange requests. A local magazine covinced him to judge a contest where the winner would pose as Lolita for a fashion shoot to be held at his own apartment. Dmitri, reflecting on his youthful stupidity, recalled that the "decidedly post-pubescent aspiring nymphets, some with provincial mothers in tow," had invaded his apartment for two solid days.

Newspaper coverage of the contest reached Dmitri's father,

who was upset enough to send a telegram to his son asking for the contest to be stopped. "The publicity is in very bad taste," Nabokov wrote Dmitri on October 7, 1960. "It can only harm you in the eyes of those who take music seriously. It has already harmed me: because of it I cannot come to Italy since the reporters would immediately pounce on me there." Nabokov was especially disappointed in Dmitri for letting "this unhealthy ruckus" overshadow his own career. Dmitri learned his lesson. From that point on, he would defend *Lolita*'s honor rather than corrupt it. But the contest mess was further proof of the ways in which perceptions of *Lolita* moved from tragedy to carnival.

BY THIS POINT Nabokov had completed a screenplay draft of *Lolita* for Stanley Kubrick. Nabokov had initially turned it down—"by nature I am no dramatist, I am not even a hack scenarist"—but while on an extended European vacation at the end of 1959 and the beginning of 1960, he relented. On January 28, temporarily ensconced in Menton, France, Nabokov wrote his friend Morris Bishop that he changed his mind about adapting *Lolita* because "a pleasing and elegant solution of the problems involved suddenly dawned on me in the gardens of Taormina."

Contract from Kubrick and his producing partner, James Harris, in hand, the Nabokovs ventured west to Los Angeles, arriving in March. Vladimir holed up for the next few months to complete the screenplay. The first draft, finished in August 1960, ran more than four hundred pages long. That draft was not used, and neither were subsequent ones Nabokov wrote before he and Véra sailed back to Europe in November. Kubrick rewrote the screenplay substantially before shooting the film the following year, though Nabokov was still given sole screenplay credit when the film was released in 1962 and he was sub-sequently nominated for an Academy Award.

What most surprised me about the original *Lolita* screen-play draft, which I read at the Berg archives of the New York Public Library, were two names that appeared in a second-half scene that did not survive in the film version, or in Nabokov's published screenplay in 1973. The names are perhaps coinci-dental, but they didn't seem that way to me. It felt more like unfinished business; that Nabokov was not through mining Sally's kidnapping for his creative pursuits.

In the scene, Humbert Humbert mentions a "Gabriel Goff," who is the subject of a gala in Elphinstone. "Goff, a black-bearded railway robber, held up his last train in 1888, not to rob it but to kidnap a theatrical company for his and his gang's en-tertainment. The stones in Elphinstone are full of Goff faces, bearded pink masks, and all the men have grown more or less luxuriant whiskers." Goff happened to be the maiden name of Sally Horner's mother, Ella.

Later in the scene, Nabokov makes a repeated reference to a "Dr. Fogg," a doctor deemed to be the best to treat Dolores's illness. It turns out "Fogg" is a disguise for Clare Quilty, who uses that alias but arrives on the scene wearing the mask of the railway robber, Gabriel Goff. Fogg, of course, was an early alias of Frank La Salle.

I could chalk up the use of these names to Nabokov's merry-trickster side, noting that "Goff" and "Fogg" are inversions of each other. The presence of doubles and masks certainly bol-sters this theory. But because the Sally Horner parenthetical reference was excised from the film script—there was no rea-son to preserve a textual reference for a visual medium, after all—this name-inversion trick read to me as if Nabokov wanted to preserve the link to Sally's story in some fashion.

JAMES MASON SIGNED ON as Humbert Humbert, while Peter Sellers and Shelley Winters were cast as Clare Quilty and Charlotte Haze, respectively. The final piece of the *Lolita* film puzzle was choosing the girl to play Dolores Haze, a search avidly covered by newspapers and magazines around the world. One gossip item speculated that Mason's eleven-year-old daughter, Portland, might be cast. Tuesday Weld, already an established television and film star at seventeen, was a serious contender, much to Nabokov's chagrin ("a graceful ingenue but not my idea of Lolita"), but she declined the role, famously saying, "I didn't have to play Lolita. I *was* Lolita."

When Sue Lyon, age fourteen, was ultimately cast, it was with Nabokov's enthusiastic approval. He did not want a girl so near to Lolita's true age for the film, and he agreed with Kubrick that a girl who looked closer to sixteen, as Lyon did, would circumvent the censors. *Lolita* could not go forward with an "X" rating, or worse, no rating at all. When Lyon began shooting *Lolita* in 1961, European newspapers followed her around taking photographs of her on set, buying food, or taking a nap. Typical paparazzi behavior, but it seemed that much more invasive because they were chasing a teenager playing the love interest of a much older man.

However Kubrick, as director, and Nabokov, as author, envisioned the reception of *Lolita* the film upon its release in the summer of 1962, they were disappointed. The infamous Bert Stern photograph of Lyon, sucking on a lollipop and wearing heart-shaped glasses, shaped public perception. So did the tagline "How Did They Ever Make a Movie of *Lolita*?" which caused a number of critics to answer: they didn't. Lyon was too old, unconvincing save for the scenes where she has transformed into the pregnant Mrs. Dick Schiller. Kubrick blamed the censors for his creative misfire. Nabokov, more generously, judged Kubrick's vision "a first-rate film with magnificent actors." While the movie did all right at the box office—$9.25 million grossed on a $2 million budget—the critical reception cast a pall.

As time went on, *Lolita* was adapted repeatedly—again as a 1997 film, as a 1981 play by Edward Albee, as a 1990s Russian-language opera, and even as a musical. The history of these adaptations, nearly all by middle-aged men, indicate how far out of touch they were from the novel's core depiction of sexual abuse. Reading *Lolita* allowed people to make their own judgments, rightly or wrongly. Seeing or hearing her sing, dance, or speak provoked far more uncomfortable responses, which led to a host of failed projects. That anyone, let alone those with a financial stake, could think visual and theatrical depictions of *Lolita* would be successful seems laughable in hindsight.

The most ludicrous idea was *Lolita, My Love,* the 1971 musical version. And yet it boasted an A-list group of creators, with lyrics and libretto by Alan Jay Lerner, who wrote the smash hit *My Fair Lady,* and a score by John Barry (of James Bond theme fame). Nabokov, who could hardly abide music, gave his approval for the musical because even he was aware of Lerner's and Barry's past successes. But the result never reached Broadway. Savage reviews of the original Boston production closed it down in early 1971, and a revived version staged in Philadelphia a couple of months later—starring future *Willy Wonka & the Chocolate Factory* star Denise Nickerson, not yet thirteen, as Dolores—yielded more disappointing notices. Nabokov had once told a disapproving interviewer that *Lolita, My Love* was "in the best of hands." Once the musical failed, he never spoke of it again.

Lolita also spawned unauthorized sequels that, in different ways, demonstrated Nabokov's mastery of difficult material, which suffered in the hands of far less talented writers. *The*

Lolita Complex, published in 1966 by an ex-con named Russell Trainer, purported to "investigate the activities of real-life Lolitas and Humberts and offers insights into an important social problem" through "case histories, professional opinions, court transcripts, interviews and police records." Trainer even thanked several of these medical professionals by name, but I could not verify that any of them existed. They are likely as fictitious as Nabokov's invented John Ray, Jr., who supplied the parodic introduction to Humbert Humbert's memoirs. Nabokov not only drew from Havelock Ellis's history of sexual deviants, but also reacted to the pervasive influence of Sigmund Freud—whose psychoanalytic theories he detested. "I think he's crude. I think he's medieval, and I don't want an elderly gentleman from Vienna with an umbrella inflicting his dreams upon me," Nabokov huffed in a 1965 interview.

The Lolita Complex was a crude cash-in, written by a veteran writer from the paperback porn mills who began his career while in prison for check fraud. Trainer's book did enough business for him to write a 1969 sequel, *The Male Lolita*, in which the faux–case history format shifted focus to young boys in power-imbalanced relationships with women. And Trainer's literary contributions might have stayed forgotten save for an improbable twist: in its Japanese translation, *The Lolita Complex* became a foundational text for the development of manga and anime, particularly the "lolicon" subgenre where little girls with big doe eyes are depicted as objects of desire and in explicit sexual situations. ("Lolicon" is a portmanteau of "Lolita Complex.")

Thirty years after *The Lolita Complex*, another unauthorized sequel took a different approach, retelling *Lolita* from Dolores Haze's perspective. *Lo's Diary*, by the Italian journalist Pia Pera, proved to be a missed opportunity. Instead of getting at the truth of Dolores Haze's dark plight, of showing her the way even Nabokov hinted at—as a clear victim, struggling to survive and maintain some sort of agency when she could never have enough power—Pera's version of Lolita depicted her as a brazen seductress, her behavior more reminiscent of Veda, the young (but not underage) daughter in James M. Cain's *Mildred Pierce*. *Lo's Diary* also suffered from years of litigation with the Nabokov estate, which blocked its publication in English until 1999.

Two years earlier, Adrian Lyne's film remake of *Lolita* arrived out of its own legal quagmire, having faced almost as many censorship issues as did Stanley Kubrick's. Lyne's film, scripted by Stephen Schiff, is quite faithful to Nabokov's novel. Jeremy Irons is almost too perfectly cast as Humbert Humbert (he later lent his voice to the audiobook edition of the novel issued on *Lolita*'s fiftieth anniversary). Dominique Swain is starkly believable as Dolores, holding her own against Irons's all-encompassing talent, and Frank Langella shines as Clare Quilty.

The cultural climate had shifted back and forth between liberal progressiveness and conservative backlash in the intervening thirty-five years, but in 1997 the appetite for a new film version was particularly low. Lyne had tried and failed to make the film for years. Once he had finally finished shooting, he faced fresh legal issues, after the passage of the Child Pornography Prevention Act of 1996, which made illegal any visual depictions of children having sex with adults—whether or not a child was involved.

Lyne battled lawyers seeking significant cuts to the film and struggled to find a distributor, which delayed *Lolita*'s opening in North American theaters by more than a year. The theatrical run was tiny (to qualify for the Academy Awards) and a prelude to an airing on the cable television network Show-time. This *Lolita,* as a result, did even poorer box office business than its predecessor. Once more, the general public did not have much appetite for seeing *Lolita* on-screen, as opposed to imagining her within the covers of a book.

More than sixty years on, the appetite for adapting *Lolita* or reviving earlier adaptations has likely subsided for good. It is difficult to see how it could be done, especially given the growing polarization of the political climate. The dark heart of *Lolita,* and the tragedy of Dolores Haze, may now be too much to transform into entertainment. It's wiser, and saner, to remember the little girl at the center of the novel, and all of the real girls, like Sally Horner, who suffered and survived.

On Two Girls Named
Lolita and Sally

oth times I met with Sally Horner's niece, Diana Chiemingo, she picked me up at the Burlington Towne
Center light rail station in New Jersey and drove us a
mile down the road to Amy's Omelette House, which does, in
fact, specialize in omelets. Diana turned seventy in August
2018. Her figure is slight and her voice does not carry, but both
convey a steely toughness. She gets to a point quickly and is not
prone to running on. Silences often stretched between us as
she considered how to phrase her answers in just the right way.

Sally is never far from her niece's thoughts. It was particularly apparent in our first face-to-face meeting in the summer
of 2016. Each of us arrived at the diner with photos to show the

other. Diana brought a stack of black-and-white images of Sally, Susan, Al, Ella, and others—her best friend, Carol, Sally's unidentified date for the evening social, probable classmates at Burrough Junior High, possible acquaintances from her last summer. Both Diana and I marveled at what a fully grown, vibrant girl Sally appeared to be. A vibrancy that had so little time to assert itself.

Then it was my turn. My photos—grainy images scanned from the *Courier-Post* coverage of Sally's rescue—were nowhere near in as good condition as Diana's trove. But I knew she needed to see the one of her, not quite two, sitting with her parents as Susan speaks to Sally on the telephone, hours after her younger sister's rescue in San Jose. Diana was startled by the photograph—she had never seen it before. Seeing her and her family all together, so long ago, made Sally's story feel fresher, more vivid. The tragic parts, but also the happier parts. Sally had come home and was part of their family again, even if it wasn't for very long.

Diana spoke of her parents, of her grandmother Ella, of her own life. The family tried to hold Sally's abrupt loss at bay with mixed results. She became, and remained, the family phantom. For a long time, Diana had no inkling of the *Lolita* connection. She'd never read the novel, so of course she would not have seen the reference to her aunt in the text. She learned of the connection when her brother, Brian, a police department evidence technician in Florence, searched online and discovered Sally's sparse Wikipedia entry as well as the essay by Alexander Dolinin.

"He was shocked," Diana told me. "I was, too. I don't know how to explain it. To think that someone is writing about your family? I was so young when everything happened, and for people to be writing about Sally—that's a really big thing."

By our second face-to-face meeting, nearly a year later, Diana had had more time to sit with the idea that Sally's story was part of a larger mosaic of girls and women who had been cruelly wronged and abused by men. Stigmas take a long time to fade. But the more Diana talked about her aunt, the more the relief, and even the joy, showed through to compensate for what she, her family, and Sally had lost.

LOLITA'S POST-PUBLICATION afterlife meant that years later, Vladimir Nabokov was still being asked about the novel, again and again, in interviews. He did not like this. The irritation is evident, leading to contradictory responses about what influenced him. He denied Humbert Humbert had a real-life basis, despite his repeated chess matches with Henry Lanz at Stanford, or his reading of Havelock Ellis: "He's a man I devised, a man with an obsession, and I think many of my characters have sudden obsessions, different kinds of obsessions; but he never existed." He denied Lolita was based upon a real girl, despite the parenthetical mention of Sally Horner. He denied any moral agenda, telling the *Paris Review:* "it is not *my* sense of the immorality of the . . . relationship that is strong; it is Humbert's sense. *He* cares, I do not. *I* do not give a damn for public morals, in America or elsewhere."

To admit he pilfered from a true story would be, in Nabokov's mind, to take away from the power of his narrative. To diminish the authority of his own art. The controlled nature of these interactions, with questions submitted in advance and responses edited after the fact, still left room for surprises— all the more because, as was customary with Nabokov, of what he chose not to say, as well as his exact phrasing of things he did say.

After one stern denial in a 1962 interview, Nabokov changed his tune a little in the near-next breath, saying that Humbert *did* exist, but only after he had written *Lolita*. "While I was writing the book, here and there in a newspaper I would read all sorts of accounts about elderly gentlemen who pursued little girls: a kind of interesting coincidence but that's about all."

This is a close-to-tacit admission by Nabokov that he knew of actual cases that bore some resemblance to his fictional world. Cases like Sally Horner's kidnapping at the hands of Frank La Salle. Nabokov references them in the text of *Lolita*, but to do so in an interview was anathema, lest listeners or readers connect the dots.

But there is no getting around the fact that Nabokov kept returning to this taboo relationship between a young girl and an older man throughout his career. That compulsion had real-life basis not only in other people's lives, but also in his own. A clue to that compulsion emerges when Humbert Humbert describes his "rather repulsive" uncle, Gustave Trapp. He thinks of Trapp again while tracking Ivor Quilty, Clare's dentist uncle, and again during his first encounter with Clare at the Enchanted Hunters hotel. (Quilty also punches through the proverbial fourth wall by signing his name as "G. Trapp" in the hotel's guestbook entry. As the German scholar Michael Maar points out, "Quilty cannot know the name.")

That uncles figure so much in *Lolita* recalls a revelation in *Speak, Memory:* that Vladimir's uncle Ruka took his then-nine-year-old nephew onto his knee and fondled him repeatedly "with crooning sounds and fancy endearments" until the boy's father called for him from the veranda. The real-life scene seems to foreshadow the famous fictional one of Humbert achieving orgasm with Dolores on his lap. Humbert, of course, believes his emission to be furtive—that the girl doesn't know.

But Nabokov, in his description, leaves it up to the reader to decide what Lolita knew.

IN *READING LOLITA IN TEHRAN*, Azar Nafisi makes the excellent point that Dolores Haze is a double victim, because not only her life is taken from her, but also her life story: "The desperate truth of *Lolita*'s story is *not* the rape of a twelve-year-old by a dirty old man but the *confiscation of one individual's life by another.*" Without realizing it, Nafisi has made the exact parallel between Dolores Haze and Sally Horner. For Sally's life, too, was forever marked by the twenty-one months she spent as Frank La Salle's captive, his false daughter, his own realized fantasy. After she was rescued, she attempted to resume the life snatched away from her. And it seemed she did, on the surface.

But how could she, when her story had been front-page news all across the country, and when those in Camden knew exactly what had happened to her and judged her—blamed her—for it? Whether she'd lived two years or many decades, whether she might have had time to move forward, even if she could not move on, Sally Horner was forever marked.

Lolita's end, dying in childbirth, is a tragedy. But Sally Horner's demise by car accident is the bigger tragedy, because it was real, and robbed her of the chance to grow up and at least attempt to move forward. In fact, Sally Horner is a triple victim: snatched from her ordinary life by Frank La Salle, only for her life to be cut short by car accident, and then strip-mined to produce the bones of *Lolita,* the only acknowledgment a parenthetical reference hidden in plain sight, hardly noticed by many millions of readers.

Over the course of researching this book these last few

years, I would ask faithful fans of *Lolita* if they'd caught the parenthetical reference to Sally Horner's kidnapping. The unanimous answer was "no." This was no real surprise. If no one caught the reference, how could they be expected to see how much of the novel's structure rides on what happened to Sally in real life? But once seen, it is impossible to unsee.

There is no simple lock-and-key metaphor to equate the tragic story of Dolores Haze to the tragic story of Sally Horner. Vladimir Nabokov was too shrewd to create a life-meets-art dynamic. But Sally's story is certainly *one* of those important keys that, once employed, unlocks a critical inspiration. There is no question *Lolita* would have existed without Sally Horner because Nabokov spent over twenty years dwelling on the theme, working it out in bits and pieces as he moved around Europe and America. But the narrative was also strengthened and sharpened by the inclusion of her story.

Sally Horner can't be cast aside so easily. She must be remembered as more than a young girl forever changed by a middle-aged man's crime of monstrous perversion. A girl who survived adversity, manipulation, and cross-country horror, only to be denied the chance to grow up. A girl immortalized, and forever trapped, in the pages of a classic novel of satire and sadness, like a butterfly with wings damaged before ever having the chance to fly.

Sally Horner, age fifteen, summer of 1952.

ACKNOWLEDGMENTS

The Real Lolita has a single author—me—but could not have been written or published without the input, advice, support, and sounding board of many people, in ways large and small. This odyssey began when Jordan Ginsberg, editor-in-chief at *Hazlitt*, replied to my March 2014 article pitch about Sally Horner's kidnapping: "Just brought this up in our editorial meeting, and it got one of the fastest and most enthusiastic 'yes' votes I've heard in a while." Eight months later, in great part to Jordan's editorial vision, the piece was published and changed the course of my professional life. Much has transpired in the intervening four years, and I remain thrilled that it all began at *Hazlitt*. Additional thanks to senior editor Haley Cullingham, whom I have loved working with and hope to do so again soon.

Transforming Sally Horner's story from a magazine piece to a book was equal parts challenging, exhilarating, exhausting, and rewarding. Shana Cohen offered invaluable feedback on the first rounds of book proposal drafts. My agent, David Patterson, has been a brilliant advocate and champion of this project, as has the entire team at the Stuart Krichevsky Literary Agency, particularly Aemilia Phillips, Hannah Schwartz, Ross Harris, and Stuart Krichevsky. Thanks also to my UK agent, Jane Finigan at Lutyens & Rubinstein.

My wonderful editors, Zack Wagman at Ecco and Anne Collins at Knopf Canada, pushed me to meet my ambitions for *The Real Lolita* and then exceed them. I am fortunate to have had such incisive and thoughtful editorial guidance from two of the very best in the business. And to Holly Harley, my editor at Weidenfeld & Nicolson in the UK, thank you for your continued support and never wavering in your enthusiasm for the project.

At Ecco, thanks to Miriam Parker, Sonya Cheuse, Meghan Deans, Megan Lynch, Denise Oswald, Dan Halpern, James Faccinto, Ashley Garland, Martin Wilson, Sara Wood (for the heart-stopping cover design), Allison Saltzman, Lisa Silverman, Andrea Molitor, and especially to Emma Janaskie. At Penguin Random House Canada, thanks to Sarah Jackson, Pamela Murray, Max Arambulo, Marion Garner, Matthew Sibiga, Sarah Smith-Eivemark, Liz Lee, Jared Bland, Robert Wheaton, and Kristin Cochrane.

Special thanks to the MacDowell Colony, for the gift of time and space to finish the first draft of the book; to Karen Riedenburg and David Dean, for invaluable research assistance; to all the archivists and institutions I visited for my research, and the sources who were generous with their time and interviews (more on them in the Notes section); and to Diana Chiemingo, who gave me her trust, faith, and belief that I could do full justice to the brief life of her aunt Sally.

Thank you to friends, family, and colleagues, a list that is by no means comprehensive: Megan Abbott, Jami Attenberg, Alice and Julian AvRutick, Louis AvRutick, Dov Berger, Liza Birkenmeier, Taffy Brodesser-Akner, Michael Cader, Steph Cha, Pamela Colloff, Julia Dahl, Hilary Davidson, Michelle Dean, Robin Dellabough, Nina Elkin, Lyndsay Faye, Dedi Felman, Charles Finch, Jordan Foster, Emily Giglierano, Juliet

Grames, David Grann, Peggy Hageman, Reyhan Harmanci, Lauren Milne Henderson, Ella Hickson, Cara Hoffman, Elizabeth Howard, Janet Hutchings, Hillel Italie, Ethan Iverson, Maureen Johnson, Rokhl Kafrissen, Stephen Karam, Leslie Kauffman, Bob Kolker, Scaachi Koul, Sara Kramer, Maris Kreizman, Clair Lamb, Michelle Legro, Katia Lief, Laura Lippman, Mimi Lipson, Lisa Lutz, Michael Macrone, Jeffrey Marks, Laura Marsh, Kyla Marshell, Chantelle Osman, Helen Oyeyemi, Bud Parr, Andrea Pitzer, Bryon Quertermous, Naben Ruthnum, Alex Segura, Deb Shoval, Kathy Smith, Erin Somers, Daniel Stashower, Adam Sternbergh, Sara Stopek, Caryn Sweeney, Vu Tran, Sharon AvRutick Wallace, Joe Wallace, Robin Wasserman, Deborah Wassertzug, Dave White, Alina Wickham, and Jennifer Young.

Lastly, thank you to my brother, Jaime; the memory of my father, Jack, who I know would have been prouder than anyone that I published this book. And to my mother, Judith, forever my hero.

NOTES

This book is based extensively on primary sources wherever available, including court documents and transcripts, prison records, legislative records, and testimony. I am grateful for the assistance of the New Jersey State Archives in Trenton, New Jersey; the Camden County Historical Society in Camden, New Jersey; the Maryland State Archives in Annapolis, Maryland; the Baltimore City Archives in Baltimore, Maryland; the City Archives and the Free Library of Philadelphia, Pennsylvania; Our Lady of Victory Center, Bishop Dunne Catholic School, and the Diocesan Archives in Dallas, Texas; and the National Archives offices in Leavenworth, Kansas; Philadelphia, Pennsylvania; and San Francisco, California.

When court documents were unavailable or lost, I relied on newspaper accounts, most notably the Camden *Courier-Post* and the *Philadelphia Inquirer*, which had the most comprehensive stories about Sally Horner's abduction, rescue, and death between 1948 and 1952.

I conducted dozens of interviews for the book, including several conversations with Sally's niece, Diana Chiemingo; one telephone conversation with Diana's father, Al Panaro, in 2014; two telephone conversations with Carol Taylor, in 2016 and 2017; and two conversations with "Madeline La Salle," in 2014. Other invaluable sources with firsthand memories of principal characters included "Rachel Janisch" and "Vanessa Janisch"; Fred Cohen and Peggy Braveman; Tom Pfeil; and Emma DiRenzo.

For the Nabokov sections, I relied on files, clippings, note cards, and letters deposited at the Library of Congress as well as at the Berg Collection, New York Public Library. Grateful acknowledgment for permission to access the Berg Collection is given to the Wylie Agency, on behalf of the Nabokov Estate, and to Isaac Gewirtz, Lyndsi Barnes, Joshua McKeon, and Mary Catherine Kinniburgh for their assistance and advice.

I also drew from the earlier work of Brian Boyd, Stacy Schiff, Andrew Field, Alexander Dolinin, and other Nabokov scholars. Schiff also generously shared her time, and advice, in a telephone conversation in April 2017, while Boyd was similarly helpful in an email exchange that same month. A telephone conversation with Walter Minton, in addition to earlier and later quotes, proved helpful with respect to the publication process of *Lolita* in the United States.

For additional historical context on Camden, I relied on *Camden After the Fall: Decline and Renewal in a Post-American City* by Howard Gillette (University of Pennsylvania Press, 2006) and the Local History: Camden website maintained by Phil Cohen at http://www.dvrbs.com.

ABBREVIATIONS

Berg: Vladimir Nabokov Archives, Berg Collection, New York Public Library, New York, NY

LOC: Vladimir Vladimirovich Nabokov Archives, Library of Congress, Washington, DC

NJSA: New Jersey State Archives, Trenton, NJ

VNAY: Brian Boyd, *Vladimir Nabokov: The American Years* (Princeton University Press, 1991)

Unless noted otherwise, all interviews were with the author.

INTRODUCTION: "HAD I DONE TO HER . . . ?"

5 no "little deadly demon": *Lolita*, p. 15.

6 It happened to the writer Mikita Brottman: Mikita Brottman, *The Maximum Security Book Club: Reading Literature in a Men's Prison*, pp. 196–197.

8 "I hate tampering with the precious lives": Nabokov, *Lectures on Russian Literature*, p. 138.

8 "It is strange, the morbid inclination": Nabokov, *Nikolai Gogol*, p. 40.

9 three increasingly tendentious biographies: The level of acrimony in Andrew Field's *VN* (1986) compared with *Nabokov: His Life*

in Art (1967) and *Nabokov: His Life in Part* (1977) is astonishing; the
falling-out between biographer and subject would make an excellent
play.

9 A two-part definitive study: Boyd's *Vladimir Nabokov: The Russian Years* (1990) and *VNAY* (1991).

10 Stacy Schiff's 1999 portrayal: Schiff, *Véra (Mrs. Vladimir Nabokov)*.

10 lifted its fifty-year restriction: Finding Aid, Vladimir Vladimirovich Nabokov Papers, Manuscript Division, LOC.

10 an earlier Nabokov story, "Spring in Fialta": *The Stories of Vladimir
Nabokov*, p. 413.

ONE: THE FIVE-AND-DIME

15 Sally Horner walked into the Woolworth's: "Camden Girl Saved
from Kidnapper in Calif," Camden *Courier-Post*, March 22, 1950, p. A1.

15 on a March afternoon in 1948: From Camden County prosecutor
Mitchell Cohen's remarks at an April 2, 1950, court hearing, reported
by the *Courier-Post* on April 3, p. A1.

16 A slender, hawk-faced man: Associated Press, March 22, 1950,
taken from the *Lima* (Ohio) *News*, p. 5.

16 A scar sliced his cheek: Draft registration card, January 1944.

17 suicide of her alcoholic husband: Death certificate of Russell
Horner, March 24, 1943.

17 Her homeroom teacher, Sarah Hanlin: *Philadelphia Inquirer*,
March 23, 1950, p. 3.

17 Emma DiRenzo, one of Sally's classmates: Interview with Emma
DiRenzo, November 13, 2017.

19 The telephone rang: Camden *Courier-Post*, March 23, 1950.

20 Ella let her concerns slide: United Press, *Salt Lake Tribune*, August 6, 1948, p. 5.

TWO: A TRIP TO THE BEACH

21 Robert and Jean Pfeffer were newlyweds: This section draws almost entirely from two newspaper reports that quoted Robert Pfeffer
at length: Camden *Courier-Post*, March 24, 1950, p. 2; and *Philadelphia Inquirer*, March 24, 1950, p. 3.

24 Ella was relieved: Camden *Evening Courier*, August 6, 1948, p. 1.

24 Detective Joseph Schultz: *Courier-News*, Bridgewater, NJ, August 6, 1948, p. 15.

25 the lodging house: The 203 Pacific Avenue address came from the 1940 census; La Salle was known to return to addresses where he had lived in the past.

25 "He didn't take any of his or the girl's clothes": *Philadelphia Inquirer*, March 23, 1950, p. 1.

26 Marshall Thompson led the search: Camden *Courier-Post*, March 23, 1950, p. 1.

26 only six months before he'd abducted Sally: Mitchell Cohen's court statement, April 2, 1950.

THREE: FROM WELLESLEY TO CORNELL

27 The year 1948 was a pivotal one: This chapter largely draws upon *VNAY*, pp. 129–135, as well as letters reprinted in Nabokov, *Selected Letters: 1940–1977*.

28 Nabokov had also traveled: Itemized road trip summaries available at "Lolita, USA," compiled by Dieter E. Zimmer, http://www.d-e -zimmer.de/LolitaUSA/LoUSNab.htm.

28 "lovely, trustful, dreamy, enormous country": *Lolita*, p. 176.

28 "Beyond the tilled plain": Ibid., p. 152.

28 marriage to Véra was once again stable: *VNAY*, p. 129.

28 had been ill: Letter from Vladimir Nabokov to Katharine White, May 30, 1948.

29 "quiet summer in green surroundings": *VNAY*, p. 131.

29 "wrinkled-dwarf Cambridge flatlet": Ibid.

30 "ends with a feeling of hopelessness": Ibid.

30 Nabokov appreciated Wilson's gift: Letter from Vladimir Nabokov to Edmund Wilson, June 10, 1948, *Dear Bunny, Dear Volodya: The Nabokov-Wilson Letters, 1940–1971*, ed. Simon Karlinsky, p. 178.

30 "I was always interested in psychology": Field, *VN: The Life and Art of Vladimir Nabokov*, p. 212.

FOUR: SALLY, AT FIRST

34 Her legal name: Sally Horner's birth certificate, issued by the State of New Jersey Department of Health, April 18, 1937, obtained from the Department of Health office in May 2017.

34 When the subject came up: Interview with Diana Chiemingo, August 2014, and again in July 2017.

34 William Ralph Swain: Susan Panaro's birth certificate listing Swain as her father, State of New Jersey Department of Health, November 1926, obtained from the Department of Health office in May 2017.

35 One subject they all fretted about: Interview with Diana Chiemingo, July 2016.

35 That's where Ella met Russell Horner: *Asbury Park Press*, December 9, 1935, p. 9, and June 9, 1936, p. 7.

35 As for Russell Junior: Social Security application, February 1937.

36 Susan remembered the beatings: Interviews with Al Panaro and Diana Chiemingo, August 2014.

36 She took Susan and Sally to Camden: Camden telephone directory, 1946.

36 Russell became itinerant: Interview with Al Panaro, 2014.

36 He lost his driver's license: "'Short Cut' Costs Autoist License," *Philadelphia Inquirer*, March 27, 1942, p. 27.

36 By the beginning of 1943: *Asbury Park Press*, March 26, 1943, p. 2.

36 Later, when it became necessary: Camden *Courier-Post*, March 22, 1950, p. 1.

37 Her mother, Susannah: Obituary for Susannah Goff, *Trenton Times*, October 31, 1939; obituary for Job Goff, *Asbury Park Press*, January 12, 1943.

37 Susan, by now sixteen: Interview with Diana Chiemingo, July 2016; interview with Al Panaro, August 2014.

37 she and Al wed in Florence: Marriage certificate, NJSA.

FIVE: THE SEARCH FOR SALLY

39 Robert and Jean Pfeffer: *Philadelphia Inquirer*, March 24, 1950, p. 3.

40 At first Marshall Thompson worked: Joseph S. Wells, "Sleuth Closes Books on Tireless Search," Camden *Courier-Post*, March 22, 1950, p. 9.

40 He had been promoted to detective: "Marshall Thompson," DVRBS.com, http://www.dvrbs.com/people/CamdenPeople MarshallThompson.htm, accessed January 16, 2018.

41 "local pugilists": Camden *Courier-Post*, January 2, 1928.

41 His musical ability was called out: Camden *Courier-Post*, November 3, 1939.

41 "quantity of sugar and cream": Camden *Courier-Post*, March 22, 1950, p. 9.

SIX: SEEDS OF COMPULSION

46 "Of the nineteen fictions": Martin Amis, "Divine Levity," *Times Literary Supplement*, December 23, 2011.

46 suggested a more likely culprit: Roper, *Nabokov in America*, p. 150.

46 "an ape in the Jardin des Plantes": Nabokov, "On a Book Entitled Lolita," *Anchor Review*, 1957 (subsequently reprinted in the Putnam edition of *Lolita* and every edition since).

47 Nabokov supplementing his writing income: Beam, *The Feud*, p. 16.

47 The short story includes: "A Nursery Tale," reprinted in *The Stories of Vladimir Nabokov*, pp. 161–172.

48 features the so-called demonic effect: "Lilith," *Poems and Problems* (McGraw-Hill, 1969), reprinted in *Selected Poems* (Knopf, 2012), p. 84.

49 A paragraph in *Dar*: Nabokov, *The Gift*, pp. 176–177.

50 When Germany declared war: *VNAY*, p. 13.

50 "laid up with a severe attack": Nabokov, "On a Book Entitled Lolita."

51 "How can I come to terms": Nabokov, *The Enchanter*, p. 1.

53 "comparable to the one afforded": Simon Karlinsky, "Nabokov's Life and Lolita's Death," *Washington Post*, December 14, 1986.

54 As he later explained: Interview with Nabokov by Alfred Appel, *Wisconsin Studies in Contemporary Literature* 8 (1967).

54 Henry Lanz was a Stanford professor: *VNAY*, p. 33; Roper, *Nabokov in America*, p. 140.

55 Nabokov, however, denied it: Field, *Nabokov: His Life in Part*, p. 235.

SEVEN: FRANK, IN SHADOW

58 A likely birth date: La Salle's age was reported variably between fifty-two and fifty-six in 1950; his death certificate lists his birth date as May 27, 1896, and his Social Security application in 1944 lists May 27, 1895.

58 Frank Patterson and Nora LaPlante: Names listed on 1943 prison

intake form, NJSA. Different parental names, as well as hometowns, appeared on La Salle's Social Security application.

58 He said he served . . . prison has no record: Prison intake form, 1943; conversations with Greg Bognich, archivist, National Archives, Kansas City, KS.

58 every time he changed aliases: "Police Record of Girl's Abductor," Camden *Courier-Post*, March 22, 1950, p. 1.

58 It is as Fogg that a sharper picture: *News Journal* (Wilmington, Delaware), August 3, 1937, p. 24.

58 He met her at a carnival: *Philadelphia Inquirer*, August 3, 1937, p. 3.

59 Which they did: Cecil County marriage license of Dorothy May Dare and Frank La Salle, July 31, 1937, obtained from the Maryland State Archives.

59 Dorothy's father . . . was livid: *Philadelphia Inquirer*, August 4, 1937, p. 2.

59 "He told me the truth": *Philadelphia Inquirer*, August 3, 1937.

60 The next morning, La Salle appeared: *Philadelphia Inquirer*, August 4, 1937.

60 La Salle was fined fifty dollars: *Philadelphia Inquirer*, August 12, 1937, p. 2.

60 arrested La Salle on bigamy charges: Camden *Courier-Post*, March 22, 1950, p. 1.

61 Dorothy sued Frank for desertion: Ibid.

61 Three Camden police officers: Camden *Courier-Post*, March 25, 1950, p. 6.

62 The five girls: Names taken from Dorothy Dare's divorce petition against Frank La Salle, *La Salle v. La Salle*, Superior Court of New Jersey, 151-246-W127-796 (1944).

62 Sergeant Wilkie swore out a warrant: Camden *Courier-Post*, March 25, 1950, p. 6.

63 La Salle pleaded not guilty: Court docket, NJSA.

63 Dorothy and Madeline had moved: Interview with "Madeline La Salle," August 2014; *La Salle v. La Salle*, Superior Court of New Jersey.

64 La Salle was paroled: Camden *Courier-Post*, March 22, 1950, p. 1; prison intake form, 1950, NJSA; draft registration card, June 29, 1944; Social Security application, June 28, 1944.

65　a forged $110 check: Camden *Courier-Post*, March 22, 1950.

65　La Salle returned to Trenton State Prison: Ibid.; prison intake form, 1946, NJSA.

EIGHT: "A LONELY MOTHER WAITS"

67　She'd found work as a seamstress: *Philadelphia Inquirer*, December 10, 1948, p. 1.

69　The case had taken on added urgency: March 17, 1949, indictment date mentioned in subsequent reports by the *Philadelphia Inquirer* and Camden *Courier-Post*, March 22, 1950.

69　Dorothy Forstein's disappearance: "Kidnapping Story Spurs Search for Wife of Forstein," *Philadelphia Inquirer*, October 23, 1949, p. 1.

70　The Friday night after Dorothy vanished: "Reward Offered for Clue to Wife," Camden *Courier-Post*, November 17, 1949, p. 24.

71　Dorothy was declared legally dead: "Lost Wife Ruled Dead," *Philadelphia Inquirer*, October 15, 1957, p. 23.

71　Ella had difficulty sleeping: "A Tree Grows, a Lonely Mother Waits," *Philadelphia Inquirer*, December 10, 1948, p. 1.

NINE: THE PROSECUTOR

73　Mitchell Cohen was appointed: Obituary of Mitchell Cohen, *New York Times*, January 10, 1991.

73　did not have enough major crime: Gillette, *Camden After the Fall*, p. 25.

73　state party's de facto leader: Camden *Courier-Post*, November 7, 1950, p. 3.

73　many jobs he held in law enforcement: Obituary of Mitchell Cohen, *Philadelphia Inquirer*, January 10, 1991.

74　In his bespoke suits: Interview with Fredric Cohen, November 2017.

74　He'd met Herman Levin: Camden *Courier-Post*, June 1, 1956, p. 2.

74　Cohen also became a theatrical producer: Ibid.; also "Music Fair Opens to 1500," Camden *Courier-Post*, June 4, 1957, p. 1.

75　early in his tenure: "Make Up in Court," *Philadelphia Inquirer*, June 24, 1938, p. 19.

75 the murder of Wanda Dworecki: Account draws from coverage in the Camden *Courier-Post* and the *Philadelphia Inquirer*, as well as *State of New Jersey v. Dworecki*, January 11, 1940, and Daniel Allen Hearn, *Legal Executions in New Jersey: A Comprehensive Registry* (McFarland, 2005), pp. 376–377.

79 Shewchuk was paroled in 1959: "Pastor Put to Death in 1940," Camden *Courier-Post*, July 11, 2000, p. 6.

79 the death of twenty-three-year-old Margaret McDade: Account draws from coverage in the Camden *Courier-Post* and wire reports from the Associated Press, United Press, International News Service, and more.

80 Howard Auld did not die: "Auld Dies Tonight as Final Pleas of Mercy Are Denied," Camden *Courier-Post*, March 27, 1951, p. 1.

TEN: BALTIMORE

84 six-year-old June Robles: Obituary of June Robles, *New York Times*, October 31, 2017, supplied the bulk of details for this section.

86 Stan visited her parents: See Christine McGuire and Carla Norton, *Perfect Victim* (Arbor House/Morrow, 1988), for a complete account of the Colleen Stan case.

86 Dugard's eighteen-year bond: See Jaycee Dugard, *A Stolen Life* (2011); Elizabeth Smart, *My Story* (2013); and Amanda Berry and Gina DeJesus, *Hope* (2015), for further information on these cases.

87 had taken a taxicab: Mitchell Cohen statement, as reported by the Camden *Courier-Post*, April 3, 1950.

87 Sally later said: Camden *Courier-Post*, March 22, 1950, p. 1.

88 around West Franklin Street: Several addresses on this street were listed in an affidavit included with *State of New Jersey v. Frank La Salle*, A-7-54 (1954).

89 rape became a regular occurrence: Camden *Courier-Post*, March 22, 1950, p. 1.

89 To enroll Sally at Saint Ann's: Affidavit included with *State of New Jersey v. Frank La Salle*, A-7-54 (1954).

89 Sally got used to the new name: *Philadelphia Inquirer*, March 23, 1950, p. 1.

90 Breakfast in hand: "GEM F: On the Road to Hell," from Mary Reardon, *Catholic Schools Then and Now* (Badger Books, 2004), of-

fered a contemporaneous account of an elementary school student
in the 1940s that proved helpful in imagining a typical day for Sally
Horner during this time frame.

ELEVEN: WALKS OF DEATH

93 Camden believed in its own prosperity: Gillette, *Camden After the Fall*, p. 38.

94 At eight o'clock that morning: This account of the Howard Un-
ruh massacre is drawn from several sources, including Seymour Shu-
bin, "Camden's One-Man Massacre," *Tragedy-of-the-Month*, December
1949; Meyer Berger, "Veteran Kills 12 in Mad Rampage on Camden
Street," *New York Times*, September 7, 1949; ". . . He Left a Trail of
Death," Camden *Courier-Post*, September 7, 1974; Patrick Sauer, "The
Story of the First Mass Murder in U.S. History," Smithsonian.com,
October 14, 2015.

95 For Marshall Thompson: "Marshall Thompson," DVRBS.com.

97 Ferry had just finished: "John J. Ferry," DVRBS.com, http://
www.dvrbs.com/people/CamdenPeople-JohnFerryJr.htm.

97 "When the other cops started arriving": Camden *Courier-Post*,
September 7, 1974. Reproduced at http://www.dvrbs.com/people
/CamdenPeople-HowardUnruh.htm.

99 Cohen walked over to the police station: Ibid.

100 He died in 2009 . . . the last survivor: Obituary of Howard Unruh, *New York Times*, October 19, 2009; obituary of Charles Cohen,
Camden *Courier-Post*, September 9, 2009.

TWELVE: ACROSS AMERICA BY OLDSMOBILE

101 Nabokov finished the 1948–1949 academic year: This account
of Vladimir Nabokov's whereabouts in the summer of 1949 is almost
entirely drawn from *VNAY*, pp. 136–144.

106 "coach in French and fondle in Humbertish": *Lolita*, p. 35.

106 "white-frame horror": Ibid.

108 "You're a detestable, abominable, criminal fraud": Ibid., p. 96.

THIRTEEN: DALLAS

112 The journey from Baltimore to Dallas: Calculated via Google Maps.

112 However they traveled: Affidavit of Nelrose Pfeil, included with *State of New Jersey v. La Salle*, A-7-54 (1954).

112 The park was designed like a horseshoe: Interview with Tom Pfeil, November 2017.

112 La Salle had changed their names again: *Philadelphia Inquirer*, March 23, 1950.

112 The trailer park was owned: Interview with Tom Pfeil, November 2017.

113 He also enrolled Sally: Reproduction of a report card included with *State of New Jersey v. La Salle*, A-7-54 (1954).

113 Our Lady of Good Counsel no longer exists: See "Our Lady of Good Counsel, Oak Cliff," https://flashbackdallas.com/2017/10/01/our-lady-of-good-counsel-oak-cliff-1901-1961/.

114 Her neighbors thought Sally: Affidavits from Nelrose Pfeil, Maude Smillie, Josephine Kagamaster, included with *State of New Jersey v. La Salle*, A-7-54 (1954).

115 She'd suffered an appendicitis attack: Camden *Courier-Post*, March 23, 1950.

FOURTEEN: THE NEIGHBOR

117 Ruth Janisch and her family: Interviews with "Vanessa Janisch," 2015 and 2016, and "Rachel Janisch," May 2017.

119 her second husband, Everett Findley: Marriage license of Ruth Douglass and Everett Findley, 1936.

119 She met husband number three: The 1940 census recorded Ruth, Findley, and Janisch all residing at the same home.

120 George and Ruth ran off: Marriage license, October 24, 1940.

121 "He never let Sally": Camden *Courier-Post*, March 27, 1950, p. 1.

121 El Cortez Motor Inn: *Philadelphia Inquirer*, March 22, 1950, p. 1; corroborated by a 1960 listing of motor courts obtained at the California Room, San Jose Public Library, July 2017.

122 Police in uniform shorts: "We'll Take the High Road," American Road Buildings Association, 1957, available at https://www.youtube.com/watch?v=wnrqUHF5bH8.

122 The friend told Sally: Camden *Courier-Post*, March 22, 1950, p. 1; *Philadelphia Evening Bulletin*, April 2, 1950.

FIFTEEN: SAN JOSE

125 On the morning of March 21: Camden *Courier-Post*, March 22, 1950, p. 1; *Philadelphia Inquirer*, March 22, 1950, p. 2; and other newspaper accounts.

126 Her brother-in-law, Al Panaro: Interview with Al Panaro, August 2014.

127 Hornbuckle had been elected: Howard Hornbuckle scrapbook, pp. 85–86, California Room, San Jose Public Library; Clerk-Recorder's Office, Santa Clara County Archives, Santa Clara, CA.

128 "Please get me away from here": *Philadelphia Inquirer*, March 22, 1950.

129 She started at the beginning: Camden *Courier-Post*, March 22, 1950.

130 Ella Horner was overjoyed: Ibid.; also *Central New Jersey Home News*, March 22, 1950, p. 8.

131 Later that day: "Sally's Mother 'Relieved,' Admits She Was 'Foolish,'" Camden *Courier-Post*, March 22, 1950, p. 1.

132 "machina telephonica and its sudden god": *Lolita*, p. 205.

133 "all a-jitter lest delay": Ibid., p. 110.

133 "Give me some dimes and nickels": Ibid., p. 141.

133 "At the hotel we had separate rooms": Ibid., p. 142.

SIXTEEN: AFTER THE RESCUE

135 La Salle was charged: The White-Slave Traffic Act, or the Mann Act, is a U.S. federal law, passed June 25, 1910 (ch. 395, 36 Stat. 825; codified as amended at 18 U.S.C. §§ 2421–2424).

135 On the morning of March 22: Camden *Courier-Post*, March 23, 1950.

136 Commissioner Marshall Hall presided: "Sex Criminal Held as Girl Makes Charges Against Him," *San Bernardino County Sun*, March 23, 1950, p. 1.

136 When police officers attempted: "La Salle Held Under Mann Act," *Morning News* (Wilmington, Delaware), March 24, 1950, p. 1.

137 Even if he raised the full $10,000 bond: Camden *Courier-Post*, March 24, 1950, p. 1.

138 Back in Camden: Taken from Sally's statement reported by the Camden *Courier-Post*, March 22, 1950, p. 1.

138 A Camden grand jury: Camden *Courier-Post*, March 24, 1950, p. 1; *Philadelphia Inquirer*, March 24, 1950, p. 1.

139 Cohen, Dube, and Thompson flew: "Cohen Flies to Calif. to Re-

turn La Salle on Kidnap Charge," Camden *Courier-Post*, March 27, 1950, p. 1.

139 On Thursday, Sally was released: "Sally Meets Mother Again After 21 Mos.," Camden *Courier-Post*, April 1, 1950, p. 1.

139 Ella waited at the airport: "Sally's Mother Waited a Long Time to Hold Kidnaped Daughter Again," Camden *Courier-Post*, April 1, 1950, p. 2.

SEVENTEEN: A GUILTY PLEA

143 Frank La Salle wasn't allowed: Camden *Courier-Post*, March 30, 1950, p. 1.

143 The solution was to transport La Salle: "Kidnap Victim Will Fly Home Tomorrow," *Oakland Tribune*, March 30, 1950, p. 51.

144 Mitchell Cohen was at the train station: Camden *Courier-Post*, March 31, 1950, p. 1.

144 La Salle, Detective Thompson, and Detective Dube: *Philadelphia Inquirer*, March 30, 1950, p. 2.

144 *City of San Francisco*: Extrapolated from sample train timetable, Union Pacific Railroad Company, Omaha, NE, Union Pacific Railroad Time Tables, April 1948, *The Cooper Collection of US Railroad History*.

144 New York–bound *General*: Times corroborated at American-Rails .com, https://www.american-rails.com/gnrl.html.

144 the trio of men: Camden *Courier-Post*, March 31, 1950, p. 1.

144 Mitchell Cohen told the press later on Sunday: Camden *Courier-Post*, April 2, 1950, p. 1.

145 Cohen arrived at the jail: "La Salle Given 30 Years," Camden *Courier-Post*, April 3, 1950, p. 1.

146 Judge Palese asked Cohen: Quoted text taken from *State v. Frank La Salle*, 19 N.J. Super. 510 (1952).

148 Because Frank La Salle pleaded guilty: Camden *Courier-Post*, April 4, 1950, p. 1.

EIGHTEEN: WHEN NABOKOV (REALLY) LEARNED ABOUT SALLY

151 Vladimir Nabokov spent the morning: *VNAY*, pp. 146–147.

151 "I have followed your example": Letter from Nabokov to Katharine White, March 24, 1950, reprinted from *Selected Letters: 1940–1977*, p. 98.

152 But as Nabokov told James Laughlin: Letter from Nabokov to James Laughlin, April 27, 1950, ibid., p. 99.

152 described in their diary: Diary entry, November 17, 1958.

152 Robert Roper . . . was certainly convinced: Email to the author, August 25, 2016.

153 "will be given a choice": *Lolita*, p. 151.

153 "Only the other day we read": Ibid., p. 150.

154 Nabokov scholar Alexander Dolinin: "Whatever Happened to Sally Horner?," *Times Literary Supplement*, September 9, 2005.

155 "the stealthy thought": *Lolita*, p. 204.

NINETEEN: REBUILDING A LIFE

157 "When she went away she was a little girl": Camden *Courier-Post*, April 1, 1950, p. 2.

157 a family outing to the Philadelphia Zoo: Film clip provided by Diana Chiemingo, with permission.

158 "She has a definite ambition": *Philadelphia Inquirer*, March 29, 1950, p. 3.

159 Ella opted for a compromise: Interview with Al Panaro, August 2014.

162 "they looked at her as a total whore": Interview with Carol Taylor, August 2017.

162 "She had a little bit of a rough time": Interview with Emma DiRenzo, November 2017.

163 Sally found refuge in the outdoors: Interview with Al Panaro, August 2014.

TWENTY: *LOLITA* PROGRESSES

165 Vladimir and Véra left Ithaca: This chapter is largely drawn from *VNAY*, pp. 200–206; see also "Nabokov's Summer Trips to the West" at http://www.d-e-zimmer.de/LolitaUSA/LoUSNab.htm.

166 "Silly situation . . . to be smitten": Page-a-Day Diary, 1951, Berg.

166 The Nabokovs changed their itinerary: *VNAY*, pp. 217–221.

TWENTY-ONE: WEEKEND IN WILDWOOD

169 Carol Taylor no longer remembers: Interviews with Carol Taylor, December 2016 and August 2017.

170 Edward John Baker drove down: *Vineland Daily Journal*, August 20, 1952, p. 1.

171 He died in 2014: Obituary of Edward Baker, *Vineland Daily Journal*, July 28, 2014.

172 "She impressed me as a darn nice girl": *Vineland Daily Journal*, August 20, 1952, p. 1.

173 Ed Baker pulled onto the highway: "Crash at Shore Kills Girl Kidnap Victim," Camden *Courier-Post*, August 18, 1952, p. 1; "Victim of 1948 Kidnaping Killed," *Morning News* (Wilmington, Delaware), August 19, 1952, p. 1.

173 The trip from Wildwood to Vineland: *Vineland Daily Journal*, August 20, 1952, p. 1.

173 Just after midnight on Monday: *Wildwood Leader*, August 21, 1952, p. 4; "W'bine Crews at 4-Vehicle Crash Scene," *Cape May County Gazette*, August 21, 1952, p. 1.

174 The death certificate: Unredacted copy of Sally Horner's death certificate obtained from NJSA.

174 The damage to her face: Interview with Al Panaro, August 2014.

175 Carol Starts was woken up: Interview with Carol Taylor, December 2016.

TWENTY-TWO: THE NOTE CARD

177 Vladimir Nabokov opened up a newspaper: Geographic location from *VNAY*, pp. 217–219.

177 The handwritten card reads as follows: Reproduced from LOC.

178 As Alexander Dolinin explained: Dolinin, "Whatever Happened to Sally Horner?"

180 "a golden-skinned, brown-haired nymphet": *Lolita*, p. 288.

181 Rather, he writes: Dolinin, "Whatever Happened to Sally Horner?"

181 how much damage he has caused: *Lolita*, p. 285.

182 Véra's diary note: Page-a-Day Diary, 1958, Berg.

182 "charming brat lifted from an ordinary existence": Letter to Nabokov from Stella Estes, quoted in *VNAY*, p. 236.

182 why Nabokov himself ranked Lolita: Page-a-Day Diary, September 17, 1958.

TWENTY-THREE: "A DARN NICE GIRL"

183 a front-page interview with Edward Baker: "Vineland Youth, Bewildered by Publicity, Describes Sally Horner as 'Darn Nice Girl,'" *Vineland Daily Journal*, August 21, 1952, p. 1.

185 After he was treated: Camden *Courier-Post*, August 18, 1952, p. 1; "Driver Held at Shore in Horner Girl's Death," Camden *Courier-Post*, August 20, 1952, p. 11.

185 not Baker's first car accident: *Vineland Daily Journal*, July 24, 1951, p. 2.

185 Sally Horner's funeral: "Private Burial Held for Sally Horner," Camden *Courier-Post*, August 22, 1952, p. 4.

185 Emleys Hill Cemetery in Cream Ridge: See https://www.findagrave.com/memorial/11035529.

185 For Carol Starts, the funeral was awful: Interviews with Carol Taylor, December 2016 and August 2017.

186 Frank La Salle made his presence known: Interview with Al Panaro, August 2014.

186 The first court hearing: "Vineland Youth Freed in $1000 Bond Following Fatal Crash Near Shore," *Vineland Daily Journal*, August 19, 1952, p. 1; "One Fined in Fatal Crash," *Cape May County Gazette*, August 28, 1952, p. 4; September session, Cape May County Court (Criminal), September 3, 1952, pp. 19–21.

186 The most serious charge: *The State v. Edward J. Baker*, Indictment No. 283, New Jersey Superior Court, Cape May County, September 3, 1952.

187 The following week: September session, Cape May County Court (Criminal), September 10, 1952, pp. 25–26; "2 Plead Not Guilty in Girl's Death," Camden *Courier-Post*, September 12, 1952, p. 10; "Motorist Held in Death of Two," *Morning News* (Wilmington, Delaware), September 15, 1952, p. 12.

187 Carol was called to testify: Interview with Carol Taylor, August 2017.

187 Judge Tenenbaum threw out the charge: January session, Cape May County Court (Criminal), January 15, 1953, p. 63.

187 He faced a cluster of civil actions: "Civil Trials Set to Begin Before Jury," *Cape May County Gazette*, May 14, 1953, p. 1; "$115,800

Damage Suits Settled Out of Court," Camden *Courier-Post*, May 22, 1953, p. 15.

188 The byzantine nature of the lawsuits: "Fatal Accident Suits Resume After Mistrial," *Cape May County Gazette*, May 21, 1953, p. 1.

188 A new hearing lasted two days: Camden *Courier-Post*, May 22, 1953, p. 15; "Consolidated Trial Suits Settled," *Cape May County Gazette*, May 28, 1953, p. 2.

188 Written beside his name: Minutes, Cape May County Court (Criminal), June 30, 1954, p. 213.

TWENTY-FOUR: LA SALLE IN PRISON

189 a writ of habeas corpus: United States District Court for the State of New Jersey, C 679-50, "In the Matter of the Application of Frank La Salle for a Writ of Habeas Corpus," December 14, 1950.

190 Hughes was so incensed by La Salle's lies: "Kidnaper Seeking His Release from N.J. State Prison," Camden *Courier-Post*, September 21, 1951, p. 1.

190 He kept on, in a lengthy series: *State of New Jersey v. La Salle*, Superior Court of New Jersey, A-7-54 (1955).

192 Tom Pfeil denied she'd ever said: Interview with Tom Pfeil, June 2017.

193 his mother's supposed statement: *State of New Jersey v. La Salle*, Superior Court of New Jersey, A-7-54 (1955).

194 Frank La Salle also wrote letters: Interview with "Vanessa Janisch," May 2017.

195 Her mother, Dorothy: Obituary, Camden *Courier-Post*, August 2011.

196 Madeline did not learn any details: Interview with "Madeline," August 2014.

197 He appealed his sentence: *State of New Jersey v. Frank La Salle*, Superior Court of New Jersey, A-343-51 (1961).

197 He died of arteriosclerosis: Death certificate, State of New Jersey Department of Public Health.

TWENTY-FIVE: "GEE, ED, THAT WAS BAD LUCK"

199 another sensational crime: "Charge Is Due Today in 'Perfect Murder,'" *New York Times*, September 2, 1952, p. 17.

199 this case got an entire paragraph: *Lolita*, p. 287.

200 The G. Edward Grammer case: Case summary is derived from *State v. George Edward Grammer* (Transcripts), George E. Grammer, 1952, Box 1 No. 3544 [MSA T 496-67, 0/2/2/39], as well as subsequent appeals, including *Grammer v. State* (1953) and *Grammer v. Maryland* (1954). The entire case file is deposited at the Maryland State Archives, Annapolis, MD.

203 openly critical of mystery novels: Catherine Theimer Nepomnyaschy, "Revising Nabokov Revising the Detective Novel: Vladimir, Agatha, and the Terms of Engagement," The Proceedings of the International Nabokov Conference, March 24–27, 2010, Kyoto, Japan. Available at http://www.columbia.edu/cu/creative/epub/harriman/2015/fall/nabakov_and_the_detective_novel.pdf.

203 called out Dostoevsky as a hack: Nabokov, *Lectures on Russian Literature*, p. 109—while this line is the opinion of the author, Nabokov's judgment "Let us always remember that basically Dostoeveski [*sic*] is a writer of mystery stories" is meant to be pejorative.

203 As Véra told their close friend Morris Bishop: Schiff, *Véra (Mrs. Vladimir Nabokov)*, p. 232.

203 stabbing murders of Dr. Melvin Nimer and his wife: Nabokov almost certainly read "Prosecutor Says Boy, 8, Confesses Killing Parents; Boy Said to Admit Killing Parents," *New York Times*, September 11, 1958, p. 1.

204 police detectives still claiming as recently as 2007: "Nimer Now" (video), *Staten Island Advance*, February 11, 2007, http://blog.silive.com/advancevideo/2007/02/nimer_now_458.html.

204 venture west one more time: *VNAY*, pp. 223–226.

TWENTY-SIX: WRITING AND PUBLISHING *LOLITA*

205 Vladimir Nabokov wrote a note: Page-a-Day Diary, 1953, Berg.

205 "a novel I would be able to finish": Letter from Nabokov to Edmund Wilson, June 15, 1951.

206 "crumpling each old manuscript sheet": *VNAY*, p. 225.

206 "enormous, mysterious, heartbreaking novel": Letter from Nabokov to Katharine White, September 29, 1953.

206 when Nabokov wrote to Edmund Wilson: Letter from Nabokov to Edmund Wilson, 1947.

206 The first time was in the fall of 1948: Schiff, *Véra (Mrs. Vladimir Nabokov)*, p. 166.

207 "Véra came to the rescue": Roper, *Nabokov in America*, p. 149.

207 "one day in 1950": Interview with Nabokov by Herbert Gold, *Paris Review* 41 (Fall 1957), reprinted in Nabokov, *Strong Opinions*, p. 105.

207 *Lolita* was ready to be submitted: *VNAY*, pp. 255–267.

208 Edmund Wilson read half: Letter from Edmund Wilson to Nabokov, November 30, 1954.

208 grew "negative and perplexed": Letter from Mary McCarthy to Nabokov, November 30, 1954.

208 Wilson's present wife, Elena: Letter from Elena Wilson to Nabokov, November 30, 1954.

209 parody piece in the *New Yorker*: Dorothy Parker, "Lolita," *New Yorker*, August 27, 1955, p. 32.

209 Nabokov joked to Edmund Wilson: Letter from Nabokov to Edmund Wilson, February 19, 1955.

209 founder and publisher of Olympia Press: Account is drawn in large part from John De St. Jorre, *Venus Bound: The Erotic Voyage of the Olympia Press and Its Writers*.

209 submitted *Lolita* to Girodias: *VNAY*, p. 265.

210 As Nabokov later recalled: "*Lolita* and Mr. Girodias," *Evergreen Review* 45 (1967), reprinted in Nabokov, *Strong Opinions*.

211 Nabokov received a letter from Walter Minton: Letter to Nabokov from Walter Minton, August 30, 1957, reprinted in *Selected Letters: 1940–1977*, pp. 224–225.

211 had succeeded his father, Melville: "Walter Minton on the House 'Lolita' Built," *New Yorker*, January 8, 2018.

212 "I thought Nabokov had": "The Lolita Case," *Time*, November 17, 1958.

212 he had all but given up: Letter from Nabokov to Walter Minton, December 23, 1957.

212 *Lolita* had been banned in France: *VNAY*, pp. 310–315.

212 Minton's letter augured a change: Letter from Nabokov to Walter Minton, September 7, 1957; letter from Véra Nabokov to Minton, September 19, 1957; De St. Jorre, *Venus Bound*, p. 144.

213 "'Don't ever open your mouth'": Undated interview with Walter Minton by John De St. Jorre, quoted in *Venus Bound*. When I spoke to Minton in August 2017, he brought up the legality of *Lolita*'s copy-

right status without prompting: "I still wonder about that damn copyright."

213 As Minton explained: Inference from Nabokov letters to Walter Minton, January–February 1958.

214 Vladimir and Véra Nabokov left Ithaca: *VNAY*, pp. 362–364.

214 "Vladimir was a tremendous success": Page-a-Day Diary, August 1958, Berg.

214 Minton sent the following telegram: Reprinted in *Selected Letters: 1940–1977*, p. 257.

215 Elizabeth Janeway's rave review: "The Tragedy of Man Driven by Desire," *New York Times Book Review*, August 17, 1958.

215 The reorder number from retailers: *VNAY*, p. 365.

215 "ought to have happened thirty years ago": Letter from Nabokov to Elena Sikorski, September 6, 1958.

216 The indefinite leave of 1958: *VNAY*, p. 378.

TWENTY-SEVEN: CONNECTING SALLY HORNER TO *LOLITA*

217 Peter Welding was a young freelance reporter: Obituary of Peter Welding, *New York Times*, November 23, 1995.

217 Welding remembered reading of Sally's plight: "Lolita Has a Secret, Shhh!," *Nugget*, vol. 8, no. 5, November 1963.

222 a *New York Post* reporter named Alan Levin: Obituary of Alan Levin, *New York Times*, February 17, 2006.

224 The Nabokovs subscribed: Manuscript box, miscellaneous clippings, 1960–1965, Berg.

226 Schiff . . . strongly advised against reading: Interview with Stacy Schiff, April 2017.

TWENTY-EIGHT: "HE TOLD ME NOT TO TELL"

229 Decades after Ruth Janisch: Account is largely drawn from interviews with "Rachel Janisch," May 2017, and "Vanessa Janisch," March 2015, March 2016, and May 2017.

TWENTY-NINE: AFTERMATHS

235 Ella had connected with a new partner: 1951 Camden telephone directory records both residing at 944 Linden Street.

236 made their union legal: California marriage records, 1965, retrieved through Ancestry.com.

236 Five years later, Burkett was dead: Death certificate, State of California Department of Public Health, 1970.

236 Diana didn't learn the truth: Interview with Diana Chiemingo, August 2014.

237 Ella settled back in New Egypt: Obituary of Ella Horner, 1998, Ancestry.com.

237 Susan died in 2012, and Al passed away: Obituary of Susan Panaro, *Burlington County Times,* August 5, 2012; obituary of Al Panaro, KoschekandPorterFuneralHome.com, February 25, 2016.

237 "Did you say that Sally Horner": Interview with Carol Taylor, December 2016; email from Robin Lee Hambleton, November 2017.

238 Edward Baker got on with his life: Obituary of Edward Baker, *Vineland Daily Journal,* July 28, 2014.

238 On the afternoon of Wednesday, May 17: *Vineland Daily Journal,* May 18, 2007.

238 The two Camden police detectives: "Wilfred L. Dube," DVRBS.com, http://www.dvrbs.com/people/CamdenPeople-WilfredLDube.htm; "Marshall Thompson," DVRBS.com.

239 Howard Hornbuckle served one more term: Obituary of Howard Hornbuckle, *Petaluma* (California) *Argus-Courier,* May 9, 1962, p. 4.

239 Mitchell Cohen's health suffered: Camden *Courier-Post,* August 30, 1950, p. 1.

239 including . . . the 1955 execution: Camden *Courier-Post,* May 4, 1955, p 1.

239 Then came his next career move: Obituary of Mitchell Cohen, Camden *Courier-Post,* January 1991.

239 Palese eventually acquiesced: Obituary of Rocco Palese, Camden *Courier-Post,* February 27, 1987, p. 19.

239 Cohen served three years: Obituary of Mitchell Cohen, *Asbury Park Press,* January 9, 1991, p. 8.

240 Véra Nabokov continued: Page-a-Day Diary, 1958, Berg.

241 went out to dinner at Cafe Chambord: The account largely draws from Véra Nabokov's November 26, 1958, entry in ibid.

241 unduly preoccupied with a *Time* magazine article: "The Lolita Case," *Time,* November 17, 1958.

241 unbylined but written by . . . Joyce Haber: Haber worked at *Time* as a researcher and reporter from 1958 through 1966. While Minton did not comment on whether he had a relationship with Haber, a former colleague recognized the writing as Haber's.

244 Comedians turned *Lolita* into late-night fodder: *VNAY*, p. 375.

244 Another bizarre stunt: Ibid., pp. 415–416.

245 "by nature I am no dramatist": Preface to *Lolita: A Screenplay*, p. ix.

245 changed his mind about adapting *Lolita*: Letter from Nabokov to Morris Bishop, *Selected Letters: 1940–1977*, p. 309.

247 "a graceful ingenue but not my idea": Nabokov, "On a Book Entitled Lolita," *Novels, 1955–1962*, p. 672.

247 "I didn't have to play Lolita": Interview in the *New York Times*, 1971.

247 European newspapers: Manuscript box, miscellaneous clippings, 1960, Berg.

248 "a first-rate film with magnificent actors": *VNAY*, p. 466.

248 gave his approval for the musical: Ibid., p. 583.

249 "I think he's crude": Interview with Nabokov by Robert Hughes, WNET, September 2, 1965, reprinted in Nabokov, *Strong Opinions*.

EPILOGUE: ON TWO GIRLS NAMED LOLITA AND SALLY

255 The irritation is evident: Interview with Nabokov, BBC, July 1962, reprinted in Nabokov, *Strong Opinions*, p. 15.

255 He denied Humbert Humbert: *Paris Review*, "The Art of Fiction No. 40," 1967.

256 After one stern denial: BBC interview, reprinted in *Strong Opinions*, p. 17.

256 "with crooning sounds and fancy endearments": Nabokov, *Speak, Memory*, p. 49.

257 "The desperate truth of *Lolita*'s story": Nafisi, *Reading Lolita in Tehran*, p. 33.

BIBLIOGRAPHY

SELECTED WORKS BY VLADIMIR NABOKOV

Laughter in the Dark (1932; first published in English as *Camera Obscura*, 1936; second, revised English-language edition published in 1938; third edition published in 1963).

Despair (1934; translated into English in 1937; second English-language edition published in 1965).

The Gift (1938–1952, translated into English and published in 1963).

The Enchanter (written in 1939, published posthumously, translated and with a preface by Dmitri Nabokov, 1986).

Nikolai Gogol (1944).

Speak, Memory (1951, as *Conclusive Evidence;* revised edition published in 1966).

Lolita (1955).

Pnin (1957).

Pale Fire (1962).

The Annotated Lolita (edited with preface, introduction, and notes by Alfred Appel, Jr., 1970; revised and updated, 1991).

Strong Opinions (1973).

Lolita: A Screenplay (1973).

Lectures on Literature (edited by Fredson Bowers, introduction by John Updike, 1980).

Lectures on Russian Literature (edited and with an introduction by Fredson Bowers, 1981).

Vladimir Nabokov: Selected Letters, 1940–1977 (edited by Dmitri Nabokov and Matthew J. Bruccoli, 1989).

Dear Bunny, Dear Volodya: The Nabokov-Wilson Letters, 1940–1971 (edited by Simon Karlinsky, 1979; reprinted 2001).

Letters to Véra (edited and translated by Olga Voronina and Brian Boyd, 2015).

WORKS BY OTHERS ON NABOKOV

Alfred Appel, Jr., and Charles Newman, *Nabokov: Criticism, Reminiscences, Translations, and Tributes*. Northwestern University Press, 1970.

Alex Beam, *The Feud: Vladimir Nabokov, Edmund Wilson, and the End of a Beautiful Friendship*. Pantheon, 2016.

Brian Boyd, *Vladimir Nabokov: The Russian Years*. Princeton University Press, 1990.

———, *Vladimir Nabokov: The American Years*. Princeton University Press, 1991.

———, *Stalking Nabokov: Selected Essays*. Oxford University Press, 2012.

Mikita Brottman, *The Maximum Security Book Club*. Harper, 2016.

Andrew Field, *Nabokov: His Life in Art*. Little, Brown, 1967.

———, *Nabokov: His Life in Part*. Viking, 1977.

———, *VN: The Life and Art of Vladimir Nabokov*. Crown, 1986.

John De St. Jorre, *Venus Bound: The Erotic Voyage of the Olympia Press*. Random House, 1994.

Michael Juliar, *Vladimir Nabokov: A Descriptive Bibliography*. Garland Publishing, 1986.

Michael Maar, *The Two Lolitas*. Verso, 2005.

———, *Speak, Nabokov*. Verso, 2010.

Azar Nafisi, *Reading Lolita in Tehran*. Random House, 2003.

Ellen Pifer, ed., *Vladimir Nabokov's Lolita: A Casebook*. Oxford University Press, 2003.

Andrea Pitzer, *The Secret History of Vladimir Nabokov*. Pegasus, 2013.

Robert Roper, *Nabokov in America*. Bloomsbury USA, 2015.

Phyllis Roth, ed., *Critical Essays on Vladimir Nabokov*. G. K. Hall, 1984.

Stacy Schiff, *Véra (Mrs. Vladimir Nabokov)*. Random House, 1999.

Marianne Sinclair, *Hollywood Lolita: The Nymphet Syndrome in the Movies*. Plexus, 1988.

Russell Trainer, *The Lolita Complex*. Citadel, 1965.

Graham Vickers, *Chasing Lolita: How Popular Culture Corrupted Nabokov's Little Girl All Over Again*. Chicago Review Press, 2008.

Michael Wood, *The Magician's Doubts: Nabokov and the Risks of Fiction.* Princeton University Press, 1997.

Lila Azam Zanganeh, *The Enchanter: Nabokov and Happiness.* W. W. Norton, 2011.

ARTICLES AND WEBSITES

Anonymous (attributed to Joyce Haber), "The Lolita Case." *Time,* vol. 72, no. 20, November 17, 1958.

Martin Amis, "Lo Hum and Little Lo." *The Independent,* October 24, 1992.

Brian Boyd, "The Year of Lolita." *New York Times Book Review,* September 8, 1991.

Robertson Davies, "Mania for Green Fruit." *Saturday Night,* October 11, 1958.

Alexander Dolinin, "Whatever Happened to Sally Horner?: A Real Life Source of Nabokov's *Lolita." Times Literary Supplement,* pp. 11–12, September 9, 2005.

Leland de la Durantaye, "The Pattern of Cruelty and the Cruelty of Pattern in Vladimir Nabokov." *Cambridge Quarterly,* October 2006.

———, "Lolita in *Lolita,* or the Garden, the Gate and the Critics." *Nabokov Studies* 10 (2006).

Sarah Herbold, "(I Have Camouflaged Everything, My Love): *Lolita* and the Woman Reader." *Nabokov Studies* 5 (1998–1999): 81–94.

Elizabeth Janeway, "The Tragedy of a Man Driven by Desire." *New York Times Book Review,* August 17, 1958.

Landon Jones, "On the Trail of Nabokov in the American West." *New York Times,* May 24, 2016, https://www.nytimes.com/2016/05/29/travel/vladimir-nabokov-lolita.html.

Erica Jong, "*Lolita* Turns Thirty: A New Introduction." *New York Times Book Review,* June 5, 1988.

Vladimir Nabokov, "On a Book Entitled Lolita." *Anchor Review,* 1957. (Reprinted in every English-language edition of *Lolita* since 1958.)

Heine Scholtens, "Seeing Lolita in Print." Thesis for M.A. Programme in Book History, Leiden University, 2005 (uploaded in 2014).

Delia Ungureanu, "From Dulita to Lolita." In *From Paris to Tlön: Surrealism as World Literature.* Bloomsbury Academic, 2017.

Dieter Zimmer, "Lolita, USA." 2007. http://www.d-e-zimmer.de/Lolita USA/LoUSpre.htm.

Dieter Zimmer and Jeff Edmunds, "Vladimir Nabokov: A Bibliography of Criticism." 2005. http://www.libraries.psu.edu/nabokov/forians.htm.

OTHER SOURCES

Amanda Berry and Gina de Jesus, *Hope: A Memoir of Survival in Cleveland.* Viking, 2015.

Phil Cohen, "Local History—Camden, NJ." http://www.dvrbs.com.

Jeffery M. Dorwart, *Camden County, New Jersey: The Making of a Metropolitan Community, 1626–2000.* Rutgers University Press, 2001.

Jaycee Dugard, *A Stolen Life.* Simon & Schuster, 2011.

Howard Gillette, Jr., *Camden After the Fall.* University of Pennsylvania Press, 2005.

Michelle Knight, *Finding Me: A Decade of Darkness, A Life Reclaimed.* Weinstein Books, 2014.

Elizabeth Smart, *My Story.* St. Martin's Press, 2013.

PERMISSIONS

Nikolai Gogol by Vladimir Nabokov, copyright © 1944 by Vladimir Nabokov, renewed 1972 by Article 3C under the will of Vladimir Nabokov.
Used by permission of The Wylie Agency and by permission of Penguin Random House UK.

Vladimir Nabokov: Selected Letters, 1940–1977, edited by Dmitri Nabokov
and Matthew J. Bruccoli, copyright © 1989 by Article 3C under the
will of Vladimir Nabokov. Used by permission of Houghton Mifflin
Harcourt.

IMAGES

Florence "Sally" Horner, age nine: Camden County Historical Society

Photograph of Sally discovered at the Atlantic City boardinghouse in
August 1948, six weeks after her disappearance: International News
Photos/courtesy of the author

Vladimir Nabokov holding a butterfly, 1947, at Harvard's Museum of
Comparative Zoology, where he was a fellow: Constantine Joffe for
Vogue/Getty Images

Mug shot of Frank La Salle taken upon the start of his prison sentence
for the statutory rape of five girls, 1943: New Jersey State Archives

Mitchell Cohen questions Howard Unruh in a hospital bed, September
7, 1949: Associated Press

Nabokov re-creating the process of writing *Lolita* on note cards: Carl
Mydans, The LIFE Picture Collection/Getty Images

Ruth Janisch, ca. 1940s: Janisch family

Sally on the telephone to her family in the hours after her rescue: International News Photos/courtesy of the author

Sally Horner and Mitchell Cohen board a Philadelphia-bound United
Airlines flight, March 31, 1950: Ernest K. Bennett/Associated Press

Sally sees her mother, Ella Horner, for the first time in twenty-one
months: Associated Press

Sally leans on her mother's shoulder minutes after being reunited: International News Photos/courtesy of the author

Frank La Salle, after pleading guilty: International News Photos/cour-
tesy of the author

Sally Horner and her older sister, Susan Panaro, in the family greenhouse: Panaro/Chiemingo family archives

A candid shot of Sally holding a newspaper: Panaro/Chiemingo family archives

Véra and Nabokov chasing butterflies: Carl Mydans, The LIFE Picture Collection/Getty Images

Carol Starts, Sally Horner's best friend, summer of 1952: Panaro/Chiemingo family archives

Edward Baker's high school graduation photo, 1950: Vineland High School yearbook, retrieved via Ancestry.com

AP story of Sally Horner's death transcribed onto a note card by Vladimir Nabokov: LOC note card, Box 2, Folder 14, Vladimir Vladimirovich Nabokov Papers, Manuscript Division, Library of Congress, Washington, DC

Image accompanying Peter Welding's November 1963 article for *Nugget:* courtesy of the author

Sally Horner, age fifteen, summer of 1952: Panaro/Chiemingo family archives

INDEX

NOTE: PAGE NUMBERS IN *ITALICS* INDICATE PHOTOS.

accidents. *See* car accidents

Albara, Ella, 35. *See also* Horner, Ella (mother)

Alice's Adventures in Wonderland (Carroll), 54

Amis, Martin, 46

Anchor Review, excerpts of *Lolita* in, 212, 242

anime, 249

"Annabel Lee" (Poe), 54

Annibale, Emma, 162. *See also* DiRenzo, Emma

The Annotated Lolita (Nabokov & Appel), 219n, 226

Appel, Alfred, Jr., 54, 219n, 226

Atlantic City (NJ), 19–20, 22–26, 25, 39–40, 138

Auld, Howard, 79–80

Baker, Edward John, *171*
background, 170–172
car accident involving, 183–187
civil suits against, 188
life after Sally's death, 238
on Sally, 183

Baker, Edward, Jr., 238

Baltimore (MD), 83–84, 86–91, 129

Belvedere Hotel (Baltimore), 88

Bend Sinister (Nabokov), 28

Benson, Jacob, 174, 183–184, 188

Berle, Milton, 244

Berry, Amanda, 86

Bishop, Morris, 29, 203, 245

Bishop Dunne Catholic School, 113

Bowen, Oliver, 60

Boyd, Brian, 9–10, 226–227

Brigantine Beach (NJ), 21–23, 39–40

Brottman, Mikita, 6–7

Bruel, Andree, 102

Burkett, Arthur "Otto," 235–236

Burrough Junior High, 158, 162

butterfly-hunting, 27, 29, 45, 103–105, 165–167, *166*, 204, 214–215

Buxbaum, Richard, 102–105

Cahill, William, 139–141, 144

Cambridge (MA)
Lolita's setting and, 105–106
Nabokov academic career in, 27–28, 29, *166*

Camden (NJ). See also *Courier-Post* (Camden)
  decline of, 94, 100
  Dworecki case, 76–79
  Forstein case and, 70–71
  La Salle's extradition to, 135–136, 138–139, 143–145, 189–190
  McDade case, 79–81
  mid-century optimism in, 12, 17–18, 41, 93–94
  mid-century teen-age life in, 169–170
  Sally's encounters with La Salle in, 15–17, 65
  as Sally's hometown, 2, 18, 36
  Sally's return to, 139–142
  statutory rape case, 61–64
  "Walk of Death" massacre, 94–100
Camera Obscura (Nabokov), 48–49. See also *Laughter in the Dark*
Cape May County Gazette, on Wildwood car accident, 187
Caprioni, Dominick, 188
captivity narratives, 84–87, 115–116, 122–123
car accidents
  Baker's (Edward, Jr.), 238
  G. Edward Grammar case, 200–202
  La Salle's hit-and-run, 60
  in *Lolita*, 108, 200–203, 220
  Pfeffer family's, 21–24
  Sally's death and, 173–175, 183–188, 221, 257
Carroll, Lewis, 54
Carroll, Thomas, 61
Castro, Ariel, 85–86
Catholic schools, 89–92, 113, 149

Chiemingo, Diana. *See* Panaro, Diana
Child Pornography Prevention Act (1996), 250
Clara S. Burrough Junior High, 158, 162
Cleveland three abduction case, 85–86
Cohen, Charles, 96–97, 100
Cohen, Maurice, 96
Cohen, Mitchell, 139
  advice for Sally and Ella, 148–149, 159
  background, 73–75
  on death penalty, 81
  La Salle's extradition, 135–136, 138–139, 143–144
  La Salle's guilty plea, 144–146, 147, 190, 192
  La Salle's kidnapping charges, 111
  La Salle's statutory rape case, 63
  life after Sally's death, 239
  murder cases prosecuted by, 75, 78–80
  Sally's return home with, 139–141
  "Walk of Death," 98–100
Cohen, Rose, 96–97
Conclusive Evidence (Nabokov), 28, 102, 151–152. See *Speak, Memory*
connections to *Lolita*. *See* real-life connections to *Lolita*
copyright laws, 210, 213–215
Cornellous (Mother Superior), 90
Cornell University
  Nabokov's academic career at, 8, 29, 101–102, 105, 165–166, 203, 205–206

Nabokov's leave of absence from, 214, 216
Courier-Post (Camden)
on car accident, 187
on Cohen, M., 41
on La Salle's arrest, 136–138
on La Salle's extradition, 137
on Sally's encounter with Pfeffer family, 22
on Sally's rescue, 131, 254
on search for Sally, 39
on "Walk of Death" massacre, 98
Covici, Pascal, 208
cross-country trips
of La Salle and Sally, 86–88, 112, 121–123, 138
in Lolita, 12, 28, 154, 178, 202, 219
of Nabokov family, 28–29, 102–105, 165–168, 177, 204–205, 214–216, 227–228

Daiches, David, 105
Dallas (TX)
Janisch family in, 117–118, 121
Sally's captivity in, 111–116, 118–123, 129, 137, 192–194
Dar (Nabokov), 49–50
Dare, David, 59–60
Dare, Dorothy, 58–65, 145, 192, 196–197
Day, Alvin, 96
The Deer Park (Mailer), 211
DeJesus, Gina, 86
Dietrich, Marlene, 106, 108
DiRenzo, Emma, 17, 162. See also Annibale, Emma
Dolinin, Alexander, 154, 178–179, 181, 218, 254

Doran, Larry, 99
Dostoevsky, Fyodor, 203
Doyle, Arthur Conan, 203
Driscoll, Alfred, 73, 136, 139
Dube, Wilfred, 139, 143–144, 238–239
Dugard abduction case, 85–86
Dworecki case, 75–79

Ellis, Havelock, 29–30, 249, 255
The Enchanter (Nabokov), 53, 221. See also Volshebnik (Nabokov)
Enoch Pratt Free Library (Baltimore), 88–89
Epstein, Jason, 208
Ergaz, Doussia, 209

Farrell, Marie, 90
Ferry, John, 97–98
Field, Andrew, 9, 30, 55, 226
Findley, Everett, 119
five-and-dime store meeting, 15–17
Fogg, Frank (La Salle alias), 58–60, 62, 246
Forstein, Dorothy, 69–71
Forstein, Jules, 69–71
Forstein, Marcy, 70
fountainists, 55
Frank J. Leonard Funeral Home, 185
Freud, Sigmund, 249

Geisel, Ted, 103
Gibbons, John, 128, 130
The Gift (Nabokov), 49–50
"Girl in the Box" abduction case, 85–86
Girodias, Maurice, 209–214
Goff, Ella Katherine, 34. See also Horner, Ella (mother)
Goff, Job, 35, 37

Goff, Susannah, 35, 37
Gogol, Nikolai, 8, 28
Gomez, Manny, 136
G. P. Putnam's Sons, 211–214,
    224, 241
Grammar, Dorothy, 200–202
Grammar, G. Edward, 200–202
Grand Teton mountains, 103–105
Guadanini, Irina, 50

Haber, Joyce, 241–242, 243
Hall, Marshall, 136–138
Hanlin, Sarah, 17
Harrie, Armand, 96
Harrie, Madeline, 96
Hazlitt (online magazine), on
    Lolita-Sally connection, 4–5
Heilfurth, Paul, 174
Hoover, Clark, 95–96
Hornbuckle, Howard, 127–129, 135,
    138, 239
Horner, Ella (mother), *140–141*
    Atlantic City "trip" permission,
        19–20
    civil suits filed by, 188
    on La Salle, 131
    La Salle's history revealed to, 26
    life after Sally's death, 235–237
    Lolita parallels, 108–109, 219–
        220, 246
    marriages of, 33–37, 235–236
    reporting Sally's disappearance,
        24–25
    on Sally's captivity, 157
    Sally's death and, 175, 185–186
    during Sally's disappearance,
        24–26, 67–72
    Sally's letters to, 20, 24, 25, 138
    Sally's rescue and, 126, 130–131

Sally's reunion with, 139–142,
    140–141
as single mother, 16–17, 18, 19,
    34, 36–37, 67–68, 71–72
testimony of, 138
Horner, Russell (father), 18, 34, 35–37
Horner, Sally (Florence)
    after rescue, in California,
        157–158
    aliases of, 89, 112, 118
    birth of, 34
    during captivity, reaching out to
        others, 122–123, 133, 155
    captivity, traveling between
        cities during, 86–88, 112,
        121–123, 138
    captivity in Atlantic City, 19–20,
        22–26, 25, 39–40, 138
    captivity in Baltimore, 83–84,
        86–91, 129
    captivity in Dallas, 111–116, 118–
        123, 129, 137, 192–194
    captivity in San Jose, 121, 125–127
    death of, 2–3, 173–175, 183–185,
        221, 257
    description of her ordeal, 128–
        130, 136–137
    family life of, 18, 33–37, 157–161,
        160–161. See also Horner, Ella
        (mother); Panaro, Al; Panaro,
        Diana; Panaro, Susan (sister)
    insights into, 84–87, 133, 155,
        158–159, 161
    La Salle, first encounters with,
        15–17, 19–20
    at La Salle's arraignment, 136–
        137, 145
    letters to her mother, 20, 24,
        25, 138

Lolita parallels. *See under* real-life connections to *Lolita*
Lolita's direct reference to, 1
love of the outdoors, 163
Miss Robinson and, 87–88, 138
neighbor's recollections of, 113–115, 121, 192–194
photographs of, *2, 25, 132, 139, 140–141, 160–161, 259*
physical description of, 1–2, 25–26, 31, 160–161
rescue of, 125–132, *132,* 135–138, *139*
reunion with mother, 139–142, *140–141*
school enrollment after captivity, 158–159, 162
school enrollment during captivity, 89–92, 113
search for, 24–26, 39–43, 69
social life of, 18, 162–163, 169–170, 171–172
subjugation of, 89–91, 257–258
Taylor on, 237–238
Wildwood trip, 169–173
Hughes, Richard, 190
Humes, Charley, 98
Hutton, James, 96

Invitation to a Beheading (Nabokov), 203
Irons, Jeremy, 250
Ithaca (NY), house inspiration in *Lolita,* 29. *See also* Cornell University

Jackson Hole (WY), 104
Janeway, Elizabeth, 215
Janisch, George, 117–121

Janisch, Pat, 117–118
Janisch, Rachel, 194–195, 229–234
Janisch, Ruth, *119*
arrival in Texas, 117–118
background, 116–120
departure from Texas, 121
La Salle's letters to, 194
Lolita parallel, 220
motivation for helping Sally, 118–121
relationship with her children, 229–232, 234
Sally's rescue and, 125–127, 146, 194–195
willingness to testify against La Salle, 139
Janisch, Vanessa, 194
Janney, Anthony, 88
Jass, Alfred, 149

Kagamaster, Dale, 112
Kagamaster, Josephine, 114, 115
Kampusch abduction case, 85–86
Karlinsky, Simon, 53
Keegan, Dick, 206–207
King, Ralph, 60
The Kingdom by the Sea. See Lolita (Nabokov)
Klots, Alexander, 103
Knight, Michelle, 86
Krim, Seymour, 218–219
Kubrick, Stanley, 245–248

Langella, Frank, 250
Lanz, Bruno, 255
Lanz, Henry, 54–55
LaPlante (La Salle's alias), 112
LaPlante, Madeline (Sally's alias), 89, 112

La Salle, Frank, *64, 148*
  aliases of, 19–20, 24–26, 58–60,
    62, 112, 246
  appeals by, 189–192
  appellate brief by, 192–194
  arraignment of, 136–137
  background, 23, 57–58
  capture of, 130
  children of, 60–63, 191–192,
    195–197
  death of, 197
  divorce of, 63–65
  extradition of, 135–136, 138–139,
    143–145, 189–190
  false narratives by, 23, 109, 130,
    191–192, 197
  funeral flowers for Sally from, 185
  grand jury indictment of,
    138–139
  guilty plea by, 145–148
  Janisch (Rachel) victimized by,
    232–234
  kidnapping charges against, 69,
    81, 111
  letters from prison, 194–195
  Lolita parallels, 152–155, 178–180,
    219–221, 246
  Lolita reference to, 1
  marriages of, 42, 58–63
  personal characteristics of,
    19–20, 57–58
  Pfeffer family helped by, 22–23
  physical description, *148*
  Sally's captivity, in Atlantic City,
    22–26, *25,* 39–40, 138
  Sally's captivity, in Baltimore,
    83–84, 86–92, 129
  Sally's captivity, in Dallas, 111–
    116, 118–123, 129, 137, 192–194

Sally's captivity, in San Jose, 121,
    125–127
  Sally's captivity, traveling
    between cities, 86–88, 112,
    121–123, 138
  Sally's first encounters with,
    15–17, 19–20
  Sally's mother on, 131–132
  Sally's sister on, 131–132
  searching for Sally and, 24–26,
    39–43, 69
  sentencing of, 148
  statutory rape case against, 26,
    61–65, *64,* 145
La Salle, "Madeline," 60–63, 191–
    192, 195–197
Laughlin, James, 152, 208
Laughter in the Dark (Nabokov),
    48–49, 208
Lerner, Alan Jay, 248
Let's Make Love (film), 244
Leuthold, Dorothy, 28, 102
Leva, Frank, 128
Levin, Alan, 222, 226
Levin, Herman, 74
"Lilith" (Nabokov), 48
Lindbergh abduction case, 84
Logan, Douglas, 128
lolicon, 249
Lolita (film), 225–227, 245–248
Lolita (film remake), 250
Lolita (Nabokov). *See also* real-life
    connections to *Lolita*
  adaptations of, 248–251, 257
  alternate ending theories, 180
  archive materials on, 10, *104,*
    177–180, *179,* 200–201,
    224–227
  car accidents, 108, 200–203, 220

completion of, 205–209
copyright to, 210, 213–215
cross-country trip in, 12, 28, 154,
    178, 202, 219
Dolores's admirable
    characteristics revealed in,
    181–182
Janisch (Ruth) on, 231–232
literary critics on, 208–209
literary inspirations, 54
"Lolita" name origin, 207
manuscript destruction attempts,
    2, 206–207
mid-century America description
    in, 28
as more art than life, 222–225
Nabokov's earlier writing
    foreshadowing, 48–50, 51–52
narrator's self-justification in, 6,
    52–53
nymphet description, 31–32,
    180–181
pedophile archetype in, 7, 31–32,
    52-55
plot and scenes from, 31,
    106–108, 132–134, 153–154,
    180–182, 256–257
popular culture references in,
    160–161
popularity of, 215–216, 240–242,
    243–245, 255
press reception for, 214–215
pseudonym consideration for,
    207–208
publication of, 209–213,
    224, 240
readers' reactions to, 5–7, 10–11,
    12, 208–209, 224, 258
rejections of, 208–209

reviews of, 214–215
sequels (unauthorized), 248–249
setting, 29, 105–106
sympathy for narrator, 6–7
telephones in, 132–134, 155
victimization portrayed in,
    241–242
Volshebnik comparison to, 51–54
Lolita, My Love (musical), 248
The Lolita Complex (Trainer), 249
"Lolita Has a Secret—Shhh!"
    (Welding), 218–223, 218
Lolita look-alike contest, 244–245
Lo's Diary (Pera), 249–250
Lyne, Adrian, 250–251

Mailer, Norman, 211
The Male Lolita (Trainer), 249
manga, 249
Marter, William, 25, 127
Marx, Groucho, 244
Mashen'ka (Mary) (Nabokov), 47
Mason, James, 247
Mason, Portland, 247
Matlack, Emma, 96
Maurer, Russ, 98
The Maximum Security Book Club
    (Brottman), 6–7
McCarthy, Mary, 208
McCord, Mrs., 25
McDade murder case, 79–80
media coverage
    of Forstein case, 69–71
    La Salle's desire to shield Sally
        from, 145, 147
    of La Salle's return to
        Philadelphia, 144–145
    of Lolita film stars, 247
    as Lolita inspiration, 152–154,

media coverage (*cont.*)
    168, 177–180, 200–203
    in Nabokov's archives, 10, *104*,
        177–180, *179*, 200–201,
        224–227
    of Sally's captivity, 152–154
    of Sally's death, 175–176, 183–184
    of Sally's disappearance, 67–68
    of Sally's mother, 67–68, 131–132
Minton, Polly, 241–243
Minton, Walter, 211–215, 241–243
"Miss Robinson" (mystery woman),
    87–88, 138
Mizibrocky, Matilda, 202
Monroe, Marilyn, 244
Mulligan, James, 98, 144
"My Heart Belongs to Daddy"
    (Cole), 244

Nabokov, Dmitri
    childhood, 50
    cross-country trips of, 28–29,
        102–105, 165–168
    Lolita look-alike contest and,
        244–245
    with Minton's wife, 242–243
Nabokov, Véra, *166*
    as academic stand-in for
        husband, 29
    background, 27–28, 47, 50
    biography of, 10
    cross-country trips of, 28–29,
        102–105, 165–168, 177, 204–
        205, 214–216, 227–228
    on Dolores's character, 182
    on *Lolita* as more art than life,
        222–225
    on *Lolita*'s popularity, 214,
        240, 244
    on Minton, 241–243
    as Nabokov's gatekeeper, 9, 215,
        223–224, 226
    on Nabokov's interest in Nimer
        case, 203
    saving *Lolita* manuscript, 2,
        206–207
Nabokov, Vladimir. See also *Lolita*;
    Nabokov, Vladimir, works by;
    real-life connections to *Lolita*
    academic career, leave of absence
        from, 214, 216
    academic career at Cornell
        University, 8, 29, 101–102, 105,
        165–166, 203, 205–206
    academic career in Cambridge
        (MA), 27–28, 29, 166
    affairs of, 28, 50
    archives of, 10, *104*, 177–180, *179*,
        200–201, 224–227
    autobiography, 28, 102
    background, 7–10, 27–28, 50–51
    biography by, 8, 28
    butterfly-hunting, 27, 29, 45,
        103–105, 165–167, *166*, 204,
        214–215
    on Carroll, 54
    cross-country trips of, 28–29,
        102–105, 165–168, 177, 204–
        205, 214–216, 227–228
    on Dolores's character, 182
    on Freud, 249
    on Girodias and Olympia Press,
        210–211
    health of, 28–29, 50–51, 151–
        152, 166
    index card writing method, *104*,
        167, 177–180, *179*, 200–201,
        203, 205, 225

on literal mapping of fiction to
real life, 8, 10–11
on Lolita, My Love, 248
on *Lolita* as more art than life, 8,
10–11, 46, 222–225, 255–256
on *Lolita* look-alike contest,
244–245
on *Lolita*'s narrator's prototype, 55
on *Lolita*'s popularity, 215–
216, 244
molestation of, 256
on mystery novels, 203
notes by, *104, 167, 177–180, 179,*
200–201, 225
on pedophilia case study, 29–30
pedophilia exploration in
writings of, 29–30, 45–50. See
also *Lolita* (Nabokov)
photographs of, *45, 104, 166*
popular culture references by,
160–161, 167
publication of, through G. P.
Putnam's Sons, 211–215
real-life crime stories and. *See*
real-life connections to *Lolita*
relocation to Switzerland, 216
on rereading books, 10
on time for writing, 102
Nabokov, Vladimir D. (father), 46
Nabokov, Vladimir, works by
Bend Sinister, 28
Camera Obscura, 48–49
Conclusive Evidence, 28, 102,
151–152
Dar, 49–50
Despair, 203
early writings of, 47
The Enchanter, 53, 221. See also
Volshebnik (Nabokov)

The Gift, 49–50
Invitation to a Beheading, 203
Laughter in the Dark, 48–49, 208
"Lilith," 48
Lolita. See *Lolita* (Nabokov);
real-life connections to
Lolita
Lolita screenplay, 245–248
Mashen'ka (Mary), 47
"A Nursery Tale," 47–48
Speak, Memory, 256. See
also Conclusive Evidence
(Nabokov)
"Spring in Fialta," 10–11
Volshebnik, 50, 51–54
Nabokov: His Life in Art (Levin), 226
Nabokov in America (Roper), 46
Nelson, Lillian, 128
Nickerson, Denise, 248
Nimer, Louise Jean, 203
Nimer, Melvin, 203–204
Nimer, Melvin, Jr., 203–204
Nugget (magazine), 218–219
"A Nursery Tale" (Nabokov), 47–48
nymphet description
in *Lolita*, 31–32, 180–181
in Nabokov's earlier writing, 46,
47–49, 51–52

Olympia Press, 209–213, 224, 240
Orlando, Samuel, 78–79
Our Lady of Good Counsel
Academy, 113

Palese, Rocco, 80, 139, 145–148,
190, 239
Panaro, Al
life after Sally's death, 236–237
marriage of, 37

Panaro, Al (*cont.*)
  Sally living with family of,
    157–160
  Sally's body identification by,
    174–175
  at Sally's funeral, 185
  on Sally's psychological state, 161
  Sally's rescue and, 126–127
  Sally's reunion with, 140–141
Panaro, Brian, 237, 254
Panaro, Diana
  birth of, 37
  childhood, 68, 71, 132, 235
  learning of Sally's captivity,
    236–237
  reflections on Sally, 253–255
  Sally living with family of,
    158–160
  at Sally's funeral, 185
  Sally's reunion with, 140–141
Panaro, Susan (sister), 160
  birth of daughter, 37
  childhood of, 35–36
  father of, 34
  on La Salle, 131–132
  life after Sally's death, 236–237
  marriage of, 37
  pregnancy of, 18, 24
  Sally living with family of, 158–160
  during Sally's disappearance, 68,
    71–72
  on Sally's father, 36
  at Sally's funeral, 185
  Sally's rescue and, 126, 131–
    132, 254
  Sally's reunion with, 140–141
Paris Review
  on *Lolita*'s real-life connections, 255

on near-destruction of *Lolita*
  manuscript, 207
Parker, Dorothy, 208–209
pedophilia
  case study of, 29–30
  La Salle and, 58
  Nabokov's fictional accounts
    of, 45–50. See also *Lolita*
    (Nabokov); real-life
    connections to *Lolita*
  pedophile archetype, 7, 31–32,
    52–55
Pera, Pia, 249–250
Pfeffer family, 21–24, 39–40, 138
Pfeil, Charles, 112–113, 193
Pfeil, Nelrose, 112–113, 192–194
Pfeil, Tom, 112–113, 192–194
Philadelphia Inquirer
  on Sally's disappearance, 25,
    39, 217
  on Sally's encounter with Pfeffer
    family, 22
  on Sally's mother, 68
Pilarchik, John, 96
plagiarism possibility, 220
Planette, Florence (Sally's alias),
  112, 118
Poe, Edgar Allan, 54, 203
Porter, Cole, 244
Prescott, Orville, 215
prisoners, reaction to *Lolita*, 7
Pulaski Highway, 88

Quinn (monsignor), 90

Ransom, John Crowe, 103
Reading Lolita in Tehran
  (Nafisi), 257

real-life connections to *Lolita*
car accidents, 108, 200–203, 220
direct reference to Sally, 1
G. Edward Grammar case,
200–203
Lanz and *Lolita*, 54–55
La Salle and, 152–155, 178–180,
219–221, 246
La Salle's sentence and, 155
media attempts to reveal, 3–5,
217–221, 222–227, 255
media coverage and, 152–154,
168, 177–180, 200–203
Nabokov on, 8, 10–11, 46, 222–
225, 255–256
Nabokov's notes, 104, 167, 177–
180, 179, 200–201, 225
Sally's captivity, direct reference
to, 1
Sally's captivity time frame, 153–155
Sally's confession to school
chum, 122, 123, 133, 155
Sally's death and, 23
Sally's mother and, 108–109,
219–220, 246
Sally's phone call for help, 132–
134, 155
of Sally's physical description,
30–31, 181
setting of, 29, 105–106
Ridgewell, Rosemary, 212, 241–
242, 243
Rifkin, John, 174
road trips. *See* cross-country trips
Robinson, Frank (La Salle
alias), 25
Robles abduction case, 84–85
Rock, Joe, 78

Roper, Robert, 46, 152, 207
Rust, Ann, 79

Saint Ann's Catholic School, 89–91
Salt Lake City writing conference,
102–103
San Jose (CA), 121–123, 125–127
Scheffler, Curt, 60
Schiff, Stacy, 10, 206–207, 226
Schiff, Stephen, 250
Schopp, Paul, 100
Schultz, Joseph, 24–25
Sears, Thomas, 186
Sellers, Peter, 247
Shapiro, Edward, 61, 70–71
Sheehan, Bartholomew, 63, 80
Shewchuk, Peter, 77–79
shop-lifting incident, 15–17
Sirin, V. (Nabokov's pseudonym), 47
Slonim, Véra, 47. *See also* Nabokov,
Véra
Smart abduction case, 85–86
Smillie, Maude, 114
Smith, Orris, 96
Speak, Memory (Nabokov), 256.
See also *Conclusive Evidence*
(Nabokov)
Stan, Colleen, 86
Starts, Carol. *See* Taylor, Carol
Stegner, Wallace, 103
Stern, Bert, 247
Studies in the Psychology of Sex
(Ellis), 29–30, 249, 255
Swain, Dominique, 250
Swain, William Ralph, 34–35

Taylor, Carol, *169*
on Baker, 187

Taylor, Carol (*cont.*)
  on *Lolita*'s connection to Sally,
    237–238
  Sally's death and, 175–176,
    185–186
  Sally's friendship with, 162–163,
    169–170, 171
Tenenbaum (judge), 187
Thompson, Marshall
  background, 40–41
  La Salle's extradition and, 139,
    143–144
  life after Sally's death, 238–239
  personal characteristics of, 41–42
  Sally's rescue and, 127
  search for Sally, 25–26, 40–43, 69
  "Walk of Death" massacre,
    connections to, 95–98
Time (magazine), on *Lolita*'s
    popularity, 241–242
Trainer, Russell, 249
Troy, Ann, 90
Troy, Mary, 90

Unruh, Howard, 94–100, 99

Vineland Daily Journal
  on car accident, 183, 186
  on Sally's rescue, 184
Volshebnik (Nabokov), 50, 51–54

"Walk of Death" massacre, 94–100
Wallace, Bruce, 145
Warner, Frank (La Salle alias),
    19–20, 24–26
Warren, Earl, 139
Watson, Donald, 61
Weiner, Jacob, 131–132
Weld, Tuesday, 247
Welding, Peter, 217–221, 222–223
Wellesley College, 27, 29
White, Katharine, 151, 206,
    207–208
Wildwood Leader, on car crash, 174
Wildwood trip, 169–173
Wilkie, John V., 61–63
Wilson, Edmund, 29–30, 206,
    208–209
Wilson, Elena, 208
Wilson, Helen Matlack, 96
Wilson, John, 96
Winters, Shelley, 247
Woodrow Wilson High School, 163
Woods, Elmer B., 188
Woolworth's, 15–16

Young, Marie, 184–185, 188

Zegrino, Helen, 96
Zegrino, Thomas, 96
Zenzinov, Vladimir, 102